OF
LOVE
AND
LIFE

OF
LOVE
AND
LIFE

Three novels selected and condensed
by Reader's Digest

The Reader's Digest Association Limited, London

With the exception of actual personages identified as such, the
characters and incidents in the fictional selections in this volume
are entirely the product of the authors' imaginations and have no
relation to any person or event in real life.

The Reader's Digest Association Limited
11 Westferry Circus, Canary Wharf, London E14 4HE

www.readersdigest.co.uk

ISBN 0-276-42997-4

CONTENTS

SHEER ABANDON

PENNY VINCENZI

What makes a young woman so
desperate that she would choose to
give birth all alone in a cleaning
cupboard at Heathrow Airport and
then abandon her baby, rather than
live with the stigma of being an
unmarried mother?
Sixteen years later that child is
determined to find out . . .

Prologue

August 1986

PEOPLE DIDN'T HAVE babies on aeroplanes. They just didn't.

Well . . . well, actually they did. And then it was all over the news-papers: GALLANT AIRCREW DELIVER BOUNCING BOY, it said, or words to that effect, and then went on to describe the mother of the bouncing boy in some detail. Her name, where she lived, how she had come to be in the situation in the first place. Usually with a photograph of her with the bouncing boy and the gallant crew.

So, *that* wasn't an option. She couldn't have a baby on an aeroplane.

Ignore the pain. Not nearly bad enough, anyway. Probably indiges-tion. Of course: indigestion. Cramped up here, with her vast stomach compressed for what?—seven hours now. Yes, definitely indigestion . . .

Didn't completely solve the situation though. She was still having a baby. Any day—any hour, even. And would be having it in England now instead of safely—safely?—in Bangkok.

That had been the plan.

But the days had gone by and become a week, and then two, and the date, the wonderfully safe date of her flight, three weeks after the birth, had got nearer and nearer. She'd tried to change it; but she had an Apex seat; she'd lose the whole fare, they explained. Have to buy a new ticket.

She couldn't. She had no money left, and she'd carefully shed the few friends she'd made over the past few months, so there was no danger of them noticing that she wasn't just overweight but that she had, under the Thai fishermen's trousers and huge shirts she wore, a stomach the size of a very large pumpkin.

(The people at the check-in hadn't noticed either, thank God; had looked at her standing there, hot and tired and sweaty, and seen simply a very overweight girl in loose and grubby clothing.)

So there was no one to borrow from; no one to help. And now she had . . . indigestion. God! No. Not indigestion. This was no indigestion. This searing, tugging, violent pain, pushing at the very walls of the pumpkin. She bit her lip, clenched her fists, her nails digging into her palms.

The boy sitting next to her frowned as she moved about, trying to escape the pain, her bulk invading his space.

'Sorry,' she said. And then it faded again, the pain, disappeared back where it had come from, somewhere in the centre of the pumpkin. She lay back, wiped a tissue across her damp forehead.

Not indigestion. And three hours to go.

They had landed; everyone was standing up, pulling their luggage down from the lockers. The moment had coincided with a very violent pain. She sat in her seat, breathing heavily.

Well—she hadn't had it on the plane.

For the rest of her life, when she read of people describing bad experiences of childbirth, of inadequate pain relief, of briskly bracing midwives, of the sense of isolation and fear, she thought they should have tried it her way. Alone, in a space little bigger than a cupboard. Her isolation absolute, her only midwife herself and her precious book, propped against the tiled wall as she lay on the floor, studying its diagrams desperately, heaving her child into the world. How could she be doing this, so afraid of pain she couldn't have a filling without a local anaesthetic.

But she did.

She managed because she had to. There was nothing else for it.

And when it was all over, and she had cleaned herself up as best she could, and wrapped the baby, the tiny, wailing baby, into the clean sheet and blanket she had packed in her rucksack (along with the sharp, sharp scissors and ball of string and large bottle of water which was the nearest she could get to sterilising anything), she sat on the floor, slumped against the wall, feeling nothing, not even relief, looking at the baby, quiet now, but breathing with astonishing efficiency, its small face peaceful, its eyes closed.

It was over. She had become a mother; and in a very short while she would be one no longer, she could walk away, herself again, free, unencumbered, undisgraced.

She could just forget the whole thing. Completely.

It was over.

The Year Before

August 1985

THEY SAT THERE in the departure lounge, consulting the same departure board: three girls, strangers to one another, the faded jeans, the long hair, the sneakers, the small rucksacks (vastly bigger ones already checked in) all marking them out as backpackers, and about-to-be-undergraduates. With school and parents shaken off, round-the-world tickets in their wallets, they were moving off; to travel a route that would take in one or all of a clearly defined set of destinations: Australia, New Zealand, Thailand, Nepal and the Himalayas, and even the States.

They were excited, slightly nervous, above all impatient for the journey to begin; constantly exchanging looks, half-smiles with one another.

It was the announcement that brought them finally together: the announcement that their flight to Bangkok had been delayed for three hours. Their eyes met, eyebrows raised, and they all stood up, picking up their bags.

'Coffee?' said one and 'Great,' said the other two, and they walked slowly towards the cafeteria.

'Here's a table,' said one of the three. 'I'll keep it—leave the bags,' and she settled at the table, studying her new friends as they queued at the counter. One of them was tall and very slim with a cloud of wild blonde hair, the other shorter and distinctly plump, with her hair pulled back into a plait. The blonde kept looking over her shoulder slightly anxiously.

'We hope it's coffee,' said the plait, as she set the tray down on the corner of the table, 'but we're not sure. It's hot and wet, anyway. Sugar?'

'No, thanks. I'm Martha,' she added, smiling quickly at each of them, pushing back a long mane of loose brown hair, 'Martha Hartley . . .'

'I'm Clio,' said the plait. 'Clio Scott. Spelt with an i. Clio that is.'

'Jocasta,' said the blonde, 'Jocasta Forbes.'

'That's quite a name. Jocasta, I mean.'

'I know. My parents were punishing me for not being a boy.'

'Did they get the boy in the end?' asked Martha curiously.

'Less than a year later. Only time he's ever arrived anywhere without a long wait. He should be here now.'

'He's going travelling with you?'

'Yup. Well, we're starting out together. It made our parents feel less nervous.' She smiled at them, pushed back her hair. 'Anyway, what about you two? Martha—any story behind your name?'

'My mother said she always identified with Martha rather than Mary, in the Bible, you know? She was the one who did all the work while Mary just sat at Jesus' feet doing nothing. My mother works terribly hard.'

'It's a nice name anyway,' said Jocasta. She had looked rather blank at the biblical link. 'Clio, what about you?'

'My parents met at Oxford, reading classics. There was a muse and a nymph called Clio. My sisters are called Ariadne and Artemis,' she added.

'And are you going to follow in their footsteps, read classics?'

'Absolutely not. I'm doing medicine at UCH.'

'I was born there,' said Martha, 'and my sister—sixteen years ago today, actually.'

'What about you two?' said Clio. 'What are you going to do?'

'I'm going to read law at Bristol,' said Martha.

'English. At Durham,' said Jocasta. 'I want to be a journalist. Tracking down stories, uncovering scandals, that sort of thing.'

'How exciting.'

'Well—I hope so. I'm told I'll spend my first five years at least covering village fêtes.'

'Josh, you made it. Amazing. Only an hour late. Lucky they held the plane for you.' Jocasta seemed suddenly less at ease. 'Here, come and join us. This is Martha and this is Clio. And this is my brother Josh.'

And Martha and Clio saw a boy who looked so like Jocasta it was almost shocking. The same wild blond hair, the same dark blue eyes, the same just slightly crooked smile.

'Hi,' he said, holding out a thin hand. 'Nice to meet you.'

'Hi,' said Martha, 'nice to meet you too.'

'You're incredibly alike,' said Clio, 'you could be—'

'We know, we know. Twins. Everyone says so. But we're not. Josh, why are you so late?'

'I lost my passport.'

'Josh—you're so hopeless.'

'I know, I know. Sorry.'

'Was Mum OK, saying goodbye to you? He's her baby,' she added to the others, 'can't bear to let him out of her sight.'

'She was fine. How was your dinner with Dad?'

'It never took place. He didn't get back till twelve. And this morning he had to rush off to a meeting in Paris, so he couldn't see me off either. What a surprise.'

'So how did you get here?'

'Oh, he put me in a cab.' Her expression was hard.

'Our parents are divorced,' Josh explained. 'Usually we live with our mother but my dad wanted—'

'*Said* he wanted,' said Jocasta, 'to spend yesterday evening with me. Anyway, very boring, let's change the subject. I'm going to the loo.'

She walked away rather quickly.

There was a silence. Josh's arrival had brought an uncomfortable tension into the group. Time to withdraw, at least until the flight . . .

Their seats were far apart, but they managed to spend some of the flight together, standing in the aisles, chatting, swapping magazines, comparing routes and plans. From Bangkok, Josh wanted to go upcountry; Martha was spending a short time in Bangkok before going on to Sydney, where she was meeting a schoolfriend. She planned to stay a few weeks there, 'working in bars and stuff' before moving up to Ayers Rock and then the rain forest and the Great Barrier Reef. 'After that I don't know, but I want to finish in New York.'

Clio was island-hopping for a few weeks and then travelling on to Singapore. 'After that, Australia, probably, but I do want to get to Nepal.'

Jocasta didn't know what she was going to do. 'Go wherever fate takes me. Start with the islands, definitely. I don't want to go north with Josh, and he wants to get rid of me as soon as he can.'

'Why don't you come to Koh Samui with me?' said Clio. 'You're sure to make friends with someone down there you can travel on with.'

'Yes,' said Martha. 'My best friend's sister, who went last year, said you keep meeting people from your own town, practically your own family.'

'God, I hope not,' said Jocasta. 'Family, I mean. I've got quite enough of mine with me.'

'I don't want to meet any of mine either,' said Clio. 'This is my first chance to do something on my own without my sisters.'

'Don't you like them?'

'I suppose so. But they're both older than me, both very beautiful and successful and they treat me like I was eight, not eighteen.'

'So, did you have trouble persuading your parents to let you come?'

'Well, my mother died when I was tiny. My sisters persuaded my father. Although they all made it very clear they thought I'd be home by Christmas, tail between my legs.' Her round little face was infinitely sad; then she smiled quickly. 'Anyway, I got away.'

'My parents couldn't wait to get rid of me,' said Martha.

'Why?'

'They just find it all so exciting. My father's the vicar of Binsmow in

Suffolk, so we have to live in conditions of unbelievable respectability. Nothing remotely racy. When I tell you I went to the cinema on a Sunday with some friends last year and at least a dozen people complained to my father, you'll get some idea of what I'm talking about.'

They digested this in silence. Then, 'And what about your mum?'

'She's just a perfect vicar's wife. Runs the WI and stuff. She's absolutely thrilled I'm going away, even though she's a bit worried.'

'How on earth did they get you, these terribly conventional people?' asked Jocasta, laughing. 'Where did you go to school?'

'Oh, just a grammar school,' said Martha quickly. 'There isn't a lot of money in a vicar's family, to put it mildly. What about you two?'

'Sherborne,' said Jocasta, 'and boarding prep before that.'

'Day school,' said Clio, 'Oxford High. I always longed to go to boarding school.'

'It isn't all fun, I can tell you,' said Jocasta. 'Loneliest place in the world if you're homesick, which I was. But I got used to it. You can get used to anything, can't you? In the end?'

She stared out of the window, clearly discouraging any further probing into her family life. The others looked at one another and started discussing an article in *Cosmopolitan* about how to have it all: career, love, children . . .

'I wouldn't want to,' said Martha. 'Have it all, I mean. Well, certainly not children. My career, that'll be quite enough for me.'

A disembodied voice asked them to return to their seats.

They spent three days together in Bangkok, three extraordinary days in which they bonded absolutely, adjusting to the soup-like heat, the polluted air, the uniquely invasive smell—'I'd call it a mix of rotting vegetables, traffic fumes and poo,' said Clio cheerfully—staying in the same bleak guesthouse on the Khao San Road.

The girls all kept diaries, writing them each night, and evolved a plan to meet in a year's time to read one another's adventures.

Jocasta inevitably took hers particularly seriously. Reading it many years later, even while wincing at a rather mannered style, she was transported back to those early days, as they moved around the filthy, teeming, fascinating city. She felt the heat again, tasted the food sold from stalls on the street, tiny chickens 'the size of a ten-pence piece', kebabs, even cockroaches and locusts, deep-fried in woks; she stared out again at the waterfalls of warm rain hitting the streets vertically, shuddered again at the shanty-town ghettoes by the river, and smiled at the incredible near-standstill of traffic that filled the vast streets all day long: the overflowing buses, the tuk tuks (motorised three-wheel taxis), hurtling through the traffic, and the motor scooters transporting families of five, or occasionally glamorous young couples.

They went to Pat Pong, the red-light district, and watched the lady-boys plying their trade—'you can tell they're men, they're much better turned out than the women'—to the post office to write to their parents to tell them where they were, checked the poste restante desk where a horde of backpackers queued to pick up letters from home, messages from friends arranging meetings. They water-taxied through the stinking canals, shocked by the poverty of the hovels where the river people lived, wondered at the gilded and bejewelled palace and temples, and visited the shopping centre, packed with Gucci and Chanel.

What none of them wrote about—with that year-off meeting in mind—was the other girls, or even Josh, but they learned a great deal about each other very quickly in those three days. That Jocasta had fought a lifelong battle with Josh to gain her father's affection and attention; that Clio had grown up miserably envious of her older sisters' beauty and brilliance; that Martha's jokey complaints about her strait-laced family masked a fierce defensiveness of them; and that Josh, easily charming, brilliant Josh, was both arrogant and lazy. They learned that Jocasta for all her wild beauty lacked self-confidence; that Clio felt herself acutely dull; that Martha longed above all things for money.

'I do plan to be really rich,' she said one night as they sat in one of the endless bars, drinking one cocktail after another, daring one another to eat the deep-fried bugs. 'And I mean *really* rich.'

And when they parted, Clio and Jocasta on their way down to Koh Samui, Josh for his trip north and Martha for a couple more days in Bangkok while deciding exactly what to do, they felt they had been friends for years.

Chapter 1

August 2000

SHE ALWAYS FELT exactly the same. It surprised her. Relieved. Excited. And a bit ashamed. Walking away, knowing she'd done it, resisting the temptation to look back, carefully subdued—she could still remember old Bob at the news agency telling her one of the prime qualities for a good reporter was acting ability.

This had been a horror to do: a baby in its pushchair, hit by a stolen car; the driver hadn't stopped, had been caught by the police fifty miles away. The baby was in intensive care and it was touch-and-go whether he would live; the parents had been angry as well as grief-stricken, clutching hands, sitting just outside the hospital door.

'He'll get what . . . three years?' the young father had said, lighting his ninth cigarette of the interview—Jocasta always counted things like that, it helped to add colour—'and then get on with his life. Our little chap's only had eight months and he could be gone for ever. It makes me sick. I tell you, they should lock them up for this sort of thing; lock them up and throw away the key—'

She could see her headline then: and hated herself for seeing it.

While she was in the middle of writing her story, her phone rang.

'Is that you, Miss—'

'Jocasta, yes,' she said, recognising the voice of the baby's father. 'Yes, Dave, it's me. Any news . . .?'

'Yes,' he said. 'Yes, he's going to be all right, he's going to pull through!'

'Dave, I'm so glad, so very glad,' said Jocasta, hugely relieved, not only that the baby was going to live, but that she was so touched by it.

Not a granite-hearted reporter yet, then.

She filed the story, and checked her emails; there was an assortment of junk, one from her brother telling her her mother was missing her and to phone her, a couple from friends—and one that made her smile.

Hello, Heavenly Creature. Meet me at the House. Nick.

She mailed Nick back, telling him she'd be there by nine, then, rather reluctantly, dialled her mother's number. And flicking through her diary, knowing her mother would want to make some arrangement for the week, realised it was exactly fifteen years to the day since she had set off for Thailand, in search of adventure. She always remembered it. Always. She wondered if the other two did. And what they were doing. They'd never had their promised reunion. She thought that every year as well: how they had promised one another and never kept the promise. Probably just as well, though, given everything that had happened . . .

Nick Marshall was the political editor on the *Sketch*, Jocasta's paper; he worked not in the glossy building on Canary Wharf but in one of the shabby offices above the press galleries at the House of Commons.

Nick met Jocasta in Central Lobby and bent to kiss her. 'I'm going to take you out to dinner,' he said, with a smile.

'My God. What have I done to deserve this?'

'Nothing. I'm hungry and nothing interesting's going on here.'

'You're such a gentleman, you know that?' said Jocasta.

In fact Nick *was* a gentleman; nobody was quite sure what he was doing in the world of the tabloid press. His father was a very rich farmer and Nick had got a double first in classics at Oxford. He had developed an early passion for politics and after an initial foray into the real thing had decided he could move into the corridors of power faster via the political pages of a newspaper. He was a brilliant investigative journalist, and came up with scoop after scoop, the most famous, if least important, of which was the revelation that a very prominent Tory minister bought all his socks and underpants at charity shops.

It had been love at first sight, Jocasta always said, for her. Nick had walked into the newsroom of the *Sketch* on her very first day there, fresh from a news agency in the West Country, and she had gone literally weak at the knees. Told he was the political editor, she had assumed, joyfully, that she would see him every day; the discovery that he only came in for the occasional editor's conference, or one-to-one meetings with Chris Pollock, the editor, was a serious blow. As was the news that he had a girlfriend on every paper. She wasn't surprised; he was (as well as extremely tall: about six foot four) very good-looking in an untidy sort of way, with shaggy brown hair, large mournful brown eyes, a long and very straight nose, and what she could only describe rather helplessly as a completely sexy mouth. Jocasta had pursued him fervently and shamelessly for several months; then they had both got extremely drunk at the *Spectator* party, and she had decided a proactive approach was the only one that was going to get her anywhere and started to kiss him with great determination. Unwilling, this time, to leave anything to chance, she then suggested they went back to her place. Nick declared himself hooked.

'I've admired you for so long, but I thought a girl who looked like you was bound to have a dozen boyfriends.'

'Oh, for God's sake,' said Jocasta, and got into bed beside him and their relationship had been finally—and very happily—sealed.

Although certainly not signed. And it troubled Jocasta. She loved Nick, and she felt, with increasing intensity, that the time had come for some proper commitment.

'So,' he said as they were finally settled at a table in Mon Plaisir. 'Tell me about your day. You look tired, Mrs Cook.'

'I *am* tired, Mr Butler.'

They had once gone to a fancy-dress party as the cook and the butler and used the names occasionally since in their emails (the more indiscreet ones), whenever a code was necessary.

'But it was OK. One tragedy, and a trivial piece on Mrs Prescott's hair. I do get so tired of doing those stories.'

'But you're so good at it.'

'I know that, Nick,' she said and indeed she was good at it; she could get into anyone's house, however many other journalists were on the doorstep. It was all part of her golden charm and, to a degree, she knew, the way she looked. If it was a choice between talking to a male reporter in a sharp suit or an absurdly young-looking girl with long blonde hair and wide blue eyes, then it was not a very difficult decision. Jocasta got more by-lines on human-interest stories, and what were known in the trade as tragedies, than almost anyone in Fleet Street. But she was weary of it; she longed to be a feature writer, or a foreign correspondent, or even a political editor.

'So—anything happen to you today?'

'I had lunch with Janet Frean.'

'Should I be jealous?'

'Absolutely not. Very nice, I'm sure, but a Wonderwoman-type politician with five children, famously pro-European, sacked from the shadow cabinet is not for me. Actually, I don't exactly like her, but she's an incredible force to reckon with.'

'So?'

'So, she's pretty sick of what's going on in the Tory party. They're all feeling depressed. Saying that the party has got everything wrong. That they'll never get in again, that Blair can walk on water.'

'So?'

'So . . . there's talk of some of them doing something about it.'

'Like what?'

'Well, like making a break for it. Backed by a few right-minded people. People who are prepared to stand up and be counted, to say this just isn't any good, we know we can do better, come and join us.'

'And do these people exist?'

'Apparently. Chad Lawrence, for a start.'

'Really? Well, I'd vote for him. Most gorgeous man in Westminster.'

'Which won't do him any harm—women voters by the dozen. And they have a couple more quite senior and high-profile people in the party on side. Most notably Jack Kirkland.'

Jack Kirkland had risen from a south London working-class family to a position as minister for education in the Tory party.

'Where is this leading, Nick?'

'A new party. A party just left of centre, but still recognisably Tory, headed up by a pretty charismatic lot, which will appeal to both disillusioned Blair and Tory voters. Saying—and it's screamingly obvious, isn't it?—"this lot's not delivering, the others can't, we will".'

'And what does this Frean superwoman want you to do?'

'Get the paper to support them. The Ed's a Tory at heart and the whole thing will appeal to his romantic nature.'

'Romantic! Chris Pollock!'

'Jocasta, he's terribly romantic. Not in your women's fiction sense, but David and Goliath, triumph of the underdog, that sort of thing. And our readers are precisely the sorts of people Frean is talking about.'

'Oh, OK. And when and how might it start?'

'They've got to get some funds together and more people on side. There'll be a lot of plotting, which'll be fun. I would say by conference time it'll all be boiling up nicely.'

His large brown eyes were brilliant as he looked at her; she smiled and took a deep breath.

'Nick,' she said.

'Yes?'

'Nick, there's something I really want to discuss with you.'

But he dodged the issue, as he always did, told her he was tired and he just wanted to take her home and curl up with her and think how lucky he was. Feebly, she gave in.

Martha looked out of her office window and saw the first streaks of dawn in the sky. She enjoyed the all-night sessions, found them exciting; and perversely she never felt remotely tired. She seemed to become high on her own nervous energy, only collapsing as she closed her front door on the day and the deal, poured herself a drink, and sank into the hottest bath she could bear—often to fall asleep and wake an hour later. People warned her it was dangerous, but Martha pooh-poohed this. It was what she did, she said, how she ran her life, it suited her, and as in so many other tenets of hers—like only eating once a day, or never taking more than one week's holiday at a time—it had always worked very well. Martha was extremely sure that what she did was right.

Although just recently she'd been having a few doubts . . .

Anyway, she had finished now; she had only to get the document typed, complete with its final changes, ready for sign-off. With the clients coming in and the deal closing at noon, it was important nothing went wrong now. It was one of the biggest acquisitions she had worked on—one financial services company taking over another—but Sayers Wesley, one of the largest, sleekest operations in London, had fought a mighty battle on behalf of their client, and won. And Martha Hartley, at thirty-three, one of the youngest partners, had been in control.

What was more, she had earned a great deal of money for Sayers

Wesley, which would be reflected in her salary in due course. Her
£300,000 salary. Her dream of becoming rich had certainly come true.

Her life was appallingly self-indulgent, and she knew it. Her apartment was dazzling, in one of the most sought-after high-rise buildings
in Docklands, with huge sheet-glass windows and coolly pale wood
floors, furnished from Conran and Purves & Purves; she owned a soft-
top Mercedes SLK, which she used only at weekends; she had a walk-in
wardrobe that was an exercise in fashion name-dropping: Armani,
Gucci, Ralph Lauren, Donna Karan, and a stack of shoes from Tod and
Jimmy Choo and Manolo Blahnik filed in their boxes in the fashionably
approved manner, with Polaroids stuck on the outside for instant recognition; and she worked on average fourteen hours every day, often over
the weekend, and had a very limited social life.

She wasn't lonely exactly, she worked too hard for that, but somewhere within her was a deep dark place, which she tried to deny, which
drew her down into it during sleepless nights. A place filled with fears of
a life that was not merely independent and successful but solitary and
comfortless, where no one would share her triumphs or ease her fail-
ures, where fulfilment could only be measured in material things and
she would look back with remorse on a life of absolute selfishness.

But (she would tell herself in the morning, having escaped from the
dark place), being single perfectly suited her ferocious ambition;
nobody messed up her schedule or interfered with her routine. Her life
was completely under her control.

A weary-looking Asian woman pushing a vacuum cleaner opened the
door to her office.

'Lina, good morning. How are you?'

Martha knew her well; she was always there at six, her weariness
hardly surprising, since this was the first of three jobs.

'I'm sorry, Miss Hartley. Shall I come back later?'

'No, no, you carry on. How are you?'

'Oh, I'm pretty well. A little tired.'

'I'm sure you are, Lina. How are the family?'

'Oh, not too bad. But Jasmin is giving me trouble.'

'Jasmin?' Martha had seen pictures of Jasmin, a beautiful thirteen-
year-old, adored by both her parents.

'Yes. Well, it's the school, really. It's a bad school. Like most schools
these days, seems to me. She was doing so well, in her last school, working so hard, getting such good marks in her SATs.'

'And now?'

'Now she's bored. Not learning anything. She says the teachers are rubbish, can't keep any discipline. And if she tries to work, she gets teased. So

already she's slipping. It's breaking my heart, Miss Hartley, it really is.'

'Lina, that's terrible.' Martha meant it; it was the sort of waste she hated. 'Can't you get her into another school?'

'All the neighbourhood schools are bad. I'm thinking of taking another job, in the evening at the supermarket. So I can pay for her to go to a private school.'

'Lina, you can't. You'll be exhausted.'

Lina's eyes met hers, and she smiled. 'You're a fine one to talk about exhaustion, Miss Hartley. Working all the nights.'

'I know . . . but I don't go home and care for a family.'

'Well, the way I see it, no point caring for them if they're all going to end up on the social. Half the teenagers on the estate are unemployed. No qualifications, nothing. Only way out of it is education. And Jasmin isn't going to get it if she stays where she is. I've got to get her out of it. And if it means me working harder, I'll work harder.'

'Oh, Lina!' God, this made Martha angry. How dare this ghastly system write off children as they did, denying them their most basic right, while swearing via their absurd league tables that standards were rising.

She wondered suddenly, wildly, if she should offer to help pay Jasmin's school fees . . . but what about all the other Jasmins, the other bright, wasted children? She couldn't help them all.

She dismissed, swiftly and ruthlessly, the thought of what she might actually do. Or at least try to do.

She checked her diary, just to make quite sure that there were no outstanding personal matters to attend to. She had sent her sister some flowers: she always remembered her birthday. It was the day they had all met at Heathrow, and set off on their travels. And she had said how determined she was to be successful and rich. She wondered if the other two had done as well as she had. And if she would ever see any of them again. It would certainly be much better not to.

Clio wondered if she was brave enough to tell him what she had done, and to tell him why. He wouldn't be pleased. Not in the least. So . . . oh, Clio, come on, pull yourself together. You may be about to get married, but you're still an individual. Go on, pick up the phone and tell him, or at least tell him you want to talk to him . . .

Her phone rang sharply, made her jump.

'Clio Scott? Hi. Mark Salter here. Just wanted to say how pleased we are that you're joining us. When *are* you actually joining us? After your honeymoon. Good. Look forward to seeing you then. Bye, Clio.'

She'd liked Mark Salter. He was a senior partner in the practice and one of the reasons she'd wanted the job so much. That, and the proximity to home. Or rather what would be home. One of the things she had based her decision on had been that the job was so near Guildford. Jeremy should like that. Surely . . .

'I don't understand.' They were sitting at an outside table in Covent Garden in the early evening sunshine; his face—his slightly severe face—was as much puzzled as angry. If you'd asked for an actor to play a surgeon, Clio often thought, he would have looked like Jeremy, tall, very straight-backed, with brown wavy hair and grey eyes in a perfectly sculpted face. 'I really don't. We agreed—or so I thought—that you'd only work part-time. So that you could support me as much as possible. And get the house done, of course.'

'Yes, I do know, Jeremy.' She waved the hovering waiter away. 'And I know I should have consulted you before I accepted. But, initially, it was a part-time job. But there were two, one full-time. And they just rang up and offered me that, and I had to make the decision. I can't understand why you mind so much.'

'If you really can't understand why I mind, then I would say we're in trouble. Serious trouble.'

Clio had a moment of panic; blind, gut-emptying panic. She picked up her glass of wine and took a large gulp.

'Jeremy! Don't say that. Please.'

'I have said it. And I mean it.'

'Well, it's ridiculous of you.' She had rallied now. 'I'm not going on the streets. I'm going to be a GP. Quite near the house we'll be living in. We need the money, you know we do—'

'Clio, being a GP is a pretty full-time job. And then you'll be on call, often at night, at weekends—'

'You work very full-time,' she said, meeting his eyes stormily. 'What am I supposed to do while you're operating six days a week? Polish the non-existent furniture? I'm a trained doctor, Jeremy. I loved my work in geriatrics at the Royal Bayswater. And now this is a wonderful new opportunity for me. Please be happy for me.'

'The fact that I work so hard is all the more reason for you to be there when I am at home,' he said. 'My work is physically and mentally very hard. I need support, and the absolute certainty that I'm going to get it.'

'Look,' she said, playing for time, knowing that she was—to a degree anyway—in the wrong. 'I'm sorry if . . . if I should have consulted you more. But I got an estimate for the work on the roof today. Ten grand, Jeremy. Just for the roof. I don't think even doing your private list on Saturday mornings is going to make that sort of money, do you? Not at the moment. When you're a senior consultant, of course.'

'And until then I have to do without your support? I see.'

'Oh, Jeremy, stop being so ridiculous.' Clio was losing her temper; that was good, it was the only way she found the courage to face him down. 'You're twisting everything. Of course I support you. My hours will be very prescribed and I won't be travelling for miles to get to work. The money I earn can go on the house, make it all happen sooner.'

'I'm beginning to think we should never have bought that house,' he said, staring moodily into his drink. 'If it's going to be that much of a burden to us.'

'Look,' she said, resting her hand gently on his, 'look, I'm really, really sorry. I never thought it would matter to you so much.' (Liar, Clio, liar; it was an unexpected talent of hers, lying.) 'Let me do the job for six months. If it's still really bothering you after that I'll leave.'

'All right,' he said finally, 'but I don't expect to like the arrangement. Now, can we please order? I'm desperately hungry. I've done three hips and four knees this afternoon. One of them really complicated—'

Clio sat back and tried to concentrate on what he was saying; a couple had settled down at the next table, both obviously backpackers, sun-bleached and skinny . . . just as they had all been. She hadn't been skinny, of course: not at first, anyway. But later . . . She often found herself thinking of the three of them at this point in the year, when London was filled with backpackers, about what the other two might be doing and how well they might get along together now.

'She would have let me go! I know she would. My *real* mother. I just wish she knew how you try and spoil everything for me.'

Helen Tarrant looked at the flushed, furious face, at the hatred in the dark eyes, and felt sick. This was the only thing she found almost unbearable, when Kate used the fact that she wasn't really her mother against her. She knew it was only Kate's age; she had been warned by the people from Adoption Support that there was bound to be trouble sometime and it would probably come when Kate hit adolescence. 'She'll idealise her birth mother, turn her into everything you're not. Just try not to let it get to you.'

Not let it get to her? How could you not, when this was someone you loved so much, wanting to hurt you, turning from you? Someone you'd cared for all her life—unlike her birth mother!—someone you'd nursed through endless childhood ailments, someone you'd comforted, petted, soothed. Someone you'd loved so much . . .

'Don't be silly, Kate,' she said, 'I don't want to spoil everything for you. You know that. I just think you're too young to go to the Clothes Show on your own, that's all.'

'I'm not going on my own,' said Kate, 'I'm going with Sarah. And I *am* going. I'm going up to my room and I don't want any supper. All right?'

'Fine,' said Helen, 'absolutely fine.' Adoption Support would have been proud of her, she thought. It wasn't a lot of comfort.

Later, after supper, Helen heard Kate crying. She knocked on the door. 'Can I come in?'

There was a pause; that was a good sign. Finally: 'Come in.'

She was lying face down, her tangle of blonde hair spread on the pillow. She didn't move.

'Sweetheart, please don't cry. Want a drink? Some cocoa?'

'No, thanks.'

The thanks were a good sign too.

'Want a chat then?'

Another silence; then, 'Don't care, really.'

That meant she did.

Helen sat down on the bed, very carefully. 'I'm sorry, sweetheart. About the Clothes Show. Next year, maybe.'

'Mum, I'm fourteen. Not four. There'll be loads of people there my age.'

'I'm sorry. Look, how would you like it if we went shopping tomorrow? Spent Granny's birthday money?'

'What, and bought some nice white socks or something? No, thanks.'

There was a silence. Then Kate said, 'Mum . . .'

'Yes?'

'I don't really hate you.'

'I know you don't, sweetheart. I didn't think you did.'

'Good. I just feel so . . . so angry sometimes.'

'Most people of your age do,' said Helen, 'it's part of growing up.'

'No. I don't mean that. Of course I get angry with you. You're so'— her lips twitched—'so *annoying*.'

'Thanks.'

'That's OK. But I mean—angry with her. With my . . . my mother. I mean, how could she have done that? How could she? I might have died, I might—'

'Lovey, I'm sure she made sure someone had found you. Before she . . . she went away.'

There was a long silence, then Kate said, 'She must have had her reasons, mustn't she?'

'Of course she must. Very good ones.'

'I mean, it must hurt to have a baby. So, to do that all by yourself, not tell anyone, she must have been very brave.'

'Very brave.'

'I wonder, sometimes, how I'm like her. In what ways. But I don't think

I'm that brave. I mean, I wouldn't have a filling without an injection.'

'Kate, you don't know what you can do till you have to.'

'I s'pose so. And then I think, what else do I know about her? Hardly anything. Except that she was terribly irresponsible. Is that what worries you about me? Does it make you extra fussy? Do you think I'm going to get pregnant? I suppose it does.'

'Kate, of course it doesn't. We would never think that.'

'Well, why are you so old-fashioned and strict then?'

'We just want to take care of you, that's all. It's—'

'I know, I know, it's a wicked world out there, crazed drug dealers and white slave traffickers on every corner. Especially at the Clothes Show.'

'Kate—' But then she saw Kate was half smiling.

'It's all right, Mum. You can't help being senile.'

'No, I can't. Sorry. You all right now?'

'Sort of. Yes. Thanks for coming in.'

Helen had reached the door, when Kate said, 'Mum, what would you think about me trying to find her?'

'Your birth mother?'

'Mmmm . . .'

'Absolutely fine, sweetheart. Of course, if that's what you want.'

'It is. Yeah.'

Thank God for the darkness, Helen thought, closing the door quickly; otherwise Kate would have seen her crying.

Sometimes, she thought, as she drank the sweet black coffee she always turned to in times of crisis, sometimes she wished she'd not told Kate the truth. How could a small person of seven—which was the age Kate had been when she had actually framed the question, 'What happened to my other mummy?'—possibly digest the news that her other mummy, her real mummy, had abandoned her in a cleaning cupboard at Heathrow Airport, leaving her without even a nappy on, wrapped in a blanket, and not so much as a note? Helen had dressed it up, of course, had said she was all tucked up in a blanket, nice and warm and snug, and that her birth mother had made quite, quite sure she had been safely discovered before going away. At the time Kate had appeared to accept it, had listened intently and then skipped off to play in the garden. Later she had come in and said, 'I've decided I probably am a princess.'

'You are *my* princess,' Jim had said, having been warned that the dreaded conversation had finally taken place.

Told that she was special, that she had been chosen by her parents, rather than just been born to them, like her sister Juliet (arriving to her parents' enormous surprise and pleasure just two years after they had adopted Kate), she had for a while been entirely happy about it, but as she grew older and sharper and the truth became balder and uglier, it troubled her more and more.

The coffee on its own wasn't working; Helen poured herself a glass of wine, and hoped that Jim wouldn't come down and accuse her of being an alcoholic like her mother. It wouldn't be a serious accusation and Jilly Bradford, Helen's mother, was very far from being an alcoholic. But she did like her gin and tonic (and indeed her red wine) and Jim, who felt, with some justification, that Jilly thought he wasn't good enough for her daughter, used the fact as a small ongoing revenge.

Her mother had been very supportive as Kate grew increasingly diffi-cult. This mostly consisted of slipping Kate ten-pound notes, taking her on shopping expeditions, 'Of course I know what she'll like, Helen, I'm in the fashion business, aren't I?' and treating her to expensive lunches at smart restaurants. Jim disapproved of the whole relationship, but as Helen pointed out, her mother was a safety valve, someone Kate could talk to if she felt she needed it.

'Why can't she talk to us, for God's sake?'

'Jim, I sometimes despair of you. The whole point is there are things she can't talk to us about. Things she thinks will upset us.'

Jim didn't argue. Helen knew there was another reason he didn't like her mother; she favoured Kate over Juliet. Which was on the face of it illogical, since Juliet was Helen's own child; but she was also Jim's, and had many of Jim's characteristics. She was a very sweet child, and extremely clever and musically gifted, but she was quiet and shy, with none of Kate's quicksilver charm, and she found Jilly rather daunting.

It had been one of the most glorious days in Helen's life—her wedding day and that of Juliet's birth being the others—when Mrs Forster from the adoption agency had telephoned to say that there was a baby who they might like to consider adopting. 'She's a foundling,' Mrs Forster had said, 'so there could be no question of her ever going back to her birth family.'

Helen had actually been reading about the baby in the papers; she had made front-page news, as such babies always did; and there had been photographs of her being held by nurses at the South Middlesex Hospital, her small face almost invisible within the folds of blanket.

'Baby Bianca,' the caption had said. 'Found by a cleaner in a cleaning cupboard at Heathrow Airport, now five days old.' It went on to say that the social services were hoping to contact her mother, who might be in need of medical attention, and appealed for anyone who had noticed anything untoward at Terminal Three at Heathrow Airport, on the night of August 16th, to contact their nearest police station.

Helen had been very nervous, driving to meet Bianca for the first time; what if she didn't feel anything for her? What if the baby started screaming the minute she saw her, sensing her complete inexperience and incompetence? But it was love at first sight; Bianca (shortly to become Kate) opened large blue eyes (shortly to become deep, dark brown) and stared up at her, waving one tiny, frond-like fist, making little pouting shapes with her small mouth, and Helen knew, quite simply, that she wanted to spend the rest of her life with her.

This had not been one of the happiest days of her life though; she poured herself a second glass of wine and tried to face the reality of that small, dependent creature who had become in some strange way as surely her own flesh and blood as her natural daughter, seeking out the woman who had actually given birth to her.

Whoever that woman was, Helen thought, and whatever she was like, she would undoubtedly want to kill her.

Chapter 2

MARTHA RAISED HER LIPS to the silver chalice and took a sip of wine, struggling to concentrate on the moment, on the fact that she was taking the holy sacrament. She never could, of course. Not completely; she had moved so far from her father's church, her parents' faith, she only went to church when she was staying for the weekend in Binsmow. It pleased them, and it charmed the parishioners; the fact that she felt an absolute hypocrite was immaterial.

She stood up now, walked slowly back to her seat, her head carefully bowed, taking in nonetheless the fact that the church was three-quarters empty and apart from a few—a very few—teenagers, she was the only person there who could be called young. How could her father do this week after week, year after year?

'Things are pretty bad around here,' her father said, as they walked home from church.

'In what way?'

'The countryside has been dreadfully hit by the foot-and-mouth business. There's an air of depression over everything.'

'Really?' said Martha. She had read about the foot-and-mouth tragedy, of course, but sheltered as she was in her glass tower in Docklands, it had somehow lacked reality.

'Yes. Poor old Fred Barrett whose family's had a farm just outside Binsmow for five generations has struggled on until now, but this has finished him. He's selling up. Not that anyone will buy the farm. And then I've got God knows how many parishioners waiting to go into hospital. Poor old Mrs Dudley, waiting eighteen months now for a hip replacement, in real pain, and still they tell her another six months.'

'Everything's a mess,' said Martha, thinking of Lina and her daughter Jasmin, 'absolutely everything.'

After lunch her sister called. Could Martha do her a favour?

'My next-door neighbour—she's a widow—needs help. Her son's car's broken down and he needs a lift back up to London. I said I was sure you wouldn't mind taking him.'

Martha felt disproportionately outraged. She did mind: very much. She had been longing for the peaceful drive back to London, with her stereo playing, catching up on phone calls, having the time to think . . . And of course *not* to think. She didn't want some spotty lad sitting beside her for three or four hours, requiring her to make conversation.

'Couldn't he get the train?'

'He could, but he can't afford it. Martha, it's not much to ask, surely. He's quite sweet, I've met him.'

'Yes, but—' Martha stopped.

'Oh, forget it,' said Anne, and her voice was really angry. 'I'll tell him he'll have to hitch a lift. You just get on back to your smart life in London.'

Martha promptly felt terrible. What kind of a cow was she turning into? 'No,' she said quickly, 'all right. But he'll have to fit in with me timewise and I'll drop him at an underground station, all right?'

'You're so extremely kind,' said Anne. 'I'll tell him then. What time exactly would fit in best with your very heavy timetable?'

'I'm leaving at about four,' said Martha, refusing to rise to this.

'Could you make the huge detour to pick him up? It would take at least fifteen minutes.'

'I'll pick him up,' said Martha.

Anne came out of her house as Martha drew up; her sniff as she looked at the Mercedes was almost audible.

'So good of you to do this,' she said. 'He's all ready. We've been chatting, haven't we, Ed?'

'Yes. Hey, cool car. It's very kind of you, Miss—'

'Hartley,' said Martha, finding herself staring at one of the most beautiful young men she had ever seen.

He was quite tall, over six foot, with rather messy short blond hair, and astonishingly deep blue eyes; he was tanned, with a few very carefully scattered freckles on a perfectly straight nose, and his grin, which was wide, revealed absolutely perfect white teeth. He looked like an advertisement for Ralph Lauren. Martha felt less resentful suddenly.

'Shall I put my bags on the back seat?' he said.

'Yes, do,' said Martha. 'Well, Anne, sorry not to have seen more of you. Next time, perhaps.'

'Perhaps,' said Anne. Her tone was still chilly.

'This really is very kind of you,' said Ed again as they pulled down the road. 'I do appreciate it.'

'That's all right,' said Martha. 'What happened to your car?'

'It just died,' he said. 'It was only an old banger.'

'So, what will you do?'

'Goodness knows.' He looked round the car. 'This is really cool. Convertible, yeah?'

'Yes.'

'I don't suppose you use this much in London.'

'Not during the week, no,' said Martha. 'Not much use for a car where I live.'

'Which is?'

'Docklands.'

'Cool.'

'Quite cool, I suppose,' she said, hoping she didn't sound like some pathetic older woman acting young.

'And you're a lawyer?' he said. 'Is that right? Do you get all dressed up in a white wig?'

'No,' she said, smiling. 'I'm not a barrister. I'm a solicitor. I work for a big city firm. Sayers Wesley.'

'Oh, I get you. You work all night, see big deals through, earn a fortune, that sort of thing.'

'That sort of thing.' She glanced at him. 'What do you do?'

'I'm just temping at the moment,' he said, 'doing some IT. It's pretty boring. But I'm going away in a couple of months. It's paying for that.'

'Where are you going?'

'Oh, Thailand, Oz, all that stuff. Did you do that sort of thing?'

'Yes, I did. It was great fun.'

'Yeah, I hope so. I should have done it before uni, really.'

'How old are you, Ed?'

'Twenty-two.'

'And what did you read?' she asked. 'At university?'

'English. At Bristol.'

'Oh, really? That's where I went.'

'Yeah?' He turned to smile at her, an astonishing, beautiful smile, then said, 'I bet you were in Wills Hall.'

'I was,' she said. 'How did you know?'

'All the posh people lived there. It was a public school ghetto.'

'I'm not posh!' she said indignantly, 'and I didn't go to public school. I went to Binsmow Grammar School. When it *was* a grammar school.'

'I went there,' he said, 'but it was a complete dump by then.'

He must be very bright, she thought, to have got into Bristol from a bad comprehensive.

They reached Whitechapel at about eight thirty. 'This'll do fine for me,' he said, 'I can get the tube.'

'OK. I'll just pull over there.'

'It's been really nice,' he said. 'I've enjoyed talking to you and so on.'

'Weren't you expecting to?'

'Well, not really. I thought you'd be . . . it would be—'

'What?' she said, laughing.

'A bit of an ordeal. Actually.'

'Well, I'm glad it wasn't.'

'No, it absolutely wasn't.' He got out, shut the door, then opened it again. He looked at her rather awkwardly. 'I don't suppose,' he said, 'you'd like to come for a drink one night?'

'Well,' said Martha, feeling suddenly very uncool indeed, almost flustered, angry with herself for it, 'well, yes, that would be nice. But I'm a bit hard to get hold of.'

'I'll try to manage it,' he said, and smiled again.

Dreadful sobs came from the room; dreadful sobs telling of dreadful grief. It was the third time Helen had heard them over the past few months. She waited a while then went in to comfort Kate.

The first two had been the result of Kate's so-far fruitless search for her birth mother. She had gone to the hospital, the South Middlesex, to Outpatients, the Maternity Unit and to the Administration Offices. They had all looked at her, she said, as if she was mad.

'I only wanted to know who'd been on the baby unit in 1986. They just said they couldn't help, I'd have to write in, so that my request could be guided through the proper channels. I mean, please!'

'Well,' said Helen carefully, 'why don't you write in?'

'Mum, they're complete morons. And they don't want to help.'

'Did you tell any of them why you wanted to know?'

'Of course not. I'm not going to look like some sad thing searching for her mother. Having everyone sorry for me.'

'Kate, my love,' said Helen, 'I think you're going to have to. Otherwise your reasons could be very dubious indeed. Just think for a minute.'

Kate stared at her; then she said, 'No, Mum, I can't. I'm not going to do that. I'll do this in my own way. I know what I'm doing.'

She did nothing for soome weeks, then she had gone to Heathrow and made for the information desk; how could she make contact with one of the cleaners?

'Do you have a name?' said the overdone blonde.

'No.'

She sighed. 'Well then, dear, how can we help you?'

'You must have a list of people.'

'Even if we did, if you don't have a name, what good would a list do? Is this a complaint or something?'

'No,' said Kate, 'no, it's not.'

'So what is it?'

'I . . . I can't tell you.'

'In that case,' the woman said, 'I really don't think I can help. Now, if you'll excuse me, there are people waiting. Yes, sir . . .'

Kate caught the tube back to Ealing and spent the afternoon in her room. That day she wouldn't even allow Helen in.

Clio loved being a GP. Absolutely loved it. Yes, it was stressful, but there was the great joy of getting to know her patients, being involved in their lives. What she had never realised before, when working in hospital clinics, was the extent to which patients relied on their GP. Especially the old people. She had one couple, the Morrises, whom she was particularly fond of; both in their late eighties, they were still managing to look after themselves at home together, an immaculately clean, ordered home. But they needed to take tablets and the dosage was quite complicated. If they didn't take their tablets, they became confused, and went on a hideously swift downward spiral.

Twice now she had received calls from social services, who reported uneaten meals on wheels. She had gone round to find Mrs Morris in her nightdress, sitting in the garden, and her husband wandering about the house trying to find the kettle. Clio had located it in the washing machine. 'Another day and God knows what would have happened to them,' she said to Mark Salter, 'but I got their medication into them, persuaded Dorothy back into the house, and called back later. They were much more cheerful, tucking into their tea, watching *Home and Away*. Anyway, I remembered those samples of tablet dispensers a rep left and filled two of them with the right dosage for a week. I'll just keep doing that.'

'You're very good, Clio,' said Mark. 'That really is over and above the call of duty.'

'Mark, think of the alternative. They'd be in a home inside a month.'

'It's ridiculous,' he said wearily. 'The carer who goes in the morning to help them get dressed could perfectly well give them the tablets, but she's not allowed to. Bloody regulations.'

'I know,' said Clio soothingly. 'But there's nothing we can do about it, Mark. And the Morrises are on my way in. It's not a problem.'

But Jeremy was a problem. It wasn't so much that he constantly, albeit gently, belittled her work, it was that he assumed it could be pushed aside on demand if he had an early night and she was still working. He made an appalling fuss when she had to do her weekends on call (only one in five); and he had a complete lack of interest in her patients and their problems, while expecting her to show an immense interest in his.

There was another problem too: one which only she knew about and which was increasing by the day. Or rather the month.

She was just packing up her things after morning surgery when Margaret the receptionist rang through. 'Sorry, Clio, but I've got Jilly Bradford on the phone. She says she wants a word. Is that all right?'

'Of course.'

She rather liked the glamorous Mrs Bradford, with her sleek blonde hair and her stylish clothes; she had come in a few weeks earlier to ask her for some sleeping pills.

'Now, please don't tell me I can manage with a hot drink and some gentle exercise before bed because I can't.'

'I should,' Clio had said, 'and it would be better for you, but we'll take it as read, shall we?'

'Do let's,' said Jilly Bradford, smiling at her.

Clio had scribbled the prescription and then said impulsively, 'I do love your jacket.'

'Oh, how kind. Well it came from the shop where I work. Caroline B in the High Street. Do you know it? The jacket's MaxMara, we carry a lot of his stuff. Although this is last season's of course.'

'It's just that I love dogtooth,' said Clio, 'and I've been looking for something to wear to a conference in October.'

'Well, when the next collection comes in, I'll give you a call.'

'That would be wonderful, thank you,' Clio had said, and promptly forgot about it.

'Mrs Bradford?' she said now. 'What can I do for you?'

'I'm just calling as promised,' Jilly Bradford's rather dated upper-crust voice came down the phone, 'to tell you the new MaxMara collection has arrived. With some very nice jackets. Would you like me to put a couple by for you? I would imagine you're a ten.'

'I wish I was,' said Clio. 'I'm a good twelve.'

'Well, his sizes are on the generous side. I'm sure you'd be a ten. When would you like to come?'

'How about this afternoon?'

Clio arrived at the shop at about two.

Jilly smiled at her and said how delighted she was to see her. 'Now, I've got your jackets here, and some tops I thought you might like. Shall I put you in one of the changing rooms and you can play around? And would you like a coffee?'

'That would be lovely, yes. Thank you.'

The jackets were both extremely nice; after a very brief struggle, she said she would take them both. 'And that black top is lovely too.'

'Right. Well, I've got your number, and in future I'll call you whenever I get anything in I think would be you. If that's all right, of course.'

'Yes, fine,' said Clio. 'I usually never think about clothes—'

The door burst open and a girl burst in: a rather beautiful young girl, with a mass of wild fair hair, large dark eyes and extraordinarily long legs in what were clearly carefully torn and faded jeans.

'Hi, Granny. Oh, sorry!' she said, seeing Clio standing by the till.

'It's all right, darling. Dr Scott, this is my granddaughter, Kate Tarrant. Kate, this is Dr Scott.'

'Hi!' said the girl. She looked at Clio, smiled briefly, then disappeared into the back of the shop.

'Kate comes to spend the weekend with me sometimes,' said Jilly, giving Clio her credit card back. 'We get on rather well.'

'Gran . . .' The girl had appeared again; she flashed another brief, brilliant smile at Clio. 'I think I'll go and get some sandwiches. I'm starving. And you haven't got any Coke in the fridge.'

'Sorry, darling. Yes, you go and get me some as well. Sandwiches, not Coke. Here's some money.'

'Thanks.' She was gone.

'What a pretty girl,' said Clio. 'She looks like you.'

'How charming of you to say so,' said Jilly. 'But as a matter of fact—'

The door pinged: another customer. Clio smiled and picked up her bags. 'I'll leave you in peace. Thank you again.'

Outside in the street she stood for a moment, looking up and down the street for the girl. There had been something about her. Something slightly . . . well, slightly familiar. She couldn't imagine what.

People often asked Martha if there had been one single thing that had done it; persuaded her to change her entire life, risk everything she had worked so hard for, and yes, she would say, there had; it had been walking into the mixed-sex ward of St Philip's Hospital where Lina lay, dying quietly and uncomplainingly of inoperable cancer of the liver, deeply distressed because she had wet her bed (having requested a bedpan literally hours earlier) and slowly just fading away, against a background of what could only be described as squalor.

Martha had done her best, of course; she had found a nurse and demanded that the bed be changed, and when the nurse had said she had no time, had walked into the small room marked 'supplies' and found some clean sheets, helped Lina into a chair and started changing the bed herself. Staff Nurse had then been summoned and she said what did Martha think she was doing? Martha told her and added, perfectly politely, that she would have thought they would be grateful for some help; adding (with truth) that she was prepared to clean the lavatory as well, that it was truly disgusting and must be spreading infection.

At which point the woman had sighed and said she knew that, and that she had been trying to find the time all day to do it.

'Surely,' Martha said, 'surely the cleaners should be doing it, not you?'

'Oh, they're not allowed by their union to touch soiled dressings or human waste. There are special people to do that, but they haven't come today yet. I—' Then someone called from across the ward to say that a patient's drip had come out, and the nurse had to leave; Martha sat stroking Lina's hand gently.

That had been June 2001; in August, Lina's friend told her, mopping her streaming eyes, that Lina had died.

'They said it was the cancer, Miss Hartley,' she said, dusting Martha's desk, 'but I think it was that her heart just broke.'

And Martha, crying too, remembering Lina's sweet, gentle face and her heroic struggle to care for her family, wondered if there was anything at all she could do to make things better for all the other people who were being failed by a country that seemed to have lost its way.

She was upset all day, performing badly in meetings, and, later that afternoon, when her friend Richard Ashcombe called her to cancel a visit to the cinema, even that seemed a major blow. 'I'm sorry, Martha; I'd completely forgotten I'm supposed to be having supper with my cousin. I can't let him down.'

'Of course you can't.' Absurdly, she could hear her own voice shaky, tearful once again at this latest blow.

'I'm sorry. But I really do have to go. Of course,' he said slowly, and she could almost hear him thinking, 'of course you could come too. We don't have all that much in common, but I know he'd like you. He's a politician, so you can share all your thoughts with him.'

'What thoughts?'

'Oh, you know, country going to the dogs, everybody being let down.'

'Do I go on about it that much?'

'Well, quite a lot. Go on, Martha, you'd be doing me a favour.'

It was an intriguing thought. 'If you really don't think he'd mind?'

'Of course he wouldn't mind. He'd love it. I'm meeting him at the House of Commons. We're having a drink there.'

'What's your cousin's name?'

'Marcus Denning.'

'The arts minister?' said Martha. She was familiar with the name.

'Shadow *junior* arts minister . . . I'll call you when I'm leaving.'

They were late arriving at the House of Commons; the traffic was so bad they paid the taxi off and walked the last quarter of a mile. As they put their coats and briefcases on the security conveyor belt she spotted Denning, clearly impatient, looking at his watch. Martha, extremely embarrassed, reached Denning before Richard, who had been asked to unpack the entire contents of his briefcase.

'I'm so sorry to do this to you,' she said, 'first crashing your evening and then being late. Richard did warn you, didn't he?' she added, seeing his bewildered expression. 'That he was going to bring me along?'

'He didn't, no. But what a pleasant surprise.' He held out his hand. 'And you are?'

'Martha Hartley. Richard and I work together.'

'Ah. Another lawyer?'

'Yes, there are a lot of us, I'm afraid.'

'Well, I'm sure we need you. Ah, Richard, good to see you. They're not carting you off to the Tower then? No lethal weapons in your briefcase?' He grinned at Richard and Martha liked him.

'Not this time. Sorry to keep you waiting.'

'That's perfectly all right. Shall we go through? I thought we'd go to the Pugin Room. The Strangers' Bar is packed. Lot of excitement over the Lords Reform.'

They turned left and walked into a room that was so dazzling, Martha literally blinked. With its glorious view of the river, the walls and ceiling covered in gilt Pugin wallpaper, and a vast chandelier hovering over the centre, it was rather like the reception area of an exceptionally grand hotel, having chairs and sofas arranged in groups, and what looked like elderly retainers carrying drinks on silver trays. Marcus steered them towards a table; someone stood up.

'Marcus, hello. What did you think about all that?'

'Absolute drivel, Hugh. Are we really expected to appreciate it?'

'I think we are. Can I get you a drink?'

'No, no, we're not staying long. I'm buying these young people dinner.' He sat down, waved across the room at someone else. 'Evening! Nice to see you.'

'This is like going for a walk round my parents' village,' said Martha, laughing.

'Oh, this whole place is a village. Something like two thousand people work here. It has everything, a florist, postboxes, a ladies' hairdresser. And you can get a drink here twenty-four hours a day, if you know where to look. That's not too much like a village, I suppose. Or maybe it is. And it runs on gossip. What would you like?'

'White wine spritzer, please.' She felt oddly at home and smiled. 'I like it here. I really do!'

They ate at Patrick's, a below-ground restaurant just along the Embankment, actually called Pomegranates. 'We all like it here,' said Marcus, as they settled at their table. 'It's fairly near the House and its other main benefit to political life is that it's just next to Dolphin Square. An awful lot of MPs live there. Used to be that mistresses were kept there, but we all have to be squeaky clean these days.'

'Hardly squeaky,' said Richard. 'A few names like Hinduja and Ecclestone come to mind.'

'Oh, I know, I know. Different sorts of scandals, that's all. A lot less attractive, I have to say. Anyway, it's a pretty depressing business to be in at the moment. Turnout at the last election was the lowest yet.'

'But you can't be surprised,' said Martha. 'Everyone feels let down, disillusioned. It's not just your party, of course, it's all of them. And at the moment there's no opposition to speak of. So of course people won't vote. Why should they?'

'You're right. And brilliant political talents are being dreadfully wasted. It really interests you, does it?'

'Oh, yes.'

'Well, you should do something—hello, Janet. Good to see you. Can I introduce my cousin Richard Ashcombe, and his friend, Martha Hartley?'

Martha looked up at Janet Frean and, as always when confronted by an absolutely familiar face belonging to a complete stranger, felt as if she must know her. It was a nice face, not beautiful by any means, but attractive, with strong features; her hair, which was auburn, was shaped into a bob. She smiled at Martha.

'Martha has some very interesting views,' said Marcus, 'you should hear them.'

'I'd love to, but I can't at the moment. I'm waiting for—ah, here he is. Evening, Nick. You know Marcus Denning, of course.'

'Sure. Evening, Marcus.' An extremely tall, rather untidy-looking young man paused by their table, smiled rather vaguely at Martha and Richard, then said, 'Janet, I hate to sound rude, but I've only got half an hour. Then I must be back in the House. Mr Mandelson is giving me a fragment of his precious time. Is Chad here?'

'No, but he will be in five minutes. He just called me. Will you excuse us?' she said to Marcus. 'And I'd love to hear your views sometime, Miss Hartley. I really would.'

Martha smiled at her, embarrassed. 'You really don't have to be polite. I'm sure my views are absolutely bog-standard.'

'I doubt it,' Janet Frean said, smiling at her. 'You don't look as if anything about you is bog-standard. What do you do?'

'She's a lawyer,' said Marcus, 'partner at Sayers Wesley. Very highpowered. Anyway, enjoy your meal.'

'Thanks. Oh, here's Chad now. Nick, come on, let's go to our table.'

'I met him once,' said Martha, staring at Chad Lawrence. 'I'm sure he wouldn't remember me, though.'

'I'm quite sure he would. Want to go over? I'll reintroduce you.'

'No, no,' said Martha, 'he looks busy. Who was the Nick person?'

'Nick Marshall. Very, very brilliant young man. Political editor of the *Sketch*. Now, are we ready to order?'

Just as (or so some say) the real action in the House of Commons is not found in the debating chamber but in the committee rooms, corridors and tearooms, the real business at the party political conferences is conducted not in the conference hall and on the platform but in the bars or at the myriad fringe meetings. Rather thinly disguised as discussion groups, sponsored by high-profile but not disinterested associations, the movers and shakers of the parties and those keen to lobby them move from hotel to hotel, hall to hall, airing and sharing their views with both the press and any interested members of the constituency parties.

That autumn at the Tory party conference in Bournemouth, where newly elected leader Iain Duncan Smith made his first lacklustre speech to the party faithful, a very large and glitzy fringe meeting had been held. On the penultimate evening, funded by Gideon Keeble, the billionaire retailer, it had addressed the question of the nanny state and its sinister and growing power over the family. Speakers had included the much-televised Lord Collins, professor in child psychiatry at Cambridge; TV agony aunt Victoria Raynsford; and Janet Frean, who, as well as being a prominent Tory MP, had the relevant distinction of having five children. Chad Lawrence had also attended and spoken passionately at the debate that followed. The meeting had been packed and it had scooped up most of the next day's headlines.

'And people have been congratulating Janet ever since,' Nick had said to Jocasta over a coffee in the conference hall. 'It would appear she has Keeble on side. Influential man, is our Gideon. Exactly what's needed.'

'For the new party?'

'Indeed.'

'It's going to happen, is it?'

'Think so. It's all looking very exciting.'

Jocasta, who was nursing a hangover, found it hard to care. 'I would have thought they'd have a name by now.'

'Well, they haven't.' Nick grinned at her. 'I've got to go. What are you going to do?'

'I think I'll go for a walk. Get some air.' She kissed Nick rather feebly goodbye and wandered out into the lobby.

God, she felt terrible; the *Sketch* had given a party the night before and she'd got incredibly drunk and ended up dancing simultaneously with a reporter from the *Sun* and a cameraman from Channel 4. She'd hoped Nick might see her and be jealous, but every time she looked for him he was huddled with a lot of dreary-looking men. Well, they looked dreary from where she was; when she'd finally fallen—or rather tripped—over, one of them had come over with Nick to help her up and sit her down at the table. He had been, she seemed to remember, quite tasty, in a middle-aged sort of way; he asked her if she was all right and then smiled at her and moved away to another group. God, how embarrassing. She really must stop drinking so much. She—

'Feeling better today?'

The voice—and the smile—swam rather hazily into her consciousness. It was Chad Lawrence.

'Yes. Yes, thank you. I'm fine,' she said briskly.

'Good. That was a nasty purler you took. I was afraid you might be a bit bruised this morning.'

She looked at him helplessly. 'Was it you who . . . who helped me up?'

'No, that was Gideon Keeble.'

'What, as in Gideon Keeble, the Billionaire Retailing Tycoon?'

'Absolutely.'

'Oh dear.'

'You thanked him very charmingly. And kissed him tenderly as well.'

'God!' This was getting worse. 'It was just . . . just my heels, they were so high.'

'Of course. Very pretty though. The shoes, I mean. Did you enjoy the party? Otherwise, I mean?'

'Yes, I did. Although . . .' Her voice tailed off.

Across the lobby was the horribly familiar figure of Gideon Keeble followed by a hotel lackey pushing a luggage trolley: at least four suitcases, a Gladstone bag, a flight bag and a suit carrier, all (apart from the Gladstone which was old and leathery) predictably Louis Vuitton. How absurd! Did anyone need that much luggage for four days?

She was about to make a run for it, when Chad hailed him.

'Gideon, hello! You off? I was hoping I'd catch you. You'll remember our young friend of last night. She was just telling me how grateful she was for your help.'

Jocasta looked distractedly up at Gideon Keeble. How could she possibly not have recognised him last night? God, she must have been drunk. He was very tall, about six foot five, and powerfully built. He was tanned and looked enormously well, as if he spent a lot of time outdoors, and he had an energy that was almost infectious; he wasn't exactly good-looking, but he had very large and brilliant blue eyes, and his dark curly hair was just flecked with grey.

'Yes. Yes, I was,' she said helplessly, 'very grateful. Thank you.'

'It was entirely my pleasure.' He had an accent just tinged with Irish and he smiled at her, a brilliant, warm smile.

'Where on earth are you going with all that luggage, Gideon, you old poseur?' asked Chad.

'To the States for a week or two. I'll call you when I get back.'

'Fine. Look forward to it. Bye.'

'Goodbye. And goodbye to you, Jocasta. May I say I enjoy your articles very much.'

'You've read them?'

'Of course. I regard it as my business to read everything I can. I especially enjoyed your piece last week about that girl in the Bournemouth hotel. The one who said the only people who'd ever properly thanked her for what she'd done for them, in five years of conferences, had been Maggie and the Prescotts.'

'Thank you,' she said, smiling at him. She got a warmth and excitement that was almost sexual when people admired her work. 'From you that's really praise.'

'Deserved. You're a clever girl,' he added. 'And what a lucky man Nicholas is. I was telling him only last night, he should make an honest woman of you.'

The blue eyes sparkled at her. He was flirting with her. How morale boosting was that? And he really was *very* attractive.

'I think he prefers me dishonest,' she said, laughing.

'Then he's a fool. Girls like you don't come along too often. With both brains and beauty. Oh, I can see my driver over there, looking extremely constipated. I think I'd better go. Farewell to you both.'

'He's very nice,' said Jocasta looking after him.

'Oh, don't be deceived,' said Chad Lawrence. 'That charm is hugely dangerous. And his temper is legendary.'

Jocasta was miserable and irritable when they finally got back to London: Nick had spent the entire journey in a huddle with a couple of other *Sketch* writers. She had thought she would be able to sleep her hangover off, but she couldn't; she just sat there with her eyes closed.

'Well,' Nick said as they got off the train, 'it seems they've made their minds up. Full steam ahead.'

'Ahead where?' she said confusedly.

'The new party. They've got some funding now. Keeble has pledged a million or two and—'

'Nick, this is fascinating, but I'm terribly tired. I think I'll just go straight home to Clapham,' she said, expecting him to argue, or at least to say he would come with her; but he gave her a swift kiss on her cheek.

'OK, sweetie, you do look done for. Call me tomorrow.'

Jocasta stared at him. 'Nick! I can't believe you just said that.'

'Said what?' He looked at her. 'Sorry, you've lost me. I thought you said you wanted to go back to Clapham.'

'I did. Only I thought you might want to come with me.'

'Jocasta, what's this all about?'

'Me, Nick. That's what it's about.' She felt like crying, or hitting him.

'I can see that. Do I come into it at all?'

'That's up to you. Look, would you like to tell me where you think we're going?'

'Well, forwards, I thought.'

'And together?'

'Obviously.'

'So . . . what exactly does that mean?'

'It means I love you.'

'You do?'

'Jocasta, you know I do.'

'I don't,' she said, 'actually. I know you enjoy my company, I know you like having me around, I think I know you like sleeping with me. But I certainly don't know you love me. Nick, we've been together for about two and a half years and you still treat me like some quite new girlfriend. I want you to say—' She stopped.

'Say what?'

'You're enjoying this, aren't you?' she said, her voice rising with her misery. 'Enjoying making me say things that . . . that—'

'Jocasta,' he said and his voice was gentle suddenly, 'I'm not enjoying it at all. It's making me feel very miserable seeing you so unhappy. But if you want me down on one knee, asking you to become Mrs Marshall, I really can't do that. Not yet. I just don't feel ready for it.'

'But, Nick, you're thirty-five. When are you going to feel ready for it?'

'I don't know,' he said. 'The idea simply fills me with terror. I don't feel settled enough, I don't feel well off enough, I don't feel—'

'Grown-up enough?' she said, her voice heavy with irony.

'Yes. Yes, that's about it. Actually. I don't. I'm sorry.'

Jocasta suddenly felt very tired. They were no further along than the last time they had had this conversation.

'Jocasta,' he said gently. He put his hand on her arm. 'Jocasta, I'm sorry that I'm an immature commitment-phobe. But I am maturing. There has to be hope. And meanwhile, why can't we go on as we are? Or is there someone else? Is that what you're trying to tell me?'

'Of course not,' she said. 'I wish there was.' She managed a half-smile.

'Well, I don't. And there's certainly no one else for me. Never could be. Not after you.' He reached out tentatively, stroked her cheek. 'Please, Jocasta, I do love you. I'm sorry if I don't make it plain enough. Now— shall we go back to Clapham, lie down and recover?'

But all through the sex which followed, lovely and healing as it was, she felt still wary, still hurt; and as she lay beside him, his hand tangling in her hair, his eyes smiling into hers, she knew that however much he said he loved her, it was not enough.

Chapter 3

CLIO'S PROBLEMS had all begun—rather absurdly—with the Morrises. They had been found in the middle of the town, wearing their nightclothes. Mrs Morris had failed to take her pills, woke up hungry, walked down to Waitrose and was found tucking sweets and crisps into her dressing-gown pocket; Mr Morris had, meanwhile, gone out to look for her, also in his dressing gown, and was apprehended, as the police called it, driving in the wrong direction down a one-way street, frantic with worry. The social services had been called and the pronouncement had been made that the Morrises were not coping and would have to go into a home.

'But they can't,' Clio said to Mark Salter, almost in tears. 'They're fine if they take their pills. I should have popped in every day.'

'Clio, stop it,' said Mark. 'The Morrises are not your personal responsibility. I can't think of anyone who'd have done what you have.'

'It's not enough though, is it?' said Clio. 'The poor old souls are going to end up in some hideous place, removed from everything familiar, and they'll absolutely gallop downhill.'

'Dear Clio, calm down. You don't know that.'

'I know it,' said Clio, 'and I'm very upset. This whole system stinks. Where are they?'

'At home. The daughter's with them, apparently.'

'Better not visit, then. I'd want to ram her mother's pills down her throat.'

'Clio, Clio.' He twinkled at her. 'That's not a nice thing to say.'

'She's not a nice woman.' The Morrises' only daughter lived forty miles away, and couldn't, or wouldn't help.

It was practice conference day, when they all met in the lunch hour to discuss patients and any problems, and it was a rather depressing meeting that day. Mark had a case even more heartbreaking than the Morrises, a young woman in her thirties with severe cerebral palsy. Her parents were elderly and could cope with her no longer; she had to be moved into a home, and the only suitable one locally was full of old people.

'She'll just sit there, rotting. With carers, the parents might have managed. But—'

They all knew about the 'but'. The bureaucracy that surrounded the carers was appalling: police vetting, a mass of paperwork, time pressures—few people were prepared to do it for £4.50 an hour.

At four o'clock, just as she was settling down to some paperwork, Jeremy phoned.

'Clio, I'm sorry. I'm going to be very late. Simmonds wants to have a meeting with me and suggested we have a meal afterwards. No idea when I'll be back. Don't wait up for me.'

Angry, useless thoughts shot into her head: why was he allowed to work late, without warning, when she was not?

Margaret came in. 'I've put all the stuff about the Morrises in this file, as you asked me. You look all-in, Clio.'

'I feel it.'

'I'm off to the pictures tonight with a couple of girlfriends. Any chance of your coming? It'd cheer you up.'

In a flurry of what she knew was rather short-lived courage, she said, 'I'd love to. Jeremy's out, so—'

'So . . . good,' said Margaret.

They saw a wonderfully distracting and amusing film, and then went for a curry. It was really fun. Clio felt much better about everything. Even Jeremy. She ought to do this more, fuss over him and his attitude to her less. He meant no harm, he was just a bit old-fashioned. She just had to keep a sense of proportion, that was all. She'd just have to be a bit firmer with him.

As she turned into the drive, she tensed. Jeremy's Audi was there and the house was a blaze of light. He always did that if she was home after him, went roaring round the house looking in every room, even the attic bedrooms, just to make the point.

She swallowed hard, went in.

'Hi.'

He appeared from the kitchen, scowling. 'Where the hell have you been?'

'I've been . . . well, I've been at the cinema.'

'The cinema?'

'Yes. Why shouldn't I?' She faced him, angry suddenly. 'You were out with your cronies. Anyway, why are you home so early?'

'Simmonds cancelled dinner. I foolishly thought you'd be pleased to see me, that we could have a nice evening together. But, as usual, you weren't here.'

Something snapped in Clio. 'Just stop it, Jeremy! Stop it. I'm not here just to run the house, and do what you tell me. You constantly diminish my job, you have no real interest in what I do, what I'm about.'

He was silent for a moment, then he said, 'Clio, I've had enough of this, quite enough. I want you to stop working.'

'Jeremy—'

'No, Clio, I mean it. I want you to give up your job. You say we need the money, but it seems to bring in precious little to me, once you've bought expensive clothes that you tell me you need. And I shall be getting more from my private work. So, tell Salter tomorrow, please.'

Clio fought to stay calm. 'Jeremy, please! You're talking nonsense. And besides, what on earth would I do all day, it's not as if—'

She stopped. She had walked into a trap. He slammed it shut; she felt the steel bite into her as harshly as if it was physical.

'As if what? As if you had a baby? I was coming to that, Clio. I think the time has come. You're not getting any younger, you're thirty-five next birthday. You of all people should know the risks involved in leaving it too late. And I would like to have a child well before I'm forty. Which doesn't leave much time.'

'But, Jeremy—'

'Yes? What are you about to tell me? That you don't want one?'

'No,' she said quietly, 'no, I do. I'd love to have a child. But—'

'But what? Is there something you haven't told me, Clio?'

'No. No, of course not.'

But there was. And he was going to have to know sooner or later. It was incredibly wrong of her not to have told him before. She stood there, staring at him, willing up the courage to say it; and failed totally.

'I agree,' she said, quietly. 'Yes. Yes, we should. Let's . . . let's try to have a baby. Before it's too late.'

What was she doing, even thinking about it? Was she completely mad? How had this managed to sweep her along on a huge, breaking wave, which had left her absolutely terrified . . . and yet wildly excited?

In reality, of course, Martha knew very well. It was a congruence of everything that mattered to her: her own ambition; an infinitesimal but dangerous boredom with the law; a sense of emptiness in her personal life; and the sheer irresistible force of four very powerful people all telling her they needed her.

It had begun . . . well, when and where had it actually begun? In that hospital ward with poor Lina dying? In the House of Commons that night, when she had found the atmosphere so beguiling? Or when Paul Quenell the senior partner had asked if she would like to become part of his team working on a new client of his, the Centre Forward Party—'It's a new political party, might interest you, breakaway from the Right—'

'Ah,' she had said, 'Chad Lawrence, Janet Frean, that lot,' and he had been so impressed by her knowledge of them that it had given her an almost physical excitement to be so carelessly close to the corridors of power. That had been a very big factor.

She had gone to the House of Commons several times to meet them, had grown familiar with its complex geography, had listened to debates from the public gallery, had slowly begun to understand how it worked. She had got to know Chad and Janet rather well, even Jack Kirkland a little. They were so hard to resist, these people, possessed of a quality she could only rather feebly call charisma, which made you want to impress and please them. And then when you did, you felt absolutely fantastic, clever and starry and—God, it was all so schoolgirly!

They had, from time to time, suggested she thought about going into it at the sharp end herself. 'You're a natural, I'd say,' said Chad to her one evening. 'You'd love it, I know you would.'

'Don't be ridiculous,' she had said. 'I don't know anything about it.'

'Rubbish. It's not rocket science. Common sense and energy are the main ingredients. And being moderately articulate, I suppose. All of which you are. You should think about it.'

And, 'You really might like to think about joining us, Martha,' Jack Kirkland had said another time, his burning dark eyes on hers. 'You'd be very good. We need new candidates desperately. Find yourself a constituency and we'll back you.'

She had said, laughing, that she hardly had time to find her own office, never mind a parliamentary constituency.

'No, no, you are not to make a joke of it. I'm entirely serious.'

How could you not respond to that?

She was sitting at her desk one morning in late January, when her phone rang. 'Martha Hartley.'

'Hi,' said a voice, 'this is Ed Forrest. I don't suppose you remember me. You gave me a lift up to London, one night last year.'

She did remember, of course: beautiful, charming Ed.

'Ed,' she said, 'how lovely to hear from you. I thought you were in Thailand or something.'

'I was. But I'm back now. And I thought I should call you. Fix a date. I said I'd buy you a drink. I felt bad, never doing it, but I kind of ran out of time. Sorry.'

'Ed, it's quite all right. I haven't been harbouring a grudge against you.'

'I didn't think you had,' he said. 'You don't seem that sort of person. And anyway, I'd really like to see you again.'

'Well, that's a lovely idea,' she said, hesitating. But—what was the harm? What on earth was the harm? 'It would be nice,' she said. 'Only it will have to be . . . let's see . . . the end of the week. Like Friday.'

'Friday'd be cool,' he said. 'Where should we go, do you think? Smiths? Or do you go there all the time?'

'Why should I?'

'I'm told lots of you City types do.'

'Well, this one doesn't. Anyway, I like it there.'

Now, how stupid was that, she thought, putting the phone down. When she could hardly find the time even to breathe?

He was sitting at a table just inside the door, in the dim light and raucous noise of Smiths, and she felt a shock of pleasure just looking at him; she had forgotten how absurdly beautiful he was. The smile, the wonderful, heart-lurching smile, was as she remembered, and the intensely blue eyes, and ridiculously long blond eyelashes.

He stood up, came forward to greet her.

'Hi. You look great.'

'Thanks.'

She wished she had worn something less severe than her black suit—

although the white Donna Karan top she had changed into was quite sexy. 'Sorry I'm late,' she said, feeling suddenly foolish.

'That's OK. I thought you probably would be late, doing lots of high-powered things.'

'Well, I wasn't,' she said and laughed. 'I was waiting for a cab and discovering my phone was very low. Which is why I didn't call you.'

'It's cool. It's good to see you. What do you want to drink?'

'Oh . . .' She hesitated. 'White wine?'

'What do you like? Chardy?'

'Um . . . yes, that'd be nice.' Actually, she hated Chardonnay.

He loped off and came back with two glasses and a bottle of Sauvignon.

'What happened to the Chardonnay?'

'I could tell you didn't like it. Am I right?'

'Absolutely right,' she said.

She felt suddenly almost scared. How on earth did he read her so well? Already?

Three-quarters of an hour later the bottle was empty, and to her infinite surprise she had told Ed about what he called 'your life-changing changes'. His response had been predictably low-key and approving— and she heard herself agreeing, as the noise and smoke level in Smiths rose, to have a meal with him.

'But I mustn't be long,' she said. 'I've got a lot of work to do.'

'What, tonight? Why?'

'Well—because it's got to be done. Sorry, Ed. I really do have to be home by around ten.'

'But you must take time to eat,' he said. 'If you don't, you'll get ill and you won't be able to work. Anyway, we've still got lots to cover.'

'I know,' she said, suddenly remorseful that they had hardly discussed him, apart from his travelling experiences. 'I want to know about your plans.'

'Well, I'll tell you while we eat.'

He had been for several interviews, since he got back: 'And today, just today I got a second interview somewhere, and I think I got the job.'

'Ed, that's great! Where?'

'With an independent television company; I want to be a researcher. And funnily enough,' he said, nibbling on a rice cracker, 'the first programme I'd be working on is about politics. So knowing a politician myself would be a big help.'

'Ed,' she said laughing, 'no way am I a politician.'

'No, but I bet you will be,' he said. 'More wine?'

It was almost midnight when they left the restaurant and Martha found herself feeling a sudden lick of desire, brief but dangerously strong, and it must have showed because, suddenly, Ed smiled and said, 'Come on. I'll take you home.'

They sat in the back of a black cab, and all the way to Docklands he kissed her, slowly, gently, at first, then harder, with a skill that she would not have expected, and she felt herself whirling into a confusion of hunger and pleasure and fear and a pure, flying excitement. And when the cab finally stopped, she wanted to ask him into her flat more than anything, but he said, 'I'll call you tomorrow. OK?' and she nodded, feebly, and said nothing.

As he paid off the cab, he turned to her and smiled, his beautiful, heart-wrenching smile, and said, 'You're totally gorgeous, Martha. Totally. Bye now.'

And so it began: she felt sometimes, not of her own volition, as if he had worked some sleight of hand while she wasn't looking. It was so ridiculous, such a totally unsuitable liaison, between this beautiful man, little more than a boy, and herself, a lot more than a girl; she didn't have time and she didn't want to get involved. But she went on and on wanting to see him. And seeing him. It was just that he made her feel so happy.

She felt uncertain a lot of the time with him. It was part of his charm. She was used to being absolutely certain; of who she was, what she wanted, where she was going. Ed questioned all of it.

'Why?' he would say. 'Why work on a Sunday, for God's sake?'

'Because the client wants it first thing.'

'And he'll leave, will he, if he gets it second thing?'

'No, of course not.'

'Well, then. Don't go to work. Come out with me instead.'

Or, 'Why? Why don't you eat more?'

'Because I don't want to get fat.'

'Martha, you're so not fat. So not anywhere near it. Anyway, would you die, or something, if you went up a size?'

'No, of course not.'

'Well, then. Have some frites. They're really good.' That had been the night she had first gone to bed with him; determined to resist, she had allowed him to argue himself into her bed.

'I just don't think it's a good idea.'

'Why not?'

'Because . . . well, because this isn't a very sensible relationship.'

'Relationships shouldn't be sensible. They should be good. Anyway, why isn't it sensible?'

'Well . . . because . . . oh, Ed, you know. You're twenty-three, I'm—'

'You're beautiful and interesting and I want to have sex with you. What's me being twenty-three got to do with it?'

'I . . . don't know.'

'Well, then. Let's go.'

As she lay in bed and watched him undressing, looked at his beautiful body, she felt a stab of terror. Suppose she was a disappointment?

But, 'You are so beautiful,' he said, sliding in beside her, pulling back the cover, studying her, 'you are just so, so beautiful . . .'

And gently, slowly, very tenderly, he was somehow all over her, everywhere, kissing her breasts, stroking her stomach, moulding her buttocks. Then he was in her, infinitely gentle, desperately slow, and then, then she wanted him terribly, and she was going to meet him, the great tangled waves of need growing higher and higher, and she thought she would never get there, reach the crest. She was struggling, fighting, desperate: and then she was there and she rode it, shouting with joy, swooping and flying, and then slowly and almost reluctantly she let it go, released it, and fell down slowly and sweetly into peace.

Afterwards, lying beside him, her body finally relaxed, fractured with pleasure, more than she could ever remember, smiling at him, half surprised at herself, half delighted, she wondered how she could ever have thought it might not be a good idea.

The Centre Forward Party had actually been launched: at the Connaught Rooms, the same location that the SDP had used a little over twenty years previously. There was no hidden agenda in this; it was simply central, large enough, famous enough and splendid enough. The trio who had made it happen, and who had equal billing—'until we're elected'—were Jack Kirkland, Janet Frean and Chad Lawrence.

They boasted twenty-one backbenchers, most of whose constituencies had agreed to let them stand under their new colours until the next election. Chad Lawrence's constituency was one of the few to force a by-election and he had won easily.

Their timing was perfect: with their slogan of 'People First, Politics Second', they had swept a rather tacky board and for a moment in history, at least, had everything going their way. Infighting and despair had swept the Tory party, and fresh horror stories about hospitals, schools and crime had beset New Labour.

Three newspapers had come down heavily on their side, the *Sketch*, the *Independent* and the *News*; others were more sceptical, but still welcomed what everyone was calling a fresh breeze in politics.

Lawrence, Frean and Kirkland were on the front pages and many of the inside ones as well. All had attractive families, wheeled out, smiling duti-fully, for photo opportunities. There was an interview with Gideon Keeble in the T2 section of *The Times*, complete with a photograph of him in front of his Irish mansion, flanked by two Irish setters, and a quote that what you needed, in both politics and the press, was, above all, courage. The City had analysed the fortunes of Keeble, and other big backers, and the extent to which they had been prepared to put their money where their mouths were; there was also much talk of anonymous donors.

On Friday, April 19th, a very big party was thrown in Centre Forward House, a new building in Admiralty Row. Apart from the politicians and the backers, a handful of City men and as many celebrities as the com-bined address books and email directories of the core team could muster were invited, together with every journalist from the world of print and radio and television. The food was good, the wine excellent, and the atmosphere heady.

Jocasta Forbes was there; she would have been there anyway, brought by her boyfriend, but her editor (who was also present) had briefed her to write a big piece about it for the gossip column the next day.

She looked dazzling, dressed in a very short black leather skirt and jacket and a sequinned top that showed most of her bosom and quite a lot of her tummy. She arrived with Nick, but promptly left his side and, inside an hour, had quotes from such disparate guests as Will Young, the public-school-educated sensation from *Pop Idol*, the Duchess of Carmarthen, resplendent in diamonds, who said it was the first political gathering she had been to since the war, and Alan Titchmarsh, charm-ingly self-deprecating as always.

After that she relaxed, drained a glass of champagne and then took another and began to wander round the room.

'Well, if it isn't my favourite reporter. How very, very lovely you look this evening. I've been hoping against hope that you'd be here.'

It was Gideon Keeble, smiling down at her, looking wonderful as always, holding a bottle of champagne in his hand.

'Hello, Mr Keeble,' she said rather uncertainly, allowing him to fill her glass. 'There are waiters to do that, you know.'

'I do know, but this is such an excellent way of extricating myself from boring people. And please don't call me Mr Keeble; it makes me feel old. Gideon, please. And where is your charming boyfriend?'

'God knows,' said Jocasta, 'but wherever he is, he's talking. And not in the least concerned with me.' She didn't mean to sound edgy, but she did; Gideon Keeble's eyes met hers.

'What a foolish young man he is. I hope he's heeded my advice now, and put a ring on your finger.'

'Not quite,' said Jocasta determinedly smiling, 'but if he had, one thing is certain, I wouldn't like it. His taste in jewellery is execrable.'

'Well, that is a serious shortcoming. I pride myself on my own. Jewellery is like perfume—it should complement the wearer's style.'

'And what would you think my style was?'

'Well, now, let me see.' His brilliant blue eyes were on her, half serious, half not. 'I think you are a diamond girl. Glittering and brilliant. But not big diamonds. Nothing vulgar. Small, intense ones. With white gold.'

'It sounds wonderful,' said Jocasta, 'but Nick isn't in the diamond league. Sadly.'

'I wasn't thinking of Nick,' he said. 'I was thinking of you. I would like to settle some diamonds on you here'—he touched one ear gently—'and a few more, let me see, yes . . . here.' And he picked up her hand and settled it in the valley of her breasts. It was an oddly erotic gesture, far more so than if he had touched her himself.

There was a silence; then she said, briskly careless, 'Well, that would be lovely. Very lovely. Now—perhaps you could tell me about a few of the people who are here. I am half on duty, you see.'

'What a shame. I was hoping to spend quite a time with you.'

'You can, if you like. Just take me round and introduce me to a few importantly famous people.'

'Very well. Do you know Dick Aoki, chair of the Jap-Manhat Bank, as it is rather disrespectfully known?'

'No. What on earth has he got to do with a new British political party?'

'Nothing. Yet. Come along, I'll introduce you.'

Martha Hartley arrived at the party very late. She had been delayed by a call from Ed, checking on the arrangements for the weekend. He had been upset that she hadn't been able to take him to the party; so upset that she had thought at first he was putting it on.

'I bet you'd be able to take one of those important old guys you know,' he said. 'I bet it's only because it's me. I'm not up to standard.'

'Ed, that is so not true. Invitations are like gold dust. I couldn't take you if you were, well, Prince William.'

'Now, why do I find that hard to believe?' he said.

She sighed. 'Sorry, bad example. But some of the partners are dying to come and can't, honestly.'

There was a silence. Then, 'OK,' he said. But, clearly, he wasn't convinced. Only a promise to spend a whole weekend in his company had mollified him. 'And you'd better not shave so much as five minutes off it.'

She promised she wouldn't.

Her main concern at that moment, however, was whether she was dressed appropriately. She had chosen a black crepe Armani trouser-suit, very simple, lent a certain pizzazz by the addition of some over-the-top diamanté drop earrings. Her brown hair in its sleek swinging bob was caught back on one side by a matching clip, and her new Jimmy Choos—perilously high, with diamanté ankle straps—made her feel sexy and daring.

When she arrived, the room was so thick with people that movement seemed impossible. Jack Kirkland waved at her, but he was deeply embroiled in conversation with Greg Dyke, a couple of people from the party's ad agency said hello and moved swiftly on; she was trying to look busy, sipping her glass of champagne, when she heard a familiar voice.

'Martha. Hi. Nice to see you. You look great.'

It was Nick Marshall; she had met him a couple of times now, but had never talked to him for more than a minute or so.

'This has been quite a day,' she said. 'You guys have all done a very good job for us. *Them*,' she corrected herself hastily.

'Martha, my lovely girl, hello.' Gideon Keeble gave her a giant hug. 'My God, you look wonderful. This room is full of beauty. We poor lowly males can only look and wonder at you.'

'Gideon, you do talk nonsense—but thank you.'

'Gideon.' It was Marcus Denning, puffing slightly, pink in the face from champagne. 'Quentin Letts from the *Mail* wants a chat. Would you mind?'

'I would not. Martha, my darling, I'll see you later. And, Marcus, you stay here and look after this beautiful creature.'

'I will,' said Marcus. 'Bit of bad news just now, I'm afraid. We've lost one of our most fervent supporters, out in the wilds of Suffolk, heart attack, poor chap. He'll need to retire.'

'Oh,' she said, 'you mean Norman Brampton.'

'Yes, that's right. How do you know about him?'

'My parents live in his constituency. My father, I'm sure I've told you, is the vicar there, knows him very well.'

'I see.' There was a long silence, while he stared at her.

'Marcus, whatever is it? Have I got spinach between my teeth?'

'No, no. I was just—thinking about something. Now look, would you mind if I asked you to chat to a couple of constituency workers? They're a bit lost here, and I don't want them feeling we don't care about them.'

'Of course I don't mind,' she said.

She was saved from too long a stint by Chad who took her arm and drew her away. 'I wonder—could we have a word afterwards?'

'Could it be now? I've got to leave early, I'm afraid.'

'OK. Look, Martha, we want you to consider taking on Norman Brampton's constituency.'

'What? I couldn't possibly. I don't have time.'

'Being an MP doesn't take that much time,' said Chad, 'especially if you're not in government. Which we just possibly may not be.'

'Oh, Chad, please! I work six days a week as it is.'

She felt as if she was falling into a deep, deep hole. She felt terrified.

'Listen, Martha, you would definitely be selected,' said Chad. 'You're a dream candidate. Local girl, well-known family, young, dynamic . . .' Chad smiled at her. 'How does it sound?'

'I keep telling you, not what I want. Anyway, I don't understand, Norman Brampton's a Tory.'

'A disillusioned one. He'd already signed up to the new policies, and persuaded a goodly quotient of his constituency committee to do the same. They don't want to risk a by-election. There's a very brisk young New Labour candidate down there—'

'Oh God, Dick Stephens.'

'You know him?'

'Not personally. My mother and her friends would like to send him to Siberia. He's very cocky, apparently. When he came to a parish do, he upset all the stalwarts by calling them by their Christian names, without being invited.'

'Martha,' said Chad, 'wouldn't you like to be an MP?'

'Well—maybe one day. Not now. I've got no political background—'

'*Please*, Martha. At least think about it. I know you'd do it well. And I know you'd love it.'

She was silent: thinking. Thinking properly, for the first time, of what it would mean. Could mean.

A new life. A new purpose to it. A chance to do something, to make a difference. A stab at real achievement, a grasp at real power, real success.

Chad Lawrence saw her hesitation, saw her thinking and said, quite quietly, 'I'm being unfair. Rushing you, pushing you. Think about it, for a day or two.'

'So . . . you think I should do it?' Martha said.

'Yeah, I do. Want some of this one? Very spicy, be careful.'

They were sitting at her small dining table, looking over the lights of London, eating a Thai meal that she had had delivered.

'Ed! Is that it?'

'I'd say so, yes.'

'But—we've hardly discussed it.'

'There's nothing to discuss, Martha. I think it's a good idea. OK?'

'Oh,' she said. She felt rather confused. She had wanted a full-blown, careful dissection of the whole thing: the risks, the advantages, her ability to cope with it. 'Well, if that's really what you think . . .'

'Of course it's what I think! I'm finding it a tiny bit tedious, to tell you the truth.'

'I'm sorry,' she said, slightly indignant. 'What would you like to talk about instead? You?'

'Well, it might make a change,' he said.

She stared at him. 'That's not fair!'

'It's perfectly fair. I haven't seen you for almost a fortnight, and how long before we got onto you? Roughly sixty seconds. Telling me about the party, about how wonderful it had been, and then suddenly remembering me and asking me politely what I'd been doing. And then back to you again, and what did I think about this thing with Chad or whatever his name is, should you do it, on and on. Somehow, you know, I don't think you ever will. You'd have to make time for it. Spare it some of your precious energy, interrupt your sacred routine. You should try thinking about something other than yourself for a bit, Martha. It might even be interesting for you.'

She felt as if he had hit her.

'I think I'd better go. I've got work to do tomorrow. You're not the only one, you know, with extra hours to put in.' He stood up, picked up his jacket from the sofa, bent and kissed her briefly.

The door slammed. He was gone. And Martha was left, staring out of the window, not sure how she felt.

Chapter 4

'RIGHT. HERE WE ARE . . .' Jilly pulled up in front of her house; it was raining. 'Now, you bring the food, darling, and I'll go ahead and open the door. Only be careful, because the path gets very slippery.'

Kate watched her walking up the path in her high heels. She had heard that accidents seemed to put things in slow motion and had never believed it; but she watched her grandmother turn to check she was following safely, then very, very slowly and gracefully, turn almost in a pirouette and skid sideways, her skirt floating up and then down again, settling round her in a sort of blanket as she fell, equally slowly, down onto the ground. And lie there, absolutely still.

'I must ask you to switch your phone off at once.'

The voice rapped across the waiting room: a bored, harsh voice.

'But I want to call my mum. That's my gran in there . . .' She indicated the cubicle where Jilly lay. 'My mum needs to know.'

'Well, you must use the public call box. Mobiles interfere with hospital equipment. You can see the notice there.'

'So where do I find a public call box?'

'There's one in the main hospital entrance.'

'Yeah, and it's not working. I've tried it. Any other suggestions?'

Everyone was looking at her now: a packed Casualty department. White-faced young families with babies, small children crying, one vomiting constantly into a plastic sandwich box; a drunk with a bleeding head, a pitifully young Asian girl, visibly pregnant, holding her husband's hand; at least three elderly couples; a couple of middle-aged men, one with his foot roughly bandaged: a sad wave of misery, pain and anxiety washed up on a hostile shore and waiting with painful patience, occasionally going up to the desk to ask how much longer it would be, only to be sent back again to sit down and wait some more. They all welcomed the diversion of the small drama.

'There's no need to be rude,' said the woman behind the desk.

'I wasn't being rude. I was asking for another suggestion. Since that one was totally unhelpful.'

Misery and anxiety was making Kate feel worse by the minute; she had expected comfort, attention and a swift resolution of her grandmother's troubles; had thought to see her tucked up in a warm hospital bed, her pain dealt with efficiently and fast. Instead her gran had been lying on a trolley in a cubicle for almost two hours, ever since the ambulance, which had come after forty long minutes, had delivered them here, just waiting to be taken to X-ray. A doctor had examined her, said it might be a broken hip or a fractured pelvis; he could do nothing until she had been X-rayed.

Her grandmother was still in her rain-soaked clothes, shivering violently, despite a nurse having promised three times to get her something warmer. Kate had offered to take her to X-ray herself, since no porter was forthcoming; they had looked at her as if she had suggested she should do a strip in the middle of Casualty.

'A porter has to do it, she can't be moved off that bed.'

'I could push it.'

'I expect you could,' said a nurse, pulling the curtains round her grandmother, 'but you don't know where to go.'

'You could tell me,' said Kate.

'I could,' she said wearily. 'But I still couldn't let you do it. I'm sorry. The porter shouldn't be long.'

Jilly was finally X-rayed at one o'clock the next morning; her pelvis was fractured, but her hip wasn't broken.

'So there's no need to operate,' said the doctor, summoned back to her cubicle. 'The pelvis will heal itself, given time. Now, then, I think as she has possible concussion, and in view of her age, we'll get her up into a ward, settle her down for the night, sort out some pain relief.'

'She's terribly cold,' said Kate, 'she keeps shivering.'

'That's shock,' he said. The nurse, standing beside him, nodded sagely. The minute a doctor appeared, there seemed to be plenty of nurses; the rest of the time there were none to be seen. They'd even managed to get her out of her wet clothes.

The doctor patted Jilly's blanket condescendingly. 'Poor old soul. What name is it? Oh, yes, Jillian. Soon have you nicely tucked up, Jillian.'

'My name,' said Jilly, and her voice was steadier suddenly, 'is Mrs Bradford. That is how I wish to be addressed.'

The doctor and the nurse exchanged glances.

When Helen and Jim arrived it was two o'clock; Kate had finally gone outside and called them, after the doctor had been.

'Where is she?' said Helen. 'Is she in bed?'

'No,' said Kate, 'she's on a trolley. They're totally useless. She was freezing to death until I made them get a blanket. She's had nothing, except for the cup of tea I got her. No painkillers, nothing. Stupid tossers!' she added loudly.

'Kate, dear, don't talk like that,' said Helen. 'Er . . . could I go and see my mother?' she asked the woman behind the desk rather tentatively.

'Of course you can,' said Kate. 'Don't ask anything, they only know how to say no.'

An old woman with no teeth cackled loudly. 'She's a right one, isn't she?' she said to Helen. 'She's put 'em all to rights round here. More guts than all the rest of us put together. You should be proud of her.'

Helen smiled rather nervously and followed Kate to Jilly's cubicle.

Kate woke up with a start; her head was in her mother's lap. She was asleep, too, her head on Jim's shoulder. Daylight was coming in through the dingy net curtains. Kate looked at her watch; it was half past six.

She sat up, walked over to the cubicle; please, please let her be gone. She wasn't; she was still there, wide awake, feverish.

'Kate! Oh, how nice to see you. I thought you'd all gone.'

'Of course we haven't gone. Oh, Gran, I'm so sorry. How is it now?'

'Painful,' said Jilly, 'terribly painful. Could you ask again for painkillers? I can't stand it much longer. And, Kate, darling, could you get me another cup of tea? Or even a glass of water?'

By ten o'clock, still no bed had been found. Kate slumped in Casualty, biting her nails. This was unbelievable. She was exhausted: how on earth did her grandmother feel? What could she do? Who would help?

And then she remembered her grandmother's nice doctor. The one who'd come into the shop that day. Surely she would be able to do something. She went into the cubicle; Jilly was dozing restlessly.

'Granny?'

'Yes?' She woke up at once.

'Granny, what's the name of your doctor? The lady who came into the shop that day?'

'Oh, Dr Scott. Yes. Nice girl.'

'Do you have her number? I thought I'd ring her. See if she can help.'

'It's in my address book. In my bag.' Her voice was slightly slurred. 'But, darling, she won't come on a Sunday. And what could she do?'

Kate shrugged. 'Dunno. But it's worth a try.'

Somewhere in the long wakeful hours (however could they be called small?) she had made the decision. She called Chad early, and said she would do it. Well, begin to do it.

'All I'm saying,' she warned him, 'is that I'll go down there with you. Talk to the constituency people, to Norman Brampton. All right?'

'All right. Martha, that's fantastic. I know we can make it work. Absolutely know it.'

Clio arrived just after two. 'I'm sorry I've been so long,' she said rushing into Casualty. 'I was on endless calls this morning. It's Kate, isn't it?'

'Yes,' said Kate. She looked exhausted, Clio thought.

'How is your grandmother? And where is she?'

'In something called HDU,' said Kate and burst into tears.

'Oh no. Look, I'll go and find out—oh, hello. You must be Kate's mother.'

'That's right. It's very good of you to come, Dr Scott.' Helen looked and sounded very tired. Jim had just gone out for a walk. He hated hospitals. 'My mother's been rushed off to HDU and then we had a bit of an upset. Kate started shouting at a nurse.'

'I wouldn't worry,' said Clio, 'they're used to it. But why is she in HDU?'

'Something about a clot. She was having pains in her legs, said she didn't like to complain and then suddenly had quite bad chest pains. Oh dear. It's all such a nightmare.'

'I'll go and see what I can find out,' said Clio, patting her hand.

Some insistent questioning of the duty doctor revealed that not only did Jilly have a deep vein thrombosis—arguably caused by the long period on the trolley—but it had moved upwards and part of it had lodged in her pulmonary artery. Clio returned to Helen and Kate and broke the news as gently as she could.

'I know it's terribly worrying for you. But she's getting the best possible care now. She's on intravenous heparin which is a wonderful drug, and the doctor will keep you informed. He's promised to come down as soon as he knows any more.'

Derek Bateson felt rather pleased with himself. He had only been working as a stringer for the North Surrey News Agency for three months and this was his third big story.

'Derek Bateson? Hi!' A slightly breathless voice sounded behind him.

Derek turned; an amazing-looking girl was smiling at him, holding out her hand. She was very tall, and she had all this blonde hair, and the most brilliant blue eyes.

'I'm Jocasta,' she said, 'from the *Sketch*. So tell me what's happened.'

'Well, this woman, Jilly Bradford, slipped last night, broke her pelvis, the usual after that, long wait for ambulance, the granddaughter was with her, then all night on a trolley, nothing happening, apart from an X-ray, then around lunchtime her leg got really painful, and she's got a pulmonary embolism. She's in Intensive Care and apparently it's touch-and-go.'

'Poor lady! And relatives? Any here?'

'Her daughter. Nice sort of woman, quiet, and the granddaughter—now she's a live wire. She tore them all off a strip earlier, for not doing anything, and she's been trouble all night according to some old biddy who's been here nearly as long. Apparently, the girl phoned Mrs Bradford's GP and she came to see if she could help. That set the cat among the pigeons—they didn't like that.'

'Do you know the GP's name?'

'Dr Scott.'

'And do you have the number?'

'Only the group practice number.'

'I'll start with that. Thanks, Derek. Is your photographer around? Just in case we need him.'

'In the pub. But we can get him any time.'

Clio was trying to concentrate on a programme about wildlife when the phone rang. 'Hello?'

'Hello. Is that Dr Scott?'

'Ye-es.'

'Hi. Dr Scott, I'm so sorry to bother you at home. My name is Jocasta Forbes. I write for the *Sketch*—'

It was at moments like this, Clio thought, that the earth really moved: moments of shock, of strangeness, even of fear, rocking you about.

'Did you say Jocasta?' she said finally, hearing her own voice shaky, odd. 'Jocasta Forbes?'

'I did, yes. Why?'

'Oh my God!' said Clio and she had to sit down suddenly. 'I can't believe it. Jocasta Forbes. So you made it, you did what you said!'

'I'm really sorry, but—have we met or something?'

'Jocasta, it's Clio. Clio Scott. Well, Clio Graves, actually. Thailand, seventeen years ago. How amazing. How absolutely amazing!'

'Clio! Oh my God. How are you? How extraordinary—'

'Totally extraordinary. All those clichés about small worlds are so true. But why are you calling me? And how did you get my number?'

'I'm doing a story about one of your patients. Mrs Bradford.'

'A story! Why is it a story?'

'Well, as I understand it, she was on a trolley for a long time and now she's quite ill. In the HDU. Tabloids like these stories. Oh, Clio, I'd so love to see you! Why on earth didn't we do what we agreed and meet when we all got home again all those years ago? Could I come round now?'

'Um, hold on a minute, Jocasta, could you? My husband's just come in.'

'Your husband! How very grown up of you. Look, ring me back in five minutes. Number's—got a pencil? Right—'

Jeremy came in, tired and irritable. 'Chaos at the hospital. Some woman's got a pulmonary embolism, supposed to have been left on a trolley, press involved, dreadful nonsense.'

'And how is she?'

'God, Clio, I don't know. Can we have that soup now?'

'Yes. Yes, of course. It's on the stove. Only . . . well, Jeremy, I'm terribly sorry, but I've got to go out again. The child with meningitis this morning—the mother's still very worried. So—'

'Dear God, I'll be glad when all this nonsense is over. All right. Don't be long, will you? This has been a dreadful Sunday.'

Clio left the house quietly, drove down the lane, stopped and phoned Jocasta.

'Hi. It's me. Look, I don't want to come to the hospital. Medical conventions and all that. Could we meet at the pub just down the road from the hospital? It's called the Dog and Fox. Saloon bar.'

'Sure. Can't wait.'

Clio saw Jocasta immediately as she hurried into the pub. She was sitting at a table by the window, smoking, reading something; she had a bottle of wine and two glasses in front of her. She looked up, saw Clio, and smiled; then stood up, pushed her mane of hair back and came towards her. And in that moment Clio knew exactly who it was that Kate Tarrant had reminded her of.

'I could sit here for ever,' said Jocasta, stubbing out her cigarette. 'Just tell me one thing. Did you stick to your plan? End up where you thought and so on?'

'No, I didn't. Not really. I often wonder what Martha's doing.'

'I heard something about her the other day. Right out of the blue. She's in politics, apparently. Well, on the edge. In with this new party. I might try to track her down. Oh dear, I must go.'

'What exactly are you going to write?' asked Clio.

'Oh, you know. Lots of sob stuff. And shock-horror, NHS fails again. Yet another old lady left on a trolley.'

'She's hardly an old lady,' said Clio. 'She's a rather glamorous sixty.'

'She is? God, I wish I could meet her. Do you think I could?'

'Absolutely not, if she's in the HDU.'

'Have you met the daughter?'

'Yes. She's very nice indeed. The granddaughter . . .' She hesitated; she was still—absurdly, she knew, for what reason for it could there possibly be?—slightly bothered by the resemblance between Kate and Jocasta. 'She's a tough little nut.'

'Yes, so I gathered. Maybe I could find her at least.'

'Maybe. Yes, it would be interesting for you.' She would be interested herself. Would Jocasta see the likeness between them? Probably not.

Her stomach lurched. She looked at Jocasta, said hesitantly, 'Jocasta, I know it's your job and everything, but, well, do you think it's going to do any good? Writing this story, putting the names of these nice people all over the paper? The hospital will hate it, I can tell you that. And—well, my husband would absolutely kill me if his name got into it. Or mine.'

'Why should his name get into it?'

'Well, he's one of the consultants there. Quite an important one.'

'OK. So why should he kill you? It won't be your fault.'

'He'd think it was. If he knew I knew you . . .'

'Well, he won't, don't fret about that. I won't use either of your names. They don't really improve the story and it's the system we're on about, not the people. Now, look, call me in a day or two. Here's my card, phone number, email address and everything.'

She leaned forward and kissed Clio. 'I'm so, so glad I found you. Don't worry about the story. Tomorrow's fish-and-chip wrapping, you know.' She always said that; it was doubly untrue, now that fish and chips were wrapped in hygienic white paper, and every story was available to be read afresh on the Internet at the press of a button or two. But it still comforted people.

Helen was dozing fitfully in the shabby discomfort of the visitors' room, and Kate was reading old copies of *Hello!*, when a doctor walked in.

She didn't look much like a doctor, apart from her white coat. She was very young and pretty, and she smiled at Kate and put her fingers on her lips. 'Kate?' she whispered.

'Yes. What is it, is Gran—?'

Jocasta jerked her head towards the door; Kate got up gingerly and followed her out into the corridor.

'As far as I know your gran's just about the same. But I'm not actually a doctor. My name is Jocasta Forbes from the *Sketch* newspaper.' She smiled at Kate; she looked exhausted, poor little thing; it must have been a terrible ordeal for her. 'How're you doing?'

'Pretty worried; they just won't tell us anything and I want to see Granny and they won't let me.'

'Well, we'll go up there in a minute, shall we? See what we can find out. I don't know how far Dr Jocasta will get, but we might make first base. Are you hungry? I've got some crisps outside.'

'Oh, yes, please. I'm starving. How did you get this far? They said the outside doors were all locked now.'

'Casualty's always open. I just walked in.'

She was great, Kate thought, wolfing down the crisps gratefully minutes later; really, really great. She liked her a lot.

Martha could hear the shock in their voices. Of all the things she had done that they found difficult to understand, this clearly topped the list.

'But, dear,' her mother said, 'of course we would be very pleased. And proud. But . . . why? I thought you loved your job.'

'I do. I do love it. But, well, just lately I've found it a bit less satisfying. And I'm intrigued by this as a . . . challenge.'

'But you don't know anything about politics.'

'Well, I didn't. But I've been working for this party, doing bits of legal work and so on, for a while. And I like what I see of it. Honestly, I'm almost as surprised as you are that they've asked me. And I'm as sure as I'm sitting here that I won't even be short-listed as the local party candidate. So it's all a bit of a farce, really. But I've said I'll give it a go.'

Only because of what Ed had said, really. Only because of the expression on his face when he left, which had looked like dislike . . .

After she had rung off she allowed herself another, proper cry.

'Oh, what fun! This is doing me much more good than all that awful stuff they keep pumping into me. There! How do I look?'

'Mummy, I'm not sure about this,' said Helen.

She sounded as exhausted as she looked; Jilly, on the other hand, was rosy and brilliant-eyed, lying back on her pillows, fluffing up her hair and contemplating herself in her small mirror.

'Not sure about what, darling?'

'You seeing this girl again. She's caused so much trouble—'

'Not for me she hasn't,' said Jilly briskly. 'If it hadn't been for her, I would never have seen you the other night. Or Kate. And then being able to tell her exactly how ghastly it was, and reading about it the next day—or was it the next, I'm rather confused now . . .'

'It was yesterday, that bit of the story,' said Helen.

'Oh, yes. Well, it did feel like revenge, of a sort. On all those stupid people in Casualty, and that dreadful staff nurse up here. And it's splendid that they've put me in this nice little room, isn't it?'

Helen was silent; her mother had been put in a side ward at the express instructions of one of the senior consultants, Mr Graves, under whose care she was, who had been incandescent with rage at the story in the *Sketch* on the Monday morning and the descent of at least a dozen other journalists and photographers on what he called his hospital. It had been a mistake that, leading as it had to a seventy-two-point headline in the *Sun* reading, 'They're our hospitals, actually, Mr Graves.'

Jocasta had visited a rather frail but animated Jilly in her room at about noon on Monday; the rest of the press had been kept out, but as the new best friend of Jilly Bradford's granddaughter, there had been no such control over her, and in any case, with her unruly hair tucked neatly under a baseball cap, nobody recognised her as the young woman masquerading as a doctor who had caused such trouble the night before, walking into HDU to check on Mrs Bradford's progress and, having ascertained it was satisfactory, telling the agency nurse in charge that she thought seeing her daughter and granddaughter for a minute or two would do her good.

'How much longer are we going to have to put up with this sort of thing?' Jocasta's emotive article had ended. 'In a health service that used to be the envy of the world? How many more patients are going to die, how many more old ladies are to be left alone and frightened, and in the case of Jilly Bradford, soaked to the skin after lying in the rain for hours waiting for an ambulance? And then denied such basic comforts as a warm bed and a cup of tea? How much longer do we all have to wait before someone takes the NHS in hand?'

Apart from finding herself described as an old lady, Jilly was entranced by the article and her starring role in it.

She was to be allowed out of hospital at the weekend, but not to her own home; she was going—with extreme reluctance—to stay with Helen for a week or two. Kate was thrilled.

'We can have a great time. I'll be chief nurse, and bring you all the champagne you want, and I'll get you loads of videos and stuff.'

'Oh, Kate,' said Jilly, patting her arm, smiling at her affectionately, 'what would I have done without you? Died, I should think. Now, Jocasta dear, I've done my best with my hair and Kate's fetched me this pretty bed jacket—will that do?'

'It's gorgeous,' said Jocasta and indeed it was, palest pink, edged with swan's-down.

Kate looked at Jocasta and smiled. 'You don't think I could be in one of the pictures, do you?'

'Kate!' said Helen. 'That's out of the question.'

'Why? Gran just said I'd saved her life. I don't see why I shouldn't. It would be so great. I might even be discovered by some model agency.'

This was her current ambition: to be a supermodel. She had confided it to Jocasta, who had actually thought she could be very successful, but hadn't said so.

'I really don't see why she shouldn't be in the photographs,' said Jilly. 'She saved my life, it's perfectly true. I'd like it very much. Jocasta, what do you think?'

'I think it would be very nice to have Kate in the picture, Mrs Tarrant,' said Jocasta, carefully. 'She's so much part of the story. I'll get the photographer in straight away. Kate, go and comb your hair. You don't want to meet the press looking less than your best.'

Kate giggled.

The photographer set up his camera. 'This'll make a great shot,' he said to Jocasta, while Jilly fussed over her hair for the umpteenth time and Kate settled on the bed beside her, putting her arm round her grandmother's shoulder. 'Probably get the front page.'

'Hope so. But get on with it—the mother's not happy, and I don't want to upset her.'

'The kid's gorgeous. You know something? She looks a bit like you.'

'God, I wish,' said Jocasta.

'Those should be lovely,' said Jocasta. 'You both looked very glamorous. Kate looks a lot like you.'

'Well, it would be nice to think so,' said Jilly, 'but unfortunately that's quite impossible. You see—'

'Mummy,' said Helen, and her voice was very cold, 'not now.'

Kate was staring at her mother; then she looked at Jocasta and smiled at her quickly. 'I'll come and see you off.'

'Fine,' said Jocasta. 'Well, goodbye, Mrs Bradford, I'm very glad you're recovering so well.'

'Thank you, my dear. And thank you for all your help.'

Kate was going to miss Jocasta; she really liked her. She wasn't scared of anyone, just went for it and got what she wanted.

'Thanks for railroading Mum. Um, could you do one more thing? Put my whole name in.'

'OK,' said Jocasta, smiling. 'What is your whole name?'

'Kate Bianca Tarrant.'

'That's a pretty name. Bianca, I mean.'

'Yeah. When I'm older I'm thinking I might call myself that. Your job must be such fun,' said Kate wistfully. 'Maybe I could be a reporter, instead of a model.'

'Well, it is fun. And you do get to meet a whole lot of people you never would normally. And hear some incredible things. But there's a lot of dogsbody work, as there is in everything. I actually think,' she said, looking at Kate consideringly, 'you'd be rather good at it.'

'Cool! Well, that's what I'll do, then. Could you get me a job?'

Jocasta laughed. 'Not at the moment. You're a bit young. Tell you what, though, we do sometimes take on people for work experience. Maybe this summer holidays, if you wanted, I could get you a week in the fashion department.'

'Oh, wow, yeah! That'd be great. Don't forget, will you?'

'I don't suppose you'll let me,' said Jocasta. 'Here, take my card.'

'Thanks, Jocasta. I'm going to miss you.'

'Me too.'

'Sorry about Mum, just then. Honestly, she's so weird. Usually she tells everyone I'm adopted.'

'Oh, are you?' said Jocasta.

'Yeah.'

'You all seem very close anyway.'

'I s'pose we are, really. To be honest, I get on with Gran best. She's such fun. My dad's all right, but even stricter than my mum, and then I've got a little sister who's just Little Miss Perfect, all clever and hard-working, with a scholarship to some posh school for her music.'

'Is she adopted too?'

'No, she's theirs. She was born after they adopted me.'

'And, do you know anything about your . . . your birth mother?'

Kate was beginning to wish she hadn't embarked on this. She certainly wasn't about to tell Jocasta—clever, cool, successful Jocasta—all the shameful, painful facts, about being abandoned in a cleaning cupboard.

'She was a . . . a student,' she improvised wildly, 'from Ireland. She was a Catholic, so she couldn't possibly have had an abortion. But she loved me and she wanted to know I was in a good home. In fact, she wouldn't let me go to the first people who wanted me, she waited until my mum and dad turned up and she was satisfied they'd look after me properly. All right?'

'Kate. It's OK. Calm down. I didn't think anything bad about your mother at all. Not for a moment. She must have been very special to have you. And very brave to have let go of you for your own sake. Now, look, it's been really fun getting to know you. Don't forget about the work experience, will you? Just give me a call when you feel you're ready. Or even if you just want to go out to lunch or something. I hate to think I'm never going to see you again, I really do.'

She probably didn't mean it, Kate thought, watching the black Golf zoom out of the car park; and they'd probably never meet again. Why should they, after all?

'Jocasta, you all right?' It was Chris Pollock; he had called her in after lunch to congratulate her on the story.

'Yes. Yes, I'm fine. Thank you. Just a bit tired, I guess.'

'Reporters aren't allowed to get tired. I've got a real beauty for you. Some poor cow's just had a baby in Holloway, while shackled to the delivery bed. Now, are you really OK? I don't want this story messed up.'

'You're such a gentleman, Chris. Don't worry. It won't be.'

She did feel tired, terribly tired. And depressed. Nick hadn't called. And she missed him, in spite of his refusal to commit himself to her. So much about Nick was right for her: he understood her, knew her completely, admired what she did. But in one way he failed her. One huge way. He might tell her he loved her, but what he did made her doubt it. And there was nothing at all she could do about it. It made her very sad.

She got home very late that night; Nick was waiting for her at her house. 'I wanted to see you,' he said, giving her a kiss. 'You look all in, sweet pea.'

'I feel it. I've had an awful day. Well, not awful. But upsetting.'

'What, steely old Jocasta, aka Lois Lane, upset? Must have been childbirth. Here, have a glass of wine. I've left you just about enough.'

'It was. You're right. I'm so phobic about it, Nick. It's so pathetic.'

'Not really,' he said, handing her the glass, 'not after what you went through.'

'Yes, it is. I should have got over it years ago.'

'A trauma's a trauma, honeybunch.'

'I know. But . . . well, anyway, this poor woman, she had a baby in prison. She was actually in chains, Nick, while she was having it. And it was an awful birth, went on for hours and hours and in the end they had to—well, I won't go into detail. But her mother did. I've got it all on tape. She was screaming and screaming for help. And the baby practically died. I just didn't know how to sit there, how to go on listening.'

'Poor baby. *You*, I mean.'

'I could never ever go through it, Nick. Not in a million years. I just couldn't. Even with all the anaesthesia anyone could offer me. I'd just start remembering and—oh God!' She started to cry, helplessly, like a child. 'Sorry, I'm so sorry . . .'

'Look at you,' he said, taking her in his arms. 'Look at the state of you. No one's going to ask you to go through it. Come on, drink that all down. And then I'm going to take you out to dinner. All right?'

'All right,' said Jocasta.

'I love you. And I'm sorry again, about—well everything.'

She stared at him. He so seldom said he was sorry. It was even rarer than his telling her he loved her. Her day and its traumas promptly faded into near-nothingness.

'I love you too,' she said. 'And I'm sorry too. Let's not go out to dinner.'

'Let's not.'

It had come without warning. Friday, the fateful Friday, had been the most beautiful day, windy and sun-dappled; although it was her last day at the practice, Clio felt oddly happy. It might not be so bad. She did after all enjoy being at home. And Jeremy would be better tempered and happier. Which would help a lot. She did still love him. She did. She knew she did.

At lunchtime, on a whim, she called him. She had had her farewell drinks at the surgery the night before, because Mark was going to be away on a course on the Friday and had wanted to be there.

'We'll miss you so much, Clio,' he had said, handing over a big scented candle and a box of chocolates. 'And this comes with all our love. You've been the most marvellous member of the team, and we're as fortunate as your patients. God knows how we're going to replace you. Well, we're not. As you know. Series of locums, right up till the end of June. Still, no doubt the practice's loss will be your gain. And Jeremy's, of course.'

Clio, eyes filled with tears, said she wasn't sure that either of those statements was correct, and said how much she would miss them too.

Jeremy had agreed to meet her for lunch: 'It would be good to get out for an hour or so. One o'clock all right with you?'

'Of course. Order me a chilli jacket if you get there first.'

She drove towards the pub singing. She could do a lot of this sort of thing in the future, make him happier. And that in turn would make her happier.

Clio got to the pub first and ordered their food; Jeremy walked in at about one fifteen, looking harassed. She waved at him.

'I've got you a drink. Virgin Mary!'

'Thanks,' he said, sitting down.

Maurice Trent, the landlord, appeared with their food.

'Here we are then. Nice to see you both. What a to-do this week, eh? Paparazzi all over the place, load of rubbish all of it. That girl you were talking to on Sunday, Dr Scott, she was one of them, wasn't she? Nice she seemed, not the sort you'd expect on a paper like that.'

Clio had often read of bowels turning to water and had scoffed at it; she knew suddenly exactly what it meant.

'What girl was that?' said Jeremy, his expression ice-hard.

'Oh, just one of the reporters,' said Maurice. 'First one down, I think. Yes, all right, all right,' he called to the barmaid who was gesticulating at him. 'Coming. You just can't get help these days, I tell you that. Enjoy your meal.'

Jeremy sat and stared at Clio, who felt violently sick.

'You were talking to one of the reporters? On Sunday? And you didn't mention it?'

'No. I mean yes. Well, not because she was a reporter. Honestly, Jeremy, I promise you. She . . . she just turned up out of the blue. I mean, she is a reporter, but we—we went travelling together years ago, when we were both eighteen. I hadn't seen her since. I—'

'And she just turned up, on your doorstep, at precisely the right moment. How very convenient for her.'

'Yes, well she rang me because I was Mrs Bradford's GP, and then she recognised my name, you know how these things happen, what a small world it is—'

'No, I don't. As far as I can remember, you sneaked out of the house on Sunday, under the pretence of making some house calls. And actually came to meet her here, and—'

'Jeremy, please be quiet. Everyone's looking.'

He turned round; it was true, half the bar was staring at them. He stood up. 'We can discuss this later. Perhaps you'd be kind enough to settle the bill.'

'Yes. Of course. But, Jeremy—'

He was gone.

Clio half ran to the bar, flung a twenty-pound note at the bemused Maurice Trent and went out into the car park. Jeremy's car had gone.

'Martha?'

'Yes. Yes, it is. Hi, Ed.'

She had literally dreamed of this, imagined it so often over the past few days, that now, she felt terrified.

'I—' There was a long silence, then, 'I just wanted to wish you luck.'

'Ed, who on earth told you?'

'Mum. She called this evening, said did I know you were going to be the new MP for Binsmow.'

Martha started to laugh. 'Oh God,' she said, 'mothers!'

'Yeah, well. You should have told me.'

'Why?'

'Well . . . because of what I said. I'm sorry, Martha. Sorry I said all those things. I was totally out of order. I can see that now.' There was a silence, then he said, 'I've missed you so much. I thought I could do without you . . . but I can't.'

'Ed,' said Martha. 'I *am* self-obsessed. I *am* a control freak. But I'm trying very hard not to be. If you hadn't said what you did, I'd have said no to Chad. Now, then, I've got an important meeting tomorrow. I've got an early start—'

'Yeah, OK,' he said, 'sorry. I just wanted to—'

'But even so, why don't you come round? We can discuss my presentation. Among other things.'

Jocasta was walking into a bar when her phone rang.

'Is that Jocasta? This is Jilly. Jilly Bradford.'

'Oh, hi, Mrs Bradford. How are you? Nice to hear from you.'

'I'm much better, thank you. I just wanted to thank you for putting that nice photograph in the paper. It was very flattering, but it will certainly disabuse everyone of the notion that I'm some senile old woman.'

'Yes, it will. I'm glad you liked it.'

'I did. Kate bought about six copies. She's the heroine of the hour at school, of course.'

Jocasta laughed. 'She's so great, your granddaughter. I think she'll do very well in life.'

'I think so, too. I hope so, anyway. She deserves to.'

There is a sensation that every good reporter knows: a kind of creeping excitement, a thud of recognition at something forming itself just out of reach, something worth pursuing; Jocasta felt it then.

'She was telling me all about being adopted,' she said.

'Was she? She obviously sensed a kindred spirit. She doesn't normally like talking about it. Extraordinary story, isn't it?'

'Well, not that extraordinary. Except that these days most girls don't give their babies up; they keep them and raise them on their own.'

'I didn't mean that. I meant her being found in that way, at the airport. Didn't she tell you that bit?'

'Well, not in any detail, no.' *Careful, Jocasta, careful . . .*

'It's so hard for her. She feels it very keenly, poor little thing. Being abandoned like that. She wants to find her mother, of course, but I think—'

Jocasta's phone bleeped warningly. 'Mrs Bradford, I'm going to have to ring you back. My phone's dying on me. If you—'

'Oh, my dear, no need. I just wanted to say thank you and—'

The phone died; Jocasta wanted to throw it on the ground and jump up and down on it. It was her own fault, of course, totally her own fault; she'd known the power was low.

Now what did she do? She could hardly ring Jilly back, on a public phone, and say, 'Now, about Kate and her adoption, do go on . . .' The moment had been lost. And it was totally and absolutely her own fault.

Jeremy came in at about eight, the taut fury, which she had grown to dread, set on his face. She smiled awkwardly, said, 'Jeremy, hello. You must be hungry. I've got some very nice jugged hare if you'd—'

'Please don't try that,' he said.

'Try what?'

'Pretending everything's normal. It simply makes it worse.'

'Jeremy, I wish you'd let me explain. I didn't say anything about the hospital or Mrs Bradford to Jocasta—'

'Jocasta?'

'Yes. The reporter.'

'I thought you met her in the pub.'

'I did. But only to talk about old times.'

'Which you couldn't have done in the house? You had to sneak off without explaining she was an old friend?'

'Well, yes. I thought you'd be suspicious, that you wouldn't believe me, wouldn't let me go.' She was beginning to feel angry herself.

'I wouldn't let you go! Is that how you see me? As some kind of tyrant? I find that immensely insulting.'

'Well, it isn't meant to be. I'm just trying to explain how it happened, why I did what I did.'

'And then you sat with her in the pub, this reporter friend of yours, and didn't even discuss the wretched Bradford woman? You expect me to believe that?'

'Yes! In fact I actually asked her not to write the story and certainly not to implicate you or me in it.'

'And that was very successful, wasn't it?'

'Actually, yes. If you read the piece you'll see she made no mention of either of us. I could get it if you like—'

'You actually expect me to read that drivel?'

'Oh, shut up,' said Clio wearily, surprising herself.

He was clearly surprised too; she so seldom went on the offensive.

'I just can't get over your deceiving me like that,' he said, changing tack. 'It was so unnecessary.'

'Well, maybe if you weren't such a bully, if you didn't treat me like some kind of inferior—'

'That's a filthy thing to say!'

'But, it's true. You *do* bully me. You don't respect what I do, you've made me give up a job I absolutely love, you're dismissive of almost everything I say, you're always in a bad temper, you blame me for everything that goes wrong in our lives. Can you wonder I didn't ask you if I could invite an old friend round for a chat? I think it's time you took a proper look at yourself, Jeremy, I really do.'

He said nothing, just stood staring at her in silence for several moments; then he turned and went upstairs to their room. She followed him; he had pulled out a suitcase and was putting things in it.

'What are you doing?' she asked. She was frightened now.

'I'm packing. I would have thought that was perfectly evident. Clearly, there is no room for me here. I have nothing to contribute to our marriage. So I think it's better I go.'

'Jeremy, don't be stupid. Please!'

'I see nothing stupid in it. You're obviously much better on your own. Doing your job, which means much more to you than I do, a job you never even consulted me over taking in the first place. I had something altogether different in mind, not a part-time wife, obsessed with her career. I had hoped we would have had a child by now, but I've been denied that as well. I wonder if you're trying to cheat me there, too. I wouldn't put anything past you, Clio.'

'You bastard!' she said, tears smarting at the back of her eyes, a lurch of dreadful pain somewhere deep inside her. 'You absolute bastard. How dare you say that!' Then, suddenly, everything shifted and she felt very strong. She looked at him, in all his arrogant self-pity and cruelty, and knew she couldn't stand another day, another hour of him. 'Don't bother packing any more, Jeremy, I'm going myself. I don't want to spend another night in this house, where you have managed to make us so miserable. I want to get out of it, and out of this marriage. It's a travesty.'

And without taking any more than her bag and her car keys, she walked out of the house and got into her car and drove away from him and their brief, disastrous marriage.

Chapter 5

JOCASTA HAD TRIED to shrug it off; to tell herself it wasn't that important, but she knew it was. An abandoned baby was a fantastically exciting story. Especially an abandoned baby who had grown up into the most beautiful girl, beautiful enough, indeed, to be a supermodel; a troublesome, beautiful girl, who wanted to find the woman who had abandoned her.

It was an absolutely wonderful story. Only—and this was where the occasional struggle Jocasta had with herself began—this could really hurt Kate: damage her dreadfully. The mother might not turn up at all and so break Kate's heart. Or she might be absolutely wonderful, claim Kate and break the Tarrants' hearts. How much better for everyone if Jocasta forgot about it, let them all be. She knew all too well the demons released from Pandora's box by tabloid newspapers, indeed by any newspaper; she saw it all the time.

But she had to get the story; she just had to.

The worst thing, Clio thought, was the feeling she had nowhere to go. That she was, temporarily, homeless. After some thought, she had driven herself to a motel and booked herself in for the night.

To her great surprise, she slept for a few hours, and woke at six, with a sense of dreadful panic and loneliness.

Now what?

She realised that she had very few close friends. Actually, she had *no* close friends. Not any more. Couples, yes, halves of couples, even, but only on a rather superficial level. Jeremy had driven a wedge between her and her previous girlfriends; expressing first hurt and later irritation if she wanted to spend time with them rather than with him. And she had never had a soul-baring kind of friendship with anyone; she supposed it was all to do with her rather emotionally starved childhood, her sense of failure when comparing herself with her brilliant sisters. She could certainly never go to them for help. Her major ambition, from the day she left to go travelling on that fateful August day, had been to show them and her father that she could manage on her own.

What she couldn't understand was why she didn't feel more unhappy. Scared, yes; lonely, yes; and desperately worried, yes. But not unhappy.

She got into her car and drove—for some reason—towards London. It seemed as good a route as any. She felt a need for coffee and turned her car into a Little Chef; the coffee was good and she suddenly wanted some toast as well. She was biting into the second slice when her mobile rang. Jeremy? Worrying about her, wondering where she was?

'Clio? Hi, it's Jocasta. I just wondered how you were, hoped that story hadn't done you too much damage.'

'Oh,' said Clio lightly, and was astonished to find she could be honest, indeed wanted to be. 'Not really. I've left my husband as a result, don't have a home any more, that sort of thing. But don't worry about it, Jocasta, not your fault.'

'Oh my God! You *are* joking, aren't you?'

'No, actually. I'm in a Little Chef on the A3 with nowhere to go, and only the clothes I'm standing up in. Oh, and no job, either.'

'My God! Oh, Clio, I'm so, so sorry. And how inadequate is that? Jesus. What happened, was it really my fault?'

'Oh, no, not really,' said Clio with a sigh. 'I mean, you might have been the catalyst—well, the story might—but it was all there, really.'

'What was all there?'

'I don't want to talk about it, Jocasta. Sorry.'

And then her calm and her bravado suddenly left her and she started to cry, huge heavy sobs; the three other people in the Little Chef all stared at her. She cut Jocasta off and fled to the ladies', where she shut herself in one of the stalls and sat on the loo, her head buried in her arms, weeping endlessly.

After about half an hour, she couldn't cry any more. She felt strangely calm. She washed her face, combed her hair and walked back into the café to pay her bill. On her way to the car, her mobile rang. It was Jocasta.

'She was marvellous. Really marvellous.' Chad smiled at Grace Hartley; they were, inevitably, in the vicarage drawing room, using the best china, with enough cakes on the tiered wooden cake-stand to feed the entire Centre Forward Party.

Chad was saying how well she'd done at the candidates meeting, even better than he'd hoped, but they wouldn't know for a while, probably not for a week, 'Just to show us at Westminster who's really in charge.'

His phone rang and they all jumped. He went out of the room, closing the door. It was obviously someone from the committee: so swift a decision must mean bad news, Martha thought miserably. It felt very bad. She had failed at something really important. Something she really wanted. And very publicly. Everyone would be so disappointed in her. She was even more disappointed in herself.

The door opened; Chad was smiling. 'Well,' he said, 'very, very good news. That was Norman Brampton. It's unofficial but—Martha, they want you! They were very impressed indeed.'

'Oh my God!' said Martha. She felt extraordinary. In that moment she could have flown. She hadn't failed. She'd done it. She had succeeded.

'Oh, that's so wonderful, darling,' said Grace. 'Well done.'

'Marvellous,' said Peter Hartley. 'We're so proud of you, Martha. And how lovely it will be to have you down here—'

'Now, you must keep this under your collective hats,' said Chad. 'Norman really shouldn't have told me. But he was quite certain.'

On her way back to London, Martha realised that her car was practically out of petrol.

At the filling station, there was something wrong with one of the pumps; it required a lot of jiggling about to get the petrol running and then suddenly it spurted out. Damn! That wouldn't do her suit any good. She finished filling the car, paid for the petrol and then went to wash.

The lavatory was predictably filthy. Paper towels littered the floor, together with some fag ends, and a tabloid newspaper balanced on top of the hand dryer. As she switched the dryer on, the paper slithered onto the floor. Martha, deciding it was in its rightful place, was about to leave, when her mobile rang; as she fumbled for it in her bag, one of her leather gloves fell onto the floor.

She swore, checked her mobile—it was Ed, wanting to know how she had got on—and bent down to pick up the glove. And there it was: the photograph. A very ordinary photograph, really, taking up about a quarter of the page; it showed a middle-aged woman, apparently in a hospital bed, and a young girl. The woman was dressed in a bed jacket and some rather incongruously large pearl earrings. The girl, who had a great deal of curly fair hair, was wearing a denim jacket and several studs in one of her ears. She had one arm round the woman's shoulders, and was smiling radiantly at the camera.

'What Katy Did', said the caption.

And Martha, crouching there on the floor, strangely compelled to read on, discovered precisely what Katy had done, which was care for her 'beloved grandmother', as she became desperately ill, after spending twenty hours in Casualty on a hospital trolley.

'But there was a very happy ending. Mrs Jilly Bradford is now recovering fast and has nothing but praise for her granddaughter's courage, as she battled with NHS staff to secure attention and treatment for her. Fifteen-year-old Kate Bianca—as she likes to be known—has ambitions to be a model. Why not a career in hospital management, Kate?'

Martha leaned over the filthy lavatory bowl and was violently sick.

She sat for a long time in a lay-by, staring at the photograph, reading and rereading the caption, calming herself by sheer will-power. Of course she was being absurd. Hysterical. The country was filled with thousands—millions—of fifteen-year-old girls. Several hundred of them undoubtedly called Bianca. It wasn't that unusual a name now. Anyway, this one, the one with the beloved grandmother (would you be that close to an adoptive grandmother?—surely not), wasn't called Bianca, she was called Kate. Bianca was just a middle name, an afterthought. And—what if she did have that hair? Millions of them had that hair, that long, wild hair. Blonde hair. No, the whole thing was ridiculous.

She put the paper in a rubbish bin, very carefully and deliberately, and texted Ed—she didn't dare speak to him just yet—then drove slowly home where she sat and watched television, an endless stream of mind-numbing rubbish. Only it didn't numb her mind quite enough; when she went to bed it was still throbbing feverishly.

There was a text from Ed. 'All hail to the new PM,' it said. 'Love you. Ed xx.' It made her feel suddenly, wonderfully better.

But not for long . . .

She stood at the window, staring out at the starry sky, wishing the night away. It would be better in the morning; everything was always better in the morning. And how often had she told herself that, almost sixteen years ago?

Clio stood on the doorstep, looking up at Jocasta's pretty little house and trying to pluck up the courage to ring the bell. What on earth was she doing here, at the worst hour of her life, paying a call on someone who was virtually a stranger? It made her feel more pathetic than ever.

She was just considering running away, when the door opened and a very tall, very thin man dressed in running gear appeared, smiled at her and said, 'You must be Clio. Go along in. I'm going for a run, so you and Jocasta can enjoy some girlie talk. I'm Nick,' he added, holding out a bony hand. 'Nick Marshall. Friend of Jocasta's. See you later.'

Clio smiled up at him. 'Thank you,' she said, and then worried that it might sound rude, to be thanking someone for going away from their own house. Or their girlfriend's house.

'Cheers, then.' He was gone, a long, loping figure, and then: 'Clio, come on in,' said Jocasta's voice and she was not only in the house, but held in Jocasta's arms, and she was crying again, and Jocasta was stroking her hair, and talking soothing nonsense and then leading her into a warm, chaotic kitchen where she sat her down and placed a large mug of coffee in front of her. And Clio stared at her and thought, as she had thought so long ago, what an amazingly nice person she was.

'Now, are you sure you're going to be all right?' Jocasta looked at Clio thoughtfully.

'Of course. I'll go to these friends in Guildford, and they'll put me up for a few days. While I sort myself out.'

'You've spoken to them, have you?'

'Of course.'

It was not a complete lie; she had called Mark Salter and explained the situation and he had said nothing would make him happier than to have her back in the practice, but that he would have to honour his fortnight's commitment to the first locum. 'I'm only sorry the circumstances are so unhappy for you.'

She had had that conversation in Jocasta's bedroom, having explained it was rather delicate; Jocasta had clearly assumed it was Jeremy, and had made a second jug of coffee. Nick had returned by then and was smiling dutifully at her. Clio had suddenly felt appalling; a burden on a lot of perfectly nice people who were trying to have a normal Sunday.

'I must go,' she said. 'Honestly, I can't take up any more of your time.'

'Of course you mustn't go,' said Jocasta, 'you're staying right there. We're not doing anything, are we, Nick?' and, 'No,' he had said, after the most momentary of pauses, 'no, nothing. In fact I've got to get back to my place and write a piece for tomorrow's paper—Chris called while I was out running.'

'Well, there you are,' said Jocasta, after he'd left. 'Think how lonely and lost I'd be without you, Clio. It happens all the time, you know, I get abandoned just like that. Anyway, we can have a nice day together.'

Clio was feeling too lonely and too dispirited to protest any further.

She tried not to tell Jocasta too much; it seemed absurdly disloyal to discuss a marriage—albeit a failed one—with someone who was not a close friend, but Jocasta was dangerously easy to talk to. She sat in silence most of the time, only speaking when a silence became just too long, and then only in the most minimal terms: 'And then . . .?' or 'So you . . .?' before waiting quietly.

Clio tried to ignore the prompts, but as the silences grew, it became very difficult, and later, eased into greater intimacy by a great deal of wine, she told Jocasta this. She laughed.

'It's one of the first things you learn, the pressure of the silence. But I try not to practise it in my personal life. Sorry, Clio.'

'It's all right,' said Clio, 'I'm sure it's done me good. In a way it's better than some mutual friend who'll feel they're taking sides.'

'Hope so. It does sound like you've done the right thing. Maybe a bit rash actually walking out, but—'

'Jocasta, if I hadn't walked out, he'd have talked me round. He's a brilliant tactician. You've no idea how often I've gone into arguments knowing I'm right, absolutely knowing it, and ended up sobbing and asking him to forgive me.'

Jocasta said nothing.

'So . . . I'm glad, really. But it's been very drastic. I wouldn't like to relive this weekend.'

'How many times has he called you?'

A very long silence; then Clio said, not looking up at her, 'He hasn't. Not once.'

'Clio,' said Jocasta, refilling her glass yet again, 'you have done absolutely the right thing. I know I shouldn't say that, but it has to be true. And—at least you haven't had any children.'

'No,' said Clio. And burst into tears again.

This time she resisted the silence.

'I think you should stay here tonight,' Jocasta said.

'Jocasta, I can't. And what would Nick say?'

'I don't give a shit what Nick says. This is my house, my life. It's nothing to do with Nick.'

'Yes, but—'

'Look,' said Jocasta, 'one, he won't come back; he's at his place, and two, if he does, that's absolutely fine. This is not the 1950s. And we haven't even started on Martha yet.'

'Martha! Have you seen her?'

'Not exactly, but our paths may cross. She wants to be an MP, according to Nick. He's met her. Says she's rather important and successful.'

'Well, she did seem very ambitious, even then. Funny thing, ambition, isn't it? It seems to be in people's genes. How about you, are your ambition genes powerful?'

'Pretty powerful. Yours?'

'More than I thought,' said Clio slowly. 'I mean, when I first married Jeremy, I thought I'd want to give it all up, but I didn't at all. I really minded leaving my job at the hospital—'

'What did you do?'

'I was a junior consultant. In geriatrics. I know it sounds rather dreary, but it isn't, it's fascinating and lovely and very rewarding. And then I really enjoyed general practice. I was so miserable the day I left. It wasn't just because it coincided with the end of my marriage.'

'So, now what?'

'Well, for the time being I can go back.'

'And long-term?'

'I don't know.'

'It might not be the best thing, going back to Guildford, where Jeremy is. Look, why don't you call those people and tell them you're not coming tonight? We've got too much to talk about, and, Clio,'—she had obviously read her face—'you weren't going there anyway, were you?'

'Not exactly,' said Clio, 'no. But—'

'Right. You're staying. Another bottle of wine, I think.'

'I . . . wondered what your plans were?'

Jeremy's voice was as she had never heard it; almost diffident, just short of nervous. Clio had answered her phone by the shampoo range in Boots; she was so surprised she practically dropped the basket.

'I'm not absolutely sure, to be honest.'

'Where . . . where are you living?'

'In a flat in Guildford. Or I'm about to be. I just signed the agreement this morning. Meanwhile I'm staying with the Salters. Look, Jeremy, I'm in Boots. It's not the place to have a conversation like this. If you really want to talk to me, we'd better meet.' She felt rather cool and in control.

'Yes. I think we should. Would you like to come to the house?'

'I'd rather not. A pub?'

'Of course. What about the one at Thursley? About six?'

Clio looked at Jeremy as he put a white wine spritzer down in front of her; he was pale and seemed very tired. He smiled at her almost nervously and said, 'Well, how are you?'

'I'm fine. Considering.'

'Good. Is it all right at the Salters'? What did you tell them? About us?'

She looked at him; he was sweating slightly. She was surprised. Why should he care so much? She supposed it was all part of his not wishing to appear in any way less than perfect.

'I told them we'd separated. I had to. Why else should I need somewhere to stay? And my job back.'

'Your job back?'

'Yes. I have to live, Jeremy. And, anyway, I love my job. There seems no reason to give it up now.'

'You decided that? Without consulting me?'

'Why should I consult you? You made it perfectly clear our marriage was over. I don't see what it has to do with you.'

'I was . . . upset,' he said. 'And I . . . I'd like you to reconsider. Well, both of us to reconsider.'

'What do you mean?'

'That we should . . . should try again.' She stared at him; this was the last thing she had expected. 'Clio, I was very hasty. I said a lot of harsh things, but I really don't want our marriage to end.'

'Jeremy, on what basis? I mean, do I still have to give up my job?'

'No,' he said quietly. 'No, you don't. That was . . . unreasonable of me.'

She stared at him. She felt very odd.

'Clio,' he said, 'I can't face life without you. I came to see very quickly that I . . . well, I do still love you. I want you back. I really do.' He waited, as she stared at him. 'What do you say?'

'I . . . I'm not sure,' she said. 'I mean it was a bit of a shock, all that. But . . . you mean I can go on working and everything?'

'Yes, you can.'

It was tempting. So very tempting. The thought of living alone, of making her own way again might be attractive in theory, but in practice it was scary. And he had made a huge concession.

'Well,' she said, 'as long as I can work . . .'

'You can work, Clio. I promise. Of course I would hope it wouldn't be for long. That we should be having children pretty soon. I mean, that is a given, as far as I'm concerned. And you too, I'm sure.'

Clio knew the moment had come, that she couldn't go on any longer, deceiving him. 'Jeremy,' she said, 'Jeremy, I'm afraid that isn't going to happen. Or almost certainly isn't going to happen.'

He stared at her, his face absolutely puzzled. 'What?'

Clio took a deep breath. 'I've got something to tell you, Jeremy, something I should have told you a long time ago.'

She took his hand and, feeling sorry for him, as she had never thought to be again, her voice surprisingly steady, she began to tell him.

Chapter 6

MARTHA HADN'T SEEN ED for almost a week. He'd been filming out of London and she'd missed him horribly. He'd called her a couple of times, but rather briefly, saying he was frantic. Had he found someone younger, or prettier, someone with curly hair and a small nose? Probably. She wanted to see him, talk to him, be with him, have him.

Her phone rang.

'I just wondered if you could give me a lift to Suffolk this weekend, Miss Hartley. I ought to visit my mum and my car's completely fucked up.'

'I hope you don't use that sort of language in front of your mother.'

'Of course I don't. Also, I have this girlfriend down there I really want to see. She's fantastic and I've been missing her a lot.'

'Well, I'll have to look at my diary. Let's see . . . Yes, I think I could just about fit you in. What? . . . Don't be coarse. Now I do warn you, Ed, I'll be horribly busy. I've got to see the Centre Forward people, I've got to do an interview with the local paper and Norman Brampton has asked my parents and me to supper on Saturday evening. I'm sorry—'

'That's OK. I could come along, say I was your secretary. Hold your microphone while you address your adoring public.'

'Yes, that's a really good idea.'

'Or I could gate-crash the wild evening at the Bramptons'. That sounds really cool. We might even be able to sneak upstairs after the dessert.'

'Yes, that's an excellent notion too.'

'Or—how about we leave early on Friday and spend the night at some luxury hotel off the M11? We could have dinner on the way.'

'Now that really is clever. You're on.'

'That's my girl. You're really living dangerously these days, aren't you?'

If only he knew how dangerously. Or rather, if only he never would.

Clio sat her new beanbag in her new sitting room and stared up at the bare windows and at the blinds still in their Habitat bags, then she wandered into the kitchen, put on her new kettle and made herself a cup of coffee in one of her new mugs and wondered however she was going to survive her new life.

Jeremy had taken it quite well, really. He had listened to her quietly and at the end they had agreed that the only thing was to part. He wanted a chance of having children, and clearly, with Clio, it was unlikely. And she was, equally clearly, not really the person he had thought she was, and although the deception had initially been minimal, indeed almost non-existent, it had grown so disproportionately fast and had become so tragically huge, that he could not contemplate trying to cope with it. Chlamydia. It was rather a pretty word. It could almost be a girl's name. It certainly didn't sound like the name of a loathsome disease. A disease that appeared to have rendered her infertile.

Of course she still didn't know if it had. There was still hope. But the last two gynaecologists had both expressed grave doubts. Her Fallopian tubes appeared completely blocked. And it was absolutely her own fault. She had slept with several men she had hardly known, and had contracted, in blithe ignorance, this awful, symptomless, unsuspected thing that had come back to haunt her when it was, probably, far too late to do anything about it. One of the things she most longed for, motherhood, was probably to be denied her, and all as a result of some foolish, irresponsible behaviour when she was eighteen years old.

Somehow, she hadn't expected sex to matter so much. She had just thought it would be a wonderful trip, meeting lots of people, seeing fantastic places. It hadn't struck her that, of course, with thousands of young people wandering untrammelled by any discipline all over the world, pleasure of every kind must include sex in a big way. No one had thought to say, 'Now look, Clio, everyone will be having sex all around you, all the time.' Or even tell her that she was very unlikely to return a virgin. Why should they? She had grown up in this uncommunicative family, repressed by her father, suppressed by her sisters, made to feel less pretty, less clever, less interesting than she really was.

She had slept with a great many boys, some of them extremely good-looking and sexy, some of them less so. Sometimes she enjoyed it and sometimes she didn't. The important thing seemed to be that she could persuade them to want her. She had become, she supposed, that much-despised creature, a slag. And she also supposed she should despise herself, but she didn't. Every time she had sex with someone, she was simply running, running away from the plump, dull, innocent person she had been.

A new Clio came home, with sun-streaked hair and a deep, deep tan. A Clio who could attract men quite easily, but who was still anxious, still eager to please, still very far from sexually confident. And the new Clio did not know, had not even considered, that she might carry a legacy from those dangerously careless days. A legacy that would damage her for the rest of her life.

'I wondered . . . I wondered if we could meet.' It was Kate's voice, rather shakier than usual. 'Have lunch or something, like you said.'

'Of course.' Jocasta smiled into the phone. 'It would be lovely. When did you have in mind?'

'Well, Saturdays are best. Because of school.'

'I can't do today. Next week? Where would you like to go?'

'Oh, I don't mind really.'

'Shall we say the Bluebird? In the King's Road? It's really fun there, specially on a Saturday.'

'Well . . . I'm not sure. Is it very expensive?'

'Kate, this is on me. I suggested it, didn't I? Do you know where it is? Right down the end, near World's End.'

'I think so, yes. I'll find it anyway.'

'Good girl. Half past one?'

'Cool.'

'Oh, Kate—'

Jocasta, don't. Don't do it . . .

'Yeah, what?'

'When's your birthday?'

'August 15th. Why do you want to know?'

'Oh, I was just thinking about your work experience, you know. OK. See you on Saturday. How's your gran?'

'She's fine, thanks. Bye, Jocasta.'

'Bye, Kate.'

Jocasta put down the phone, and sat staring at it for quite a long time; then very, very slowly, as if someone was physically holding her back, she called up the *Sketch* archive site on her computer and typed in August 15th, 1986.

Carla Giannini was one of the great tabloid fashion editors. She understood precisely what fashion meant to tabloid readers: not hem lengths and fabrics and cut, but sex. She ignored the collections and the couture designers. Using up-market photographers she had them shoot sharp trouser-suits and dresses from Zara, Top Shop and Oasis, shoes from Office, jeans and knitwear from Gap, on young, long-legged, bosomy models, who preened themselves on her pages, saucer-eyed and sexy.

Carla had her own office, just off the newsroom, and Jocasta's desk was nearest to it. They were not exactly friends, but they fed each other cigarettes and quite often compared their extraordinarily different problems at the end of the day in the nearest wine bar.

Carla's major problem was finding girls to photograph. She liked real girls, not quite off the street, but singers, actresses, designers, anyone with more of a story to them than their statistics.

She felt all her birthdays had come at once, therefore, when she was walking past the Bluebird Café at lunchtime one Saturday and saw Jocasta sitting at a table, talking earnestly to one of the most beautiful young girls she had seen for a very long time.

'No,' said Jocasta. 'No, no, no, Carla. You can't, OK?'

'But, Jocasta, why not? She's *gorgeous*. Beautiful. Actually, she looked a bit like you—she could have been your younger sister.'

'Yeah, right,' said Jocasta. And then, 'Funny, Sim said that as well. Oh shit.' She stared at Carla and prayed she hadn't taken in what she had said. Her prayers were not answered.

'Sim? Sim Jenkins the staff photographer? Jocasta, has this girl got anything to do with that story about the old woman on the hospital trolley? She's not the granddaughter, is she?'

'Yes, all right, she is. But her parents are very protective of her. They didn't want her in that shot. Anyway, she's not sixteen yet.'

'Why are they so against it?'

'I suppose they mistrust newspapers. Quite right too. So you are not to do anything, Carla. Absolutely not to. We're talking important things like people's lives here. Not just some cruddy fashion pages.'

'I don't do cruddy pages,' said Carla with dignity.

'Anyway, I must go,' said Jocasta, standing up, pulling her tape recorder out of her drawer. 'I've got to go and interview this girl— woman—I used to know. Well, I didn't know her really. I travelled with her for a few days when we were eighteen.'

'Hi.' Kate, waiting for her bus, looked up from her *Heat* magazine. Nat Tucker stood in front of her. His black hair was cut very short and he was wearing baggy combats and a white sleeveless T-shirt. He looked fantastic. Why did it have to be today, here, with her in her school uniform? Thank goodness she'd taken her tie off.

'Hi,' she said again, pulling her headphones out of her ears.

'You all right?' he said.

'Yeah. Yeah, cool, thanks.'

'Still at school?'

'Yeah. Doing my exams, aren't I?'

'S'pose so. Want a lift home?'

'Oh . . .' She swallowed hard, simply to delay her answer, not sound too eager. 'Well, maybe. Yeah. Thanks.'

'Car's round here.' He jerked his elbow in the direction of a side road, started walking. Kate followed him. This was amazing. A-mazing.

'You've got a new car,' she said, looking at it admiringly.

'Yeah. It's a Citroën. Citroën Sax Bomb.'

'Great,' said Kate carefully.

'My dad got it into the workshop, let me do it up. Like the spoiler?'

'Course.'

'It does hundred and eleven,' he said, with an attempt at nonchalance. 'I upgraded the ignition and that. And the sound's great.'

'So . . . your dad let you have it for nothing?'

'No,' he said indignantly, 'I have to work for him, don't I? Well, get in. Here, give us your bag.'

He threw her school bag into the boot, and got in beside her, switched on the stereo. The street was filled with the thumping rhythms of So Solid Crew. He started the engine, pulled away with a screech.

'Where d'you want to go?' he asked.

'Oh, Franklin Avenue, please.'

'So . . . what you going to do next? After the exams I mean?'

'Don't know. Go to college, I suppose.'

'What?' His voice was incredulous. 'You get out of school and go straight back in again?'

'Yes. Well, I want to do A-levels.'

'Yeah? What for?'

'Well . . . to go to uni?'

'What for?' he said, clearly genuinely puzzled. 'I haven't got any GCSEs even, and I got a good job, plenty of dosh.'

'Yeah. But, Nat, I can't go and work for my dad like you. I want to work for a newspaper or a magazine, something like that.'

'What, as a model or something?'

'No. A writer. Why should I be a model?' she said, stretching out her legs, surreptitiously easing her skirt a little higher.

'Well . . . you've got the looks. Make lots of money that way, you could.'

Kate was silent; this was beyond her wildest dreams.

He turned into her road, pulling up with a screech of brakes. He left the stereo running. She could see her grandmother looking out of the window. God. Suppose she came out, asked to be introduced to him?

'I must go,' she said. 'Thanks for the lift.'

'Want to come out Saturday?' he asked. 'Clubbing over Brixton?'

Kate felt herself starting to blush with excitement. This was unbeliev-able. Nat Tucker was asking her out.

'Well . . .' She managed to wait a moment, then said, 'Yeah, thanks.'

'I'll pick you up. Nine-ish. OK?'

'Yeah. OK.'

The effort of keeping her face expressionless, her voice level and uninterested, was so immense she found it hard to breathe. She was halfway up the path when he called her.

'Don't you want yer bag?'

'Oh. Oh, yeah. Thanks.'

He got out of the car, pulled it out of the boot, slung it over the gate.

'Cheers. See you later.'

Kate was incapable of further speech.

'Hi, Martha! Blast from the past. It's me, Jocasta.'

'I think I'd have known that,' said Martha. She smiled, a charming, courteous smile. 'You look just the same. Do come in.'

Jocasta walked into the apartment. It was quite simply stunning. A mass of ash-blond wood flooring, huge windows, and a minimal amount of black and chrome furniture. 'This is gorgeous,' she said.

'Thank you. I like it. And it's near to my work.'

Martha was gorgeous too: in a cool, careful way. Very slim, wearing dark grey trousers and a cream silk shirt. Her skin was creamy too, with just some eye shadow and mascara and a beige-brown lipstick. Her hair—brown, shining hair, streaked with ash—was cut into a sleek bob.

'Which is where?' she asked. 'Your work, I mean?'

'I'm a partner with a City law firm. At the moment.'

'Oh, OK. Fun?'

'Not exactly fun. I like it though. Can I offer you coffee?'

'Yes, that'd be great.'

'Fine. Just excuse me a moment. Make yourself at home.'

She disappeared. Snooty cow, thought Jocasta; and recalled that other Martha, slightly nervous, eager to be friends, mildly defensive about her background. She had been so polite, so eager to please. What had changed her so much? Clio had hardly changed at all.

And she had been fun. Undoubtedly fun. The very first night in Bangkok, they'd all huddled together in one bed, the three of them, screaming at the cockroaches that had appeared when they put the light on, and then she'd pulled a bottle of wine from her bag and they'd shared it, drinking from the bottle, giggling.

'Right. Here we are.' Martha had appeared again, with a tray set with white cups, a cafetiere, milk jug, a bowl of brown sugar lumps. Jocasta almost expected her to put a bill down on the table in front of her.

'Thanks. So . . . cheers.' She raised her coffee cup. 'It's good to see you.'

'And you.'

She was very still, Jocasta noticed, still and self-controlled. She was also, clearly, very nervous. It seemed strange, when she was so patently self-confident. Well, that was what interviews were about. Finding out.

'Tell me,' Martha said, 'what's your brother doing? Is he a barrister?'

'God, no,' said Jocasta, 'much too much like hard work. No, Josh works for the family company. He's married. Got two little girls.' She smiled at Martha. 'So . . . you went to Bristol Uni, did you?'

'Yes, I did.'

'What degree did you get?'

'A first. In law. Look, is this part of the interview? Because I did say—'

'Martha,' said Jocasta as patiently as she could, 'I'm just playing catch-up. I'll tell you all about me if you like. And Clio.'

Martha seized on this. 'How is Clio?'

'Not very happy,' said Jocasta. 'She's getting divorced. She's doing very well at her job, though.'

'That's so sad. About her divorce, I mean. Have you met the husband?'

'No. He sounds like an arsehole.' She smiled expansively at Martha. 'He's a surgeon. Arrogant. She's better off without him. Mind you, I did upset him.'

'I thought you hadn't met him?'

'I didn't. But I wrote about his hospital. He didn't like it.'

'I don't suppose he did,' said Martha. She picked up her cup of black coffee. Her hand was shaking slightly, Jocasta noticed.

'But she's just the same, dear little Clio—remember how we started calling her that, on the second day in Bangkok?'

'No, I don't think I do,' said Martha.

Clearly, she was going to block any attempt at reminiscence.

'Anyway, did you do what you said, do Oz, and end up in New York?'

'You have an amazing memory,' said Martha. She paused. 'Oz, certainly. I didn't see much of the States. Look, Jocasta, I don't want to be rude, but I don't have an awful lot of time. So maybe we should start.'

'Of course. Fine. Well, look, let's start with a few basic facts.'

'Like what?'

'Oh, you know, what you do, how you got drawn into politics. Then we can do some details. It's a very good story, I think.'

She watched Martha slowly relaxing, growing in confidence as she took control, presented what was obviously a carefully rehearsed story. And it was a good one, from a spin point of view: the death of the office cleaner, her longing to do something to help, her growing involvement with Centre Forward, her returning to her roots.

'And . . . what about your personal life?'

'My what?' She had flushed scarlet. 'Jocasta—'

'You'll be moving to Binsmow. I just thought if there's a man in your life, he might not like that. It's a pretty radical step. Or does he live there?'

'No. I mean, I don't have a man in my life. Not . . . not an important one. Just a few good friends.'

'That's lucky. Or maybe it isn't.'

'I'm sorry, I don't know what you mean.'

'I mean, it may be lucky for your political plans, but wouldn't you like to have someone?'

'I really don't want to comment on that.'

'Oh, OK. Well, from what you've seen of it, is politics sexy?'

'Again, I don't quite know what you mean . . .'

'Oh, Martha, come on, all that power, all those secrets: husbands living away from home, nubile secretaries and researchers at every corner. I find it very sexy, and I'm only on the edges of it!'

'Perhaps that's why,' said Martha coolly. 'I can only tell you I have no personal experience of that kind of thing.'

Jocasta gave up. 'I remember you being rather shy when we first met. So, how different are you today from the young Martha? The one I went travelling with?'

'Jocasta,' said Martha, 'I don't want to go into all that.'

'Why not? It's such a sweet story. Three girls from school, meeting by chance, setting off round the world, and then meeting up again years later, each of us quite successful. It's too good not to use, Martha. It's not unsavoury or anything, it just makes you sound more colourful and interesting. I mean, it was a defining experience for me. Wasn't it for you?'

'No, I wouldn't say it was.' She was growing agitated. 'Look, I don't want it used. I said that I didn't want this to be a personal article.'

'Did you do a lot of drugs or something?' said Jocasta.

'Of course I didn't do a lot of drugs!'

'Well, I did,' Jocasta said cheerfully. 'And I got ill as well. Horribly ill. Dengue fever. I ended up in hospital and spent the worst night of my life listening to a young Thai girl in labour. She died.' Jocasta shuddered, then her thoughts returned to Martha. 'You never had anything like that? Never had to go to one of their hospitals?'

'No. I didn't stay long in Thailand at all. I went off to Sydney.'

'When was that?'

'What?'

'I said when did you go to Sydney? Don't look so scared, I just wondered. I was there in the January.'

'I'm really not very sure. It's so long ago. Jocasta—'

'And then did you go up to Cairns? And the rain forest?'

'Yes, for a bit. It was wonderful.'

'And you really didn't feel that year changed you much? It didn't affect what you might now call your political philosophy?'

'No,' said Martha firmly, 'no, it didn't. I'm afraid I really do have to go in a minute, Jocasta—'

'So, what is your political philosophy? Can you encapsulate it for me?'

Martha was caught unawares by this sudden return to safe ground.

'Well, yes. It's that people, all people, ought to be given a chance. Lots of chances. Good education, decent health care, reasonable living conditions. No one should be written off, abandoned to—to his or her fate.'

'That's really nice,' said Jocasta smiling at her sweetly. 'I like that. Thank you. Thank you so much, Martha, you've been great. I can do a nice piece about this. You're going to come out looking squeaky clean.'

'I don't know why you should say that,' Martha said, a spot of high colour on her cheeks. 'Why shouldn't I come out squeaky clean, as you put it? I hope you're not going to imply the reverse.'

'Of course I'm not! Calm down.'

'I'm perfectly calm. It's just that you—well, this is a new game for me.'

'Of course. But—'

'Excuse me,' Martha said suddenly, 'I've just remembered something.'

She stood up and walked, very quickly, out of the room—and that was what did it for Jocasta. Turned over the memory: one that she had long ago decided was not a memory at all, but a mistake, a case of mistaken identity, made as she was pushed and jostled in a swarming, stinking street. She sat reviving that memory and waiting for Martha to return.

She was quite a long time. Jocasta heard the loo flush, and then a tap running. When Martha came back in, she had renewed her lipstick and resprayed her perfume.

'I'm sorry about that,' she said, 'I had to check an email.'

'That's all right,' said Jocasta. 'Well, I must go. And I promise you faith-fully the article will be nothing but positive about you. You and the party.'

'Thank you. Right. Well, I'll have to trust you.'

'Yes, you will. Bye, Martha. And we must have a threesome one evening, you and me and Clio. Such a shame we all lost touch. Still, we've found each other now.' She walked to the door, then turned and smiled. 'Please don't worry about the piece.'

She saw Martha relax. 'I won't,' she said, and smiled back. For the first time she looked more friendly, less aggressive.

Jocasta took a deep breath. This was the moment. 'I just remembered something,' she said. 'You didn't go back to Bangkok, did you? That year? In . . . let me see . . . in late June?'

The smile went completely. Martha looked—what did she look? Angry? No, worse than that. Terrified, trapped. As she'd looked that day.

'Go back? Of course not. I told you, I went to the States—I went home from there—'

'I must have been mistaken then,' said Jocasta, her voice at its sweet-est. 'I thought it was unlikely. But I thought I saw you there. I went back that way, you see. It was outside the station, Bangkok station. I called your name. Quite loudly, but whoever it was just walked away.'

'Well, I expect she did,' said Martha. 'If her name wasn't Martha.'

Of course it had been Martha. She knew in that moment as certainly as she knew anything. And Martha knew she knew.

So why was she lying about it?

Kate couldn't ever remember being so angry. How could they do this to her, how dare they? The most important thing in her whole life and they were wrecking it for her.

'I just don't believe you're doing this to me,' she kept saying.

'We're not doing anything to you, Kate,' Helen said, 'except trying to look after you.'

'Oh, right. So you do that by not letting me go out for a few hours with my friends?'

'Kate, we're not talking about your going out for a few hours with your friends,' said Jim. 'You're going to a club in one of the most crime-ridden neighbourhoods in London—'

'The whole point about clubs in Brixton,' shouted Kate, 'is they're cool. What do you think's going to happen to me, for God's sake? That I'll take some Ecstasy and die? That I'll be beaten up? End up on the streets? I'm going with Nat. He'll look after me.'

'No,' said Jim. 'You are not going with anybody, and that's my last word.'

Kate glared at him, then left the room. Very shortly the familiar thud of her music filled the house.

Jilly heard Kate come downstairs when everyone else had gone to sleep. She heaved herself out of her bed in the dining room and went into the kitchen; Kate was making a cup of tea.

'Hello, darling. Make one for me, would you? I'm sorry about your date with your young man.'

Kate turned a swollen face to her. 'Oh, Gran,' she said, 'what am I going to tell him?'

'Maybe I can help,' said Jilly. 'I've always been very good at lies.'

They came up with the best they could manage: that Jilly was going home that weekend and Helen had insisted Kate went too, to look after her. Kate rang Nat and struggled with this, but he wasn't impressed.

'Can't you tell them you won't? That you're coming out with me?'

'Not really,' said Kate sadly.

'OK. Fine. See you around.'

His phone went dead. Kate went upstairs and cried.

Chris Pollock came storming across the newsroom and threw Jocasta's copy onto her desk.

'What the hell do you think this is? If it's your idea of a profile, Jocasta, you'd better go and find another paper to put it in. I'm not printing this crap. It's dull, it's uninformative, it's got no life—'

'Bit like the subject,' said Jocasta, under her breath.

'What's that?'

'Nothing. No. I'm sorry, Chris. I didn't think much of it myself.'

'Well, what the fuck did you turn it in for then? And this old picture of her. Off some leaflet or other. I mean, give me strength! I'm not running this unless you can get more out of her, or give it a decent angle. Preferably both.' He walked off, shouting across at the picture desk.

Carla came out of her office. 'What was that about?'

Jocasta told her.

Carla looked at her thoughtfully. 'Show me the picture.'

'Here. She's a thousand times better looking than that. Great figure too.'

'Well, darling, we're looking at the answer, aren't we? She can be my fashion feature next week. It's a great story. We can dress her for her new life. Then your copy won't matter.'

'Oh, thanks,' said Jocasta.

'No, honestly, darling, it's a great idea. Let me talk to Chris, then you can ring the bitch.'

'And then he said'—Jocasta paused, refilled her glass for the third time in twenty minutes—'then he said I'd better find another paper to put the story in. I can't believe it. I mean, it wasn't *that* bad. It's not fair, it really isn't.'

'Well, I don't think you can say it's not fair. The thing is, sweetie, you turned in a bad piece. By your own admission.'

'Thanks,' said Jocasta, glaring at him. 'I thought I might get a bit of comfort and reassurance from you, not a lecture on journalistic standards. You're supposed to be on my side, or so I thought.'

'I *am* on your side.'

'Oh, really? You could have fooled me. I've been waiting around for days to see you, and you were away for the weekend with your bloody mother again. Two weekends in a row you've been up there.'

'For two good reasons. Rupert's birthday and then Mummy and Pa's anniversary. Anyway, you were invited. And actually, I found it quite difficult, explaining why you couldn't come for a second time.'

'Oh, well, I'm so sorry, Nick. Sorry I make your life difficult. It's just that sitting around in a freezing dining room, while everyone talks about the hunt ball, isn't quite my idea of fun.'

'Jocasta, you're being very unpleasant. It's not like you.'

'I feel unpleasant. You're not being very nice either, saying I shouldn't file lousy pieces.'

'I said nothing of the sort.' He smiled at her. 'You're being ridiculous. Come here, let me give you a hug.'

'I don't want a hug,' she said, and to her horror, she started to cry. 'I want you to be there for me, when I need you—'

'I *am* there for you.'

'Nick, you so are not! You just go on and on your own sweet way, doing exactly what you please, working all the hours of the day and night, seeing your friends, going home to mummy, and just coming round here when you feel in need of a fuck!'

'That's a filthy thing to say!'

'It's true. And I'm sick of it. If you really cared about me, you'd have made some sort of commitment by now—'

88

'Oh, so that's what this is all about. The fact I haven't gone down on one knee and put a ring on your finger.'

'No. Not entirely. But—'

'Jocasta, I've told you. I would if I could. But I don't feel—'

'You don't feel ready. And when do you think you might? When you're forty? Fifty? I'm absolutely sick of the whole thing, Nick, I really am. I feel so . . . so unimportant to you.'

'Well, I'm sorry to hear that,' he said, picking up his car keys.

'Where are you going?'

'I'm going home. I'm not going to listen to any more of this.'

'Good!'

And he walked out, not slamming the door, as she would have done, but shutting it very slowly and carefully behind him. Jocasta picked up a heavy glass ashtray and hurled it at the door. It gouged out a chunk of wood before falling onto the tiled floor and shattering. She was standing there, staring at it, when her mobile rang. She looked to see who it was: Chris Pollock. Now what had she done?

'Jocasta? I want you on a plane to Dublin. Tonight if you can manage it. Gideon Keeble's daughter has run away from school with a rock star. You know Keeble. Don't come back till you've got the full story, OK? I don't want a repetition of that fuck-up with Martha Whatshername.'

'There won't be,' said Jocasta.

It was one of the longest days Kate could ever remember. And the most miserable. Nat had taken another girl, Bernie, to Brixton in the Sax Bomb and she hadn't stopped going on about how he'd looked so fit in his combats and vest, how he could really, really dance and how they'd been there till five in the morning. By the time Kate got home she was beside herself with rage and resentment.

She went up to her room, turned on the radio and lay down on her bed. It was so unfair. So totally, totally unfair. Everything was shit. Nat would never ask her out again, not now. She was branded as a poor sad creature still under her parents' thumb. She hated everyone. Nobody was on her side. Even Jocasta seemed to have forgotten about her.

Suddenly angry with Jocasta as well, she decided to ring her. She dialled Jocasta's mobile. It seemed to be switched off. Funny, she'd told Kate that she couldn't do her job without it; maybe it was out of range. Or . . . maybe she was at the paper. She could try there.

Endless ringing; on and on it went without being answered. Obviously she was away on a story. She was just going to ring off, when a voice said, 'Hello, Jocasta's phone.'

'Oh, hi,' said Kate, nervous suddenly. 'Is . . . is she there?'

'No, I'm sorry. Jocasta's away for a few days.' It was a nice voice, slightly foreign, quite deep. 'Can I take a message?'

'Um, no. No, it's OK. I'll ring again. Could you tell her Kate rang.'

'Kate? Is that Kate Moss?'

'I wish,' said Kate. 'No. Kate Tarrant.'

There was a brief but quite noticeable silence, then the voice said, 'The girl with the granny? At the hospital?'

'Yeah.'

'How is your grandmother now?'

'Oh . . . she's fine, thanks.'

'Good. Yes, I think I saw you the other day, having lunch with Jocasta at the Bluebird. Would that have been you? Long blonde hair?'

'Yes, that's me,' said Kate.

Then the voice said, 'You know, I wanted to meet you. I told Jocasta I thought you could perhaps be in one of my fashion features. My name is Carla Giannini, I'm the fashion editor of the *Sketch*.'

'You did?' Kate's heart began to pound. 'Do you really think that?'

'Well, I think you might photograph very well. I couldn't say, until I've done a few test shots. But I think it's more than possible. You should come in and see me one day.'

'Do you mean that?'

'Of course. Look, think about it and give me a ring. Maybe tomorrow? I'll give you my direct line.'

'Yeah. Yeah, that'd be great. Thanks.' Wow. WOW! Cool, or what? God. That would change Nat's mind. A model. In the newspapers. Wow!

Carla put the phone down and then smiled at it. Good. Very good. Jocasta wouldn't like it, but that was too bad. She had no claim on Kate. And Carla had pages to fill.

She'd quite enjoyed doing the shoot with Martha Hartley. She hadn't been nearly as bad as Jocasta had made out. A bit . . . reserved. But she was a lawyer. And she was certainly very attractive, and she wore the clothes—a suit, a jacket and an evening dress all from Zara—very well.

Half an hour later, as Carla had known she would, Kate called her.

Jocasta stood at the gates of Gideon Keeble's glorious house, and waited, along with two dozen other reporters, a large clutch of photographers and cameramen, and the duty policeman. She had been waiting for some time now, about twelve hours; it was the first crucial thing you learned as a reporter (or a photographer) to do. Nobody exactly enjoyed it, but nobody minded either; there was great camaraderie.

Dungarven House was almost a fortress on a hilltop. It was surrounded by a twelve-foot wall, and the southernmost tip of the estate was bounded by a lake; the only access from the far side was by boat.

Their radios told them that retailing billionaire Gideon Keeble was inside and that Fionnuala Keeble, his beautiful fifteen-year-old daughter, had run away from her convent school with rock musician Zebedee and had still not been found. Her mother, now Lady Carlingford, was on her way back from Barbados where she lived and was not available for comment. It was generally agreed that if Fionnuala was found, she would be returned to her father at Dungarven House.

Jocasta returned every so often to her hire car, which was parked a quarter of a mile or so down the lane, to check her emails. As darkness fell on the Cork countryside, she could only try to imagine what fear and anger Gideon Keeble must be experiencing over the disappearance of his beloved only daughter.

She looked at her screen as she typed her thoughts, and sighed. That copy wasn't going to redeem her in Chris Pollock's eyes. Give me a break, she said, looking up at the half-moon just rising now in the soft dusk sky. Please, please give me a break.

God, she wanted to pee. She'd have to go and find a bush—again. She shouldn't have drunk all that coffee.

She stood up gingerly, pulling up her trousers; she really was getting terribly cold. Maybe she should go for another walk, get her circulation going. If she walked down the lane she wasn't going to miss a car. She set out briskly; and after about ten minutes she saw a tiny pinprick of light coming towards her. It was fairly steady, not the up-and-down movement of a walker's torch. And certainly not a car. There was complete silence. So what—oh, of course! It was a bicycle. A farm worker perhaps. But why should he be coming up at this hour? She waited, almost holding her breath, and the light suddenly swerved off the lane and disappeared. Or rather went off to the right. Its rear light bounced up and down now, but proceeded quite steadily; it must be a track of sorts. Jocasta decided to follow. It was probably a wild-goose chase . . . but then there was a muffled cry and a curse and the light went out.

Jocasta walked cautiously over to the dark heap that the bike and its rider had become. 'Hello?' she said. 'Are you all right?'

There was silence.

She was right up to the heap now. It took shape. It was a boy of about fifteen, sitting on the ground, rubbing his ankle. He had a canvas bag beside him.

'Are you all right?' she said again.

'Sure I'm all right.' The accent was strong.

'Good. I thought you might have hurt yourself.'

He tried to stand up and winced. 'Fock,' he said.

'You have hurt yourself. Want me to look?'

He shook his head.

'Funny night for a bike ride,' she said.

No reply.

'You on your way up to the big house?'

'I am not. Making my way home. Down there in the village.' He pointed down into the darkness.

'Strange, you seemed to be going in the opposite direction. Anyway, you won't get home in that state. Would you like me to drive you?'

'No, thanks.' He stared at her. 'You one of those reporters?'

'Yup.'

He hesitated. Then, 'You won't write about me, will you?' he said.

'I might,' said Jocasta. 'Depends.' She looked at him consideringly. 'Quite a good night for poaching, isn't it? Just enough moonlight.'

'I am not going poachin'!'

'Well, you certainly aren't any longer,' said Jocasta. 'I think you'd better let me fetch my car and take you home. I swear I won't tell anyone.'

He looked down at his ankle. 'OK,' he said finally.

'One thing in return. How do you get into the grounds?'

There was a long silence, then the boy said, 'Follow this track right up to the wall. Follow round to your right. Few hundred yards along, there's a big tree. One of the branches hangs over the wall.'

'Right,' she said. 'I'll get the car.'

Twenty minutes later, she was back, having dropped the boy home. She parked her car quite a lot further down the hill. She didn't want any of the others getting on her trail. She pulled a torch out of the car, slung her rucksack onto her back, and then shut the car door very quietly. She started walking up the lane again, looking out for the track.

Right. Here was the wall. To the right, he had said, a few hundred yards . . . Tree, tree, where was the bloody tree?

There! Right there, just in a curve of the wall. Not too bad to climb, either, until she was level with the top of the wall, standing on a very strong branch with a helpfully placed parallel one to hold on to.

Then it got worse. She could step onto the wall quite easily, but she then had to get down on the other side and it was a good twelve-foot jump. Onto grass to be sure, but nonetheless it looked like a long way down. And there was absolutely no sign of the house, so she had no real idea of the direction she should walk in. Shit. She should have bought a map of some kind. And suppose Keeble had dogs roaming the grounds?

'Oh, for fuck's sake,' she said aloud, then unhitched her rucksack and threw it down. Finally, wondering in the slow motion of fear if this would be the last thing she ever did, she jumped after it.

'You sound absolutely terrible, love.'

'I feel absolutely terrible. I don't think I can stand it much longer.'

It was so unlike Helen to complain that there was a silence; everyone stopped what they were doing and stared at her.

Helen did feel appalling. She had had bronchitis after Christmas, which appeared to have recurred. Over the past few weeks, she had coughed repeatedly, night after night, went short of sleep, had a constant headache.

'Have you been taking your antibiotics?' asked Jim severely.

'Yes. Of course. He might as well have told me to eat sugar lumps.'

'Might have been better, love. You're skin and bone. It's all this worry, I'm sure. Your mother, the publicity, all that. It's been a big strain on you. I'm sure you'll feel better soon.'

'Dad!' said Juliet. 'Is that the best you can do? What about taking Mum away for a few days? See she has a bit of sunshine.'

'Where do you suggest I take her, the South of France or something?'

'Yes. Why not? It'd be lovely down there now.'

'I dare say it would. And my name's Midas. Do you realise what it would cost just to get down there?'

'Forty-five pounds each,' said Juliet firmly. 'Look, it says so here in the newspaper. EasyJet to Nice. Forty-five pounds.'

'It does sound a lovely idea, Jim,' said Helen.

They all stared at her; she so seldom asked for anything for herself.

'And who's going to look after you two?'

'We could go to Gran,' said Kate. 'We both could, as it's half term.'

'Oh, go on, Dad. Live dangerously,' said Juliet.

Helen giggled, which triggered a spasm of coughing.

Jim looked at her, then at Juliet. Then he said, 'Well—I'll look into it. Give me that paper. I might look on the web as well.'

Jocasta found herself at the back of the house; it was beautiful, classic Georgian, with wonderful tall windows reflecting the moonlight and a terrace running its full length. She walked towards the terrace, wondering for the first time what on earth she was going to do next. Should she knock on the door? Should she try to get into the house?

She suddenly felt almost embarrassed. She walked quietly along the terrace, looking into a series of rooms: a drawing room dimly lit, what appeared to be a library, in semidarkness, the walls lined with books; then a couple more rooms in total darkness and then—then what was obviously a study. The light in there was quite bright. Very traditional, it was book-lined again, with two leather chairs either side of a fireplace and a huge wooden desk housing, incongruously, a large computer, a laptop, a fax machine and several telephones. As she watched, Gideon Keeble came into the room, talking into a mobile. He sat down at the desk, then suddenly switched the phone off and sat staring at it. Then he put it down, very slowly and gently, folded his arms on the desk and buried his head in them.

Jocasta watched him, paralysed, feeling like the worst kind of voyeur, probing into an intensely private grief. She was actually contemplating stealing away, when a door further along the terrace opened and an Irish setter puppy, about six months old, bounded up to her, leapt up and licked her face. It was followed by an older dog, its mother, she guessed, barking, almost sternly, and as she patted and stroked and tried to hush both dogs, she saw Gideon stand up and walk to the door, clearly calling someone, before he disappeared. As she stood petrified, both dogs now barking loudly and relentlessly, he came out through the side door. He was carrying a flashlight, which he shone along the terrace; she stood there, frozen like a rabbit in the headlights of a car, braced for abuse, for fury, for outrage, watching him walking towards her, very slowly. But as he reached her, he said, in tones of absolute good nature, as if she had just wandered into a restaurant or some other very public place where he happened to be, 'Why, it's Jocasta Forbes, isn't it? What a pleasant surprise.'

'And you found her *where*?' the photographer, Marc Jones, asked Carla.
'In a restaurant.'
'Jesus. I can't believe nobody got there first.'
It was late in the evening; Marc had just returned with the test shots of Kate. Carla was waiting for him with a bottle of wine.
'I know. It was just lucky,' she said modestly. 'So, how are the shots?'
'Sensational.'
He flung a sheet of black and white contacts down on the desk; Carla pulled a magnifier out of a drawer and bent over them. They were remarkable. Despite having been in the studio herself when the pictures were taken, she saw something that had not been apparent before: the strange alchemy between subject and lens that occasionally takes place, an extra dimension, indeed almost another person. A nervous schoolgirl had walked into the studio; and there in front of them now was a gangly, wild-haired beauty, with an absolute knowledge of her own sexuality and how to confront the camera with it.
'Very, very lovely. Got any colour?'
'Yeah, I'll put them on the light box. They're great, too. It's the dark eyes and the fair hair. When are you going to use her?'
'Next week, probably.'
'Great.' He grinned. 'Just give me a date. What's the fashion story?'

'I thought we'd let Kate choose her own. I'll take her to Top Shop, Miss Selfridge, Kookai, and let her loose. That street fashion thing is a story in itself. I'll have to speak to the parents, of course. She's not sixteen yet. But it should be OK. I can't think why not.'

Jim had managed to book a week in a three-star hotel near Nice; Helen was torn between excitement and guilt and worry at leaving Kate at such an important time in her life.

'If you fail these exams, you won't get a second chance, you know. You need good grades for Richmond, and—'

'Honestly, Mum, I'll revise. I swear. Even if Gran lets me off, Juliet won't, she'll probably call the hotel and tell you if I stop for more than five minutes.'

'I won't!' said Juliet indignantly. 'Anyway, I'm doing that music course, don't forget. You can bunk off as much as you like.'

Martha pounded the running machine, sweat pouring off her; her legs throbbed, her lungs felt close to explosion. The demons that had attacked her in all their horror as she knelt in that filthy lavatory, vomiting into the disgusting bowl, had left her again, banished almost entirely. Almost.

She had finished. Target achieved. She stepped off the running machine, staggered to the shower. Now she could go back to her apartment, have a herbal tea, sort out her clothes for the morning, listen to some music and do some background reading for a meeting. She'd told Ed she couldn't see him. Not tonight. Tomorrow they had a date though. It was their four-month anniversary. Four months since they'd first gone out. Four months of being astonishingly happy.

Happiness was not an entirely familiar condition to Martha. She knew about achievement, about meeting her own standards, about success. But happiness: happiness was something else. Happiness was unexpected and uncontrollable; happiness was an entirely new set of values.

Ed had taught her that as he had led her into love. She did love him, she knew that. She had resisted it for a long time. She was frightened of love. It scared her. It was risking too much, giving too much away.

In addition, her first tentative courtship of her own constituency was proving as satisfying to her as she had hoped. Local politics might well be dull, but it was also a genuine opportunity to help the underdog, and to give people a voice. But above all (and this was what she found most exciting), it was a fight for hearts and minds. She was battling not only for them, but also for herself, to persuade them to give her power, power to help them more.

The article she had been so fearful of had become a bland fashion feature, with the copy little more than an extended caption, gratifyingly generous about her political career and pleasingly flattering about the Centre Forward Party. Chad would be very pleased. She had liked the pictures too. Martha was not vain; her appearance was simply one of her assets, one that she used and worked hard to improve, but no more than that. Nonetheless, the publication across a double-page spread in a national newspaper of three extremely flattering photographs of herself, wearing very nice clothes extremely well, was quite a pleasing prospect.

'I'm so sorry,' said Jocasta, 'so terribly sorry.'

'And what are you sorry for,' Gideon said, 'exactly?'

'I'm sorry about being here. I feel so . . . so awful.'

'Oh, that's perfectly all right,' he said. 'You are doing your job and I have to admire your initiative. You must tell me where you made your break-in, though. I didn't realise it was so easy.'

'It wasn't easy!' said Jocasta, mildly indignant. 'It was very difficult. I had to climb a huge tree and then jump down that massive wall—'

'Now, I hope you are not looking for sympathy,' he said. 'That would really seem a little unreasonable of you.'

'No, of course not,' she said. 'Sorry, Gideon. And I'm so sorry about your daughter. About Fionnuala. You must be terribly upset.'

'I'm not in the least upset,' he said. 'It takes more than a naughty daughter to have any effect on me.'

She was reminded of her own father. He would have dismissed the whole thing thus, as a naughty, childish prank, no more, not a desperate cry for help. She began to like him less.

'You haven't heard from her?'

'Now, would I be telling you if I had?' He smiled, a polite smile.

'No, of course not.' This was a nightmare; what was she going to do?

He sat, drumming his fingers on the arm of his chair. 'It might be an idea if you gave me your mobile. I'm sorry if I appear discourteous, but I really would prefer you not to file any stories just at the moment.'

Jocasta flushed. 'Of course,' she said. She pulled her mobile from her rucksack and handed it to him.

'Thank you. Now, if you will excuse me, Jocasta, I have work to do. Do let Mrs Mitchell know if you want coffee. She's just along the corridor.'

'Yes, of course,' she said, 'thank you.'

Should she make a run for it? For the front gates, climb over, forget her scoop? Anything would be better than this. And then she heard it: first the distant whirring, then the increased beating of helicopter blades, cutting through the silence.

Gideon stood up, white suddenly, his face very drawn. He looked out of the window onto the lawn behind the house; Jocasta stood up too, and in the sudden brilliant light that flooded the area, watched the helicopter land, saw the pilot jump down, and then shortly after, a slight figure wearing trousers and some kind of large jacket follow him and run under the spinning blades towards the house. It must be Fionnuala.

Gideon didn't move; just stood there, staring out. As the figure reached the terrace, she stood still herself, looking up at the house, and then began walking swiftly towards the side door. Not Fionnuala, but her mother, Aisling. Mrs Mitchell appeared on the terrace, and walked towards her; they stood together for a moment or two, then walked back towards the house. Finally Jocasta couldn't bear it any longer.

'Aren't you—aren't you going to go and meet her?' she said; and Gideon gave a great sigh, almost visibly shook himself and then walked silently and very slowly out of the room.

Chapter 7

KATE HAD BEEN LOOKING at the pictures of Martha Hartley in the *Sketch* on and off all day. She looked sleek and self-assured. 'Dressed for success', it said, right across the centre spread. 'Is Martha Hartley the future face of politics?' And then, under the headline, several extremely nice photographs of the future face. And figure. Kate grinned. If her pictures were as good as that, it would be awesome. She'd have the last laugh then, all right. And it would be this space; Carla had said when she called, that she'd like her to be in the Saturday paper.

'Next Saturday, if possible. Are there any days you could get away from school early? Say by lunchtime.'

'Any day,' Kate had said. 'It's half term.'

'Wonderful! Then how about Tuesday? And we could go out on Monday and pick out some things you like for the pictures. I thought I'd let you choose your own. Oh, and, Kate, do bring one of your parents along with you to the session—I wouldn't want them worried in any way about all this.'

'They're away,' said Kate, 'for a week.'

'Oh, I see,' said Carla, thinking that there must indeed be a God.

'I could bring my gran,' said Kate. 'She's looking after my sister and me next week. She's got a clothes shop and she's really cool.'

'Fine. Well, tell her to call me if she has any queries.'

Janet Frean read the piece about Martha Hartley; she didn't normally take the *Sketch* but a very excited Jack Kirkland had faxed her a copy of the spread. He called her half an hour later.

'Didn't she do well? Got all the points across. Very professional, I thought. Considering it's her first exposure to the press.'

'Indeed,' said Janet. 'And, yes, she does look extremely nice. Pity she talked about her personal dresser: could alienate a few people. But she'll learn. And it's only a detail.'

'What's so great about her,' said Jack, 'is that she's young and success-ful herself. Out in the real world. Not much of that in politics today. I think she's a real find.'

'Indeed,' said Janet. 'Jack, you must excuse me, I've got a line of people waiting for their breakfast here.'

Bob Frean, who was actually serving up the family breakfast, wondered what the loud crash was that emanated downstairs from the study and sent Lucy, the fourteen-year-old, to find out. Lucy came back grinning.

'She's fine,' she said. 'In one of her strops, that's all. Threw a paper-weight right across the room. She says she doesn't want any breakfast.'

'Fine by me,' said Bob.

'Darling, it's terribly exciting!' Jilly looked at Kate's flushed face, looked down at the newspaper with the pictures of Martha again. 'And I can see it would be lovely for you, but, well, I really don't know what your par-ents would say. I think maybe you should wait until they get back—'

'Oh, no!' said Kate, who knew very well what her parents would say. 'Granny, it can't wait. Carla said it was really important we did it this week, that otherwise it wouldn't be for ages, and anyway, then I'll be doing my exams so God—I mean goodness knows when it could be. They'd probably forget about me altogether. Oh, please, Granny, please say yes! It's such a brilliant chance for me. And, honestly, this woman's so nice, and she wants you to come with me. She says to call her with any questions you've got. She gave me her mobile number, said any time. Gran, please. *Please.*'

'Oh, well, that's a little different,' said Jilly. 'She's obviously a nice, responsible woman. But only if you go upstairs immediately afterwards and do at least two hours' revision. And then I'll test you on it. And don't call me Gran—you know I don't like it.'

'Sorry, Granny. And of course I'll work now,' said Kate earnestly.

Carla Giannini did seem to be an extremely nice woman: clearly interested in and concerned for Kate and her future.

'I really think she has the making of a model,' she said. 'I'll send you a few back copies of my pages, together with the photographs of Kate.'

'That would be kind. But is there really that much hurry? My daughter and her husband are away, as you know, and I would like to get their permission for this.'

'I can see that, of course,' said Carla, sympathetically, 'but next Saturday would be ideal. I have girls booked for the next four weeks, so it would mean going forward a long way. When, as I understand it, Kate'll be doing her exams. Naturally, I don't want to interfere with those . . .'

'That's very understanding of you.' Jilly liked her more and more.

'So I would have a problem if I had to pull Kate out now. Would it be possible for you to email your daughter, or speak to her on the phone?'

'I might be able to speak to her, yes.'

'Wonderful. But . . .' Carla hesitated. 'I will need to know by tomorrow at the latest, I'm afraid.'

Helen phoned on Saturday evening: they were having a wonderful time, the hotel was nice, the weather was beautiful, and Jim was taking her out to dinner at some very pretty restaurant down the road.

'I just lay by the pool all afternoon, and I'm coughing less already.'

'I'm so glad, darling. That's wonderful. And you mustn't worry about us, we're fine, and Kate is working really hard. There's just—'

'Oh dear, Jim's making faces, says we'll lose our table. Thank you once more. I'll ring again in a day or two.'

'Yes, but—'

'Mummy, I must go. Sorry. Love to the girls.'

Well, thought Jilly, she'd done her best. It wasn't her fault if Helen didn't have time to discuss things with her.

She called Carla Giannini the next day and told her she hadn't been able to ask her daughter about Kate. 'But I do feel quite happy about it myself.'

'Good. I'm so delighted. Now, would you like to come shopping with us tomorrow? Picking out the clothes for Kate to wear? You could make sure they were all quite suitable.'

'Oh, I don't think so,' said Jilly. 'I still get rather tired. And you'll have more fun without me.'

Chris Pollock was becoming seriously anxious about Jocasta. It really was very unlike her, this silence. He was in his office late that Sunday night when the call came.

'Hi, Chris. It's me, Jocasta.'

'Jocasta, where have you been? And what do you think you're playing at? And where's the bloody story?'

'I've been here. In Ireland. In Gideon's house.'

'In Gideon Keeble's house? My God, Jocasta, that must be some story. You've been there all this time?'

'Yes. And I'm really sorry, Chris, but there isn't going to be a story. Not from me anyway. Well, you can say Fionnuala's safely home again, but that's all. And the other thing is, Chris, and I'm truly sorry about this too, but I'm afraid I'm going to give in my notice.'

Jocasta had been quite frightened, that first evening. Sitting there, trapped in the vast house, living out this extraordinary adventure, with no idea what she should do.

She had drunk a cup of tea that Mrs Mitchell had brought her and wolfed down the biscuits that had accompanied it on the tray, had begun to study the books that lined the walls—wonderful, wonderful books, some of them first editions. She then moved on to the stack of CDs on the other side of the room: church choral music, through Mozart, and Mahler, into jazz, swing, and thus to the present, to Bruce Springsteen, Bob Dylan and 'My God, Leonard Cohen,' she said aloud.

'And what is so surprising about that?' she heard Gideon's voice asking her and she swung round and smiled at him and said, 'I absolutely love him. He's so . . . so wonderfully dismal. Not many people do. We're in a very small minority you and I.'

'Sondheim?' he asked.

'Adore him.'

'Opera?'

'Don't get it.'

'Bob Marley?'

'Of course.'

'Well,' he said, 'we are clearly made for one another. Musically, if in no other way.'

She looked at him nervously. He wasn't smiling.

'Now, I have come to see if you would like a bed for the night. We have a few to spare.'

'Well, I am tired. But . . . what's the alternative?'

'There isn't one,' he said. 'I'm not going to let you out yet. I'm sorry.'

'It's all right. I can see you can't.'

She accepted with absolute equanimity his low opinion of her. She had broken into his house, in order to steal something of infinite importance and delicacy, his relationship with his runaway daughter, and she had no right to feel even remotely indignant.

'Very well, then. Good night, Jocasta. I hope you sleep well. And—I hope you will forgive me—I have disconnected the land line. So there would be no point your trying to make any calls.'

'Fine,' she said.

The room was on the second floor, high-ceilinged, shuttered, and very cold. Mrs Mitchell, who clearly thought Jocasta a trollop, ushered her in, asked her if there was anything she might be wanting and left again very swiftly. Jocasta undressed with great speed, fell into bed and went straight to sleep.

She awoke, literally shivering; it was six o'clock. She got out of bed, folded back the shutters and realised why: the windows were wide open. Expecting a wonderful view, she could see only thick, grey mist; and it was raining. She shut the windows, pulled her clothes on—good reporter that she was, she had things like clean knickers and a tooth-brush in her rucksack—then went stealthily downstairs. No one was about, not even the dogs.

The kitchen was vast, and warmer than the rest of the house, thanks to an extremely elderly-looking cream Aga. She filled the vast kettle, managed to find a slightly chipped mug, took some milk out of the 1950s-style fridge, and went to the back door. She looked along the ter-race; it was so drenched in mist she couldn't even see the end of it, and the rain was growing heavier. She went back inside.

There was a phone ringing, quite persistently. Did that mean he had reconnected the land line? Now that was worth investigating. At least she could make a quick call to Chris. She followed the sound down the corridor. Of course! It was coming from Gideon's study. She slipped inside the room and closed the door. She waited for four more rings and then picked up the receiver. Silence.

'Hello,' she said cautiously, and then, 'Mr Keeble's residence.'

'Who's that?' The voice was young, light, cautious. Fionnuala? Jocasta Forbes, this is the scoop of your career.

'A friend of . . . of your father's. Shall I get him?'

'No, thanks.'

A voice, Gideon's voice, cut in, saying 'Hello? Hello?' and then the phone went dead.

She stood there, still holding the receiver, feeling oddly frightened. She was just putting the phone down, wondering why she wasn't doing it more quickly, when the door opened and Gideon came in, wearing nothing but a white towelling robe; he was barefoot, his hair wild, his face white, his eyes black with fury.

'What the hell are you doing in here?' he demanded, and for a moment she thought he was going to hit her. 'How dare you? Get the hell out. Now.'

'I wish I could go. Unfortunately I seem to be a prisoner here.'

'And what do you expect? Breaking into my home, prying into my most personal life? What do you think you're doing?'

'I'm doing my job,' said Jocasta, calm now, astonished at the extent of it. 'Which does consist, unfortunately, of prying into people's personal lives. I'm sorry, Gideon, very sorry, and I'm actually not enjoying it. Any of it.'

'I had thought better of you,' he said, his tone full of contempt.

'Oh, really? And why should that be? I seem to remember your congratulating me on some of my stories when we met at the Tory conference last autumn. What's changed, Gideon? I'd really like to know.'

He stared at her and then said, still icily hostile, 'So, who was that?'

'It was your daughter.'

'And what did she say?'

'Not a lot. She asked who I was. I said I was a friend of yours. I offered to fetch you.'

'And?'

'And she said . . .' she hesitated, 'she said, "no, thanks". And rang off.'

His face changed; she saw that she had hurt him. Then, 'Well, thank you for that, Jocasta. Depriving me of a chance to speak to my daughter.'

'Gideon, I didn't deprive you. She didn't want to.'

'And what were you doing answering my phone?'

'It was ringing,' she said. 'No one else was answering it. I assumed you and your wife must have left again.'

'I was in the shower. My wife—or more accurately my ex-wife—was no doubt on her own telephone. Speaking to her husband. Anyway, Fionnuala has been found, by the police. At Belfast Airport. Mr Zebedee is in police custody, although as Fionnuala is swearing he hasn't touched her, I doubt if he will remain there for long. So very soon you can go and write your wonderful story. Now just get out of here, will you? Right out.'

As she reached the door, she turned to look at him. He was slumped at his desk, staring at the phone, and she saw him dash his hand across his eyes. 'Gideon,' she said, tentatively. 'I'm so sorry for you.'

'Well, you have a strange way of showing that,' he said. 'No doubt Mr Pollock said to you, "You know him. You can get into his house. You can make him talk." Or words to that effect. Am I right?'

'Yes. Yes, you are, I'm afraid.'

'And you thought, no doubt, something along the lines of, "Well, yes, I can. He fancies me. I can get him to talk." Didn't you?'

'Yes, Gideon, I suppose I did. And I'm very, very ashamed of myself.'

'It's such a pity,' he said. 'I liked you, Jocasta. And, yes, I did fancy you. Who wouldn't?'

'I'm sorry. I feel absolutely . . . wretched,' she said.

'Well, I suppose that is something,' he said and gave a look of such dislike she felt sick. 'Now, I really would rather you left me alone.' He turned away from her, and Jocasta was reminded of countless similar incidents, when her father had ordered her from his presence, had made it plain he wanted none of her, and she felt, suddenly, a rush of courage, and knew what she should say to him.

'Gideon, there are other things I'm sorry about.'

'And they are?'

'Fionnuala,' she said quietly. 'I feel very sorry about her. And for her.'

'And what do you know about it? What right do you have to feel sorry for her? I really think you should stop this, Jocasta. I am in no mood for ignorant comment.'

'It's not so ignorant,' she said. 'I know something of what Fionnuala feels. Well, not exactly, of course. But I know how it is to be her.'

'I don't think you do,' he said. 'Be very careful, Jocasta.'

'I can't, Gideon, if being careful means not telling you what seems to me so obvious. What might help. I also have a father who is rich and high profile. Who I hardly ever saw. Who seemed to have no interest in me. Except when I did bad things, of course. My father was empire-building, making money, moving round the world. There wasn't any room for me.'

'I'm sorry you had such an unhappy childhood, Jocasta. You must write about it some day.'

'Oh, shut up!' she said and, horrified, found herself on the edge of tears. 'Look, don't you see—you have a daughter who doesn't know you. Who probably thinks you don't care about her. Who feels your business is much more important to you than she is. Can't you see how much that hurts? Can't you see it makes her want to do anything—anything at all—to make you take notice of her?'

'Oh, please,' he said, 'at least I acknowledge my daughter. Your father seems to deny your very existence. You'll be telling me next he abused you. That seems to be a prerequisite for successful young people of today.'

'You bastard!' she said and then the tears did come, strong, choking tears, and the memories with them, crashing in on her, horrible, miserable memories. She sat down on a chair, folded her arms across her stomach, bending over them as if in physical pain, sobbing helplessly.

'I'm sorry,' he said. 'I shouldn't have said that. Please forgive me.'

She said nothing, continued to sob. He sat down beside her, put his arm round her shoulders, tentatively. She shook it off.

'Did he? Is that what he did?'

'No,' she said, shaking her head. 'Of course not. Well, not sexually. I never quite know what abuse is,' she added with a watery smile.

I mean, does it have to be sexual? Or even physical? It's such a hazy area. Ironic, isn't it, and me a tabloid journalist.'

'It is indeed. I would personally define it as something permanently damaging. Which I am clearly guilty of. In your court at any rate.'

'I don't think you are,' she said slowly. 'My father was cruel, terribly cruel, and I know you're not. I'm not comparing the two of you, just our situations, Fionnuala's and mine.'

'Well, I think I deserve a few lashes. I have clearly made what is known here as a complete dog's dick of fatherhood.'

In spite of herself, she giggled.

'That's better. Do you want to talk about your father? It might help. It might even help me. You never know.'

'He just bullied me,' she said, 'right from the beginning. Not physically, he never hit me once, but he mocked me, put me down, and then laughed and said it was a joke. And there was endless comparison with my brother, Josh. "Why can't you be more like your brother?" he'd say. God, that'll be engraved on my heart. I tried and tried to please him but it never worked. I can't ever remember him saying anything kind to me.'

'And you've no idea why he disliked you?'

'Some drunken old uncle of ours told Josh our mother had trapped him into marrying her, got pregnant on purpose. He certainly hated her. Which is probably why he hated me, if the story's true. I've often thought he'd just planned to have the son, and then leave her, and I was a daughter and he was stuck with her, waiting for the boy. The minute Josh was born, almost, he left her.' She managed a weak smile. 'I'm sorry,' she said. 'I never in a million years meant you were like my father.'

'Well, that is a relief,' he said, 'considering how much you dislike him. Now, would you like a good strong cup of tea? With a lot of sugar. My mother's remedy for everything.'

'No. No, thank you.' She was silent, then, 'I shouldn't have said all those things to you. It was nothing to do with me.'

'I dare say it was good for me,' he said. 'One of the things about being an important person . . .' he smiled at her, to show that it was intended as a joke, 'is that very few people are brave enough to tell you the facts of life. The real ones, that is. And you live in a rather comfortable little bubble, thinking how clever you are and how right about everything. So, you've possibly done me a great service, Miss Jocasta Forbes. And Fionnuala, too. Now I must go. Aisling is going down to collect her and bring her back here. So that we can find out what's actually happened.'

'I see. Well . . . you can't arrive at a police station dressed like that.'

'Oh, I'm not going,' he said, 'she has made it very plain she doesn't want me there. She'll probably spit in my face if I turn up.'

'Gideon!' said Jocasta. 'You haven't taken in a word of what I've said. Go, for God's sake. If she spits in your face, at least while she's doing it she'll know you could be bothered to come.'

He stared out at the mist. 'I don't know if I should,' he said.

'Oh, get a grip,' said Jocasta, and she was smiling at him now. 'Go on. Go and get your clothes on.'

He came back in ten minutes; he was wearing one of his perfectly cut tweed suits, under a long Barbour. He looked very stylish: a caricature of a country gentleman. 'I've shaved as well,' he said, 'the better to receive the spittle.'

'Good. I promise you it'll be worth it. Is she really coming back here?'

'Yes.'

'Good. Then I might meet her.'

'Jocasta, you must go. I can't detain you any longer. People will be worried about you. And you have a story to write. I'll tell Mrs Mitchell to take you, when she goes down to the village. I'm sure your car will still be there.' He bent down and kissed her briefly on the top of her head.

It was late afternoon when they came back. Jocasta was watching from her bedroom window. The drenched grass gave way a little as the helicopter landed; Gideon got out, then Aisling, and then he turned and reached up his hand to the top of the steps. A girl got out: slight, dark-haired, dressed in jeans and a leather jacket. That was all Jocasta could see: except the way she shook her father's hand off and then stalked ahead of him towards the house, after her mother.

Two hours passed; there was the sound of shouting, predictable words, slung out like stones: 'After all we've done,' 'How could you be so stupid?' 'You've ruined my life!' 'I hate you both.'

Phrases drifted into her head; it was a perfect story, with every possible element in it: not merely love and lust, but riches, power, beauty, and wilful youth. Even, should she care to mention it, her own incarceration.

And then she saw them, walking across the lawn, Aisling and Fionnuala, with Gideon following behind them; the blades began to spin, and mother and daughter ran under the wind and climbed into the helicopter. Slowly it lifted, tilting dangerously, then began to climb. All that could be seen was a small white circle in the window, a face, Fionnuala's face, looking down. Gideon waved, and—please, please, Jocasta thought, wave back, please—but the circle did not move and there was no sign of any response. He turned again and walked back towards the house, looking as if he was the last person left in the world.

Jocasta turned also, and for the first time since early that morning, left her room.

He was in the study, as she had known he would be, staring at his laptop screen, his huge hands moving with odd deftness over the keyboard. She tapped on the door.

'Not now, Mrs Mitchell,' he said.

'It's not Mrs Mitchell. It's me.'

He swung round, his eyes red-rimmed. 'Why haven't you gone?'

'Oh—Mrs Mitchell didn't want to take me. How did it go?'

'What?'

'I said how did it go?'

'Not well,' he said, 'not well at all . . . But I really don't want to discuss it, I'm afraid. You must have quite enough for your piece. Especially if you've been here all day.' He looked at her and said, 'Are you sure Mrs Mitchell refused to take you? That you haven't just stayed here, gathering material all this time? Because—'

'Gathering material for what, Gideon?' she said.

'Your story,' he said, 'that's what. Your bloody, undoubtedly brilliant, story. Are you happy with it now, Jocasta? I expect you are.'

'Oh, very happy,' she said, 'and it is undoubtedly brilliant.'

'Well, good. But I hope you're not going to ask if you can file it from here. There are limits, you know, even to my good nature.'

'Of course,' she said, 'I realise that. And there are limits to even my ruthlessness. There is no story, as far as I'm concerned. OK?'

'What?' he said, staring at her. 'What did you say?'

'I didn't realise you were that decrepit,' she said, smiling at him, moving slowly across the room towards him. 'I didn't realise your hearing was faulty. I said'—she was quite near him now—'I said, there is no story. Not from me, anyway.'

'I don't understand.'

'Then your brain must be failing as well. And your animal instincts, come to that. I can't do that to you, Gideon, I just can't. It's perfectly simple, I just care about you too much. Now, you'd better get that'—she gestured towards his ringing phone—'it might be important. I'll leave you in peace. I'll be in the next room, if you want me.'

A few minutes later he came in. He sat down beside her and studied her as if he had never seen her before. Then he reached out his hand and pushed back her hair, leaned forward and kissed her, very gently.

'Thank you,' he said. 'I can imagine what that cost you.'

'Not as much as you might think.'

'Oh, really? I'm surprised.'

'Well, you don't know me very well, do you?' she said. 'Not yet, anyway. Who was that on the phone?'

'It was . . . it was Fionnuala.'

'Oh, really? And what did she say?'

'She said . . . she just said, "Hi, Dad. Thanks for coming today."'

'That sounds quite a lot to me,' said Jocasta. 'Now, I wonder if I could go for a walk? I've been shut indoors all day. And . . .'

'I would say that was absolutely your own fault,' he said, and he kissed her then, very softly, on the mouth, leaned back and smiled at her. 'And I wonder if you would allow me to join you? I think we have rather a lot to talk about . . .'

'I do, too,' said Jocasta.

'Well, I think that's enough.' Carla smiled at Kate.

They had had a wonderful morning, combing Top Shop, Oasis and River Island. The last two had been a bit of a rush, as Kate had promised Jilly she'd be home by soon after lunch to get on with her revision. Kate had chosen almost everything herself, some things that Carla wouldn't even have considered herself, but which looked wonderful on.

'I think so, too,' said Kate. 'I'm so excited. What time do you want us?'

'As early as possible. I've ordered a cab and I've booked someone from Nicky Clarke to do your hair. Now, let's get you onto your tube. I don't want your grandmother worried. She's terrific, Kate. You look a bit like her, too. Same colouring.'

'Pure coincidence,' said Kate.

'Why?'

'I'm adopted,' said Kate. 'Look, I'd better go. It's been great, Carla. Bye!'

Carla looked after her thoughtfully as she disappeared down the escalator, a whirl of blonde hair and long legs. Adopted? That was interesting. Another dimension to the story, perhaps. She must find out more.

Nick was walking along the Burma Road, as the Westminster press corridor was known ('Because everyone ends up there,' he had explained to a breathlessly interested Jocasta what seemed a lifetime ago), when his phone rang. He looked at the number; it was her. She had finally deigned to contact him, then. He had heard, of course, from Pollock, that she had not only failed to deliver what would have been the most brilliant piece, but that she was leaving the paper.

'As from now. It's so unlike her, so unprofessional. I suppose you know what it's all about?'

'Of course I don't,' said Nick. 'I don't know anything at all. I've been trying to contact her, but her phone's been switched off.'

'Do you think she's with Keeble?'

'I suppose it might be a possibility,' said Nick, and just saying the words was like drawing teeth.

And now here she was, on his mobile, several days after disappearing, several days of not caring for his anxiety, his concern.

'Yes?' he said shortly.

'Nick? Did Chris tell you?'

'He did. I have to say I'd have expected to be your first port of call.'

'Sorry, Nick, but I had to tell Chris about the story. And then, well, I wanted to think.'

'What about?'

'About what I was going to say to you.'

'And it didn't even occur to you that I might have been worried out of my mind? So, what are you going to say? What are your plans?'

'I'm going to stay here for a few more days.'

'So am I to infer you're there with Gideon Keeble? I mean actually *with* him? In his—' He stopped. He couldn't bring himself to say the word 'bed', it hurt too much. 'In his house?'

'Well, yes, I am. Obviously.'

'Obviously? I don't understand quite why it's obvious.'

'Nick, I couldn't do the story because of . . . of Gideon.'

'But the story was *about* Gideon. You might just have realised that. Before you left even.'

'Yes, I did. But I didn't care then.'

'What, so in forty-eight hours from not caring about him at all, you cared so much that you've thrown your entire career away?'

'Well, it's a bit more complicated than that,' she said. 'It wasn't just about Gideon. I realised what harm I could do to his family.'

'Oh, how touching!' he said. 'You've developed a social conscience!'

She was silent. Then: 'Sorry, Nick. I'm very sorry.'

'Jocasta, how can you turn your back on—on us? How can you throw away a long and very happy relationship just like that? On a whim.'

'It wasn't just on a whim. It absolutely wasn't.'

'Oh, really? Dare I assume this has something to do with my refusing to trail down to the altar after you?'

'Actually,' she said, 'I'd be trailing after you. You obviously haven't been to many weddings, Nick. But, yes, just something. In a way.'

'How fucking pathetic,' he said, and cut her off.

Carla was in the office, looking enraptured at the pictures of Kate that Marc Jones had taken. The girl seemed to leap off the page, alive, carelessly confident, quite, quite beautiful.

Now, what was she going to write about Kate? She wasn't really particularly interesting. Just one of a million other fifteen-year-olds. Best to concentrate on that. 'An extraordinary ordinary girl,' she wrote, 'who could be working in a branch of Top Shop, or—' No, it wasn't good enough. It just wasn't.

Her door burst open; Johnny Hadley, the diary editor, came in, looking flustered. 'Carla. Hi. Look, do me a favour, would you? I'm frantic, got to check a couple of things for the lawyers. I'm running a nice story on Sophie Wessex. A few months ago, Jocasta interviewed some woman in the powder room at the Dorchester Hotel, who said how sweet Sophie was, how she always had a kind word for everyone. It never ran, so could you have a rummage in her desk, see if you can find it. It would just make a nice bit of background. God, who's that? Looks a bit like Jocasta, wouldn't you say? Or am I imagining it?'

'No,' said Carla, glancing down at the pictures of Kate, 'I've thought it myself. She's my latest discovery. Yes, all right, Johnny, I'll bring the piece in if I can find it.'

She went out to Jocasta's desk and pulled out the top drawer; nothing in that but a stack of old tapes, some rather dubious-looking lipsticks and a packet of Tampax. The next one looked more promising: cuttings from the paper, a few drafts of articles. Nothing about Sophie Wessex.

'Oh my God!' said Carla. She sat down suddenly, at Jocasta's desk, and began to read a set of pages.

It was *exactly* what she had been looking for. Only it wasn't an article about the chatelaine of the toilets at the Dorchester. It was something quite, quite different. The photograph of Kate Tarrant with her grandmother in hospital attached to a print-out from the *Sketch* archives, and another from the *Mail* and yet another from the *Sun*, about a baby, abandoned at Heathrow Airport. On August 15th, almost sixteen years ago. A baby whom the nurses who cared for her had named Bianca . . . and whose mother had apparently never been found.

Chapter 8

'OH, NO,' WHISPERED HELEN, 'oh, no, please no,' as she read the story, read it again, and again, and then sitting there, white-faced under her new tan, concentrating on the extraordinary pictures of Kate, as if by ignoring the words enough, she could will them away.

Jim, literally speechless with rage, was pacing up and down the kitchen, pausing occasionally to bang his fist on the back door; and Jilly, the one most responsible for the horror, sat in the dining room, too shocked even to think.

When Gideon found Jocasta, she was sitting on the grass by the lake, still and stunned, holding the paper close to her, wondering how such a thing could possibly have happened, and cursing Carla with a venom that surprised even her.

Clio, doing a Saturday-morning surgery, was shown the article by the receptionist. 'It mentions Mrs Bradford,' she said excitedly. Clio sat in her room, reading and rereading it, wondering how much Kate had contributed to the story herself, and hoping against hope it had been nothing to do with Jocasta. And wondering, too, how Kate's mother, her real mother, would be feeling when she saw it, as she surely must.

Nat Tucker read it as he sat in his mother's kitchen, ignoring his father's exhortations to get on down to the garage, and wondering not only if he should call Kate or just go round and see her, but how he could never have realised how totally gorgeous she was. And, with a sensitivity that would have surprised most of his mates, and the whole of his family, thinking that it couldn't be that great, having the fact you'd been abandoned in a cleaning cupboard splashed all over some cruddy newspaper.

Martha saw the story trailed on the front page of the *Sketch* while she was out on her early run: 'The abandoned baby: now tipped as the latest face in fashion. Meet Kate Bianca, modelling for the first time in the *Sketch* today.' She read the story, put the paper, folded neatly, into a rubbish bin, ran back to her apartment, showered and dressed in one of her constituency suits, and drove down to Binsmow. She arrived, as promised, at the vicarage at eleven thirty, did a brief legal surgery, and at one thirty went to a school Summer Fayre. That evening she and her parents attended a charity concert in Binsmow Town Hall, where she bought five books of raffle tickets and won a bottle of bubble bath. She left Binsmow early next morning, after going to early Communion and then breakfasting with her mother, who was engrossed in the story of Kate Bianca, the abandoned baby, which had found its way into the *Sunday Times* as well as the *Mail on Sunday*. She agreed it was the most dreadful thing to abandon a baby and that she couldn't imagine anyone doing such a thing, then drove back to London and her apartment, where she spent the day working. In the evening she went to the gym, where she did a spinning class and swam thirty lengths of the pool.

Ed Forrest, who had left four messages on her land line, several more on her mobile and a couple of text messages as well, asking her to call him to discuss, among other things, a trip to Venice he had organised, was first hurt, then annoyed and finally seriously anxious, when she failed to answer any of them.

And Kate, her golden, dazzling day turned dark and ugly, sat in her bedroom, the door firmly locked, crying endlessly and silently, and feeling more wretched and ashamed than she could have believed possible.

Clio decided she should ring Jocasta.

Her mobile was on message. Clio left her number, asked her to call, and was still wondering if she could actually be bothered to make herself anything more than a sandwich, when Jocasta rang.

'Hi, Clio. It's Jocasta. How are you?'

'Fine. I just saw the article about Kate and—'

'It was nothing to do with me, Clio. Honestly. Well, only in the most indirect way and, well, actually I've left the *Sketch*.'

'You've left? Why?'

'Oh, bit of a long story. Look, I'm in Ireland at the moment, about to fly to London. I'm going to try to see Kate, because I do feel responsible. In a way.'

'Jocasta, you're talking in riddles.'

'I know. Sorry. Look, if I haven't been beaten up by the Tarrants, could we meet this evening? It'd be good to talk it through with someone who knows Kate. Would you mind?'

'Of course not. Don't be silly. Just call me.'

'Is that Mrs Tarrant?'

'Yes?'

'Mrs Tarrant, you don't know me, but I think I could be Bianca's mother. You see, I left a baby at the airport seventeen years ago . . .'

Helen thought she might be sick. 'Sixteen years,' she said sharply.

'What? Oh, I'm sorry, I thought it said seventeen.'

Helen slammed the phone down and burst into tears; and greatly against her will, she called Carla Giannini.

Carla had called first thing, bright and confident. Weren't the pictures lovely, didn't Kate look great, they must all be so proud of her.

'Would Kate like to speak to me, I wonder?'

'No,' said Helen in a quiet, numb voice, 'no, I'm sure she wouldn't.'

'Well, later, perhaps. Tell her I've had several offers for her already.'

'What sort of offers?'

'Modelling agencies. Of course, that is all entirely up to you.'

'I'm so glad something is,' Helen said icily.

Carla ignored this. 'There is one thing, Mrs Tarrant. One thing I should warn you about. You could get calls. From women claiming to be Kate's mother. We've had a couple already. Now, I would advise you to let us handle these for you. Put any calls on to us. It's—'

'I don't want you to handle anything for us,' said Helen, and she could hear the loathing in her voice. 'Please leave us alone.'

And she put the phone down, very carefully. What was she going to do? How were they going to get through this? How?

After two more phone calls from women, Helen realised, very reluctantly, that they couldn't do it alone.

Carla was brisk and efficient. 'Just redirect them all to us.'

'And suppose . . . suppose one of them was genuine?' The words hurt her to speak them. 'How would we know?'

'Well, we would ask for proof of some kind. Is there anything that you know, about the way Kate was abandoned, that wasn't in the story?'

'Yes, there is one thing. She wasn't wearing a nappy.'

'That will do,' said Carla. In fact it would do wonderfully well. No one would expect a baby to be left without a nappy on.

Half an hour later, there was a ring at the door. Helen answered it. It was Nat Tucker. The Sax Bomb stood at the gate, its engine still running, its sound system at apparently full volume.

'Oh,' she said. 'Nat. Hello.'

'Mornin',' he said. 'Kate in?'

'Er, she is,' said Helen, 'but I'm afraid she's not very well.'

'Oh, right. Just tell her I came then. And that I saw her photos in the paper.'

'Fine. Yes. Of course.'

'Nice, aren't they?' he said. 'She looks great. Well, see you later.'

And he ambled down the path, pulling a packet of cigarettes out of the pocket of his extremely low-slung trousers. Helen and Juliet, who had heard his voice, stood staring after him.

'How sweet,' said Juliet, 'how really, really sweet. Wait till I tell Kate.'

Helen caught her arm. 'Juliet, you are not to tell Kate.'

Juliet stared at her. 'Why on earth not? He's the one person in the whole world, probably, who can make Kate feel better just now.'

'Don't be ridiculous,' said Helen.

'It's true! She only did it to make him notice her. She'll be so pleased he came round. And don't you realise, half of what's making her so upset is thinking everyone'll know that her mother just, well, just threw her away, as she sees it. If Nat Tucker doesn't care about it, she'll be so much happier. So I'm going up to tell Kate and you can't stop me.'

Kate was wondering how she could ever leave her room again; ever face a world that knew what had happened to her, that must be either despising her or feeling sorry for her or even laughing at her, when Juliet called through her door that Nat had come to the house, had wanted to see her, had said she looked great: it was like—well, she didn't know what it was like. Like being given a present. She opened the door, let Juliet in, and sat on the bed, staring at her.

'Did he really? Come here?'

'He really did. He's so sweet, Kate. Honestly. It can't have been easy for him. He obviously does like you a lot. Why don't you call him?'

'Yes. Yes, I might. Later. God, Jools, think of that. He actually came. Came here. That is so cool. Tell me again exactly what he said. Exactly . . .'

Helen recognised Jocasta; she was looking nervously from behind the curtains in the front room at the growing crowd at the gate. She turned to Jim. 'It's Jocasta. You know, Jocasta Forbes—'

'I'll tell her to bugger off,' he said.

'Jim!'

'Well,' he said, his tone weary, 'she was where it all began. No doubt she told that other woman all about Kate. I don't want her here. And if we let her in, those other vultures will follow her. Or try to. Here's another, looks like a photographer. Oh, Helen, what are we going to do?'

'I think we should let Jocasta in,' said Helen bravely. 'My mother said it was nothing to do with her. And I think she might be able to help.'

'It was totally awful,' Jocasta said to Clio later, over a glass of wine. She had arrived on Clio's doorstep, pale and very shaken. 'None of them believed me. Kate refused even to see me. She just said she thought she could trust me. That she thought I was her friend. Shouting through her door at me. Oh God, Clio, what a mess. What have I done?'

'Nothing, I thought,' said Clio.

'Well, I did do one thing,' said Jocasta. 'I looked Kate up in the archives. Her grandmother told me she'd been abandoned, and Kate had told me when her birthday was. I printed the story off. It was in all the papers at the time. About Baby Bianca being found.'

'And then what?'

'Then Kate told me all about it herself when we had lunch at the Bluebird. She thought that if I wrote about it, her mother might come and find her. I certainly wasn't going to do anything without her parents' permission, but I put all the print-outs in my drawer. I shouldn't have. If I'd thought for five minutes, I'd have shredded them. But, well, I didn't know I was going to leave. I didn't know that cow Carla was going to go through my desk. Oh, Clio, what am I going to do?'

'I don't know,' said Clio, 'but I'm sure Kate will calm down.'

Jocasta's mobile rang. 'Hi,' she said. 'Oh, hello, Gideon. How absolutely lovely to hear your voice. No, everything's not all right. It's ghastly. Look, I'll call you later. I'm with a friend. An old friend.' She smiled at Clio. 'Yes, you would like her. A lot. She's really, really normal. We went travelling together. With that bitch Martha I told you about. What? Oh, that's wonderful, Gideon! I might stay in London, till you get back. I don't think I can cope with Mrs Mitchell on my own. Yes, I will. I promise. I love you too.'

'Who was that?' Clio asked.

'Gideon Keeble. He's Irish and quite famous—owns dozens of shopping malls all over the world and God knows what else. Several houses. He's had umpteen wives and he's got a nightmare teenage daughter, who he's just off to see in Barbados, to buy her some polo ponies.'

'*Some?*' said Clio, incredulously.

'Yes. One is nothing like enough, apparently. Anyway, he's older than me and a complete workaholic and it's all completely unsuitable. And I am totally, totally in love with him. I've left Nick, given up my job, given up my whole life here. Just to be with Gideon.'

'Goodness,' said Clio, 'he must be very special.'

'He is. I can't imagine how I could ever have thought I was happy until now. I feel—oh, I don't know—as if my real life has only just begun.'

All she had to do was keep completely calm. Nothing could happen, if she did that. No one could possibly think she had the slightest connection with this rather sensational story in the tabloid press. There was no connection. None at all. The only person who might think there was anything disturbing her was Ed, because he had been so close to her. But he couldn't be any more. He would have to be out of her life. And then she would be safe. As long as she kept calm. Perfectly calm.

Kate called Jocasta. She sounded very shaky.

She said she was sorry she'd been so rude to Jocasta and that she totally believed that Jocasta had had nothing to do with the story.

'I was just upset. It was all such a—a shock.'

'Of course it was. I was so sorry for you. The pictures were lovely,' she added carefully.

'Yeah, well. Pity about the rest. But it's not so bad, I s'pose. I don't have to go to school at the moment, because I'm on study leave, so I can avoid the really cowy girls. But I need your help really badly, Jocasta. All these women keep ringing up, saying they're my mother, about a dozen of them now, and I'm so scared one of them really is my mother, after all this, and I'm going to miss her. I just don't know what to do.'

'Well, I'm sure the paper will be keeping names and so on.'

'Yes, but I need to—to know,' said Kate desperately. 'I can't lose her now. And what about the model agencies, what should I do about that? Mum is so totally no use, and Dad's gone ballistic, and Juliet said we should ask you. Could you help, do you think? Please, Jocasta, please.'

Jocasta was so touched by this plea that she was half inclined to rush straight over to Ealing and the Tarrants, but she called Gideon and he had wiser counsel.

'You can't do it, Jocasta. You're too involved and the responsibility is just too much. Now, listen, I have the very man for you.'

'Gideon's such an angel. You can't imagine,' Jocasta said to Clio. 'He's so kind and so concerned for me. I'm so lucky. Just wait till you meet him, Clio, you really will love him, I promise.'

'I'm sure I will,' said Clio carefully.

She was staying the night in Jocasta's house in Clapham. The next day she was meeting her old friend, Beaky, a professor at the Royal Bayswater Hospital, who had let her know that there would soon be a consultant's job coming up. General practice in a country town was fine, if you had a life outside it; she didn't, and she already felt the loneliness beginning to bite. She had told Mark, hating to deceive him when he'd been so kind, that she had to see her solicitor about her divorce, which was true, for she had arranged that too.

'Meanwhile, you're going to meet a friend of Gideon's who's going to sort Kate out. His name's Fergus Trehearn.'

Fergus Trehearn was Ireland's answer to Max Clifford, Jocasta explained to a rather bemused Clio. 'You must know about Max Clifford,' she added, seeing Clio's puzzled face. Clio said humbly that she didn't and when she had heard what Max Clifford did—'He sort of manipulates everybody including the press'—she said she was surprised that anyone should want to.

'Oh, Fergus is a complete sweetheart, apparently,' said Jocasta, 'and Kate certainly needs him. She—they just can't cope with it all. Fergus will take the whole thing on, sorting all these women out, getting Kate the best contract with a model agency, deal with offers from other papers and magazines for her story—'

'She won't want anything like that, will she?' said Clio.

'Not at the moment, no. But the thing is, you see, as far as the media is concerned, Kate will be Abandoned Baby Bianca for the rest of her life. Any story about her will refer to it and maybe one day, who knows, she might want to tell her story. And if her mother turns up . . . well, that could be huge. Anyway, she needs her interests protected. Fergus will stop unscrupulous people taking advantage of her. And her parents. Anyway, I said Fergus should come to my house. You don't mind, do you?'

'Of course not,' said Clio bravely.

The last thing she wanted was to have to meet some flashy gold-medallion man and listen to him talking about manipulating the press.

But it was not a medallion man who sat in Jocasta's untidy sitting room, listening carefully to her as she talked. It was someone charming and courteous and well dressed, in a linen suit. He was in his early forties, tall, slim, and extremely good-looking, with close-cropped grey hair, and very dark brown eyes. He was Irish, garrulous and funny, and she found it hard not to like him. Jocasta introduced her as her brilliant friend who was a consultant physician and he appeared duly impressed, even as she protested and said she was nothing of the sort.

His manner, as he listened, was concerned, and sweetly interested. It completely belied the ruthless opportunism that drove him.

'He will be perfect for Kate,' Jocasta said to Clio happily, after he had gone, 'and make her lots of money. Isn't he a sweetheart?'

'Look,' said Martha, 'I'm sorry. I can't go away to Venice. Not at the moment. I don't know why you can't accept that.'

It had taken her all day to bring herself to make this call; and every word that she said hurt more than the last. She kept seeing him, sitting there, confused, bewildered by the change in her, and she didn't quite know how to bear it. But it had to be done.

Suppose he'd read about it, said he couldn't imagine anyone doing such a thing. Or said how dreadful, how awful the mother must be.

No, it was very clear. The need for control was back. And to be in control, you had to be independent, answerable to no one. Ed loved her. And she loved him. And love was powerful, when it came to secrets. Huge, dangerous secrets. It saw them, it found them out.

She took another deep breath. 'So, I can't go to Venice. Is that all right?'

'Of course it's not all right! Two days ago you said you could.' Ed's voice was very quiet. 'You couldn't even be arsed to call me all weekend, didn't return my calls. Don't you care that I was worried out of my skull? Don't you?' His voice was cracked with pain.

'Yes, of course I care, Ed, but as I told you, I—'

'You're made of fucking stone,' he said, 'you know that?'

She was silent for a moment. Then she said, 'Ed, I really don't like being abused like this. If you can't cope with my life and the way I am, then we would do far better to end this whole thing.'

'What whole thing?'

'Our relationship, of course.'

'Relationship!' he said. 'You call what we have a relationship? Right now, I'd call it a load of bullshit, Martha. You tell me what to do and say and think, where to be and when, and I'm finding it extremely tedious all of a sudden. OK?'

And he slammed the phone down.

Martha replaced her receiver and sat for a long time, just staring at it. Wanting more than anything to pick it up again, fighting the instinct to say she was sorry, she hadn't meant it, and she loved him, wanted to see him. But she couldn't. It was too dangerous.

By the end of the weekend, Kate was feeling better. She couldn't help it. It had been an awful shock, and she still felt hideously ashamed that everyone knew what had happened to her, that everyone must be pointing her out, saying that's the girl whose mother just threw her away, and yes, it was horrible to have trusted someone like Carla and then found yourself just totally let down. It was appalling to think that one of those women who had phoned up might be her birth mother, and that she was having to wait quietly when the most tumultuous discovery in her life might be within reach. But it was also quite nice, she had to admit, to have not just the *Sketch* but papers like *The Sunday Times* describing you with words like beautiful and dazzling, and to see your pictures in them, as well.

And to have model agencies ringing up, asking you to go and see them, and even magazines, asking if they could come and interview you—that was pretty cool.

And then there was Nat. It had almost been worth it all, to have Nat calling her twice a day and taking her out in the Sax Bomb and saying what about going to the Fridge this Saturday. Given everything that was happening to her, it seemed a little absurd for her parents to try to stop her. They had compromised on a 2 a.m. latest return; Nat had said that it was cool. The thing they didn't understand—that nobody seemed to understand—was what a nice person Nat was. The first thing he'd said when she'd got in the car was, 'You all right?' and, 'Yes,' she'd said, yes, she was fine, thank you. And he'd said, 'I meant about the story in the paper, like, about your mum,' and it had completely wiped her out, that he'd understood how she might be feeling.

Then he leaned forward and started to kiss her; he was a very good kisser. They were parked under some trees; it was terribly romantic.

Clio felt very tired when she got home. The meeting with Beaky had been wonderful; he had told her how much she had been missed and how he hoped that she would apply for the consultant's job.

'I've got a very good team at the Royal Bayswater,' he said. 'Keen, clever, mostly young. You'd fit in jolly well, Clio. We've got a couple of research projects going, we're doing some trials with a new Alzheimer drug and we've got a wonderful new psychiatric chap.'

'It does sound wonderful,' she said wistfully, 'but—do you really think I'm up to it?'

'Clio! Is this really the brightest new consultant in the department for years talking? You do put yourself down, dear girl, and you really mustn't do it. I wouldn't suggest you apply, if I didn't think you were absolutely up to it, as you put it. As far as I can see, you're the perfect candidate. You're familiar with the hospital and the workings of the department, you did very well when you were here, everyone liked you—and from what you tell me, you've done a lot of geriatric work while you've been in general practice.' He patted her hand. 'We need you.'

She left him, promising to apply, and made her way to her solicitor's office. She had been warned it would be wretched and it was. It was one thing to agree, however sadly, that your marriage was over; it was quite another to find yourself picking over the balance sheet of that marriage. She had agreed that she wouldn't contest the divorce and had expected a certain generosity in return; but Jeremy was even querying her right to a share of the house, claiming she had walked out on a marriage that she had entered into under false pretences.

'Don't worry, Mrs Graves, they all start like this.' Her solicitor smiled at her encouragingly. 'He'll come down.' She passed Clio a tissue from the box on the desk between them. 'It's horrid. I know.'

Martha got out of the cab, went into her building, pressed the lift button. She felt just a little better. No journalist had rung her; and after three days, it didn't seem likely that they would.

The only thing was, of course, how much she was still hurting over Ed. It was like the pain of a burn, searing, shocking, beyond the reach of any analgesic. But it would pass. It had to.

Her doorbell rang. She pushed the buzzer. 'Yes?'

It was Ed.

She stared at him as he stood in her hallway, thinking with complete irrelevance that he looked absolutely wonderful, wearing an open-necked white shirt and jeans, like someone in a film.

'I want to know what's going on,' he said. 'Something's happened, Martha, hasn't it?'

'Nothing's happened,' she said, fists clenched, meeting his eyes with considerable courage, for what might he read there? 'Nothing's happened at all. I'm just . . . just terribly busy.'

'Martha,' he said quietly, 'I love you. I know you really rather well. I know every inch of you. Literally. I know how you are when you're happy and when you're upset and when you're stressed and when you want sex, and I know when you want to talk and when you want to be quiet and when you're feeling tired and mean. And I know something's happened to you—I *know* it. This is not about you being busy. It's about you being scared. What are you scared of, Martha? You've got to tell me. What have you done? Nothing you did could shock me, or upset me, unless it was falling in love with someone else. I'd have to get over that, but at least I'd know. Is that it, is there somebody else?'

'No,' she said, shakily, 'there's no one else.'

'So, what is it?'

And just for a moment she wanted to tell him. Just to get it over, just to know that someone else knew this awful, dreadful, shocking thing.

But she couldn't.

'Nothing's happened,' she said finally.

'Oh, Martha,' he said, 'I wish you could trust me. I shall find out, you know, somehow. I won't leave you alone until I do, and I won't leave you alone, even then. I think you need me.'

'No,' she said, summoning up all her will. 'No, I don't. I don't need you, Ed. And you certainly don't need me.'

'That's where you're wrong,' he said, 'I do need you. We need each other. I'm going now. But don't think I'll give up. I love you too much.'

And then he was gone.

She was awake all night. She had set her alarm for five, but she watched the hours, the quarter hours; she felt appalling fear, her heart pounding, her stomach churning. She had never felt so alone: not even in that dreadful tiled room, in appalling pain, pushing her baby out in abject terror.

When Martha began putting on weight, she told herself it was all the food she'd been eating and the beer she'd been drinking. It was a well-established fact of travelling that you lost weight in Thailand and piled it on again in Oz. But this was different, her arms were still stick-thin, and, forcing herself, with a supreme effort of will, to look sideways at herself in the bathroom mirror at the Avalon Beach Hostel, she could see a distinct doming of her flat stomach. She told herself that she was just being hysterical. Just the same, she went into the Avalon chemist, bought a pregnancy-testing kit, locked herself in the bathroom the next morning to use it. A distinct blue ring told her she was pregnant.

Terrified, she gathered all her courage together and went to the doctor in Avalon. He was young, brisk, cheerful and very Australian. 'Let me have a look at you and then we'll know what we're talking about.'

He was quite a long time, gently palpating on her stomach, doing an internal. A nurse stood watching, her face expressionless.

'All righty, Martha,' he said finally, 'you get your clothes on. And then we'll have that talk.'

He told her she was about five months pregnant. 'But I can't be,' she said, her mind flying back in hot, black panic to Koh Tao, five months earlier. 'I've had periods, one just about a month ago.'

'Can still happen. Was it quite light?'

'Well . . . quite.'

'How long did it last?'

'About . . . about two days.'

'Martha, I'm sorry, that's quite common. Have you had any nausea?'

'A bit. But not every day, just, well, for a few days. I can't be pregnant, I really can't.'

'Are you telling me you haven't done anything to get pregnant?' he said, his blue eyes twinkling at her.

'Well, I have. But only . . . only once.'

'It only takes once. I'm sorry, Martha. There really is no doubt. When was this one time?'

'At the end of October.'

'I'm afraid that exactly adds up. Exactly.'

'I'll have to have a termination,' she said immediately.

'Martha, I'm very sorry,' he said, and his voice was gentle and almost hesitant, 'it's much too late for that.'

Chapter 9

CLIO HAD APPLIED for the job of consultant geriatrician at the Royal Bayswater. It had taken a lot of courage; she knew how devastated she was going to feel if she didn't get it. Just the same, she knew that staying in the Guildford practice wasn't what she needed any more. She did love it, but she really wanted to get back to London.

She still hadn't said anything to Mark, but she was taking Beaky's advice and had organised a few days off to visit the other hospitals in the Bayswater group.

'Borrow my house,' Jocasta had said promptly when she heard. 'I'm going to New York. The people next door have the key.'

Clio arrived in the early evening, and within ten minutes felt at home. As she was was coming downstairs, her mobile rang.

'Clio? Clio, it's me, Jocasta. How are you?'

'I'm fine. Just arrived at your house. How's New York?'

'New York's wonderful. Really wonderful. Listen, I've got some news. Big news. We're married. Me and Gideon.'

'Married! But—'

'Don't but. We just did it. Went down to Vegas, actually. Anyway, I'm Mrs Gideon Keeble now. How cool is that?'

'Very cool.'

'Well! Don't you have anything else to say? Like congratulations?'

'Of course I do. Of course. I'm absolutely so happy for you. Both of you. Give my love to Gideon, won't you? Tell him he's a lucky man.'

'I will. Anyway, we'll be back in a week, and we're going to give the most ginormous party. Keep everything clear, won't you?'

'Of course I will,' said Clio. 'And . . . many, many congratulations.'

Mrs Gideon Keeble. How insane was that? As Jocasta might have said.

Jocasta would actually have said it was reckless, daft even, if she'd read about it in the papers: someone of thirty-five, someone independent and ambitious, marrying a millionaire—well, a billionaire, actually—of fifty-one, who had three ex-wives and a difficult daughter. She'd have said it must be for his money, that she couldn't possibly fancy him, that the sex must be rubbish.

Well, she did fancy him: a lot. He was very fanciable. Amazingly so, for someone of his age. The sex was, well, it was fine. Not specially, incredibly interesting, but maybe older men didn't do interesting. Anyway, she'd had plenty of interesting sex with Nick. It wasn't important. It was good and she really, really enjoyed it. They both did.

And she certainly didn't miss her job; she found Gideon much more interesting and rewarding, and being his wife much less demeaning and demoralising than doorstepping unhappy people.

She wasn't sure what she was going to do all day, but there were so many possibilities. She wanted to see a lot of the world. She wanted to entertain all the immensely interesting and famous people that Gideon seemed to know. She wanted to talk to him for ever.

So here she was, sated with happiness, with two days of shopping to do, and then home to England. And their wedding party.

The date of the party was set for June 22nd at Gideon's Berkshire house.

The guest list currently stood at three hundred and rising; Jocasta had agonised over whether or not to invite Nick. She knew he wouldn't want to come, but she could hardly exclude him from an invitation.

She rang him up, said how she'd love him to be there; he was short with her, thanked her, said he was going home to the country that weekend, but that he hoped she would be very happy. Jocasta put the phone down and cried for quite a long time.

The formal invitations to the Keeblefest, as Gideon persisted in calling it, went out in the last week of May. Jocasta had hired a party planner, Angie Cassell, a silvery stick-thin blonde, and in a few days she had caterers, menus, marquees, bands and DJs lined up. 'I think we should go for a Gatsby theme,' she said. 'The costumes are sooooo flattering.'

Jazz bands, bootlegger bars, speak-easy style dining tents, and gun-toting gangsters in spats and trilbies roaming the grounds sounded fun.

'And what about an ongoing ten-minute crash course in the Charleston,' said Jocasta, 'from a professional, so people aren't afraid of trying?' Angie clasped her hands together and cried, 'Perfect!'

Clio's first emotion on getting her invitation was panic. All those glittering people, all knowing each other, all those wonderful costumes. Could she be ill? Yes, that would be the best thing. She could accept and then phone on the morning with a stomach bug.

She wrote a formal acceptance, feeling pleased with herself; Jocasta called the next day, saying she wanted Clio to come the night before.

'I know it'll be difficult for you to get here and someone'll need to hold my hand through the day. What are you going to wear?'

Clio said, trying to sound delighted, that she would hire something.

'Well, look, I've got a sweet girl making me something. Would you like her to do one for you?'

'Won't that be awfully expensive?' said Clio.

'No way,' said Jocasta airily. 'This is fake stuff, cheap as anything.'

Clio tried very hard to believe her.

Chad Lawrence was going to the party, of course. The entire Centre Forward Party—or at least its major players—had been invited. Jack Kirkland, who hated parties, called Martha Hartley to see if she would like to go with him. His irritation when she said she couldn't go, that she was away that weekend, was profound.

'Martha,' he said, 'you are *not* away that weekend. You are going to the party. This is a three-line whip. *You* are going. We are *all* going. Now do you want to come with me, or would you like to bring someone else?'

Martha, sounding rather shaken, said she would like to go with him.

Bob Frean was dreading the party. He could cope with Janet's political career, her ferocious ambition, and her absences from home . . . just. What he objected to was being dragged into it. He did it, occasionally, when he had to. But this was different; this was social. The kind of thing he most loathed.

Fergus Trehearn was euphoric at being invited. It was exactly the sort of occasion he loved best: glamorous, fun, high profile, and crawling with media. He would have a wonderful night.

Fionnuala Keeble, with wisdom beyond her years, refused the invitation. She did it by text message to her father, which made him smile.

Josh was longing for his sister's party. His wife, Beatrice, had thrown herself into it, suggesting that they went as Scott and Zelda Fitzgerald, and had even hired a (fake) Bugatti for them to arrive in.

Ronald Forbes, after carefully considering the invitation to his only daughter's wedding party, sent a note accepting, telling her he hoped she and Gideon would be very happy and enclosing a very large cheque by way of a wedding present. He knew it was a meaningless gesture: as meaningless, indeed, as his acceptance, which he had absolutely no intention of honouring. Nevertheless Jocasta was pleased.

'I never thought he'd come, I really didn't.'

'Well, there you are,' said Gideon, giving her a kiss.

Several days after the mass of invitations had been sent out, Jocasta had the idea. 'I'm going to ask Kate Tarrant,' she said to Gideon.

'What on earth for?'

'Because she'd love it. And it would sort of make up for all the trouble I've caused her. I'll tell her to bring her boyfriend. Actually, I'll ask her parents as well, I think; that'll reassure them. Oh, and her grandmother.'

'Her grandmother! Jocasta, what on earth are you doing inviting grandmothers to your parties? Unless it's to make me feel young.'

'Gideon, I swear you could fancy Kate's grandmother. She's really glamorous. And I'd love you to meet Kate. Do you really think it's a bad idea?'

'I think it's a terrible idea,' said Gideon. 'But I can see you're going to do it anyway.'

Clio was still wrestling with her hair when the first cars started coming up the drive. She had a wild desire to run away; Jocasta would never miss her now—she was standing on the steps of the house in a state of high excitement, greeting, kissing, laughing, hugging.

A massive marquee stood just to the rear of the house, with lanterns strung across the trees above it; there was a jazz band on a platform on one side, and a white grand piano, complete with pianist in white tie and tails, on the other. A fountain, made of outsize champagne glasses, played on the terrace, and beside that stood Gideon's pride and joy: a black and silver twenties Chevrolet; a photographer was on hand for any guests who might wish to pose in it. Several cocktail bars, complete with barmen, were dotted about the grounds; a flashing sign on a gleaming black-and-silver Art Deco-style structure said 'Casino', and next to it, something that declared itself to be a cinema. Men in Al Capone suits and slouch hats carried trays of drinks, and gangsters' molls, with too much make-up and floozies' curls, offered cigarettes and lighters. After dinner, and before the dancing, there was to be a treasure hunt, a great twenties craze.

And now the party was about to come to life; the guests, all the brilliant, famous, distinguished guests would appear, and Clio felt as close to terrified as she could ever remember. The dressmaker had done her proud. She was wearing a pale blue chiffon dress, ankle-length with a drifting skirt, set off with long ropes of pearls; and her hair lent itself perfectly to the period, curved obediently into marcel-like waves, held back from her face with a pair of diamanté clips.

But her spirit didn't quite match it. Whoever could she talk to, who on earth would she know? God. What a nightmare. She couldn't do this, she really couldn't.

And then she had the idea. She could leave now. No one would miss her. Least of all Jocasta. She could call for a cab once she reached the lane that led to the house; it would be easy.

Deciding to stay in her costume—she might meet Jocasta on the stairs or something if she changed—she picked up her bag and cautiously opened her door. The corridor was deserted. She was almost at the bottom of the stairs, when she heard her name.

'Clio, hello! How lovely to see you.'

It was Fergus Trehearn, smiling up at her, wonderfully handsome in white tie and tails; he came up to her, caught her hand and kissed it.

'You look marvellous. A real twenties femme fatale! What a lucky man I am, to have caught you on your own.'

She smiled at him rather feebly, wondering what she might do next.

'Would you like to take a turn round the grounds with me? Or do you have a beau waiting for you to join him? I expect you do.'

'Fergus, I don't have any beau anywhere,' she said laughing, 'and I'd love to take a turn with you. I've been sitting in my room, feeling scared.'

'You ridiculous woman,' he said, 'what do you have to be scared of? It's going to be fun, just you see if it isn't. And did you know we're on the same table for dinner? With old Johnny Hadley, diary writer on the *Sketch*. He's the best fun and has so many scurrilous stories. We'll all have a wonderful time together.'

'Good heavens,' said Jilly, 'just look at those lights and that fountain over there, how marvellous. Oh, now there is Jocasta. What a dress!'

Jocasta stood on the steps of the house, with Gideon, wearing a dress that was a faithful copy of a Chanel, vintage 1924. It was ankle-length chiffon, in palest grey, with a layered petal-like hem, the fabric printed in a spiders' web pattern in a darker grey. When she raised her arms, wings unfolded from the dress in the same floating fabric, falling from her fingers; she looked like a shining, glittering star.

'Jilly, how perfectly wonderful to see you! You look younger than ever. I want you to meet my husband, Gideon Keeble. Helen and Jim, it's so nice of you to come, and where is the lovely Kate? Kate, darling, come and give me a kiss. You look wonderful, and who is this handsome man you've got with you?'

'Nat Tucker,' said Nat, holding out his hand.

'Hello,' said Jocasta. 'Now, do go through there, all of you, and you'll be looked after.'

'She's very nice-looking,' said Nat, the first to take a glass of champagne, leading the way through the arch of flowers that led across the side of the house and down to the wonderland below.

'Isn't she? And nice too,' said Kate, following his example, sipping at her glass, aware that people were staring at her. 'Oh, look, a cocktail bar and there's another; this is going to be really cool! Let's explore.'

'Well, he's certainly pushed the boat out for her, hasn't he?' said Josh. He and Beatrice were settling themselves at their table for dinner: the family table, with Gideon and Jocasta, Gideon's brothers and their wives and Jocasta's godmother and her husband, substituting for Ronald Forbes, who the day before had said he would be unable to attend. Jocasta had changed the table plan through a blur of tears.

The marquee slowly filled, the buzz of conversation rising and falling as people moved to their tables, greeting people on the way; it was almost half an hour before everyone was seated.

'They really have thought of everything, haven't they?' said Jack Kirkland to Martha. She smiled.

'Indeed. It's been quite wonderful.'

So far it really had been fine; Jack had been a marvellous escort, courteous and attentive, introducing her to anyone who would listen as one of Centre Forward's brightest stars; Janet Frean, rather surprisingly dressed in tie and tails herself, her auburn hair slicked back—'Well, I don't like dresses'—had been warm and friendly.

Sitting next to her was Chris Pollock, the Editor of the *Sketch*, whom she had liked enormously when she met him at the Centre Forward launch. Chad Lawrence was on her other side; she asked him where his daughters were.

'Oh, there's a younger contingent down there,' he said, gesturing towards the other side of the marquee. 'They're having a wonderful time. Too many cocktails, I'm afraid, but it's that sort of night, isn't it?'

Martha agreed. She would have liked a little more champagne, but she knew she couldn't afford to. She needed to be very watchful.

Towards the end of the meal, Gideon stood up. He smiled round the vast space, raised his hands for silence, picked up a microphone.

'No speeches, I've promised Jocasta. Except for two things: thank you all for coming. It's been a wonderful night—so far. I'm told it is yet extremely young. Not being quite that myself, I am hoping I can last a little longer.

'And I just wanted to tell you all, our friends, our very good friends, how much I love Jocasta and how happy she has made me.' He reached down and took her hand; a chiffon wing spread itself across the space between them. 'I don't know what I've done to deserve her, but I only hope I can make her as happy in return.'

Jocasta promptly started to cry; Gideon leaned over and wiped her tears tenderly away with his fingers.

'She's like that,' he said, 'terribly predictable.'

A roar of laughter went up. As it died again, he said, 'Next on the programme is the treasure hunt; each table has a list of clues. First back here wins. I shall be waiting patiently. Good luck.'

'Martha—isn't it?'

'Yes. Yes, it is. Hello, Josh.'

'Hello. Wonderful to see you.'

'And you.'

'Who'd have thought we should all be reunited at a bash like this?'

'Who indeed?'

'What are you doing these days? Law, isn't it?'

'Law, yes. And a foray into politics. And you?'

'Oh, working for the old family firm. Are you married?'

'No. You?'

'Oh, I'm married. Yes. Very much so. Two children as well. Girls. Dear little things.'

'And is your wife here?'

'Yes. Somewhere.'

'Well, I must be getting back to my table. Nice to see you, Josh.'

'Nice to see you too. Very nice dress,' he added.

'Thank you.'

Well, that had been all right. She'd got through that. No awkward questions. He still looked pretty good, a bit heavier, maybe, and possibly a bit less hair, but you could still just about see the golden boy there.

Yes, it had been fine. She needn't have worried about that.

'Who was your smooth friend?' It was Bob Frean's voice; Janet had proved a rather enthusiastic treasure seeker and been missing for ages.

'Oh, Jocasta's brother, Josh,' she said carefully.

'I didn't know you knew them that well.'

'I don't really. Not any more. I met them when we were young.'

She was beginning to feel a bit panicky; she smiled at him feebly.

'Do you want to go over to the casino? Or have a dance, even?'

'I'd love to go to the casino,' she said. She had learned, when she was feeling like this, that the trick was to keep moving.

'Come on, then.'

They walked slowly away from the table and she felt better already.

'Well, my ex-star reporter, how is married life treating you? Is it really better than the *Sketch*?' Chris Pollock had invited Jocasta to dance; they were walking towards the disco.

'It's wonderful,' said Jocasta. 'Truly.'

'You don't miss it at all?'

'Not at all. Honestly.'

'Well, I suppose I should be happy for you. But we certainly miss you. The newsroom is not the same without your legs—'

'Chris! That is so chauvinist.'

'Sorry. I was born that way. And the paper is not the same without your by-line and the stories beneath it.'

'Really?'

She stopped suddenly, looked at him; and for a moment she knew she did miss it, missed the excitement, the pursuit of stories, the absurd panics, missed the rhythm of a newspaper's day.

'Well, maybe just a bit,' she said finally.

'Thought so. Young Nick misses you. That's for sure. He's a man with a broken heart.'

'Well,' said Jocasta, 'if he hadn't been such a commitment-phobe, maybe it needn't have been broken.'

'Are you telling me,' he said, his eyes dancing with malice, 'you married Gideon on the rebound?'

'No, I am not. Of course I'm not. Don't put words into my mouth.'

'Sorry, darling. Only teasing.'

'Martha! It is you, isn't it? How lovely!' A girl was standing in front of her; a small, slender girl, holding the hand of a rather handsome man with close-cropped grey hair. 'I'm Clio. I hoped I'd find you.'

She would never have recognised her: tubby, shy Clio, transformed into this pretty, sparkly woman. She managed to smile.

'Yes, it's me. Hello, Clio. I thought you might be here. This is Bob Frean. Bob, this is Clio Scott. We knew each other when we were younger.'

'We went travelling together,' said Clio, smiling. 'I've been so impressed with everything I've read about you, Martha. Especially the political bit. Are you in politics, Bob?'

'Thankfully not. But my wife is.' He looked uncertainly at Fergus.

'Oh, I'm sorry,' said Clio, 'this is Fergus Trehearn.'

'Hi,' said Fergus.

'So, where are you off to?' asked Clio. 'The cinema? The disco?'

'The casino,' said Bob Frean. 'I'm no dancer, I'm afraid.'

'Well, it's worth looking in at the disco,' said Clio, 'honestly. Just put your head in. We're going that way, we're off to the cinema next, they're showing *The Jazz Singer*.'

'How marvellous,' said Bob Frean. 'I don't think I can resist that. Martha, fancy a movie?'

'No,' said Martha hastily. Here was her escape: she could disappear, call a cab, she'd surely done enough for the wretched party for one evening, she could get out safely, before—

'Clio, dear! You look marvellous. And Fergus, how nice!'

A glamorous woman was hurrying towards them.

'My goodness, Mrs Bradford,' Clio said, 'how lovely to see you.'

'What a party, Clio!' said Jilly. 'I didn't think they did them like this any more. So generous of Jocasta to invite us all. But I'm sorry, I'm interrupting your conversation—'

'No, no, it's fine,' said Clio. 'Mrs Bradford, this is Martha Hartley, an old friend of mine and Jocasta's. Martha, this is Mrs Bradford—'

'Oh, Jilly, please. How do you do, Martha? I was just off to look in the disco—such fun to watch.'

'I said the same,' said Clio. 'Come on.'

'Do you mind, Martha?' said Bob. 'It sounds like fun.'

'Of course not.'

They stood just inside the disco, taking it in, the strobe lighting, the gyrating bodies; the music was very loud. Martha suddenly felt dizzy; she put out her hand to steady herself on one of the tables.

Bob Frean noticed. 'Do you want to sit down?'

'No, no, I'm just a bit hot. Maybe I should go back outside—'

She did feel very dizzy; she sat down abruptly.

And then it happened.

'Gran! Come and dance. Come on, I'll show you.'

'Darling, no. I couldn't possibly—'

'Oh, hi, Dr Scott. I didn't know you were here. Isn't this cool, isn't it great? Are you enjoying yourself?'

'I certainly am.'

She must get outside. She must.

She was tall, this girl in a silver dress, tall with long, long legs and wild fair hair. She looked like—she looked just like . . .

'Fergus, come and dance with me? I'm having such a good time. Come on—' She twined her hand in his, started to pull him towards the dance floor, walking backwards, laughing. She heard him say, 'Kate, Kate!'

Kate. Kate.

The room spun, the music seemed to roar; it was hot, poundingly hot, she was going to faint, it was all blurry now, blurry and far away.

She managed somehow to stand up. 'Sorry. Must get outside.'

Away from her. Away from having to look at her.

'You look awful, Martha.' Clio's face was concerned. 'Jilly, could you find some water?'

'Darling, get a glass of water, would you?' Jilly called to Kate. 'Miss Hartley isn't feeling well.'

'Sure,' said the girl. She ran to grab a glass, followed them outside.

'Thank you, darling. Here you are, Martha, dear, drink this. Just little sips. That's right. Deep breaths.'

'You look better, Martha,' said Clio. 'Less green. Good. It really was awfully hot in there.'

'Oh, dreadful,' said Jilly Bradford. 'Of course you don't notice it,' she added to the girl with the flying hair. The girl called Kate. So near she could touch her. 'Martha, have a little more water. That's right. I don't think you've been introduced to my granddaughter, have you? This is Kate, Kate Bianca Tarrant as she likes to be called these days. Kate, darling, this is—Oh my God. Clio, she's fainted!'

How on earth had this happened? She was in bed in a room in Jocasta's house, with no chance of escape. She felt more alone and more frightened that she had ever been in her life.

Everything had changed suddenly, she realised. That was the most frightening thing of all. She couldn't deny it all any longer. The child she had left behind was no longer Baby Bianca, totally anonymous, for ever a baby; she had become Kate, a beautiful sixteen-year-old girl. She had been in the same room as her, breathed the same air, seen her, watched her, almost touched her; she had become reality.

She sat up, bolt upright, feeling the panic coming back, the breathlessness, the sweating. 'God,' she said aloud, 'God, what do I do?'

And then the door opened and Janet Frean came in.

Martha was so pleased to see her, a friendly, reassuring person, that she burst into tears. Janet sat down on the bed, held her like a child and told her to cry as much as she liked. Which Martha did, and for quite a long time: helpless, uncontrollable tears; and Janet just sat there, in complete silence, except for the occasional soothing, hushing noise, until finally Martha stopped crying and lay back on her pillows.

'I'm so sorry,' she said, 'so terribly sorry.'

'Martha,' said Janet, smiling at her gently, 'Martha, stop apologising. Please. You've done nothing wrong.'

'Oh, but I have. That's the whole point, Janet. You don't understand.'

'Do you want to talk about it? Nothing seems as bad once you've shared it with someone, it's a fact. And I would say I'm totally unshockable. Having five children and spending a great deal of my life at Westminster has done that for me, at least. Try me. Try talking about it. Please, I can't bear to see you like this. Tell me what it is.'

And suddenly, she did. She had to. She couldn't fight it all any longer.

Chapter 10

'OH, LOOK AT THIS PICTURE of Kate!' Clio passed the *People* across the table. 'Doesn't she look sweet? And the boy looks rather handsome too.'

'He *is* rather handsome,' said Jocasta. 'And he's a poppet. Who else did they get? God, the nights I've spent with the paps, outside rich people's gates. And now they're my gates and I'm inside.'

It was half past ten. Gideon had already swum and had been making coffee for hours; people were drifting down to the kitchen, including several of Gideon's brothers. Jocasta embraced them all fondly; she had long since given up trying to work out which of them was which. Beatrice, considerably the worse for wear, huddled behind the newspapers. Josh, most unfairly full of beans, had already been for one walk and was suggesting another.

'I think I should check on Martha,' said Clio.

She came back in five minutes. 'She's gone,' she said. 'Is that strange behaviour, or what?'

'Very strange,' said Jocasta. 'How did she get away, anyway?'

'She said she got a cab. She's left a note,' said Clio holding it out. 'It's very polite, so sorry to have put us to so much bother, thanking us for all our kindness, but she had to get home.'

'She is the strangest girl,' said Jocasta. 'I think she didn't like it that we'd all seen her out of control. I never met anyone quite so tight-arsed in my entire life.'

Martha had spent the entire day in a desperate effort to calm down. She felt terrible: her pulse was racing, her heart pounding. She tried to tell herself she was being absurd, that there was nothing wrong; she was in no danger of any kind. But she was. She had committed an act of unbelievable folly; she had done what she had never even considered doing. Obviously it would be perfectly all right, obviously. Janet Frean was the kindest, most dependable woman, and, more important, absolutely discreet. There was no way she was a gossip, no way she would talk to anyone about what Martha had told her. Of course she wouldn't.

The phone rang and Martha let the answering machine pick up the call. It was Ed. He had taken to calling her every other day or so, asking her how she was. They would chat. It was all very agreeable, only it hurt more than she would have believed.

'Hi, it's me. Just rang to see if you enjoyed the party. I saw the pictures. Why none of you? I'll call again . . .'

Maybe it was Ed she should have told. At least she knew he loved her, wished her well. Why did she tell Janet, who she didn't know at all? Not really. Who might even now—oh God! Of course she wasn't. Of course—

The phone rang again and the answering machine picked up. This time it was Janet. 'Hello, Martha, only me. Wondering how you were.'

Her voice was warm, friendly, gentle. Martha felt better at once and picked up the phone. 'Hello, Janet,' she said, and she could hear the relief in her own voice. 'How kind of you. I'm fine, really. Much, much better. And thank you again for last night, you were wonderful.'

'My dearest girl, it was nothing. You needed to talk. You couldn't have kept that to yourself for ever. It's an intolerable burden. God knows how you've coped all these years. You're clearly making yourself ill. And I'd like to think talking to me helped—just a little.'

'It did, Janet, it really did.'

Liar, Martha, it didn't help, it's frightened you horribly.

'I feel deeply honoured that you confided in me. Showed me that kind of trust. And I won't betray it. I swear to you, Martha.'

'I must fly.' Gideon leaned over to Jocasta and kissed the top of her head. She was burrowed into the pillows of the vast bed. 'See you in forty-eight hours. Love you.'

'Bye,' said Jocasta, still half asleep.

She got up an hour later, stared out at the garden. It was a beautiful day. So, what was she supposed to do? Walk? Do a little light weeding? Swim in the pool? Alone? All day? Shit, this was pathetic. There was so much she wanted to do. Find a new house for a start. A house for them. For her and Gideon. Well, she could do that. She'd call up all the estate agents in . . . in where? They had houses in the best places in England already. Why buy another?

'Oh shit!' said Jocasta aloud. People never thought of this, people who weren't rich. She certainly never had. When you could have everything, nothing was right, nothing was good enough. Not just houses, but clothes. Shopping was about choices, about decisions, what suited you best, not about having whatever your eye lighted on.

Well, maybe she should do something completely different. Find some new challenge. Like—learn to fly. That'd be something to get excited about, get the adrenaline pumping. That was the main problem: she wasn't making adrenaline. Or rather her life wasn't.

Jocasta felt her heart literally lurch. Had she, after all, been completely sensible, giving up her job? Should she have hung on for a bit? Until . . . well until what? Until she had a family, people would say. But she wasn't going to have a family. She absolutely wasn't.

The old adage about marrying in haste and repenting at leisure drifted into her head. She had been Mrs Gideon Keeble for just over a month and she was already not entirely happy about it.

By five o'clock that afternoon, with the first of a dozen flying lessons booked for the next day and a silver BMW Z3 on order, she was still depressed. Depressed and almost frightened.

'Now, Kate,' Rufus, the photographer, said. 'I want you to think about nothing at all. Just empty your head. Just . . . be. Be you. Before any of this happened to you.' She nodded. It was quite difficult, thinking of nothing at all. After three more tries, she was getting upset. Rufus suddenly rushed out of the studio, then came back with a pile of magazines, *Seventeen* and *Glamour* and *Company*.

He gave her one. 'Right. Read it. Really read it, find something you're interested in, OK?'

She nodded; opened *Glamour*, which was her favourite, and flicked through it. And found an article on how you'd know if you were in love. She was always wondering if she was in love with Nat.

'I've got something.'

'Good. Now sit there, on that stool, where you were before, that's right, and read it. Really read it.'

It was easier than she'd expected She was just into the second question, wondering if what she felt when Nat kissed her was exciting, very exciting or totally off the scale, when Rufus said, 'Kate!'

She looked up, not sure what he might want. The camera flashed.

'OK,' he said. 'Carry on.'

After three more, he came over to her, with some Polaroids. 'There,' he said, 'how's that?'

Kate looked; she could have been her own younger sister; almost no make-up visible, her hair just tumbled over one shoulder. She looked slightly surprised, sweetly confused, her dark eyes wide and questioning, her pale lips just parted.

'It's glorious,' said Rufus. 'Can you do that again, do you think?'

'Oh, yes,' said Kate, confident now that she knew what he wanted.

Next day, Smith made their offer: a three-year contract for Kate to be the face for their new young range, Smith's Club, for a million dollars a year. The terms of the contract would include a publicity tour in both the States and the UK, as well as public appearances at Ascot and Smith's Lawn polo. Fergus told them he would have to discuss it with Kate and her parents and that he would get back to them.

'Martha? Martha Hartley?'

'Yes?'

It was Malcolm Farrow, head of publicity at Centre Forward House. A request had come through for her to appear on *Question Time* that week, Clare Short had pulled out at the last minute and they'd like Martha.

'Oh God.' She felt absolutely terrified. 'They should have Janet Frean,' she said. 'Obviously. Please, please tell them to ask her.'

Farrow said, rather awkwardly, 'We did suggest her, of course. But they said they'd rather have you.'

'Well, I can't do it,' said Martha flatly. 'I'm frantically busy here, and anyway, I don't want to. And I couldn't, I'd be useless.'

'Martha, you'll be marvellous.'

'What would Janet say?'

That was the worst thing: too hideous to contemplate. How Janet must be feeling: turned down for *Question Time*, the most desirable slot on television for a politician, in favour of her. Not Janet Frean, experienced professional, but Martha Hartley, inexperienced amateur. She'd want to kill her. She'd want to—oh God, what might she want to do? What might she do?

The waiter eased a salmon steak onto the plate, poured the juices from the pan over it, all with great care, and then leaning over Nick in order to place the vegetables carefully on the table, said very quietly, 'Mr Marshall, there's something in your jacket pocket.'

'Thanks. Thanks very much.'

Nick was lunching in the press dining room with one of the boys from the Foreign Office; he excused himself as soon as he decently could and walked slowly out of the dining room. His jacket was hanging on a coatrack. He picked it up casually, went into the gents', and sat down in one of the stalls.

There was a note folded neatly in the inside pocket of the jacket, marked Confidential. A classic way of imparting information.

I'd love to have a chat with you sometime, it said. *I've got some stuff you'd find really interesting. Maybe you could call me on my mobile.*

It was signed 'Janet Frean'.

Clio caught the two thirty to London—just. Plenty of time to get to her interview at the Royal Bayswater. She sank into the corner of the compartment, trying to get her breath back, rummaged in her bag for a comb. No comb. Lucky she had a small one in her make-up bag, she could—'Shit,' she said aloud. No make-up bag either.

This was grim. Well, maybe she could get something from Boots on Waterloo Station. No, she wouldn't have time. Oh God . . .

The journey from Waterloo to Bayswater was not easy. Cab? Dodgy, and she didn't have much cash on her. The tube then: Lancaster Gate was the nearest, then she could get a cab from there. If there was one.

Her phone bleeped. A text message from Fergus, saying 'Good luck with the interview. Hope you're wearing the wedding party dress.'

She texted back 'Thanks vv much. I wish. Look terrible. Clio.'

He texted back at once. 'Why?'

'In a rush. Forgot make-up. Might not make it.'

It was passing the time at least. Was this train going slowly? No, it must be her imagination. It was a fast train . . . a fast train going slowly.

'We apologise to customers for any delay. Due to signal failure at Waterloo, this train will terminate at Vauxhall. Customers are advised . . .'

Shit shit shit! She just wasn't meant to get this job. She wasn't. She might as well—

Her mobile rang. 'Clio? It's Fergus. Is anything wrong?'

Fergus had said he would meet Clio at Vauxhall: 'I can cut across London, easily. Across Vauxhall Bridge, up Park Lane, you'll be there in a trice. Don't worry.'

She had protested, said he must have other things to do, like work, but, 'Nonsense,' he said. 'I'm as free as air this afternoon. Anything else I can do for you?'

'Well . . .' She hesitated; it seemed an awful lot to ask. 'Well, actually, Fergus, if you could just—'

He must like her; he must.

They pulled in to Vauxhall station at 3.35 and he was waiting for her outside the station, grinning, holding a Boots bag.

'Oh, Fergus!' said Clio, giving him a kiss. 'You are an angel.'

'Not quite, come along now, you can do your face as we go.'

At five to four they were at the car park that was called Park Lane.

'Clio, hello!' It was Beaky's secretary. 'Are you in the building?'

'No,' wailed Clio, 'I'm at the bottom of Park Lane. Stuck! They're not running late or anything, are they?'

'Fraid not. Dr Smartarse—I didn't say that—your only real rival is in there now. Due to come out any minute. God, Clio, shall I warn them?'

'I think you'd better,' said Clio.

At a quarter past four they were approaching Sussex Gardens; the traffic was still crawling.

'I think you'd be quicker legging it from here,' said Fergus. 'I'll park and come and find you. Good luck. I'll be waiting.'

They all looked at her very coldly when she went into the room. Even Beaky. There were five of them: some familiar, some not. The chief executive of the hospital, an outside assessor, the clinical director, one of the other consultants—and Beaky.

'I'm so, so sorry,' she said, sinking onto the chair they indicated. 'I can explain if you like . . .'

'Not now,' said the administrator. 'I think we have been delayed enough. If we could just begin . . .'

Astonishingly, once she started, she felt coolly together; all her facts and theories marshalled, her experience summoned, made to seem clearly relevant. She answered all their questions smoothly and easily, expressed her view that as much a part of geriatrics as medicine was the social side, the importance of enabling elderly people to continue in the community by way of careful monitoring, drug therapy and support from the social services. She had done some research of her own on late-onset diabetes and on stroke management, was absolutely up-to-date on treatment, both in the UK and the States. She could see that impressed them. And finally, she expressed her personal view of the frustration of the carers, prevented from giving out drugs by red tape and meaningless regulations.

'I know this is more politics than medicine,' she said, 'but it is so important. I firmly believe we would see smaller clinics here, fewer beds needed, less pressure on the homes if we could only overcome it.'

She was never sure afterwards when it had gone wrong: when the hugs and kisses outside the hospital, the sense of warm euphoria and sweetly shared triumph at being offered the position ended, and the chill began. He had even bought her some flowers. 'I knew you'd earn them,' and insisted on driving into Covent Garden—'perfect place to celebrate'.

Fergus had ordered a bottle of champagne.

'Here's to you, Consultant Scott.' Fergus raised his glass to her. 'I'm very proud indeed to know you.'

'Thank you. A whole bottle! Fergus! Your eyes are bigger than your stomach. As my nanny used to say.'

'Your nanny! How very grand,' he said. 'Where I come from your nanny is your gran.'

'Fergus. I only had a nanny because I didn't have a mother,' said Clio. She could feel herself blushing. Had that been it? She had certainly felt awkward suddenly, less happy.

'You had no mother?'

'No. She died when I was a baby.'

'That's terribly sad.'

'Not really. I know that sounds dreadful, but I never knew her, I didn't know any different. Anyway, that's not what I want to talk about. Oh, Fergus! I'd never have done it without you. Never. I just don't know how to thank you.'

'You don't have to,' he said, 'I feel rewarded enough that you got it. You were a long time,' he added. 'I was beginning to wonder if you'd popped out the back way.'

'Fergus! Of course not. There's a lot to discuss at these boards, you know, it's not just like a simple interview—' She stopped, fearing she sounded condescending.

'I dare say. The only interview I ever attended was for the position of filing clerk. It lasted about two and a half minutes. Since then, I've just wheedled my way into places.'

'I'm afraid wheedling isn't a recognised interview technique for doctors,' she said. Damn. She'd done it again. She smiled at him, still afraid it sounded schoolmistressy.

'Yes, well, our worlds are obviously pretty far apart,' he said. And this time he didn't smile back.

She had begun to feel panicky. It couldn't all go wrong today. Not now. Not after all he'd done.

136

'You were so kind, Fergus,' she said. 'So, so kind.'

'Now let's not OD on the praise,' he said. 'It was just what any friend would do.'

A friend. Any friend. That was how he saw her. He had just been helping a friend.

'And what are you doing this evening?' he said.

'Oh, just getting back.'

'But, do you have to?'

'Oh, yes,' she said quickly. She didn't want him to feel he had to amuse her, go on helping her to celebrate. She'd imposed on him enough.

'Right. Well, I must get back to the office too.'

'You certainly must. I've robbed you of hours of useful occupation.'

'Debatable, I'd say. That it was useful. Not like being a doctor.' He sounded defensive. 'But it was a pleasure helping you. It really was.'

A long silence, then, 'Can I give you a lift to Waterloo?'

'Oh, no. Honestly. That would be too kind. I'll get a cab. I don't think I could walk another inch.' She stood up. 'Thank you again for the champagne, Fergus. And for everything.'

'I'll see you to your cab.'

'There's no need.'

'I know that,' he said and his voice was slightly impatient. 'But I will, just the same. I have been properly brought up, you know. Even if I didn't have a nanny.'

Where had it all gone, she thought, all that happiness, all that triumph, all that closeness? How had she managed to wreck that, and so quickly? God, she was a disaster. Completely hopeless.

'Here's a cab,' he said.

'Thanks, Fergus. I do hope—' What did she hope? Nothing that wouldn't sound boring. 'I do hope you get everything done.'

Now, how crass was that?

'I will,' he said.

She got into the cab, leaned forward. 'Waterloo,' she said and turned to say goodbye—only he had wrenched the door open, was climbing in beside her. 'Fergus, what—'

'I want to talk to you,' he said. 'Get to the bottom of this—this personality change you go through. One minute you're you, all warm and chatty, and the next all buttoned up. What is it, what do I do?'

'It's not you,' she said quickly. 'Really it isn't, it's me.'

'What do you mean, you?'

'I can't explain,' she said wretchedly, and she felt, to her horror, the tears well up and she fished in her bag for a tissue and blew her nose.

'Hay fever,' she said by way of explanation.

'I don't see any hay,' he said, taking the tissue away from her and wiping her eyes tenderly. 'Come along, Clio, tell me what's wrong, please. Otherwise'—he looked out of the window; they were on Waterloo Bridge now—'I shall throw myself into the river.'

Clio giggled in spite of herself, and then sniffed unromantically. 'Well, it's just that—'

'That what? Are you in love with someone else?'

'No, no, it's nothing like that—it's just that I'm so . . . so dull. And middle-aged and—'

'What are you talking about?' he said, looking genuinely mystified.

'I'm dull, not exciting. Serious. Not like the people you know and—'

'Which entrance?' said the driver.

'Oh, Eurostar will do,' said Fergus. 'Clio, I love your company—I adore your company. You're so interesting and thoughtful—'

'Oh, yes,' she said, 'very exciting that makes me sound.'

'It is to me, you silly bitch,' he said.

She stared at him. 'What did you say?'

'I said you were exciting, to me. I find you very exciting. And today I was so proud of you and—'

'Yes, but what else?'

'I said you were a silly bitch. OK? I'm sorry.'

'Seven quid,' said the driver.

Fergus fumbled in his wallet, pulled out a tenner, thrust it at him.

'That's all right, keep it.'

'Fergus, that's terrible,' said Clio, shocked by this piece of wanton extravagance. 'You can't just give him three pounds—'

'I can. Of course I can. Come on. OUT!'

She got out: meekly followed him into the Eurostar building, and then up the escalator. At the top he turned and faced her.

'Look,' he said, 'I don't know how I can convince you that I like being with you. That I find you terribly attractive. You're driving me mad. What do you want, woman? A signed declaration? Here'—he pulled a sheet of paper out of the small filofax he kept in his pocket—'here you are. *I, Fergus Trehearn, find you, Clio Scott*—don't know what your married name is—*incredibly exciting and interesting and desirable and I would like to remove all your clothing right here.*' He tore the paper off, handed it to her. 'There. Will that do? Now then, we'd better go and find your bloody train.'

Clio stood very still and stared, first at him, then at the piece of paper. Then she said, 'Fergus, I don't want to get the bloody train. And I don't have to. I want to stay with you. And I want you to remove all my clothing. As soon as possible. Only not just here, maybe.'

Chapter 11

MARTHA LEFT WORK at two; the BBC was sending a car for her. She sat watching the clock as it crawled the last half-hour. This must be like waiting for the executioner, she thought. She had a fat bundle of briefing material, sent over from Jack Kirkland's office, which she knew more or less by heart, and she had the day's papers to read in the car.

At five to two the phone rang; she let her answering machine pick it up. It was Ed. 'Hi, Martha. I just discovered you're on telly tonight. Mum told me. Cool. Good luck. And—'

Suddenly she wanted to speak to him. Terribly.

She grabbed the phone. 'Hi, Ed. I'm here. Just leaving now.'

'Yeah? How do you feel?'

'Terrible. Absolutely terrible. So frightened, you can't imagine!'

'Is this the cucumber-cool Miss Martha Hartley, prospective parliamentary candidate for Binsmow? Martha, don't be scared, you'll be fine.'

'I won't be fine, I know I won't.'

'Would you like me to come?'

'What? To Birmingham?'

'Is that where it is? Cool, I love Brum. They have some great clubs there, we could go out afterwards.'

'Ed, I'll be in no state to go clubbing.'

'OK, we'll just sit in the greenroom and watch the reruns. Do you have anything planned for afterwards?'

'Suicide,' she said.

'Terrible waste. Look, I mean it; I will come if you want me to.'

She was silent for a moment, then, 'I'd absolutely love it,' she said simply. 'It would make all the difference. But I don't know if you'll be able to get in.'

'I'll think of something. If I can't get in, I'll wait in reception and watch you on the monitor.'

'Oh, Ed.' Her eyes filled with tears. God, she'd missed him. And God alone knew what she was doing, letting him back into her life. It was hugely dangerous; she was over-emotional, frightened, she might say or do anything. It was also exceedingly selfish. But . . . she'd worry about that afterwards.

139

Nick was beginning to feel frustrated. So far he'd been listening to Janet Frean for an hour and a half and he'd got nothing from her but a lot of rather dull policy statements and a bit of banging on about her personal hobbyhorses, like NHS reforms.

'We have to get rid of the managers,' she was saying now, slightly pink-faced. She had begun to drink during the main course and had actually had rather a lot. 'I tell you, Nick. Those managers are a far bigger obstacle to NHS efficiency than lack of funds. And Centre Forward's policy of less interference would extend above all to that sort of thing.'

'Yes,' said Nick. 'Absolutely.'

'Anyway,' she said, picking up her glass, 'anyway, Nick, that's enough of the politics. How would you like a bit of gossip?'

'I'd love it. Political gossip?'

'Well, you could say that. It concerns a politician. An up-and-coming one. It's quite a story . . .'

They were in position, sitting at the table. Martha was at the end, two away from David Dimbleby, next to a rotund Tory. He was being very nice to her and so was Dimbleby. They were all trying to put her at her ease, but there was no escape and she felt dreadfully sick. And she hadn't heard from Ed. What had happened to him, for God's sake? Probably decided not to come after all: well, she deserved it.

'Right, we're going to put a dummy question to each of you, to get the sound levels,' said the floor manager. 'Martha, you first. How do you rate your chances tonight?'

'On a scale of one to ten, zero,' she said, and everyone laughed. For a brief moment, she felt better. And then much worse again.

What would happen if she just couldn't think of anything to say? Some wild card might come up. The researchers were moving about among the audience now, getting questions, deciding which ones to take. These were then written down, but that was only for Dimbleby's benefit. He kept the paper covered, so that the people on either side of him couldn't get a preview. The first the panel knew was literally when the questions were put.

She took deep breaths, trying to calm her heaving stomach.

And then she heard one of the cameramen calling her name quietly.

'Martha. Over here.'

She looked at him, at Camera Two or whatever it was. The man was grinning at her, and gesturing just below the camera. There was a large hand-lettered sign there.

Hi, Martha. Go for it! Ed xxx.

She laughed aloud—and suddenly everything seemed much better.

'Nick! Why on earth are you ringing me at this time of night? I'm in bed. What? No, alone. Gideon's out. No, of course you can't, I'd be in the divorce courts—what? WHAT? My God, Nick. Yes, of course. Come at once. I'll let you in. Sure, bye.'

Clio was in the kitchen when her mobile rang; Fergus had demanded a cup of cocoa before they went to bed.

'Hello? Jocasta! No, I'm making cocoa. Oh, shut up. We don't all live on champagne and—no, I'm listening. What? WHAT? My God, Jocasta. My God!'

An hour later, she and Fergus had arrived at Kensington Palace Gardens; Gideon was still out.

'I'm glad you're here, actually,' Jocasta said, hugging them both. 'Me being alone in the house with Nick is just a tad compromising. Cocoa? Or something even more exciting? Just look at the two of you, I think it's so wonderful!'

'Cocoa will do fine,' said Fergus, smiling at her, 'and we think it's wonderful too. And it's all because of you.'

'Aw, shucks,' said Jocasta. 'Now, come on, Nick's in the drawing room. I'll go and get the cocoa.'

She came back with a tray. She looked absurdly out of place in the vast room, Clio thought, with its heavy brocade curtains, its embossed wallpaper, its chandeliers, its Antique (with a capital A) furniture, dressed in nothing but an oversized T-shirt, padding across the (no doubt priceless) Indian carpet in her bare feet. It somehow seemed to sum up the whole marriage; she didn't belong here, it didn't suit her. But then—Gideon did, Clio told herself firmly. He suited her perfectly. And she suited him. That was what mattered . . .

'Well, all I can say, Nick,' said Jocasta, putting the tray down, 'is that Martha was very lucky Janet chose to tell *you*. Not someone from the *Sun*. Or the *Mirror*. It'd be in tomorrow's paper, no messing. I s'pose it's because we—I mean the *Sketch*—had the exclusive on the Baby Bianca story. What did you say to her, anyway? I presume you've got it on tape?'

'Yes. In my pocket, right here.' He patted it. 'I just thanked her for giving me the story, said I wasn't sure what would happen next, then legged it as fast as I could. I was terrified she'd change her mind, ask for the tape back. Not that it would have made any difference, but she's obviously a bit deranged.'

'Is she?' asked Clio. 'Why do you say that?'

'It's a very odd thing to do. If she wanted to discredit that party of hers, she's going the right way about it. Yet she talks about the party as if it was another child she adores. I don't understand it. Anyway, what do we do next? What do I, in particular, do next? Chris would have my balls if he knew I was sitting on this. And she could be talking to the *Sun* right now. I could have just been a rehearsal. God, what a mess.'

'We have to tell Martha,' said Jocasta, 'absolutely have to.'

'So, what do we do?' asked Nick. 'Ring her, say, "Oh, hi, Martha, nice performance, and we know you're Baby Bianca's mother"?'

'And there's another thing,' said Jocasta. 'Who's going to tell Kate?'

'Well, Martha must,' said Clio, 'of course. My God. No wonder the poor girl fainted.'

'What poor girl?' said Jocasta. 'Martha? You're not saying you're sorry for her, I hope?'

'Of course I'm sorry for her. Just think what she's been going through for the last sixteen years. I think it's one of the saddest stories I ever heard.'

'Me too,' said Fergus.

Jocasta looked at him thoughtfully. 'This relationship with Clio is turning you soft, Fergus. Now, come on, who's going to make this call?'

Martha was half asleep in the car, her head on Ed's shoulder, when her mobile rang.

'Oh, let's just ignore it,' she said sleepily. 'It won't be anyone I want to speak to. Probably Jack, having yet another orgasm.'

Kirkland had already rung twice, the first time to congratulate her in general terms, the second to say how brilliantly he felt she had put the party philosophy over. Chad and her parents had also called.

'Yeah, OK. Speaking of orgasms, I hope you're going to be a bit more alert than this when we get home.'

Martha turned to him, pulled his face down to hers, and kissed him with great thoroughness.

'That's on account. A sort of down payment. I feel very, very alert in the relevant department.'

They had discussed staying in Birmingham, but Ed said he had to be in London first thing.

'And my car overheated all the way up. Hate to drive it down now.'

'We can both go in the Beeb car, and drive up and get yours on Saturday. Oh, no, I'll be in Binsmow. Well, Sunday, then. No, I've—'

'How about dawn on Wednesday week?' Ed laughed.

'You're on.'

'You were fantastic, you know. Really, really good.'

'I wouldn't have been,' she said, 'without your message. Oh, Ed, what on earth was I thinking of, keeping you away from me all this time?'

'If you can't answer that,' said Ed, 'there's no hope for any of us. When are you going to tell me the reason?'

'I'm not.'

They reached Canary Wharf just before two.

'I'm sorry,' she said, as they walked in the door, 'I just absolutely have to have a shower. I was sweating like a pig under those lights.'

'The cool Ms Hartley sweating? I don't believe it. All right. Tell you what, I'll join you. How would that be?'

'Heavenly,' said Martha.

At that moment the land line went, and the answering machine cut in.

'I want to come with you,' said Ed.

'No, Ed, you can't. I'm sorry. It's too complicated. But I will be back, I swear, and I'll tell you everything then.'

'All right.' He sighed. 'But I don't like you driving. You're exhausted, you're upset—'

'I'll be all right. Promise.'

'Suppose I drive you over, wait outside?'

'No, Ed. I might be hours.'

'I've waited weeks for you already,' he said. 'What's a few more hours?'

Jocasta opened the door; she had put on some jeans under her over-sized T-shirt and looked about seventeen. She smiled at Martha.

'Hi. Come in. Is that—' She peered out at the car. 'Is that someone with you?'

'Yes, but he's waiting outside,' said Martha, 'I don't want him with us while we talk.'

'Oh, OK.'

She led the way into the drawing room. Fergus had left. It had been agreed that this was best handled by the three of them.

'Hi, Martha. How are you? You were so good tonight,' said Clio.

'Thanks. First and last time, I guess.'

She managed a smile: a cool, slightly sad little smile.

'I'm sorry about this, Martha,' said Nick, holding out his hand.

She took it. 'Not your fault.'

They all sat down again.

'Look,' Martha said suddenly, 'this is a bit hard for me. I don't really want to talk to all of you at once.'

'That's fine,' said Jocasta. 'We're only all here because—well, because Nick knew I'd be able to get hold of you. And it was obviously urgent. God knows who else she might have told.'

'It's not in the other papers,' said Clio quickly. 'We went to Waterloo and got them, so we've got a few hours at least. Days hopefully.'

'But, it's got to happen, I suppose? Got to come out?'

143

She sounded vulnerable at last.

'I would say so, yes. I'm so sorry.'

'No, no, it's very nice of you to try to help, I haven't exactly been very friendly to you.'

'Well, we know why now,' said Jocasta.

'Anyway,' said Clio, 'we felt that—perhaps—you might find it easiest to talk to me. I'm a doctor, after all. Hippocratic oath and all that.'

'Actually,' said Martha, 'I think I would like to start with you, Clio. If the others don't mind.'

'Of course not,' said Jocasta. 'We'll be in the kitchen if you want us.'

'I cannot believe I've been so stupid,' said Martha suddenly, 'telling that bloody woman. I mean, why her?'

'It was at the party, wasn't it?' said Clio. 'You were obviously very distressed. And you had just been confronted by it all. Literally.'

'I suppose so. But—oh God. Oh God . . .'

She dropped her head into her hands and began to cry. Clio went over and sat next to her, put her arm round her.

'Look, why don't you try telling me about it? When you're ready.'

And Martha sat there with Clio, in the quiet drawing room, already growing light in the midsummer dawn, and started. Because she had done it just a few weeks earlier, it was easier than it might have been, but she still had to force every painful, difficult word out.

'So, how long were you in Bangkok?'

'About two and a half months. I thought I'd go mad. But, actually, it got better. I stayed downtown, on the left bank of the river, there's a kind of ghetto of cheap guesthouses. I went to the markets a lot, tried to eat properly, and just waited for the baby to be born. I sort of hoped I could have it there, by myself.'

'By yourself! You thought you could have a baby all by yourself?'

'Well, yes. I mean, people do. I'd bought a medical book in Australia, so I knew exactly what to expect. I knew all about cutting the cord and everything. I bought some sharp scissors and some strong string—'

'God, how brave you must be. But—what did you plan to do with the baby, Martha? Afterwards? What did you think would happen to it?'

Martha met her eyes with great difficulty. 'I'd decided to take it to the Bangkok Christian Hospital. I thought I could leave it there, by the main door, and it would be found by someone, and be well looked after. I'm sorry, Clio, I can see you think it's appalling of me, but it wasn't really a baby to me. It was something dreadful that I'd done, that I had to leave behind. So I could go home, and everything would be all right again.'

'Yes. Yes, I see.'

'But the baby just wouldn't come. I tried everything—walked miles, sat in a hot bath . . . I could never have got another ticket, the cheap flights were all booked for weeks ahead. So I thought, well, I'll just have to go and sort something out when I get back. And then—well, it started on the plane. I crawled off the plane at Heathrow and headed for a lavatory. I saw this room on the way in marked "Staff Only". It had cleaning stuff in it, and a sink, and just room for me to lie down . . . and I had her there. It was, well, awful. But I didn't have any choice. If anyone had known . . .'

'Martha, couldn't you possibly have told your parents?' Clio's voice was very gentle. 'Had the baby adopted after that, fine, but at least told them, got some help?'

'No. I couldn't. Well, I can see now, that just possibly I could have done, but then—Clio, you don't know what Binsmow's like. I was the vicar's daughter. I'd have brought disgrace on them . . .'

'You're talking like a Victorian novel,' said Clio, and smiled for the first time. 'Bringing disgrace on them?'

'But I would have done. The whole parish respected my father so much, he would never, ever have recovered. I honestly believe that he would never have lived it down. And they were so proud of me, you see, getting into Bristol, doing law. How could I have failed them, said, "Sorry, I'm not what you thought, I'm not your darling innocent daughter, I've done something terrible, I've had a baby."'

'So . . . how did you feel? When you left her?'

'Well, I rested for a bit, and . . . and cleaned myself up, and then I thought, That's it, it's over, I've done it, and I held her for a while and then wrapped her up in a sheet and a blanket I'd bought for her in Bangkok, and laid her in a sort of trolley basket thing with towels in it. And then I went and sat on a bench just opposite, and waited until someone found her. I was worried because I'd not thought to get her any nappies; I thought she'd pee on the blankets. After all that, and I was worried about a bit of pee. Anyway, a woman cleaner found her and came out of the room calling for help and there was a lot of fuss, of course, and then a policewoman just took her away.'

'Didn't you feel upset?'

'Honestly? No. Just relief. I thought, She's safe now, and that's all I felt. I'm sure you must think I'm dreadful, but I didn't feel sad, or any of the things you might expect. Later on, yes, but not then.'

'I don't think you're dreadful,' Clio said. 'I'm just so sad for you. And full of admiration that you could be so brave.'

'I told you, I had to be. I went to a YWCA hostel in Hayes; I had just enough money, and I slept a lot and looked after myself as best I could.'

'Didn't you get milk?' asked Clio very gently.

'Yes, I did.' Tears welled up again. 'I wasn't expecting that. It was awful. That did make me cry. I kept thinking, This was meant for her. It was horrible. And quite painful. I bought some pad things at Boots and stuffed them in my bra. After a few days it dried up.'

'And . . . and your parents didn't suspect anything?'

'Why should they? I'd put on some weight, of course, but I'd bought caftans and those fishermen's trousers, so I wore them. I was very tired, but that was to be expected.'

'And how did you cope? Didn't you feel unhappy at all?'

'Well, in a way, yes. But I knew she was all right, because I read the papers. So I just buried it and got on with my life. Worked hard, did well. It all helped. And developed into the control freak you see before you. But, in private, I'd remember her suddenly, remember what she looked like, remember holding her, specially on her birthday. But even that was like something that had happened to someone else, not me.'

'Oh, Martha. What a story.'

'It is quite, isn't it? And then all these extraordinary coincidences that have brought us together. That was such a terrible day—there she was in the paper, abandoned Baby Bianca. I did go a bit strange then.'

'And now?'

'Now I don't know,' she said. 'I really don't know what now. I mean, it's the end of my life as I know it.'

'Martha, no, it isn't!'

'Yes, it is. Look at me, a highly paid lawyer. Abandoning a baby is a criminal offence, you know. You can get ten years in jail for it. And, worse than that, I'm a prospective parliamentary candidate. For Binsmow, where my father's the vicar. You have to sign something saying there's nothing in your past that would cause your party any difficulty or embarrassment, you know.'

'Yes,' Clio said quietly, 'yes, I can see you're right. Martha—the father—did he ever have any idea?'

'No,' she said quickly. 'I couldn't possibly have told him.'

'Because?'

'I don't want to go on with this,' she said. 'Sorry.'

'All right. But what about Kate? She's going to have to know.'

'I know. How on earth is that going to be done? Who's going to tell her?'

'Well, I thought . . . you should,' said Clio, very gently. 'You're the only person who can help her understand.'

Martha stared at her. 'I really don't think I can do that,' she said.

'Poor you. Poor, poor you.'

Ed's voice was very quiet and gentle. Taking courage from it, Martha forced herself to look at his face. It was tender, concerned, there was no judgment, no shock, even. It was as if she had told him someone dear to her had died. She supposed, in a way, that was right: the cool, efficient, hyper-successful Martha had died; and in her place was someone flawed and very frightened, someone who had done something so shocking and shameful that she had kept it hidden for sixteen years.

She looked at him and smiled tenderly. 'I love you,' she said simply. 'I really, really love you . . .'

Nick was walking through Central Lobby when he saw Janet Frean.

'Look,' she said, 'our conversation last night . . . you haven't run the story today, I see.'

'No, I needed to do some more research on it.'

'Well, don't leave it too long. I'd hate to see it wasted and I'm sure the *Sun* would love it.'

'I'm sure they would.'

'So, why didn't she come herself?' asked Kate. She was white and very shocked, sitting close to her mother, holding her hand.

'I—we—'

'Who's we?'

'Me, and Clio and Martha herself, we all felt it best if I told you,' said Jocasta. 'You know me, you can yell your head off at me and I won't mind. And your mum and dad know me too. It just seemed more sensible.'

Kate nodded. 'So—does she want to see me?'

'Kate, of course she does,' said Jocasta, hoping devoutly this was true. 'But she wants you to get used to the idea. I mean, she's a complete stranger to you, isn't she?'

'Yeah . . . Yeah, she is.' She sat in silence for a moment, then, 'What's she like, Jocasta? I mean, what sort of person is she?'

'Well, I don't really know her either. We all went travelling together when we were a bit older than you are now, and I suppose we spent a week altogether in each other's company. Fast-forward sixteen years and I've met her only a couple of times since. Very briefly.'

'But . . . do you like her?'

'Yes, I think so.'

'And she's never told anyone at all?'

'No one at all. Except this madwoman, and that was at the party.'

'But . . . had she seen about me in the paper?'

'Well, yes.'

'So why the fuck didn't she come and see me then?' She was angry now, two spots of colour high on her cheeks.

'Kate, there's no need to swear,' said Jim.

'Yes, there is! She's a cow, a stupid, stupid cow. I hate her! I hate her already. I didn't like her at the party, and now I like her a whole lot less. Seems to me the only reason she's come clean now is because she's got to. Because she's scared it'll all be in the papers. Not because she gives a toss about me, not because she wants to see me. Cow!' She folded her arms across her chest. 'Well, you can tell her I don't want to see her. Ever.'

'One thing,' said Ed, 'does the . . . the . . . well, does he know?'

'No,' said Martha. 'No. I never told him anything.'

'But you know who he was?'

'Ed—'

'Look,' he said, and for the first time there was irritation, something raw in his attitude, 'look, I've been OK so far. Like totally on your side. I think I have a right to ask a few questions, don't you?'

'Of course you do. But—I can't answer that one. I'm sorry.'

'What, you don't know who it was?'

'I do know who it was. Yes. But I don't intend to talk about him. Ever.'

There was a long silence. Then, 'Seems to me it means you don't trust me. Unless you're still in love with him, that is.'

'I am not still in love with him. I never was in love with him. It was just . . . just something that happened. By the time I knew I was pregnant, I had no idea where he was.'

'But now you do?'

She was silent.

'You do! For Christ's sake, Martha, don't you think you should tell him? Don't you think she'll want to know?'

'Who?'

'Who? The girl. Kate. Your daughter. God! This is beginning to get to me, Martha. Don't you think she has a right to know who her dad is?'

'I don't know,' she said. 'Does she?'

'For fuck's sake,' he said. 'Look, I need to be on my own for a bit. Suddenly I can't cope with this. I'll see you later. I'll call you, OK?'

'OK.'

She watched him go, her eyes blurred with tears, wishing she could tell him.

She had been half asleep on the boat, coming back from Koh Tao to Koh Samui. The boat was rickety, even by Thai standards—very basic. She slung her rucksack onto the huge pile with all the others.

The trip was quite long, over three hours, and a wind had come up. Martha, who was a good sailor, had drifted off to sleep, lulled by the rise and fall of the boat; she woke once to see her rucksack tumble onto the mailbags on the lower deck. She tried to haul it back up, but she couldn't reach it, and went back to her corner. They were about thirty minutes from the jetty at Hat Bophut, when she heard his voice.

'Hi, Martha! I only just realised it was you. Your hair's different.'

She sat up, slightly dazed, and saw him, smiling down at her. 'Hi! Oh, the braids? Yes, I had it done on the beach. Were you on Koh Tao?'

She wasn't remotely surprised to see him; that was the whole thing about travelling. People came into your life, you became involved with them, and then you parted, to meet up with them again months later, in an entirely different place.

'Yeah. Been diving. You?'

'Just snorkelling. Lovely, though.'

'Isn't it? And where now?'

'Oh, back to Big Buddha Beach for a few days and then I've got a vague arrangement with some girl to move over to Phuket.'

'It's lovely there. And Krabi. You been north yet?'

'Yes, it was amazing.'

'Isn't it? May I sit here?'

She nodded; he smiled, slung his rucksack down on top of Martha's and the mail pile, and offered her a cigarette. Martha shook her head.

'So, where are you going now?' she asked him.

'Oh, up to Bangkok for a few days. Girl I knew quite well was in a scooter accident on Koh Phangan, pretty badly hurt, she was taken up there. Here, Martha, can you smell burning?'

'Only your cigarette.'

'No, it's not that. I'm sure I—Christ! Look, look at that smoke!'

She looked; there was a thick grey cloud pouring out of the engine room. Nobody seemed terribly concerned; the guy who was driving the boat smiled determinedly and there was a complete absence of anyone else who might have been considered crew. The smoke grew thicker.

'Shit!' he said. 'I don't like this. Bloody flames now!'

Martha was suddenly very, very frightened. These boats, old and battered, usually had one life belt at most. She looked towards land, at the comforting white curve of the beach, and the stern towering figure of Big Buddha, and felt better. They were surely near enough to swim to shore if necessary. She said so.

'No way, that's at least a mile and this is shark territory. Shit, shit, shit!'

Everyone was beginning to panic now, pointing at the flames, shouting at the captain, who was continuing to steer his boat doggedly towards the land, even though the fire was obviously out of control.

And then . . . 'Dunkirk,' said Martha pointing. 'Look!'

A small armada of longtail boats, their deafening diesel engines at full throttle, was setting out from the shore. One pilot per boat with two small boys perched at the stern of each.

One after another the longtails pulled up alongside the burning boat and people scrambled over the side and down into them. The flames were increasing all the time and there was still a slight swell; some people were clearly terrified, screaming and crying, but the boatmen remained calm, urging and coaxing them along.

The backpackers left the boat last; being inherently courteous. Martha, hiding her terror, was in the very last one.

As the longtails made in convoy for Bophut, the captain and a boy were struggling to rescue some of the luggage, while the flames began to consume the boat in earnest. Martha gazed at them trustingly; they would surely get her rucksack, they surely, surely would. And then, knowing that even just five minutes later they would have been in very, very real danger, found herself crying.

They stood on the shore watching as the boat went up like a fireball. Martha had stopped crying but she was shivering violently.

'Hey,' he said, coming over to her, putting his arm round her shoulders, 'you're cold. Here, have my sweater.'

He put it round her.

'I think I'm a bit shocked,' she said. 'I mean, if it had happened even half an hour earlier we'd be dead.'

'I know. But it didn't happen half an hour earlier, and we're not dead. Think of it as an adventure. Hey now, here's baggage reclaim. And, Martha . . . who are the lucky ones? I see both our rucksacks, nobody else's. And you know why? They came in on the mailcoach. Look!' It was true; four mail sacks and two rucksacks had been brought safely in to land. The rest of the luggage was clearly at the bottom of the sea.

'I feel so guilty. It seems so unfair.'

'Not unfair. But we were lucky. Look, I happen to have rather a lot of money on me—my dad cabled me some extra. Why don't we treat ourselves to a night in a hotel?'

'Sounds lovely. But I don't have any money. You go on your own.'

'I don't want to go on my own. I want you to come with me. I might have nightmares. Don't look at me like that—two rooms, no hidden agenda, honest. There's a really cool luxury beach resort near Chaweng, Coral Cove. And let's get a cab, none of your bus rubbish.'

Martha still felt terrible; she knew he was rich—it was patent from various things he had said—and their shared adventure had indeed made her feel as if he was an old and extremely close friend, or even a relative. She suddenly had a sense of total unreality.

'It sounds wonderful,' she said. 'Thank you.'

There is something about being in a very expensive hotel that is the opposite of character forming. There is a strong sense, born at the reception desk, that the servility and cosseting on offer are an absolute right, to be maintained at all times.

Martha, who had been brought up to regard frugality as the ultimate virtue and arrogance as the ultimate vice, found herself settled by the flower- and fern-fringed pool at the Coral Winds Hotel, a mere sixty minutes or so after unpacking her rucksack (while picking her way through the bowl filled with peaches and grapes supplied to her room by the management and sending down her crumpled and grubby shorts and T-shirts to the hotel express laundry), waving at the pool boy and asking, just very slightly irritably, if her second cocktail was on its way.

Having received a profuse apology, along with the cocktail, she sipped it briefly and then stood up, walked to the edge of the pool and dived neatly in, swam a length or two and then walked languidly back to her place and lay down again.

'Hi,' he said, appearing from inside the hotel. 'You OK?'

'Absolutely,' she said, 'thank you.'

'Excellent. Me too. What's that you're drinking?'

'A Bellini.' She spoke as if she drank them quite often; she had only ordered it because it was at the top of the menu. It was extremely nice.

'Ah, one of my favourites. I'll join you. I thought we'd have lunch here. They do a very good club sandwich, I'm told. Would that suit you?'

'Perfectly,' she said.

Lunch was brought and they ate it in a companionable silence.

That evening they wandered along the beach in the soft darkness; every hundred yards or so was a restaurant, candlelit tables set on the sand, a stall of fresh fish laid out on ice and a barbecue alight to cook it. They sat down, ordered barracuda, and while they waited for it, drank iced beer and watched the water lapping on the shore.

'This is the life,' she said. 'What a lovely day it's turned out to be. I feel quite, quite different.'

'You seem quite different from how I remember you,' he said.

'Oh, really? Well, I'm just the same.' Really she wasn't; she was no longer Cinderella but the princess and, until the clock struck and they left in the morning, so she would remain.

After dinner they walked slowly back to the hotel. There was a jazz singer in the bar, and they sat and listened to her, while drinking more cocktails. 'Honestly,' said Martha, 'I've drunk more today than I have in the last three months.'

'It suits you,' he said. 'Have another, have a Bellini, that's what you've become, a Bellini girl, I've enjoyed the transformation.'

'Thank you.'

That was what had done it, that one more drink. One more Bellini. She had become tipsy, silly, more and more confident.

So that, when they were walking to their rooms, and he leaned forward and kissed her gently, saying, 'It's been really fun,' she responded rather more enthusiastically than she had intended. She sensed his slight shock, then his pleasure; and then he took her hand and led her along the wooden, palm-fringed walkways towards their bungalows and it was just the shortest step to becoming one of those carelessly confident girls who took sex, along with all the other pleasures, not especially seriously.

'You're absolutely gorgeous,' he said the following morning, just before dawn; before he left for the airport in one of the hotel limos and she became Cinderella again. 'Really, absolutely, I had no idea at all . . .' And it was so wonderful to be told that, and by someone so beautiful himself. It had been fun while it lasted, and so very unlike her, but now it was over. She had no illusions about that. But she wasn't about to become boring, buttoned-up Martha again until she absolutely had to.

Martha knew she had to tell her parents. She couldn't risk it any longer. Just because the story hadn't been in the paper today, or yesterday, it didn't mean it wouldn't be tomorrow. Nick was being wonderful, but there were other papers, and Janet wasn't going to wait for ever.

She felt very bad. Ed had not come back. He had called, saying he needed time to think, that he did love her, but he really needed to know more. 'It's not fair, otherwise. I think I've a right to know who this bloke was. Give me a bell if anything changes. I'm not going anywhere. But I do need a bit of help over this one.'

So she had phoned her parents, said she was coming up, that she needed to talk to them.

'Well, that'll be lovely, dear,' Grace had said. 'When will you be here?'

'Oh, quite late, around nine or ten.'

'Lovely.'

No, it won't be lovely, Martha thought, it will be dreadful. But there seemed absolutely no alternative. It had to be done. Too many people knew already, quite apart from the press. There was no knowing what Kate might do, for instance.

And then she rang.

'This is Kate Tarrant. I'd like to come and see you. In about an hour. I presume you'll be there?'

'Yes,' said Martha rather weakly, 'yes, I'll be here.' And rang her parents again and told them she'd be much later; to go to bed and she'd see them in the morning.

'Hi,' said Kate. She was dressed in jeans and a T-shirt that showed a great deal of her flat stomach. Her hair was tied back, and she wore no make-up. She was a lot taller than Martha.

'This is Nat Tucker,' said Kate. 'He's a friend of mine.'

'Hello, Nat,' said Martha. 'Do come in, both of you. What can I offer you, a drink or something?'

'Nothing, thanks,' said Kate. She walked in, looked round. Nat followed her.

'Very nice,' Nat said, breaking the frozen silence. 'Good view.'

'Thank you,' said Martha. 'Would you . . . would you like to sit down?'

Nat dropped onto one of the low, black leather sofas; Kate stayed on her feet, turned to face Martha.

'I want to know who my father is,' she said. 'That's all. Nothing else. Unlike you, he might actually want to meet me.'

Martha had not really been expecting this; not at this stage. 'I'm . . . I'm afraid I can't tell you that.'

'No? Why not? Don't you know?' The dark eyes were very hard. 'Was it, like, a one-night stand?'

She's bound to be angry, Martha thought, bound to be hostile.

'I . . . just can't tell you,' she said.

'Yeah? Are you still in touch with him, then?'

'No. I'm not. But he has no idea. And I don't think it's right to—to tell him now. After all these years.'

'Oh, you don't think it's right? I see. You think it was right to leave me though, do you? Just left, along with a bit of cleaning fluid.'

'Kate—'

'And you thought it was right not to come and see me, when it was in the paper and everything, and you could have done it so easily. That was fine, was it? Funny idea of right and wrong you've got! You left me there, a newborn baby, all alone, I could have died—'

'I waited,' said Martha, 'I waited until I knew you'd been found, that you were all right—'

'Oh, you did? Well, that was really good of you. I s'pose you thought that was that, did you?'

'I—'

'You never thought how I might feel, later on. Knowing my mother, my own mother, just wasn't interested in me. What do you think that's like? To be so not wanted. So not important. Don't you think that must be totally horrible? Anyway, luckily for me, I've had a real mother, a proper mother. *She* cared about me. She still does. I reckon I'd have been better off with her, anyway. I don't know what kind of mother you think you'd have been, but I can tell you, you'd have been shit!'

153

'Kate,' said Nat mildly, from the depths of the sofa.

'She'd have been shit,' said Kate looking at him briefly, then turning back to Martha. 'So I should be thanking you, really. For getting out of my life. Anyway, I don't want to carry on with this, it's totally pointless. But I do want to know who my father was. So if you'll just give me his name, I'll leave you in peace.'

'Kate, I'm really sorry, but I'm not going to do that. I can't.'

She looked at her steadily, trying to equate this girl, this beautiful grown-up creature, with the tiny baby she had left behind.

'I'm sorry,' said Kate, 'but don't you think you owe me anything?'

'Of course I do. But . . . not that.'

'You cow,' Kate said. 'You stupid cow.'

Nat stood up. 'Kate, there's no need for this. It isn't helping. I'm sorry,' he said, addressing Martha, 'she's not usually so rude.'

For some reason this amused Martha: so much so that she smiled, almost giggled. She supposed it was a relief from the tension.

Kate walked over to her and slapped her hard across the face.

'Don't you laugh at him,' she said, 'he's worth a million of you.'

'Kate, I wasn't laughing at him,' said Martha, shocked. She put her hand up and touched her face. 'I was laughing at . . . it doesn't matter.'

'Like I don't,' said Kate. 'Like I don't to you. Not at all. Like I never have. Just something to get rid of, I was, wasn't I? Why didn't you have an abortion? Tell me that. That would've been much better, wouldn't it?'

And she started to cry, great noisy sobs, that got louder and louder; Nat tried to calm her, but it was hopeless. She went on and on, beating her clenched fists helplessly against her sides; and then collapsed onto the sofa, her head buried in her arms, her hair showering over them.

Martha looked at her, and felt a stab of sorrow to see her like this, in such grief, in such pain. She sat down beside her, put an arm rather tentatively round her shoulders; Kate shook it off viciously.

'Don't! Get off me.'

But that feeling, that stab of feeling, had given Martha courage. 'Could you just listen to me, just for a little while?' she said.

'What, and you try to explain? No, thanks.'

But she had at least looked at her, while sniffing and wiping her eyes on the back of her hand; it was a contact of sorts. Martha went to fetch her some tissues; she took them without a word.

'I think we'd best go,' Kate said to Nat, 'there's no point staying here.'

'Don't you think it might be an idea, Kate, to listen to what she's got to say?'

'No,' said Kate briefly, 'I don't. Only thing I want to hear from her is my dad's name. Come on, Nat, let's go.'

She walked over to the door; she had trouble with the lock. Martha followed her, undid it for her.

'I'm so sorry,' she said, meeting Kate's eyes. 'I know it doesn't mean anything to you, but I am, truly sorry. I wish you'd let me talk to you.'

'You could have done that months ago,' said Kate. 'It's too late now.'

And she and Nat were gone.

Martha hadn't realised how tired she was until she was on the A12. Maybe she should stop, stay at a motel, and drive on in the morning. She could call her parents and tell them, so they wouldn't worry. She dialled their number. The answering machine cut in. She knew what that meant: they were watching television. *Casualty*, probably. They never heard the phone from the sitting room. Damn. And they seldom checked the answering machine until the morning. She left a message anyway, saying she might find a B&B and come on in the morning.

She felt terrible. Really terrible. The encounter with Kate had shaken her horribly. For some reason, she hadn't expected quite so much hostility. Naive really.

Martha knew it was crazy, but she rang Ed. She felt so lonely, so besieged by fate; losing him now when she had found him again, albeit so briefly, was almost unbearable. She was beginning to wonder why she was being protective of—of him. She certainly didn't owe him anything. But—she did. It was ripples in the pond—the wider they went, the worse it got, the more people were hurt. 'Hi, Ed, it's me.'

'Hi. Where are you?'

'About an hour from Binsmow.'

'Yeah?' The voice was polite, no more. 'Going to see your parents?'

'Yes. And to tell them.'

'Yeah?'

This was awful. She had only heard his voice this hard once before and that had been the night of their terrible row, when he had gone for her, told her how cold and controlling she was. She threw caution not just to the winds, but into outer space.

'I'm scared, Ed. So scared.'

'Of what?'

'Of hurting them. That's how it all began.'

'Yeah. Well, I'm sure you'll manage.'

'Ed—'

'Yes, Martha?'

'I'm missing you.'

'Well, I miss you too. But, like I said, there are limits. I can't cope with all this shit, you know? About the father.'

'I know, but—'

'Are you going to tell me or not?'

'No, Ed, I'm not. Not yet, anyway. I wish you could understand—'

'Sorry, but I can't. You never change, do you, really? You just call me in when you need me, focused entirely on yourself. You're still doing it.'

'I'm not!'

'Martha, you should listen to yourself. On and on, round and round like a bloody cracked record. Saying how you don't want to hurt your parents, that was how it all began. Assuming that I'll just drop everything, to listen to you. Well, I'm busy right now. I'll call you in a day or two.'

She managed to say goodbye, and then started to cry, the tears blurring her eyes. She had to stop. Together with her tiredness, it was a fatal combination. She pulled across to the inside lane, meaning to draw up on the hard shoulder. She missed the fact that a slip road was coming onto the A12 from her left; a large lorry, being driven only a little too fast, was coming down it, its driver momentarily distracted, himself, by a call from his girlfriend. He pulled out to try to avoid her, hit her anyway, and skidded right across the width of the road, taking the Mercedes with him.

Chapter 12

'MARTHA'S VERY LATE,' said Grace Hartley, switching off Michael Parkinson and moving into her bedtime ritual of cushion-plumping, cat-ejecting and newspaper collection, 'I hope she's all right.'

'I'm sure she is. I'll just go and switch off my computer, read through that sermon again, and see if she's called.'

He came back, smiling. 'She's probably going to stop on the way. She said she's tired, so she may book into a motel and be here for breakfast.'

'Well, I'm glad she's so sensible. You go up, and I'll make the tea.'

'Is that the Reverend Peter Hartley? I'm sorry to ring you in the middle of the night, sir. This is the police. I'm afraid there's been an accident . . .'

He put the phone down and looked at his wife. Her eyes were wide with fear. He didn't need to tell her.

'Is she alive?' she said. 'And where is she?'

'She's alive. But in Intensive Care. In Bury St Edmunds Hospital.'

'Well, let's go,' she said, climbing out of bed, very calm, reaching for the clothes she had laid out for the morning, as she always did. 'Quickly, Peter. She needs us.'

As he pulled on his own clothes (adding his clerical collar; it could be very useful, he had discovered), Peter Hartley started to pray silently. He could pray while he did anything: drove the car, did the supermarket shop, weeded the garden, tidied his study. He didn't stop until they reached the hospital. And then prayed that they were not too late.

It was eight o'clock in the morning. Martha had survived the hours of surgery for a ruptured spleen, but her blood pressure had dropped alarmingly with the blood loss, and the surgeon had told the Hartleys that at one stage he had been really quite worried. But, so far, so good.

'So, is she all right now?'

'I can't quite say for sure. Sorry, but I don't want to mislead you. She has lost so much blood and her pulse is very erratic. There's always a fear of secondary infections. But we're pumping her with blood and antibiotics and other things, and she has no head injuries. Anyway, she's been lucky, so far. I should go home and get some rest if I were you.'

Grace wondered if he had any children and decided not; if he had, he'd never have suggested anything so absurd. And Peter thought of the hours of prayer he had sent up for Martha, and knew that it had not just been luck that had seen her through.

'We'll stay,' they said, simultaneously.

'Fine. Well, it's up to you. Coffee machine down the corridor. Try not to worry.' And he was gone.

Peter had phoned his curate at seven, and asked him to take the Communion service. 'And the rest, actually, I'll be here all day.'

The curate said that would be the least he could do and that of course he would include prayers for Martha at every service.

Which was how Mrs Forrest, who had gone to early Communion, learned about the accident. She was very upset.

Ed was eating his usual Sunday-morning breakfast—a doughnut and a coffee in Starbucks—when his mother rang.

'Edward? Are you busy, dear?'

'No. Not at all. You OK, Mum?'

'I'm fine. I've just been to church.'

'Oh, yeah? How was the Rev?'

'He wasn't there. That's why I'm ringing. Andrew took the service.'

'Yeah? Cool.' He took a large bite of doughnut. Hardly worth a phone call—she'd obviously not got enough to do.

'Yes. Poor Mr Hartley was at the hospital.'

'The hospital? What's wrong with him?'

'Nothing, dear. But I thought you'd want to know. It's their daughter, the lawyer. Martha, you know.' The doughnut was turning to something very unpleasant in Ed's mouth; he spat what was left of it out into his napkin, took a swig of coffee.

'She's been in a terrible accident. A car crash. She's still alive at the moment. But it's very serious, apparently. Anyway, I wanted to tell you, because I knew you'd met her. She drove you up to town once, didn't she? Very kind, that was. They're such a lovely family.'

'Yeah, I know that. Can you . . . can you tell me a bit more, Mum?'

'Well, not a lot, dear. She had a collision with a lorry. Last night. Her car was under it, apparently. She's had surgery and she's in a critical condition, Andrew was saying. Poor girl. After all she's trying to do for Binsmow as well, with her legal sessions—'

'Surgeries,' said Ed automatically. 'They're called surgeries. What hospital is she in, Mum, do you know?'

'Bury. She's in Intensive Care. You sound quite upset, dear. Did you ever see more of her?'

'A bit,' said Ed, and put the phone down.

A bit. Quite a bit. All of her, in fact. All of her lovely, skinny, sexy body; all of her tough, awkward, fierce mind; he knew every mood of her, knew her loving, knew her laughing, knew her angry, knew her— very occasionally—calm. Usually when they had had sex.

And now she was lying in Intensive Care, her body crushed and broken, dangerously, critically ill. Her car under a lorry: last night. After he had spoken to her, after he had been so cruel to her. She had rung him for help and he had refused it. It could all have been his fault.

Ed suddenly felt terribly sick.

'Jocasta, this is Ed. Ed Forrest. Martha's friend.'

Of course. The gorgeous boy. Nothing had surprised them all more than Martha's choice of boyfriend. They'd expected some buttoned-up lawyer, and had met instead this easy, beautiful creature who seemed far too young for her. Who clearly adored her.

'Oh, hi, Ed. What can I do for you?'

'I don't know,' he said, 'but I thought you ought to know . . . Martha's had a terrible accident. A car crash, she . . . she's in Intensive Care. I don't know much more than that.'

'Oh, Ed, no! I'm so sorry.'

'I'm going up there right away,' he said, 'to see her. But I thought you should tell Nick . . . sorry, I can't remember his name, the journalist—'

'Yes, yes, of course.'

'So he can tell that woman. Get her off our backs, I mean. She won't do anything now, will she?'

'I shouldn't think so,' said Jocasta quickly. 'God, how awful. Where is she? Which hospital?'

'Bury St Edmunds. So, quite a way. I must go.'

'Of course. Ed, give her our love. I'm sure she'll be fine. And don't worry about Janet Frean. We'll deal with her. I'll call Nick right away.'

'Thanks.'

Janet? This is Nick Marshall.'

'Oh, yes?'

'Janet, Martha's had an accident. A car crash. She's very seriously hurt. I imagine this changes everything, for the time being.'

'Of course. How dreadful. Yes, we'll speak later.'

Actually, Janet thought, it would make the whole story more brilliant still. Give it an added edge. A poignancy even. She could see it now. Yes. It would work very well. As long as Martha lived, of course. Which she would, obviously. Nick was exaggerating the seriousness of the accident to buy himself more time. She really didn't see him doing the story now.

Ward F was very quiet; even hospitals seemed to respond to the mood of Sunday mornings. Ed ran along the corridor, desperately trying to find anyone, anyone at all.

He saw a door marked ITU. He tried to open it, but it was locked; there was a bank of numbers on the door. Bloody combination lock. Shit. He hammered on the door.

An irritable face appeared.

'I think my girlfriend's in there. Martha Hartley?'

'If she is, you certainly can't see her. This is ITU. No visitors.'

'Oh, God. Please, PLEASE!'

'I'm sorry, no. Please wait outside, and someone will help you.'

'But . . . Oh, Mr Hartley. How are you? I mean, how is she? I mean—'

Peter Hartley's face was ravaged with grief. 'She's not very well, Ed,' he said simply. He showed no sign of surprise at seeing him. 'Couldn't you let this young man in, Sister? It can't make any difference now . . .'

Bob Frean stood in the doorway of Janet's study. His face was very cold, very blank. 'Janet—'

She raised her finger to her lips, put her hand over the receiver.

'Sorry, talking to the *Sun*. Won't be long—'

Bob walked forward and put his hand on the receiver.

'Bob! What are you doing, you've cut me off!'

'Good,' he said, 'that was what I intended. And before you ring them back, I have just one thing to say to you, Janet. If you tell the *Sun* anything at all unpleasant about Martha Hartley, I shall tell them a great many unpleasant things about you.' He smiled at her, quite politely, and then turned and walked out again. Janet sat staring at the telephone, listening to his footsteps going along the corridor.

Martha was on the bed, her eyes closed; she looked perfectly peaceful, her face slightly swollen and bruised, but no worse. Tubes seemed to be coming out of every part of her; drips hung above her on both sides of the bed, one delivering blood, the others, he supposed, drugs of some sort. A bank of monitors to her right blinked various incomprehensible messages: the one comfort he could find was that there was no dreadful straight line on any of them: the line so familiar to viewers of hospital soap operas, signalling, as it did, the end of a story.

But this was not a soap opera and this was not a story line. The person on the bed was Martha, his Martha, who he loved more than he had ever even realised. And who it seemed he was about to lose.

He looked, panic-stricken, at the Hartleys. Grace was very calm, sitting by the bed, her eyes fixed on Martha's face, Peter was holding one of her hands. Ed moved round the bed, and carefully picked up the other hand.

'Can I—am I allowed to speak to her?' he said, very quietly, remembering, from his own father's death, that hearing was the last sense to go.

'Yes, of course,' said Grace.

She sat there watching him now, as he bent down, totally unselfconscious, and said gently, 'Martha, it's me. Ed. I'm here now.'

If this was *Casualty*, Grace thought, Martha's eyelids would flicker, she'd move her head, she'd squeeze his hand. But it isn't, it's real life and none of those things will happen.

And Peter thought, If she recovers now, it would be a miracle. And struggle as he might, in that moment he didn't believe in miracles.

Ed was still talking in the same gentle voice. 'Martha, I'm so sorry. What I said last night. So sorry. I don't care about Kate. I don't care about any of it. I love you, Martha. Very, very much. I really, really love you.'

And then it happened, against every possible expectation, and Grace and Peter watched, awed, as Martha's eyelids did indeed flicker and she turned her head, just very slightly. No more than a hair's-breadth but enough to be seen, in Ed's direction, and a glancing shadow of a smile touched her face; and two great tears, Ed's tears, fell on the hand that had, almost imperceptibly, squeezed his.

It was only a small miracle: but in some ways it was enough.

Afterwards, real life came swiftly in again: and the line on the monitor grew straight and Martha's story was written gently out of the script. But Ed, who had both worked and experienced the miracle, felt, as he bade her farewell, just a little comforted.

'I don't know why I feel so upset,' Jocasta said. She was sitting in Nick's flat in Hampstead, weeping; his arms were round her, and he was tenderly stroking her hair. 'It's not as if I'd been close to her, or anything. I suppose it was Kate; she came with Kate, in a way. It's so sad.'

'It is sad,' he said, 'dreadfully sad. I can't believe it, not any of it.'

'But at least Ed got there. That's something. He was so distraught, Nick, I can't tell you. He said he was going to stay with his mum tonight, in Binsmow, and he'd see us tomorrow. He said'—she swallowed hard, sniffed loudly—'he said he thought they'd like us to be at the funeral. He said we'd done so much for her. I wish.'

'Well, we tried,' said Nick. 'We did our best. I think Janet must be feeling pretty bad.'

'I bloody well hope so,' said Jocasta.

'Oh, it's so, so sad,' said Clio. Her eyes were red with weeping; like Jocasta she couldn't quite work out why she was so upset. Fergus told her it was because she was so tender-hearted, but she knew it was more than that. In a few short weeks Martha had wound her way into their lives, just as insistently as if they had had the annual meetings they had promised one another all those years ago. She kept thinking of Martha living with her dreadful secret, and she thought that Martha was, without doubt, the bravest person she had ever met.

Jack Kirkland called Janet Frean.

'It's about Martha. Dreadful thing. She's died.'

There was an endless silence: then: 'Died!' The word shot from her, very loud.

'Yes. I'm afraid so.'

'But I thought—Jack, are you sure?'

'I'm very sure. Nick Marshall just rang me.'

'Nick Marshall! What's it got to do with him?'

'Oh, she and Jocasta were friendly, as you know. They went travelling together when they were girls. Anyway, she died. Around lunchtime today. Janet—are you all right?'

The line went suddenly dead. Puzzled, he rang off, waited for her to ring him back. When she didn't, he called Chad Lawrence.

Half an hour later, he rang again. Bob Frean answered the phone.

'Oh, hello, Bob. I was talking to Janet about half an hour ago, and we were cut off. May I speak to her?'

'I'm afraid not.' Bob sounded awkward. 'She's not very well.'

'Oh, I'm sorry. She does too much. I thought she sounded rather odd when I told her about Martha. She was very fond of her, of course.'

'Indeed.'

'I wanted to speak to her about the funeral. Obviously we should all go. It's at Martha's father's church in Suffolk; he's taking the service, poor man. Next Monday. I know Janet will want to come.'

'Yes, of course. I'll tell her. I'd like to come myself, if that would be all right. I was very fond of Martha.'

'Perfectly all right, yes. Well, give Janet my best.'

Bob went into the bedroom he and Janet shared occasionally. Most of the time he slept in another room, on the next floor. She was lying on the bed, staring up at the ceiling, ashen-faced, very still. She looked almost lifeless herself.

'That was Kirkland.'

She said nothing.

'It was about the funeral. Martha's funeral.'

Silence still.

'It's next Monday. I said we'd both go.'

'I can't go,' she said, her voice as expressionless as her face.

'Janet,' he said, 'you're going.'

Gideon Keeble found himself very moist-eyed when Jocasta told him the news. 'Silly old fool that I am,' he said to her, 'but she was lovely, and so charming and clever. What a waste, what a dreadful waste.'

Jocasta agreed.

'The funeral's next Monday, Gideon, will you be able to come? Will you be back? I'd so love it if you would.'

'I'll be there.'

'Thank you. I love you, Gideon.'

'I love you too, Jocasta. Where are you, incidentally? I've been calling the house.'

'I'm at Nick's,' she said, without thinking.

'I think I'd like to go to the funeral,' said Kate.

Helen stared at her. She was pale, but otherwise composed, not hysterical. 'Kate, love, are you sure?'

'Yes, of course I'm sure. Perfectly sure. Why shouldn't I be?'

'But, you didn't know her,' said Helen, realising the absurdity of this statement, even as she made it.

'Mum! I know that. But I'd like to say goodbye to her. Properly. I . . . well, I wasn't very nice to her when I met her. I feel bad about it.'

'Oh dear.' Helen sighed. She wasn't at all sure about this. For all sorts of reasons. Not least—'Kate, what do you think Martha's family will think about it? Won't they wonder who you are?'

'I'll tell them I'm a friend of Jocasta's, that I met Martha through her. I've thought of that.'

'Oh dear,' said Helen again. 'Kate, I don't think I can go. Even if you do. It would be very difficult. I don't expect you to understand, but—'

'Oh, Mum!' Kate's expression suddenly softened; she put her arms round her mother. 'Of course I understand. Of course you don't have to come. I'll go with Jocasta. And Fergus will be there. I'll be fine.'

'Beatrice . . . I know this might sound a bit odd, but I think I'd like to go to Martha Hartley's funeral.'

'Really? Why?'

'Oh, hard to explain. I'd just like to. No need for you to come.'

'No, it would be out of the question anyway. Well, I suppose if you want to, Josh. It seems totally out of proportion to me—'

'I know. But—oh, I don't know, it's just that she's the first, the very first of our generation to go. I still feel quite shocked. I'd met her, and I'd like to . . . to acknowledge the fact.'

'Fine. You go. I'm sure Jocasta will be pleased.'

The night before the funeral, Gideon phoned from Seattle. 'Jocasta, my darling, I'm going to fail you. I can't get there in time for tomorrow.'

She felt disproportionately angry and upset. 'Why? What's happened?'

'Some kind of breakdown in air-traffic control. So I can't even charter anything. Darling, I am so, so sorry. I've been trying to get something sorted for hours. I didn't want to ring you until I knew it was hopeless.'

'Yes, well, now you have,' said Jocasta.

'Darling one, don't sound so angry.'

'I *am* angry. If you'd left a day earlier, as you should have done, anyway, to be sure of getting back in time, you'd be here by now.'

'Jocasta, I haven't exactly been on holiday out here, you know.'

'I do know, and I shouldn't think you ever will be. Oh, never mind. I'll get by without you. Everyone else is coming. Even Josh.'

'Josh? Why should he be going? He didn't know Martha, surely?'

'He did. Briefly. He was with us when we first went travelling. And he met her again at our wedding party. Anyway, he wanted to say goodbye. Pay his respects, he said. Don't worry, Gideon, I'll be fine.'

'Jocasta—' But she had put the phone down.

The funeral was to start at two. By just after one, cars began to fill St Andrew's Road. By one thirty, people were standing awkwardly about outside, greeting those they knew, smiling uncertainly at those they didn't. At twenty to two, they moved into the church.

St Andrew's was not a large church, but it was not a small one, either; by ten to two it was full. The older members of the parish had come in force, all wanting to say goodbye to the little girl they had watched grow up; and Martha's constituents too, wishing to show their gratitude for the help she had given them so freely, albeit for so brief a time.

And then there were the Other People, as Grace called them to herself. The people from London, carloads of them: a large contingent from Sayers Wesley, all marshalled in by a stony-faced Paul Quenell. The Centre Forward Party had come in force: Jack Kirkland, of course, and Chad Lawrence and his wife; Janet Frean, horribly pale and haggard-looking, with her husband, and then another whole row of party members, other candidates, and the secretaries from Centre Forward House. And an Asian family: a beautiful teenage girl and an embarrassed-looking boy, and their father, smiling awkwardly. Lina's family, come to show their respects to Martha for what she had tried to do for Lina.

And finally, her friends: Jocasta, with a stricken-looking Kate, Clio, Josh, Fergus, Nick, all filing in together: Ed saw them first, as he walked in behind the coffin, together with Martha's father. They gave him courage as he heard the awful words, in Peter Hartley's voice: 'I am the resurrection and the life,' and wondered in bewilderment how they could possibly apply to the person he had loved so much, who was lying in this flower-drenched coffin, with his own wreath set beside her parents' larger one, a ring of white roses with the words: *Martha, my love always, Ed* on the card, written in his own untidy hand.

The elderly organist, who had played at Martha's christening and confirmation, was pouring his heart into Elgar's 'Nimrod' for her. Nick, sitting with Clio and Fergus, looked at the two rows of politicians—the only people he knew properly here, apart from Jocasta—and wondered what Martha could have found in these self-seeking, power-obsessed people that could have lured her under their spell. What was it about politics that people found so irresistible, and worth sacrificing so much for? If she had resisted them, then she would, very probably, have been alive today. He tried not to dwell on that; it was too awful.

Paul Quenell was standing up now, moving to the lectern; deeply touched to have been asked by Grace and Peter to read from St Paul's letter to the Corinthians. He only hoped he would not fail them.

It was with the words 'the greatest of these is charity' that Ed's heart felt as if it might explode with pain. He gripped the pew in front of him and bowed his head, fighting back his tears; Jocasta, who was sitting behind him, reached forward and placed her hand on one of his shoulders to let him know she was there and wept too.

And then, praying for enough strength to do it, Peter Hartley spoke the briefest of eulogies.

'You must forgive me,' he said, 'if I am unable to finish this. But with God's help I will. I want only to say a very few words of farewell to Martha. She was not, in any case, an effusive person, as most of you know. But she was a remarkable person, and even allowing for some natural prejudice, strong as well as gentle, kind as well as ambitious, brave as well as tender-hearted. She was a perfectionist, as many of you will also know, and hard at times to live up to. Grace and I were always immensely proud of her, and although it was sad to lose her to the big city, and her high-flying career, we could see that was where she belonged. But this year she had come back to Binsmow, and was working for the community in a new way, in her guise as a fledgling politician. Who knows what might have happened to her? Maybe a future second woman prime minister grew up in this parish and in the house next door. We shall never now know. But what we do know is that while she was'—his voice shook—'while she was with us, for that too-short a time, she failed no one. Not her family, not her colleagues, not her friends. And we all loved her.

'There could be no better epitaph. Thank you all for coming to say goodbye to her. My wife and I thank you from the bottom of our hearts.'

Kate was aware of something strange happening to her, which had begun as they first went into the church, a little melting of the cold around her heart. This mother of hers, this woman who had abandoned her as a baby and pursued her own interests, had begun to change. That cold and selfish person she had imagined couldn't have earned all this. There must have been a different Martha, a kind and generous one, who meant a great deal to a great many people. Who were those Asian people, for instance? And who was that gorgeous bloke, sitting and crying in front of them? He was quite young, maybe a brother or something. She must have been better than Kate had thought. Not all bad. And her poor mum, she looked really nice, and her dad too. That had been brave, standing up and saying all that. She looked at Jocasta, and at Clio, Martha's friends, her real mother's friends; they were both crying and it sobered her. They were both so nice, so cool: how could they have cared so much about the monster she had created in her head?

If only she'd known her, if only she'd been a bit nicer that day.

Bach's Toccata and Fugue in D minor filled the church now from the organ loft. Clio, clutching Fergus's hand, saw the pallbearers pick up the coffin and turn very, very slowly, as if in a dream. And then the coffin began to move, slowly, so slowly down the nave, the flowers spilling over it, the sunlight streaming so determinedly in. She would always remember Martha in sunshine, Clio thought, only not here, not in this church, but on a sun-drenched white beach. And then she looked at Ed, his eyes red-rimmed and still full of tears, moving off behind the coffin, and thought she had never seen such pain on so young a face. And then Martha's mother, she supposed it was, leaning on a young woman's arm, her other daughter obviously, sobbing in a dreadful silence.

She looked at Josh, standing next to Jocasta, Kate between them. They could almost be a family, they all looked so alike. And then everything moved into slow motion . . . *Kate looks so like Jocasta . . . I can't tell you who the father is* . . . and then it was there, right there, as it had been all the time, in front of their eyes. And she looked again at Jocasta and Josh, standing there together, and Kate so like both of them, and Clio knew in that moment, and with an absolute certainty, who Kate's father was.

At half past eleven that night, an ambulance arrived outside the Frean house. Janet had taken an overdose: whether or not it was too late to save her, nobody could say.

Chapter 13

'MY DARLING, could we have a little talk?'

Jocasta was lying in bed, watching Gideon while he dressed. This was increasingly a pattern; she had nothing to get up for, so she would wait until he had gone, and then lie in the bath for anything up to an hour, making non-plans, as she thought of them, to fill her day. It was actually quite nice, the watching; she would comment on his clothes, he would consult her on which tie he should wear, and tell her what he was doing for the rest of the day. On a good morning he would suggest what they might do in the evening, or even (occasionally) for lunch; he had been in London now for over a week and said he had at least another two there, before a big trip to the States she was to accompany him on.

'Goodness, Gideon,' she said, 'when my father said things like that, it meant I was in serious trouble.'

He smiled at her, came over to kiss her. 'Not trouble at all. But—'

Jocasta was beginning to feel irritated. 'Gideon, do come to the point.'

'Sorry. Right. It goes like this. I want to give a couple of big dinner parties within the next month. In London. Mostly business, but a few friends. Could you liaise with the housekeeper, Mrs Hutching, on menus and so on. I'll do the guest lists, obviously—'

'I'm sorry?'

'I said I'll do the guest lists.'

'Why?'

'Why? Well, I just told you, these are mostly business affairs. I have to do them.'

'You said a few friends.'

'Yes, I know, but I meant—' He stopped.

'You meant *your* friends?'

'Well, yes. But I very much hope they will become our friends.'

'What's wrong with mine?'

'Jocasta, please. There's nothing wrong with them, but most of your friends wouldn't fit in with a large, rather serious dinner party with a lot of middle-aged people.'

'And would I?'

He looked at her. 'You're different,' he said awkwardly. 'You're my wife.'

'So you're stuck with me at this rather serious dinner party, which I won't fit in with? Thanks!'

'You're being difficult.'

'I am not being difficult. And I would venture to suggest that if you want to have a dinner party, which I won't enjoy, you should have it at a restaurant. Or in your boardroom. Or I'll go out.'

'Oh, for God's sake,' he said, irritable himself, now, 'I think we'd better stop this. I'll speak to Mrs Hutching myself.'

'Yes, and give me the dates and I'll make sure to be out.'

He looked at her with intense dislike and slammed the bedroom door without saying another word.

She lay in her long bath, wondering what non-plans she could make for the day, feeling miserable. What was she supposed to be, some kind of secondary housekeeper? She didn't know anything about that sort of thing: menus, guest lists, table linen, not even flowers, not really. It wasn't what she was about.

So, what was she about? She really didn't know any more. She got out of the bath, wrapped herself in her bathrobe and, greatly to her surprise, she started to cry. She felt so useless. So lost.

She got dressed, went down to the kitchen, made herself some coffee and drank it quickly, before Mrs Hutching could appear and offer her breakfast, ask her if she'd be in for lunch—God, it was awful, not living in your own house—when Nick called her. She was so pleased to hear from him, she burst into tears.

'What on earth's the matter?'

'Oh, nothing. Just me. Sorry. Rewind, yes, Nick, nice to hear from you, how are you?'

'I'm fine,' he said. 'I rang you because I had a clearout at the weekend and I found a few of your things. Wasn't sure what to do about them.'

'What sort of things?' She felt rather bleak suddenly, seeing his bright white flat, with its tall ceilings, looking over Hampstead Heath, where she had spent so much time over the past few years.

'Oh, you know. Jewellery mostly. And a few bits of rather expensive-looking lingerie—'

She thought he might have wanted to keep that, as a memento. The tears started again.

'Jocasta, is something wrong?'

'Oh, Nick, I don't know what's the matter with me. I feel sort of incompetent. I don't know how to be a good wife. I don't know about running houses and telling staff what to do. It's not me.'

'Well, sweetie'—the endearment slipped out—'it's got to be you, don't you think? You've married someone who wants you to do those things. He's a high-maintenance husband, he needs a highly maintaining wife.'

'Well, he's got the wrong one.'

'Jocasta, you've married him, for God's sake!' He sounded angry. 'Look,' he went on, 'I don't think this is a very healthy conversation.'

'Why not?'

'If you don't know why not, you are truly stupid, Jocasta. It isn't healthy and it isn't very kind.'

'Who isn't it kind to?'

'To me, for crying out loud,' he said and there was a note in his voice she had hardly ever heard before. 'Can't you see how hideous it is for me to listen to you wailing about your marriage and what a mistake it seems to be, when I still'—he stopped—'still care about you? Just grow up, Jocasta. For God's sake. Try thinking about someone other than yourself for a few minutes, why don't you?'

When Gideon got home that evening, an immense bunch of flowers in his arms, Jocasta was sitting in the kitchen with Mrs Hutching, a sheaf of menus fanned out between them. She got up and went into his arms, kissed him fondly.

'I'm so, so sorry about this morning,' she said.

'Me too. So very, very sorry.'

Mrs Hutching gathered up her menus and hurried upstairs to her flat.

'Hi, Fergus, it's Kate.'

'Hello, Kate, my darling. How are you?'

'I'm fine. But I've made up my mind. I don't want the Smith contract.'

'Right.' Fergus tried to suppress the slug of disappointment. 'Right, I see. Are you sure?'

'Absolutely sure. I know it's a lot of money and everything, but I just can't cope with the rest of it.'

'Like what, Kate?'

'Oh, you know, the publicity. It'll all start again, just as it's beginning to die down. Asking me about my mother and everything. And now I know . . . well, I can face it even less. Sorry.'

'That's all right, I understand.'

Fergus counted to ten silently. This was a nightmare. Silly, arrogant little thing, imagining she could play games with these people, tossing a three-million-dollar contract down the drain as if it was a used Kleenex. Who did she think she was? Naomi Campbell?

Jocasta was trying very hard now to be a good wife. She was too frightened not to be. She had to make this work, she just had to. She had rung Nick to apologise for whining at him that day. He was friendly but brisk, said it was fine, and had all her things biked back to her with a perfectly nice but cool note. She felt rejected and miserable for days.

Anyway, she felt she was getting somewhere with learning to be Mrs Keeble. It was bound to take time, to settle into all this; she'd get used to it. Of course she would.

And then it happened.

It had started quite gently: he asked her to go on a business trip with him in a few weeks' time. It wouldn't be the most exciting event in the world, he said, it was a three-day weekend for captains of industry in Munich. 'But I think you'll enjoy it,' he said. 'There's quite a nice spousal programme, lots of shopping and sightseeing—'

'A what?'

'A spousal programme. Surely you know what that is.'

'Actually, Gideon, I don't. Sorry to appear so simple.'

'What a very sheltered life you've led. It's what wives do while the husbands do business.'

'What, all together? Me and the other wives? A load of old trouts? Oh, Gideon, don't make me, please!'

'I'm not making you,' he said, his face developing the rigid look that she knew prefaced a loss of temper, 'I'm saying it would be very nice for me, and helpful too.'

She was silent.

He sighed, then said, 'This marriage seems to be turning into a bit of a one-way street, Jocasta.'

'And what's that supposed to mean?'

'I mean it only goes the way you want. For God's sake, you don't have to do much—'

'Oh, really? Not sort out your meals and your housekeepers and wait quietly until you deign to come home, and—'

'I don't consider that very onerous. Actually. In return for—'

'In return for what, Gideon? Do tell me.'

'In return for quite a lot. Like that'—he indicated a pile of unopened bags in the corner, from Harvey Nichols, Chanel, Gucci—'and flying lessons and cars—'

'Oh, so it's a credit and debit arrangement is it, our marriage? I hadn't realised that. Well, let me see, perhaps we should set a price on a few things. How much for two hours, just waiting for you to come home for dinner, a whole morning sorting out your wardrobe—'

'Jocasta, don't be childish!'

'Don't say that to me! It's a disgusting thing to say. Insulting, horrible.'

'This is a disgusting argument.'

'I'm sorry, but you started it. Talking about what I did in return for your fucking money. And talking about fucking, what about sex, Gideon, is there a price on that? How should we set that, how much does a high-class tart earn these days? I'm sure you know.'

'Can we just stop this horrible conversation?' he said.

'No, I don't think we can. I want to get it sorted out.'

He came over to her, his face heavy with rage; she really thought he was going to hit her. She stood up quickly and knocked over her bag; a bundle of credit card slips fell out. He picked them up, started going through them.

'Don't do that, Gideon, please. They're mine, nothing to do with you.'

'Unfortunately, they almost certainly are. Look at this, thousands of pounds all on a lot of rubbish—'

'Well, I'm so sorry. I'll take it all back tomorrow.'

'And—lunch for two at the Caprice. Pretty pricey, even by their standards. Champagne, eighty pounds. Who did you share that with, Jocasta? Nicholas Marshall?'

'No,' she shouted, 'no, no, no. It was my mother, actually.'

'You took your mother to the Caprice and bought her vintage champagne? I find that very hard to believe.'

'Ask them,' she said, handing him her mobile. 'Go on, check up on me. Do you really think I'd take Nick to the Caprice if I were having an affair with him? Why on earth should I be having an affair with anybody?'

'Let's just say your behaviour doesn't inspire confidence,' he said.

Jocasta went upstairs, and packed a rather minimal bag, containing none of the new clothes she had bought, and then went down again, and into his study.

'I'm leaving,' she said, 'and I'm not coming back until you apologise.'

Gideon said that he had absolutely nothing to apologise for.

'I've just been a device, as far as I can see, to make Nick come to heel. Well, I don't like it, Jocasta. I'm not prepared to put up with it.'

Jocasta called a cab—for how could she take her new car?—and directed it to Clapham.

Nick was packing; the parliamentary summer recess had begun and he was going home for a couple of weeks to stay with his parents.

He pulled down the battered old leather Gladstone bag from the shelf in his bedroom and tipped its contents out on the bed. This was always an interesting moment; he could never be bothered to finish unpacking when he got back from the trips the paper sent him on—usually to follow sundry politicians around the globe—and this evening's yield, following a trip to Washington in the early spring, was no exception. A couple of half-read paperbacks, three American newspapers, a pair of socks—clean, thank God—and some gold cuff links his father had given him. Thank God for that—he'd thought he'd lost them.

And a tape recorder, still in its box; a present from Jocasta for the trip, with tiny tapes; one was labelled 'Play me'. Curious, he slipped it into the machine and pressed play. Jocasta's voice came out: 'Hello, darling Nick. This is your devoted—well, fairly devoted—girlfriend, wishing you *bon voyage* and *bonne chance* and all that sort of thing. Have fun, but not too much, and don't forget the Hershey bars. [Of course he had.] Love you loads and loads and thank you for the best time last night. Lovely dinner, lovely everything; kiss kiss.'

Nick played it again, and then again. Thinking about her, about how that tape was just like her, sweet and funny and loving. And thinking how much he had loved her. Still loved her. And that he really hadn't been very nice to her, last time they had spoken. Still less so when he'd sent her stuff back. It was terrible to think of all that love, evaporated into coldness and distance. For ever.

He picked up the phone and rang her.

Jocasta was lying in bed, feeling extremely sorry for herself. She had had a lonely weekend, and had sent out for a curry on Saturday evening; it had been the first meal she had eaten for days, and she gorged herself on it, and washed it down with an entire bottle of rather rough red wine. Whether it was the curry, the gorging, or the wine, she had been extremely ill much of Saturday night and most of Sunday. She was only just beginning to feel better. And still terribly lonely.

Nick's voice was, therefore, even more irresistible than she might have expected.

'Hi,' she said carefully, 'it's lovely to hear from you.'

'Hello, Jocasta. I—just thought I'd make sure you were all right.'

'I'm fine, yes. Thank you. That's very sweet of you.'

'You sound a bit—tired.'

'I had some bad curry on Saturday night.'

'I'm sorry. I wouldn't have thought curry of any kind would be on the menu for Mrs Gideon Keeble.'

'No, well, obviously it wouldn't normally. But he was . . . he was out, and I just fancied it. You know. Um—where are you, Nick?'

'Just packing. To go down to Somerset for a couple of weeks. And I found the tape recorder you gave me. In my bag.'

'Oh, yes. I hoped it'd be useful. Obviously it hasn't been, if it's still in your bag.'

'Oh, it has. Of course it has. And I played the tape you put in for me. Again, I mean. It was very sweet, and I just wanted to thank you.'

She could remember making the tape and sending it to him, just before the whole drama had begun, Centre Forward, Gideon, Kate, Martha. God, it had been less than a year.

'So, where are you?' Nick asked.

'Oh, at home,' she said without thinking.

'What, at the Big House?'

'Of . . . of course.'

'And you're really all right? Happy?'

'Terribly happy,' she said. 'Yes, thank you. Oh, hang on, Nick, there's someone at the door. Won't be a minute.'

Nick sat there waiting; he could hear the roar of traffic in the background, a police siren, hear her saying, 'Yes, that's for me, thank you, do I need to sign, fine, there you are,' heard the door slamming, heard her walking back across the wooden floor—the wooden floor? Roar of traffic? Answering the door herself?

'Jocasta, where are you?'

'I told you—'

'I know what you told me,' he said, 'but I don't recall traffic roaring up and down Kensington Palace Gardens. I would have thought staff would take in parcels. And I seem to remember a lot of carpeting everywhere, and quite a distance from the front door to anywhere.'

There was a silence. Then she said, 'I'm in Clapham, Nick. I've just come to collect a few things.'

'So why lie to me about it?'

'Oh, I don't know. It seemed simpler.'

'Jocasta, what's happened? Please tell me.'

She wouldn't let him come to Clapham; it was too dangerous. She said she'd meet him in Queen Mary's Garden in Regent's Park. It had been a favourite place of theirs, in the early days, halfway between both their houses. She looked at him sitting there on a bench, his long rangy body stretched out in the sunshine, his untidy brown hair flopping into his eyes, and thought how she missed him more every single day, and that even this was not exactly sensible. She sat down beside him. He gave her a kiss.

'That allowed?'

'Of course.' She smiled at him, and told him some of what had happened, very unemotionally.

'I'm really, really not complaining, Nick,' she said carefully. 'I can see a lot of it was—is—my fault. Most of it. But it just isn't working—just at the moment. It might still. I hope so.'

It was a lie, of course. She didn't think so at all. She just couldn't let Nick think it was over, that she was throwing herself at him, expecting to be taken back.

He was very sweet, very unreproachful. He said if that was the case then he certainly wouldn't want to be the cause of it not working out; he said he would like always to be her friend, her best friend; he said he missed her terribly.

'I miss you too,' she said, 'so yes, let's be friends. Best friends.'

She stood up, smiled down at him, and had just managed to say, 'Well, I must be getting back then,' when she felt suddenly terribly dizzy and faint. She swayed visibly and had to sit down again, her head between her knees.

And after that, it was only a very short—and logical—progress to his car and thence to his flat. He bought some food on the way, good, bland, binding food, he said firmly, eggs and bread and some Vichy water—'full of minerals'. And then he cooked her an omelette, made her some toast, and—well, somehow after that, there they were, alone, in his flat, and try as she might, she couldn't remain unemotional and said she thought she should go. To which he suddenly said, quite sweetly, that she should never have left him, and that reminded her exactly why she had, and she got angry and told him.

'I loved you,' he said. 'So much.'

'And how was I to know that?'

'I kept telling you.'

'But you didn't show me,' she said. 'You never showed me.'

'Oh, this is ridiculous!' he said. 'I couldn't show you then, not how you wanted. I didn't know—' He stopped.

'Didn't know what?' she asked, but he wouldn't answer her, just turned away and looked out of the window, and then suddenly it was the old situation starting again, and she couldn't bear it and she said, very wearily, 'I must go.'

'Yes, I think you should. I'll call you a cab. I'm very sorry, Jocasta. For all of it. I hope it works out for you, I really do.'

'Thank you,' she said.

'Can I kiss you goodbye? Old times' sake?'

'Old times' sake . . .'

He bent to kiss her on the cheek; only somehow she moved and his mouth met hers instead. And—that was that, really.

They were naked before they reached the bedroom. She flung herself back onto the bed, holding out her arms to him, saying his name over and over again, hearing him saying hers, both of them talking fast, feverishly, 'Want you, missed you, love you,' and then his mouth was everywhere on her: her throat, her breasts, her stomach, her thighs, and hers on him, moving over him, frantic for him, a great tangle of desire growing and growing in her, pushing at her. She pushed herself onto him, crying out as the sensations grew, journeying through some dark, wonderfully difficult place, reaching for the light at the end of it, feeling herself growing, clenching, climbing, struggling and then yes, yes, that was it, the height, the peak and she was there, shouting, yelling with triumph and then she felt him come too and she came again, in great warm, easy, spreading circles, until finally she fell into a deep, sweet peace.

'Now what?' he said, and his brown eyes, smiling into hers, were very sweet, very tender.

'God knows,' she said and went suddenly and happily to sleep.

Jocasta had said goodbye to Nick and gone home. He had not argued, had not tried to detain her. It was all rather unnerving.

He simply told her he would always love her, that he would always be there for her, and then agreed that the best thing for both of them was for him to go home as planned and for her to go back to Gideon.

'And I certainly don't see any need for foolhardy confessions, or anything like that.'

'Of course not,' she said, bravely bright. 'It was just a bit of—of lovely, naughty fun.'

But when she got home to Clapham, digested what had happened, thought over what he had said, she felt a disappointment so crushing she could hardly bear it.

She would have been comforted and totally astonished over the next few days, had she heard him talking endlessly to his favourite brother, telling him how much he still adored Jocasta, loved her more than ever, indeed, but that she had made it very plain she was still hoping to salvage her marriage and it would be dreadfully wrong of him to do anything to scupper that.

Clio spent Sunday with Jocasta in Clapham. She found her in an odd mood, on an emotional seesaw, overexcited one minute, tearful the next. There had been another very ugly row the day before; Gideon had demanded that she meet him to try to have a reasonable discussion about what they were going to do next, and Jocasta had said it wasn't possible to have a reasonable discussion with a person so unreasonable that he was actually unstable; each confrontation was infinitely worse than the last, making that one seem comparatively pleasant, almost an exchange of views.

Right in the middle of telling Clio this, Jocasta burst into tears, and when Clio asked her if there was anything particularly the matter, said there was, but she couldn't talk about it.

In the end, Clio gave up and said she must go home.

'Oh, please don't go,' said Jocasta. She had been talking to someone on the phone, sounding increasingly hostile. 'That was Josh. He's threatening to come round; he thinks he can make me see sense, as he puts it.'

Josh arrived an hour later, and sat telling Jocasta that she was being immature and unrealistic.

'I thought you loved Gideon?'

'I do. Well, anyway, I thought I did. But I can't live with him; he's a monster, leading a monstrous life. It's much better this way. Let's talk about something else. What's in that bag?'

'Oh, I found some old pictures of Thailand.'

'Now you're talking,' said Jocasta. 'Let's have a look.'

He pulled them out: batch after batch, in no kind of order, shots of the steaming jungle up in the north, shots of elephants, of monkeys, of the hill villages, the sweet, smiling children; of the temples and palaces and floating markets and canals in Bangkok. 'God, I can smell it just looking at them,' said Clio.

And then there were shots with people in them, some occasions they remembered. 'Look, there we are at the airport,' said Josh, 'all of us, that nice old chap took it, remember?'

Frozen in time, smiling, tidy-looking, everything ahead of them.

'Poor Martha,' said Clio, studying her. 'God, if we'd known . . .'

'Best we didn't,' said Jocasta soberly.

And then there was island life, hundreds of people, most of whom they couldn't remember, smiling, hugging each other; lying on the beaches, sitting in the boats, swinging on ropes over lakes, swimming under waterfalls, elephant riding, snorkelling.

'God, it was all fun,' said Jocasta, 'such, such fun. Hey, Josh, what's this? Posh hotel, or what? And who's this? Martha? By that amazing pool? And on that terrace? Josh, you never told me about this?'

'Didn't know that was there,' said Josh, flushing a dark red, and went on rather hurriedly to explain that he'd bumped into Martha leaving Koh Tao; there'd been a fire on the boat and they'd all nearly drowned. 'No, it's true, I'm not making it up.' They'd both felt pretty rough, and he'd had plenty of money on him, so they'd gone to a hotel near Chaweng, stayed there one night . . .

'Mmm,' said Jocasta, her eyes dancing, 'you dark horse. You never said. When was that? You obviously had lots of fun. Is that why you wanted to come to the funeral?'

'No. Well, sort of. I mean . . . yes, it was, actually.'

'I think that's very sweet.'

Clio had been praying for some bell, however faint, to ring in Jocasta's head. It clearly wasn't going to. She had to do it. And it was now or never. She took a deep breath, and said, 'Josh, when exactly was that?'

'I don't know,' he said. 'Does it matter?'

'Yes. It . . . could.'

'Why?' Josh asked.

'Well . . .'

'Clio,' said Jocasta, 'what are you on about?'

'I—well, I was just thinking about . . . about Martha. That's all.'

'What about her? Except that she was obviously a darker horse than we thought. I mean—with Josh! And never telling us. And—oh my God! You don't think—I mean—Josh—oh my God!'

'What?' he said irritably. 'What's the matter with you both?'

'Just tell us when you and Martha had your little . . . fling.' Jocasta was speaking very slowly. 'It's terribly important.'

'Well, it was before Christmas, definitely, because I was in Malaysia then. Must have been October, yes, it definitely was, because I was on my way up to Bangkok, to see my girlfriend. Well, not exactly my girl-friend, but we had been pretty involved, and she was in hospital, she'd had a scooter crash on Koh Phangan, and I had my birthday up there, my eighteenth, I do remember that.'

Jocasta looked at Clio. 'So that's October 26th, his birthday. And Kate was born in the middle of August, so it would have had to have been November, wouldn't it?' said Jocasta.

'Sorry,' Clio said. 'Kate was nearly three weeks late. Martha told me. That was the whole point, why she was here when she had her. So the end of October would be just right.'

'What are you two going on about?' asked Josh. 'You've lost me.'

'Josh,' said Jocasta, filling his glass to the brim, 'drink that. You're going to need it. You really are . . .'

Josh had hardly slept. He felt he would never sleep again.

It seemed to him it was impossible to do the right thing. He either had to tell Beatrice, who would be horrified, and what on earth would the girls make of it, suddenly having a big sister? Or he could just not say a word and simply live with this awful, oppressing piece of knowledge.

And then there was Kate. Kate his daughter. The vision of her kept rising before him. The girl at the funeral, so lovely, so funny, was his daughter. He had a grown-up daughter.

How could you start being a father to someone you'd met for the first time at that age? She was grown up, processed, done.

And what would she want? This new, problematic daughter? Jocasta and Clio had both told him she was very upset by what had happened to her; that she had been searching for her mother, ever more confused.

'She just wants to know where she belongs,' Clio had said, 'where she came from, if you like. She loves her adoptive parents dearly but they can't supply the answers. And Martha's death has been yet another blow. She didn't provide any answers, either.'

When the clock struck four, Josh went downstairs to make himself a hot toddy.

Beatrice had been absolutely wonderful; Josh had called her from his office at midday, unable to stand it any longer, and asked if they could meet after work for a drink.

'What on earth for, Josh? Why not at home?'

'Because I've got something I want to talk about and I don't want the girls around. Or anyone, come to that.'

They met in the American bar at the Connaught. Beatrice arrived, looking rather pale. She clearly thought Josh was going to tell her he had met someone else.

'Which I suppose, in a way, he had,' she said to Jocasta, brightly.

The news had been so extraordinary and so shocking that she had found it difficult to find an appropriate reaction at all. What exactly did you say, when your husband told you he had just discovered he had a sixteen-year-old daughter? 'How nice,' or 'I can't wait to meet her'?

None of them seemed right. Beatrice sat and looked at him, at this person she really did love, this charming, good-looking person, and found that her overwhelming emotion was sympathy.

'For heaven's sake, Josh,' she said quite sternly, 'a lot of seventeen-year-old boys sleep around. That was just incredibly unfortunate.'

'Yes,' he said, 'I suppose it was.'

'I can't imagine why Martha didn't tell you.'

'Nor me.'

'Or her parents.'

'Indeed.'

'I suppose she just felt she couldn't.'

'I suppose.'

'What a sad, sad story.'

Of them all, Kate had had the worst of it and she deserved the best now. She was a child and they were adults; if Josh found the situation distressing and she found it painful and Kate's adoptive parents found it difficult, that was their problem. Kate must come first, and they should all do what was best for her. It was perfectly simple.

Helen had taken the news with remarkable calm; so much had happened to her over the past few weeks that she would hardly have been surprised if Jocasta had told her Prince Charles was Kate's father. Or Brad Pitt. Or David Beckham.

Josh actually seemed a fairly happy option. At least he was someone they had all met and Kate liked.

'I suppose that explains the similarity between you and Kate,' she said to Jocasta.

'Yes, it does.'

She agreed that Jocasta and Josh should tell Kate together.

'It will come much better from you. And he can answer lots of her questions. Including, hopefully, about Martha.'

She still found it difficult to refer to Martha as Kate's mother.

She told Jim, who was less pleased.

'Public school, I suppose,' he said, irritably. 'Like his sister.'

Helen opened her mouth to tell him not to be so silly and shut it again. She knew what this was about: what she had been through a few weeks earlier. Fearing rejection, criticism, comparison. Most of all comparison.

'I don't want him coming here,' he said, abruptly.

'Jim! He's bound to come here, if Kate likes him. Be sensible,' she said gently. 'Whatever he's like, and however much or little Kate likes him, you really don't have to worry. She knows who her father is and it's not him. Not really.'

'Yes, it is,' he said and walked out of the room.

They took Kate out for a meal: to the Bluebird.

She had walked in looking stunning, not, for once, in jeans, but a long, bias-cut floral skirt, and a white T under a denim jacket, her hair hanging loose over her shoulders. Heads had turned.

'Oh God,' said Josh.

Jocasta patted his arm encouragingly. 'It'll be fine.'

They both stood up as Kate reached the table, kissed her.

'This is so nice of you,' she said. 'I've been looking forward to it.'

'So have we.'

There was a slightly awkward silence. 'Let's choose,' Jocasta said, 'then we can relax.'

'Glass of wine, young Kate?' said Josh.

'Yes, please.' She grinned at him. 'It's really weird, you calling me young Kate. It makes you sound like some elderly uncle. Which you're not.'

Another awkward silence. Jocasta hadn't expected this, had expected Kate would chatter away as she usually did.

'I finally decided about the contract,' she said, into the silence. 'Did Mum tell you? Or Fergus?'

'No, what did you decide?'

'Not to do it. Now I'm really worried it was the wrong decision. I mean, it's just so much money to say no to. Think what it could have done for us all, me and Mum and Dad. And Juliet, of course. She's going to be very expensive with her music.'

'Well, I'm sure your mum and dad would rather take care of everything, anyway,' said Josh. 'They wouldn't like being indebted to you.'

'I hadn't thought of that. If there'd been no question of that money, they'd be finding a way to pay for her somehow, wouldn't they?'

'Of course.'

She smiled at him. 'Thanks for that. I feel a bit better now. I've been feeling so down.'

'Sweetheart, I'm sorry,' said Jocasta. 'What sort of down?'

'Well, you know.' She looked at Josh, clearly uncomfortable at discussing it in front of him, even though Jocasta had told her that he knew about Martha being her mother. 'The usual. Like I said to you, no further forward really.'

'No?' said Josh. 'But you know who . . . who your mother was now.'

'Well, yeah. But she's . . . well, she's gone, hasn't she?'

Jocasta decided this was getting too heavy too soon. She changed the subject. 'I'm thinking of going back to work.'

'Really? Why?'

'I miss it.'

'I thought you would,' said Kate. 'You're much too clever to be sitting around all day, waiting for your husband to come home.'

Josh laughed. 'Beatrice would agree with you. She doesn't wait for me.'

'No? What does she do?'

'She's a barrister.'

'So she must be pretty clever.'

'She is. Cleverer than me, I can tell you that.'

There was another silence; then she asked Josh, 'You've got kids, haven't you? What sort of a dad are you?'

Josh took a very deep breath. 'What sort of a dad am I?' he said. 'Well, that's a very interesting question. I try to be a good one. I like to be with my children a lot. Um—Jocasta, what sort of a dad would you say I was?'

Jocasta had heard the deep breath, had heard the cue also.

'Pretty good, I'd say,' she said. 'Really pretty good. Now, Kate, when you've finished that, let's go, shall we? Go for a walk or something?'

She looked at them, clearly puzzled by this swift ending to the meal. She had been looking forward to the pudding. 'OK.'

They called for the bill, which Josh paid in silence. He couldn't remember ever feeling so frightened. He led the way outside.

'I've got my car,' he said, 'let's go down to the river, shall we?'

'Cool car,' said Kate. It was a Saab convertible and he put the hood down. At the river, he parked it, rather recklessly, on a yellow line, on a corner. 'It'll be OK,' he said. 'Come on, let's walk.'

He pulled Kate's arm through his and Jocasta did the same. Kate looked at them both and smiled. 'We look like a family,' she said.

'Funny you should say that,' said Jocasta.

'Why?'

'Well, now, Kate, this is going to be a shock.' They were down on the river walk now. 'Let's sit down,' said Jocasta, indicating a seat. 'Come on. Kate, darling, hold my hand. Josh, this is your story. Off you go.'

She sat in silence, listening, looking up at him intently and occasionally at Jocasta. He stumbled along: it was difficult. He told her that he and Martha had been quite close, had done some travelling together (he and Jocasta had agreed that a one-night stand was not an attractive notion) but that afterwards he had moved on to Australia, and she hadn't been able to get in touch with him.

'No mobiles, you see. All we had were poste restante addresses, and nobody knew where anybody was going to be, or when.'

She said nothing.

'And I think, then, she decided to manage on her own,' said Jocasta, 'she was a very independent lady. That much you must have learned. And as I told you the other day, she felt she couldn't tell her parents.'

'That's so weird,' Kate said, 'I've thought about that so much. About feeling it was worse than just . . . just leaving your baby, I don't understand it, still.'

'I know,' said Josh, 'it does seem jolly odd. I think you just have to accept it. Martha obviously felt they wouldn't have been able to stand the shame and so on, because he's a vicar.'

'This is so much the sort of thing I wanted to talk to her about,' said Kate sadly. 'Only she would have been able to help me make sense of it. And what did I do, the one time I met her? I just shouted at her and said all I wanted to know was who my father was.'

'And what did she say?' said Josh.

'She said she couldn't tell me. She said he—you—didn't know and she didn't think it was right to tell you after all these years.'

There was a silence. Then Kate said, 'I was shouting at her. A lot. I wish I hadn't now. She said, Could you just listen to me, just for a little while. I said no and left in a strop. I wish I had,' she said and started to cry, 'let her try. It might have helped.'

They all sat there for a while, staring at the river, then she said, 'The thing is, though, that whatever she said, it comes down to the same thing: she was ashamed of me, ashamed of having me. That isn't very nice to know.'

'Well, I'm not,' said Josh and put his arm round her, kissed the top of her head. 'I'm very proud.'

When she got home, Helen and Jim were reading. Helen smiled at her; Jim didn't look up from his paper.

'How was it, dear?'

'It was fine. I s'pose Jocasta told you, he's my dad. Her brother Josh.'

'Yes, yes, she did. But we thought they should tell you. How do you feel about that? Oh dear, what a silly question.'

'No, it's not. When I've got used to the idea, I think I'll be quite pleased. He's nice. I mean really nice. And he came to tell me straight away, the minute he knew. I think that's lovely. Not like her. Still—' she added, 'I even feel a bit better about her, now.'

'What's he do, then?' said Jim. 'This paragon?'

'Jim,' said Helen warningly.

'He works for his dad. He doesn't like it much. He wishes he'd been a photographer.'

'His dad seems to pay him plenty of money,' said Jim. 'Nice car that.'

'Yes, it's cool.'

'Well, I expect you'll be seeing a lot of him now,' said Jim, 'now you've found him.'

'Quite a lot, I expect, yes. I hope so, anyway.'

She looked at Jim and then went over to him and wriggled onto his knee, put her arms round his neck.

'He is very nice,' she said, 'and he's quite good-looking and I can see he's fun. But you're my dad. You so are still my dad.'

Chapter 14

CLIO WAS DUE TO START at the Royal Bayswater on October 1st; plenty of time to work out her notice, find somewhere in London to live. And go on a little holiday.

Only, Fergus had called and said he just might not be able to make it.

'Oh, Fergus! Why on earth not?'

'I might just have got a very hot new client.'

'And that takes precedence over our holiday. Great!'

'Clio, I'm sorry, but I have to be practical. If I don't work, I don't get paid. I haven't done at all well lately, you know. Kate's let me down—'

'Fergus! I think that's stretching things a bit. She's a little girl. She's been through no end of an upheaval. She needs support, not pressure.'

'Of course. But it is difficult, you know, you arrange things, and we're not talking chicken feed here, this is big money, important assignments, and everything goes hang on the whim of a sixteen-year-old.'

'Exactly. A sixteen-year-old. Anyway, who or what is the client?'

'Oh, it's another rent-boy story. Been totally screwed in both senses by his manager, he's a singer, and now the bastard's—'

'Fergus, please don't go on. *That's* what's coming between us and Italy?'

'Yes. It's work, Clio. It earns me my crust and, as I've said before, I don't know any other way. I can't, unfortunately, get a highly paid job as a hospital consultant, and be a pillar of the community, as you can.'

'Oh, for God's sake,' said Clio, 'don't start that!'

And she put the phone down.

Half an hour later, she rang to apologise, but got the answering machine. She decided not to leave a message.

Jocasta was wandering rather aimlessly round the supermarket, when it hit her. Hit her with the force of a rather large truck. And left her almost physically reeling.

Come on, Jocasta, concentrate. Coffee, tea, better get some milk; the last lot had been off. Bread, got that. Toiletries—shampoo, soap, Tampax and—that was when it hit her.

Now, this was absurd. One day, one day late: well, two. Actually, she could remember that last time so clearly, it was just before she had walked out on Gideon, that terrible, terrible Thursday. Two days was nothing. Nothing.

Actually, though, it was, when you were so regular you could literally set the clock by it. Well, that was the pill of course. No need to worry, she was on the pill. You didn't get pregnant on the pill. You just didn't. Unless you forgot to take it. Which she never, ever did.

Or—and this was the second ramming by the truck—or you had a stomach upset. Which she had had. A truly terrible one. Throwing up, diarrhoea, the lot, for two days. And hadn't even taken the bloody thing for one day. Actually, two. She decided there was no point, especially as she wasn't having sex.

Only . . . she had. Hadn't she? Sex with Nick, amazing sex with Nick, a few days after the stomach upset, right bang in the middle of her cycle.

Oh God. Oh—my—God!

Now, calm down, Jocasta. She could do a test. You could do them on the very day your period was due, and it was something like ninety-eight per cent accurate. She'd go to Boots and buy a test, and take it home and it would be negative and then everything would be all right and her period would probably start straight away.

Jocasta stood in her bathroom, her heart thudding so hard she felt her body could hardly contain it.

The instructions were very clear; you had to hold the end of the stick thing—it looked a bit like a thermometer—into your pee for five seconds and then keep it pointing downwards for one minute. There were two little windows at the other end of the stick. At the end of the one minute, a blue line should appear in the end window and then you could read the result window. A plus meant pregnant, a minus not.

She timed the five-second dip into the pee she'd collected, and then dipped what they called the absorbent sampler into it. And then waited. For one minute. In one minute she'd be fine, in one minute a nice neat minus sign would tell her she was not pregnant, and—God! It was there!

A little blue plus sign. Plus. Not minus. Plus meant pregnant. She was plus something. Plus a pregnancy. Plus a baby. Plus Nick's baby.

She felt very odd. Very odd indeed. Not entirely as she would have expected. The thing that she had dreaded for years had happened and she felt shocked and horrified; but she felt something else, as well. Awed. That it could have happened. That she and Nick could have made a baby. They had made love and made a baby. Something that was partly her and partly Nick. It was an extraordinary thought.

Only she must get rid of it. Obviously.

Quite apart from the fact she could never, ever have a baby, what on earth would Nick do or say, if he knew? Nick, who still couldn't contemplate any sort of commitment, not even living together, certainly not getting married. How would he react to the news that he was going to be a father? It was absolutely unthinkable.

She decided to go to see Clio.

Clio, of course, gave her all the wrong advice.

Like she shouldn't do anything too hasty. Like was she really sure it was Nick's. Like she ought to tell Nick.

'Tell Nick! Clio, are you mad? Of course I can't tell Nick. He'd be horrified, he'd run away, he'd hate it, he'd hate me. No, I must just—just have a termination as soon as possible and—'

'Jocasta, I really think you should tell him. If you're really pregnant and it's really his, you should tell him.'

'But why?'

'Because it's his baby, too. It's wrong not to. It's a terrible thing to do, just deciding to get rid of a baby, without telling its father.'

'Clio, you don't know Nick and I do. He would not want a baby. He doesn't even want me. And if you're even contemplating telling him yourself, you'd better just stop right away, at once, you've got to promise me not to, promise, Clio, all right, now, at once, on your life—'

She was crying now; Clio went over to her, put her arms round her.

'Of course I won't tell him. I promise, on my life, I won't.'

Jocasta's gynaecologist confirmed the pregnancy.

'If I was just having the termination,' Jocasta told Clio on the phone, 'I could have what they called a con-op, first a consultation, then the termination, all on the same day. But as I want to be sterilised, they'll counsel me, as they call it, and then book me in for another day. But there's no problem. I can do it.'

It sounded terrible to Clio. 'What did she say about telling the father? Does he have a right to know?'

She knew he didn't, but she was hoping Jocasta's mind might have been at least alerted to the possibility.

'She said I didn't have to, and he couldn't stop me having the termination. It's totally up to me. So—in about ten days, with luck. Will you come with me?'

'I don't think I can,' said Clio and slammed the phone down.

She found it hard to believe that, even in her manically self-absorbed state, Jocasta could be asking her to go with her to get rid of her baby. Could be so grossly insensitive not to have remembered Clio's grief on the subject of her own infertility. It hurt almost more than she would have believed.

The phone rang again almost at once: she picked it up, feeling remorseful. She had misjudged her; Jocasta had phoned to apologise . . .

'Clio, don't know what happened then. Look, I've heard from Gideon, he wants to see me, to discuss things. I'm absolutely petrified, he wants me to go round to the house tomorrow afternoon. Can you come up afterwards?'

'No,' said Clio, 'I can't. I do have a life of my own, you know, Jocasta. I can't actually drop everything, just whenever it suits you. Sorry.'

There was a silence: then Jocasta said, her voice absolutely astonished, 'OK, OK. Easy. I thought you'd want to help.'

Clio said she was getting a bit tired of helping, and put the phone down for the second time.

Jocasta drove up to Kensington Palace Gardens. She had dressed very carefully, in a short black linen shift that was just slightly too large for her. She knew her boobs were slightly bigger than they had been and she was terrified Gideon would notice. Notice and guess.

She knocked on the door tentatively; Mrs Hutching opened it, smiled at her rather awkwardly. 'Hello, Mrs Keeble.'

'Hi,' said Jocasta.

'Mr Keeble isn't here yet. He asked me to give you tea in the garden room. He said he wouldn't be long.'

'Lovely. Thank you.'

As she walked through the hall, she glanced at the letter rack; there was a postcard in it. A sepia-tinted postcard. She pulled it out. It was a picture of Exmoor and it was Nick's writing.

'This is for me,' she said. 'Why didn't you send it on?'

'I don't think it is for you, Mrs Keeble. It's addressed to a Mrs Cook. It's certainly this address. I thought perhaps one of the agency cleaners we have in August might claim it—'

'It's OK. It's from a friend of mine. A sort of joke.'

'Oh, I see. I'm so sorry.'

'It's OK.'

OK? When she had been waiting to hear from him for two and a half very long weeks? Why hadn't she thought of this: of course Nick would have written to her here. He thought she was living here.

*Dear Mrs Cook, Thank you so much for a very pleasant afternoon. I
enjoyed it enormously. It is wonderfully beautiful down here; I know you
don't admire the countryside, but the moors are amazingly lovely. The
air is so very clean and clear; I wish I had been able to persuade you to
join me here occasionally in the past. With every good wish, James Butler.*

She slipped it into her bag, feeling much happier, and went into the
garden room to wait for Gideon—who was actually very nice, friendly
and courteous. He said he was sorry things had got so bad between
them, that he had never intended it and he saw himself as at least partly
to blame. He had been doing a lot of thinking, and if she wanted a
divorce, then he would not contest it, however sad he might feel. He
was sure they could come to an amicable arrangement over a settlement.

'I don't want a settlement, Gideon,' she said. 'I don't want anything.
Nothing at all. Really. I couldn't possibly take any money from you.'

'Of course you could.'

'I couldn't. Honestly. I really, really don't want anything.'

'Jocasta—'

'No, Gideon, I don't. I feel bad enough already.'

There was a silence, then he said, 'Well, you may change your mind.
You look tired, are you all right?'

'I'm absolutely fine,' she said quickly.

How on earth would he react, if he knew she was pregnant? With
another man's baby, the ink on their marriage licence hardly dry? Or
thought it might be his? It was terrifying. God, she was a disaster!

'Good. I would really like you to have something. So if you change
your mind—'

'I won't,' she said, 'I know I won't.'

'Well, at the very least take the clothes,' he said. 'They are clogging up
cupboard space and they don't suit me at all.'

She smiled. 'Gideon, this is so sad. We should just have had an affair.'

'But you didn't want an affair,' he said, 'you wanted a marriage. Come
along, Jocasta, admit it.'

'I admit it,' she said.

'But I encouraged you.'

'Yes, you did. And most of the time, it was great, great fun.'

'I'm so glad you thought so,' he said. 'I enjoyed it, too. Most of it.
Now, drink up your tea, and then you must excuse me. I'm—'

'Going away tomorrow,' she said and laughed. 'Oh, Gideon. I'm so
sorry. I behaved so badly.'

'I behaved badly, also. And I am sorry for it. Well, it was a short marriage but mostly a merry one. Thank you for coming today. I just
wanted us to part friends.'

'Friends it is,' she said and went over to his chair, bent to kiss him. 'Goodbye, Gideon.'

'Goodbye, Jocasta. And I would be hugely grateful if the press didn't hear of this just for a little while.'

'They won't. I promise.'

They wouldn't. The press getting hold of it was the last thing she wanted. Especially one member of the press.

Just the same, Nick had sent a postcard. Had clearly been thinking about her. That was nice.

The minute she got into her car, she called his mobile; it was not Nick who answered.

'Hello. Pattie Marshall. Can I help?'

'Oh, sorry, Mrs Marshall. It's Jocasta here.'

'Hello, Jocasta.' The voice was very cool; they had never liked one another. 'I expect you're wondering why I'm answering Nicholas's phone. He's broken his right radius—'

'What's that?'

'It's one of the bones in the forearm.'

'I'm so sorry. Is he all right?'

'Yes, he's fine. He fell off a horse; bit of a shame. It isn't serious, but he's asleep at the moment.'

'I'm so sorry. Please give him my . . . my best wishes. And thank him for the postcard. When . . . when will he be back in London?'

'Oh, not for a couple of weeks, I should think. I'll get him to call you. Are you at home?'

'Yes,' she said. 'I'm at the Big House.'

When Nick woke up, Pattie Marshall told him that Jocasta had called and sent her best wishes. And that she was at the Big House.

At the Big House—not leaving it. He'd lost her—again.

This time tomorrow it would be over. Just—over. She wouldn't be pregnant any more. Fantastic. She looked down at her stomach; it was totally flat. It was impossible to believe there was anything alive in there, certainly not a baby. A child. Hers and Nick's child.

She wondered what on earth Nick would say, if he knew: if he knew she was pregnant. He'd be terrified: absolutely terrified. He'd want to just run away. And what if he knew she'd had a termination without telling him? Well, that was a bit tricky. He might be cross. He might say he had had a right to know. But he still wouldn't want it. So it was certainly infinitely better he didn't. The only person who did know was Clio, and she'd never tell. Nick was still down in Somerset. She was sorry he'd broken his arm, or whatever it was, but it was . . . lucky.

So what was troubling her? She wanted to be rid of the—pregnancy. She would never have to worry about another. She'd have her life back.

It was just a bit—sad.

Nick woke early. It had been a hell of a drive back to London from his parents' home, but he'd done it, and fallen exhausted into bed in Hampstead, at midnight. But the pain in his arm had woken him up; he struggled into the kitchen, took a couple of the painkillers—they were bloody strong, made him feel quite woozy—and made himself a cup of tea. Maybe he should go for a walk; clear his head. God, he'd be glad when he could run again; at the moment it jarred his arm too much, destroyed the pleasure. Yes, he'd go for a stroll, buy the papers, come back and have breakfast and then head down to Westminster. There was bound to be something going on; and it would be good to be back.

He walked down to Heath Street, bought *The Times*, the *Guardian* and the *Daily Mail* dropped in at the deli for some croissants and went home.

He was halfway through one of the croissants when a feature in the *Mail* caught his eye: 'Holiday Getaway Gear', it said, and was a piece about what to wear when travelling and how to look as good—or as bad—as the rich and famous. Lots of shots of people leaving airports, over the past few days—Madonna, Kate Moss, Jude Law, Jonathan Ross—and Gideon Keeble. Terrifically well dressed as always, in a linen suit and Panama hat. Bastard.

The captions said where they were all going: mostly to the sun. Workaholic Keeble, as they called him, was off to Melbourne on a business trip. No Jocasta in sight. Not famous enough, he supposed. Or maybe she hadn't gone; maybe she was still in London, in that absurd mansion. Or down in Wiltshire, was it? Or Berkshire?

He could ring her, tell her that he was fine, back in London.

He called her mobile. It was switched off.

Well, best leave it then. Only . . . maybe he could try the house. Just see if she was there. Why not?

He dialled the Big House; a foreign voice answered. A Filipino-sort of a foreign voice. 'Mr Keeble's residence.'

Slightly odd phraseology. Surely it was the Keeble residence now?

'Good morning. Is Mrs Keeble there?'

'Mrs Keeble? No, Mrs Keeble not living here now. She—'

There was a sort of scuffle at the end of the line; then Mrs Hutching— he recognised her voice—said, 'Good morning! Can I help you?'

Nick's heart was doing slightly peculiar things.

'Mrs Hutching, isn't it? Good morning. You won't remember me, but I'm a friend of Mrs Keeble's, Nicholas Marshall. I wanted to speak to her.'

'I'm sorry, Mr Marshall, she isn't here. She's away.'

'With Mr Keeble? Or in the country?'

'I'm not sure. I'm sorry. If you would like to leave a message—'

Nick left a message and then put the phone down. He felt slightly dizzy. Must be the pills, of course. But—the first woman, she'd said Jocasta didn't live there any more. And Mrs Hutching had sounded pretty bloody odd, as well.

Shit. Had Jocasta actually left Gideon? She'd have told him. Surely. And if she hadn't told him, the outlook wasn't too good for him anyway.

Nick stood up, walked up and down his small kitchen a couple of times and then rang Clio. She'd know. She'd tell him.

Jocasta couldn't sleep and was in the middle of a walk on Clapham Common when she felt faint. She sank rather dramatically onto her haunches, dropped her head in her arms and tried not to panic.

'You OK?' A girl, a jogger, had stopped, was bending over her. Jocasta looked up at her, tried to smile and then threw up onto the grass.

'Sorry,' she said, 'so sorry. Yes, I . . . well, no, I don't feel too good. Have you got a mobile?'

'Sure.' She rummaged in her bum bag, handed her phone to Jocasta. Even making the call was almost beyond her.

Clio felt dreadful. She was the worst liar in the world. She had done her best, had stumbled through her story that she hadn't seen Jocasta for a while, that she didn't know if she was still with Gideon and that she didn't know where she was. It had been totally pathetic. Nick had actually said that. He'd said, quite nicely, 'Clio, that is just so pathetic. Of course you know where she is. Come on. At her house? Look, I can see you're protecting her for some reason. She probably made you swear not to say. So if you don't say anything I'll assume it's Clapham, OK?'

Clio was dutifully silent.

Nick got into his car and set out for Clapham.

You are just so stupid,' said Beatrice severely, helping Jocasta up the steps of their house and into the sitting room. 'You should have told us before.'

'I couldn't,' said Jocasta wearily, dropping onto the sofa. 'I just couldn't bear to talk about it. Or think about it. Bit like Martha, I suppose.'

'I think you're a little better off than she was, poor girl. I presume Gideon knows about this?'

'Well—'

'Jocasta! I can't believe this. Of course you must tell him.'

'It isn't Gideon's baby,' said Jocasta. 'It's Nick's.'

Nick stood outside Jocasta's house alternately ringing the bell and banging on the door.

After five minutes he decided to let himself in. Even if she wasn't there, he might get some clue as to where he might find her. Or what had happened. Thank God he had never given the key back.

She wasn't there: but she had clearly only just left. Her duvet was flung back, there was the usual incredible mess in her bedroom, several used cups piled up by the dishwasher.

God, his arm hurt. So, so much. They'd obviously known what they were talking about, telling him to rest it. Bloody agony. And he'd left his pills behind, of course. Jocasta always had plenty of painkillers; she was a bit of an addict. He'd take some of hers, have a cup of tea and wait for her. He put the kettle on, went to the cupboard under the bathroom basin.

It was a shrine to her messiness; two or three Tampax packets, a very exhausted-looking toothbrush, a mass of hair bands, a spilt box of cotton buds, a half-empty bottle of mouthwash, an enormous bottle of vitamin C tablets and—what was this? God in heaven, what was this? It couldn't be—no, it wasn't—yes, it was, it really indubitably, really horribly was, a pregnancy-testing kit.

What was this, what had been going on here, what had she been doing, why hadn't she told him? Absurd, ridiculous, pointless, cretinous questions. Was the baby Gideon's? Must be, it surely, surely couldn't be his . . . could it?

Josh was still asleep, when Beatrice rang. He'd had a bit of a night with the sales force in the Midlands office and his head was agony.

'Josh, it's Beatrice. Look, I've got something to tell you. You are coming back tonight, aren't you?'

'Of course.'

'Right, well, Jocasta will be there.'

'Jocasta! Why?'

'She's pregnant.'

'Pregnant!'

'Yes. And, wait for it. It's not Gideon's. It's Nick's. And she's clearly planning a termination.'

'Nick's! How terrible. Can't we stop her?'

'I'm not sure. But the point is, he doesn't know. And he really should. She swears he wouldn't want it, but he ought to have a chance to say so himself. He can't stop her legally, of course, but, anyway, do you have his number?'

'I think so.'

'Try to reach him. I must go. I'm due in court in an hour.'

'Nick? This is Josh.'

'Josh! Thank God. Maybe you can help. I'm terribly worried about Jocasta, I don't know where she is and—'

'She's at our house.'

'At yours?'

'Yes. Now the thing is—oh God, this might be a bit of a shock, Nick, but she's . . . well, she's pregnant. Sorry to spring it on you, but—'

'I did . . . think she might be,' said Nick. 'I just found some tests. I'm at her place now. But, why are you ringing me?'

'Because it's yours.'

'Mine?' said Nick and he felt as if he was falling through a large silent space, with Josh's voice echoing in the heart of it. 'My baby? Are you absolutely sure?'

'Well, Jocasta is. She told Beatrice.'

'Good God,' said Nick. 'Dear, sweet Jesus.'

'Yes. And she's about to have a termination.' There was a silence. 'Nick? You still there?'

'Yes. Yes, I'm still here.'

'Nick, I'm so sorry. Bloody awful thing to hear out of the blue. But Jocasta's at our house, if you want to stop her.'

'Of course I want to stop her, for God's sake!'

'Well, call her. Got the number? I think you really have to put your skates on, Nick, and—'

But Nick had already cut him off.

'Miss Forbes, isn't it? Yes. And you're booked in for . . . yes, a termination this morning? And a sterilisation.'

The nurse smiled at her encouragingly.

'Yes,' said Jocasta, 'that's right.'

'If you'd like to come with me, I'll take you up to your room. We can do your admission; check everything's in order, ask you to sign the consent form, all that sort of thing. You've had nothing, since six o'clock, to eat or drink?'

'No, I haven't.'

'Good. Now I think we'll start with taking your blood pressure.'

'I'm sorry, Mr Marshall, but Jocasta's gone.' The nanny at Josh's house was clearly anxious. 'Yes. She left about . . . oh, I don't know, about half an hour ago. I'm sorry, I didn't— What? In a cab. Yes. No, it was a mini-cab. I have no idea, I'm afraid— Oh, hang on, he's left a card. I can't stand the way they always do that, can you? Oh, sorry, yes, Clapham Cars, does that ring a bell? Yes? Well, the number's—'

191

'Would that have been a Miss Forbes?'

'I would imagine so. Yes.'

'Let me see. She changed the booking, from Haines Road, to Old Town pick-up . . . yes, here we are. She's booked to Gower Street. The GG & O Clinic, Gower Street, it was. Just down from UCH. Pick-up this afternoon, time to be confirmed.'

'Thank you,' said Nick, 'thank you so much.'

'Kate, my darling, come along in. You're looking perfectly gorgeous, as usual. How are you?'

'I'm good, thanks, Fergus. Now who's that—excuse me, sorry—'

It was extraordinary, the way the young responded to their mobiles, Fergus thought, as if every call was crucial, far more crucial than anything else they might be involved in. And they didn't seem to think breaking off whatever conversation they were having was remotely antisocial.

'Sorry. I'll switch it off now. That was Ed. You know Ed? Martha's boyfriend.'

'I do. Rather handsome, as I recall.'

'Handsome or what! Yeah. Anyway, apparently Mrs Hartley, that's Martha's mum, she's really low. And I wrote to her. I was thinking, you know, that she was my gran really, another gran, and she seemed really lovely, and I felt so sorry for her, and Mr Hartley said my letter had really cheered her up, can't think why, and could Ed let me know. It's a pity we can't tell them, in a way—'

'I do hope you won't,' said Fergus anxiously, 'I don't think that would be a good idea, at all.'

'Fergus! I'm not that stupid. Anyway, I've come to talk about the contract with Smith. I think I should sign it, I feel so different now and—'

Nick roared along Gower Street. He had to find the clinic. Right at the top it had been, the man had said. Where was the bloody place?—ah, there. No meters of course, only double yellow lines everywhere.

He abandoned the car and faced a traffic warden who asked him what he thought he was doing. 'Saving a life,' he said.

The man had clearly heard this before. 'I'll have to give you a ticket,' he said.

'Great. Fine. I'd really like that. Just go ahead.'

The warden started to write the ticket, shaking his head.

And there it was, a discreet, very freshly painted door: with GG & O Clinic on a brass plate. GG & O—what sort of bloody nonsense was that? He pushed on the bell; the door opened with a self-important burr.

There was a reception desk in the hall, with a vast urn of flowers on it; to the left of the urn was a smiling young woman in a navy suit.

'Good morning,' she said. 'How can I help you?'

'By telling me where . . . where my wife is,' said Nick. He somehow felt they'd be more helpful if he assumed husband status. He sat down breathing heavily. He felt rather odd.

'Would you like to give me her name?'

'Keeble. Jocasta Keeble.'

'And who is she seeing today?'

'I'm afraid I can't tell you. I don't know.'

The woman started to press the keys on her computer.

'Keeble, you say. No, I don't have anyone of that name this morning.'

'Well, how about Forbes?'

'Forbes, Forbes . . . oh, yes. Yes, here she is. Good. If you'd like to sit down over there, I'll let Mrs Miles know you're here. Do help yourself to tea or coffee.'

'I don't want any coffee and I certainly don't want Mrs Miles. I want my . . . wife.'

'Mrs Miles is looking after your wife today. Please try to be patient— hello? Susan, it's about a Mrs Forbes. One of Mrs Miles's patients. Her husband is here. Is she in theatre? Ah, yes, I see. Thank you.' She sat back in her chair, gave Nick an even more gracious smile.

'I'm so sorry, Mr Keeble. Your wife has already left.'

Nick walked very slowly back to the car. It had been clamped. He decided he couldn't sort it out yet; he would just leave it.

He felt rather sick and terribly tired. Apart from that, nothing; not sad, not angry, just . . . nothing. His arm hurt. He hailed a cab, directed it to Hampstead. He sat in it, staring out of the window, trying hard not to think about Jocasta and about the baby she had just thrown away. He failed. His mind felt as if it would never think of anything else again.

It would have been absolutely terrifying: it would have meant not only commitment, absolute commitment, abruptly and forcibly entered into, but a new and entirely different life. There would have been no period of adjustment for the two of them, no time to learn to live together, no time for him to come to terms with his new condition. He would have had to make the leap from single man to husband and father, with scarcely time between to take breath. It would have been very, very difficult. But—it was what he would have wanted.

And as he sat there, astonished at the sadness of it, of what he had lost, they had both lost, he leaned forward and tapped on the window and said to the cabby, 'Could you change that, take me to Clapham, instead. Please.'

Nick stood looking at Jocasta's little house for a moment, listening to the taxi drive away. He felt almost frightened to go in, but he knew he had to see her, face her. He raised his finger and pressed the bell. There was quite a long silence. And then he heard her voice.

'Who is it?'

'Nick.'

A moment's pause, he could sense her shock. Then he heard the chain being undone, watched the door open, saw her.

She looked dreadful. She was very white and her eyes were red and swollen with crying. Her hair hung lankly round her face, and she was twisting a handkerchief in both hands.

'Hi!'

'Hello.'

'Do you want to come in?'

'If I may.'

'Of course . . . Would you like a cup of tea?'

'No, thanks. How are you feeling?'

'Terrible.'

'Ah.'

There was a long silence, then she said, 'Excuse me,' and rushed out of the room. He heard various unpleasant noises coming from the lavatory. She emerged, finally, whiter than ever. 'Sorry.'

'The anaesthetic, I suppose,' he said.

She looked at him sharply. 'You know?'

'Yes, I know. I've just come from the clinic.'

'From the—Nick, who told you?'

'I'm quite a good detective,' he said. 'It's part of being a journalist. As you know.'

'Yes, but—'

'Oh, I had a little help.'

'From Clio, I suppose?'

'No. Not from Clio. She wouldn't tell me anything.'

He looked at her and shook his head.

'Why on God's earth didn't you tell me? Don't you think I had a right to know? About . . . about a baby that wasn't just yours, but mine as well. Ours. How could you decide all on your own what was best, for . . . for all of us? It was terribly arrogant and it's made me terribly, terribly unhappy.'

'Unhappy?'

'Of course. Jocasta, I love you. I love you so much. How could you think I should have no part in all this?'

'Nick . . . Nick, you don't mean . . . you don't mean you'd have wanted me to have a baby?'

'Of course I'd have wanted you to have our baby. I might not have chosen it, just now. But that doesn't mean I'd have wanted you to . . . to throw it away. Given the choice. Of course I wouldn't.'

'Oh,' she said, 'oh, I see. Yes.'

'And I can't begin to think how you could have done that. Without talking to me.'

'No. No, indeed. Well . . . well, you see, the thing is—'

'The thing is, what? I don't think I can cope with any justifications.'

'You're not going to get any. The thing is, Nick,' she said, slowly and very gently, 'actually, it is rather a fine thing I've done. I think.'

He stared at her. 'What do you mean?'

'I mean I couldn't do it,' she said, 'not in the end. I just couldn't. I got into that room, and I lay there, thinking, really thinking, about what I was doing, what was going to happen, and then after a bit, I just got up and left. So . . . I'm still pregnant. What are we going to do about that?'

Clio looked, with great foreboding, up at Jocasta's windows. She was terrified of what she might find. It wasn't going to be easy. She was actually finding it very hard. That someone, especially someone she was fond of, could so carelessly—literally—discard a baby, hurt her a lot. But—Jocasta's reasons, however tortuous, had seemed insurmountable to her; and it was Jocasta they had to look after now.

Very tentatively she pressed the bell. After a few minutes, she heard Jocasta's voice. 'Hello? Who is it?'

She sounded remarkably cheerful; she looked remarkably cheerful, as she opened the door. She was very pale, but—yes, cheerful. She was recovering very fast, Clio thought, and tried to suppress her irritation.

'Hello, darling Clio. Come in, it's so lovely to see you.' She led the way into the sitting room.

'Well, how do you feel?' Clio asked.

'Dreadful. I keep being sick.'

'Oh, Jocasta, I'm sorry. You've been very unlucky. The anaesthetics don't usually do that, these days.'

'Don't they? I wouldn't know.'

'What?'

'I said I wouldn't know. I didn't have one.'

'You what? You mean, they didn't give you anything?'

'Nothing. Nothing at all.'

'Jocasta—' Clio looked at her; her eyes were sparkling in her white face, she was smiling.

'I didn't have it. I didn't have the termination,' she said. 'I'm still pregnant. I can't think how I'm going to cope with it, but I am. I just walked out. Told them not to do it, just as they were coming in to get me. They were awfully cross,' she added.

Clio felt as if someone had just given her irrefutable evidence that the earth was flat. She sat there, staring at Jocasta, trying to work out what she felt. Finally she started to cry.

'Clio, darling, don't, don't, I know it's hard, but—'

'No,' she said, going over to her, giving her a hug, 'it's not hard. Not at all. You getting rid of it was hard. I'm really happy for you.'

'Oh, good. Because I'm happy for me too. Very happy. I'd be ecstatic, if I could stop being sick. Serves me right for being so snooty about it.'

'Yes, maybe it does. Have you told Nick?'

'Yes. He came round.'

'What did he say?'

'Clio, he was happy about it. He was actually excited. And until he knew it was all right, he was terribly upset. I can't quite believe it—'

'Jocasta,' said Clio, 'I hate to say this, no, I don't hate to say it, I'm enjoying saying it, but I did tell you so!'

Where is Nick?' she said, half an hour later, after she had made Jocasta some camomile tea.

'He's had to go and sort out his car—it got clamped. Silly bugger,' she added fondly.

Her mobile rang. 'Hi, Kate. How are you—oh God,' she handed it to Clio, 'I've got to go back to the loo. Sorry.'

Clio made sympathetic faces and said, 'Kate, it's me, Clio.'

'What's the matter with Jocasta?'

'She's . . . got a tummy bug.'

'Oh, no. Poor thing. I'll come round and see her, shall I, bring her some flowers? I've got Nat with me, we're in Clapham, just down the road from her, we've looked it up in the *A to Z*.'

'Kate, I really don't think—'

But she had rung off.

Jocasta was surprisingly pleased by the prospect.

'I'd love to see her. Honestly.'

'And Nat? Are you sure?'

Well, maybe just for a minute or two. I know why she's coming, she called me yesterday: it's about the Smith contract. She's changed her mind, she's going to do it.'

'Oh, yes?' said Clio. She didn't think she wanted to hear about Kate and her contract. Her contract and Fergus.

Thinking about Fergus made her feel suddenly terrible. She was happy for Jocasta, of course, and for Nick, but here she was, alone again. Very alone. She hadn't heard from Fergus since their argument over the holiday.

Kate came in, looking radiant, holding a large, but rather inelegant bunch of flowers.

'Darling, they're lovely,' said Jocasta.

'I hope so. We got them from the garage. Nat chose them.'

'They're lovely. Thank you, Nat.'

'That's OK. Sorry you're not feeling so good.'

'You know something?' said Jocasta. 'I'm feeling perfectly wonderful!'

'Really?' said Kate. 'Clio said you had a tummy bug.'

'Oh, did she? No, I haven't got a tummy bug. I'm going to have a baby, Kate. What do you think about that?'

Kate stared at her. 'I think that's really cool. You'll be a great mother. Gideon must be pleased.'

'It isn't Gideon's,' said Jocasta carefully. 'Gideon and I are getting divorced.'

Kate looked very confused. As well she might, Jocasta thought.

'So whose is it then?'

'It's Nick's.'

'Nick, who used to be your boyfriend? Who came to the funeral?'

'The very one.'

'Oh.' She digested this. 'So . . . are you going to marry him now?'

'Probably. He's a bit anti actual marriage. But he seems very keen on the baby.'

'Well, that's a good thing, I s'pose . . . I'm sorry about Gideon, though. I really like him.'

'Oh, Kate, so do I. But it's all right. We should never have got married in the first place. It was a stupid mistake. Mostly on my part. And we're still good friends.'

'Cool.' She was clearly baffled; out of her depth. Jocasta decided she should change the subject. 'Now, tell me all about your contract,' she said. 'Have you actually signed it, and when are you going to start with them?'

'I'm not,' she said. 'I didn't sign it. Fergus told me not to.'

'Fergus told you not to?'

'Yeah. I was all set to, went in to see him for a meeting and he told me not to. He said I just didn't realise what I was letting myself in for, he said it would start all over again, with the press and that, and—well, he just wouldn't let me. I'm really relieved now,' she added. 'Even in spite of the money, deep down I didn't want to.'

'Yes, well, money isn't everything, is it?' said Nat.

'It absolutely isn't. Clio, where are you going? Clio—'

Clio drove as fast as she could to Fergus's office. She prayed he'd still be there. This wasn't something that could be settled on the phone. As she reached the North End Road in Fulham, and his building, she saw him standing at the first-floor window, staring down at the street. He looked terribly unhappy. She parked the car, and ran across the road, pressed her finger on the bell.

He was a long time answering it. Supposing he'd seen her, supposing he didn't want to let her in, or see her?

Finally he spoke on the intercom. 'Who is it?'

'It's Clio. Please let me in.'

'Oh, OK.' He didn't sound exactly pleased to hear her voice. She took a deep breath, pushed on the door, and ran up the stairs. He was sitting in the reception area, and looked at her rather coolly.

'Hello.'

'Hello, Fergus. I've come to . . . to apologise to you for all those things I said about you being cynical and trading on people's misery.'

'I see.'

'Yes. It was terribly wrong of me, I had no right to say any of them.'

'No.'

This wasn't going very well. Maybe she'd hurt him too much for him to forgive her. Oh God.

'Fergus, I . . . Fergus, I really, really want you to know that I . . . I . . . well, that I care about you so, so much. I've missed you terribly. I was thinking only today how much I missed you, that I shouldn't have been so stupid and—'

'That's all right,' he said, staring at her, his face expressionless.

This was terrible. She really had upset him, beyond redemption. Well, it served her right. She was a pompous, self-righteous woman; she didn't deserve someone as lovely as Fergus. She should have trusted him, she should have known better. She looked at him again. Still the frozen face.

'Well,' she said finally, her voice trembling, 'well, that's all I came to say. It needed to be said, I thought.'

She turned towards the door. If she could only get out without crying, that'd be something.

'Where are you going now?' he said.

'I don't know. Home, I suppose. Home to Guildford.'

'You are not,' he said, 'you are most definitely not.'

'What?'

'You're staying here with me.'

'Staying here?'

'Yes,' he said, 'staying here. I love you.'

'You love me?' she said.

'Yes. I love you. Love you an awful lot. You silly bitch,' he added.

'Grace, dear, we've got some visitors.' Peter Hartley's voice was slightly tentative. 'Can I bring them up?'

'Oh—oh dear. I'm not sure. I'm very tired.'

'We won't stay long, Mrs Hartley.'

'Oh,' she said, and they could all hear the pleasure in her voice. 'Oh, Ed. How nice.'

'There's two of us,' said Ed. 'I've brought Kate with me.'

It had been arranged on the spur of the moment; he had called Kate to tell her that he was going to see Martha's parents and she said that she'd like to go with him.

'It's a long way, Kate.' Ed sounded doubtful.

'Doesn't matter. Nat could bring me. He's got some new wheels for his car and he wants to show them off.'

'Yeah. What's he got then?'

'Saxo.'

'What, the bomb?'

He sounded very impressed; they cared more about their cars than anything, Kate thought.

'Yeah.'

'Wow. I couldn't . . . hitch a ride, could I?'

'Course you could. He loves showing it off.'

'Well, OK, then. Thanks.'

She was a one-off, Ed thought, switching off his phone. Absolutely totally gorgeous and funny and really quite bright. He liked her a lot. Of course, he could never fancy her. Not really. She was Martha's daughter and that made it unthinkable. But somehow, she comforted him. Made him feel just a little less desperate. She wasn't Martha, but . . . in a funny way she was. Part of her. Literally. There was something about her voice, for instance, that was Martha. And when she giggled, that was Martha, too. And her eyes, those huge dark eyes, they were Martha's eyes. It ought to hurt and in a way, it did. But in another, it absolutely didn't.

'Hello, Mrs Hartley,' said Ed. 'You remember Kate?'

'Yes, of course I do. It's very good of you to come, dear.'

'It's cool. Here, we brought you these.'

Helen had chosen the flowers and they were beautiful.

'How sweet of you. Peter, go and put them in water, love. It's a long journey you've done,' she said to Kate.

'Oh, not really. My boyfriend brought me. In his car. He's gone shopping for it,' she said hastily, clearly anxious that Grace shouldn't feel she should ask the boyfriend in, as well. 'It needs a new trim, or something.'

'Oh, I see.' She looked at her. 'How old are you, Kate?'

'Sixteen.'

'You're still at school?'

'Yes.'

'And what do you want to do?'

'I think I want to be a photographer. Then again, I might be a lawyer.'

'A lawyer! My goodness. Like Martha.'

'Well, yeah. And Ally McBeal.'

'Who, dear?'

'Ally McBeal. She's a lawyer on TV. You ought to watch it, it's good.'

'I'll look out for it. And how is Jocasta? That's right, isn't it?'

'Yes, that's right,' said Kate, 'she's fine. She's going to have a baby.'

'A baby! How lovely. I'm so pleased.'

'Yes.' She paused, looked at Ed for a moment, then said, 'She sent you her good wishes and she said—'

'Yes? What did she say?'

'She said,' Kate said, smiling with great sweetness at Grace, 'she said to tell you that, if it's a girl, she's going to call her Martha.'

PENNY VINCENZI

Penny Vincenzi embarked on her storytelling career at the age of nine, when she wrote her own magazine called *Stories* on her mother's old typewriter, making carbon copies and selling them at school for two old pence each. 'It was not a best seller, but it taught me some valuable lessons,' Penny remembers. 'The crucial one being that every chapter should end on a cliffhanger so readers would have to buy the next one!'

After a career in journalism, working on such magazines as *Cosmopolitan, Vogue, Tatler, Woman's Own* and *Options*, Penny was persuaded to write a novel and has now written eleven best sellers, producing sales of over 3.5 million copies worldwide. 'I was a journalist and thought that the best fun, until I discovered that making it all up was much better.'

Sheer Abandon took Penny nearly two years to write, 'which is longer than usual, partly because I was taking it a little slower and having a bit of a rest, and partly because the research was so complex.' To research the backpacking adventures of her three characters, Jocasta, Clio and Martha, Penny travelled in Thailand with her youngest daughter. 'We didn't see nearly enough,' Penny told me, 'but we managed Bangkok, Koh Samui and Koh Pangnan. It was quite amusing because I insisted that we slept in huts on the beach and went on the studenty boats, which we did . . . for a day or two. Then I rather felt we'd done that, and we hurriedly repaired to the nearest five-star hotel. We had huge fun, but more importantly got the flavour of the place, which you can't get without going there. I talked to lots of students and even went to a club on one of the islands, where they all clearly thought I was older than God . . .'

Like Martha in the novel, Penny Vincenzi has always been intensely interested in politics and was involved with her local SDP party in the 1980s. 'I think it's the single most absorbing thing, maybe because it touches on every aspect of our lives. I love the intrigue and the gossip, too, and life in the "Westminster Village", where they all spend their days. Certain issues concern me greatly: education, health, the things that distressed Martha in the book and drove her into politics. Incidentally, a lot of the politicians I interviewed in my research thought the Centre Forward Party—the one I invented for the book—was a terribly good idea, and I am waiting for someone to call and ask me to form it . . . but so far, no call. How strange!'

Penny has been married for thirty-six years and has four daughters and four grandchildren. 'I'm a family person and, as an only child myself, I'm delighted that I have created this big family. We have a cottage in the Gower Peninsula in Wales, which has to be one of the most beautiful places in the world. I work there often, overlooking the sea, and it is in the garden there, under an old apple tree, that we have the most wonderful family lunches.' It is also here that Penny loves to walk her dogs on the beach and where she loves to surf, 'strictly modest boogie board variety,' she states. 'I love working, indeed I suppose I'm a workaholic, but I have to be busy doing something all the time. I have a saying "don't let the day slip away", which drives my family mad, as I chase them out of bed, down to breakfast, onto the beach. I want it written on my gravestone: "Not a day slipped away."'

Jane Eastgate

The Golden Cup

MARCIA WILLETT

As Honor Trevannion's life ebbs away, she makes one last request: a collection of letters she wrote over fifty years ago must be found . . . but only by her beloved granddaughter, Joss.

But when the letters come to light, they unleash a tide of guilt and emotion that threatens to overwhelm everyone Honor loves.

PROLOGUE

THE TWO FIGURES, leaning together beneath the bare boughs of an ancient beech, were barely distinguishable in the fading, wintry light. They stood quite still, a smudge of darker grey against the high granite wall that separated the sheltered garden from the sloping meadow. As he stared across the frosty grass he heard the arched, wrought-iron gate open with a clang and saw a young woman pass through, closing the gate carefully behind her. He straightened, recognising her from the brief glimpse he'd had earlier when he'd called at the house. A soft plaid was wrapped about her shoulders and she wore green gum boots beneath a long, knubbly-textured skirt.

The donkeys plodded to meet her with their familiar head-dipping gait and she spoke quietly to them, holding out her hands, bending down so it seemed as if she might be kissing their suede-soft muzzles. He hesitated—longing to call out to her, to make a connection with her—but his courage failed him. Instead, he pictured her as he'd first seen her as she'd come in through a door half hidden in the shadows at the back of the hall: a straight, uncompromising glance from beneath dark, level brows, her arms crossed over something that she held to her breast—a book? or a box?—and an air of wariness. She'd paused, watching, listening, and then had vanished through another door, leaving him with the older woman who'd smiled with such sweetness and sympathy.

'I *am* sorry. It would be quite impossible for you to see Mrs Trevannion today. She's got this wretched chest infection on top of everything else. If only we'd known that you were coming.'

'I wrote to Mrs Trevannion,' he'd answered quickly, unable to hide his disappointment. 'I sent a copy of a photograph with the letter. I think—I'm really hoping—that she knew my grandmother's sister way back during the war. She emigrated to the States in 'forty-six, my grandmother, and then they just lost touch. We were so excited when my mother found the wedding photograph, all four of them together, the names on the back of it clear as clear. Hubert and Honor Trevannion . . .'

'I'm afraid she's been too ill to answer any correspondence. A broken ankle, you see, and now this infection.' She'd frowned a little, crushing his enthusiasm kindly but firmly. 'Perhaps in a week or two . . .'

'I'm only here for the week,' he'd told her, dismayed, 'staying over at Port Isaac. I've been interested in this for a long time now and the photograph was a real find . . .'

Once again, at the mention of the photograph, he'd sensed a faint withdrawal.

'I don't see how we can help you at the moment.'

He tried a different tack. 'What a magical little valley this is; so secret and so green. And what a great name for a house. "Paradise". You really do have strange names in Cornwall, don't you? Indian Queens, Jamaica Inn.' He shook his head as if in amused puzzlement. 'And then there are all those saints. But I love "Paradise". And it certainly looks like it is one.'

'We think so too.'

Her courtesy was as blank as a stone wall and, in the end, he'd given her his card and she'd promised to contact him, smiling farewell, closing the door quietly.

As he stood at the five-bar gate watching the donkeys, he tried to be rational, persuading himself that Honor Trevannion was probably very ill; that the older woman and the young one were too concerned with her well-being to have time to spend with an unexpected stranger hunting for an ancestor. He hunched his shoulders against the chill of the evening and rested his arms along the top bar of the gate. The shadowy group at the far side of the meadow was hardly visible now as the twilight, creeping across the grass and thickening beneath the trees, blotted away the glimmerings of sunset and dimmed the last bright reflections slanting from the west. He frowned, still thinking about the interview. Had he imagined that slight tension? A reluctance to discuss his letter and the photograph?

He heard again the metallic clang as the gate closed: the young woman was gone and the donkeys had moved into the small open-fronted barn. Frustrated, he walked back to the disused quarry where he'd parked his car and drove away.

206

PART ONE

THE GRASSY TRACK from the meadow twisted between rhododendrons as tall as trees, whose woody arms, stretching along the hard, bare earth, were supported and propped upon deep-rooted, knuckly elbows. The tough, lance-shaped leaves shivered in the chilly, gently shifting air and, at the edge of the path, clumps of snowdrops gleamed dimly in the gathering shadows. Light shone suddenly from an upstairs room and a figure stood with arms wide-stretched, pausing briefly to look out, before the brightness was quenched by the sweep of curtains drawn swiftly across the windows.

By the time the young woman had reached the garden door, kicked off her boots and crossed the hall to the drawing room, Mousie had come downstairs and was piling wood onto the open fire.

'So there you are, Joss.' There was an odd note of relief in her voice. 'I wondered where you'd disappeared to.'

'I took some apples to the donkeys.' She sat on the wide fender, curling her toes in their thick, cosy socks, relishing the warmth from the flames that licked with greedy yellow and orange tongues at the rough-sawn logs. 'How is Mutt?'

'Sleeping peacefully. I shall take up a tray of tea and sit with her for a while. Would you like to join us?'

Joss shook her head. 'I'll go up later and read to her. Who was that man who was here just now? What did he want?'

Mousie hesitated. 'He's an American tracking down a relative. He seemed to think that your grandmother might have known his great-aunt during the war.'

'And does Mutt know her?'

'I haven't asked her,' answered Mousie crisply. 'Do you want some tea?'

'I'll come and get mine in a minute, just leave it in the pot.' Joss smiled at the small upright figure, whose high-necked jersey was slung about with several pairs of spectacles on long pieces of cord. 'You know I can manage perfectly well if you want to go home, Mousie.'

'I know that, my darling.' Mousie relaxed visibly. Her slate-blue eyes were bright and warmly affectionate beneath the unruly crest of soft white hair. 'But perhaps just one more check to make sure that she's settled.'

Joss chuckled. 'Hopeless,' she said. 'It must be all those years of nursing and being in charge. Old habits die hard. I'm qualified too, you know. OK, I know I'm not a *proper* nurse, but I can lift Mutt and I promise you that some gentle massage will really help now that her foot is out of plaster.'

'And you also know very well that I am *not* prejudiced against osteopathy,' said Mousie firmly. 'I have no anxiety about you looking after your grandmother; I'm just rather worried about the chest infection.'

Her eyes were anxious again and, watching her, Joss felt a stomach-sinking fear. 'We have to give her time,' she said. 'It was a bad break and this infection isn't helping. She'll be fine, Mousie.' It was almost a plea for consolation and Mousie responded to it swiftly.

'Of course she will, my darling. And having you here is the best medicine she could have.' She smiled mischievously, her sense of humour returning. 'That and the massage, of course.'

Left alone, Joss drew her feet up onto the fender, rested her chin on her knees and began to think about the good-looking American. She'd been attracted by the eagerness that had informed his gestures and expression, and was already regretting her own wariness. How simple—she told herself now—to have joined in the conversation; offered him some refreshment. They might have had some tea together and he could have shown her the photograph of his long-lost great-aunt. She felt frustrated by this new constant need for wariness that clamped her tongue and inhibited her gestures. Relationships with her family had become more complicated since she'd moved out of the bedsit in Wadebridge to stay at Paradise while she renovated the cottage at the end of The Row. Yet how could she have foreseen that a childhood friendship would flower so abruptly into a love that must be kept secret?

'Tea's made,' Mousie called on her way upstairs.

Joss went out into the hall, pausing to revel in the atmosphere of this house that she loved so dearly. It was such a perfect place, elegantly proportioned with high sash windows. Mousie's voice could just be heard, murmuring comfortingly beyond the closed bedroom door, and Joss wondered whether her grandmother had once known the American's great-aunt, way back when they'd both been young. She understood his interest in this vanished relative. Her own heart was more at home here in this valley of St Meriadoc, where her mother's family had lived for centuries, than in her parents' house in Henley or the London flat where her father spent most of his working week.

Still thinking about the young American, she poured tea into a mug and carried it back to the fire.

Upstairs, Mousie removed the tray, saw that Mutt was dozing again and looked about the room. The porch room, given its name because it was situated directly above the front door, looked south across the secret, sheltered garden to the lane and the hillocky, gorse-edged little fields beyond. A sturdy wisteria grew beneath the window, so that in early summer the scent from its grey-blue flowers drifted into the room through the open casement. Here, on a June evening, Mutt could watch the full moon, egg-yolk yellow, rise above the distant thorn trees at the head of the valley. Now, a small but cheerful fire burned in the grate, safely contained behind a tall meshed guard, and a pretty painted screen had been set so as to shield the elderly woman in the bed from the brightness of the tall lamp set on a gate-leg table near the window. It was at this table that Mousie kept her vigil and it was piled with books and the paraphernalia of letter-writing.

She stood for a moment, her back to the bed, squaring the loose sheets of a letter she'd been writing before folding them into the leather blotter, collecting stray pens and a pencil and putting them into a blue and white ceramic jar. Presently she slid the print from beneath the blotter and stared down at it. It was evident that it had been copied from a photograph, as it bore the marks of scratches and creases. She'd recognised it at once: in 1941 her cousin Hubert had sent an identical photograph from India to his aunt Julia in Portsmouth.

He'd written:

I was deeply horrified and sad to hear about Uncle Hugh and the loss of HMS Hood. But I am so pleased that you're going to St Meriadoc to be near Mother and Father. . . I can't wait for you all to meet Honor, she's a darling. Give my love to Mousie and Rafe . . .

Even now she could remember the shock and misery she'd felt at this news coming so soon after the death of her father. From her earliest memories she'd loved Hubert with an overwhelming devotion, willing herself to grow up quickly, imagining the glorious, much-dreamed-of moment when he would see her as an adult and realise that he'd loved her all the time. It was Hubert who had given her the nickname 'Mousie' and, though he had teased her, he could always make her laugh: there was no one else like Hubert. She'd gazed at the face of Hubert's new wife, smiling mistily beneath the charming, silly hat slanted over one eye, and had silently, bitterly, hated her. As the war dragged on, news had filtered back to St Meriadoc from India: Honor had given birth to a son, Bruno, and, three years later, to a daughter, Emma. Mousie was seventeen when they'd heard that Hubert was trying to book a passage to England for his wife and children in an attempt to protect them from the riots and upheaval of partition. He'd planned to follow them when his discharge came through, later in the year, but he had died of some kind of food-poisoning just days before his family were due to sail and Honor—whom Hubert had nicknamed Mutt—and the children had come back to Paradise alone.

Mousie slid the photograph beneath the blotter and moved back to the bed, sitting in the low upholstered armchair so as to be nearly on the same level as Mutt.

'Poor Mousie.' The words were barely stronger than a breath and Mousie had to bend closer to catch them. 'What a nuisance I am.'

'Not a bit of a nuisance.' She took Mutt's weakly outstretched hand and held it warmly between both of her own. 'You're getting better by the minute. And Joss will be up soon to read to you.'

There was a little silence while the logs crumbled together in a soft ashy explosion of flames.

'Odd, wasn't it,' Mutt murmured, 'both of us being nurses?'

'It was all Hubert's fault,' Mousie answered lightly. 'You know how he was my hero when I was small. Once he'd qualified as a doctor I was determined that I would train to be a nurse. I was always foolishly pleased that he knew I'd started my training before he died.'

Mutt stirred restlessly, turning onto her back. 'I might try to sleep again,' she said.

Mousie watched her thoughtfully for a moment before putting the handbell beside her on the quilt, and going quietly away.

As Joss entered the porch room later that evening she felt a sense of pleasure at its peaceful, elegant comfort, although, privately, she preferred her own room at the back of the house, which looked north towards the high rugged cliffs. At night she could hear the restless, rhythmic sighing of the waves, as they pried and dragged at the resisting rocks with foamy fingers, and tumbled hugger-mugger into the caves. Now, the cold, frosty night was closed out behind thick, velvet curtains and her grandmother's room was quiet.

Joss glanced towards the bed and its motionless occupant and, seized by sudden terror, moved quickly. Mutt opened her eyes as Joss stooped beside her, feeling for the thin wrist, checking the light, fast pulse. She grimaced, as though guessing at her granddaughter's momentary fear and mocking it.

'I'm still here,' she murmured.

'Yes.' Joss silently expelled a breath of relief. 'So you are.'

They smiled at each other, the deeply special love that had defined their friendship from the earliest days flowing between them. She and

Joss had always been a team: occasionally defying the middle generation and making their own fun. Joss touched the thin hand lightly with her lips. 'It's nearly time for your medicine,' she said, 'but I wondered if you'd like some massage first?'

'Mmm.' Mutt acquiesced readily, accepting what she recognised was an offering of love as well as relief and comfort. It was she who had enabled Joss to become an osteopath, taking her side against her father's prejudice and helping out financially, and now she reaped the benefits. 'Did I hear the telephone?'

'You did.' Joss edged her carefully into position. 'Mum's coming down tomorrow.' She took a small bottle from the bedside table, tipped a little oil into the palms of her hands and then began to knead the muscles with dextrous, confident gentleness. 'She'll stay down at The Lookout with Bruno but she'll be up to see you as soon as she can.'

Mutt showed no change of expression at this proposed treat; her concentration was fixed elsewhere.

'Did someone call here earlier?'

Joss hesitated, wondering if her grandmother knew about the American and his photograph, realising that she must have heard the ringing of the doorbell. It was not in her nature to dissemble, however, and she could see no harm in a truthful answer.

'There was an American here who's trying to trace his great-aunt. He has some idea that you might have known her during the war.'

She was turning her again and saw a spasm of pain pass across the old woman's face and paused, watching her anxiously. 'Did that hurt?'

Mutt shook her head, frowned and began to cough convulsively. Joss lifted her, cradling her thin frame in one arm while pouring medicine into a plastic measure with the other hand. Presently, the attack over, Joss laid her back carefully, supporting the injured leg on a pillow.

'I must wash my hands,' she told her. 'Shan't be long.'

Left alone, Mutt rolled her head on the pillow, staring across at the table where Mousie had been sitting just a few days ago, opening the morning post.

'Great grief!' she'd said, amused. 'There's a letter here from a young fellow who wants to know if you've ever met his great-aunt. He's enclosed a photograph.' There'd been a moment's silence and when she'd next spoken, her voice had been different, tender and hedged about with emotion. 'How extraordinary,' she'd said. 'Remember this, Honor?' and she'd got up and come over to the bed, holding out the print.

The shock had been very great: to see her own youthful, merry face laughing out of that little group of friends, recalling with a sharp twist of painful joy that happy day and the grief and fear that followed after—

these sensations had deprived her momentarily of any rational thought. It was some moments before she'd remembered the letter Mousie had read aloud to her.

'I can't see him,' she'd cried apprehensively, cutting across something that Mousie was saying. 'I simply can't. It's all too painful, too long ago,' and Mousie had calmed her, agreeing that she wasn't fit enough yet for visitors, and had given her some medicine to soothe the wretched cough that racked her.

Now, waiting for Joss to return, she thought of something else—a foolish, secret thing, long forgotten—and fear crept and tingled in her veins. But the medicine was beginning to have an effect and, instead, she grew drowsy. She imagined she was in India again, visions and noises jostling her confused memory; the pungent, acrid smells; brown bodies and bright bougainvillea; soft, warm dust and relentless heat.

The telephone shrilled suddenly in the hall below, and was silenced abruptly as Mousie lifted the receiver. Mutt cried out in her sleep and Joss, sitting beside her, raised her eyes from her book and watched her.

'I've just been thinking whether I ought to stay up at the house,' Emma's quick, light voice was saying into Mousie's ear, 'instead of with Bruno. If Mutt really is, well, *really* poorly with this chill, Mousie, perhaps I should be a bit more available. It's just that I don't want to butt in on Joss. She's been in charge since her grandmother broke her ankle. She and Mutt have always got on so well, haven't they?'

Mousie smiled, picturing Emma hunched over the telephone, gesturing with her free hand: warm, scatty, lovable.

'You'll be fine with Bruno,' she assured her. 'The Lookout is only ten minutes away and Honor isn't in a dangerous condition . . .' She remembered the doctor's words and bit her lip. 'Although, given her age, we should be prepared—'

'That's what Raymond's been saying,' Emma cut in, anxiously. 'That I should be with her. You know he doesn't have much confidence in Joss. He can't be doing with all that alternative medicine stuff.'

Mousie's lip curled. She could well imagine that Raymond Fox would prefer it if his wife were to be very much on the spot at this critical time. 'Tell him not to get too stressed about Honor,' she answered drily. 'I think you're very wise to leave Joss in charge here. You can assure Raymond that she's more than capable and Honor feels very comfortable and safe with her.'

'Bless you, Mousie. I'll tell him. The trouble is that he can't take on board that she's grown up, and it's not as if she's a qualified nursing sister like you are, although I keep telling him that she's done brilliantly. Of

course, Father was a doctor and Mutt trained as a nurse so I expect she
gets it from them. . .'

'Joss is fine,' said Mousie firmly, 'and Raymond should be proud of her.
She knows exactly what she's doing. She's very professional.'

'You are such a comfort,' said Emma fervently. 'I'm hoping to be down
in time for lunch. It'll be heaven to see you all. My dear brother is only
quite pleased at the prospect of my arrival; he's wrestling with a tricky bit
of the book, apparently, and I can tell by his voice that he's totally
wrapped up in it. Never mind. It'll do him good to have a bit of distraction. Give everyone my love.'

Mousie felt a fleeting sympathy for Bruno as she replaced the receiver
and returned to the drawing room. Mutt's love for quiet, formal elegance
informed each room in the house and nowhere more than here and
in the small parlour where she sat to read or work. Here, two small,
comfortable sofas were set at right angles to the fireplace and a third,
longer, sofa made the fourth side of the square. The tapestry that Mutt
stitched away at each evening by the fire, lay half completed on the rosewood table behind the long sofa.

Mousie went to a corner by the fire, picked up her big carpetbag and
sat down on one of the sofas. Carefully she drew out the photograph
with its accompanying letter and looked at the four laughing faces:
Hubert and his wife and another couple.

The American had written:

> It was a double wedding because the four of them were such close
> friends. My grandmother remembered that both girls were nurses but
> thinks my great-uncle ran some kind of company in India. It's all a bit
> vague but my great-aunt's maiden name was Madeleine Grosjean. I
> know that the two sisters were very close, but shortly after my grand-
> mother moved to the States there was complete silence from the Indian
> end. From enquiries made at that time it seemed that Madeleine and
> her family had just disappeared. We suspect that they died during the
> unrest in 1947.
>
> Perhaps, by that time, you and Dr Trevannion had already returned
> to the UK. It would be terrific to find out the truth and I hope you might
> spare me a moment if I were to visit next weekend, say on Saturday
> around three o'clock?

She folded the letter and stared ahead, remembering Honor's arrival at
St Meriadoc. By 1947, Hubert's mother was dead, his father rather frail,
but they'd all done their best to make the travellers feel at home: the
small Bruno, so like his father, dazed by the events of the last two
months, and sweet Emma, too young to understand what had happened

but good-naturedly ready to embrace her new family. From the first moment Mousie had adored the children—but as for Honor . . . Mousie sighed regretfully. There had always been some kind of barrier between them, a reserve that Mousie had found impossible to breach. She'd feared it might be the result of her own love for Hubert, and had worked hard to overcome it, but she had never succeeded. She hadn't even been able to use the silly nickname that the children used: to Mousie she was always 'Honor'.

She heard footsteps on the stairs and bundled the letter and photograph back into the capacious bag so that by the time Joss opened the door Mousie was sitting with the newspaper open, apparently absorbed, relaxed and comfortable beside the fire.

Travelling the familiar road past Launceston, turning off at Kennards House, waiting for a sight of the distant, shining sea, Emma talked aloud for company, encouraging herself: nearly there now, nearly home. Despite the very early start she felt alert, full of energy and looking forward to seeing her family—especially Joss and Bruno.

'And dear old Mutt,' she said aloud. She was anxious about her mother's condition but her anxiety sprang from the fact that she felt so useless with ill people: not like Mousie, who had the knack of being caring and practical.

'She looks terrible,' Emma had cried privately to Mousie, the last time she'd seen Mutt. 'She looks so frail and old.'

'She is frail and old,' Mousie had answered with her sharply humorous look that always comforted Emma. 'She's nearly eighty and she's had a bad fall. What did you expect?'

'Well, she's always been so'—Emma searched for the right word—'so independent.'

'True,' agreed Mousie wryly, 'but independence is tricky when you can't walk and you're in a very confused state.'

The thing was, thought Emma, as she drove through Delabole, that it had been much more than a shock to see the cheerful, capable Mutt confined to her bed and under sedation. It was as if a secure, reliable point of reference had been destroyed overnight and she'd found herself adrift, untethered.

She passed through St Endellion and Porteath, turned right into the lane that led down to St Meriadoc and pulled abruptly into a gateway. Opening the car door she stepped out into the pale sunlight, delighting in the familiar scene. Startled sheep with lambs at foot stampeded away over the field, their cries echoing in the cold, clear air as she gazed across rough, open land to the cliffs. By climbing a few rungs of the gate, so that she could stare down into the steep valley, she could make out the slate roof of the house surrounded by tall shrubs and trees; to its west lay the tiny, scooped-out bay with the disused boatyard and a row of cottages which, together with The Lookout perched on the cliff above it, made up the estate known as St Meriadoc. Mutt referred to this quiet, secret valley as 'the golden cup'; a phrase taken from George Meredith's poem about a lark, which she'd read to them as children. Emma could still remember a few lines of it:

> *And ever winging up and up*
> *Our valley is his golden cup*
> *And he the wine which overflows . . .*

She'd always loved to look down on it like this, coming home from school or, later, from London.

'Why do you want to stop here?' Raymond would ask impatiently, on visits during those early years of marriage. 'We'll be there in a minute.'

And there was no answer, she told herself. At least, no answer that she could give to *him*. Her brother Bruno understood that feeling of glorious anticipation when, for a moment, you'd postpone the excitement of being a part of that scene below and look down on all the promise to come.

'Never mind,' she'd mutter, acceding as usual to his will—Raymond was so mature, so sensible—and he'd reach to pat her knee, unaware of her shrinking from his physical presence and his values.

'Silly girl,' he'd say with patronising affection, while she'd press her own hands between her knees and pretend to be absorbed by something beyond the car window. Moments later, however, she'd be reminding herself of his sound qualities—a rather clumsy kindness allied to a natural tendency to protect; his ability to provide the necessary comforts while carefully husbanding his resources—qualities, Mutt had pointed out, that were just as important as mutual passion. Twelve years her senior, good-looking and already successful, he had seemed so glamorous to her inexperienced twenty-year-old eyes, and his determined pursuit had been very flattering. Remembering, Emma made a little face; the point was that once Bruno had announced his engagement to the waif-like gamine Zoë, a photographer's model, Emma had felt rather left out of things. Zoë had a way of making her future sister-in-law feel clumsy and raw, and Raymond had been conveniently at hand to soothe this sense of inadequacy.

'You can't marry him,' Bruno had said flatly, after the first meeting with Raymond.

'Mutt really likes him,' she'd said stubbornly. 'She thinks he's reliable and steady.'

'*Reliable?*' Bruno had stared at her in disbelief, shaking his head. 'For God's sake, Em! Do me a favour.'

Now, still thinking about the ensuing quarrel, Emma climbed back into the car and drove down the steep, winding lane, slowing when she reached the boatyard beside the row of cottages and finally pulling into the disused quarry opposite.

The cheerful tattoo, thumped out on the car's horn, roused Rafe Boscowan from his work and drew him to the upstairs window.

'It's Emma,' he shouted to his wife. 'I'll go.'

Pamela continued to sit at the kitchen table, carefully peeling vegetables, a look of expectant pleasure lighting her face. She heard Rafe reach the bottom of the stairs, open the door and shout a welcome, and then turned in her chair as they came in together. She could smell Emma's flowery scent, felt her face taken between gentle hands and her cheek kissed: a little pause—and she knew Emma was studying her closely.

'You look so good, darling. Such a pretty jersey—and a new haircut? I love the blonde streaks.'

Pamela's hands went straight to her head: how like Emma to notice the change. 'D'you approve? Rafe says it's good but I'm not sure I can trust him to tell me the truth. Olivia said I was looking dowdy so I decided to brighten myself up a little.'

Rafe and Emma exchanged a glance: the eldest of the Boscowan children was not noted for her tact.

Pamela smiled into the tiny silence. 'No Slips,' she said with the devastating acuity that had developed with her blindness. 'I know that Liv can be outspoken but she's quite right: I mustn't let myself go.'

Emma touched Pamela's shoulder; in the Boscowan family, the word 'slip' in that context stood for 'Sly Looks in Private'—meaning an exchange that Pamela could no longer see—and they all tried to keep to the rules that her blindness should in no way be exploited.

'I promise you,' Emma said, 'that it looks really good.'

Rafe lifted the board of peeled vegetables away and took some glasses from the dresser. 'You'll have a drink?' he asked. 'I told Bruno to come down and join us but he probably won't notice the time. Mousie will be in soon.'

He poured some wine, took a glass to the table and lightly placed Pamela's fingers around the stem. Emma wandered about happily: inspecting the latest photograph of Olivia's new baby, peering from the window, talking all the while. The row of cottages was only a few feet from the sea wall and the kitchen was filled with grey, watery reflections, giving a sense of light and space to the long low room with its beamed ceilings and thick, stone walls. Emma sighed with contentment; just so had it looked when Aunt Julia had welcomed the small Emma with homemade fudge, although now the old range was gone and the kitchen had been modernised so that Pamela could make her way about with confidence.

Watching her now, Emma was reminded of a younger Pamela, who'd flitted about carelessly, bending to deal with the small Olivia who tumbled at her feet. It was evident that Pamela's blindness had brought her and Rafe even closer, deepening and strengthening their relationship, yet Emma was filled with sudden sadness for all that Pamela had lost.

Rafe's sister, Mousie, came in. She held out her arms in welcome, and Emma went gratefully towards the warmth of Mousie's embrace.

Bruno emerged from his small, book-crowded study, glanced at his watch and grimaced guiltily: twenty past two—lunch would be over down at The Row. Taking comfort in the fact that his family would understand, and suddenly aware that he was very hungry, he went to the fridge. Nellie—the happy result of an unscheduled mating between a Border collie bitch and a golden retriever—who lay stretched on the cold slates of the kitchen floor, roused herself and looked hopeful.

'Lunch is a bit late today, old dear,' murmured Bruno, putting a large, half-full tin of dog food, some eggs and a piece of cheese on the draining board. 'Sorry about that.'

Yet he felt elated by his morning's work, conscious of a sense of well-being that was the result of translating his ideas successfully onto paper through the medium of his computer.

Built as a folly by a Victorian ancestor, Bruno found The Lookout, with its fantastic view of the bay and the ice-green sea beyond, to be the perfect place to write his books: a series inspired by his own family, historical faction beginning with a Trevannion who'd fought for the King during the Civil War. Today he was completely preoccupied with an engineering Trevannion who'd worked with the great Sir Joseph Bazalgette on the main drainage system for London.

It was fortunate, thought Bruno as he fed Nellie and grated some cheese, that the Trevannions of the eighteenth and nineteenth centuries had been so prolific: plenty more characters to keep him busy for a few years yet. Lucky, too, that his present family was so tolerant regarding his time-keeping. He was halfway through his omelette when Emma came in.

'You are useless,' she said, regarding him affectionately. 'Utterly useless. Where were you today? Mousie said that you were probably halfway down a sewer in Victorian London.'

'And she was absolutely right.' He stood up, reaching across the table to embrace her. 'Sorry about that.'

She bent to fondle Nellie's soft, floppy ears, happy to be in this place where she was most able to be herself. At intervals in her busy social life—the daily round in Henley and entertaining Ray's business clients at lavish dinner parties in the London flat—it was always a bit of a relief to be with Bruno. He looked just as he always did: relaxed and comfortable in dark brown cords and a fisherman's navy-blue jersey. As a concession to the February chill he wore a red silk scarf wound round his neck. Emma had given him the scarf for Christmas. She suspected that he was wearing it today simply because it had been the first thing to hand at the precise moment he'd noticed he was cold.

'Love the scarf,' she observed brightly, testing him.

So do I,' he answered blandly. 'Do you want some coffee or are you going up to see Mutt first?'

'I'm going straight up.' Her expression grew more serious. 'How is she? Mousie is doing that sort of guarded "We have to remember that she's nearly eighty but I'm sure she's going to be fine" stuff.'

Bruno forked up the last piece of his omelette and gave his plate to Nellie to lick. 'I saw her yesterday just after lunch,' he said. 'To be honest I don't feel qualified to make a judgment. Sometimes she's lucid, if frail, and at other times she's wandering. I think a lot depends on when she's had her medicine. Joss is wonderful with her.'

Emma's face brightened. 'I can't tell you how thrilled I am that it's working out. It's so good for her to be able to help with Mutt. Raymond's still utterly dampening about her work and they seem to have a row every time she comes home.'

'Not much change there, then,' observed Bruno. 'And how is Brer Fox?'

Emma shrugged, clearly torn between the luxury of telling the truth and the tug of silent loyalty, and Bruno, knowing from past experience that loyalty would be temporarily abandoned, decided that now was not the moment for a heart-to-heart.

'Go up and see Mutt,' he said, not waiting for an answer. 'Stay and have tea with Joss and I'll see you later.'

She hesitated, anxious at what she might find up at the house. He watched her thoughtfully, knowing how difficult she was finding Mutt's deterioration since her fall.

'Tell you what,' he offered casually, 'Nelly and I need a walk, we'll come with you over the cliff path. Or were you going to drive up?'

'No, no.' She shook her head quickly. 'That would be good. As long as I'm not taking you away from your sewers?'

'Bazalgette designed other things too,' he told her. 'Putney Bridge for one. But don't worry, you're not distracting me. I need to think out a few things and the walk will help.'

Joss closed her book, paused to check that Mutt was sleeping soundly, and slid quietly out of the room. She'd heard voices, kept low but still audible, the scrunch of boots on the gravel drive beneath the window, and had no wish for anyone to disturb her grandmother.

As she reached the turn in the stairs she saw that her mother had come in and was taking off her coat in the hall below. The expression on Emma's down-turned face, the little frowning look of mingled worry and fear, checked Joss's step and she paused in the shadowy corner, fixed by a familiar mix of emotions: tremendous affection for her mother intertwined with occasional bursts of irritation at Emma's refusal to stand up for her own principles against her husband. Joss could not remember at what point in her life she'd become aware of her father's acquisitive, insensitive brand of morality, but she'd soon learned that no one outside his immediate family was allowed to benefit from, share in, or receive any portion of his—not inconsiderable—wealth. Even when it came to Christmas or birthday presents, his jovial, 'And what did that cost, I wonder?' or, 'And does Mummy really want another scarf?' managed to spoil all the pleasure she'd had in saving for and choosing the gift.

It was such a relief, once he'd left Henley for the London flat each Monday morning, to revel in four days free from his bantering criticism. Joss suspected that it was these few days of freedom that enabled her mother to cope with those small humiliations in front of her close friends and his regular lectures on thrift. Joss found it hard to believe that her mother could be truly happy with her father.

'How can you bear it?' she'd cried to her mother, after he'd discovered that Emma had lent a very close—but unreliable—friend some money and Joss had witnessed the scene that followed. 'How can you stand his meanness?'

'He's been a good father to you, darling,' she'd answered with her usual loyalty. 'I know that he can be insensitive, which at your age can be difficult to deal with, but you mustn't be too hard on him. He's made sure that we both have absolute security . . .'

'But everything he gives has a price tag. With him, nothing's unconditional, is it? He has to have a return.'

'Security is very important to him; you'll understand that better when you have children of your own. After all, Joss, everything he has will be yours one day.'

'I don't want it,' she'd answered childishly. 'I'll earn my own money.'

How hard she'd worked to earn money during her training—refusing to take a penny from her father, who jeered at any kind of alternative medicine—taking on jobs in bars to pay for any extras. It was Mutt who'd believed in her. Without appearing to take sides, Mutt nourished and encouraged her granddaughter and gave as much financial help as she could. Emma, caught between them all, worried for her daughter's physical ability to cope with her extra jobs as well as her degree.

'You'll kill yourself before you start,' she'd said. 'You look exhausted, darling. Why can't you just ignore him? Underneath all that nonsense he's anxious for you. Look, let me help you . . .'

'I can't, Mum,' she'd said, hating herself for causing the misery on her mother's face. 'I shall manage.'

Bruno's generosity had been life-saving on occasions.

'I suppose Mum's been getting at you,' Joss had said ungraciously once or twice—but his wry look always managed to call her own smile into being. 'Sorry,' she'd mutter. 'It's just I can't take anything from either of them when I know how much he despises what I'm doing.'

'Just take it, girl, and don't be so prickly,' he'd advise, pushing a cheque or some notes into her bag. 'I promise you I hold no brief for Brer Fox's views, and my money's my own to do what I like with.'

'Why?' she'd asked him once—just as she'd asked her mother. 'Why did she marry him, Bruno? He's just . . . so *not* Mum. She's so warm and kind and loving, and he calculates everything. What did she see in him?'

He'd been silent for a while. 'You have to remember,' he'd answered at last, 'that, for women, marriage was much more important thirty years ago than it is now. Your father was a very good-looking, successful fellow and Mutt approved of him. She saw—with justice—that he'd look after her daughter and so she encouraged him. Emma had no experience to fall back on and was rather flattered by his absolute determination to have her. The fact is, Joss, that nobody can judge a marriage. However close you are to it, you'll never understand what makes it work or see the million tiny invisible strands that hold a couple together. Emma is very loving and very loyal—to both of you—and it's not for either of us to judge her. Just don't make it more difficult for her.'

Now, standing in the shadowy turn of the stairs, Joss's heart speeded with remorse and love.

'Hello, Mum,' she said, hurrying down. 'Did you have a good trip?'

Emma hugged her daughter warmly. 'No problems at all,' she said. 'How's Mutt?'

'Sleeping. I was just going to have a cup of tea and then we'll take some up for her. How long can you stay?'

'Oh, for a few days at least. Your father's up in London at the flat, meetings and so on. You're looking very well, Joss. I thought you'd be feeling the strain. Mousie told me that you're being such a help to her. So, anything new?'

'Actually,' Joss said slowly, 'rather an odd thing happened yesterday. Someone came looking for a relative. He was hoping that Mutt knew her out in India . . .'

'Who is Lottie?'

Emma stood with her back to the fire, leafing through the new paperback edition of Bruno's most recent book. Receiving no answer to her question, she glanced towards the kitchen and raised her voice a little.

'Bruno? Did you hear me? Do we know anyone called Lottie?'

There was the noise of the oven door being shut, water gushed briefly and, when he finally appeared, Bruno was drying his hands on a rather ragged towel. 'Sorry. Lottie?' He shook his head. 'Why do you ask?'

'Something Mutt was saying earlier.' She held the book up. 'Nice cover. Looks good, doesn't it? Very modern.'

He took it from her. 'I'm very pleased with it,' he admitted. 'Apparently the back list is going to be packaged in the same format.' A pause while he turned the paperback over in his hands, studying it. 'So what was Mutt saying?'

'Oh, she was rambling rather.' Emma kicked at a smouldering log and bent to take another from the big basket beside the hearth. 'Joss mentioned the name too. I wondered if it might have anything to do with this American who was here yesterday.'

Bruno put the book down carefully on the long table that stood at the back of the room, facing the bay window.

'I haven't heard about an American,' he said. Rather mechanically he began to tidy the table. 'What did he want?'

'He wrote, so Joss said, saying that he's looking for a relative who might have been out in India at the same time as Daddy and Mutt. He sent a photograph of this aunt, or whatever, with the letter to see if Mutt recognised her and then he turned up yesterday afternoon hoping to have a chat with her.' Satisfied with the blaze, Emma perched on the arm of the sofa. 'Joss wondered whether it might have stirred up some memories for her.'

'And did Mutt recognise this . . . relative from the photograph?' asked Bruno, after a moment.

Emma shrugged. 'From what I can gather, Mousie's playing it a bit low-key. She wouldn't let the young man see Mutt but I think she read his letter to her. Joss said Mutt called out Lottie's name several times in her sleep.' She frowned. 'It sounds odd but it kind of rang a bell.'

She looked at him hopefully, but he shook his head. 'Not with me,' he said firmly. 'And if you want a bath before supper you'd better get a move on.'

When she'd gone, collecting up various belongings, pouring a glass of wine to take upstairs with her, Bruno stretched out a hand to Nellie—but it was an automatic gesture and his thoughts were elsewhere.

Emma is not yet four years old when she first asks that question. Halfway up the cliff, out of breath from the steep climb, they sit together on spongy, springy turf, staring over the silky surface of the bosomy sea that gently lifts and swells below them. A fishing boat chugs north, heading towards Port Isaac, and Bruno gulps down deep breaths of delicious salty air, feeling the cool breeze tugging his hair. He looks sideways at Emma: her hair is fine and fair as candy floss and the sun shines through it so that she appears to have a halo. Her pudgy fingers pluck at the grass and her gaze is fixed, thoughtful.

'Who is Lottie?' she asks him.

Abruptly, Bruno allows himself to fall backwards on the turf. He closes his eyes, not only against the sun but also to keep the question outside. There were so many questions when they first arrived in St Meriadoc nearly two years ago.

'Goodness!' Aunt Julia cried, half amused, half shocked. 'Why do you call your mother "Mutt"? Does she allow it?'

He felt panic rising inside him as memories of that last dreadful week in India edged back into his consciousness.

And dear Mousie smiled at him—oh, how he loves Mousie!—and said, 'You're just like your father. He always gave people nicknames, do you remember, Mother? It was Hubert who called me Mousie.'

'But "Mutt",' Aunt Julia murmured, 'it sounds so disrespectful,' and it was Mutt, herself, who said, 'Oh, I'm used to it now. It was his way of saying "Mother" when he was very small. Please don't worry him about it. He's been through quite enough, poor little fellow . . .'

As he lies in the sunshine, the sun hot on his face, Emma prises with her small fingers at his tightly closed eyelids. He rolls away from her, over and over, and she scrambles after him, shrieking with laughter, her question forgotten.

The smell of stewed fruit, spilling over the side of the saucepan onto the hotplate, brought Bruno back abruptly to the present. He cursed beneath his breath and hurried out to the kitchen, where he snatched up the saucepan and dropped it hastily on the draining board. Then he opened the oven door to check the stew and turn the potatoes, which were baking in their jackets on the shelf beside it. Closing the door again, he began to assemble knives and forks but he was preoccupied: part irritated, part anxious. It was difficult, almost impossible, at this critical moment to detach himself from the world he was creating, to re-engage with reality, and part of him resented Emma's arrival and the need to entertain her. He longed to be alone: to go back into his study to pore over old documents and books.

Yet it had seemed churlish to refuse Emma's request to come and stay when Mutt was ill and Mousie already stretched in caring for her. Bruno paused, his hands full of clashing spoons and forks, anxiety gnawing in his gut. Just how ill, he wondered, was Mutt? Unease edged his mind towards sealed-off places and reminded it of voices long since silenced.

The gurgling and splashing of the bath water pouring away, forced him to concentrate on the present, and by the time Emma appeared, the table was set, candles were lit, and Bruno was opening a can of dog food with Nellie in close attendance. Emma sighed contentedly and topped up her glass from the bottle on the long sideboard, looking affectionately at the familiar scene. A modern oil painting of the harbour at Port Isaac hung on the whitewashed stone wall alongside a charcoal drawing of The Lookout, clinging to the precipitous cliff. She turned to look at the huge, framed, black-and-white photograph, that hung over the sideboard, opposite the big granite hearth. It showed a Paris boulevard, passers-by stepping round the pavement café, a Citroën parked at the kerb. The girl's head was turned a little aside, chin up, but the long, narrow eyes looked straight at the camera; indifferent yet provocative.

Bruno came in carrying the casserole dish, saw the direction of Emma's gaze and hoped that they were not about to embark on a discussion of his ex-wife.

'Dinner is served,' he said cheerfully with a mock bow. He lifted the lid and plunged a spoon into the lamb stew, used a threadbare linen napkin to put a hot potato on Emma's plate. The warm room seemed to close in a little, leaning as if to listen, and Emma settled comfortably into a chair, ready now for confidences and gossip.

Mousie woke early in her cottage at the end of The Row. The room brimmed with quivering sea-light and she lay still, savouring the cosy comfort of warm blankets, watching the milk-blue sky beyond the window. Except on those wild nights, when a northwesterly gale whipped the sea halfway up the cliffs and drove rain against the cold glass panes, she hated to sleep with the curtains closed.

This morning, she let her thoughts drift between the duties and pleasures of the day ahead: Joss would be off to Wadebridge, busy with her patients all day, so she would go straight up to the house after breakfast; seize the opportunity of some time alone with Emma; write and post the birthday card for Tom, Olivia's eldest. What a relief that Emma would be able to stay with Honor while she caught up with a few tasks.

It was odd, thought Mousie as she pulled the bedclothes more closely around her shoulders, that the arrival of the young American had filled her with such a strong sense of apprehension. After all, there was no reason why he shouldn't pursue his quest and the photograph was certainly an important lead. It was such a shock to see it again, after so many years, and it was obvious that Honor had been affected by it too.

Mousie was pierced by remorse. Why had she never quite been able to drift into the habit of calling Honor by the foolish little nickname? There was still something that blocked such familiarity between them. Thinking now of the numbed, bewildered little family when they had first arrived in England, she could remember how she'd watched Honor with a clear, cool eye, ready to disapprove.

After the long sea passage, Honor seems disorientated—confused by this homecoming to an unknown home, keeping her children close.

It is as if, thinks Mousie, Hubert's young widow has been silenced by her grief, made dumb by sorrow.

'She won't talk to me,' Mousie says to her mother. 'Not properly. And she seems afraid to let the children out of her sight.'

'Think back to how we were when Daddy was killed,' advises her mother. 'I know it's six years ago now but remember how we all clung together? They are suffering from shock and it takes time to recover from these dreadful things. And, after all, Honor is a stranger here. When we came back to St Meriadoc we'd looked upon it as a second home ever since you and Rafe were babies. Honor knows only what Hubert has told her.'

And Mousie, ashamed of her jealousy, tries harder—inviting Honor to accompany her on walks and to talk about Hubert, but any encouragement to share the past is met with resistance. Honor, it seems, simply cannot bear to dwell on what she has lost. Yet Mousie notices that Honor spends long periods talking to Hubert's frail, elderly father. She comes upon them sitting beneath the lilac trees in the Paradise gardens. Uncle James is in his old steamer chair, Honor is half turned towards him, her face animated.

'He specialised in tropical fevers . . .' she is saying. 'He was quite brilliant. Everyone loved him . . .'

Bruno leans against her knee, his face bright, as if through her words his father lives again, while Emma staggers about the sunny lawn, wrenching pink-tipped daisies from the grass. The old man watches Honor, a smile pulling at his lips.

At her approach, the small group seems to solidify into watchfulness.

Uncle James peers towards her beneath the sweet-scented flowers and Honor instinctively holds Bruno close against her side. Only Emma is untouched, shouting with pleasure at the freedom of the garden.

'Hello, Mousie,' Honor calls; she uses the nickname with no apparent effort or awkwardness, yet Mousie still feels excluded from intimacy, and the moment never arrives when she is able to return the compliment. Only Bruno and Emma use the cheerful little name that links the three of them to the past.

The shrill, insistent bell of her alarm clock shocked Mousie fully awake and drove her from her warm nest, shivering into the bathroom. Her cottage was small and neat: just the right amount of space for someone who was positively Franciscan in her minimalist needs. It was because of this trait that Hubert had nicknamed her when she was a child; her liking for small nooks and odd corners, combined with her horror of excess—large portions of food, too many belongings—had inspired him. His son Bruno, taking up the tradition years later, referred to her little cottage as 'The Wainscot'.

Mousie grinned as she pulled on warm trousers and a thick jersey. Bruno was so like Hubert and she loved him very dearly; but then Bruno was so easy to love. Mousie sighed, regretting the readiness to criticise that had so defined her early relationship with Honor.

Next door, Rafe and Pamela clattered about, each interrupting the other as they discussed the exciting prospect of the arrival of their son, George.

'Just for one night.' Rafe picked up the postcard, received yesterday, and read the words out loud again. '"A quick dash to see you all. Penny and Tasha won't be with me." Let's hope he has a good run down.' He cracked eggs into a white china bowl and switched on the coffee percolator. 'It's odd that he's coming on his own.'

'It's a bit of an upheaval just for one night'—Pamela rationalised her disappointment, excusing Penny—'when you've got a baby to organise. Perhaps Penny thinks it would be nice for us to have him to ourselves.'

She wished that she was able to see the faces of her grandchildren. Mousie and Rafe did their best to describe them for her: Mousie was very good at it, painting in the tiny details of each child, remarking on the likeness to a parent or some other relative, until Pamela was able to form an idea of the faces of the new members of her growing family.

'See if you can catch Joss before she goes off to Wadebridge,' she said suddenly to Rafe. 'Perhaps she could come in for some supper. I can smell burning. Is the toast stuck again?'

Rafe dealt briskly with the toaster, shared the scrambled eggs between two plates and carried them to the table, ducking automatically as he passed beneath the heavy beams. The two middle cottages of The Row had been converted into one larger dwelling and, when his mother, Julia, died, Rafe had moved back into it with his young wife and their baby daughter, Olivia. His view was that the quiet beauty of St Meriadoc more than made up for a higher salary and career opportunities upcountry. Pamela, already pregnant with Joe, gazed at the cottage, the shining sea, the tumbling cliffs, and agreed with heartfelt gratitude.

'It's so beautiful here,' she'd said. 'I've loved being in Exeter—and I know you'll find sixth-form colleges a bit different from university lecturing—but, oh, Rafe, this valley is *such* a place to bring up children. It's good of Mutt to let us have it so cheaply. She could earn much more money letting it to holidaymakers. Or I suppose she could sell it?'

He'd shaken his head. 'Probably not. I don't know how Uncle James left the estate but I imagine it would have passed from Hubert into some kind of trust for Bruno and Emma. We don't come from that side of the family. Uncle James's wife was my mother's sister and they took us in during the war when Father died. Well, you know the story.'

Watching her now, as she reached for the toast, her fingers testing the side of one of the small pots of conserve for the raised shape of the orange—marmalade, today, rather than strawberry jam—he felt such love for her. He did everything possible to enable her, suppressing the early instinctive reaction to protect, quickly seeing how much could be done to give back some of the freedom this swift descent into blindness had snatched from her. They'd stride arm-in-arm together over the windy hills, plunging down into the sheltered lanes, pausing so that she could identify the birds—'I can hear a robin . . . and there's a buzzard somewhere.' He'd put a creamy crown of honeysuckle into her hand and watch her frown of concentration smooth into delighted recognition as she held it against her face, breathing its heavy evocative scent, reliving long-ago sunny afternoon walks.

The light on the percolator glowed red and he stood up to pour out two cups of coffee.

'Odd, though,' her voice from behind him echoed his own secret thought, 'that George sent a card. I wonder why he didn't ring us?'

Mutt woke to confusion and a clutching fear. The letters must be found and there was something else . . . Joss was bending over her and, gazing up at her, Mutt seemed to be looking at herself when young; those level brows, that short, straight nose and the widely curling mouth, these features had all been there in the photograph Mousie had shown her. She felt hot and weak; dimly she perceived danger lurking: for herself and

226

for Joss. She clung to Joss's hands as if she were her rescuer. 'The letters,' her voice creaked and cracked. 'My letters, darling.'

Her granddaughter's hands were blessedly cool, her short hair— cropped below her ears and falling over her hazel eyes—was brown and shiny as seaweed. The old woman in the bed was stilled briefly by the clean, calm beauty of her young face. She lay back on the pillows and tried to marshal her thoughts, breathing as deeply as she could while this terrible band of pain gripped her chest.

Joss watched her anxiously, concerned by the wheezing sound that whistled between her grandmother's lips. She wished that Mousie would arrive and, still holding Mutt's hand, glanced surreptitiously at her watch. Yet she maintained her outward calm and managed to smile.

'Mousie will be here soon,' she said rather cheerfully, as if it were to be a social visit. 'Would you like some cordial? I suppose we'd better get the nasty bit over first.'

She took the small plastic measure of medicine and Mutt swallowed obediently, choking a little, and relaxed against Joss's arm. Her panic subsiding a little, Mutt inhaled more slowly; she knew now exactly where her letters were. The temporary relief from pain brought the clearing of her mind.

'Will you do something for me?' She watched Joss pour the cordial. 'It's private. Just between you and me. Do you promise?'

'Of course.'

Joss's instinctive response was to comfort rather than to bind herself, but the old woman sensed this and struggled up a little. She sipped at the cordial impatiently, almost out of politeness, then held the glass away from her mouth with trembling hands.

'No more. It's important, Joss darling. A real promise.'

Joss stood the glass back on the tray. 'I'll do what I can, Mutt,' she said, puzzled by such urgency. 'But Mum will be here soon. Wouldn't it be better—'

'No.' She shook her head, vehemently. 'Only you.'

'OK. I'll do my best.' Joss sounded dubious.

'Find the letters,' muttered Mutt. 'Don't tell anyone. Promise.'

The hand she stretched out was hot, and Joss nodded, frightened by her grandmother's terrible urgency and this descent into breathlessness.

'I promise,' she mumbled.

It was with great relief that she heard the front door click shut and Mousie's voice calling from the hall below. She shouted an answer and her grandmother opened her eyes again, fighting the familiar confusion, clinging to this new comfort.

'Don't forget,' she whispered as her granddaughter bent to kiss her.

Half running down the drive, Joss felt unhappy and very anxious. Part of her was pleased that Mutt had not told her where the letters were: clearly she could do nothing without that information yet she had made the promise. Was it right to keep something private between them at this stage of her grandmother's life? What could it be that must be kept secret from her own children?

Joss forced herself to slow down. Out in the lane she gasped in lungfuls of freezing air, heard the iced-over puddles splinter beneath her feet. The black hawthorn twigs were rimed with frost and, in the ditch, a rabbit's sudden flight crumbled last year's crisped, brittle leaves to powder. At the field gate she stopped, climbing a rung or two, feeling in her big bag for the apples she'd bought for the donkeys, Rumpleteazer and Mungojerrie. These were the latest in a long line of animals from the sanctuary, who'd come to enjoy the peace of the meadow here at St Meriadoc. They came towards her, breath steaming, heavy heads nodding, and she spoke quietly to them, stroking their velvety muzzles and pulling at their ears.

She finally reached the quarry and her car in a much more positive mood. Mutt was feverish, she reminded herself, silly to get so upset.

Across the road Rafe had appeared, calling from the door, and Joss turned quickly, fumbling with her keys.

'George is coming down,' he was saying. 'Only for the night but Pamela says that you must come in and have some supper.'

She nodded, pointing at her watch and miming the need for haste, and climbed into the car. It was like sitting in a fridge but the engine started at the third go. Driving carefully, heading away from St Meriadoc towards Wadebridge, she grappled with this new complication. Her love for George was still the best-kept secret in the world. Only she and George knew of it and, though her instinct assured her that he loved her too, his marriage made it impossible for him to acknowledge it openly. Oh, how she loved him . . . Joss gave a cry of fear as she pressed down incautiously on the accelerator and the back wheels slipped across a patch of ice.

Concentrate, she told herself. Forget Mutt. Forget George. Think about the morning ahead.

She liked to be at the practice early, at least half an hour before the first patient was due to arrive or the telephone started to ring. By sharing rooms—renting a consulting room and a waiting room on the ground floor at a dentist's practice—she had the benefit of the place always being clean and warm, of having other personnel in the building, and even a share in the car park. She was hopeful that her practice would grow and, meanwhile, the income derived from working as an assistant to a well-established osteopath in Bodmin for two days a week helped with the bills.

Who was first on the list this morning? Joss took a deep breath and began to focus her mind on the day ahead.

'There goes Joss.' From the curved living-room window of The Lookout, Emma could see across to The Row as well as far out to sea. 'The sun is just touching the roofs. Ray always says that it's a shame that we don't get much sun down here in the valley in winter.'

'Yes, I can well imagine that Brer Fox would blow up some cliffs to make a place more attractive to the masses and earn himself a fast buck. It's impossible for him to appreciate the countryside unless it's in the terms of property development.'

Emma moved back into the room, hugging her long fleecy robe more tightly about her generous figure.

'He is rather tiresome at the moment,' she admitted. 'You know, talking about what he'd do if Mutt . . . well, when Mutt dies.' Her worried expression trembled into distaste.

'Do about what?' Bruno was sitting at the table, spooning porridge from a large bowl. 'He hardly ever sees her now. What difference will it make to him?'

During breakfast he'd been mentally blocking out his next chapter, but, once again, reality was forcing him into an anxious awareness.

'Well, not much,' she agreed, shrugging, 'but you know what I mean. Oh, I'm well aware of what you think about Ray, but you'd have to be supernaturally disinterested not even to consider what would happen, wouldn't you?'

'I don't see why anything should change.' He put the bowl down for Nellie to lick and stood up. Anxiety battled with the overwhelming need to get back to his own internal world and he felt restless and edgy. 'Why are we talking about Mutt dying, anyway? She's broken her ankle and now she has a chill. Is it really serious? Mousie hasn't said so.'

Emma stared at him thoughtfully. 'Odd, isn't it?' she observed. 'We've been coming here all these years, me and Zoë, and then Olivia and Joss too, whenever we've been in trouble. And you've sorted us out and got us kick-started again. But with Mutt it's like you just don't want to accept that she's old and frail and ill.'

'It's not the same at all,' he answered irritably. 'Let's not get onto that one, shall we? Won't Mousie be waiting for you?'

Emma burst out laughing. 'Ten out of ten for subtlety, dear bro. But yes, I must get a move on. Are you coming up to the house with me?'

He hesitated. 'Will it be a bit much for Mutt? All of us at once? Tell her I'll be up about tea-time as usual . . .' He frowned, feeling guilty.

'And anyway, you want to work,' she prompted, grinning.

He grinned back at her. 'I don't have a wealthy spouse to support me. Only an ex-wife who still thinks it's my duty to bail her out of trouble at regular intervals.'

Emma's smile died, the old, familiar protectiveness aroused. 'Zoë has absolutely no right to exploit your good nature. Why should you have to support her when she walked out on you? What about all those other lovers she's had?'

'Give it a rest,' he said, hands raised, palms outward. 'I'm not in the mood. Go and get some clothes on before Mousie phones up wondering where you are.'

She trailed away, retying the belt on her robe, her expression sulky, resenting Zoë's presence in their lives.

The room seemed to settle and expand a little around Bruno now he was alone again. He strolled over to the window and, hands in pockets, stared down towards The Row and, beyond it, to the corrugated iron structure of the old boathouse. Under its roof, at the top of the slipway, was his old boat the *Kittiwake*. Another smaller sailing boat sat nearby on a trailer. George owned the *Enterprise*, and Bruno wondered if there might be time for them to get out for a sail at some point while George was down. He glanced seawards: the sea, flat as a shelf, was banded with bars of silver, and there was no breath of wind.

He found that he was thinking about George: how he'd come upon him, standing with Joss one hot afternoon last summer, high up the valley beside St Meriadoc's Well, listening to a lark singing high above them. There'd been some tension between them that caught his attention. They'd smiled at him in a dazed kind of way, and he'd suddenly realised why, much to the whole family's puzzlement, Joss didn't get serious with her boyfriends . . .

'See you later.' Emma was waving to him from the doorway, her sunny good humour restored. 'Enjoy your trip down London's sewers. No, Nellie, you can't come this time. Sorry, old girl.'

Bruno began to collect the breakfast things together, relieved that the subject of his ex-wife had been avoided for once. From the very beginning Zoë and Emma had crossed swords and his loyalty to each had been severely strained. He piled the dishes beside the sink, let Nellie out for her morning potter and allowed his mind to flow back into its natural channels of creativity. However, now that he was able to return to his own world he felt that, mysteriously, it was closed to him. All he could think about was Zoë: bringing her home to Paradise and introducing her to Mutt before taking her down to show her The Lookout.

At twenty-three, just out of naval college, he is well aware that Zoë is outside his experience; he cannot take his eyes off her. Conscious of his admiration, she slightly exaggerates her movements, swinging her hips in the tight black miniskirt, crossing her legs in long black leather boots. The Mary Quant bob suits her thick black hair. Zoë always wears black: she is sophisticated and sharply aware of her image. Not quite as famous as The Shrimp or Twiggy, she is, nevertheless, much in demand: a waif-like gamine with an air of weary boredom; a black-eyed stare that challenges. There is nothing naive about Zoë.

She is impressed, however, by St Meriadoc, lying in its sheltering valley, and the fact that, one day, Bruno will inherit this charming little estate elevates him in her estimation.

'Nice, darling,' she says, wandering round the big room with its curving window, digging a crumpled packet of Sobranies out of her bag. 'So this is your pad?'

He hurries to light her cigarette with the smart Dunhill lighter she's given him for his twenty-third birthday. 'Yes,' he says. 'Yes, The Lookout is mine.'

That's how it's always been. 'You can have The Lookout,' Emma says, 'and I'll have Paradise,' although neither of them takes it too seriously.

In his final year at school, Bruno works hard redecorating The Lookout so that his friends can come to stay. It's good to get away from the constraints of the house and have some fun, and Mutt is very understanding. She allows him to take down some unwanted furniture and discarded curtains, enough to furnish it adequately. He celebrates his twenty-first birthday with a party at The Lookout, with his fellow officers from the naval college.

'We had a ball,' he tells Zoë casually. 'Drank too much and went swimming off the slipway at midnight.'

'Great,' she says indifferently, turning from the window. She grinds out her cigarette in the hastily proffered ashtray, her eyes on his. 'So what's the scene upstairs?'

Though grateful for the experience gained on various runs ashore in Holland and Sweden, Bruno is almost relieved when they hear a door slam and Emma's voice echoing up the stairs. He mutters apologies, tucking in his shirt, hurrying down to meet her.

'Mutt said you'd be here,' she says. 'I can't wait to meet Zoë.'

'I was just showing her round upstairs,' he says awkwardly.

Zoë descends the stairs slowly, aware of Emma's fascinated gaze, meeting Bruno's eyes with a secret smile. While Bruno introduces them he senses antagonism on both sides: Zoë lets Emma see that she thinks her unsophisticated and of little account; Emma is knocked out of her stride by such sophistication coupled with barely concealed indifference. For the first time Bruno is caught between two women—between, on one side, strong physical desire and, on the other, deep affection and loyalty—but at twenty-three there is no contest.

'You can't marry her,' cries Emma. 'She's all wrong for you. Don't be confused by sex.'

But he *is* confused by it: confused, drugged and drowning in it. Zoë is chosen to market a famous brand of cigarette and her image is to be seen everywhere: staring down from posters and out of the shiny pages of popular magazines. The photograph becomes an icon and he feels excited and overwhelmed each time he sees it.

She gives him the huge framed copy, which hangs in The Lookout, as a wedding present.

'Mutt looks better today,' said Emma hopefully. 'Don't you think so, Mousie? She seems calmer and her mind is surprisingly clear.'

She was busy at the ironing board, pressing and folding sheets with swift, economical movements, while Mousie sat at the kitchen table, peeling and dicing vegetables for soup.

'The antibiotics are helping,' she said—yet she felt that it was something more than that; as if a burden had been lifted and Mutt had relaxed for the first time in several days. Mousie looked thoughtfully at Emma, who was now ironing one of Mutt's nightgowns.

'Did Joss tell you about our American pilgrim?' she asked lightly.

'Yes, she did.' Emma set the iron on its rest. 'A rather good-looking chap, I gather, who was trying to track down an aunt.'

'Great-aunt,' said Mousie, almost absently. 'Does the name Madeleine Grosjean ring any bells?'

Emma frowned. 'I don't think so. Was that her name?'

'Apparently. He said that she knew your parents out in India.' Mousie deftly scraped the last peelings into some newspaper. 'She might have been a nurse.'

'Oh, well.' Emma shrugged. 'That's a closed book to me. I wasn't quite two when we came home.'

'Mmm.' Mousie seemed distracted. 'Did you ever see any photographs?'

'Mutt's got a few photos but those little black-and-white snapshots aren't very revealing, are they? Bruno and I have each got a very nice cabinet-size photo of Daddy taken when he first went out.'

Mousie stood up, carried the vegetables to the sink, rinsed them and turned them out into a large saucepan containing a rich, meaty stock.

Emma sighed in pleasurable anticipation. 'It's nice, isn't it?' she said spontaneously to Mousie. 'Being together like this, I mean. The clean smells of the ironing and delicious food cooking on the Aga, and having a good old gossip. Bruno would say that it all goes back to the hunter-gatherers. All those millions of years with women gathering and spending all that time together while the men were off hunting.'

Mousie slipped an arm about Emma's shoulder and gave her a little hug but she was not distracted by Bruno's theory. An idea was growing in her mind and for some reason she was afraid of it.

'Have you ever seen a photograph of their wedding?' she asked. 'Honor's and Hubert's? It was a double wedding, you know. Hubert sent us a photograph. My father had just been lost with the sinking of the *Hood* and we came back to St Meriadoc. One of the cottages was empty so we were able to move in. You know all that, of course, but it was at that time that Hubert got married and sent the photograph.'

'I love all these stories about the family.' Emma folded a nightgown and placed it on the pile of crisply laundered items. 'How terrible it must have been for you all, Mousie. I do wish I could remember more. Do you know I can hardly even bring Grandfather to my mind? But then he died quite soon after we got home, didn't he? Thank goodness we had all of you. It must have been such a comfort for Mutt to come back to a ready-made family, especially when she'd lost her own parents so tragically in the Blitz.'

'We were very lucky,' agreed Mousie. 'All of us.' A pause. 'So you haven't seen the wedding photograph?'

Emma looked at her curiously. 'Have you still got it?'

'Not the one Hubert sent to us. Or, at least, if we have I don't know where it is. I just wondered if Honor might have had one somewhere. The American sent a copy of it. It was very odd, seeing it again after all these years.'

'I'd love to see it,' said Emma. 'Joss didn't show me the photograph, she just said he'd called.'

Mousie went out of the kitchen, crossed the hall to the drawing room, and picked up the large carpetbag which was lying beside an armchair. She stood quite still for a moment, the photograph in her hand, before returning to the kitchen.

'There.' She laid the print on the table and Emma bent over it eagerly. 'Have you seen it before?'

'Never.' Emma was smiling. 'Those ridiculous hats! But don't they look happy and—good gracious, Mousie, doesn't Joss look just like Mutt at that age?'

'That's what struck me,' agreed Mousie. 'It was quite a shock . . . Do you recognise the other woman at all?'

Emma picked up the photograph, holding it towards the light.

'I don't know.' She looked puzzled. 'There's something about her . . . Isn't it odd, though, Mousie—'

The sound of Mutt's handbell sounded through the house and the two women tensed.

'I'll go,' said Emma. 'I'll shout if I think you should come up.' She dropped the photograph on the table and disappeared, running up the stairs. Mousie picked up the print and stared at it.

She thought: I wonder what happened to Madeleine Grosjean.

George Boscowan parked his car in the old quarry and sat for a moment, summoning up the courage to break the news to his parents.

'You have to tell them,' Penny had said. 'No, I can't come with you. I just can't face them. Sorry, George.'

'Please, Penny.' He'd made another effort. 'Look, I don't have to stay in the navy if you hate it that much. Of *course* I can imagine how much you miss your family, especially when I'm at sea. Look, we can all go to New Zealand. Why not? Make a new start together.'

'Are you crazy?'

She'd stared at him in such horror that he'd realised with a shock that the idea of him being with her in her own country, among her own people, was completely unacceptable to her. Mentally she'd already moved into a new life; a life where her lover, Brett Anderson, had usurped him. It was because Brett had broken off their engagement that Penny had come to England in the first place. Now he wanted her back.

'I think I must have been in love with him all the time,' she'd said pathetically. 'Only I *did* love you, George. And I still do. Oh, this is terrible. Can you love two people at once?'

Yes, he'd wanted to shout. Yes, you bloody can. I should know. But you can at least try to fight it. Instead, he'd grimaced bitterly, feeling betrayed by her readiness to break up their marriage.

'Brett left you before,' he'd said, 'he might do it again. And what about Tasha? How often am I going to see her with you in New Zealand?'

'You don't see her much now,' she'd answered unforgivably, upset by his pain but determined not to give an inch, 'you're away at sea so much.' And then, seeing his expression: 'I'm sorry, George,' she'd said sadly but with finality. 'I just belong back there with my family and friends—and with Brett. Tasha needs to be with me. Please, George, if you really love her you'll do what's best for her.'

He'd felt so angry by this manipulation of his love for her and their baby that he'd been obliged to walk out: striding away from the little house on the edge of Meavy village, climbing up onto the moor. Staring westwards into Cornwall, where the sunshine showered shafts of gold upon the distant hills, he'd thought of Joss—and felt the balled fist of guilt deep in his gut. It was Joss who'd listened while he'd poured out his worries that Penny missed her family, was lonely when he went to sea; Joss, with whom he had fallen suddenly in love, between one glance and the next, realising that his feelings for Penny were a dim reflection of this shattering experience. However, he'd been determined that it should not affect his commitment to Penny and their baby.

Now, he reached for his overnight bag, took a breath to steady his nerves, climbed out of the car and walked towards The Row.

As George opened the door, Pamela could sense at once that there was something wrong. Nevertheless, she smiled steadily into the darkness, waiting for him to come to her and kiss her; putting up her hands to clasp his shoulders, to touch his hair. His lips grazed her cheek, his 'Hi, Ma' was a warm breath in her ear, and then he'd moved away.

'What a morning,' Rafe was saying cheerfully. 'You must have got away early, George. We weren't expecting you quite yet. Have you got snow on Dartmoor?'

Pamela could hear the sounds of coffee being prepared, the screech of chair-legs as George sat down, the exchange of pleasantries, and she tensed, waiting for the blow to fall. Already she'd mentally rehearsed the possibilities: financial difficulties? Well, they'd certainly extended themselves when they'd bought the cottage in Meavy. Perhaps they'd come seriously unstuck and needed help. Her mind ranged to and fro, wondering how she and Rafe might raise money. They'd managed to save a small amount over the years, but the sum wasn't going to stretch far.

Perhaps Penny was lonely and had asked George to resign his commission? The trouble with that was, what could George do outside the navy that would earn him the same kind of money to support his family and the mortgage?

Pamela realised that an uncomfortable silence had fallen and grew instantly alert, listening: the kitchen clock ticked with an unnatural loudness, the sea whispered unceasingly from beyond the window.

'Look,' George was saying, 'I expect you've both guessed that this isn't just a friendly visit. The thing is . . .'

The thing was, apparently, that he and Penny had decided to separate, things weren't working out; they'd agreed that it was the best way and that Penny would be returning to New Zealand.

Rafe murmured something—she could imagine his shocked expression.

'Darling,' she said shakily. 'Oh, George, this is terrible. You've always seemed so happy. And what about Tasha . . . ?' Her voice trailed away uncertainly. Oh, how petty her former anxieties—so easily surmountable now, compared with the reality—had been.

Rafe was attempting to ease his son's path through the thickets of explanation: perhaps Penny had been too much alone or had George . . . ?

Pamela pressed her lips together, resolutely holding back the questions that she wanted to shout at him. If only she could see his face, read between the lines.

'Is there someone else?' she asked sharply—and heard George's swift intake of breath. 'No Slips,' she cried. 'Not now. What is it, George? What has happened to make you take this step?'

He was able to answer this honestly and did so. 'Penny was engaged before she came to England,' he told them flatly. 'The man, Brett Anderson his name is, broke it off and she came here to start a new life. Well, he's turned up again and she's decided that she's loved him all along and that she fell for me on the rebound. She says that her life is with him and her family in New Zealand.'

'But what will happen to Natasha?' Rafe was asking. 'Surely Penny can't expect you to give your child up so easily?'

His short laugh had no mirth in it. 'I'm between a rock and a hard place,' he said. 'I can't keep her, can I? How would I look after a three-month-old baby? And even if I could think of some way round it, would it be fair to her? Penny has a big family to support her . . .'

He stopped abruptly and Pamela, knowing why, felt quite unreasonably as though she had let him down.

'Oh, darling,' she said sorrowfully. 'I am so sorry. We're not much use to you, are we?'

'Don't be silly, Ma,' he said harshly. 'It's not your fault. It's simply that we have to face facts. I haven't got anyone who could look after Tasha while I'm away at sea and I don't know what the hell I'd do if I came outside. Tasha is better off with her mother than with strangers.'

Pamela was struggling with a variety of emotions: anguish for her son; despair at the thought of losing her grandchild; a momentary hatred of Penny, of whom she'd been so fond. She knew that George was loyal, independent, straight-talking, yet something nagged at the back of her mind; something was missing.

'It must be really serious'—she was feeling her way—'for Penny to react so drastically. She must feel very strongly to be doing this.'

'She does feel strongly,' said George after a moment. 'She says that she never stopped loving Brett, although she really did think she had. When she saw him again she realised the truth of it.' She sensed his shrug, heard his sigh. 'Well, I can understand that.'

She was onto it like a hound on the scent: *this* was what she'd been feeling for, this tone that indicated a true understanding of Penny's situation. Alongside the bitterness ran sympathy: the very real sympathy of someone who was struggling with the same dilemma. She responded to it instinctively. 'I think George should take his things upstairs and then have a serious drink,' she said. 'We all need to re-group.'

She waited, listening to George's departure, his footsteps on the stairs, then stretched her hand to Rafe who took it, holding it comfortingly.

'Telephone Bruno,' she told him urgently. 'Tell him to get hold of Joss and cancel supper. Tell him why if you have to. Hurry, before George comes back.'

Bruno picked up the message when he left his study to make himself some lunch. He kept the telephone in the kitchen, permanently on answerphone with the bell switched off. Now, he saw the red winking eye and pressed the PLAY button. Rafe's voice sounded odd: deliberately kept low, as if he feared to be overheard. Bruno listened, his brow furrowed with surprise.

George had a problem and it was best that Joss didn't come to supper: Could Bruno contact her and warn her off?

As he cut bread for a sandwich, Bruno pondered on this message. He had an unwelcome premonition that he might have guessed the possible reason for George's problem. Presently he telephoned a number. Joss answered in a flat voice, which indicated that she was with a patient.

'Sorry to interrupt,' he said. 'Message from Rafe. Supper seems to be off. George isn't on form.' He heard her breathing rather quickly. 'Make sense to you?' he asked lightly.

'Yes,' she said shortly.

'I thought it might.' He hesitated. 'Want to come in on your way home?'

He could hear her thinking about it: a desperate, almost violent mental exercise with half her mind still on her patient.

'May I?' she asked. 'Thanks, Bruno. About six?'

'Great,' he replied. 'See you then.'

Nellie had brought her toy to his feet, a brightly coloured rubber bone with a tinny bell in it that Bruno detested. She looked from it to him, tail wagging, flopping ears pricked hopefully, and he kicked it across the kitchen. She leaped after it, paws scrabbling, seizing it with delight. Now, after Rafe's message, Bruno decided that a walk would probably do them both good and, with luck, it might start the creative juices flowing again. Anyway, he wanted to see Mutt.

Emma was alone at Paradise. Mousie had gone to Polzeath to do some shopping, she told him, and would look in later on.

'We are so lucky to have her,' she said. 'Joss is doing what she can but

237

she has to keep her practice going and, after all, darling old Mousie is so experienced. Mutt seems calmer today, we both think so, though she's very weak. The doctor will be calling in a bit later. Go and talk to her.'

He went upstairs, relieved that he was able to have a moment alone with Mutt, wondering how he might broach a very difficult subject. He closed the door quietly behind him and stood for a moment, seeing that her eyes were closed. The sight of her, frail and tiny in the big bed, affected him powerfully. He remembered her as she'd been only a few months ago, at the end of the summer: still sailing with him in the *Kittiwake*, working with Rafe in the garden, walking over the cliffs and along the valley. She'd looked after them all: Paradise and the valley would seem empty indeed without Mutt's presence.

Trying to conceal his emotions, he crossed to the bed and kneeled down beside her, kissing her soft, wrinkled brow. He took her hand and shook it gently. She turned her head slowly on the pillow.

'Everything was for you and Emma, wasn't it?' she asked. He leaned close so as to hear her feeble voice. 'But now I want Joss to have Paradise.'

'Is that how you've left it in your will, Mutt?' he asked. 'Have you been explicit about the estate?'

She frowned as if remembering something, her eyes sliding away as if she could no longer meet his own. 'I've been a fool.' She took an uneven breath. 'Forgive me.'

'Nothing to forgive,' he told her firmly. 'Remember how happy we've been. You kept us together as a family.'

Tears squeezed beneath her papery lids and she clutched his hand tightly. 'You'll look after them, I know that,' she whispered with difficulty. 'But I did so want Joss to have Paradise.'

He leaned forward to kiss her. 'I promise to look after Joss,' he said clearly, his lips close to her ear.

Before she could answer, the door opened and Emma appeared. Bruno sat back on his heels as she approached the bed and, releasing the thin hand, stood up and walked away to the window.

'I think she should rest now.' After a few moments Emma joined him, speaking in a low voice. 'I'll come and sit with her for a while but shall we go downstairs and have a cup of tea first?'

He followed her down to the kitchen but he knew that, in his present mood, it would be quite impossible to sit cosily over the teacups.

'Do you mind if I crack on?' he asked. 'Poor old Nellie needs a walk and I'd like to get a bit more work done. We can have some time together after supper.'

She responded at once to the suggestion: those after-supper times with Bruno were terribly important to her.

'I might be a bit late, though,' she warned him. 'I don't know what time Mousie will be back but I said we'd have something together here.'

'Doesn't matter,' he said. 'Whenever. Come on, Nellie.' But, at the door, he hesitated, suddenly conscious of Emma's fears and anxieties. 'Are you going to be OK?' he asked.

'Of course I am.' She was touched by his concern. 'To tell you the truth I rather like being here on my own. It's so peaceful.'

He stooped and kissed her cheek, turned quickly away, and she watched him stride off down the drive, surprised at this unusual display of affection. She thought: He's upset by the way Mutt looks. I expect he wants to be on his own for a bit to come to terms with it.

But Bruno wasn't thinking about Mutt. He was remembering how, thirty years before, Emma had introduced him to the young Raymond Fox.

It is a warm evening in June and the big windows are open to the swelling sea. The room is washed by golden light and full of sweet, fresh air. Fiddling with a dish of olives, wishing that Zoë would appear, Bruno checks his watch for the third time. It is at his suggestion that Emma is bringing Raymond to The Lookout. Instinctively, Bruno has arranged this meeting on his own ground: Emma's descriptions of Raymond Fox, twelve years her senior, make him sound formidable. Already he is the junior partner in a company of City stockbrokers, he has inherited a highly desirable town house in Henley and owns a flat in London.

With his short-term commission ended and his first book attracting attention, Bruno need not feel overshadowed by such a reputation. Nevertheless, there is an air of contest here. As he pours himself a drink he hears their voices: Emma's light and rather breathless; and the pleasant baritone accompanying it, measured, calm, confident.

He lets them come in to him, Emma leading the way and calling out as they pass through the kitchen, and the next minute they are here. She makes the introductions, cheeks flushed with that odd blend of pride and defiance, while Raymond holds out a large square hand. His handsome face is oddly lacking in expression, as if it has been carved from brown, lightly pitted wood, and his light grey eyes are watchful.

'Nice little place,' Raymond says, strolling to the window. 'Damp in the winter, though, I should think, isn't it?'

'The whole of Cornwall is damp,' answers Bruno coolly, 'winter and summer alike.'

He pours Emma's usual gin and tonic and holds the bottle questioningly towards Raymond.

'Got any Scotch?' he asks genially—as if he doubts that Bruno will be so sophisticated—and Bruno pours some malt whisky into a tumbler, his mouth compressed into a thin line of irritation.

'Very narrow little cove, isn't it?' Raymond remarks, sipping his drink, peering downwards. 'Not easy to sail from, I imagine.'

'Not very,' answers Bruno. 'Apart from anything else there are very dangerous rocks right across the entrance.'

'Pity.' Raymond frowns judicially. 'But you could make a nice little killing if you were to knock down that old boatyard and build a hotel.'

It is at this moment that Zoë makes her entrance, coming down the stairs, yawning, her black eyes taking in the scene. Her feet are bare, she wears one of Bruno's shirts and little else, and she looks bed-rumpled and terribly sexy.

Emma's face grows sulky and cross, Raymond's hands go instinctively to his tie and Bruno chuckles inwardly.

'Hello, love,' he says. 'All dressed ready for dinner, I see.'

Zoë's eyes wander over Emma's pretty frock and Raymond's London suit and, although she doesn't speak, Emma feels frumpy and Raymond overdressed. He steps forward, however, undiminished by her glance and introduces himself.

'And I know who you are,' he adds playfully, though she has made no effort to tell him her name.

She turns away from him, reaching for the drink Bruno has poured for her. 'Everyone knows who I am,' she says indifferently. 'You didn't say we had to dress up, darling.'

Emma stares at her. 'You weren't coming up to dinner like that, were you?' She laughs, an artificial sound. 'Honestly, Zoë. Mutt would have a fit, you know she would.'

'Well, of course not,' Zoë says impatiently. She yawns again. 'I'm going to have a bath,' she says, trailing away, carrying her drink, pausing to stretch on tiptoe so as to kiss Bruno.

'Hurry.' Bruno pushes her towards the stairs, still amused at the performance, grateful for the distraction that has pre-empted a row between him and his putative brother-in-law. He sees trouble ahead.

'You can't marry him,' he tells Emma later.

'Mutt really likes him,' she says stubbornly. 'She thinks he's reliable and steady.'

'Reliable?' He shakes his head in disbelief. 'Do me a favour, Em.'

'What's wrong with being reliable?' she bristles. 'Why don't you like him?'

'Because there's no real warmth in him,' he answers after a moment. 'You need to feel safe emotionally in marriage, Em.'

'You mean like you and Zoë?' She can't resist the cutting retort: the taunt is bitter but well observed and he has no answer for it.

It was dark by the time Joss arrived back at St Meriadoc. She was later than usual, having fitted in an appointment at the end of her surgery hours: a farmer complaining of a low backache. He'd never been to an osteopath before and, as she'd welcomed him in, he'd looked rather wary. Now, driving down the narrow lane to The Row, she chuckled as she remembered the farmer's reaction to the manipulation. He'd first looked alarmed and then laughed almost gleefully at the sound of the clicks, and he'd been very ready to make another appointment.

She parked the car at the quarry and remembered with a shock that George was here. Anxiety replaced her sense of satisfaction with a good day's work and she slid silently from the car, closing the door as quietly as she could, lest Rafe or Pamela should appear. As she crossed the road and climbed the track to The Lookout, she told herself that it was foolish—that whatever might happen between George and Penny, she had done nothing of which to be ashamed—nevertheless, unease dogged her and she was glad to see the light shining out from the window.

Bruno poured her a glass of wine and she sat down in the bentwood rocker, suddenly at ease. She heaved a great sigh and stretched a foot to Nellie, who was lying on her back in front of the fire.

'Good day?' asked Bruno. 'Getting the hang of it now?'

She smiled up at him gratefully; he knew how anxious she'd been because, to begin with, she'd worked so slowly. 'I'm getting better,' she told him. 'Working a half-hour list at the practice in Bodmin is giving me confidence and I'm beginning to get a few referrals.'

Bruno sat down on the sofa and Nellie immediately leaped up gracefully beside him, curling against his side. Joss rocked herself, sipping with pleasure at the chilled Sancerre. They sat for a while in companionable silence, watching the flames flaring and dying, while, in the background, Billie Holiday's husky voice singing 'No More' created an atmosphere of bittersweet melancholy. Joss, listening to the gravelly, sexy voice, wondered why it was that, once you fell in love, it seemed that every love song might have been written for you personally.

'Since your supper plans have been cancelled,' said Bruno at last, 'can I offer you something or will you go up to the house and join Em and Mousie?'

'Oh, yes, I think I will.' Her face clouded. 'Sorry about that message, Bruno. You must have wondered what's been going on.'

He shrugged. 'Just a tad. I gather that George has a problem. I imagine it's to do with Penny.'

Joss stared into the fire while he watched her consideringly: from childhood her style had been a blend of countrified bohemianism that appealed to Bruno. On anyone else the mole-coloured needlecord shirt worn with a long charcoal-striped flannel skirt, embroidered at the hem, and the whole outfit finished off with leather ankle boots might have looked strange, but Joss carried it off with casual elegance.

'The thing is,' she said suddenly, 'that Penny wants to go back to New Zealand. She misses her family terribly and having the baby has made that longing worse. She just wants to be back at home among all the old familiar things. I can understand that, can't you?'

'Oh, yes.' Bruno answered readily. 'Home is always best when we're miserable or hurt. I suppose she and George haven't been together long enough for her to feel that her home is with him?'

'Well, he's been at sea quite a lot and they've only known each other for two years, anyway.' A pause. 'And there's something else,' she added.

'Ah yes,' he said. 'I had a feeling there might be.'

She looked at him quickly. 'You guessed, didn't you? I wondered after that day you saw us up in the valley at the well, but it's not like you might think it is.'

Bruno smiled to himself, guessing that Joss's inherent honesty wouldn't allow her to dissemble. 'You don't have to tell me,' he told her gently. 'It's between you and George.'

'The thing is,' she said again, 'I love him. I've tried not to but there it is. But I've never tried to influence him, I've just listened.' She looked at him anxiously. 'There's nothing wrong in that, is there?'

He grinned at her, quirking an eyebrow. 'Depends how you listened.'

She laughed, as he'd meant her to.

'And do you suspect George of transferring his affections from Penny to you?'

She shook her head and then paused. 'I think George loves me,' she replied honestly, 'but he wouldn't have let it make a difference if Brett hadn't come back into the frame.'

'You've lost me now,' he said. 'Who's Brett?'

Joss explained. 'And now Penny wants out. It's awful, really. Deep down inside me a tiny voice is shouting "Yes! Yes!" and punching the air because it means we can be together, but it's so complicated. What happens about Tasha?' She sighed. 'I suspect that Penny has finally pulled the plug and that's why George is here. Can you imagine anything more terrible than telling your parents this kind of news?'

She glanced at Bruno after a moment, saw that he was looking particularly sombre, and looked at her watch. 'I'd better go. You won't say anything to anyone, will you, Bruno?'

'Don't be daft,' he answered impatiently, getting up to go out with her. 'Do you want me to come up to the house with you?'

'No, I'm fine. It's a bright night, not properly dark at all. And thanks.'

She stood on tiptoe to kiss his cheek and he watched her walk away, swallowed up by the shadows, before he turned back into the house. Sitting down again, leaning forward to reach for the poker, it seemed that he heard other voices echoing in the shadows.

I might as well tell you that I'm pregnant.

Bruno stabbed so savagely at the logs that showers of sparks burst and exploded against the smoke-blackened stone. Dropping the poker, he picked up his glass again and closed his eyes.

'I might as well tell you that I'm pregnant.' Zoë's voice is flat, and she huddles her dressing gown around her as she sits in the rocking chair, one knee crossed over the other. Her black hair, usually so shiny, is lank, and her bare legs and feet look bird-thin and sharp-boned.

Bruno sits down on the edge of the sofa, elbows on knees, his hands clasped. 'But that's wonderful,' he says, though he sounds tentative because of the expression on her face, the glum voice. 'It's fantastic.'

'Is it?' She raises her head and stares at him, her expression almost contemptuous. 'Wonderful for you, perhaps. Not for me.'

'Why not?' He leans forward to kiss her; her body is a frail cage of bones beneath his hands and he is moved by a protective tenderness. She responds for a moment and then draws back, smiling at him, reaching for the inevitable Sobranie.

'Pour me a drink, darling,' she says, and she curls back in the chair, staring into the fire as she lights her cigarette.

He pours some wine, wishing that they could both be celebrating with a shared joy. For a moment he allows himself to think about being a father. His heart bumps with excitement and terror at the prospect and he wonders if either of them is ready for such a huge responsibility. His hands tremble as he sets down the bottle and lifts the glasses, and he is washed through with a happy pride. As he passes her the glass, he bends to touch his lips to her cheek, and she smiles again, veiling those cat-like eyes. She draws her feet up beneath the dressing gown and sips at the wine, flicking ash in the direction of the hearthstone.

'The thing is,' she says, and her voice is full of confidentiality, 'I've been offered this part in a film.'

He watches her, trying to hide his dismay. 'What kind of part?' He is careful to keep his voice fairly neutral.

'It's the old marital triangle thing with a bit of a twist. I would be cast as the other woman,' she answers. 'It's a very new film company but I think they're going places.' She hesitates, not looking at him. 'So you can see why the prospect of a baby isn't exactly a brilliant one just at the moment?'

He stares at her, disbelievingly. 'But need it make a difference? How far'—he glances at her thin frame—'how many months are you . . . ?'

'Two months.' She looks sulky and he is seized with fear. 'By the time we start filming it will be showing. These projects take ages, darling, you know that. I can't risk it.'

'What do you mean?'

She glances at his white angry face and looks away again.

'It's OK for you. Nothing need ever interfere with your career. I'm not ready to abandon mine yet. But I don't want to go to some back-street abortionist. You'll have to help me, Bruno.' Her voice changes, wheedling, persuasive. 'Please, darling. I might never get another chance like this and we can have a baby any time.'

The row that follows is so deeply destructive that Zoë leaves for London early the next morning. Later, she tells him that the pregnancy was a false alarm, but he hears through friends that someone has helped her to get rid of the baby. The film is never produced and Zoë's career as a film star suffers the same fate as their baby.

When, a few months later, Emma says, 'I'm going to have a baby, isn't it wonderful?' Bruno feels as if something sharp is being twisted agonisingly deep inside him.

Before the end of the following year Zoë has left him for the first in a long line of lovers.

By the time supper with Mousie and Joss had finished, and Emma reappeared at The Lookout, Bruno was stretched full length on the sofa with Nellie asleep on the floor beside him.

'How was it?' he asked without getting up, raising a tumbler half full of whisky in a kind of salute, and then resting it again on his midriff. 'How's Mutt?'

Emma dropped her coat on a chair and sat down in the rocker. The tone of his voice alerted her to the fact that he was having a 'downer', as they both called it, and she wondered if he'd at last faced the fact that Mutt might not be much longer for this world.

'The doctor called in earlier,' she said. 'He says she might have some fluid on her lungs but he's convinced that the best place for her is in her own home with her family nearby.'

Bruno sat upright. 'Should I go up to see her?' he asked anxiously.

'Heavens, no.' She was quite emphatic about it. 'Mousie will have settled her for the night by now and Joss has promised to telephone if she thinks it's necessary. We'll go up together first thing in the morning.'

'OK.' He sat for a few seconds, staring at nothing in particular. 'You must be very proud of Joss, Em,' he said at last. 'She's a great girl.'

She warmed to his praise, but now knew what the trouble was all about. At regular intervals he had downers when he thought about Zoë and the baby she'd refused to have. Her own pregnancy, coming so close on Zoë's, had caught him off guard and he'd told her about that evening and described the row that had followed his refusal to assist in the destruction of his own child.

Now, watching him, Emma was unable to think of anything that could be of comfort. Instead she said warmly, 'I'm terribly proud of Joss. It's lovely to see her with Mutt. I know I shouldn't say this, Bruno, but I have this dream of Joss living at Paradise. After all, she could have her patients to the house, couldn't she? That old back road to the house could be reopened so that patients didn't have to drive through St Meriadoc.'

'I feel we're jumping the gun a bit, don't you?'

She looked guilty. 'Oh, I'm not wishing Mutt's life away. Of course I'm not. Anyway, it's just as much her dream as mine, I promise you.'

'Have you any idea what's in her will?'

Emma shook her head. 'But it was always settled, wasn't it? You have The Lookout and The Row and I have Paradise.'

'I suppose Mutt might have other ideas. You might get The Row and the boatyard.'

'God, I hope not,' said Emma involuntarily. She glanced quickly at Bruno but he'd leaned forward to stroke the recumbent Nellie and wasn't looking at her. 'It's simply that Ray would be a pain in the neck,' she said, laughing a little, making light of it. 'You know how he's always said that we should pull down the old buildings and build a hotel there.'

'But since that means destroying the quality of life for everyone in The Row, I imagine he'd see that it's not an option.'

'Well, Ray thinks that Rafe and Pamela and Mousie would be just as happy in new bungalows in Polzeath.' She sighed. 'He has no idea. The trouble is he's such a juggernaut once he's got an idea in his head.'

'He wouldn't want to sell Paradise?'

She hesitated. 'Probably not as long as he thought Joss was getting it, but you know Ray.'

'Yes,' he answered grimly, 'I know Ray. And, as I've said before, none of it is his to do anything with, either now or in the future.'

'I know that,' Emma said rather crossly, 'but it's not that easy.'

He let her talk, but although he made all the right responses, his thoughts were busy elsewhere and his heart felt constricted with anxiety and dread.

With supper over and Emma gone off to The Lookout, Joss and Mousie cleared up together. Mousie washed the dishes, while Joss dried and put away, as they talked over the events of the day together. Joss had got

245

herself into a yawning fit, eyes streaming, and Mousie put a sympathetic arm about her shoulders.

'Go and run a hot bath and soak for a while,' she suggested. 'You look exhausted and I'm not surprised. I'll go and get your grandmother settled for the night and then you can both get some rest.'

Gratefully, Joss agreed to this plan, returning Mousie's hug before trailing away upstairs. Mousie finished tidying the kitchen and crossed to the drawing room to gather her belongings together, pausing to put the photograph carefully at the back of her capacious carpetbag. After that initial look at the wedding picture, Emma had been moved to fetch other albums of photographs from the bookcase and, while they'd waited for the doctor's visit, they'd turned the pages together.

'Old photographs are so sad,' Emma had sighed. 'All that hope and innocence. And somehow more poignant in black and white, don't you think?'

Now, as she picked up her reading spectacles and slung them round her neck, Mousie wished she could identify this anxiety that touched her heart with icy fingers: it was something that stretched back to those early days after Mutt's arrival at St Meriadoc, something to do with her silent wariness. Mousie drew out the letter from the young American and stared down at it. What had happened to Madeleine Grosjean?

The name had meant nothing to Emma but it suddenly occurred to Mousie that Bruno might have the answer. Perhaps if she showed him the photograph it might jog a memory. Again, that tiny tug of fear. Of course, she could simply consign the letter and the photograph to the fire, and that would be the end of it, yet she had the feeling that they hadn't heard the last of the young American. She glanced at the signature at the foot of the page: Dan Crosby. She remembered the enthusiasm and hope in his face and the set of his jaw. Perhaps it would be more sensible to discover the truth as far as it was possible, so that they were ready for him.

She thought about Mutt. 'I think that time is short,' the doctor had told her, 'though at this stage there's a narrow line between getting better or worse. One can never quite tell. Anyway, there's nothing more could be done for her if we were to get her into hospital and, in my opinion, this is where she needs to be—at home with her family nearby.'

Perhaps it had been wrong to allow Emma to go back to The Lookout, but Mousie hadn't wanted to frighten her or Bruno and she felt that tonight Mutt should be left in peace with her granddaughter. Having made this decision she went upstairs and into Mutt's bedroom.

The fire had burned low and the room was shadowed, but Mutt was awake, stiffening eagerly as she watched the door open—as if she were waiting for someone. Mousie crossed to the bed and stood looking down at her. Questions crowded to her lips, but the sight of the elderly, frail woman aroused her compassion and prevented her from asking them. Instead she said: 'I'm going to give you your medicine and settle you comfortably and then I think I shall go home, Honor. Will you be happy with Joss to look after you?'

She saw a slight sagging of the thin, square shoulders, a relaxation of the old bones, as if Mutt were in some way relieved, and Mousie smiled mischievously as she held the small measure to her lips.

'Glad to see the back of me, are you? Well, I don't blame you.' She laid Mutt back against the pillows and made certain that the ankle was supported. 'You've probably had more than enough of my bullying and fussing over the last six weeks.'

'No, no. Not that.' Mutt reached out a hand and Mousie took it. 'Nothing like that. Thank you for everything, Mousie.'

She hesitated as if wanting to say more and then shook her head, denying herself the luxury, but she looked distressed and the pressure on Mousie's hand increased.

'I should like to thank you too,' Mousie told Mutt. 'Not many people would have been as generous as you've been, Honor, to me and all my family, letting us stay in our cottages at ridiculous rents. Don't think we're not grateful.'

She realised that there was a ring of finality in her words, as if she might not have the chance to say these things after this evening but, before she could decide how to proceed, Joss came in behind her. Mousie turned to her with relief, the difficult moment over, and explained that she was on her way home. She kissed Mutt, everything easy and natural again with Joss looking on, said good night and went away downstairs.

Left alone with her grandmother Joss knew, even before Mutt spoke, the words that she would say.

'Have you found the letters, darling?'

Joss shook her head, praying for some kind of release from her promise, wishing that Mousie had not gone home.

'In my desk.' She closed her eyes. Joss hesitated and Mutt's eyes opened suddenly. 'Give me a kiss before you go.'

Joss touched the dry lips with her own, trying to hide her anxiety, smiling down at her grandmother.

'I'll be in later when I've found them,' she said. 'Ring the bell if you need me.'

'Bless you, darling. It's all for you, remember.' Mutt sounded drowsy. 'I want you to have Paradise.'

Joss paused at the door, but Mutt seemed to be falling asleep, and she went out, closing it quietly behind her. She descended the stairs slowly and crossed the hall to the small parlour. The roll-top desk stood squarely beneath the window and Joss pulled the curtains across the black, cold glass panes before sitting down.

The bottom left-hand drawer was full of catalogues—Mutt had shopped a great deal by mail order in the last few years—but in the right-hand drawer were some battered brown files with the words *School Reports* scrawled across them. The first file was headed 'Bruno', the second one 'Emma', and they were wedged firmly down in the drawer so that she had to tug at them to get them out. Beneath them was a pile of letters, some loose but neatly folded, others pushed into envelopes.

With her heart beating painfully Joss drew the papers out, recognising her grandmother's handwriting. Not love letters, then, unless they were Mutt's own, returned to her. Joss was struggling with herself, trying not to look at them, but knowing that she must at least see to whom the letters were written. They were a piece of Mutt, these letters: they contained her thoughts and were part of her history. It would be impossible just to consign Mutt's words to the flames without glancing at one or two of them. She picked up an envelope and held it under the anglepoise lamp. 'Mrs Vivian Crosby' . . . She selected another one and then another; they were all addressed to the same person.

One of the open letters was dated 30th June 1947 and headed simply 'Paradise'. Her eyes fled across the words, skipping whole sentences, frightened of what they might discover, yet unbearably curious.

> Vivi, darling,
> I write these letters in the evenings when the children are in bed. To be honest with you, Vivi, the real problem is that, once you start down a road like this, things carry you along with them . . .
> Oh, Vivi, this is the exhausting part. I have to be so vigilant. And the real danger comes not from him but from Hubert's cousin Mousie . . .

Puzzled, Joss glanced swiftly through the rest of the letter and then reached for another.

> Darling Vivi,
> This is the last letter I shall write to you, exactly one year since I first arrived at Paradise. I suppose if I am to fully commit I must finish with Madeleine Grosjean. After all, she disappeared out there in India . . .

Impatiently she seized another. It was quite short, describing a black-berrying outing and a picnic with Bruno and Emma, but it was the last page that caught Joss's attention.

Anyway, a good day here in Paradise. I wonder if ever I will show it to you. Oh, what joy to imagine you here, if only I could see you face to face, Vivi, and explain it all properly. You would understand, I know you would.

God bless you, darling.

All my love,

Madeleine

Holding the page in her hand, Joss stared ahead, brow furrowed. *Madeleine.* Her grandmother's names were Honor Elizabeth yet these letters were certainly in her handwriting. And she'd already mentioned Madeleine Grosjean . . . Confused, Joss began to sort the letters, checking the dates and stacking them into some kind of chronological order, resisting the temptation to pick one out at random. Once she'd achieved this object she went upstairs and into the porch room. Mutt was sleeping deeply, her face peaceful. Joss went back down to the hall and then crossed into the kitchen, where she filled the kettle with water. As she waited for it to boil she paced to and fro, debating with herself.

Presently she carried her mug of tea back to the study. Here, in this quiet room, where Mutt's presence and influence were most to be found, Joss opened the first letter and began to read her grandmother's story.

PART TWO

Paradise
St Meriadoc
Cornwall
8th June 1947

Vivi, darling,

Yes, this is where I am. In Paradise. Will you ever believe the things that have happened to me? To be honest, I don't know where to start my story—or at least *how* to start. In one way it seems very adventurous, romantic, the stuff films are made of, and then again, it could look shabby and underhand. Now that I need to write it down, the adventurous feeling is fading and the *wrongness*—and the danger!—

of what I have done presents itself more forcefully. I am masquerading as another woman, you see. I am no longer Madeleine Uttworth—or Madeleine Grosjean, that was—I am Honor Trevannion. And Lottie is no longer Charlotte Uttworth but Emma Trevannion.

They died, you see—first Hubert, then Emma, then Honor—in Karachi on the way to catch the boat. Hubert hadn't yet been discharged and he was coming back to Multan but he was determined to get Honor and the children away. They were to spend a week in Karachi so that Honor could do some shopping, spend their last few days on holiday together, but then Hubert fell ill. I think it was botulism, probably from some tinned food. It was certainly quick enough. Honor managed to get a telephone call to the hospital in Multan asking me to come to them, to help her with the children. I packed my few portable treasures and caught the first train out. Oh God! I shall never forget that journey, the crush of people, the noise and the heat.

By the time we got there, Hubert and Emma were dead and Honor was ill. There was a young Indian doctor with her, rather out of his depth and very relieved to see me. He promised to return in the morning but by then Honor was dead. He made out the certificate and hurried away again, leaving me to deal with everything else.

It was Honor who told me to use the tickets to get us back to England. I'd been in such a dither wondering what to do (I'd written to you by now, of course, but I just had this feeling, though your letter was very practical and charitable, Vivi, that you couldn't quite see me and Lottie fitting in with your new life in America) and, as you know, things are bad in India: riots, killings, and Multan in particular is a trouble spot. In March the Army was brought in and introduced a twenty-four-hour curfew. Honor begged me to get Bruno back to Cornwall. 'It is what Hubert would have wanted,' she said. 'He'd want you all to be safe.' He'd been so unhappy about Lottie and me staying on. He was such a super person, Vivi. So alive, so confident, and so generous.

Poor Bruno, poor little boy. He'd lost all his family in a matter of days and we were all that he had left. Lottie and me. I was frightened about what would happen to the three of us—and then, quite suddenly, the way seemed so clear. There, in that hotel room where Hubert first became ill, were all their papers: the tickets, the Trevannion family passports. My idea was that we should actually become that family, the three of us together. I thanked God that they'd called me Mutt. M. Uttworth, do you see? Muttworth. Mutt. It was Hubert who'd started it and Bruno thought it was terrific fun—even Lottie chanted Mutt, Mutt, rather than Mum, Mum.

I explained to Bruno that someone might take him away from us if they didn't believe I was his mother—oh, I wasn't deliberately trying to frighten him, Vivi, I really thought we might be separated and I wanted to get us out. The means to escape was right there under my hands with Hubert's and Honor's blessing.

Perhaps I should have gone to the Commissioner and explained or talked to the purser on the ship, but I didn't. I kept thinking: Let's just get home and then I'll try to think more sensibly about all this.

Somewhere in the Indian Ocean Lottie became Emma. Remembering to call her Emma wasn't too difficult for Bruno—she was so like his own little sister that he'd often muddled their names—but it was very hard for me. Then, when I saw Paradise, Vivi, I knew I'd made the right decision. Bruno is back where he belongs and I shall look after him and love him as if he were my own son.

How I wish I could see you and meet your American husband. Will it ever happen? God bless you, darling.

Your loving sister,

Madeleine

> Paradise
> 17th June 1947

Vivi, darling,

When I read my letter through I realised I hadn't told you about the actual homecoming. I wondered whether to post it just as it was but I decided to add some more so that you can get a fuller picture of what happened and see how I finished up here at Paradise.

I fully intended to give myself a day or two, once we got to Liverpool, to reconsider the whole situation. What I didn't expect was to be met at the dock. There we were, struggling with cases, ~~Lottie~~ Emma screaming her head off, and suddenly this man appeared. His name was Simon Dalloway. He swept us through Customs and into a taxi.

'Hubert asked me to get you sorted out this end,' he said. 'I've only just heard the sad news. I am so terribly sorry . . .'

Something like that. I can't remember his exact words, I was too shocked. Fortunately, so was he. Apparently the purser had explained the whole situation about Hubert's death to him and he took over: sent a telegram to Cornwall, hurried us away. That's when it first began, you see. Now it was impossible to admit the truth. And what about Bruno? I'd promised Honor that I'd look after him and I love Bruno as if he were my own child.

Simon was very gentle with us all, putting my confusion down to grief. I let him shepherd us all on to the train bound for Bristol. He'd got the tickets, organised a hamper, and I realised that Honor would have known that this had all been planned for her and the children. Simon had booked us into the Royal Hotel for the night before the final leg of the journey to Cornwall. At dinner, with the children in bed, he talked about St Meriadoc—and the pitfalls began to open at my feet—but I decided that it was only right to escort Bruno home, and perhaps there was still time to tell the truth.

I can imagine your face, Vivi. It was always you, wasn't it, who stopped me plunging into trouble. I thought of writing to you the first time Johnny disappeared but I felt ashamed and couldn't bring myself to admit to you that he had let us down. Sensible, steady people don't seem to realise that when you've been a fool you don't need anyone to rub it in. When I received your answer to my letter, back there in Multan, I sensed your anxiety; that you didn't really want your destitute sister and her child rocking the boat of your shiny new life. I didn't blame you for that. Despite writing to each other and exchanging photographs over the last eight years, we'd drifted a bit, hadn't we? Me, with my missionary zeal, rushing away to be a nurse in India, and you joining the WAAF when war broke out. Neither you nor Mother approved of my going to India, did you? Honor said that her people felt exactly the same. She was an only child and her parents were killed in the Blitz. When you wrote to tell me that Mother had died of cancer Honor was such a brick. What would she think of me now? I wonder. I'm sure she'd see that I'm thinking of Bruno.

Do you remember *Goblin Market*, Vivi? You were Lizzie, weren't you: 'full of wise upbradings'. And I was Laura, tempted by forbidden fruit. I still have the copy you gave me for my fifteenth birthday. It was one of the few things I brought from Multan in my hastily packed bag.

My love, darling,
Madeleine

Paradise
30th June 1947

Vivi, darling,

I write these letters in the evenings when the children are in bed and Hubert's father is in the drawing room reading the newspaper or listening to the wireless. I haven't posted the other two letters yet. Silly, isn't it? It comforts me to write to you, like this. I've decided to bring you right up-to-date and then send all three letters off together.

Arriving here with Simon, it seemed suddenly impossible to explain the situation. Hubert's father, James, was so pleased to see us all and so overcome by the sight of the children. Over and over again he'd touch Emma's hair or tip Bruno's chin so as to look at him. 'Just like Hubert at that age,' he'd say. And you could see that he was struggling to keep back the tears.

The children were like a breath of new life to him. There was never quite the right moment to explain to him at the beginning and, as each day passes, it becomes more and more impossible.

We don't talk too much about Hubert: James is typical of the stiff-upper-lip generation: nothing is to be talked about that might be classed as emotional. But he loves to hear about Hubert's hospital work. That's easy for me, of course, because I worked with him for six years, but I still have to watch what I say and this is the exhausting part. The real danger comes from Hubert's cousin Mousie. I had no idea that there would be other people apart from Hubert's immediate family—and I knew that he was an only child and that his mother had died—so you can imagine the shock to find an aunt and two cousins living ten minutes away! The aunt is a kindly soul and Rafe is a fairly standard fourteen-year-old boy, still at school, but his older sister, Mousie, is a different proposition. She watches me, as if puzzled, and I am frightened of her.

'You!' I hear you cry. 'You've never been frightened in your life.' Oh, but that was before I had my baby, Vivi. Once you have a baby you have a hostage to fortune and nothing is ever the same again. But now I have found Paradise and I can tell you that it is worth the struggle. The house is part of a small estate, hidden in a sheltered valley. From the main road, a long deep lane plunges down between two grassy banks, high and straight as a wall with a wild thorny hedge on top, until it reaches a little U-shaped cove. On the seaward side, there's a boatyard that is no longer used and next to it a row of four cottages, called—imaginatively—The Row. Just one big step from the door, is the sea wall. This is the north coast, Vivi, and the houses turn their backs to the wild Atlantic. Across the road from the cottages there is an old quarry and high up in the valley is St Meriadoc's Well: a tiny, bubbling spring half buried in tall, feathery grasses. The spring grows into a stream that runs down towards the sea and beneath a little bridge that divides this cove with its row of cottages and the boatyard from Paradise and The Lookout—a Victorian folly built on the cliff. Beyond the bridge, the path splits into two: one branch goes up to The Lookout, and then on across the cliffs, and the other takes you along the lane and through the big gateway into the driveway to Paradise, which is now my home.

Imagine, then, a Queen Anne house, grey stone washed white, slate-roofed, set among a tangle of rhododendrons. The rooms are cool and elegant: drawing room and dining room on either side of the long hall and behind them the kitchen—square, roomy, looking north—and a charming little parlour behind the drawing room, which James uses as an office.

He lets me sit here at this old desk to write my letters. I call him James, Vivi. I tease him a little, very gently, and his back is a little straighter, his eye brighter, because of it.

He's calling for me, Vivi. I'd no idea it was so late.

All love, darling,

Madeleine

She puts down the pen and looks about the room, folding the letter hastily and tucking it into the writing case. She is beginning to grow used to the fact that she owns very little—she brought so few belongings with her from Multan. She has Honor's things, of course: this writing case is among these, along with her gold fountain pen. Mutt screws on its lid just as James appears, pushing open the door, smiling half enquiringly, half apologetically.

'Not interrupting anything?'

'Heavens, no.'

Her smile is warm with affection and he beams back at her gratefully; she is quick to love, this girl of Hubert's, and her presence is already easing his loneliness. His son's death has been far more of a blow than he will ever show, but the arrival of his son's family is a blessing.

Mutt gets up and walks to the door, where she slips a hand within his arm, and wishes that she were not deceiving him. 'I think we need our nightcap,' she says, drawing him into the room. 'Just a tiny one for me, of course, but it helps me sleep.'

'Well, of course it does.'

This last drink ritual was a solitary affair when Margaret was alive; she'd go upstairs, leaving him beside his fire to brood over the events of the day while she prepared herself for bed. He misses her dreadfully, of course he does, but he admits to himself that this is rather fun: Honor perching on the corner of the desk and watching him while he measures out a finger of whisky.

Inside herself, Mutt is marvelling at the little scene: can it be true that she is sitting here with Hubert's father? She imagines how his face would change if she were suddenly to say, 'Listen, I'm not really Hubert's widow. It's all a terrible mistake . . .'

Instead she is comforted by a sense of rightness, of being where she truly belongs. It seems so much like home, this lovely valley, and already she has a strong affinity with this dear old man. He is very like Hubert, although the thick black hair is now white. His thin, clever face is still lively and the brown eyes have a twinkle.

She smiles, filled with tenderness, and he smiles back at her, raising his glass as if in salute.

Paradise
12th July

I'm feeling very low tonight, Vivi. James has gone out to dinner with some friends, and I'm alone for the first time at Paradise. You'd think, wouldn't you, that I'd be glad to be alone? No pressure, no need to think before I speak; nobody to put on an act for; but the truth is, actually, I feel unbearably lonely. The children are in bed and I've had a couple of whiskies and, just suddenly, I felt the need to talk to someone who really knows me, so that I don't have to pretend.

Oh, Vivi, Honor was dark and had brown eyes. Mine, as you know, are hazel but, thank God, the Customs man only glanced at the passport photograph and I'd tilted a hat over my eyes, and carried Lottie in my arms as a kind of shield. She hates to be carried and I knew that she'd struggle and scream and in the end everyone was glad to push us through. I mustn't call her Lottie. I only do it when I'm tired.

Vivi, I feel so guilty. What am I doing here? Why ever did I think I could pull this off? Some woman turned up here this morning, her husband was one of Hubert's chums, thought I'd like to go over for lunch and so on. I was terrified that I might slip up. She began to talk to Bruno, saying how like his daddy he was, asking how old his little sister was and I can't forget the expression on his face. I sometimes kid myself that Bruno thinks Lottie is his sister, that he's forgotten Emma.

Anyway, I burst in with some nonsense and distracted the woman, but I can't get over it. If I can't bring myself to call James 'Father', how can I expect so much from this poor little boy? How he must resent me for trying to take his mother's place, yet I know that he loves me and I think he would miss me if I were to go. In an odd kind of way, James protects me. He's made it safe for me. He's the angel standing at the gate of Paradise with his flaming sword, except that I'm still inside even though I've eaten of the tree of knowledge.

I think I've drunk too much whisky and I'd better get to bed before James comes home and finds me like this. Good night, darling.

Joss put the letter aside and then picked it up again, folding it mechanically. There was too much here to understand all at once. *Mutt wasn't Honor Trevannion.* Yet Joss was distracted from the sheer shock of this by other impressions that were affecting her so powerfully. Mutt's dilemma, her warm personality and humanness, struck Joss forcibly. She could identify with this young woman who'd taken such a chance, torn by doubt and fear, yet driven by some deep-down conviction that what she was doing was right.

Mutt's granddaughter caught her breath: how had Mutt dared to risk so much? She tried to picture the atmosphere of terror in India in those hot, unstable days, and envisage the long voyage home. What must it have felt like, giving your daughter a different name and a new persona? And this child, Joss was obliged to remind herself, was her own mother—who wasn't Emma Trevannion at all but Lottie Uttworth.

And what about Vivi, to whom Mutt wrote with such intimacy and affection? Was Vivi still alive, out in America, imagining her sister and daughter long dead? Clearly Mutt's letters had never been posted . . .

Unable to grasp it all, Joss reached for the next letter.

Paradise
Thursday morning

Much better today, Vivi. This morning I feel confident again that I am doing the right thing. Bruno gave me such a hug after breakfast and I held him very tightly and just whispered, 'I know how much you must miss Mummie and Emma, darling. I'm just trying to look after you.' And he looked at me, Vivi, so solemn and kind, and he said, 'It's all right, Mutt. I'm glad you're here.' Oh, I felt such a flood of relief and gratitude, as if he'd given me absolution.

It is so odd being called Honor. I hoped that the children's nickname for me might be taken up by everyone but Mousie can't bring herself to use it. I am afraid of her, Vivi. She watches us as if some instinct warns her that something is wrong but she doesn't know what it is. I become nervous when she is with me and I retreat into silence. Aunt Julia puts my shortcomings down to grief and encourages Mousie to be kind and patient. And poor Mousie is trying very hard to deny all her instincts and to be sweet to me. She is puzzled but because of Bruno she doesn't come near the truth of it. I feel horrid, holding her at arm's length like this, but what am I to do?

Mousie must have loved Hubert so much; she knows everything about him, his passions and his dislikes, his tricks of speech and his habits. Yet she can't have been much more than a child when she last saw him. He wrote to her from time to time but, with the war and the distance between them, communication was very patchy. Luckily there aren't too many photographs: they have the wedding group—remember the one I sent to you?—and also a family one with Bruno as a baby. This is more worrying because Honor isn't wearing a hat, but fortunately she is gazing down at the baby.

I said at once: 'Gosh, I looked so much younger then, didn't I? But of course it's nearly five years old.'

I felt so ashamed of myself, Vivi. Thank God Bruno wasn't there.

Mousie has several snapshots of Hubert before he went to India and one or two little keepsakes, which she treasures. She has a knack of keeping me on my toes. I have no idea about countless tiny things which I should have known after six years of marriage. It became clear fairly early on that he'd never mentioned me by my nickname, which is a terrific relief, nor by proper name, as far as I know.

I haven't really explained about Johnny, have I? I don't know how to go about it, I suppose. Looking back, he was such fun, so happy-go-lucky, and very good-looking. His name sounds French, I know, but he was very English. Hubert and Honor were a bit cautious about him and I know you would have said that he wasn't 'sound'. As you know, he did something in tea—he had an office in Lahore. I think that they felt he should have joined up once the war was really under way instead of disappearing on business for weeks at a time. Once Lottie was born he simply vanished more often and for longer periods.

At one point we wondered if he'd been killed, but after a while we heard some rumours about him setting up with another woman. Well, I'd had to face the fact that there were other women, Viv, and I'd begun to suspect that he was a gambler as well. Then I discovered that the rent hadn't been paid for months. Hubert and Honor bailed me out, as usual. They were such good people. I often think about Honor. She was so straight, so sweet. I imagine her looking at me from the shadows as I walk in the Paradise gardens with Bruno. She'd have wanted him to be looked after by someone who knew him as a baby.

I can hear the children's voices; they've been with Aunt Julia and Mousie down at The Row.

God bless, darling.

Madeleine

She stands watching from the kitchen doorway. The little group have walked up from The Row over the cliff path, Emma being wheeled by Aunt Julia in the little collapsible pushchair that hasn't been used since Rafe was a small boy. Now Mousie kneels before Emma, smoothing the child's fair, tangled blonde hair and dabbing with a handkerchief at some smears upon her cheek.

'Sit still,' implores Mousie, but she is laughing and she gives Emma a kiss on her rosy cheek before standing up with a gesture of resignation.

'Your sister,' she says to Bruno, 'is a little monkey.'

Just for a second his expression freezes into a kind of still watchfulness and then he looks at Emma and smiles.

'She can't help it,' he tells Mousie with a rueful tolerance. 'Daddy used to say . . .' He hesitates awkwardly and Mutt comes swiftly to his aid.

'Have you had a lovely time?' she cries, as if she has only at that moment appeared in the doorway. 'Poor Mousie.' She smiles sympathetically at the younger girl. 'Are you exhausted yet?'. She sits on one of the kitchen chairs and puts an arm about Bruno, giving him a quick hug, her heart beating fast.

These are the moments she dreads. She is filled with guilt each time she sees the expression on Bruno's small face change from innocence to uncertainty, hating this need to be continually on guard. Emma climbs onto a chair, hoping that there will be a pot of jam in Aunt Julia's capacious bag and looking eagerly for the little cakes that her aunt brings out with a flourish. Mousie steadies Emma as she screams with delight and the chair rocks unsteadily beneath her.

'She screamed all the way home,' says Bruno, almost admiringly—and indeed he is impressed by Emma's cheerful determination to have her own way. 'She doesn't like riding in the pushchair unless she's tired,' he explains to Mousie and Aunt Julia. Emma has no words yet to explain this, but he knows exactly how she feels. 'She likes to be in charge.' She and Mutt have always been part of his world and he is prepared to go to any lengths to keep them with him.

'Tea-time,' says Aunt Julia firmly—and Mutt breathes a huge silent sigh of relief and her hold on Bruno relaxes.

Paradise
3rd August

Vivi darling,

Simon came down to stay for a long weekend. He comes at intervals to see everyone, which I think is rather sweet of him, and James is so fond of him. They talk about Hubert and the things he and Simon used to get up to, and James relives it all over again. Simon and Rafe took us out sailing—they keep a boat in the old boatyard—and we took it in turns with the two of them: Mousie with Bruno and then me with Emma, who sat so still next to me as we skimmed across the silky silvery water, out past the sharp black rocks. The clean, fresh wind fled past me, tingling on my skin. Oh, how I loved it.

Simon said, 'I expect you didn't get much chance to sail in India,' and I was able to reply confidently, 'No, none at all.' He said: 'Hubert would have missed that,' and I just nodded—and then prayed that there was no record anywhere of Honor suffering from seasickness!

On Sunday afternoon we went picnicking up the valley to the Saint's Well. Fuchsias grow wild here and there are butterflies everywhere. Bruno made a dam in the stream while Emma paddled, being very splashy and noisy and refusing to hold Mousie's hand.

I wondered if Mousie might be attracted to Simon but she made no sign of it; no sidelong little glances, no showing off or flirting. She's training to be a nurse in Truro but she seems younger than her age and I am fearful that she might find herself trapped here with her mother and uncle. I know that when we were seventeen, Vivi, we'd have wanted a bit more from life than this group of older people, even in a paradise like this one. If someone like Simon had shown up when we were her age we'd have fought over him like cats.

He's awfully attractive. Quite tall, very tough-looking, nice hands. He shows no interest—not that kind, anyway!—in Mousie. Perhaps it's because he's known her for ever. I'd like to take her in hand. Her hair is light brown with gold and reddish lights in it, but she bundles it into a plait without much care. Eyes a lovely, dark slatey blue and a clear, creamy skin, but no touch of make-up, not even a little slick of lipstick.

She was aware of Simon and me lounging on the rug by the stream, while Rafe helped Bruno with his dam and Emma paddled. It was so good, there in the hot sun, with the cold clear water bubbling out of the well and a lark so high that we couldn't see him but could only hear his golden voice.

'There he is,' Simon cried suddenly, and he leaned, pointing upwards, so that his bare arm brushed my cheek.

Oh God, Vivi. That warm touch of his skin against mine, I can feel it now. My heartbeat was all over the place, and he looked at me, just one look, and then got to his feet and strolled over to the dam.

'Pretty good,' he said. 'You'll make an engineer yet, young Bruno.'

I couldn't have moved, my legs wouldn't have supported me. But that's quite natural, isn't it, Vivi? After all, I'm only twenty-seven and it's not wicked, is it, to be attracted to a man? Of course, I can quite see that everyone here, including Simon, would see it as disloyalty to Hubert's memory. But the truth of it is that I've been alone for nearly a year and I do get so lonely. I was grateful when Emma stamped up out of the stream and simply threw herself on top of me, all damp and warm and shrieking with delight. It broke the tension and I was able to pull myself together.

Simon shows me what I'm missing, Vivi. But I'm not going to start regretting things. I'm so lucky to be here, with kind people and my baby safe.

I miss you so much. And Honor and Hubert too. I feel that I've lost you all at one stroke.

I love you, darling.

Madeleine

MARCIA WILLETT

Paradise
15th August 1947

Have you wondered, Vivi, how I am managing for money? Well, there was some for the journey that I have eked out very carefully, but James has realised the embarrassment and is coming to my rescue. He won't hear of my working—he insists that the children need me here—but he has opened a bank account for me and gives me a small allowance and, this was a shock, has begun enquiries into Hubert's pension. I had a jolt of terror when he talked about that.

'Do you have Hubert's death certificate?' he asks.

Well, yes. I have all three death certificates. Honor's and Emma's are taped carefully between the backboard and the paper cover of *Goblin Market* along with my own papers. I sent a telegram back to Multan saying that Dr Hubert Trevannion and Mrs Madeleine Uttworth and her daughter had died of botulism and that his wife and children were on their way home to England.

I had to think quickly but I've always been good at that, haven't I? Once I was married to Johnny I needed to be able to get us out of scrapes quite often—and without warning—and I learned to think on my feet. To begin with I adored him and it didn't matter, but once Lottie was born I didn't want muddle and cheating for her.

Honor and Hubert managed to balance their lives and I envied them so much. Sometimes I feel that I've become a part of Honor's and Hubert's lives and that some of their goodness and wisdom is rubbing off on me. Honor was so wise and practical, whereas I used to try to be all things to all men.

Honor and Hubert loved me, though. That always surprised me.

'Look after the children if anything happens to me,' Honor would say. We'd promise each other that we'd do that—it was terribly important out in India in those times to know that we had each other. And, at the end, I was the one Honor sent for and she knew I'd get to her.

I brought with me what I was standing up in, but not much more, and rationing is so strict that I have to wear Honor's clothes. I've explained to everyone that I lost weight after Hubert's death and I'm using his mother's sewing machine to take in seams and I've had to let down the hems.

'Have you got taller too?' Mousie asked—and all I could think of to say was that I felt it was a bit of a change from short skirts. Goodness, I feel so frightened at times.

Are you living like a queen in America, Vivi? I hope so, darling.

All love,
Madeleine

THE GOLDEN CUP

Paradise
30th August

I woke early this morning, Vivi. Leaning from my bedroom window and looking out beyond the gardens, I could see tall, fragile trees—spindle-limbs and feathery arms—drawn in a smudgy charcoal against the soft, dense mist that rolled up the valley from the sea. And now the scene is washed in gold, as the sun edges up over the rim of the world, and dazzling light floods along 'the golden cup'—our valley—and into the shadowy corners of the garden.

When Margaret, his wife, died, James moved into his dressing room at the back of the house. He says he likes to hear the sea on wild nights, and all his things are there, but I feel rather guilty having this wonderful room as my own.

We had a touching little ceremony yesterday (Honor's birthday—I can't tell you how unreal it all was) when he offered me one or two precious items of Margaret's jewels: a double string of pearls with matching earrings, a pretty garnet necklace set in silver, a few rings—one diamond, a ruby, and a charming sapphire engagement ring.

'I know she'd have been so happy for you to wear them,' he said, rather gruffly. I kissed him and said I would be very touched to have them. But you can imagine, Vivi, how I felt! I tell myself that it will all be passed on to Bruno and so, in the end, it will be as it should be—but then I wonder how Emma will feel when that day comes and nothing is for her.

I can hear her upstairs singing to herself in her cot. She's a happy child, warm and loving, and she and Bruno adore each other. I'm beginning to believe that Bruno is trying to forget about India.

In his own room, listening to Emma's imperious shouts, Bruno brings the story he is telling himself to a good stopping place and wonders if there will be time for a walk to The Lookout before tea. He loves the strange old house on the cliff and it features in many of the stories he makes up in his head. His grandfather James has told him about wreckers and smugglers, and he weaves these tales together with the things he remembers about India. Sometimes, if it is a really good story, he acts it out as a game that can last for days. The grown-ups often have roles, although they don't know it, but Emma is too young to play.

He can hear her now, singing loudly as she tramps up and down in her cot. He hears Mutt coming upstairs, and he thinks about the little scene yesterday, when Grandfather gave her Grandmother's jewels. He is getting used to these moments when Mutt gets flustered. 'Flustered' is an Aunt Julia word and it means exactly how Mutt behaves when the

India story crashes into the Paradise story. He can understand why Mutt has her own pretend game and he is happy to play it with her. Much though he loves Aunt Julia and Mousie and Rafe, he couldn't bear to be without Mutt and Emma. Even when he deliberately reminds himself that Mummie and Daddy and baby Em are gone for ever, the knowledge that Mutt and Emma are here with him makes it not quite true. It's as if they have all become mixed together.

Sometimes, now, Mummie and Mutt seem to be one and the same person, just as Emma—who was once called Lottie—now seems to be baby Em too. He is glad that Daddy is just Daddy and can be talked about with Mousie or Grandfather, even though he has to be careful that it doesn't lead on to other things. He wonders how Mutt manages and sometimes hugs her to show that he understands.

Bruno climbs off his bed and goes into the nursery where Mutt is lifting Emma from her cot, and he feels safe and happy.

Paradise
15th September

Such fun, Vivi. Simon is here for a few days. We're all so pleased to see him. Did I tell you that he's a GP with a practice in Exeter and spends one day a week at the Royal Devon and Exeter Hospital? It's nice because it means that I can talk intelligently to him about his work.

It is clear that he takes his duties as godfather to Bruno very seriously, and asked me all about schools and so on. Well, you can guess my reaction as these new pitfalls opened up before me. I had no idea where Hubert had been at school, but thankfully James stepped in with, 'Well, of course he'll go to Truro just as Hubert did,' and then they were off, discussing schooldays, and giving me a chance to pull myself together. Thank God that Bruno's not five until December, which gives us another year to prepare for that first ordeal. On the other hand Emma has her second birthday while Simon is with us. Can you imagine how odd it is, Vivi, to celebrate your child's birthday on the wrong date? Lottie was born on 13th October, and now will spend the rest of her life exactly one month older than she really is. I tried not to think about it and, despite the rationing and the difficulties of buying anything really good, she had a splendid party.

When the cake was brought in with the candles alight Emma positively screamed with excitement. Bruno helped to blow out the candles and then Simon produced his present. Two tortoiseshell kittens, Vivi, the prettiest you've ever seen. It was so clever of him to bring two because, the moment he saw them, Bruno's eyes simply shone with joy.

'One each,' Simon said firmly. 'I expect you to take care of them, Bruno, until Emma's a little older.'

It was good to see Bruno going off with Simon to find a box for the kittens to sleep in and an old blanket. I wished that I'd thought of it earlier. It's exactly the thing to distract Bruno and give him responsibility.

When I looked in on Emma later that evening she was fast asleep with a blissful smile on her face.

Once Bruno was in bed Simon took me out to dinner at one of the hotels in Polzeath and we danced.

She puts down the pen and rests her elbows on the desk, wondering how to continue. Simon will be leaving very soon, to drive back to Exeter, and yet she needs this small respite from him; from all of them. The letter is an excuse—'Long overdue,' she says ruefully. 'Must catch the evening post'—and she slips away, hoping that if she tries to put down the events on paper it might help her to see things more clearly.

The light knock makes her jump and as Mousie puts her head round the door Mutt hurriedly shuffles the paper away, turning with a smile.

'I wondered if you'd like me to take your letter to the post?' Mousie smiles back at her. 'I've got my bicycle with me and I'm off home now.'

'That's very sweet of you.' Mutt makes a face of comical despair. 'You know, I still haven't finished it. Utterly hopeless but I'm simply not in the mood. Thanks, anyway.'

Mousie nods and leaves her sitting there but she frowns to herself as she slips on her cardigan and goes through the kitchen and out into the dusk. She reflects on Honor's reaction; how she tried to hide the letter. As Mousie hoists herself into the saddle, freewheeling down the drive and into the lane, she wishes that they could be friends. Intermittently she catches glimpses of a different Honor, light-hearted, warm, funny. She guesses that Simon sees this other Honor too, and is very much attracted to her. Today there has been an odd restraint between them as if they are afraid of showing too much of their true feelings to each other and to the family.

In the drawing room at Paradise Simon is rather put out when Mutt murmurs something about a letter and slips away. He has been hoping for a few minutes alone with her and he feels frustrated.

Soon Mousie says that she must go home; she has been helping to bath the children and put them to bed. After she's been gone for a decent interval, Simon begins to indicate that he too must be on his way. James glances at the clock and begins to get to his feet.

'No hurry,' says Simon quickly. 'I've got to get my bags down. I'll look in when I'm ready to go.'

James nods, settles back in his chair and picks up his newspaper.

Simon goes out into the hall. He hears a noise on the landing and, glancing up, he sees Bruno staring down at him. 'Hello, old chap,' he says quietly. 'Got a problem?'

Bruno comes slowly down the stairs, one step at a time. His hair is peaked and his eyes are wide and confused. Simon goes swiftly up to him and sits down on a stair near the top.

'Bad dream?' he asks sympathetically—and when Bruno nods, he slips an arm round him and gives him a hug. 'Want to tell me about it?'

Bruno shakes his head but sits beside Simon, leaning against him. As they sit together Simon looks down into the hall, holding the child gently but mentally planning ahead. He is interested in cardiovascular research, which might mean studying abroad in America or Australia. He wonders how Bruno would react to another move after such an upheaval and whether he would resent being taken from his father's home to a far-off country. Emma is too young to remember her father, and he has no doubts that she will adapt very readily, but Bruno is an imaginative and sensitive child and it might be difficult for Mutt to explain her new allegiance . . .

Simon grimaces to himself. He's jumping the gun a bit, taking a lot for granted, but he could tell when he was dancing with her that she wasn't indifferent to him. Oh, they behaved very properly, but underneath all that he felt her response to him. He mustn't rush her, he reminds himself—that could be fatal—but she is too warm, too much in love with life to spend the rest of it as a widow here, and she's intelligent, that's so important, and can talk about his work.

He smiles reminiscently. When he took her out she'd looked so beautiful in her strange-coloured frock, apparently unaware of the other men's admiring glances, but the really good thing was that they had a wonderful time together. At first they were tongue-tied with a kind of shyness, but once they'd had a drink they'd loosened up. They'd laughed at the same things and he loved the naughty twinkle in her eye that mocked the other rather stuffy couples, so upright as they danced.

'This has been such fun,' she'd said at the end of the evening. But then she'd got that stricken look, probably remembering Hubert, and he'd had to remind her that she was still young and was allowed to be happy. He was very restrained and he could see that this was winning him points. She was so grateful that he'd found the kittens and brought them along for the kids.

'Bruno wants to call them Pipsqueak and Wilfred,' she told him.

Remembering, Simon looks down at Bruno, who leans against him, relaxed now and half asleep.

'OK now, old chap?' he asks.

Bruno nods and Simon takes him back to his room, tucks him in and goes to fetch his bag.

In James's study, Mutt stares at the sheet of paper, rereading the last sentence but quite unable to continue with the letter. Now it is Simon's turn to knock, telling her that he must be on his way back to Exeter, and she folds the sheets into the writing case and comes out to him, shutting the door behind her.

Later

It's over a week since I wrote that last sentence, Vivi. You'd have guessed at once that it wasn't as casual as it sounded just written down like that in one easy sentence.

Oh, the heaven of dressing up in something pretty—another of Honor's frocks but this one made of a dark prune-coloured silk and only needing a little effort to make it fit properly. Thank goodness that Mother made us work hard at our dressmaking.

Simon looked so handsome in his dinner jacket. He has very dark hair and disturbing brown eyes. We took each other by surprise, once we were dressed up, and suddenly we both felt shy, and it wasn't until we'd had a drink or two that we began to relax. I began to ask about his work, which I find fascinating.

It was a typical seaside hotel, with an orchestra playing behind the potted palms and the guests rather staid and polite, so that quite suddenly I felt a terrible desire to giggle. Then I told him how clever he'd been over the kittens, and how Bruno wanted to call them Pipsqueak and Wilfred.

And then we got up to dance. A week later and still I don't know how to describe the sensations I had when he put his arms round me. He's one of those dancers that hold you very close but not in any way suggestively. He stooped slightly above me so that his cheek was almost touching my hair. Beside the other terribly formal men—chins held high, hands planted firmly in the middle of their partners' shoulder-blades—he had an intimate, sophisticated kind of shuffle and I wanted the music to go on for ever.

When we sat down I was very quiet and he looked a bit anxious and asked if I was OK. I said lightly, 'Oh, just memories,' and his expression changed as if he'd suddenly recalled that I was Honor Trevannion, a grieving widow of just a few months. But that wasn't what I wanted and I couldn't bear to think he was suddenly despising me, and just blurted out, 'I can't tell you what it means simply to enjoy myself again. It's heaven here in Cornwall, but there's so much I miss.'

I stopped then, Vivi, because I'd been going to say that I missed my work, and that particular camaraderie I'd had with Honor and Hubert, and I could see myself getting into difficulties. I knew that there was so little I could tell him—or anyone, apart from you—about those years.

Simon put my hesitation down to a different kind of confusion. 'You've had a terrible shock in frightening circumstances,' he said, 'but you're still young and you must give yourself the chance to be happy.'

'Oh, I am happy,' I reassured him. 'As happy as I can be, anyway, in the circumstances,' I added quickly. 'Everyone's so kind to me.'

He smiled at me, then—oh, such a smile, Vivi—and said, 'I'm sure they are.'

I felt myself blushing, and he held out his hand to me and I followed him back onto the dance floor without another word. They were playing 'Ev'ry Time We Say Goodbye' and he held me just the same as before but I was convinced that he could hear my heart hammering. If he did then he gave no sign of it, and when we went back to our table he began to talk about some research he's working on and it restored us both to normality—well, nearly.

I tried to think of how Honor would have reacted to Simon and exactly how much Hubert had told his old friend about her. I can't imagine the Hubert I knew sitting down to write lengthy letters to anyone— though I know that he did do just that occasionally for Mousie—and if Honor ever wrote to his family then no one has told me about it.

This is the problem, Vivi; this waiting for the unexpected to jump out at you. That brief time with Simon, when both of us forgot everything except our two selves, was the most wonderful relief. The trouble is, I daren't forget that I'm *not* myself. I'm not Madeleine Grosjean, not even Madeleine Uttworth. I'm Honor Trevannion.

We said good night sensibly—he just touched my cheek with his lips—and then we had a nightcap with James. And that's that.

Love, darling,
Madeleine

Joss got up from the desk. She felt stiff and tired and she was aware of an inclination to weep. She'd given up all attempts to assess the rights and wrongs of Mutt's actions and had given herself wholly to the narrative of the letters. Oh, how often she'd imagined the luxury of such a relationship with George, knowing that it must be denied while every instinct cried out that it was right. How well she could imagine that light brushing of Simon's warm bare skin against Mutt's cheek and the mad, wild heartbeat.

Joss took a deep, shaky breath and went out, through the hall and into the kitchen, where she filled the kettle. She made some coffee, imagining the young Mutt dressing for the dance: turning before the looking-glass, assessing herself in Honor's made-over frock. She imagined Mutt, filled with apprehension, while Simon waited downstairs in the drawing room, handsome in his dinner jacket. She could identify with that breathless excitement, forbidden yet irresistible; the delicious shyness breaking out into giggling and wild, foolish happiness.

And then we got up to dance . . .

Joss shivered, hugging herself. 'George,' she muttered with wistful despair. 'Oh, George. I do love you.'

Paradise
2nd October

How you would have laughed, Vivi, if you could have seen us today. It would have taken you back to our childhood: Indian summer days in the hot, dusty Wiltshire lanes, picking blackberries for Mother. The juicy fruit, each one like a cluster of shiny black pinheads, was picked with care; even Emma was allowed to help, although she invariably squashed the fruit between her small fingers and her mouth was stained purple by the time we'd finished. Honeysuckle is still flowering in the hedges and I picked a crown, delicate and pale, and threaded it through the buttonhole of my shirt.

We were allowed a little treat for our labours: a picnic by the Saint's Well. Aunt Julia had managed some little fairy cakes, milk for Bruno and Emma, and a Thermos of tea. I think that she had saved all her fat and sugar rations to make these things for the children, who loved the little party, although Emma had to be forcibly restrained from paddling in her shoes and socks.

We left Aunt Julia at The Row and crossed the little bridge to Paradise. Bruno always likes to visit The Lookout. It's more like a light-house with its great bowed window curving out over the sea. For some reason it fires Bruno's vivid imagination and he uses it as a kind of play-house. We didn't have the key with us so he had to content himself with running up the rocky path to peer in at the kitchen window while we waited in the lane. Coming home across the meadow, clouds of tiny white moths fluttered up from the long damp grass: Emma reached for them, trying to catch them, chuckling with delight.

I've had a letter from Simon. It was simply to thank me for the week-end, saying how lovely it was for him to spend some time away from his work in a family atmosphere. Right at the end he suggested that I might accompany him to the wedding of a friend of his: he makes it very clear that he'll be staying with this friend—Simon's to be the best man—and points out that, while I might not like the idea of being left to my own devices while he's doing his duty, the rest of the time could be rather fun. He says he'd book a hotel for me, organise the travelling, and wonders if we might go to the theatre.

Anyway, a good day here in Paradise. I wonder if I will ever show it to you. Oh, what joy to imagine you here, if only I could see you face to face, Vivi, and explain it all properly.

God bless you, darling.

All my love,

Madeleine

Paradise
23rd October

Knowing how clear-eyed and practical you are, Vivi, it will surprise you to read that I actually spent several days considering Simon's invitation. You would have said at once, 'You can't possibly go,' having seen the complications immediately. I think I knew too, but I wanted to go so much, Vivi. I could imagine it all so clearly: the opportunity to dress up a little, the fun, the company of people of my own age. I'd had that moment with him, you see; that moment of stepping apart and being simply us—Simon and Madeleine. I wasn't anyone's mother or widow, I wasn't pretending to be another woman, I was just me.

I did actually believe that I could go to London. I went into my bedroom to look at a tussore silk suit—Honor's, of course—which might be pressed and tweaked into respectability. I was trying it on, humming 'Ev'ry Time We Say Goodbye', when Bruno suddenly came through the doorway behind me. I didn't turn round. We simply stared at each other through the mirror and I could see that he was looking at the suit. Do you know, Vivi, I was simply unable to speak: I couldn't think what to say to him. He disappeared as silently and quickly as he'd arrived and I sat down on the edge of the bed, still in the suit, and faced the fact that I wouldn't be going anywhere.

I changed out of the suit and went straight downstairs to reply to Simon's letter. I wrote things like, 'It's rather too soon to trust myself on such an emotional occasion' and, 'I think I might feel a little out of my depth among so many strangers' and then I went to look for Bruno.

It was a still afternoon, after a week of wild gales from the west, and the garden had that peaceful, waiting atmosphere of late autumn. I saw Bruno at once. He was riding Hubert's old tricycle down the drive: elbows akimbo, feet pedalling furiously. At the gate he turned the handlebars sharply, so that the gravel flew beneath the rubber tyres, and then he stopped: head on one side, legs straddling, he held a long, earnest conversation with nobody I could see. Presently he took hold of the handlebars again and came back up the drive at great speed. I stepped out of view, only reappearing as he reached the house.

One glance at his flushed, eager little face told me that he was in the grip of some exciting game of his own invention, a world away from me and Honor's silk suit, and I felt quite weak with relief. I saw a moment's confusion in his eyes, as the two worlds collided, and I smiled at him.

'I think there might be Cornish splits for tea,' I said to him, 'with blackberry jelly and clotted cream. I hope Pipsqueak and Wilfred haven't got at the cream. Shall we go and see?'

He slipped from the saddle, watching me, and I went down on one knee and held out my arms to him.

'I love you,' I told him—oh, how I hugged him—'and I want you to be happy.'

'I am happy, Mutt,' he said, quite seriously as if to reassure me. 'I love it here with you and Emma and all the family.'

And he took my hand, Vivi, and we went into the house.

As he dips toast fingers into his egg, Bruno is thinking about how he felt when he went into Mutt's bedroom and—for one heart-stopping moment—saw Mummie standing with her back to him. The suit had triggered off so many memories that he'd been knocked off balance: the Paradise world colliding with the Indian world. Then he'd seen Mutt's face in the mirror and he'd felt relieved but confused and he'd run away again quickly. He'd known that if he'd allowed it he might have burst into tears, because the memories were making him remember all the people and things that he'd lost, but another part of him was already making up a story that distracted from the hurt. He'd let himself go along with the story, finding his tricycle and dashing off on it, acting out the story while it unwound itself in his head. When Mutt had appeared he'd almost forgotten what had happened earlier. She'd hugged him.

'I love you,' she said, 'and I want you to be happy.'

He knows that this is quite true and he tried to comfort her, explaining that he is happy here with all the family round him.

Now, eating his egg and watching Pipsqueak and Wilfred playing on the floor, he knows that he wouldn't want anything to change.

Paradise
December

It's nearly Christmas, Vivi, and more than six weeks have passed since I wrote that last letter: a month of storms and rain and influenza. Poor Bruno's birthday passed almost unnoticed and we intend to make it up to him at Christmas. Goodness, I am exhausted and I've lost some weight, rushing between The Row and Paradise, but it was good to be useful and to try my nursing skills once more. Mousie will make a very good nurse, that's certain, and Rafe is such a blessing.

I don't have to tell you, dear Vivi, that I've always got on better with the male of the species. They are less complicated than we are — 'And,' I can hear you saying rather tartly, 'much more susceptible.' Well, yes, I can't deny that. I think Rafe has a bit of a crush on me at present — it's very touching. Fifteen is such an uncomfortable age for a boy, although Rafe is very independent and mature. With no father he has had to grow up quickly and Julia sees to it that he shoulders the family responsibilities in his father's stead.

There's something missing in me, Vivi. I never acquired that maturity that implies superior wisdom because, between one day and the next, I happened to become an adult, or a married woman, or a mother. When does this magical transition take place? Honor had that adult quality, a kind of gravitas that made you feel safe with her, yet she could be fun too. Sometimes, when I wear particular items of her clothing, a little of the gravitas rubs off on me like fairy dust. In her tweeds I feel a little more ready to deal with emergencies.

Well, I am Honor Trevannion now. I have her name, her clothes, her home and her son, and it's only fair to try to do as she would have done with them all.

I discovered something else, Vivi, once I'd made the decision about Simon's invitation. I can't send you these letters, can I? Perhaps I knew that too, but couldn't face it. Writing to you is my lifeline to the truth, to what I really am, and I'm afraid to cast it off in case I forget the truth and lose myself utterly. I think we all long to have one person in our lives who truly knows us and, despite everything, loves us unconditionally. But how can I send the letters? Will you feel you must tell your husband and, if you do, what then? At night, alone, I rack my brains and try to see a way out. I long to go to Mass this Christmas. But if I were to make my confession how could I go on afterwards, still living a lie? What I really want is to be given a blessing on what I am doing here at Paradise.

I think about you, dear Vivi, and wonder what you're doing this Christmas.

Paradise
15th January 1948

I've just reread my last letter, Vivi, and, despite its rather dreary note, we had a delightful Christmas, with a tree and charming homemade presents for everyone — and Simon brought a goose. Did I say that he was coming for Christmas? James invited him and I have to admit that he added considerably to the fun. It was good to be home for a traditional Christmas and Bruno was enchanted. I wish you could have seen him carefully examining the tree decorations, the same ones with which Hubert had decorated the tree when he was the same age as Bruno is now: delicate, frosted glass balls in different shapes—an owl, a clock, a mouse—and Victorian papier mâché bells, hand-painted red and green, with tiny clappers. There were little carved musical instruments and birds, and each branch held its own candle. When they were lit on Christmas Eve, and we brought the children into the darkened drawing room to see the finished tree, the gleaming, magical look of it took my breath away. Simon and James stood one on each side, beaming proudly, and I have to say, Vivi, that I was glad of the shadowy darkness. Looking at the children's awed faces—one of those rare occasions when Emma is silenced by events too great for her—I thought of Honor and Hubert, and I wept.

Fortunately, Emma's silence, never very long-lived, was broken by the sight of the angel at the top of the tree and her demanding to be lifted up to look at it. I could see Simon watching me across the room but, surprisingly, it was Mousie who slipped an arm about my shoulders and gave me a hug.

It was one of those moments in life where you can go deeper in with someone, move the relationship on to a different plane and allow it to grow, and I can't tell you how I longed to do it. Yet as we looked at each other I felt fear. Of all the family, Mousie is the only one whose intuitiveness tells her that something is not quite right. It would be impossible to come really close to her and be able to hold anything back.

I couldn't risk it. I returned her hug and made some remark about the children—but we both knew. She smiled at me and went to Bruno, leaving me alone. For a moment I didn't know what to do, where to go: I was outside the magic circle, cold and alone. Then Simon was beside me, offering me a glass of sherry, murmuring something, bringing me to life again. His intuition—different from Mousie's—tells him that I am not indifferent to him.

Simon would give me true companionship and it's clear that he wants his own children. He would be wonderful with Bruno and Emma; it would mean friendship with other people of our own age and simple, ordinary fun. I'm in love with Simon, Vivi.

A Happy New Year, my darling.

Paradise
19th February

I'd forgotten how melancholy the English spring can be, Vivi. I sit in the drawing room looking out into the twilight, a wood fire crackling behind me, watching the sky change colour: patches of gun-metal grey, robin's-egg blue, salmon pink. The lawn is frosted with a light scattering of snow, icing the snowdrops and crocus that are flowering in the grass, and I can hear a thrush singing amongst the camellias. A blackbird flies swift and low over the silent garden, alighting with its stuttering, warning cry on a bleak, bare branch, and there are lambs crying in the fields below the house. Quite suddenly the crimson sunset colour drains out of the sky and I see the thin beaten-silver disc of the moon tangling amongst the black twigs of a thorn tree.

This is Paradise, Vivi, and the serpent is a worming, gnawing creature called Discontent: the sting of the wasp, the smarting of the nettle, the piercing of the thorn, all belong to him. Do you think that God punishes us? I don't. We punish ourselves by imagining that He thinks like we do. On evenings like this I catch a glimpse, just a glimpse, of what He is offering us.

Sorry, Vivi. I find that, more and more, I have to talk things through with myself so as to try to understand my feelings. It's best when I sit and write to you like this. I hear your voice and imagine what you would be saying to me.

I love Simon.

We took Bruno to the pantomime at Bodmin for his belated birthday treat; he'd never seen anything like it and his eyes never left the stage. He sat between me and Simon—Mousie and Rafe and Aunt Julia further along the row—and Simon laid his arm along the back of Bruno's seat, oh, so casually and naturally, so that his fingers were just resting on my shoulder.

As I stared sightlessly ahead, unmoved by Aladdin's plight, I thought about Honor and how she would have reacted. It was a pointless exercise: Honor would never have allowed herself to be in such a position. I clapped in all the right places, hands held high, smiling brightly, and bent solicitously to Bruno to explain the plot to him from time to time.

I knew that Simon was watching me, admiring me in my motherly role, approving my love and tenderness for my son. Honor's son. Bruno's rapt excitement, the way he clutched me when the genie shot up through the trap door, also held me steady. I love him too, Vivi, which makes it all so terribly complicated.

I imagine that I hear your voice telling me that it was already complicated, that my life could never be simple again. I make up little fairy stories for myself, in which everything comes right in the end and we live happily ever after.

The serpent whispers in my ear and tells me that I can have it all, that I need only to stretch out my hand to take it, and his restless whispering drowns out the silence where God lives.

It's evening now. The moon is sailing free of the thorn tree, its cold light silvering the frosty grass, and the trees cast black shadows across the drive. I can hear James coming out of his office, ready for a drink.

Today would have been my birthday, Vivi, and I would have been twenty-eight.

Love you, darling.

Simon can barely keep his eyes from her. She looks so beautiful but tonight there is a remoteness about her that both attacks his confidence and fuels his determination. The presence of the family is frustrating and he senses that she is holding him at arm's length. Simon grimaces ruefully to himself: 'arm's length' is exactly the right phrase. He is unable to resist stretching his arm along the back of Bruno's seat so that his fingers just touch Mutt's shoulder.

Bruno is far too preoccupied with the pantomime to notice what his godfather is doing but Mutt is aware of him: Simon knows that. She isn't responding this evening as she has done in the past, though. She's particularly maternal this evening, her whole concentration bent on ensuring that Bruno is enjoying himself on his birthday.

There's something different, though: a new coolness has quenched the warmth of her personality. He finds himself studying her covertly across Bruno's head. She watches the stage, apparently totally absorbed, unconscious of his stare, and he moves his fingers so that they touch the thin material of her frock and the warm shoulder beneath it. Suddenly he is aware of Mousie, further along the row, watching him. He smiles quickly and shifts in his seat, folding his arms across his chest.

Although he laughs and applauds in all the right places, he is thinking hard, planning ahead: somehow he must find the opportunity to be alone with her again.

Later

I never told you what James gave me for Christmas, did I? He's not a man for gifts—in these strict days of rationing it's a problem anyway— but he presented me with his wife's tapestry frame. I rather prefer this kind of gift, something special that has been used for years within the family, and I was absolutely thrilled with it. I see the evidence of Margaret's work all over the house: an impressive set of chair covers in the dining room, a big medieval-type tapestry on the landing, and smaller charming flower studies in lovely, plain frames.

James was so pleased at my reaction. I've taken the frame and set it up in the dining room. He is so good to us; it can't be easy having two small children suddenly wished upon you, yet he manages very well.

He told me yesterday that, after his death, the two farms would have to be sold to pay the death duties. You can imagine my shock at this

273

subject so casually introduced into the conversation. I said I didn't want to talk about his dying and he smiled, such a sweet, Hubert-like smile, and said that he didn't actually have it in his diary but that we needed to discuss certain things.

'Everything goes to you and the children,' he said. 'No change there. Of course, if you were to marry again . . .'

He hesitated and I knew that he was thinking about Simon. I felt my face grow hot and my stomach churned about.

'I shan't marry again,' I answered.

I said it so quickly, with such certainty, and immediately afterwards I felt a great peace begin to fill me.

'You're very young to make that decision,' James said. He looked so kind, so understanding. 'You don't have to rule it out but if you were to do so then I would make a new will. The estate would revert to Hubert's children to be held in trust until they come of age.'

I saw then that he wouldn't want Paradise and St Meriadoc being passed on to any children I might have by Simon, and this whole wretched deception came clearly into my mind. He wouldn't want Emma or me to have any of it either, if he knew the truth of it, and my brief moment of peace was shattered.

'It was simple for me and Margaret,' he was saying, 'having only one child. My dear, forgive me for speaking about it but I want to leave you safe if I can, and not in the hands of Bruno's wife or Emma's husband, so it will all come to you and I shall trust you to leave it to Hubert's children. I've arranged a trust for their school fees but, beyond that, you'll be hard pressed, I'm afraid. There are the rents from The Row, of course . . .'

'I have my pension,' I said quickly. 'We shall be fine. Please don't worry.'

'The place is in good heart,' he said, 'I've seen to that.'

So Paradise is to be mine, Vivi, but not just yet. I had a letter from Simon this morning. He's beginning to press me a little, suggesting a visit to Exeter. He's coming down for Easter.

What shall I do?

Paradise
23rd March

We've been down to The Lookout today, by the cliff-path. The day starts with thick mist drifting smoke-like from the sea, blotting out the waxy faces of the magnolia, misting the windows. Suddenly a breeze ripples through the garden, tearing the cloudy vapour apart and revealing a patch of tender blue sky. An unexpectedly violent downpour, and then the wind begins to rise and the clouds are whirled away. We set out at last in brilliant sunshine and vibrant colours: the icy green of the wild sea, the gold of the forsythia—all is vivid where, an hour before, all was grey and dim. After the sheltered garden, the cliff-path is high and exposed: the wind tears past us, whipping our hair into our mouths and stinging our eyes. Our clothes are whirled about our legs and we have to shout to one another to make ourselves heard. I pick Emma up, since she can make no headway on her short legs, and, with Bruno clinging to my free hand, we stare down through the flying creamy foam to the heaving, billowing water smashing onto the rocks below.

We are quite grateful to reach the relative peace of The Lookout, to watch the magnificent drama of sea and sky from the window.

'I love it here,' says Bruno, staring out, arms resting on the broad, low sill. 'I shall live in The Lookout when I grow up, with Pipsqueak and Wilfred. You and Emma can be at Paradise and I shall come here.'

'That's a good idea,' I answer lightly, 'and Emma and I will come to visit you.'

'We'll have tea at the table here,' he says, his face lighting up at the prospect, pointing at the big deal table which faces out towards the sea, 'and then we'll sit by the fire and tell stories. Are we going to light the fire today?'

This is a big treat. James has given us permission to light the fire in this enormous room: it helps to air the house, he agrees, as long as we make sure it's properly out by the time we leave. Bruno and I set to with twigs, matches and paper spills and soon we have a blaze going.

'You could live here too,' says Bruno out of the blue later, fearful perhaps that I have been hurt. 'Only who would live at Paradise?'

'Well, of course, Grandfather will be there,' I tell him cautiously.

'But not for ever,' he answers anxiously. 'Grandfather is old and sometimes he isn't very well. You'll be there too, won't you, Mutt?'

And out of nowhere, Vivi, I hear Honor's voice saying, *You'll look after the children if anything happens to me and Hubert, won't you, Mutt? You know I'd have Lottie.*

'Of course I shall be there,' I answer Bruno. 'I promise.'

Emma who, with the aid of a chair, has managed to climb up onto the table, somehow tumbles off and sets up a great wailing. We both rush to rescue her and the moment passes in a necessity to get out the picnic in order to distract her. The amazing blue-green light from the sea and sky reflects in her wide eyes and, watching her, I am seized with the familiar terror that every mother knows.

How would it work for Emma if I were to marry Simon and have other children? Would he love her as if she were his own? I try to imagine him living with us at Paradise and somehow I can't: he won't

275

fit into the picture. He is passionate about certain areas of research, has already talked about working abroad, and I try to imagine explaining all this to Bruno: why I am marrying Simon and why we are moving on again instead of staying at Paradise. He has returned to the window and his small, immobile figure seems to be part of the scene. He belongs here, Vivi, and I have promised him . . .

I wonder if you have children too. I'm sure you have: perhaps a son who is a small edition of your husband, Don, or a little girl who looks like you used to once. Everything changes once you have a child.

Apart from all that, Vivi, how could I risk marrying Simon? Imagine how easy it would be to make a mistake once the barriers were down and my guard relaxed. If I can't trust his love enough to tell him the truth now, then I certainly daren't take the chance of him discovering it later when there would be even more complications.

I hope he'll believe me when I tell him that I don't love him.

This time Joss was not quite able to hold back her tears. Some level of her consciousness continued to assess with dismay the threat these letters posed to her own security yet she still held the true realisation at bay, enthralled by the predicament of her grandmother's journey. Joss was impressed at the development of Mutt's self-knowledge, her brave—if utterly human—way of dealing with her hopes and fears.

She didn't need to read any further to know that Mutt's and Simon's love had had no future: Mutt had made her bed and must lie in it alone. With the true compassion of fellow feeling, Joss picked up the dwindling sheets and began to read the last remaining letters.

Paradise
29th March

It's done. He went back to Exeter this afternoon and now, although it's late, I simply had to write about all this. I'm in such an odd state, Vivi: exalted and trembly and foolish because he told me he loved me. He took me by surprise, you see. Mousie had taken the children down to The Row after lunch on Saturday so that I could paint and hide the Easter eggs. James had gone down to Home Farm, and Simon was expected in time for dinner. I was listening to the wireless, and quite suddenly the door opened and there he was.

Oh, Vivi, it was disastrous. I forgot my plan; forgot about being distant and sensible; forgot that I was Honor Trevannion. I simply sat there, my paintbrush held aloft, beaming at him with delight. I just said 'Hello' or something silly like that, still smiling at him, with my heart all over the place and thinking how dear he was. It was quite the stupidest thing I've ever done. He responded in the most natural way.

He closed the door behind him, came round the table and kissed me.

Fool that I am, Vivi, I responded to that too. It was the shock, you see. I'd planned it all out in my head how it would be. I was going to be distant and calm and then make it clear that I'd been thinking things over and seen that I'd given him quite the wrong impression. I was very fond of him, but I didn't have any intention of marrying again.

Instead here he was, in the kitchen, kissing me. He pulled me to my feet, paused briefly to relieve me of my egg and paintbrush and then continued where we'd left off. I remembered my plan far too late but eventually controlled myself enough to draw away from him. There was embarrassment on both sides.

It needn't have been like that. It could have been so nice if I hadn't made up my mind that I couldn't go through with it. It would have been so easy to smile at him and show him that it was quite all right; to make it clear that he wasn't taking liberties but only responding naturally to the signals I'd given him over the last six months. In those brief moments I saw so clearly how wonderful it might be with him: love as well as passion and our minds tuned to the same pitch. It seemed to me, at the time, that it would be criminal to kill something so good.

No gold stars then, Vivi, if you'd guessed that I didn't do it properly. I did the cowardly thing of telling him that I wasn't ready to fall in love again while giving the impression that if he hung around long enough I might change my mind. I apologised for leading him on—naturally he said at once that it was his fault—and muttered something about being lonely and finding him very attractive. Mousie arrived at the garden door just as he'd begun to say that he'd wait for as long as it took and I was saying that I had no plans to marry again. Fortunately we heard her in enough time to compose ourselves, I was back at my egg-painting before she actually appeared, and Simon was saying loudly that he'd take his bag up, was he in the usual room and so on, and suddenly it was all over.

I've lost everything that was important to me—but I have gained Paradise.

The Easter egg hunt is great fun although Emma cannot quite get the hang of it. Once Bruno has found the first egg—balanced carefully in the lower branches of the wisteria—she expects them to be anywhere she chooses to look and there are wails of disappointment punctuated by shrieks of delight. Rafe is there to help them, to guide them towards the painted eggs, while pretending to be as amazed as they are each time one is discovered. Rafe is enjoying himself. Often he finds Mutt at his elbow, reminding him where she has hidden the eggs, and they laugh together at the sight of Emma staggering purposefully in Bruno's wake, screaming encouragement. She is just as happy if he finds one, possessiveness having been entirely left out of her character, and anyway he shares them scrupulously between the two of them.

'Because she is too small,' he says seriously to Rafe, 'to find them on her own.'

Bruno's sharing of the painted eggs with Emma is not totally altruistic: his natural generosity is assisted by the knowledge of the present that Simon has brought with him from Exeter. He puts his hand into the pocket of his shorts and feels the shape of the little red bus.

'After all,' says Simon, 'you *are* my godson, old chap. We men have to stick together.'

Bruno can see that Simon is happy too, which is good, but it is to Rafe he instinctively turns now. With Rafe he feels the same sense of security he has in the company of Aunt Julia and with Mousie.

'That sister of yours,' says Rafe feelingly—and Bruno laughs too, shrugging and rolling his eyes just as he's seen the grown-ups react to her escapades.

Watching Mutt swinging Emma into the air he feels a deep sense of belonging.

'Time for tea,' Mutt is calling—and they all set off together towards the house.

Paradise
9th April

I had a letter from Simon a few days ago. It was beside my breakfast plate and James watched me as I opened it, though he pretended to be absorbed in his own letters. It occurs to me that the chemistry I described, zinging between me and Simon during that weekend, might have been obvious to other people too, and I feel anxious and guilty. I wonder what James thinks of me, having told him I wouldn't marry again, and I fear that he might misunderstand and disapprove in some way. In an effort to appear calm and unaffected I helped Emma with a few mouthfuls of her porridge and cut the top from Bruno's egg before I opened the envelope.

We eat breakfast in the dining room, and sometimes the sun streams in, circling Emma's head with a fuzzy golden halo and smoothing the gleaming rosewood of the oval table to a deep richness. It glints on gold-leaf patterns of the china teapot and strokes its way over the silky stitches of Margaret's big wall tapestry. Its warmth blesses and cheers us, making us eager for the day ahead and nourishing our plans.

The morning of Simon's letter it was raining. The dirty grey sky leaked with an unrelenting drizzle and the room felt bleak. We'd had a warm spell—the spring comes and goes, tantalisingly showing us her glories and then retreating behind a sharp shower of hail or a wild gale from the west—and this sudden reversion to winter was depressing. Emma was grizzling—as irritatingly persistent as the rain outside—and Bruno was asking if we could walk over to The Lookout after breakfast.

'If it clears up,' I said to Bruno, and opened Simon's letter.

To my horror I saw that my hands were trembling, and I quickly laid the sheets on the table beside my plate, my eyes scanning the lines of cramped writing. It was a sweet letter, Vivi, apologising for taking advantage of my 'vulnerable state' and telling me that he'd fallen in love with me. He went on to assure me that Hubert would be pleased to think that we might be gaining comfort from each other.

I looked up and saw that James was watching me. There was such far-seeing wisdom and affection in his eyes that fear clutched at my stomach. I knew that I couldn't bear to see disillusionment and disgust in those eyes and that I had no choice but to follow my chosen path.

I smiled at him. 'A bread-and-butter from Simon,' I said lightly, 'thanking us all for such a lovely weekend.' Folding the sheets and stuffing them back into the envelope I wiped Bruno's fingers. 'I think Bruno's right. We should visit The Lookout and give it an airing. What sort of morning have you got, James?'

'Oh, an office morning for me, I'm afraid.' He drank up the last of his tea and pushed back his chair. 'Humdrum, boring old paperwork.'

He slipped away and I smiled at the children. These two were now my life, my work, my whole future.

After lunch I wrote back to Simon while the children were resting and James was nodding over the newspaper. I sat at the dining-room table and wrote to him that there was no future for us, that my mind was quite made up, and that, having experienced true love and companionship, I knew that I didn't love him in that same way. I asked him not to pursue it but added that I hoped we would always be friends.

Don't think it was easy, though, Vivi. I hated it. All that morning while I was winding the children into scarves and pushing their warm little feet into gum boots I was mentally writing that letter. Phrases and sentences jostled about in my head as we went down the drive, Emma jumping with passionate glee into every puddle, and I rehearsed it a thousand times as we lit our little fire and Bruno chatted non-stop to me and to the variously imagined friends with which he peoples his life.

Aunt Julia came up to Paradise after tea, as she sometimes does, to help to bath the children and put them to bed. I left her reading a story to them and slipped away up the lane to post the letter at the box up on the Polzeath road. I stood by the postbox for a good five minutes holding the letter in my pocket. I prayed then, Vivi. I prayed for guidance and wisdom so as to do the right thing for all of us, and all the time I was held by a kind of peacefulness that remained with me all the way home.

Aunt Julia finishes Bruno's story and tucks him firmly into bed. 'Good night, Bruno,' she says. 'Sweet dreams,' and hurries downstairs.

James is reading peacefully in the drawing room but he looks up as she comes in and sets his book aside: her expression indicates that all is not well. Julia closes the door and sits down on the sofa.

'I'm worried about Honor.' She comes straight to the point. 'She seems rather *distrait* and I can't help wondering whether she's fallen in love with Simon. What do you think?'

This is straight talking, even for Julia. It is true that during the Easter weekend he began to notice that Honor and Simon were sharply aware of one another, and when his letter arrived earlier in the week James was unable to ignore her reaction to it.

'A bread-and-butter from Simon,' she'd said lightly—but he'd seen how her hands trembled.

He feels such compassion for her, imagining how wretched she must feel to be torn between several loyalties. James suspects that Honor believes that Hubert's children should grow up here at St Meriadoc and he wonders how Simon would approach the tricky situation of assimilating himself into this place and taking over his old friend's family.

He stirs, aware of Julia's eyes fixed upon him.

'I think it is a possibility,' he begins cautiously. 'But even if she has I don't see what we can do about it.'

'It would be quite wrong for Bruno to be uprooted again,' Julia says strongly. 'He is just beginning to recover from his father's death and I think it would be disastrous for him to adapt all over again to a new father and away from his family. Emma's too young to be a real problem, but even she is settling so happily here.'

'But what can I do about it?' asks James helplessly. 'I can't forbid them to fall in love. I've already explained to her that, should she marry again, the estate will be held in trust for Bruno and Emma. She said that she had no intention of marrying again and I believed her.'

Julia frowns. 'Even so, watching them over Easter I would have said that there was something between them. Simon is a charming, attractive man, but I don't want her to make a mistake.'

James looks at her curiously. 'Don't you like Simon?'

'Oh, he's a nice enough fellow. She could go further and fare worse but I don't want her rushed into anything.'

'Perhaps you could speak to her,' James ventures.

She shakes her head. 'We're not on those terms. Despite her natural friendliness Honor still keeps herself a little distant from us. Fair enough, I'm not a one for messy emotions all over the place either. That's why you should approach it from the point of view of the will.'

'I don't know how I should start,' says James wretchedly. 'Good grief, Julia! What could I say? I'm not her father.'

'You are the children's grandfather,' she says—but she can see his dilemma. 'We need something which will make her review the situation carefully.' Julia pauses, raising her hand warningly, and presently Honor comes in through the hall. She smiles at them almost dreamily as if possessed of a great inner contentment.

'Whoever called this place "Paradise" is right,' she says. 'It's the most beautiful place in the world. I can't get over how lucky I am to be here.' Her smile becomes more practical and she looks with great affection upon the older pair. 'I'm going to get the supper.'

They remain silent, until they can hear movement in the kitchen, and then James raises an eyebrow questioningly and Julia shrugs.

Paradise
12th April

He came to Paradise yesterday while the family was at church. I met him at the top of our valley by the Saint's Well. He telephoned, Vivi. I had a feeling that he wouldn't just accept the letter and after a day or two I began to feel edgy. The sense of peace wore off and I felt tense and expectant. Each time the telephone rang I jumped and trembled—and then, at last, it was Simon.

'I'm coming down,' he said at once. 'I'd like to see you on your own, Mutt. Don't argue about it, please. Just give me this one chance. I have an idea . . .'

His idea was that I should miss Matins, giving a headache as an excuse, and meet him high up in the valley. He could leave the car up on the Polzeath road and walk down the track.

'I'll see you by the well just after eleven,' he said, and hung up.

I see now that it would have been wiser simply to explain to James that Simon had proposed and I had refused but I complicated matters further by going along with Simon's plan. As soon as they'd set out for church I slipped away. All the way along the valley I was thinking about that picnic where it had first started, this thing between us.

He was waiting for me. It was a chill, dank morning, no larks singing, and he stood with his hands thrust down into his pockets. He was nervous, of course, defensive, but his posture was aggressive and that helped me. He watched me walking up our valley, his head lowered slightly, his face expressionless.

I felt quite strong and in control of myself. The help I was already getting from Simon's unwelcoming stance was reinforced by the way he began by calling me Honor.It reminded me of the children and my responsibility towards them, of dear old James and the family, and even of Honor and Hubert themselves.

There was no magic by the Saint's Well that morning: only the clear, cold sound of the water, and all the passion that had flamed between us in the kitchen at Easter was now quenched into a cool exchange. He behaved as if a chasm lay at our feet and he spoke to me across it. He talked about the future he'd planned for us: he has been offered a research post at the Baker Medical Research Institute in Australia and he described a new life for us all, free from sad memories of the past. The more he spoke the deeper and wider the chasm grew until, confused and angry, he accepted defeat, turning away with a gesture of frustrated farewell before striding off towards the Polzeath road.

I can hardly remember getting back to Paradise but quite suddenly I felt weak, no longer upheld by that inner strength I'd had at the well, and I lay down upon my bed. The children found me there, bringing me flowers picked in the lane, and Emma scrambled up beside me and patted my face with her soft, pudgy hands, crooning a little song. Bruno stood stiffly beside the bed, his face taut with anxiety.

'Are you really ill, Mutt?' he asked.

I roused myself and managed to smile at him reassuringly.

'Just this wretched head,' I said. 'Don't worry, darling.'

And then Aunt Julia came in, bringing me a hot-water bottle and an aspirin, and shushing the children, and after that there was silence. It was then, with my defences weak, that I wept Vivi, cradling the hot, comforting bottle in my arms. I wept not only for myself and Simon but also for Hubert and Honor and Bruno and all that we'd lost.

Much later, I got up, washed my face, put on some make-up, brushed my hair and tied a bright yellow and blue scarf over it. When I opened the drawing room door, Julia, James and Bruno were seated at the table in the window playing Monopoly. They turned and their welcoming expressions warmed my heart and gave me courage.

Bruno scrambled down and came to me. 'Are you better?' he asked.

'Quite better,' I answered. 'And when you've finished your game we'll go for a walk over the cliffs to The Lookout.'

I sat down on the sofa where Emma was curled, fast asleep, her smooth limbs carelessly disposed, her flushed face peaceful. Sitting there, watching her sleep, listening to the murmuring voices from the table, I made my commitment once and for all.

All the morning, while he is in church and on the walk home, Bruno is worried about Mutt. She says that she has a headache but he senses something more, and he feels anxious. When they get back to Paradise and find her in bed he is filled with fear: the memories press in on him and he can recall how Father fell ill, then baby Em, and then Mummie; lying amongst the damp, crumpled sheets too weak to comfort him. His throat seems to close up with tears and he knows that he simply couldn't bear it if anything were to happen to Mutt. He stands beside the bed, stiff with fright, his bunch of flowers wilting in his clenched hand.

'Are you really ill?' he asks her, and though she tells him that it is just the headache he doesn't believe her.

Aunt Julia hurries him and Emma out of the bedroom, telling him that Mutt needs to rest. He can barely swallow any lunch and afterwards Aunt Julia and Uncle James play Monopoly with him while Emma falls asleep on the sofa. And then suddenly she is there, opening the door and smiling at them, and his relief is overwhelming.

'Are you better?' he cries, and she says that she is quite better and that later they'll walk over the cliffs to The Lookout.

Julia watches Honor as she sits down beside the sleeping Emma. Her older, wiser eyes see the result of bitter weeping that the make-up and the gay headscarf cannot quite disguise and there is something in Honor's down-turned face, as she looks at her sleeping child, that rends Julia's heart. She tries to analyse the expression—resolve?

Suddenly, Honor glances up. 'Do you know I quite forgot to tell you that Simon's been offered a research post in Australia. Very exciting for him but very sad for us,' she says lightly. 'You won't be seeing much of your godfather from now on, Bruno, but I'm sure he'll write to you. We shall miss him, won't we?'

James and Julia study the board with great concentration, answering Bruno's questions about Australia, and, presently, when Emma wakes up, the children set off to The Lookout with Honor.

At last James and Julia look at each other.

'I think we underestimated her,' says Julia after a long moment.

James nods in agreement and begins to put away the board.

'She's a good girl,' he murmurs. His instincts have not played him false: Paradise will be safe in her hands.

Paradise
8th June

Darling Vivi,

This is the last letter I shall write to you, exactly one year since I first arrived at Paradise. These letters to you contain the only record of who and what I truly am, and the truth of what happened, but if I am to fully commit I must also finish with Madeleine Grosjean. After all, she disappeared out there in India.

A man arrived at the door the other day—just a stranger who had lost his way while out walking the cliffs—but I was filled with a sudden unreasoning terror. Supposing Johnny were to try to track me down, through Honor and Hubert, or suppose you and Don made some enquiries? I imagine that the news that Lottie and I died in Karachi with Hubert has filtered back and that nobody will bother to question it. Nevertheless, it made me see that I am still vulnerable.

I must become Honor Trevannion. I must allow her firm kindness, her decisiveness, her strict way of loving gradually to sink into my character. I've managed quite well so far but I cannot afford any distractions.

So no letters, Vivi. I must do without the comfort of sharing with you. I shall miss you. When I lie awake at night wondering how I shall answer Bruno when he's old enough to ask the question: 'Why did you pretend to be my mother?' then I shall wish that I had you to help me through.

I hope he'll understand the way those decisions were taken and how the smallest deception can entrap so quickly.

I think he will understand. There's something wise about Bruno, some grace which is far beyond his years, which even now casts its healing over me. When he smiles at me, hugs me—knowing the truth as he does—I feel as if I have been granted absolution.

And there's something else, Vivi, I cling to when I feel myself, Madeleine, being slowly but inexorably rubbed out. I remember words that Sister Julian read to us at the convent.

> Do not fear, for I have redeemed you,
> I have called you by name; you are mine.
> When you pass through the waters, I will be with you;
> And when you pass through the rivers,
> They shall not overwhelm you . . .
> Do not fear, for I am with you.

If He knows me by my name then nothing else really matters, does it?

There will be so much I shall want to tell you: all those small but significant events that shape the pattern of our lives as our children grow up. I shall be thinking of you, Vivi, and wondering if you will be telling your own children about the fun we had. Perhaps I am already an aunt, and Emma has a cousin she will never know.

I love you, darling. That will never change.

Your sister,
Madeleine

PART THREE

BRUNO COULDN'T SLEEP. Emma had gone yawning upstairs hours ago and still he paced the big room, lights switched out and curtains open to the clear night, while Nellie watched him from the sofa. As he walked to and fro, or paused to stare out into the darkness, he wrestled with the problem that now confronted him. How was he to juggle the complications of the inheritance with the need to protect Emma?

In all his conversations with Mutt down the years, she'd pleaded with him that Emma should never know the truth: that somehow, after her death, the deception should be maintained.

'You belong, Bruno,' she'd said. 'This is your home and these are your family. I know that what I did would seem unforgivable to most people but you've always understood why I did it, haven't you, darling? What do you think Emma would feel if she discovered that she didn't belong here? Or that you weren't her brother?'

Her very real distress had never failed to move him. Despite the terrible loss of his own family he'd always been able to understand her dilemma and why she'd acted so impulsively fifty years before during those last terrible days in Karachi. Even now he could remember his overwhelming relief when she'd appeared in their hotel room with Emma jabbering cheerfully in her arms. The thought of being without Mutt, who was that vital living link between the unknown future and the shocking past, was not to be borne.

Only he, watching her down the years, had sensed Mutt's struggle. Some instinct told him that her guilt would never let her rest. She had looked after them all and the valley had become her true home. Her creative spirit expressed itself in the Paradise gardens, where she and Rafe had worked so tirelessly, and in her tapestry work that now adorned the local churches. He knew, too, that sailing was her greatest pleasure: that as the gap between the boat and the shore widened so this joyful spirit, passionate and carefree, shook off the shackles of capable widow and mother.

It was odd, thought Bruno, that he should be the one who knew her best and loved her most. Because of her he'd had to deny the memory of his own mother and sister, to accept and live the deception into which she'd plunged them. Yet from the earliest days he'd been aware of her hard-won courage. As Emma grew up he'd seen the same qualities in her that he still glimpsed in Mutt. She too was passionate, given to laughter, generous. She loved Paradise, adored Bruno and Rafe and Mousie. After she was married she'd come racing down to Cornwall at every opportunity, insisting that St Meriadoc was her real home and where she most belonged.

Bruno and Mutt had almost quarrelled over Raymond Fox. This was the first time his sympathy for Mutt had given way before a genuine sense of anxiety for Emma. He'd already had a shouting match with Em, each of them deriding the other's lack of taste when it came to choosing a marriage partner, and later he'd gone up to Paradise to have it out with Mutt. Now, listening to the sea's rhythmic *shush-shush* against the rocks below the window, he saw the scene in his mind's eye as clearly as if it were being enacted on the black glass in front of him.

'She loves him,' says Mutt, not looking at him, opening the drawers of her desk and closing them again with a bang.

'Emma loves everyone,' he answers impatiently. 'I've never known a girl like her for needing to love someone and to be loved in return.'

She turns then, staring at him almost fearfully across the back of the chair. 'But she's always known how much we've loved her, hasn't she?' she asks anxiously. 'Oh, Bruno, do you think that she's missed having a father? More than we realised?'

'I've no idea,' he answers, not in the mood for soul-searching. 'The point is whether this wretched Fox loves her, and in my opinion he doesn't. He's a cold, calculating type. She won't be happy with him, Mutt.'

He sees her expression change from worried introspection to thoughtful consideration of his words. 'He's steady,' she says at last. 'He won't do anything foolish or make a fool of her with another woman.'

His laugh is short and explosive. 'You're dead right about that,' he answers crudely. 'He wouldn't know what passion was if it struck him.'

'You're young,' she says quietly. 'You can't imagine what it's like to be abandoned or to have no security. I don't want that for Emma.'

He studies her, realising that he knows very little about Mutt's own past except in relation to his own family. Some tacit agreement from those early years has cast a cloak of silence over the years in India.

His irritation subsides a little, but he has no intention of giving way yet. 'Emma will never be abandoned while I'm alive,' he says, 'but even the fear that she might be doesn't mean she has to marry a man like Raymond Fox. He's wrong for her,' he insists stubbornly.

'That's what she says about Zoë. That you married her for all the wrong reasons. I did question it myself, if you remember, but you answered—quite fairly—that you had the right to do what you liked with your own life. Emma feels exactly the same.'

'So you have actually discussed it with her?' he asks lightly. 'That you think that she might be marrying for the wrong reasons?'

He watches her averted face, sees her bite her lip. The silence between them is stretched, tense.

'We've talked about it,' she answers evasively at last. 'Of course we have. She's in love with him and he loves her.' Her chin goes up a little higher, her back is a little straighter, and his heart sinks. 'After his fashion Raymond has given his heart to Emma. She'll be looked after and he'll be a loyal husband and a responsible father.'

'Sounds like fun,' he says, his voice brittle with defeat. 'You don't think that a bit of passion might be nice or even some kind of meeting of minds?'

The silence this time is of a different quality. Something else has joined them in the parlour, something that softens Mutt's expression. When she speaks her question takes him completely by surprise.

'Have you heard from Simon recently?' she asks. 'It seems a long time since you had any news of him.'

'Yes,' he says, confused. 'Well, I had a letter a month or two back. He sent a photograph of the twins with Tessa on the beach at Bondi. I meant to show it to you.'

She turns to look at him. 'Don't be too harsh on me,' she says gently. 'Passionate people need a framework of stability. Emma loves the good things of life and she likes to share them. She will be able to entertain for Raymond, give parties, dress well. And there will be times when Raymond's stolidity and lack of imagination will be invaluable to Emma. She'll use them as a defence against her own mistaken passions. Friends and enemies will blame him and she'll be loved for herself.'

'It doesn't sound a particularly honest way of going on,' Bruno says.

Mutt gets up and comes to him with arms outstretched. 'It's so hard to get it right for other people,' she says almost desperately. 'Especially when you love them. Should I have stopped you from marrying Zoë?'

He puts his arms about her. 'You didn't have a hope,' he says. 'You're quite right, Mutt. Why do we think we can get it right for other people when we get so much wrong for ourselves? If Emma's made up her mind there's no more to be said about it.'

A door opened upstairs and Bruno tensed, listening to water gurgling in the cistern and footsteps overhead. Presently Emma's bedroom door closed and there was silence. All at once he made up his mind. He took

Nellie through to her bed in the kitchen and shrugged into his coat.

'Stay,' he told Nellie, ignoring her beseeching expression. 'Good girl.'

Shutting the door gently behind him, he paused to glance towards The Row, where all was dark and quiet, then set off up the cliff-path towards Paradise. When he arrived at the front door, he pushed it open and stood for a moment in the hall, considering. Some instinct had brought him over the cliff to Paradise but now he waited, uncertain of the next move. Thinking about Mutt, remembering the past, he'd forgotten about Joss. Even as he thought about her, the parlour door opened and she came out into the hall.

At her gasp of surprise and alarm he raised his arms. 'Sorry,' he said. 'I wasn't thinking. I had a feeling about Mutt and just came on up. Sorry to frighten you.'

She came towards him, out of the shadows, and he saw that she was struggling with some strong emotion. Bruno reached out and took her by the shoulders. 'What is it? Is it Mutt?'

Joss shook her head and then nodded. 'Yes, I suppose it is in a way.' Her eyes, blurred by tears and shock, slid away from his.

Without speaking he led her into the drawing room and pushed her gently into the corner of the sofa. Carefully, he piled charred logs and embers together, then, picking up the bellows, puffed life back into the fire. Huddled on the sofa, her hands pressed between her knees, Joss watched him silently while her tired brain rocked with the effort of assimilating this new knowledge: Mutt had been living a lie all these years, yet Joss's heart went out to her and tears rose once more to her eyes as she recalled the words her grandmother had written so long ago.

Bruno laid down the bellows and looked up at Joss, but a quick glance at her troubled face gave him no assistance. Somehow, he intuited, the trustful ease with which she'd always approached him was damaged. Still crouched, he swore silently and then rose to his feet in one quick movement, thrusting his hands into his pockets.

Suddenly he remembered Emma's remark about the American. 'Perhaps you've found something,' he hazarded, rather as if they were playing some kind of guessing game. 'Maybe it was a photograph.'

She swallowed, biting her lips, but still avoiding his eyes. His hands clenched into fists as frustration rose inside him. 'Come on, Joss,' he wanted to say, 'help me to help you.' But her white, unhappy face and restless eyes restrained him. There was an uneasiness about her that suggested guilt and suddenly he had an idea.

'I suppose you haven't by chance come across a copy of Mutt's will?' he asked lightly. 'I must admit it would simplify things if you have.'

She stared at him then. 'Would it? I can't imagine how.'

Her voice was almost childishly defiant and she shrank back into the cushions as he came to kneel beside the arm of the sofa.

'Come on, love,' he said. 'Don't play games. Tell me what you've found.'

'Letters,' she said, eyes wide and dark. 'I wasn't going to read them and then I found I simply couldn't resist. Mutt asked me to find them . . .'

Her voice trailed away into silence and he frowned.

'Letters? What kind of letters?'

'She wrote to her sister but never posted them. They explain it all. How she came here and who she really is.'

Bruno closed his eyes for a second. 'Christ!' he muttered. 'I don't believe it. *Letters!*'

They stared at each other. His shocked expression restored her as nothing else could have done and she drew her legs up into the sofa, leaning closer to him.

'I can't take it in,' she told him. 'Nothing is what I thought it was. I just couldn't grasp it to begin with but, after a while, how it affected me—all of us—didn't matter so much as what I felt about Mutt.'

She hesitated, as if hoping for some response, perhaps encouragement, but Bruno remained silent. There was something else in his face besides horrified disbelief: he was angry.

'Letters!' He swung himself to his feet and went across to the fire. Picking up the poker he stabbed it furiously against the logs. 'All these years of secrecy and remembering to think twice before I speak, and meanwhile she writes it all down in bloody letters and leaves them lying about. I can't *believe* it.'

Huddled in the sofa, Joss watched him anxiously. Despite her own shock when she'd looked at Bruno in the hall and thought, But he isn't my uncle and nothing is what it seems, she'd still felt an overwhelming compassion for her grandmother.

'They weren't lying about,' was all she could think of to say in defence of Mutt. 'They were underneath lots of things in a drawer'—but she knew that it was a feeble protest.

'In a drawer,' he repeated contemptuously. 'Oh, well, that's perfectly all right. No one is going to be looking for anything in a drawer, are they?'

She got up and went to him, taking his arm. 'You need to read them,' she said. 'They aren't just casual letters dashed off for fun. It was Mutt's way of retaining her identity and trying to assuage her guilt. I can understand that. I expect she just couldn't bring herself to destroy them.'

Bruno was watching her unsympathetically. 'What about *my* identity?' he asked. 'All my life I've denied my mother and sister. I've lied and prevaricated and thought it worth it for certain reasons. And now it's blown wide open, all gone for nothing, because Mutt has an urge to commit her qualms to paper. Why letters? And if you write letters, why not post the bloody things? Perhaps she *has* posted some and other people know the truth.'

Joss dropped his arm. 'It's not like that. You must read them, Bruno. Remember that she just asked me to find them and if I hadn't read them nobody would be any the wiser.' She suddenly had an inkling of what it must have been like for him. Any guilt she was experiencing was quenched by her instinct that this was the right course to take. 'Please, Bruno, just keep an open mind until you've read them,' she pleaded. 'Don't judge her until you've done that.'

He took a deep, barely resigned breath and nodded. 'OK. Where are they?'

'I'll get them,' she said quickly. 'They need to be read in order. Build up the fire and I'll make some coffee.'

She hurried out, down the hall and into the parlour. As she sorted and piled the letters her hands shook and she paused at one point, listening, wondering if she'd heard Mutt's bell. There was only silence.

Bruno was sitting beside the fire, leaning forward, hands clasped loosely between his knees. Joss dragged forward a small table and placed the letters on it. He glanced at them and then at her.

'Sorry, Joss.' His voice was gentler. 'It's been one hell of a shock for you too.'

She nodded, biting her lip. 'I'll get that coffee,' she said.

In the kitchen she was seized with a sudden fit of shivering. Part of her was with Bruno reading the letters, willing him to empathise, other thoughts jostled to the forefront of her mind as she waited for the kettle to boil. Her mother: what would she say if she knew? Well, she must never know. The secret must be kept.

Joss stared round the kitchen, trying to come to terms with the fact that she and her mother and Mutt had no right to be here. It was impossible to take it in.

Suddenly she needed to see Mutt. Perhaps now her grandmother might be awake again and she, Joss, could somehow indicate that she knew the truth and that, whatever had happened in the past or might happen in the future, Joss's love for her was unchanged.

She made the coffee and took it into the drawing room. Bruno didn't look up; his face was set and absorbed. Joss slipped out again and up the stairs. She hesitated at the door to Mutt's room, her heart banging, and then gently turned the handle and went inside.

Mutt wasn't there. Joss could tell at once that the room was empty even before she saw the lifeless figure on the bed. Mutt was gone and it was too late.

Bruno set the last letter aside, sitting for some moments in silence before glancing at Joss, curled in the corner of the opposite sofa. He'd been hardly aware of her presence, but now he saw how pale she was. He'd been moved by the letters but not surprised by the revelations of Mutt's dilemma. She'd turned to him too often down the years for him to be unaware of her need for his 'absolution', as she called it. Now, he could only be grateful that he'd given it unstintingly and continued to reassure her. He'd known the real Mutt who'd hidden behind the cool, sensible façade of widowhood; known the light-hearted, compassionate woman who fought with her own devils of guilt and insecurity.

The real surprise to Bruno was that touching record of the brief flowering of love between her and his godfather. Of course, it had been ended and Simon had emigrated to Australia while he, Bruno, was still a small child, yet he felt almost hurt that she'd never spoken of it. Now he saw how lonely she must have been. He felt a great need to see her.

'You were quite right to insist that I read them,' he said to Joss. 'And you've been sitting there all this time, poor love, trying to come to terms with all this. Look, we'll talk, I promise, but first I need to see Mutt. Can you manage—'

'She's dead,' she said. Tears suddenly ran from her eyes and streamed down her cheeks. 'Mutt's dead, Bruno.'

'But when?' he cried, leaping to his feet as if even now he might not be too late. 'You said she was asleep.'

'She was,' she whispered, gazing up at him. 'But I went up when you began to read the letters and she'd gone. She looked so calm that I'm sure she must have died in her sleep.'

Her eyes were red and swollen and he knelt down and put his arms about her. She began to weep again, turning her face into his shoulder. He held her gently, his mind working on several different levels: controlling his own grief, remembering certain extracts from the letters still fresh in his mind. Why had Mutt not asked *him* to find the letters? Why on earth entrust the task to Joss and risk so much?

'What are we to do?' he murmured aloud.

She released herself and blew her nose. 'I just can't believe it. It's been such a shock,' she muttered. 'And now with Mutt gone . . .' She hid her face in her handkerchief briefly and then scrubbed her cheeks. 'I can't take it in that we don't really belong here. Me and Mum and Mutt are impostors.'

Bruno stood up and went back to the sofa near the fire. He looked calm but his mind leaped desperately to find words that were both true and comforting.

'You are exactly who you've always been,' he said. 'You are Mutt's granddaughter and Emma's daughter. Nothing has changed there. As for your relationship to me—well, all I can say is I've always thought of Emma as my sister. We were all so close, you know. Your mother and my sister were much the same age and, given that I had to lose my mother and my sister so tragically, imagine the comfort of having Mutt and Emma, who were already like family to me anyway.'

'But you were angry,' she reminded him. 'When I told you about the letters, you were angry.'

'Of course I was angry.' His own banked-down emotions flared briefly. 'We had an agreement, Mutt and I, that no one would ever know. I'm gutted about Mutt too. To be honest, I can't quite think straight. How are we going to deal with it now that you know? It's no good my saying that as far as I'm concerned nothing has changed, is it?'

Joss frowned, trying to wrestle with the problem, her heart heavy. 'It's difficult,' she began haltingly, 'because part of me wants to say that Mum mustn't know. It's bad enough for *me* but it would simply finish *her* to know that she's not a Trevannion and that this isn't her home.'

'Of course it's her home,' said Bruno impatiently. 'She came here when she wasn't two years old. Where else would be her home?'

'Yes, but you know what I mean.' Joss leaned forward. 'Mum's been lied to all along the line. Hubert wasn't her father, you aren't her brother, this isn't her inheritance. Paradise and St Meriadoc belong to your family, Bruno, not mine. Mousie and Rafe have more right to it than we do, so how do we get round that?'

He was impressed by her grasp of the situation, her self-control, and felt a sense of relief that he could share this responsibility with her.

'It was quite wrong of Mutt to ask you to deal with the letters.' He decided to start at the beginning of this new turn of events. 'She might have guessed that you'd read some part of them, even if only by mistake. A line or a phrase would be bound to catch the eye.'

'Perhaps she thought I'd be too honourable to look at them.' Joss bit her lip.

'For goodness sake, don't let's do that kind of hair-shirt stuff,' said Bruno impatiently. 'The only thing that makes sense to me is that Mutt decided it was time that you knew the truth.'

Joss was comforted by Bruno's almost brutal response but unable to go along with his reasoning.

'No.' She shook her head. 'Mutt was very anxious that the letters should be found. Probably the American's visit frightened her and she wanted them to be destroyed. She trusted me.'

'But did she actually tell you not to read them?' Bruno ignored the tremor in her voice. 'The more I think about it the more I feel that she wanted you to know the truth about her. I know you and she were very close but she must have seen the risk. That's not a criticism, Joss. Mutt knew all about the weaknesses and temptations of human nature. I think some subconscious desire was driving her.'

'It might be so.' Joss was willing herself to believe it. 'But what now? Do we carry on as if nothing has happened? How has Mutt left things in her will?'

He shook his head. 'I don't know.'

'She should have left everything to you but I can see that would arouse suspicion. Do you think that she might have left Paradise and The Lookout to you? That would be good, wouldn't it? After all, if only The Row was left to Mum, nothing need change. I'll rent my little cottage from the estate just as Mousie and Rafe do theirs. That would be OK, wouldn't it?'

He smiled a little at her eagerness to maintain the status quo without benefiting. 'Your father always wanted to develop the boatyard,' he said. 'Knock down the old shed and build a hotel.'

'That's crazy,' she answered at once. 'It's not possible. Oh.' He saw her catch his meaning. 'You mean he might try to persuade Mum . . . Oh, no.' She shook her head, horror in her eyes. 'He couldn't. It would ruin the cove and anyway, it wouldn't be his to develop.'

'If the boatyard and The Row should be left to Emma,' Bruno said gently, 'we must consider every eventuality.'

'But what about Mousie and Rafe?' she protested.

'*What* about Mousie and Rafe?'

Mousie's voice echoed in from the hall, cheerful and rather amused, and they heard the front door close behind her. It was nearly five o'clock.

Joss remained in her chair, momentarily paralysed by shock and fear, while Bruno swept the letters into a pile beneath the cushioned seat of the sofa. He rose quickly to his feet and went out into the hall.

'Mousie,' Joss heard him say, 'it's bad news, I'm afraid. Dear old Mutt is gone. Peacefully in her sleep, but poor Joss found her. We were just deciding how to let you know.'

A brief silence.

'Well, I can't say I'm terribly surprised.' Mousie's voice was barely audible. 'Poor Joss. We're never prepared for it, somehow. Perhaps I should have stayed after all, but I had a feeling that Mutt wanted to be alone with Joss tonight. Did Joss telephone you?'

'Come and see her.' Bruno avoided the question. 'She's still suffering from shock, I think.'

Joss took a deep breath. Her limbs were stiff, her head ached, and she found that she was shivering again. She stood up carefully and tried to smile at Mousie as she came into the room.

'Poor darling.' Mousie put her arms about her and rocked her as if she were a child. 'Poor Joss. Goodness, how cold you are. Come over to the fire and get warm. I'll go upstairs to see her.'

She glanced warningly at Bruno, who obediently piled more logs onto the embers and reached for the bellows, smiled reassuringly at Joss and disappeared.

'This is terrible,' whispered Joss rapidly as soon as she'd gone. 'I've lost my bearings. How can I go on like this now that I know the truth?' She leaned forward. 'How on earth have you managed all these years?'

He sat back on his heels, watching the flames, his face bleak. 'Try to remember that it was rather a *fait accompli* as far as I was concerned. You don't have much control at four years old, you know. And anyway, it was what my mother wanted. No, no,' he saw her expression, 'not that Mutt should impersonate her but that she should bring me back here. Mutt and Emma became my family. How could I expose them even if I'd wanted to? And at what point? When I went to school? My twenty-first birthday party? When I got married?' He gave a mirthless chuckle. 'Mutt offered me this house when I got married but I didn't want it. Had I accepted it, it might have made things simpler now. I could have passed it over to you without any questions asked. After all, that's Emma's dream. Mutt's too. Those were almost her last words to me. "I want Joss to have Paradise".'

'But how could I have Paradise now?' she asked him almost angrily. 'It would be quite wrong . . .'

She fell silent as Mousie came hurrying down the stairs and into the drawing room. 'A good, peaceful slipping-away in her sleep.' Mousie glanced at Joss. 'Bed for you,' she said firmly. 'Hot-water bottle, a couple of paracetamol. Go on up while I do the hottie.'

They went out together. Bruno waited for a moment and then slipped upstairs and went into the porch room.

'You knew I'd be angry, didn't you?' he murmured, as he stood looking down at the peaceful, care-smoothed face. 'And I was. Letters! Good grief!' He took her hand, touched it with his lips. 'I'm glad I read them, though.'

He stood for a moment, still holding her hand, his gaze inward as he remembered passages from her letters, until he heard Mousie going into Joss's bedroom. Tucking Mutt's hand beneath the cover, he gave her one last kiss and left the room. He hadn't reached the hall before Mousie was behind him, following him downstairs.

'No point in dragging the doctor out this early,' she said. 'I'll make some tea, I think.' She looked at him, gauging his weariness and strain.

'It's always a shock, even when you're half expecting it. You didn't tell me earlier. Did Joss telephone you? Was she worried about Mutt?'

He shook his head. 'I couldn't sleep and suddenly I had a very strong feeling that I should be here. I was too late to see Mutt, but at least Joss had some company after the shock of finding her.'

'I'm glad,' said Mousie. 'Perhaps I should have stayed but as I said, it seemed to me that Joss and Mutt should be here together.'

'I think you were absolutely right. From what I can gather something very special happened between them earlier on.'

'Oh, that's good,' she answered with impulsive warmth. 'They were so close, those two, and Joss brought her a great deal of comfort. Anyway, you look exhausted. Go home and try to get some sleep before Emma wakes. There's nothing more you can do here.'

There was no alternative but to let himself out into the grey morning. A damp breeze touched his face and a soft mist wreathed and curled through the branches of the rhododendrons. Hands thrust into the pockets of his jacket he walked quickly down the drive, anticipating Emma's reaction, persuading himself that Mousie would not find the letters. He wished now that he'd seized his chance when Mousie had gone to deal with Joss's hot-water bottle, but he'd had no plan as to where to hide them and feared to be caught red-handed.

He tried to empty his tired mind, to think about Mutt: immediately grief closed up his throat, making it difficult to swallow, and suddenly he saw how very much he would miss her. Despite his anger, the letters had touched him deeply and his heart was weighted with sadness and loss.

He let Nellie out and went to revive the fire, all the while bracing himself to the task of telling Emma that her mother was dead.

George woke early, pulled on his long tartan dressing gown and went downstairs. Rafe was already up. He'd made some coffee and was drawing back the curtains. 'Weather's changed,' he said. 'Pity. I was enjoying the nip in the air and the sunshine. Did you manage to sleep?'

'On and off.' George took his mug of coffee gratefully. 'The trouble is that this problem gets between me and everything else.'

An uneasy silence fell between them, as Rafe swiped at the draining board with a cloth, wishing he could help George through to some kind of conclusion or at least convey sympathy and encouragement. He, who had spent his life teaching and enabling, felt at a loss to help his own son.

George sensed his father's frustration and felt equally impotent. He swallowed some coffee and went to look out of the window, racking his brains for some remark that would ease the tension. The sea slopped untidily at the cliffs; grey and unfriendly as dishwater.

'I was wondering if I might get a sail in while I'm here.' George said the first thing that offered itself. 'Sailing helps to clear the mind somehow.'

Rafe came to stand beside him at the window. 'Not much wind.'

'No, and anyway I ought to be getting back.'

Rafe slipped an arm along his son's broad shoulders, gave him a hug. 'You know you are always welcome here. Just stay in touch.'

'Of course I will.' George finished his coffee. 'Will Ma be OK?'

'Your mother will be fine. She just wants what is right for you.'

'If only we knew what that is it would be a start. Relationships are so complicated.' He shook his head as if baffled. 'Penny seemed quite happy in London. She'd settled in so well, had a good job. Perhaps I should never have asked her to give it all up and move down here.'

'Perhaps,' said Rafe carefully, 'she was trying to make things work; to take her mind off . . . whatever his name is.'

Some odd kind of delicacy made him unwilling to name Penny's lover but George had no difficulty with this.

'Brett,' he said, supplying the name without any particular emotion. 'You could be right. I'm beginning to believe that he's been around for longer than I'd realised.'

Rafe studied his son. There was no sign of any real jealousy: no bitterness. 'What do you *really* want, George?' he asked. 'Given a free choice?'

George chuckled. 'How do you spell it, Pa?' he asked. 'First things first. I want to make certain Penny and I have done everything we can before we chuck it in.'

'And then what?' asked Pamela from behind him.

'I'll take that step when it comes.' He bent to kiss her. 'Good morning. I'm going to dash off, Ma. I want to tell Penny that you've been told, as she asked me, and that you are very sad but not angry.'

'You're clearing the decks,' she said thoughtfully.

'If you like.' He looked amused at the expression. 'Will you tell Joss I'm sorry not to have seen her?'

'Joss?' she asked quickly.

There was a brief silence.

'And Mousie,' he said evenly, 'and Bruno and Emma and Mutt. I've got a few days' leave only.'

'You must do whatever you have to,' she said, putting her arms round him. 'Just stay in touch, my darling. Give our love to Penny and Tasha, and remember that we're here if you need us.'

'I know that.' He held her tightly for a moment. 'Thanks, Ma. I'll phone when I get home.' He disappeared upstairs while Pamela stood quite still, her head bent thoughtfully.

'I was just bringing you some coffee.' Rafe spoke normally, an ear cocked towards the stairs. 'What did you mean,' he lowered his voice, 'about clearing the decks?'

'Just a feeling I have.' She held out her hand and he put the mug into it. 'He never did like muddle, did he? He always wanted things cut and dried. Well and truly off with the old before on with the new.'

'Any more clichés?' Rafe asked drily. 'You sound surprisingly cheerful about it this morning.'

'Oh, Rafe, I think I am,' she answered. 'I think . . . oh, dear, I can feel another cliché coming on. I think I can see a light at the end of the tunnel.'

At The Lookout, Emma was staring miserably at the fire, her arm round Nellie, who sat beside her on the sofa. 'So suddenly,' she murmured. 'I can't believe it. And poor darling Joss there all alone with her.'

'It could have been much worse,' Bruno said, hearing the conventional uselessness of the words but too tired to think of anything original.

Tears suddenly streamed down Emma's cheeks and she wiped at them with the back of her hands.

'I wish you'd woken me up,' she said. 'When you went.'

'It wouldn't have made any difference,' he told her. 'I didn't see her alive either.'

'I must go and see Joss.' She made as if to move but sank back again, as if defeated by the heaviness of grief.

'I told you that she's asleep,' he reminded her. 'Mousie will get her off to work but she needs to rest.'

'Surely she doesn't have to go to work,' protested Emma. She laid her cheek against Nellie's head. 'They'll understand, won't they? Poor Joss . . .'

'She'll want to go.' Bruno had never been able to convince Emma of the work ethic. 'And quite right too. Work is the best thing for her. It'll take her mind off things. Why don't you go up to Paradise and see how Mousie is coping, and then you'll be able to have a word with Joss when she wakes up? I need a shower and a shave and then I'll follow you up after I've told Rafe and Pamela.'

She glanced at him, grateful for his presence. 'You look exhausted,' she told him anxiously. 'Why don't you try to snatch an hour's sleep?'

'I might,' he said. 'I'll see how I feel after I've showered. As long as you're OK?'

She nodded, although her lips trembled a little. 'It's just so hard to believe she isn't there any more.'

He watched her go out, mopping her eyes. Bending to stroke the recumbent Nellie, he wondered if Joss had found an opportunity to move the letters to a safer place, and pondered how and when he might transport them away from Paradise.

Joss woke suddenly. She heard the front door close and voices, muffled, in the hall. She huddled beneath the bedclothes, dredging up the courage to face the day. So much had changed, despite Bruno's reassurances that she was still exactly the same person she'd always believed herself to be. Emma was her mother, Mutt had been her grandmother, true enough; but there was no link now to Bruno, Mousie and Rafe.

She rolled onto her back and fear stiffened her muscles as she thought about her mother and the complications that lay ahead regarding the will. How could she, Joss, now accept anything from the estate and how could she approve her mother inheriting above Rafe and Mousie, especially if her father were to interfere? She knew his ways: if her mother were to inherit the boatyard then he would try to convince Emma that the development of the cove would be in everyone's best interests: that Mousie, as well as Rafe and Pamela, and all their family would share in the profits. Joss could well imagine how difficult it would be for Pamela to resist once she was shown how the development would bring such financial help to her children.

Olivia and Joe had never had the passion for the valley that she, Joss, and George shared. They would be unmoved by the fact that The Lookout's prospect would become a noisy holiday centre. It would be Bruno, the true inheritor and only legitimate beneficiary, who would suffer most. The tranquillity and privacy that he valued so much would be destroyed.

It was quite wrong that this destruction should be instigated by someone who had no rights at all over the estate that belonged to Bruno's family. How, Joss asked herself, would she be able to remain silent if all this were to happen? Perhaps, after all, a time might come when it would be necessary for the truth to be told and the letters shown. They must be kept in a safe place, just in case.

The thought of the letters brought her upright and onto the edge of the bed. She wondered if Bruno had managed to conceal them while she and Mousie were out of the drawing room. With luck he would have carried them away to The Lookout and hidden them in his study, which was generally considered out of bounds.

As she brooded on their whereabouts the door opened and Mousie came in, carrying a mug of tea. She set it down on the bedside table and touched Joss lightly on the head. It was at once affectionate and encouraging, and Joss smiled at her.

'Emma's here,' said Mousie, moving to the door, 'just in time to see you before you go off to Bodmin. I've made some porridge.'

Joss nodded, not quite trusting herself to speak. She picked up the mug and drank the hot, reviving tea. It seemed impossible that, only a few hours ago, she'd believed that her new knowledge would not affect the relationship between her and George. It could not change the past, this was true, but how would she manage now? Sometime today she would see him. Joy mixed with fear churned in her gut. She finished her tea and went to have a shower.

Downstairs, Mousie was comforting Emma, explaining that Mutt had died peacefully in her sleep.

'But she seemed so much better,' said Emma tearfully. 'If I'd known I would have stayed here last night.' Emma's tears spilled over again.

'But you couldn't have known. None of us could. She might have got better and then had another fall. And what then? Would you have moved down here to be with her, just in case?'

'She'd have hated that.' Emma blotted her cheeks with a tissue. 'She was very independent.'

'Quite. And she had Bruno, who saw her every day, and the rest of us nearby. And don't forget that she's had Joss with her for the last few months.' Mousie stirred the porridge.

'Yes, I do realise that.' Emma tried to smile. 'Sorry, Mousie. I'm being pathetic.'

'It's always a shock.' Mousie touched her shoulder and put a mug of coffee beside her. 'Even when you're expecting it, you never get used to the finality of it. Coming to terms with the fact that your chance to have one more joke, share a hug—whatever it is—is gone for ever.'

Mousie turned away to hide her own emotion and Emma's eyes filled with tears again.

'Sorry,' she said again. 'I think I'll go up and say goodbye to her, Mousie.'

She hesitated and Mousie smiled at her encouragingly.

'I think you should,' she said. 'Joss'll be down in a minute . . .'

Emma stood up, preparing herself for what might lie ahead. She met Joss in the hall. Shocked by the look of suffering on her daughter's face, Emma forgot her own loss and hugged her tightly.

'You did so well, darling,' she told her warmly. 'How wonderful that you've been with Mutt these last weeks. You gave her so much happiness.'

Joss smiled rather wanly but gratefully. 'Are you going to see her? Would you like me to come with you?'

Resisting the urge to cry 'Yes! Yes, please!' Emma shook her head. 'I'd rather be alone,' she lied. 'Just this last time.'

Joss watched her go upstairs, then went swiftly into the drawing room. She went straight to the sofa, lifted the padded seat and gave a sigh of thanksgiving: the letters were gone.

George had already set out and Joss was on her way to Bodmin by the time Bruno arrived in The Row to tell them the sad news.

'Oh, Bruno, I am so sorry.' Pamela stretched out a hand towards him and he took it between his own.

'She'd made a bit of a comeback yesterday'—he gave her hand a squeeze then let it go—'but I think it was all too much for her to recover from: the fall and then that infection. I'm sorry I've missed George.'

There was an uncomfortable silence; then they spoke together.

Rafe: 'Things are a bit tricky for him at present . . .'

Pamela: 'I don't see why Bruno shouldn't know . . .'

'No need to say anything,' said Bruno quickly—too quickly. 'None of my business. I just wondered if he'd gone back to sea or whether he might be here for the funeral.'

'He's got some leave,' said Rafe awkwardly, 'just a few days but I'm sure he'll be down. He was very fond of Mutt.'

'We all were,' said Pamela sadly. 'And we're very grateful to her. There's no way Rafe and I could have afforded to live in a place like this if she hadn't been so generous about the rent. Nor could Mousie.'

Another silence. Bruno, unable to reassure them that nothing would change, said nothing.

'Poor Joss,' said Pamela, sensing some embarrassment and seeking a change of subject. 'Such a shock for her. Well, for all of us, of course . . .'

'Absolutely,' agreed Rafe quickly. 'What a pity George dashed off before we could tell him.'

'Never mind,' said Bruno. 'There's nothing he could do. Well . . . I'd better get up to Paradise. Sorry to have been the bearer of bad tidings . . .'

He almost added, 'when you've got enough on your plate already', but remembered, just in time, that Joss had told him in confidence about George and Penny. He hesitated, then raised a hand in farewell. He could only hope that Rafe and Pamela would put his odd behaviour down to grief. He'd been too quick with his reply and shown no surprise—or concern—that George might be having problems.

With Nellie at his heels, he crossed the narrow bridge and walked swiftly up the lane. When he arrived at Paradise, he let himself in through the garden door and paused in the hall, listening to the low murmuring of voices from the bedroom above, before passing into the drawing room. He went quickly to the sofa, lifted the padded seat and gave a sigh of relief: the letters were gone.

George had travelled fast through the quiet lanes to the dual carriageway and was already turning off the A30 at Launceston onto the road to Tavistock. As he travelled, his mind was busy on several different layers and he barely noticed the familiar landmarks. Passing over the Tamar he glanced briefly downstream where the mist smoked along the river and wreathed itself between the tall trees that clung to the steep, high banks.

He drove carefully through Milton Abbot, picking up speed again as he left the village. In his mind's eye, he could see Joss's face: dark winged brows above hazel eyes, the straight little nose and wide curling mouth. If only they hadn't lost touch during that crucial growing-up time they might not be in this terrible situation now.

Taking the back lane out of Yelverton, he approached the little cottage. Penny's hatchback was in the single parking space beside the house. He pulled in tight under the thorn hedge, reached for his grip and climbed out. The front door led immediately into the sitting room, which was empty. He glanced through to the long narrow kitchen, and then shouted up the stairs. 'Hello. I'm back.'

Even as he climbed the short steep staircase he knew that she'd gone. He looked into the two bedrooms and checked the bathroom, and the certainty grew. The rooms were too tidy: there was none of the usual clutter that seemed to spawn and spread in so small a house. Going back downstairs, he was increasingly aware of a sweet, sickly smell which, as he returned to the sitting room, was suddenly intolerable.

He opened the window, breathing in cold, fresh air, and saw the pot of hyacinths. Penny had bought the bulbs in Tavistock market just before Christmas and put them on the window sill. Now, the blue, bell-shaped flowers were fading, but their scent was still strong in the airless cottage. He carried the bulbs through to the kitchen to give them some water and saw an envelope, pinned down on the kitchen table beneath a coffee jar. He stood the jar back on the shelf and opened the letter.

I am just so sorry, George, but this is the only way I can do it. It seems underhand—and it is, of course—but there's no point in it dragging on any longer. Brett was staying in Yelverton and came to get me and Tasha as soon as you'd gone yesterday. By the time you read this we'll be on a flight home to New Zealand.

It was wrong of me to marry you, George, knowing that deep down I still had feelings for Brett. I actually did believe that making the commitment of marriage would finally exorcise any love I had for him. It didn't work like that and, anyway, a year later he came to find me. I shouldn't have deceived you then but I was so mixed up because part of me *did* love you.

The fact is Brett and I should never have split up, we know that now, and I'm really sorry you've been hurt by our mistakes. But there's no point in going on compounding the wrong. Also I've missed my home and family terribly; it's just where I belong.

301

The other thing I have to tell you is that Natasha is Brett's child. You probably won't believe this, you'll think I'm trying to get away with keeping her, but it's true. I went to London just after you'd gone back to sea a year ago and that's when I met up with Brett again. I'm afraid we got carried away but by then I'd had my period and that's how I know she's his. Even then I didn't admit it because I still wasn't sure I could trust him. You don't have to believe me, there are other ways of testing it, but I hope you will and let us go peacefully.

Sorry, George, and thanks for all the good times.

She'd scribbled something that had been crossed through several times, and then written her name and he guessed that she hadn't quite known how to finish it. After a moment, he lifted the phone and dialled his parents' number.

'Hi, Ma,' he said when his mother answered. 'I'm here but Penny isn't. She's done a runner with Brett, taking Tasha with her and leaving a letter saying that it's all over. They've gone back to New Zealand.'

'Gone?' She was clearly shocked. 'Oh, George . . .'

'Bit of a conversation stopper,' he agreed. 'Sorry if I sound callous, Ma, but I don't quite know what the form is for this.'

'Of course not,' she said quickly. 'I don't know what to say to you and you probably need time to adjust. I have to tell you, though, that Mutt died last night. Poor Joss found her. You can imagine what a shock it was for her. She telephoned from the practice in Bodmin and I thought she seemed disappointed to have missed you . . .'

She talked on, trying to get them both through this difficult moment, but George suddenly felt as if he'd been thrown a lifeline.

'Look, there's nothing I can do here,' he told her. 'If it's OK with you I think I'll come straight back. Maybe I can be useful.'

'Oh, do,' she agreed warmly. 'It would be wonderful to have you here. Only, drive carefully. You're probably in shock.'

Once he'd hung up he stared round the kitchen, feeling some kind of responsibility for this little cottage, which once had been their home and was now silent and unwelcoming.

He saw now that the hyacinth flowers were not just fading but beginning to decay, their petal edges brown, and he was filled with a terrible sadness. He took the pot out and put it in a sheltered place in the back porch: later the bulbs could be planted under the hedge in the garden and next spring they would flower again.

By the time Bruno got back to The Lookout he was feeling the effects of twenty-four hours with no sleep. The day had been busy, emotional, and he'd been grateful for Mousie's calm professionalism. She'd got them through it all: Mutt's body taken away by the undertakers, plans made for the funeral, Emma held steady by a hundred and one tasks.

'I shall stay here with Joss until the funeral,' she'd told Bruno when the rector had gone and the tea things were washed up and put away. 'Ray will be down tomorrow so Mousie and I are going to Polzeath to do some shopping and then we'll make up beds. Why don't you go home and try to catch up on some sleep? You look exhausted.'

He'd been glad to take her advice. Collecting Nellie from the kitchen, he'd walked back over the cliff, although the dense vapour-like mist made it impossible to see very far. He felt it press damply upon him—obscuring familiar landmarks, deadening sound—chill and cheerless.

Once inside, he went to light the fire in the sitting room in an attempt to lift his own spirits and saw the red light of the answerphone blinking. Joss's voice was expressionless, her message brief, as if she'd realised that Emma might well be with Bruno when he listened to it.

'Glad you found those letters. Is it OK if I drop in on my way home about five? See you later.'

Bruno pressed several buttons and replayed it: no mistake. Mechanically he went about the task of reviving the fire, piling the charred logs together on their bed of hot ash, working the bellows until the heart glowed red. Nellie nudged at him, pushing her nose beneath his arm as he sat on the leather pouffe beside the flat granite hearth, sitting close to him as he put an arm about her neck.

Once the wood was well alight, he went out into the kitchen with Nellie prancing at his heels and, all the while he prepared her supper, he was thinking about Joss's cryptic message. *Glad you found those letters.* There was no question in his mind which letters—did she imagine that he had them? He glanced at his watch: nearly twenty minutes to five. The telephone rang and he snatched up the receiver before the answerphone could click into play.

'Hi,' said Rafe. 'Sorry to trouble you, we can guess what a dreadful day it's been for you, but we wanted to say that George is back and ready to be of any use.'

'Thanks, Rafe.' For a moment Bruno couldn't remember where George had been and why he was back. His brain simply refused to function properly. 'That's kind.'

'Pamela is asking if you'd like to come over to supper?'

Bruno hesitated. 'I don't think I will. I'm going to try for an early night. Emma's staying up at Paradise with Joss. I have to say that Mousie has been fantastic, Rafe.'

'Well, she's had plenty of experience.' He took the praise of his sister lightly. 'Don't forget we're here if you need us.'

He rang off and Bruno stood for a while in thought, then he went out to the kitchen. Despite the earliness of the hour he poured himself a stiff whisky and went to sit beside the fire in the sitting room, waiting, with Nellie curled beside him on the sofa.

Joss arrived just before twenty past five.

'Beastly weather,' she said, as Bruno led her into the sitting room to sit on the sofa and warm her hands at the fire. 'It was horrid driving through the lanes. I see that George is back.'

'George is back,' Bruno agreed, sitting down opposite Joss, 'although I don't know where he's been, and what's all this about the letters?'

She stared at him. 'George went back to Meavy,' she said slowly, taking one thing at a time, 'and it's a bit odd that he's come back so soon.' She frowned. 'You must have realised what I meant about the letters. They weren't there so I imagine that you were able to get them last night when Mousie and I were upstairs.'

'No.' He shook his head. 'I'm afraid that's not so. Do you mean that you haven't got them?'

'Of course I haven't. I told you. When I got downstairs this morning they'd gone.'

'But that's impossible,' said Bruno. 'Wait a minute.' He closed his eyes, recalling the scene. 'When Mousie arrived, I put them under the seat . . .'

'Maybe Mum found them. Oh my God . . .!'

'I've been with Emma all day,' said Bruno impatiently, 'and she hasn't given the least impression that she'd found a cache of letters.'

'There's something else,' Joss's hazel eyes were wide with fear. 'I thought about it when I got to work. What happened to *Goblin Market*?'

He stared at her blankly. 'To what?'

'Mutt's book,' she prompted him impatiently. 'The one she treasured so much. She said that the death certificates and things were hidden in the back of it.'

'Christ,' murmured Bruno softly. 'I hadn't given it a thought. You'll have to find it, Joss. Damn and hell, what was Mutt thinking about?'

'She probably wasn't thinking at all.' Joss defended her grandmother. 'It was only right at the end, when the American came, that she suddenly remembered the book and letters. Where can they be, Bruno?'

'Let's not panic.' He saw that it was time to be reassuring. 'Go on up to Paradise and have a look round but don't make Emma suspicious. Shall you go over to see George?'

'George?' For a brief moment it seemed that she had forgotten George. 'Oh, Bruno, I don't know what I shall do about George.'

The telephone rang and Bruno took up the receiver.

'I was wondering if Joss is with you?' Emma's voice was anxious. 'She said she'd be home by five and the fog is really thick now.'

'She's right here, Em.' Bruno made his voice light, cheerful even. 'She's on her way up to you now.' He replaced the receiver and looked encouragingly at Joss, eyebrows raised.

When Joss had gone he sat down again by the fire, waiting. He heard Mousie come in through the kitchen and into the sitting room. She dropped her bag down beside him on the sofa, but remained standing, and presently he looked up at her.

'So where do we go from here?' he asked.

'So where do we go from here?' Rafe was asking Pamela. George had arrived back at St Meriadoc just before four o'clock and now, nearly two hours later, had gone upstairs to have a bath. Rafe and Pamela sat opposite each other at the table. 'And what about Tasha? Do you believe she's not George's baby?'

Pamela was silent for a long moment. 'I think we must let it go,' she said at last. 'If Tasha had been older, or George had been able to spend more time with her, it would be a different story. Penny adores Tasha and I think she knows that she'll get everything she needs in New Zealand. I think it would be wrong to fight it and especially now that there's a doubt over who her father is.'

'It's a pity that it's all come together,' said Rafe. 'Penny going off and poor old Mutt . . .'

'Oh, no,' answered Pamela quickly. 'It will get George and Joss over any awkwardness. They won't have too much time to think about themselves and the guilt and all the other emotions. Life will just make them get on with it. Much better.'

'If you say so.'

'I do say so. Although I did feel for Joss this morning when she telephoned. She simply couldn't hide her disappointment that George had gone. I expect it was coming on top of Mutt. They were very close.'

'Poor Joss. I can't believe I never guessed. She's a good girl, Pammie.'

'She's a darling,' agreed Pamela warmly, 'and I can't wait to tell her how thrilled we are about her and George.'

'You won't say anything.' He sounded shocked. 'I mean, not before George has . . . Dammit, we don't even know we're right, do we?'

'Of course we're right,' she answered serenely. 'And of course I shan't say anything. What do you take me for?'

Rafe let out a sigh of relief and got up from the table. 'I don't care where the sun or the yardarm is,' he said. 'I need a drink.'

'Perhaps George will go up to Paradise and see her and Emma later on,' mused Pamela. 'I wonder how they're managing.'

From the moment Joss had arrived, Emma hadn't stopped talking. Words streamed from her mouth as earlier the tears had streamed from her eyes: the undertakers . . . so friendly and kind . . . Mousie, such a tower of strength . . . the rector had been so sweet . . . made them laugh about things that had happened in the past . . . her own wedding . . . Joss's baptism . . . then, after he'd gone, trying to get ready for Ray . . .

Talking eased her grief, shaping it into something manageable, holding misery at bay. 'And I've been looking everywhere for Mutt's address book,' she said. 'I've searched high and low—'

'Searched?' The word pierced the numbness that occluded Joss's brain. 'Did you . . . find anything?'

'Not a thing.' Emma sounded exasperated. 'Every time I got started there was some kind of interruption.'

'I think I know where it might be.' Joss tried to sound casual. 'Can you manage supper? I'll have a look while you're getting it ready.'

'Of course I can.' Emma got up, only too ready to be distracted.

After she'd gone, Joss tried to collect her thoughts. She looked round the room, then went quietly through the hall into the parlour. There was no sign of anything that might contain the letters and she crossed to the bookshelf, glancing quickly at the titles, knowing in her heart that Mutt would never have put *Goblin Market* in such an obvious place.

Of course, she might have removed the papers and certificates at a later date and put them somewhere else . . . Hastily she pulled out the drawers of the desk, checking each one: no letters, no *Goblin Market*. The address book was lying on the table, beneath a piece of tapestry. With a little cry of relief Joss seized it up; with luck this would deter Emma from further searching for the time being.

The telephone rang and she heard Emma hurry out into the hall to answer it. Quickly Joss took up Mutt's big carpetbag and riffled through it. 'We're fine,' Joss heard her mother say. 'Good idea . . . We'll see you in the morning then . . . Yes, I'll tell her that.'

Joss came out of the parlour, holding the book, just as Emma replaced the receiver.

'Bruno,' she said. 'Just checking we're OK. He's going to have an early night. Oh, and he said to tell you that he found those letters he was telling you about.' She raised her eyebrows at Joss's blank expression. 'Mean anything to you?'

'Yes,' said Joss quickly. 'They were something to do with his book. I'm glad he's got them. And look what I found.'

She held up the address book and Emma gave an exclamation of relief. 'Good,' she said. 'We'll check through it together. I wondered if you'd like a drink?' she offered. 'I thought it might do us good. There's some Rioja in the larder, probably Bruno's choice. What do you think?'

'Great,' said Joss. 'Good idea.' She sat down by the fire, dazed. Bruno had found the letters—but where? Before she could puzzle it out Emma arrived with the drinks and there was no chance for further thought.

'Sorry for the interruption, Mousie,' Bruno said. He sat down again in the corner of the sofa. 'It would have been cruel to leave Joss worrying. So you've read the letters . . .' He leaned forward, forearms resting along his thighs, his hands loosely clasped, needing to create an atmosphere of intimacy. 'Let's start right at the beginning. You heard us talking as you let yourself in . . .'

Mousie was sitting on the pouffe with her fingers laced round her knees, her expression guarded and watchful, but she began quite readily.

'As I opened the front door I could hear your voice. You were talking about the boatyard and The Row, and Joss said words to the effect of, "Oh, no. That would be wrong. What about Mousie and Rafe?" At this point I guessed you hadn't heard me come in and I thought it would be less embarrassing all round if I made my presence known. I called out to you and there was one of those pregnant silences and, as I glanced through the half-open door, I saw you gather up a heap of papers and sweep them under the cushion. I was a bit surprised and I wondered if you'd actually realised that it was me—it could have been Rafe, he's got a key—and then you came out and told me about Honor . . .'

She paused, hesitating over the name, and Bruno at last recognised the emotion she was trying to conceal; an emotion he'd experienced himself earlier: Mousie was angry.

She took up the story again. 'It wasn't until after you'd gone that I made myself some coffee and went into the drawing room. In your hurry to conceal the papers one of them had caught on the chair and was hanging down below the cushion and I remembered that odd scene when I'd first arrived.' She hesitated. 'I felt it was sensible to gather up whatever it was and put it all safely out of sight. The trouble was that when I lifted the seat the sheets of paper were all over the place and I had to collect them almost individually. It was impossible not to catch a glimpse of some of the writing.' A pause. 'I recognised it,' she said at last, 'but what really caught my attention was the name at the bottom of the letters. Madeleine.' She looked at him directly. 'It was the name that the American, Dan Crosby, had written in his letter. Madeleine Grosjean was his great-aunt and he was trying to find her.' She shook her head sadly. 'And to think that all the time we talked, he and I, she was lying upstairs. Mutt knew it, of course, when I read the letter to her. "It's too late," she said. Imagine what she must have been feeling. Vivian's

grandson looking for her and not being able to acknowledge him . . .
And then there was the photograph.'

'Photograph?' Bruno frowned, trying to remember.

'I think it started with the photograph,' Mousie said, 'all those years
ago when Hubert got married. I loved him, you see, in that romantic,
intense way that little girls fall in love with older men. I was twelve or
thirteen and he embodied everything I admired. I used to dream that
when he came back from the war I'd be grown up and he would fall in
love with me. And then we had the letter saying that he was married
and enclosed with it was the photograph.' Her chuckle contained no
mirth. 'I know it sounds foolish but it was such a shock. It was just
before we came back to Cornwall. Your grandfather let us have the cottage—well, you know all that. Anyway, I was fascinated by this picture
of the girl Hubert had married. I was jealous of her in her silly little hat,
and looking so pretty and happy. I studied her closely and I hated her.'

There was a longer silence and, after a while, she looked at him again.

'I'm sorry, Bruno,' she said sadly. 'I'm talking about your mother, your
real mother . . .'

'Go on,' he said gently. 'It's OK.'

'Well, the years passed.' Mousie took a deep breath, remembering.
'And then we heard that you were coming home, Honor and the children, with Hubert following on later. You can imagine how we all felt
when we heard that he had died.' She shook her head. 'And then you
arrived, the three of you, they took you all in with open arms, but I . . .
all I could feel was that something was wrong. Well,' she shrugged,
'you've read the letters. I reacted exactly as she recorded it and I wonder
if my intuition was based on the photograph. It was years since I'd
looked at it, and when I saw the copy of it that the American boy sent, I
realised what it was that had troubled me. The girl who came home with
you and Emma wasn't the girl who was standing with Hubert in the
photograph. It was a double wedding, you see. Honor and Hubert with
Madeleine and Johnny Uttworth. I tested it out on Emma and she said at
once, "Doesn't Joss look just like her grandmother?" And so she does.
Joss looks very much like Madeleine did then.'

'And you think that your suspicions were founded on that?'

Mousie nodded. 'Yes, I do. And they were compounded by Honor's
behaviour. She guessed that I sensed something was wrong and her guilt
made her nervous. But she was right when she wrote that it was you
who prevented me from coming near the truth. While you treated her as
if she were your mother it would never have occurred to me that it
could be otherwise.'

'And that's what's making you angry?'

Her look was swift, surprised, and then she laughed. This time there was genuine mirth in the sound and Bruno relaxed a little.

'Yes, I was angry. I've felt so guilty all these years because I could never totally accept her. And now I see that actually my instincts were right and I'd been duped. Nobody likes to be fooled, do they?'

'I'm sorry, Mousie . . .'

'Oh, my dear boy, it's not your fault,' she said at once. 'I can understand the position you were in and the burden you've carried all these years. How you've managed, Bruno, I can't imagine.'

'Mutt described it very well, I thought,' he answered. 'The trouble is that generally we never quite remember the way things actually were at the time. There have been moments when I wondered why I went along with it but, luckily for me, I *can* remember what it was like in India then: the atmosphere of violence and the overwhelming sense of terror. I can still feel the stifling heat and the fear and then Mother falling ill. When Mutt walked into that hotel room with Emma in her arms she was like an angel straight from heaven. I often wonder what would have happened to me if she hadn't turned up.'

'I am so sorry,' Mousie said gently in her turn. 'I was very fond of her, you know, and she was very good to me. And to Rafe.'

'She used to try to convince herself that nothing was different, no one was suffering, because she was here. She offered me Paradise when I got married, but I never wanted it, and you and Rafe seemed perfectly content. At the end she told me she wanted Joss to have Paradise.'

'So what will happen now?'

Bruno shrugged. 'It's more difficult,' he admitted, 'now that Joss knows. It will be hard for her to accept anything from the estate but Emma would soon smell a rat if Joss holds out.'

Mousie looked puzzled. 'But surely you don't intend to continue to keep this a secret?'

Bruno stared at her. 'Emma would be shattered if she knew,' he said. 'You know how she loves it here and how proud she is of her family. She'd feel she doesn't belong, that the whole thing's been a charade.'

'I think you underestimate her,' said Mousie strongly. 'Once she gets over the shock, Emma will accept that she is a part of us all. How could it be otherwise after what has happened over the last fifty years? You can't possibly go on now as if nothing has changed. And you don't know Joss very well if you think she could live a lie and remain as whole and happy as you have been. Up until now nobody but you has suffered from the deception and you have counted it worth the pain. Joss will never be able to be natural with any of us from this time forward.'

'But it's Joss who is insisting on it,' he told her almost angrily. 'Joss is adamant that Emma shouldn't know, and as for the will . . .'

He paused and Mousie looked at him shrewdly.

'Do you know how your grandfather left the estate?' she asked.

Bruno shrugged wearily. 'He would have left it all to Mutt, I suppose.'

Mousie shook her head. 'Wrong. Uncle James would have left it to Hubert's wife. The estate should have come to you fifty years ago. The tax was paid then, you shouldn't have to pay again. Think about it.'

'I can't think about it,' he said at last. 'I got no sleep last night and my brain won't work.'

'You need to sleep,' she agreed. 'But you should find the will and that book with the death certificates hidden in it, Bruno. Raymond arrives tomorrow and then your problems will really begin.'

George walked up to Paradise as soon as he'd finished breakfast. A light southwesterly breeze was lifting and shredding the mist so that the sun gleamed fitfully between trailing skeins of candy-floss cloud. He paused at the field gate. The donkeys were across the other side of the meadow, grazing quietly, and he stood for a moment watching them, deeply and gratefully aware of this new sensation of freedom but fighting a sense of guilt at having been presented with it so easily. Soon he would see Joss, able at last to tell her his true feelings.

He went on up the lane to Paradise, passing between the granite pillars on to the drive. Small clumps of snowdrops, heads drooped, glimmered moony-pale amongst the rhododendrons, and a tide of purple crocus flooded the small lawn with their darkly vivid colour.

Feeling that under the circumstances a certain formality was in order, George avoided his usual entry through the garden room and knocked instead at the front door. Emma answered it, opening it wide when she saw who it was, beaming at him affectionately.

'How nice to see you, George,' she said.

He kissed her lightly. 'I'm so sorry about Mutt,' he said. 'I came to see if there was anything that I could do.'

'That's very sweet of you.' A sudden flash of speculation quenched the sadness in her eyes and he braced himself to deal with her curiosity. 'Is Penny with you?' she asked brightly. 'How is she? And Tasha?'

Joss had come out of the kitchen and was standing by the door in the shadows at the back of the hall, watching him. George met her eyes above Emma's head and was shocked by the anxiety in her face.

With an effort, George turned his attention to Emma. 'They aren't with me,' he answered shortly. Then raised his hands, as if making a reluctant decision. 'You might as well know that Penny has taken Tasha back to New Zealand. She's decided that they will be happier there.'

Joss had already turned aside, probably to hide her expression of relief, but Emma's eyes were round with shock.

'But, George,' she gasped. 'Gone back to New Zealand? My goodness, I can't believe it.'

'I'm sorry,' he said. 'Coming on top of Mutt it's a bit much, isn't it? The trouble is, there's no other way to break this kind of news.'

He glanced rather helplessly towards Joss, who came forward to put an arm round her mother. He guessed that she didn't want her mother to know that his news was not too much of a shock to her.

'Come into the kitchen,' Joss said. 'We've just finished breakfast but there's some coffee in the pot.'

'It's Joss's day off,' said Emma, allowing herself to be led back into the kitchen, 'and I was trying to persuade her to have the morning in bed.'

'I couldn't rest,' said Joss quickly. 'I'm too tensed up, I suppose.'

'Perhaps a walk would do you good,' George suggested, keen to get her to himself, longing to explain the happenings of the last twenty-four hours. 'We could take the donkeys. You know how they love a stroll.'

For one brief moment Joss's face lit up with pleasure, but as he watched her he saw the light die from her eyes and felt ashamed that he'd put his own needs before her grief.

'Perhaps later on,' Joss told him. 'That would be good.'

Emma, distracted but still curious, raised her eyebrows. 'Why not now?' she asked. 'It would do you good. You don't have to worry about me. I've got plenty to do, and your father will be arriving later.'

George took his coffee, noticing that Joss's hand trembled slightly. He looked at her, trying to catch her eye so as to exchange one of those private signals they'd shared since childhood, but she evaded him. It was as if the current of affection that flowed so naturally between them had been switched off and he felt a real sense of loneliness. He realised that ever since he'd left the cottage at Meavy he'd been needing to share the news with her. He saw, however, that it couldn't be quite as he'd imagined it and he quickly assessed this new situation.

'Later will be fine,' he agreed, as if Emma hadn't spoken. 'Meanwhile, there must be something I could do. How are you off for logs?'

Joss looked at him gratefully. 'Actually, we've managed to use up all the smaller ones,' she said. 'If you could split some of the big ones . . . ?'

'Not a problem.' Maybe she would come and talk to him while he was working. 'I'll finish my coffee and then go out to the woodshed.'

'I still can't get used to the fact that we won't hear her bell ring.' Emma's eyes filled with tears. 'It seems so impossible . . .'

Before either of them could comfort her they heard the sound of an engine, a car door slammed and the front door was tried by someone who clearly expected it to be unlocked. The knocking that followed was loud and impatient. Emma got up and hurried into the hall.

'Ray!' they heard her exclaim. 'I wasn't expecting you for another hour.'

George and Joss stood together in silence, listening.

'I didn't see much point in hanging around.' His voice, booming round the hall and echoing up the stairs, was as insensitive to grief and death as his knocking had been and George felt Joss wince. 'This damned fog held me up but it began to clear as I got nearer to the coast.'

'I'll crack on with the logs.' George spoke quietly. He caught Joss by the shoulders and held them for a moment as if to reassure her. 'You know where I am if you need me.' He bent to kiss her cheek, reached for his jacket and slipped out through the garden door just as Emma and Raymond entered the kitchen.

Once he'd gone, Joss took hold of the back of one of the chairs as if for support. She hadn't been prepared for the difficulty of seeing George again, knowing as she did now that she wasn't the person she'd believed herself to be. It was as if, until this point, she and George had been all of a piece; not only because of similarities of mind and taste, and their love for this small valley hidden away on the north Cornish coast, but through blood and bone and family ties. Now, the truth divided them.

Sympathetic though she felt towards her grandmother, Joss was conscious that neither Mutt nor her descendants had any right here at Paradise and, the moment she'd seen George, she'd been struck by the impossibility of pretending otherwise. Even the news that Penny had gone didn't have the power to affect her as it would have done forty-eight hours earlier. Only her mother's grief and distress was preventing her from getting into her car and driving as far away from St Meriadoc as she could. Perhaps, after all, it *was* different for Bruno. Whatever the deception, he was at least a Trevannion. He belonged.

As her parents came into the kitchen Joss braced herself anew to deal with the weight of her knowledge. She was hardly aware of her father's brief kiss, seeing only his familiar, assessing glance around as he sat down at the table.

'All this will soon be mine', his look seemed to say. There was a faint but unmistakable air of anticipation in his expression that made Joss shudder. His acquisitiveness had always repelled her; now, with her new knowledge, it appalled her.

'When's the funeral?' he was asking. 'You said the undertakers had been, dear?'

Joss stared at him. She hated the way he called them both 'dear'; there was a lack of intimacy about the word, as if he used it because he felt an endearment was appropriate to his wife and daughter without it really mattering what it was.

'I'll make some fresh coffee.' Emma hurried to the percolator.

Joss could see that her mother was on edge, prepared for a falling-out between her husband and daughter, and instinctively adopting a cheerfulness that might, with luck, placate the two of them.

'The rector thought Monday but he's going to telephone this morning.' Emma paused in her coffee-making and shook her head. 'I simply can't take it in,' she added miserably.

Raymond stretched out his large, square hand and patted the piece of Emma he could reach. 'She's had a good run for her money, dear,' he said, not unkindly. 'At least she hasn't suffered.'

'She suffered quite a bit in the last few weeks, actually,' Joss said. 'The break was quite a bad one.'

Her father smiled. 'I'm sure you were a great help,' he said, as if she were ten. 'All that expensive training must have come in very useful.'

'She was wonderful.' Emma was defensive. 'Mousie said so.'

'Ah.' His eyes became watchful. 'And how is Mousie?'

'She's fine,' her mother answered briefly. 'So how long did the drive take you?'

The question was so clearly meant as a diversion that Raymond didn't bother to answer it: his fingers tapped out a rhythm and his eyes were speculative. 'Did you manage to get a look at the will?' he asked, following out his own train of thought.

'No.' Emma glanced uneasily at Joss. 'No, of course not. Won't it be with Mutt's lawyer?'

She managed to sound quite indifferent and Raymond frowned.

'It might be anywhere,' he answered irritably, 'but I'd like to see it.'

'Why?' Joss couldn't contain herself. 'Do you think Mutt might have left you something?'

He looked at her consideringly, as if reminding himself that she was grieving for her grandmother. 'I have to look after your mother's interests,' he answered almost genially. 'Surely you must see that?'

Various retorts jostled at Joss's lips but now none of them was relevant. She let go of the chair-back and smiled at her mother.

'No more coffee for me,' she said. 'See you later,' and, taking up her plaid shawl, she let herself out quietly, closing the door behind her.

Emma pulled out a chair and sat down at the table. She began to pour coffee, her lips compressed, her eyes anxious.

'So you haven't seen the will?'

It was as if the exchange with Joss hadn't taken place and Emma stirred irritably.

'I've already told you I haven't. Why should I? Honestly, Ray, you're so tactless.'

He shrugged the criticism away. 'Have you thought where the Inheritance Tax will come from this time?' he asked. His voice was softer now, almost meditative. 'When your grandfather died there were farms and land to sell but now there's nothing except Paradise itself. Or The Lookout and The Row. It'll be a tidy bit to pay. We're probably talking at least a hundred thousand.'

He saw that he had her attention; her face was shocked. 'A hundred thousand *pounds*?'

He raised his eyebrows at her amazement. 'Why do you think I've been suggesting for years that Mutt should hand some of the estate over? If she'd given Bruno The Lookout and passed Paradise to you we'd have saved a fortune.'

'But surely we won't have to sell Paradise?' She gazed at him fearfully. 'You know I've always wanted it for Joss.'

Raymond drew down the corners of his mouth. 'Well, it might have to go. The estate might have to come under the hammer and then, when it's all sold up, you and Bruno would share out the remaining money.'

'But that would be dreadful.' Her eyes were huge with shock. 'I can't believe that could happen.'

'Oh, my dear,' his laugh was indulgent, 'you clearly haven't had any dealings with the Inland Revenue. Of course,' he pursed his lips thoughtfully, picking up his coffee cup, 'there might be another way, if only I could get a look at the damned will.'

'How would it help?' she asked tremulously. 'Just looking at it can't alter the facts, can it?'

'It can't alter the facts,' he agreed, seeing she was now on his side, 'but we can be prepared. 'Look'—he leaned forward, conspiratorially, smiling at her—'why don't we see if we can find the will? You are entitled, as her only daughter, to read it, especially if it's been left here in the house. I suppose you've no idea where Mutt might have kept it?' He tried to keep his voice casual, though he was willing her to get on with it. 'In that old desk in her parlour is as good a place to start, I suppose.'

'I suppose,' she agreed wearily. 'I'll go and have a look.'

She got up and went out and he heard the parlour door close behind her. He stretched with relief and poured himself some more coffee, resigning himself to patience.

Joss could hear the thud of the axe as she slipped down the drive. Her one thought was to see Bruno; he was the only person with whom she could now feel entirely at ease. She told herself that she needed time to adjust and that a moment or two with Bruno would give her a breathing space. Also, she wanted to know where he'd found the letters. Last night, after Emma had gone to bed, she'd continued her search for *Goblin Market* in the parlour, but she'd been unable to bring herself to root around in Mutt's empty bedroom so soon after her death. Now she wondered if she should have ignored her finer instincts. Her father, she was certain, would not be so nice: he or her mother might now start to look for the will and come across *Goblin Market* quite by accident.

She wondered what George was thinking, whether he'd finished the logs and was puzzled by her disappearance, and gave a small groan of despair. He must have been surprised that she'd taken his news so coolly, merely offering him coffee and sending him out to split logs.

She saw that her knowledge would lie between them like a sword, cutting them off from each other, and more especially so if there should prove to be unfair provisions in the will. It would be intolerable now if she or her family were to benefit at Rafe's or Mousie's expense, and the arrival of her father had crystallised her fears into reality.

The sight of Bruno, standing in the great bow of the window and staring out to sea, filled her with an overwhelming relief. She waved to attract his attention and he raised a hand, turning back into the room as he came to meet her.

'I haven't found *Goblin Market*,' she told him as soon as she entered the kitchen. 'At least, it's not in the bookcase in the parlour or on the shelves on the landing. I couldn't bring myself to go into Mutt's room.' She followed him into the sitting room and sat down at the table.

'I have a feeling that it'll be somewhere less obvious,' he said calmly. 'In the desk, perhaps, where the letters were?'

'I looked there,' she told him. 'Very quickly because Mum kept coming in and out and then, when you telephoned, I was able to have a better chance. And now Dad's arrived.' She paused. 'Where *were* the letters?' she asked.

'Mousie found them,' he told her gently. 'It had to be her, didn't it, when you think about it? She heard us talking about it when she came in and saw me bundle the pages under the seat. Later on she remembered the scene and was afraid that the wrong person might discover whatever it was we were hiding. When she took them out they scattered all over the place and, without meaning to, she saw enough to puzzle her.'

'Oh my God.' Joss pressed her fingers to her mouth.

Bruno nodded. 'Mousie was already . . . well, curious. You read in the letters that Mutt feared that Mousie knew something. The long and short of it is that she read the letters and now she knows the truth. And it doesn't matter a damn to her,' he added quickly. 'Why should it? Oh, she feels irritated that she's been taken in for all these years but, having read the letters, she understands Mutt's dilemma and, as far as you and Emma are concerned, nothing's changed at all.'

'But *everything's* changed,' she cried angrily. 'It's crazy to say that.'

'Look.' He sat down at right angles to her. 'Remember that nobody has lost out financially because of what Mutt did. On the contrary, she looked after Mousie and Rafe and kept the estate going when my grandfather died. As for me, Emma has been as close as any sister could have been, and a very good friend. Think how lonely I would have been without them. And you, Joss, have been as dear to me as any daughter I might have had. If it had been I who had been Mutt's son would you feel differently about me now? Would you love me less or look upon me as a usurper? Do try not to see it purely in terms of blood and family ties.'

'I can't help it,' she said miserably. 'When Dad turned up this morning and started talking about the will before he'd been there two minutes, I saw how different he is from all of you. I felt we were intruders, the three of us, sitting in the kitchen at Paradise as if it were ours.'

She sounded calmer, however, and Bruno watched her thoughtfully, trying to assess her state of mind, gathering up his courage.

'Mousie thinks that Emma should know the truth,' he said. 'Her view is that the burden will be too heavy for you,' he said, 'and I think she's right. She says that it's not fair to you and that we are underestimating Emma. Mousie believes that if we were to show her the letters she'd understand, just as we have, and be able to come to terms with it all.'

'I don't agree. I think she'll be gutted.'

Yet her voice was less confident and he watched the inward struggle reflected on her face and decided on a different approach.

'Seen George?' he asked, almost as if he were changing the subject.

'Oh.' It was a cry almost of pain. 'He came up to Paradise and told us that Penny and Tasha have gone back to New Zealand, and I couldn't think of anything to say to him. Not just because Mum was there but because it was all different between us. In the end Mum gave him some coffee and then he went out to split logs.'

'"All different between us",' repeated Bruno thoughtfully. 'Yet you still don't think that the truth should be told?'

She stared at him almost fearfully. 'I don't know,' she said at last, 'but, anyway, not until after the funeral.'

'OK.' Bruno sighed, frustrated. 'But it's going to become very awkward if Emma finds the will and Brer Fox starts laying down the law. We must get hold of it first. Of course it might be with Mutt's lawyer . . .'

In the hall, the telephone rang and he got up to answer it.

'Hello, darling.' The gravelly voice, matured by years of Sobranies and

Scotch was unmistakable. 'It's me. Zoë. You'll never guess where I am.'

Bruno put his hand across the mouthpiece, thinking furiously. When he spoke to her, his voice was curt.

'Wait a minute, will you? I've got someone with me.'

He placed the receiver beside the telephone and went back to the sitting room.

'It's Zoë,' he told Joss. 'Bloody awful timing but par for the course.'

'I've got to go back, anyway.' She got up at once. 'They'll all be wondering where I've gone and I have to see George.'

She looked so intimidated by the prospect that he gave her a brief hug. 'Courage,' he said.

She smiled at him. 'Thanks, Bruno.' She pulled her plaid about her and he went with her to the door. 'Shall I tell them you'll be up later?' she asked.

He hesitated. 'I'm not certain when,' he warned, 'but don't worry. I'll be there sometime this afternoon.'

She nodded again, and went away, and he returned to the kitchen.

'Do I hear a woman's voice?' Zoë sounded amused.

'Joss,' he answered briefly. 'So where are you?'

'I'm at Rock, darling.' She sounded almost as surprised as he was. 'Can you believe it? And at this time of the year too. I told you that Jilly and Tim bought a cottage here, remember? Apparently there were rumours of burst pipes during the cold spell, so I drove her down to check it out. How about I come over for lunch?'

Bruno closed his eyes in despair. 'The timing isn't good,' he said with difficulty. 'Mutt died in the early hours of Tuesday morning and . . . well, you can imagine the rest.'

'Oh, darling, I'm sorry.' She sounded it too. 'Fancy old Mutt gone!' A tiny pause. 'When is the funeral?'

'I don't know yet.' He felt edgy, suspicious. 'Probably early next week. Emma's down and Brer Fox has just arrived. There's a lot to sort out.'

'I'd really like to see you, darling. Especially now. Look, I can be with you in half an hour and I won't keep you long.' A pause—then her voice altered. 'Are you writing?'

He laughed mirthlessly. 'Are you kidding?'

She chuckled. 'Poor darling. Has reality kicked in? Never mind. We'll have a drink together, don't bother about the food. See you.'

The line went dead and he cursed long and hard.

George wheeled the barrowful of logs round the side of the house and parked it beside Raymond's BMW. He came into the kitchen just as Emma appeared at the other door leading from the hall.

317

'I can't find it in the parlour,' she was saying to Raymond. 'Only this parcel with Bruno's name on it. Oh, hello, George. Are you ready for some more coffee after all that hard work?'

She dropped the parcel on the table and went to wash up the mugs. Raymond murmured a greeting, but all his concentration seemed directed towards the package. It was clear too that Emma was feeling slightly uncomfortable, as if George's appearance was inconveniently timed. From where he was standing George could recognise the handwriting. It was Mutt's: *For Bruno James Trevannion. Personal and Private.* And across the bottom was printed one word: CONFIDENTIAL. The brown paper parcel was tied with string.

Very slowly Raymond turned the parcel over, his thick forefinger idly probing the knots, although he still wore an almost indifferent expression, as if he were brooding on something else entirely and the parcel was simply an object to fiddle with.

Beside him, George felt Emma stiffen: waiting and watching. He realised that she was prepared for Raymond to open the parcel and was bracing herself to prevent him.

Instinctively, George went to fill the kettle. He smiled at Emma. 'I think I do need a shot of caffeine after all that effort,' he said. 'Is Joss anywhere about? She might like some.'

'I don't know where she is.' Emma had relaxed a little but was still distracted. 'I'll give a shout up the stairs.'

'She went out.' Raymond sounded very certain. 'I heard the front door close about half an hour ago. Perhaps she's with the donkeys.' He gave George a friendly glance. 'Emma can make the coffee if you want to go and find her.'

George smiled back at him. 'She might be anywhere,' he answered casually. 'I expect she'll be in soon.' He took a mug from the cupboard, feeling Emma hovering beside him uncertainly, wondering if he were imagining the tension. After all, why on earth should Raymond want to open a parcel addressed so clearly to Bruno? It was more with a sense of mischievousness, rather than any self-righteous intention, that he sat down at the table and openly turned the parcel as if to read the writing for the first time, pulling it across the table.

'For Bruno, I see,' he said conversationally. 'Did Mutt leave it for you to give to him?'

Emma didn't see Raymond's swift upward look of warning.

'It was in her desk,' she said, puzzled. 'Odd really. It was at the bottom of a folder containing Bruno's school reports.'

'Really?' George was beginning to enjoy himself. 'Why were you reading his old school reports? Bit late in the day, isn't it?' He chuckled at his own feeble joke. 'I'll take it down to him, if you like.'

Raymond's large square hands reached for the parcel slowly, as if George had drawn it to his attention and he too were now reading the writing for the first time. As he turned it, he moved it almost unobtrusively back to his own side of the table.

'No need to bother,' he said. 'I expect he'll be here soon.'

'Oh, it's not a bother,' answered George cheerfully, preparing for a little light-hearted contest with Joss's father. 'I shall be going past his door.'

'You haven't had your coffee yet.' Raymond's hands were now clasped together and resting on the parcel. He leaned forward, his broad shoulders hunched. 'There's no hurry.'

George met his cold, blue-grey stare and was aware of an odd stirring of unease. He was glad to hear the kettle boil, to have an excuse to get up from the table to make the coffee. He was convinced now that Raymond shouldn't have the opportunity to examine the contents of the parcel, yet he was powerless to prevent him. He saw exactly what Joss meant when she'd talked about her father's juggernaut tactics.

'He just goes straight on,' she'd said. 'He fixes his eyes on his goal and never wavers for a second. If you get in his path you simply go under with everything else. I used to get cross with Mum for giving in to him, but as I grew up I realised that withstanding him is like trying to stand up to a hurricane.'

Now, as George sat down again at the table and picked up his mug of coffee, he wondered what he would do when he'd be obliged to get up and go out to deal with the logs. He was certain that, on his return, the package would have disappeared and he would be in no position to question either Emma or Raymond about it. He prayed that Joss would return before that moment came. He would draw her attention to the parcel and suggest that they walk down together to deliver it.

His gasp of relief was almost audible when the front door opened and light footsteps hurried up the stairs.

'There's Joss.' Emma's voice was brighter, as if she too were relieved. 'I wonder where she's been.'

George kept an eye on Raymond as the door opened and Joss and Mousie came in. Raymond rose swiftly to his feet and in one smooth movement conveyed the parcel to the dresser behind his chair, pushing it beneath a newspaper so that it was half hidden, even as he was saying, 'Mousie, my dear, how nice to see you,' and giving her a kiss. It was so adroit, so clever, that George was almost breathless with admiration.

He looked at Joss, her eyes bright with some recent excitement, and he was filled with love and longing for her. She smiled at him across the kitchen yet he could still feel the barrier between them. With a jolt of fear he wondered if he'd mistaken this new reticence in her: that it was nothing to do with Mutt's death. After all, they'd never spoken openly of their feelings—he'd been too committed to his marriage for that to be possible. Perhaps Joss was not ready to see Penny's defection in the light of an opportunity for her own happiness—and his.

With this sudden loss of confidence and his preoccupation about Joss, he forgot the little scene with the parcel. Mousie was explaining that she'd left a book in the drawing room and had come up to collect it, meeting Joss on the way, and Emma was insisting that she should have some coffee.

'I'll get on with the logs,' George said. Suddenly he felt depressed, knowing that his new freedom was an empty gift without Joss to share it. He passed close to her, but politely as a stranger might, and she touched his arm.

'Sorry I dashed off,' she murmured. 'Things are a bit difficult. But it's not *you*. Honestly.'

'I'm glad about that.' He smiled, his heart lifting. 'See you later.'

He went out, comforted by this little exchange, and began to fill the log basket, carrying the wood in a plastic container between the wheelbarrow and the drawing room. It wasn't until later, as he wheeled the empty barrow back to the shed and went in through the garden door to the kitchen, that he remembered the package.

Raymond Fox was seated at the table, the women milling about him. Lunch was being prepared and Mousie was being pressed to stay and join them. There was no sign of the parcel.

George debated with himself and then spoke to Emma as she emerged from the larder. 'I'll be off now,' he said, 'or I'll be late for lunch. Shall I take that parcel for Bruno?'

'Oh, don't worry about that.' She seemed edgy. 'Joss says that he'll be up later on.'

He nodded and turned to Joss. 'If you feel like a walk later,' he told her. 'I'll be down at the field to take the donkeys out at around two o'clock.'

Zoë slipped into the kitchen, quiet as a cat, dropped her overnight bag in the corner by Nellie's bed and hesitated by the inner door. Her black eyes took in the simple preparations for lunch: some rolls standing on a rack ready to be warmed in the oven and soup in a saucepan by the stove. As she listened for a moment, wondering if Bruno was alone, she shivered and wished she'd brought warmer clothes. She'd forgotten how cold it was on the north coast.

No voices, no sound at all that she could hear; she took a few paces back, she closed the door with a bang and called out: 'Hello, darling. It's me.' She passed through the kitchen and into the sitting room just as Bruno emerged from his study.

'I'm sure I'm being a nuisance,' Zoë said, putting up her face to be kissed, first one cheek and then the other, 'but there's no need to look *quite* so unwelcoming.'

'Am I?' He chuckled. 'Well, I warned you that your timing is bad.'

She shrugged. 'My timing is always bad.'

'I'm surprised to see you in north Cornwall in February, Zoë,' he said. 'I would have thought that the Maldives were more your scene.'

'And how right you are, darling. The trouble is it was Cornwall or nothing.' She shivered again. 'I always forget how cold it is here. No wonder you keep that fire going right through winter.'

'Wait a minute.' He ran up the stairs and reappeared with a scarlet pashmina. 'Emma keeps it here for the same reason. She won't mind if you borrow it.'

Zoë raised her eyebrows disbelievingly. She suspected that Emma would mind very much, but she wrapped the shawl about her thin frame and perched in the rocking chair beside the fire, watching Bruno as he piled on more logs and fanned the wood into leaping flames.

'I am so sorry about Mutt. I liked her, you know.' she said suddenly.

'So you said earlier.' Bruno sat down on the sofa. 'She liked you too.'

She quirked an eyebrow. 'Don't say it like that, sweetie. Some people do. Odd, isn't it? Mutt didn't make judgments—that was what I liked about her. She never made me feel raw and young.'

Bruno laughed out loud. 'You? Raw? Come off it.'

She laughed with him. 'I was born old,' she admitted, 'but it didn't do me much good, did it?'

She watched him, huddling the pashmina round her thin shoulders, out-staring his assessing look.

'You had a good career. You were internationally famous.'

She made a gesture that disposed of the past. 'We've said all this before. It's history. How's life here at St Meriadoc?'

'Just as it usually is.' He stood up. 'Like a drink?' It was a rhetorical question. 'Well, actually *not* as it usually is, for the obvious reasons. Emma's here, of course, and Brer Fox arrived earlier this morning.'

'They're up at the house?' She deliberately made the question light but was relieved by his answering nod. 'Brer Fox must be rubbing his hands with glee.' She took her glass and grinned up at him. 'You'll have to watch him, won't you?'

'Why?' Bruno sat down again on the sofa and then cursed as a sharp barking was heard. 'Hang on. That's Nellie back from her afternoon walk to the Paradise gardens.'

He went out and she heard the back door open. Nellie came gambolling in, tongue lolling, delighted to see a guest, and Zoë quickly put her glass out of harm's reach and stretched a hand to pat her.

'Careful,' Bruno said. 'Her feet are wet. Here, Nellie. *Here*. On your rug.'

Nellie leaped onto the end of the sofa and curled onto her rug.

'She's such a nice, smiley person,' said Zoë, watching her. 'I wish I could have a dog but the flat's far too small. I sometimes long for a puppy. What fun it would be!'

'You'd hate having a puppy,' answered Bruno at once. 'The sheer relentlessness of it would kill you. It's a bit like having a child . . .'

He paused, picking up his glass, his face suddenly bleak.

Damn, thought Zoë. Damn, damn, damn. Just the wrong note to strike. 'Well, you're right, of course,' she said aloud. 'I have this unfortunate character which always lets me down when it matters most. So how is Emma taking it? I bet old Brer Fox has got the valuers in already.'

Bruno grinned unwillingly. 'I haven't seen him yet,' he admitted, 'but you're probably not far out.'

In the silence that followed, she sipped thoughtfully at her wine. 'I suppose it's share-out time,' she suggested casually. 'But you've always expected it, haven't you? You and Emma knew how it would go. I can hear her now: "You have The Lookout and I'll have Paradise." The thing is'—she shifted in the chair—'neither of you talked about the rest of it.'

She decided to press him a little; he could warn her off if he wanted to. 'How has Mutt left it, do you know?'

He glanced at her as if deciding what to tell her. 'I haven't seen the will,' he said slowly, 'but I'm hoping that the boatyard won't be left to Emma. That could be tricky.'

'Tricky?' She gazed at him in disbelief at such an understatement. '*Tricky*? Brer Fox would turn the cove into some kind of leisure complex. What would you do about it?'

Bruno shrugged. 'What *could* I do about it? Of course there's the Inheritance Tax to be paid.' He rubbed his fingers reflectively over his jaw. 'Something will have to go.'

Zoë settled back into the chair, tucking the pashmina more firmly around her. 'If Mutt has left the boatyard to Emma, then finding money to pay the Inheritance Tax will give Brer Fox just the handle he needs.'

'Possibly. There are a few problems, though. It will need planning permission, of course. Perhaps we'll have to sell Paradise. Anyway'—he seemed to pull himself together, abandoning the confidences—'I'd offer you another drink but if you're driving it wouldn't be very sensible.'

'Well, that's just it.' She wriggled a little, looking rather forlorn. 'I've got a problem, darling.'

He looked amused. 'No change there, then. What is it this time?'

'I was hoping that I could stay for a day or two.'

His expression changed so swiftly from amusement to surprise that she pretended dismay. 'Oh, don't look like that, darling. The truth of it is that Jilly rather used me as a cover so that dear old Tim didn't smell a rat and now I find that she's invited Greg Allen too. Three is definitely a crowd and I'm hoping that you might rescue me just for a few nights. I know, it's not a good time,' she said quickly. 'But, please, Bruno, I'll keep out of your way.'

'Oh, do me a favour,' he said crossly, standing up and pushing his hands into his trouser pockets. 'I wasn't born yesterday. What is really the problem?'

She hesitated, curled back in the chair as she stared up at him. 'I've got a serious cash-flow problem,' she said rapidly. 'They've switched off the power at the flat, the bastards, and it's freezing. When Jilly said she was thinking of coming down I offered to drive her if she paid for half the petrol. I thought I'd come on to you and ask if you'd help.'

'I'm flattered,' he said drily. 'You don't normally feel the need to drive all this way to ask for money. A telephone call usually does the trick. What's so different this time?'

She looked away from him. It had been worth a try but she might have guessed that he'd see through her.

'The truth is that I've got in a bit of a muddle.' She reached for a cigarette, breathed in a lungful of smoke and visibly relaxed. 'The thing is,' she began again, 'I thought I had some work lined up and then it fell through. Anyway, I'd got deep in on the strength of it, maxed the credit cards and so on, fallen behind with the rent. Well,' she pulled a face, not looking at him. 'If you must know, I've borrowed from all my chums and I can't bear the humiliation of hearing their voices when they know it's me on the phone. Jilly said she'd pay the petrol if I drove her down, but Tim will be arriving on Saturday and they'll go back together. To be honest, darling, I haven't got anywhere else to go.'

Mousie leaned on the field gate, some withered apples in her pocket and Mutt's will tucked into the shabby leather bag slung over her shoulder. She'd managed to resist Emma's invitations to lunch, finishing her coffee and hurrying away as soon as she could, and now she took a moment to catch her breath. It was after breakfast this morning that she'd thought of the place where the will might be; a place where Mutt had put personal papers, letters and cards that she'd treasured. Oddly, this wasn't in the desk in her parlour but in a drawer in her dressing table. During those early days after her fall, she'd asked Mousie to bring something—a letter from Emma, perhaps—from the drawer and it had been obvious that it was here she kept her special correspondence.

As soon as Mousie remembered it she decided that she would go up to Paradise and take a look. She saw Raymond's car sweep past, driving up to the house, and realised that she might need to have a plan: she'd say that she'd mislaid a book. After all, she'd spent a great deal of time in Mutt's bedroom and had more excuse than any of them—except for Joss—for gaining access to it.

Now, standing at the field gate with the will safe in her bag, she smiled to herself. As it had turned out, Joss had given her all the cover she'd needed, waiting on watch in the hall while she, Mousie, had run lightly upstairs and found what she was looking for.

The donkeys came plodding to see her, heads nodding, blinking their extraordinary eyelashes. They jostled each other for prime position and she held out the apples and promised them a walk.

'Later,' she told them. 'Joss will be down, later.'

As she stroked their long ears she wondered how Joss would deal with the discovery of her true identity. There would be moments, of course, when the sudden thought of it would knock her off balance. She'd had just such a moment when they'd met earlier at the bottom of the path to The Lookout.

'I've just been to see Bruno,' Joss had said. 'Are you coming up to Paradise?'—and then, quite unexpectedly, her face had been washed by a tide of vivid colour as if she'd just remembered who she was—and, even worse, that Mousie knew her secret. It was a purely instinctive response to put an arm around the girl and give her a quick, brief hug. Joss had stood stiffly in the embrace, as if too dismayed by her knowledge to return it.

Mousie had released her and stepped back. 'I can't tell you,' she had said, 'what a relief it was to read those letters. But I have to apologise. I had no right, of course.'

Joss had flushed an even brighter red. 'I had no right, either,' she answered wretchedly. 'Mutt told me to find them, not to read them.'

'Oh, but what a responsibility.' Mousie had shaken her head sympathetically. 'I didn't have even that excuse. I recognised her writing, you see, and then saw the signature: Madeleine.'

'That was it,' Joss had cried eagerly. 'That's what got me too.'

As they set off together towards Paradise, Joss explaining why she'd read the letters, Mousie experienced a fear that, if the truth were not told to everyone, Joss might spend the rest of her life apologising because she felt that she had no right to be at St Meriadoc any longer.

'But isn't it better,' she asked, when there had been a lull in Joss's explanations, 'that we should all know the truth? I, for one, am glad to know. It's been a trouble to me ever since Mutt came back from India.'

Gently, quietly, she repeated what she'd told Bruno the previous evening, explaining her misgivings and telling how she'd regretted the withholding of her trust. They reached the field gate and it was natural to stand there, watching the donkeys while they talked.

'I'd felt so guilty about it, you see,' she told Joss. 'Putting it down to childhood jealousy and castigating myself for being so foolish. Then, once I'd read the letters, I was angry because I felt that I'd been right to be suspicious, after all, and that your grandmother had deceived me.'

Joss turned then, meeting her eyes bravely. 'And now?' she asked.

Mousie chuckled. 'Oh, my dear, now I just regret allowing it to come between us all our lives. Once I'd thought about the letters—even while I was reading them—I felt a huge sympathy for the position your grandmother was in. She was brave, resourceful and compassionate and I'm sure you must feel very proud of her. I just wish that the shadow of suspicion on my side, and the fear on hers, hadn't stunted our friendship. I think Bruno had the right of it when he told me that Mutt and Emma saved his life. For the last fifty years she looked after us all.'

'And now?' Joss asked again. 'Bruno says you think we should tell Mum the truth.'

'I do. Lies cast long shadows. I think you'll find that out for yourself.'

Joss turned away, her face miserable. 'I don't think Mum will be able to deal with it,' she said.

'Let her read those letters and judge for herself,' Mousie said firmly.

'She'll feel we don't belong here any more.' Joss was only just able to control the trembling of her lips. 'I don't want her to feel that but, at the same time, it would be wrong for her—or me—to inherit anything.'

'You *do* belong here,' Mousie replied. 'We all love you. Nothing changes that. Try to see what your mother and you mean to Bruno. You *are* his family, Joss, as much as I am or Rafe and his brood are.'

'But my father isn't.'

Mousie sighed. 'Raymond has never made any effort to be a member of the family,' she said truthfully. 'He has no wish to be. I agree that it would be quite wrong if he were to exert undue influence now over the estate. That's why I think the truth should be told.' She paused. 'I think I know where the will might be. It would be a good idea if Bruno could keep it until he's ready to let it be made public. Will you cover for me if I go up to Mutt's bedroom and look for it?'

Joss was only too ready to assist in the suppression of the will.

'Do you think *Goblin Market* might be there, too,' she asked eagerly. But Mousie shook her head regretfully. The drawer was too shallow.

They had gone on together, entering Paradise like two conspirators, Joss punching the air in silent triumph when Mousie reappeared on the stairs brandishing the will in its brown envelope. All the while she was drinking coffee, talking to Emma and Raymond, it had been as if the document were burning a hole in her leather bag.

Now, still leaning on the gate, Mousie allowed herself to think about Mutt and to grieve for her. How strange, how moving, it had been to read about Uncle James and her own mother, Julia. Now she saw herself, all those years ago, though Mutt's eyes—young, rather priggish, critical—and recalled that moment at the Christmas party when her offer of friendship had been rebuffed. She saw now that the withholding of the foolish nickname had been her way of keeping her own pride intact.

Silently she gave tribute to Mutt, grateful for all she had done for Bruno and for all of them, and then, giving the donkeys a final pat, she set off for The Lookout: the sooner Bruno took the will into his own keeping the happier she would feel. She climbed the steep path, let herself into his kitchen, and was calling out to him before she caught the murmur of voices.

Bruno met her as she came in, his broad shoulders blocking the other end of the big, light-filled room. His look was warning but his voice was natural and welcoming.

'Hello, Mousie,' he said. 'Look who's here.' He stood aside and she saw Zoë, sitting by the fire. 'You're just in time for a drink.'

Emma closed the front door behind Mousie and stood for a moment, giving herself time in which to think. She was still confused by what Raymond had tried to explain to her earlier about Inheritance Tax, anxious now that with Mutt gone, things here at St Meriadoc would change. Her heart was squeezed and wrung with grief and she gave a tiny sob, quickly putting her fingers to her lips as if to stifle the noise as Joss came out of the kitchen.

'I thought I'd go upstairs for a bit to catch up on some notes ready for tomorrow,' Joss said. 'Lunch is nearly ready but there's just something particularly important I'd like to deal with, if that's OK?'

Emma saw that Joss had hesitated at the foot of the stairs, watching her, and she pulled herself together. 'Of course it is,' she answered. 'I can manage lunch. I'll give you a shout.'

On an impulse Joss crossed the hall and gave Emma a quick hug. 'It'll be OK, Mum,' she said seriously, rather as if she were making a promise, and Emma smiled back at her; grateful for that warm, unexpected gesture.

'Of course it will,' she agreed bravely.

She watched Joss leap the stairs, two at a time and, taking a deep breath, went back into the kitchen. Raymond was standing at the dresser, moving and folding a pile of newspapers, his face set into frowning, angry lines.

'The damned thing's gone,' he said abruptly as soon as he saw her. 'It's simply disappeared. Did George take it, after all?'

She shook her head, looking puzzled, but her heart jumped anxiously. 'Do you mean the parcel? No, he offered but I didn't take it up.'

'When Mousie and Joss came in I thought it was best to put the package out of sight. I put it on the dresser. Just here. Now it's gone.'

'Perhaps Mousie saw it and decided to deliver it.' She shrugged, collecting knives and forks together, beginning to set the table for lunch. 'Anyway, what did you intend to do with it? You could have hardly opened it yourself.'

The silence went on for far too long. She stared at him, pretending disbelief, and he coloured a little.

'I was merely going to check that the will hadn't been put in with other things, that's all.' He almost sounded defensive. 'Don't forget you have just as much right to see Mutt's will as Bruno has. A quick glance would have forewarned us and nobody would have been the wiser.' He could sense her resistance. 'The sooner we decide how the tax is to be paid the better. At least, I imagine you don't relish the idea of selling Paradise to meet it, do you?'

Emma hid her twinge of fear, raising her chin as if in defiance at his threat. 'I've been thinking about that and I still don't quite see what could be done about it, even if we knew the contents of her will. It's horrid, talking like this when we should be mourning Mutt.'

Before he could answer her Joss came downstairs again and Emma braced herself. Instinctively her voice lightened and her lips smiled, as if this air of determined cheerfulness might act as a restraint to the natural antagonism between Raymond and Joss.

'Lunch,' she announced brightly, as a further distraction—but already Raymond was questioning Joss about the parcel.

'Did you see a package,' he was asking, 'wrapped up in brown paper and string? It was here on the dresser.'

'A package?' Joss shook her head indifferently. 'No. Was it going to the post?'

'No.' Raymond sat down again at the table. 'Your mother came across it when she was looking for something else. It contained something your grandmother had wrapped up long ago by the look of it. It was addressed to Bruno.'

Emma set the fish pie on the table and began to divide it up.

'To Bruno?'

Joss's voice was sharp and Emma hid a sigh. Now it would all come out and there would be an argument. 'Never mind about it now. Is that enough for you, Joss?'

'It was . . . oh,' Raymond was measuring the size of the parcel, squaring the air with his hands, 'about so big. You didn't see it, then? It's rather important that we know what's inside it.'

Joss shook her head. She looked shocked, almost frightened, and Emma snorted with silent indignation, in sympathy with her daughter. No doubt she'd already guessed that her father had intended to open it.

'But where did you find it?' Joss didn't seem interested in the plate that Emma handed to her. 'What were you looking for?'

'Your mother was looking for Mutt's will,' answered Raymond smoothly. 'She came across this parcel and we wondered if the will might be inside it.' He was getting on well with his pie; nothing deflected Raymond from his food. 'Now it's disappeared.'

'But *where* was it?' Joss asked again.

'It was in Mutt's desk.' Emma answered the question. 'She kept our old school reports in one of the drawers and it was in a folder that had Bruno's stuff in it.'

She saw that Joss was staring at her in some kind of horror and she was obliged to remind herself that she had every right to sort out Mutt's things. Nevertheless, she felt a creeping guilt in the face of Joss's reaction.

'We *do* have to find the will, darling,' she said gently. 'Apart from which, Bruno ought to have his parcel, whatever it is.'

'But where is it?'

Joss now seemed almost as anxious about its whereabouts as Ray was, and Emma breathed deeply, trying to contain a rising irritation.

'Shall we finish lunch?' she asked lightly. 'Then we can all have a look for it. Mousie might well have taken it away with her, thinking she was doing us a favour.'

'Yes, that's possible.' Joss seemed to relax a little.

Emma sighed with relief and cast about for a harmless topic of conversation. 'It was so kind of George,' she began at random, 'to come up and help this morning. But what a shock about Penny taking Tasha and just going off like that.'

She saw, with relief, that Ray was not interested in George's domestic problems but was wrapped up in his own thoughts. Joss had picked up her fork and was eating her fish pie with a studied concentration.

'I always thought,' continued Emma, 'that she was hiding something. Oh, I know she missed her family and her country—well, that's only to be expected and nobody would blame her for it—but I have a feeling that there's more to it than that.'

Although she was quite used to conducting these monologues at family mealtimes, in an attempt to keep the sparks from flying, she was surprised at Joss's complete lack of response. She piled some more pie onto Raymond's plate and glanced invitingly at Joss, who shook her head with a little smile.

'I think we shall hear that there's someone in New Zealand. It wouldn't surprise me at all,' Emma prophesied, finishing her own lunch and debating whether she should have another small helping.

Joss shifted suddenly, as if she might speak, glanced anxiously at her father and instead took another forkful of pie. Emma frowned to herself. Clearly Joss didn't wish to have a discussion about George and Penny in front of Ray and she felt a stab of curiosity. Of course, George and Joss had always been very close . . .

Emma put down her fork. She looked again at her daughter, who had bent her head over her plate and was eating quickly, as if nothing mattered but to finish her lunch. Emma saw that her cheeks were stained with colour and, as she watched the flush deepen, several things clicked smartly into place.

'Delicious, dear.' Ray had finished his second helping. 'Anything left? What was that you were saying about George?'

Emma scooped the last of the pie onto his plate and stood up. 'I was saying that he is a dear, good fellow and that he and Joss are taking the donkeys out for a walk this afternoon.' She nodded sharply at Joss, who was now staring at her in surprise, and then began to fill the empty dish with hot water. 'Didn't I hear you fix a time with him, darling? It's nearly two o'clock and I don't suppose you'll want any pudding. Only fruit salad, I'm afraid, Ray, but there's cheese if you want it.'

Joss stood up, hovering indecisively by her chair.

'Off you go, then,' Emma said briskly. 'George will be waiting.'

They exchanged a look, encouraging on Emma's side, confused but grateful on Joss's, and she went out. Emma sighed with contentment, her spirits rising.

'I can't manage anything else at the moment, dear.' Raymond patted her arm. 'There's nothing to beat that local fish. Delicious.'

'Thank you, darling.' Emma beamed upon him. 'Now, why don't you go and relax in the sitting room and I'll bring the coffee in to you? It will be nice to have a moment to ourselves. Here, take the newspaper . . .'

To her great relief he disappeared obediently and Emma crossed swiftly to the dresser. She opened a drawer, checked that the parcel was well hidden and, taking a pile of cloths from another drawer, covered it more securely. She was determined that there should be no arguments, no fighting or bitter words, until after Mutt had been laid peacefully to rest. Whatever the parcel might contain could wait a few more days. Satisfied that it was out of harm's way, she closed the drawer gently and went to make some coffee.

George arrived at the field gate a few minutes after Joss had entered the meadow from the garden. Her relief at seeing him was so overwhelming that she was glad to be able to busy herself getting the donkeys into their head collars, smiling briefly at him, but feeling unnaturally shy.

'Which way shall we go?' It was clear that he was trying to pretend that nothing had changed between them. 'Up the lane and back down the valley? I'll take the Teaser.'

He took Rumpleteazer's halter and set off across the meadow, leaving her to follow with Mungojerrie. This was the usual form: the Teaser always liked to lead. Down the lane they clopped, over the narrow bridge and past The Row. The wind was stronger now, whipping up the choppy surface of the water into white spumy frills, while the sea birds swooped and drifted high above in strange, ever-changing patterns, crying mournfully. The sea roared as it advanced, pounding over the rocks and against the cliffs with ceaseless energy.

The tide and the wind combined made conversation impossible and, as she led Mungo up the narrow lane, climbing and winding inland now, Joss was thinking about Mutt and the letters, remembering particularly the passages about Simon and trying to imagine what would have happened if Mutt had told him the truth. Would he have recoiled from her in horror, as she'd feared, or would his love for her have given him the compassion to understand? As they passed between the high grassy banks, studded now with delicately pale primroses and shiny-bright celandines, Joss wondered whether Mutt had ever regretted that Sunday morning's work by the Saint's Well.

When George glanced back at her, checking their progress, she knew at once that the barrier was still between them. *Lies cast long shadows.* She could never be easy with him again until he knew the truth. Smiling back at him, nodding that all was well, she sighed heavily and deeply inside herself. In that moment when her father had entered the kitchen at Paradise she'd known that it would be impossible to continue to protect her mother from the truth, but it was also impossible to imagine any scene in which she might be told. Remembering her own reaction as she'd read the letters, Joss shrank at recommending the same process.

Watching George's familiar stride, Joss recalled how comforting Bruno and Mousie had both been and how easy, with them, to feel that nothing terrible had happened after all. She was still herself, Joss Fox; unchanged and still loved by those she valued most. If Bruno and

Mousie felt like that about her after this startling revelation then why should George feel any different?

She saw that he was waiting patiently at the point where the lane widened and she hastened to catch him up.

'They're going well, aren't they?' he said cheerfully. 'Are you OK?' But she was seized with compunction at his expression. Even he couldn't hide the misery and confusion he felt at the unexplained obstacle that prevented the usual flow of affection between them.

'Oh, George,' she said, clutching Mungo's halter in both hands, 'no, I'm not OK, but I don't quite know how to deal with it.'

He looked relieved at once, glad that at least the acknowledgment of this obstacle was out in the open. 'Is it to do with Penny leaving so suddenly?' he asked.

'No, it's not that. It's nothing to do with you and Penny at all.'

'You said that earlier.' He frowned anxiously. 'But if it isn't to do with me or Penny, then what is it?'

'It's to do with me,' she said quickly. 'It's something you haven't known about me. I'm not . . . what you think . . .'

As she shook her head in frustration at the inadequacy of her words, an engine could be heard in the lane ahead.

'We can't talk here,' George said. 'We'll go through the field at the top and then down the valley. We can let the donkeys off there for a bit.'

The delivery van came round the bend, slowed at the sight of the donkeys, and the driver raised his hand as he drove on down the lane. As Joss and George crossed the wide field, bordered by hedges of furze and blackthorn, the wind tugged at their hair and jackets so that they bent against it, hauling the donkeys forward to the shelter of the valley.

It was so much quieter down by the stream. The last of the clouds were being bundled away to the east and the sun burst out suddenly as they released the donkeys. They could hear the bubbling spring and Joss thought of that long-ago picnic, when Mutt had heard the lark's falling, tumbling song, and how, as Simon had pointed upwards to him, he'd brushed her cheek with his arm and she'd fallen in love with him.

George reached into his pocket and brought out a Bounty bar: one piece each, which was just as it had always been since the first time they'd been allowed to go off together without a parent to supervise. They'd always shared. Now, he held the piece of chocolate out to her, smiling his familiar smile, but there was a shadow in his eyes.

Folding her plaid to make a cushion she drew him down beside her on the stone where once her grandmother had sat with Simon on a hot August afternoon fifty years before, and slowly, haltingly, she began to tell him her story.

Rafe watched the little procession go past The Row while Pamela listened to the clop of the donkeys' hoofs.

'How do they look?' she asked. She waited patiently for his answer, her fingers trailing lightly over the delicate tassels of some catkins held in a pottery jar.

'They have a slightly muted look,' Rafe answered. 'Rather like they used to be on the last day of the holidays. George is leading Rumpleteazer, and Joss is following with Mungojerrie as usual, but there's a dejected air about the party.'

Pamela frowned, picturing the scene. 'I don't think he's had a proper chance to speak to her yet, do you? I know he said at lunch that he'd told them this morning but it's one thing giving the bare facts to Emma and another explaining properly to Joss.'

'And Raymond was there, which couldn't have helped.' Rafe came away from the window and sat down beside her at the table. 'This news, coming on top of Mutt's death, will probably knock Joss sideways.'

'She'll find it very hard,' agreed Pamela, 'to be truly happy for herself at this particular moment. At the same time, I thought she would be pleased to hear the news.'

There was a little silence.

'I suppose,' said Rafe dubiously, 'that we could be wrong?'

Pamela shook her head. 'All my instincts tell me that this is right,' she said. 'But there are other aspects to it, Rafe. Did you ever think what might happen once Mutt was gone? With the estate, I mean.'

'Well, I assumed it would go on much as before. It will be left between Bruno and Emma, I imagine. I have wondered whether Mutt might have left the house to Joss. They've been so close, haven't they. Why, what were you thinking of, particularly?'

Pamela grimaced, as if undecided as to exactly what she had in mind. 'It might not be quite that straightforward,' she said at last. 'What about Inheritance Tax, for instance? Supposing something had to be sold off to pay it? Perhaps there's some difficulty that Joss knows about which might be a bit embarrassing for her just at present.'

'Difficulty?'

'Well, we've taken it a bit for granted, haven't we, that nothing would change for us in The Row, yet Raymond has made no secret about his idea of developing the boatyard.'

'He'd never get permission for it. Anyway, do you really think Emma or Bruno would sit by while we and Mousie had our lives ruined?'

'I hope not,' answered Pamela feelingly. 'I just wondered, that's all.' She stretched a hand to him and he took it, holding it closely, while they sat together in silence.

Walking down the steep path from The Lookout, Bruno was aware of the change in the weather. The bitter northeasterly wind had backed to the southwest, the ice in the muddy tracks had melted, and the turbulent air was soft and warm. He carried a parcel under his arm that he settled more firmly before glancing back briefly at The Lookout, where Zoë stood in the window, staring out at the sea.

He crossed the narrow bridge and stopped at the first cottage in The Row, knocking at the door before opening it and passing inside, calling Mousie's name just as she appeared. From the tiny hall the stairs rose steeply to the floor above. He hung his jacket on one of the hooks beside the door before following her into the one big downstairs room. A counter with cupboards beneath it separated the kitchen from the living area: two dark green, wing-backed chairs, one on either side of the Victorian grate where a coal fire burned, and an oak gate-legged table set in the window looking seawards.

'I'm sorry I couldn't talk earlier.' He put the parcel containing Mutt's letters on the table. 'You saw the difficulty. I'm hoping you'll look after these for the time being. I'm not saying that Zoë is unprincipled but it's probably best to keep temptation out of her way.'

'Then I expect that you'll feel the same way about this.' Mousie held out the long brown envelope. 'It was in Mutt's dressing-table drawer.'

Bruno breathed a sigh of relief. 'I guessed that you'd found it when you said that there was something you needed to discuss with me. You had the look of someone who'd pulled off something clever. No sign of *Goblin Market*, I suppose?'

She shook her head regretfully, watching him draw the paper from its envelope. 'The drawer isn't deep enough for a book. I can't imagine where that can be. My real fear is that Emma will find it. You can imagine the shock if she should come across it and those death certificates are still where Honor hid them.'

'Mmm.' He was only partially listening to her, reading swiftly over the paper. 'This is better than I feared. She's left The Lookout and the boatyard to me and Paradise to Emma. It was witnessed by the vicar and his wife. But it's clear that the question of Inheritance Tax never occurred to her. Or maybe she hoped that Brer Fox and I might pay it between us.'

Mousie snorted. 'Not even Honor would think Raymond could be that philanthropic.' She gave a rather sad little shrug. 'I suppose, given one didn't know the truth, that development is the obvious way to go.'

'Not if I can help it.' Bruno folded the will and pushed it back into the envelope. 'I think we sit on this until after the funeral.'

Mousie looked at him, then insisted. 'You agree, though, that Emma should be told afterwards?'

He hesitated, putting the will with the letters, folding them together in Mousie's bag. 'Yes,' he said at last, almost reluctantly. 'For Joss's sake. I agree with you that unless Emma is told, Joss will never be able to be open and natural with the family again. And I'm hoping that you're right and that we are underestimating Emma's reaction.'

'She must read the letters,' said Mousie firmly.

Bruno sat down in one of the wing-backed chairs. 'What will happen now, Mousie?'

'If the truth can be proved, I can't see why everything shouldn't turn out well.' She glanced at him sharply. 'What does Zoë want at this particular moment?'

'She wants shelter until she moves into a new flat . . . Why? What did you imagine she wants?'

Mousie shrugged. 'It's just rather neat timing, isn't it?'

'Oh, come on.' Bruno stared at her. 'You don't think she'd heard about Mutt? Good God! Where? How?' He shook his head. 'I really don't think that's why she's here. I might be land-rich but she'll realise that there won't be much cash in it. Zoë's not really devious or grasping, you know. I'm sure her turning up now is just a coincidence.'

Mousie's expression indicated a doubtful acceptance. 'Fair enough. Forget Zoë and concentrate on Raymond. You've got to be prepared that he won't believe those letters. Or, at any rate, he'll try to contest their validity.'

'But how can he? I'm here to tell everyone it's the truth.'

Mousie laughed. 'It's clear that you're no detective writer,' she observed. 'Who stands to gain from the letters? You do. Of course you're going to endorse them. I've no idea whether they'd stand up in a court of law but you'll need those death certificates.'

Mousie dropped a hand on his shoulder. 'Trust me,' she said grimly. 'Raymond won't give in that easily and it could get very messy and upsetting for Emma and Joss. This is the sort of thing that would come between us all and do much more damage than the truth. We must find *Goblin Market* and the certificates to back up the letters.'

'That's all very well,' he answered impatiently, 'but where do you suggest we start to look while Emma and Brer Fox are up at Paradise? You were damned lucky to lay your hand on the will so easily, Mousie. It could take days to go through the house in an attempt to find the book. What do we say that we're looking for and how do we discourage them from joining in the search?'

'I know, I know.' Mousie held up a placating hand. 'Of course, Joss will be keeping her eyes open for it.' She paused for a moment. 'If all goes according to plan, what will you do with Paradise?'

'You mean will Joss live there?' He smiled at her association of ideas. 'The real obstacle would probably be Joss herself. She'd find it difficult now to look upon it as her home when there's Rafe's brood with a more legitimate claim.'

'Unless, of course, she's living there with one of the brood.'

He looked at her quickly. 'Do you know about Joss and George?'

She chuckled. 'My dear Bruno, I've known about Joss and George since they were children. It was a pity that he ever married Penny but now, so Rafe and Pamela tell me, it's all over and she's gone back to New Zealand. I don't think it will be too long before Joss and George do what they should have done five years ago. Why shouldn't they live at Paradise? It's exactly what Mutt would have wanted.'

'As long as we can persuade Joss that she still belongs here.'

'I think George will do that for us,' promised Mousie. 'After all, if she marries him she'll be a part of the family, won't she?'

Bruno stood up and pushed the bag towards her. 'Will you look after this for me?' he asked. 'Keep it safe until it's needed.'

For answer, she unlocked the cupboard beneath the glass-fronted bookcase built into the recess beside the fireplace and put the bag inside. 'Quite safe there,' she said, locking the door again. 'Now all we need is *Goblin Market* and the rest of the puzzle.'

Raymond drove away early the next morning, shortly after Joss left for her practice. Emma waved the car down the drive and then straightened her shoulders, enjoying a familiar feeling of relief now that Ray was gone. She pulled a strand of encroaching ivy away from the wall, smiling with pleasure at a patch of primulas almost hidden in the long grass, her confidence growing, reassuring herself that it was quite right to keep the parcel hidden. She'd stuck with her theory that Mousie had seen it and carried it off to Bruno, and had managed to talk Ray round to her own point of view: that the parcel had been wrapped up too long ago to contain the will. It was much more likely to be something that had belonged to their father, Hubert, which Mutt had decided should be passed on to his son after her death. Ray had reluctantly accepted this reasoning, but then had insisted on another search—including Mutt's own room, which had produced nothing. Finding a card she'd sent recently to Mutt, she'd suddenly been so overcome by grief that Ray had insisted she sit down while he'd made a pot of tea.

He *could* be kind, dear old Ray, and that was what most people didn't understand about him: they didn't see the side of him that he showed only to her and occasionally to Joss. He *was* irritating, pompous and self-seeking. In the beginning, she'd been humiliated, identifying herself with his behaviour, trying to explain it away while making light of it. Nevertheless, there had been many moments in their marriage when they'd been quietly happy together. Yesterday afternoon had been one of those. He'd brought her tea, made just how she liked it, and comforted her in his own kindly way as they'd sat there before the fire. And then Joss had returned. She had come into the drawing room, hesitating in the doorway, and her expression had been one of joyous exultation.

Emma had automatically risen to her feet. 'Darling,' she'd cried. 'Here you are.' She'd gone towards her, unable to think of anything else to say, almost dazzled by that look of happiness.

Joss had looked from one to the other, as if not knowing quite where she was. 'Hello,' she'd said uncertainly.

Unaware of anything unusual, Ray had simply grunted a greeting and picked up his newspaper, but Emma had taken Joss by the arm and led her into the kitchen where she'd pushed her down into a chair.

'Now,' she'd prompted her, refilling the kettle. 'You've had a lovely time with George and the donkeys . . .'

'Yes,' agreed Joss happily. 'Oh, Mum, I have.' She'd stared about her, as if she'd never seen the kitchen before. 'I love him. I've always loved him and now it's all right.'

Remembering those words, Emma began to understand how bad it must have been for someone of Joss's open, truthful temperament to be in love with a married man. How hard to keep her love hidden while continuing to nourish the friendship that had been so important to them both since childhood. Now, it need be a secret no longer.

'If only Mutt had known,' Emma had been saying. 'Oh, she'd have been so thrilled for you, darling. She loved George so much . . .' And she'd seen Joss's expression change, as if she'd remembered something, and the familiar, slightly wary look had come down like a mask.

As she stamped the mud from her shoes at the front door, Emma guessed that it had been the remembrance of grief that had been the cause of that change. In the hall, Emma paused. She'd planned to go down to The Lookout and had even considered taking Bruno his parcel, provided that he promised that—whatever it contained—he should not discuss it with Ray. As soon as she'd heard that Zoë was with him, however, she'd been seized with her usual irritation and now had no intention of allowing Bruno to open the package beneath Zoë's ironical black-eyed gaze. No, it could remain where it was, but she would go down and have coffee with them and be as polite as was possible. Suddenly she was seized again with the joyful thought of Joss's happiness that even the prospect of Zoë couldn't tarnish.

Smiling to herself, she went to get her coat.

Dan Crosby parked his car in the old quarry, reached for his briefcase and climbed out. He glanced at the other three cars, trying to remember whether they were the same ones he'd seen last weekend and hoping that the young woman might be around. He told himself that it was unlikely on a Thursday afternoon, that she'd almost certainly be at work, but he'd been unable to resist another trip to Paradise.

As he walked away from the car, crossing the narrow bridge, he felt that the name was entirely appropriate. He hadn't looked directly at the row of cottages, in case it seemed as if he were prying in through their windows, but he did take a moment to stare across at the strange house perched on the cliff with its outflung window. It must be pretty wild up there with an Atlantic gale blowing.

He passed on up the lane and paused at the field gate; the donkeys watched him consideringly while he called softly to them, clicking his fingers encouragingly. They came towards him with their peculiar head-dipping amble, and he pulled their long ears and rubbed their soft noses, remembering how the young woman had talked to them and fed them and how he'd felt such a strong sense of empathy with her.

'I haven't got anything for you,' he told them—but they stood patiently anyway, glad of the company.

Presently he left them, walking on up the lane and through the gate-way, his heart jumping nervously now as he braced himself for another meeting with the small woman with the keen eyes. He'd prepared an opening gambit—that his holiday was nearly over and that he couldn't go back without one more visit—and he held the briefcase a little tighter under one arm as he knocked on the door, ready for another rejection.

He found himself confronting someone quite different: a pretty, friendly woman with fair hair tucked behind her ears, rather plump but nicely so.

'I do hope I'm not disturbing you,' Dan said. 'I was hoping to see Mrs Honor Trevannion. I know she's been ill . . .'

The woman's expression stopped him, her eyes were brimming with tears, and his spirits sank again.

'Mrs Trevannion died in the early hours of Tuesday morning,' she told him sadly. 'She was my mother.'

'Oh my God,' he said softly. 'I am just so sorry. I had no idea, please forgive me for troubling you.'

'No, no, it's quite all right.' She seemed to recover a little. 'Is there anything I can do?'

He hesitated and then gestured helplessly. 'Well, OK. I sent Mrs Trevannion a photograph of her wedding taken with my great-aunt. A double wedding. They worked together out in India, apparently, and then my great-aunt stopped writing. I had hoped I might learn a little more about her. She seemed to disappear round about the time of India's Independence and, by that time, my grandmother—her sister— had married and moved out to the US. We found this photograph of a double wedding with their names on the back—'

'Oh, I've seen that,' the woman interrupted excitedly. 'Mousie showed it to me. I remember now her telling me that you'd sent it. Look, why don't you come in and have a cup of tea? I'm just making one.'

'Well, that's real kind.' He still felt awkward lest his enquiries were out of order at such a time. 'I have to go back to London at the weekend . . .'

She was welcoming him in, introducing herself: Emma Fox. They shook hands and he held up the briefcase, feeling foolishly shy. 'I have some more photographs here. Perhaps you'd like to see them? Were you born in India, Emma?'

'Yes, I was but I can't remember much about it, I'm afraid.' She was leading him across the hall. 'Do you mind if we go into the kitchen while I make us some tea?'

'Not at all.' He looked about him appreciatively. 'What a lovely house it is. Well, the whole place is so beautiful. It surely is Paradise.'

She beamed at him so warmly that he smiled back at her with real affection: he felt the oddest sensation that he'd known her always.

'Mousie showed me the photograph,' she was saying. 'It was a nice one of Mutt, though, and she looked so much like Joss.'

'Joss?' He sat down at the table and watched her prepare the tea. She took a cake tin from the larder and edged the Victoria sponge onto a flowered plate.

'Help yourself. Take a big piece.' She provided him with a plate and a fork. 'Joss is my daughter. She's an osteopath and she's been living here with her grandmother for the last few months. She's absolutely devastated by her death.'

'I think I've seen her.' He cut himself a piece of cake, beginning to enjoy himself. 'Not to speak to, though. Dark-haired and very pretty?'

'Well, I think she's rather special.'

Joss's mother spoke proudly and Dan's heart warmed to her.

'She's not here today?' he asked hopefully.

Emma shook her head. 'She's at her practice in Wadebridge today. She won't be home much before six o'clock.'

He could see her hesitating, wondering whether to suggest that he should stay on to meet Joss.

'Would you like to see the photographs?' he asked tactfully, hoping to rescue her from her dilemma. 'I've only got the one wedding photograph, I'm afraid, but I suppose that there's a faint possibility that you might remember something. My great-aunt, Madeleine, had a daughter who would have been about your age. Her name was Lottie.'

She'd put the teapot on the table now, and was watching him open the briefcase.

'How odd,' she said slowly. 'Lottie. That name certainly rings a bell.' She sat down opposite him, looking puzzled. 'D'you know, Mutt spoke that name only a few days ago in her sleep. She called out several times. "Lottie. Lottie." She seemed distressed . . . Good heavens. Do you think she knew something about what might have happened to Lottie?'

They stared at each other across the table, the briefcase between them, a few photographs already lying there beside his plate.

'If my great-aunt and your mother were such close friends that they had a double wedding,' Dan observed, 'it wouldn't be surprising.'

Emma picked up the photograph. 'This is the photo I saw, isn't it?'

'That's the wedding.' He gathered a few more together, ready to pass across the table to her. 'This is the original and there are the names on the back. That's how I managed to track you down. Trevannion is not a common name and Madeleine had written somewhere that you all came from Cornwall. My grandmother remembered that.'

She smiled at him. 'Is she still alive, your grandmother?'

A shadow touched his face. 'She died last year. She was a great old girl and I promised her I'd try to find out what happened to her sister. She got quite intense and upset about it. She said once that, if she'd been a bit more generous, Madeleine and Lottie would have come to her after the war and perhaps then they'd have still been alive. She felt that they must be dead, you see, because the letters stopped coming. It's crazy,' he said slowly, 'but I just feel I'm trying to put it right for her, as far as I can.' He shrugged. 'I can't bring them back to life but I just want to try to lay a few ghosts.'

'I wish I could help you.' Her sympathy was evident and she reached across and she took the photograph, holding it up. 'It's just so amazing to see the likeness. That's so like Joss. Do you recognise her?'

He stared at the face smiling out at him. He hadn't seen Joss smile but the likeness was certainly very strong.

'Yes,' he said. 'I see a likeness to the young woman who was here last Saturday. But this is very odd . . .'

He hesitated, frowning in consternation, and Emma turned the picture back so that she could look at it again.

'Now I remember why I said it was odd last time,' she exclaimed. 'How strange! Do you see? The brides are with the wrong grooms. Mutt isn't standing with Hubert. I wonder why. Do you think it was for a joke?'

He was silent for such a time that she looked up at him enquiringly.

'It would seem a bit weird,' he said slowly, 'to do that for a wedding photograph you were planning to send back home to your own folk, wouldn't it? Unless you explained the joke, of course. Madeleine just wrote the words "Me and Johnny with Hubert and Honor Trevannion" on the back. See?' He took another breath. 'Is this the lady you call Mutt?' He pointed. 'This is your mother?'

Emma nodded, still frowning. 'Yes, that's Mutt. How extraordinary. It *must* have been a joke, surely?'

'The thing is . . .' He bit his lip, his face worried. 'The thing is,' he began again, 'that this lady you call Mutt is my great-aunt, Madeleine.'

They stared at each other, perplexed, tea and cake forgotten.

'But how can it be?' asked Emma, reasonably enough. 'There's a muddle somewhere. Why do you think *she's* your great-aunt and not the other woman? I still think it was taken as a silly joke and the wrong photograph got sent home to your family.'

'No, no.' He shook his head very positively. 'Look here. See this one.'

He held out another photograph to her across the table. The young woman was seated, staring straight at the camera, a baby cradled tenderly in her arms with its long gown trailing over her knee. Behind her a tall, fair man looked down on both of them with a proud smile.

'But that's Mutt.' Emma was clearly taken aback. 'Who is the man with her? And could that be Bruno?'

She turned the photograph to read the writing on the back: *Me and Johnny with Lottie. Lahore 1945*. The writing was Mutt's.

Silently, feeling nervous now, Dan passed another snapshot to her. The two girls, clearly sisters, stood arm-in-arm, beaming at the unknown photographer; the younger girl's hair was cut short and the resemblance to Joss was even more marked. Slowly, Emma reversed the snapshot: the faded ink was blurred but clear enough to read the words: *Vivian and Madeleine in the garden. 1936*.

She looked at him, clearly frightened, and he stared back at her with distress; he hadn't been prepared for this.

'What does it mean?' she asked, her voice trembling a little. 'I don't understand it.'

'Neither do I.' He tried to keep his voice level. 'Do you have any photographs of your mother taken out there in India when she was young? Or when she was a child?'

Emma shook her head, her brow furrowed, shuffling the photographs as if they were cards and studying them.

'I don't understand it,' she said again. 'This is Mutt, you see. But who is the man, Johnny? And who is Lottie? Can she have been married before she met my father? Maybe she was a widow . . . No, that doesn't work.'

'Not with the wedding photograph as evidence,' he agreed. 'This man you see her standing with is Johnny, isn't it? It's the same man. Yet Hubert Trevannion is in the same photograph with them.'

Emma stared at it. 'Then who is this woman?' she asked.

There was a short silence; Dan heard the front door open and close again quietly and someone came into the kitchen behind him.

Emma gave a cry of relief and Dan stood up quickly, recognising the woman, feeling as guilty as if he were a thief, gaining access under false pretences.

'Mousie,' Emma was saying, her words tumbling out in a rush, 'something so strange is going on here.' She gestured with the photographs. 'We simply can't understand it.'

Dan knew that the woman called Mousie could hear the panic in Emma's voice and he was relieved when she smiled quite calmly, giving him a little nod of recognition but concentrating on Emma.

'I can guess that it must be very confusing,' she said. 'I had a feeling something like this might be happening so I've brought some letters to show you. Will you come with me, Emma? They'll explain any confusion. We'll leave Mr Crosby to his tea and cake just for a moment'—she flashed him a quick reassuring smile—'but this is rather private.'

Emma got up, looking puzzled and frightened, but she went readily enough. The door closed behind them and Dan sat down again at the table. He reached for his tea but his hand trembled so much that he set the cup back in its saucer and he continued to sit in silence, waiting.

'So what was that all about?' Pamela stood in the archway to the kitchen, mug in one hand and cloth in the other, listening as the front door banged shut behind Mousie. 'What's going on?'

'I have no idea.' It sounded as if Rafe had moved to the window. 'She's dashed in next door . . . Ah, here she is again. She's got a parcel with her and she's crossing the bridge . . . and going up to Paradise.' He turned back into the room. 'I wonder who this young man can be to cause so much consternation.'

'She said he was an American, didn't she?' Pamela put the cloth and the mug on the table. 'I didn't quite catch what she said. As soon as you said she was back from Polzeath I went to put the kettle on.'

'Well, she came in and put our shopping on the chair, and then she made some joke about the quarry becoming a national car park, or something. That's because of Zoë's car being there, I suppose, and she asked who the visitor was. I told her that I didn't recognise him but that I'd seen the car there last weekend. I told her that it was a tall young man with very dark hair and that he had a briefcase. I suppose I thought

341

he might be someone to do with the funeral arrangements.'

'But she cried out, didn't she?' asked Pamela. 'That's when I came through.'

Rafe frowned a little. 'She cried, "Oh, my *God*, it's the American boy with the photograph." Something like that. And then she said, "And Emma's at Paradise alone." Her face turned pale and she had a look . . .'

'What kind of look?' she asked, after a moment.

'When she was a girl Mousie seemed to get ideas about things or people. Not seeing into the future or anything like that, just very strong intuitions. Mother didn't encourage it, she thought it was fanciful, but I saw it as a rather useful gift. Anyway, that's what she looked like just now. As if she'd had a premonition.'

'Do you think she's guessed about Joss and George?' wondered Pamela, imagining Mousie in this new light.

'I expect so.' He gave a rueful chuckle. 'Probably you and I are the only ones who didn't.'

She chuckled too. 'The thing is that they've been in and out and under our feet all their lives so we've taken their relationship for granted. And so had they.' She sighed with pleasure. 'He sounded so happy, Rafe, when he was telling us last evening.'

'He *looked* happy, so different from when he went out to meet her, but sort of shocked, as well.'

She picked up quickly on this remark. 'I felt that, too, but I thought it could simply be relief that it was settled so quickly with Joss. She might easily have held him off until the divorce was through, or in case Penny changed her mind; something like that. I imagined that he was still trying to come to terms with his good luck: one minute despair, the next joy.' She laughed. 'Or am I being crazy?'

'No,' answered Rafe slowly. 'Not crazy. He's back.' Rafe was at the window. 'I think Joss will have to take her car up to Paradise tonight at this rate. Mousie's right: it's beginning to look like a car park out there.'

'How does he look?' asked Pamela.

Rafe grinned. 'Like a man who's just had lunch with his sweetheart. Full of himself, beaming away like an idiot, two foot taller than when he went off to Wadebridge . . .'

They were both laughing when he came in and he laughed too, for sheer happiness.

'Whose is that car?' he asked. 'Got a visitor?'

'It's rather odd, actually,' Rafe answered. 'It was here last weekend. A young man with a briefcase got out and went up to Paradise and then Mousie came in and when I described him she went screaming after him.'

'But why?' George went to stand beside his father, staring out at the car as if it might answer the puzzle. 'Emma's up there, isn't she?'

'Rafe thinks that Mousie had a premonition that something was going to happen and when she heard about this young man she shot off,' Pamela explained jokingly to George. 'Make any sense to you?'

When he made no reply Pamela turned towards him, surprised, and Rafe said sharply, 'What's going on, George?'

In the silence that followed, Pamela heard him take a very deep breath like someone about to dive into fathomless water. 'It's not my secret,' George said, 'but Joss said that I could tell you, although we were going to wait until after the funeral. It's about Mutt.'

'About *Mutt*?' Pamela groped for a chair and sat down in it.

'I'll tell you,' George said, as if coming to a very important decision, 'but you mustn't say a word to anyone until after the funeral.' He and Rafe sat down too. 'You won't believe it, I promise you. It starts when Mutt and the children came back from India. The fact is that she wasn't Honor Trevannion at all. Honor died with Hubert and their daughter Emma in Karachi.' He grimaced into the shocked silence. 'It doesn't sound possible, does it? I'll try to tell you how it was just the way Joss told me but, remember, I can hardly believe it myself.'

He began to tell the story carefully and faithfully, trying to recall the words Joss had used as they'd sat together beside the Saint's Well, while Pamela and Rafe listened in disbelieving silence.

Mousie telephoned Bruno just after Zoë had trailed away upstairs for her afternoon rest.

'I'm at Paradise.' Mousie's voice was low and guarded. 'The young American Dan Crosby is here, and he and Emma have been looking at photographs.'

'Oh my God,' he said involuntarily.

'My reaction exactly,' she said drily. 'I hope you won't be angry but I've given her the letters to read. It was the only way, Bruno, believe me.'

'I believe you,' he said, after a moment. 'How is she?'

'I've put her in the parlour at Mutt's desk. It seemed the right place for her to read them, somehow, but I think you should be here. She might suddenly need some support. When you get here I'll take Dan down to my cottage and tell him the truth about it all. I think it's best he's not here when Emma comes out.'

'I quite agree,' he said quickly. 'I'll come straight up.'

He left Nellie sleeping peacefully and walked quickly up to Paradise. He let himself in quietly and went into the kitchen. The young man got quickly to his feet. Bruno held out his hand, smiling at him, and introduced himself.

'I'm Dan Crosby,' replied the American, 'Madeleine Grosjean's great-nephew. I am just so sorry.' Dan gripped the hand gratefully. 'You have to believe that I had no idea about all this.'

'How could you know?' Bruno glanced at Mousie. 'Have you managed to tell Dan the whole story?'

She shook her head. 'Only the bare bones. I think he should come home with me and have some tea and then I can explain it to him properly. He's as shocked as we are.'

'I certainly am. I feel terrible.' Dan's face was grey, as if with fatigue, his eyes blank. 'And at a moment like this too . . .'

'The time was right, Dan,' Bruno told him gently. 'Don't feel badly. Good will come of this now, I'm sure of it. It means a new start for us. For all of us. Go and have some tea with Mousie and we'll meet later on.'

'You're very kind.'

Dan stumbled out after Mousie, the picture of misery, and Bruno stood alone, his mind focusing on Emma. He glanced at the photographs scattered on the table and, with a jolt to his heart, saw his mother and father smiling up at him.

Picking up the wedding picture he scanned their faces, trying to remember them like this: young, laughing, happy. Only flashes from the past—his father swinging him high above his head, his mother's voice singing a nursery rhyme—rewarded his effort. His father's face was familiar—Bruno had a portrait photograph of him from about this time—but his mother's he barely recognised. He stared at it, feeling guilty, as if he had connived in the sudden despatch to oblivion of her and his little sister's memory.

Bruno sat down at the table, folding his arms in front of him, willing up the memory of that hotel room: his father and sister dead and his mother lying in bed, too weak to comfort him. How strong and bright Mutt's sudden presence in contrast; how encouraging the feel of her arm round him as she'd knelt with him beside his mother's bed. Her relief at the sight of Mutt had been palpable.

'Do exactly as Mutt tells you,' his mother had told him. 'Promise me, darling,' and he'd promised, the tears clotting in his throat, and all the while Mutt had held him steady.

Afterwards, on the voyage home and here at St Meriadoc, he'd learned to weave the memories of India into stories, retreating further and further from the unbearable reality.

Bruno rested his chin on his arms, still staring at the photograph, and it was here Emma found him.

She'd finished the last letter with tears streaming down her face, piling the letters together and looking about the familiar room without quite knowing what she was doing. She sat at the desk, the words fresh in her mind, the image of the young and vulnerable woman still clearly before her.

'Mutt,' she murmured from time to time. 'Oh, Mutt,' and then wept again with despair and love.

She got up and wandered about the parlour, touching an unfinished tapestry, imagining her mother at the desk writing to the sister she would never see again, then went almost blindly out into the hall. Through the half-open kitchen door she saw Bruno's shoulder and bowed head and she went in to him.

'Oh, Bruno,' she cried. 'Poor, darling Mutt. Oh, how I wish I'd known this before she died.'

He got to his feet and put his arms about her, gaining solace from her embrace and allowing the shadows of the past to slip gently away. She looked up into his face and saw his compassion and affection for her.

'It was how she wanted it,' he comforted her. 'Don't cry, Emma.'

'What a shock.' She took his proffered handkerchief and wiped distractedly at her cheeks and eyes. 'I can hardly take it in. Yet while I was reading the letters she seemed so alive. When I'd finished I couldn't believe she wouldn't walk in. I wish I could tell her that I think she was brave and that I love her. All those years of secrecy.' She took hold on her emotions and tried to control herself. 'And you, Bruno. However did you manage it? I know it wasn't right of her to put such a burden on you when you were so small but, all the same, I can't help but feel for her.'

'And so did I.' He shook her gently by the arms. 'I regret nothing. She did what was right at the time. It's no good looking at it with hindsight. She's showed us exactly how it was, and why she did it, and all of us— Mousie, Joss, you and I—we all accept her reasons.'

Emma sighed shakily and he helped her down onto a chair.

'Joss knows,' she said, wonderingly. 'And Mousie. She explained to me before I read the letters and said that you were waiting until after the funeral to tell me.'

'That was how Joss wanted it.' He sat down opposite. 'She was afraid for you.'

Emma's eyes brimmed again. 'I thought of her just now. Opening the letters all alone that night. Mousie said she's been so brave. Poor Joss. What a shock for her, and then going up to find Mutt had died. Thank God that you were here, Bruno.' She put her hands to her face, massaging her eyes with her fingers. 'I can still hardly take it in. Is it wrong to say that I feel proud of her? Of Mutt, I mean?'

'You should be proud of her,' he agreed. 'She saved my life. You both did. I often wonder what would have happened if you hadn't turned up then. Can you imagine a small boy of four, left alone in Karachi, with all my family dead? You and Mutt *were* my family.'

She stared at him. 'We're not brother and sister,' she said slowly. 'I'm just taking that in. You aren't my brother.' She shook her head. 'And I'm not Emma but Lottie. I asked you about Lottie, do you remember?'

He shrugged helplessly. 'What could I do? I'd promised Mutt.'

'Oh, I'm not blaming you,' she said quickly, 'but she called my name at the end, Bruno. Do you think she was remembering?'

'Probably. After all, she remembered the letters that had lain hidden all those years.'

A short silence.

'If Joss hadn't read them, would you have ever told me?'

Bruno was silent for a moment. 'I would have kept my promise to Mutt,' he said at last.

She gave him a little smiling shrug. 'Well, it's no longer relevant,' she said. 'But if there had been some sort of trouble over the will, say that Ray had tried to force his plan to develop the boatyard, would you still have kept Mutt's secret?'

He made an odd snorting noise. 'I don't know. It would have become very difficult should Pamela and Rafe have been in any danger of losing their home. As it happens the problem doesn't arise. I've read her will now and Mutt has left Paradise to you, just as we thought she would; and The Lookout, The Row and the boatyard are left to me. She clearly hadn't thought about Inheritance Tax.'

'Ray was worried about Inheritance Tax,' Emma said. She frowned, puzzled. 'I suppose Dan's arrival reminded Mutt of the letters. Poor fellow. It's sad, isn't it, that after all his efforts he didn't get to see Mutt? But why ask Joss to find the letters? Why not you?'

'I have a theory about that,' answered Bruno. 'I think that when Mutt told Joss about the letters, subconsciously she was hoping they'd be read.' He laughed drily. 'God, I was angry when Joss told me. All these years of secrecy and all the time the letters had been lying there for anyone to find.' He paused. 'Joss has coped remarkably well.'

'George has helped,' murmured Emma with a wistful smile. 'I always hoped that Joss would have Paradise. Well, things have changed, haven't they?'

'I have great hopes that she and George will live at Paradise,' he told her gently. 'The way I see it, Emma, you still have rights, because of all that you and Mutt have done for us, and I hope to honour that. But, if we're talking legally, then, yes, things have changed.'

'Ray will have a fit.' She managed a laugh. 'So what will happen now?'

He explained to her how his grandfather's will could be re-proved to prevent paying Inheritance Tax twice, and she listened intently while he explained his idea of giving Rafe and Mousie their cottages, to save future tax, and his wish to leave the rest of the estate to Joss and George.

'I look upon them as my children,' he told her. 'Anyway, I promised Mutt I'd look after Joss and I intend to do it, if she'll let me.'

Emma looked at him with gratitude. Her eyes were full of tears. 'Bless you, Bruno,' she said. 'What can I say?'

Before he could answer they heard someone open the front door and shut it with a slam, as if it had slipped from nervous fingers; and then quick footsteps crossed the hall.

Joss rushed into the kitchen, her cheeks flushed, her eyes bright with anxiety. 'Mum,' she said anxiously. 'Are you OK? Mousie caught me on the way home . . .'

Emma was on her feet, her arms wide, and they held each other tightly. 'Oh, darling,' she said, half laughing, half in tears, 'what a shock it was. We've just been talking it over and I'm still all of a tremble. However did you manage so bravely?'

Joss held her at arm's length, studying her. 'You're really OK?' She let out a great gasp of relief. 'Thank God, then. Mousie was right.'

'Mousie?' Emma looked puzzled.

'I was afraid you'd be really devastated but Mousie said that I was underestimating you and that you'd admire Mutt for her strength and courage and you wouldn't mind.'

'And she was right.' In her daughter's presence Emma was quickly regaining her composure. 'I think that Bruno might be right, too, in suggesting that subconsciously Mutt was hoping you'd read the letters and there would be no more need for secrecy.'

'Do you really think so?' Joss looked almost shocked. 'I wish I could believe it. And you really don't mind?' She glanced anxiously at Bruno.

'We've talked about re-proving the original will,' he told her, 'and we're agreed on how we can go forward. However, it would help enormously if we could find *Goblin Market* and the certificates. At least we can look now without upsetting anyone. I wish I knew where to start.'

'Oh.' Emma's eyes flew wide with the shock of a sudden realisation. 'I bet it's in the parcel.'

Before their astonished gaze, she went to the dresser, took out the package and pushed it across the table to Bruno. He untied the string with difficulty, trying to control the trembling of his fingers. The paper cover was illustrated with strange Rackhamesque figures. He opened it carefully, first removing the envelope attached to the back cover with a strong paper clip.

'It's a first edition,' he said, examining it reverently. He passed the book to them, opened at the title page so that they could read the inscription: *To my sister Madeleine On her fifteenth birthday With my love, Vivian.*

Emma turned the pages with gentle fingers, Joss watching over her shoulder, while Bruno read the letter.

Paradise
June 1948

My darling Bruno,

This is for you when you grow up because you should have the things inside it in case of some emergency in the future. I should have liked this book to go to Emma but I wouldn't be able to explain the inscription and so it might cause trouble. Keep it safe.

Please forgive me if I have done you any harm, my dear boy. I have only wished to make you happy but, as you get older, you'll find we damage others quite by mistake.

Thank you for your love, it means a great deal to me. I hope you know how much I love you in return.

Mutt

Deeply moved, Bruno stood up, smiling with some difficulty, folding the letter in with the other documents.

'I'm going to leave you now,' he said rather abruptly. 'I'd like to have a look at these documents, and you both need some time together. I'll come up tomorrow morning. Oh, and the book is for you, Emma. Mutt says so in this letter.'

'It's just as bad for him,' said Joss after he had left. 'Poor Bruno. All those memories.'

Emma turned back to the book, rereading the writing on the title page, and then picked up a photograph from the table. Together they looked at Madeleine and Vivian, smiling happily in the sunny garden, and then at each other.

'Oh, darling,' said Emma shakily, 'what a day it's been.'

Mousie was watching the sunset. The wind had died to a gentle breeze and the western sky was scorched and stained with a vivid crimson fire. Dazzled by the spectacle she sat peacefully, reviewing the last few hours with a kind of contentment. It had taken Dan some time to understand Madeleine's story and Mousie had needed all her tact and authority to make the account true yet acceptable to him.

Still shaken by the turn of events, but trying to come to terms with this new light shed upon his great-aunt, he'd gone away with the hope that the result of his search was not the disaster he'd first feared.

'It was time,' she'd told him. 'Bruno was right about that. I'm so sorry that you didn't meet Madeleine. You must read the letters, Dan. They'll tell you far more about her than I can.'

'I meant no harm coming here,' he'd said remorsefully. 'Quite the opposite. I hoped I could go home with some positive news about Great-Aunt Madeleine, even though it was too late for Grandma Viv.'

'It was too late for both of them,' she'd answered, 'but not too late for us. You haven't done us harm, Dan, trust me. And you won't go back home empty-handed, after all, but with a whole new family. And, if I know Emma, she'll want to know all about you and Mutt's relations.'

It was to his credit, she thought, that he took his leave when enough had been said on either side. Mousie was relieved to see him go, feeling strongly that Bruno might arrive before too long.

He came at last, knocking on the door and then calling her name as he entered the hall. She continued to sit at the table, waiting for him, and presently he laid the envelope in front of her.

'Emma had this all the time,' he said. 'She found it in the drawer where Mutt had put the letters, but this was wrapped up in a parcel and addressed to me. She was waiting until after the funeral in case it contained something that might cause trouble between me and Brer Fox.'

'Was *Goblin Market* with it?' Mousie did not touch the envelope.

'Yes, it was just as Mutt said. She'd written me a letter . . . Well, you can read it for yourself.'

He sat down, while Mousie took the sheet of paper and felt for her spectacles, resting his elbows on the table and staring seawards. He sat quite still while she read the letter.

Presently Mousie took off her spectacles and folded the paper, wondering just how difficult it would be for him to see those official reports of his family's deaths after so many years of denial. A long silence fell between them. The light was fading now, shadows gathered in the corners of the room, and one brilliant star hung low over the horizon.

'It was a very terrible thing,' Mousie began gently, 'that you should lose your whole family in one savage blow. Yet, even out of such terrible tragedy, good can come. Your childish instinct to blend fact and fiction, which was so necessary to your survival, released in you the gift of story-telling. The way you combine the dry bones of history with the colour and drama of fiction is a wonderful talent that brings delight to many thousands of people. Hubert would have been so proud of you.' She took the envelope and opened it, leafed through the certificates and put them to one side. 'It's right that you should have them, so that your grandfather's will can be re-proved without any fuss,' she said, 'but they have no further use. None of it was your doing; you had no choice. Let them go, Bruno.'

He looked at her. 'I think I've begun to do that. Up at Paradise in the kitchen, while Emma was reading the letters, I saw the wedding photograph and realised that I could hardly remember my parents, or my sister, either. And then Emma came in and, while comforting her, in some odd way I felt released from the guilt. It was odd because, although I *was* comforting her, she brought me comfort too, and I was reminded of Mutt appearing in that hotel room and how I felt then. I hope she knew how much I loved her.'

He took up the certificates, looking at them with a lingering compassion, and then put them back into the envelope, thinking of Mutt's words to her sister: *There's something wise about Bruno, some grace which is far beyond his years . . . When he smiles at me, hugs me . . . I feel as if I have been granted absolution . . .*

He didn't feel particularly wise, but he was glad that he'd been able to give her such comfort in return for the stability and love she'd always shown to him while attempting to keep her promise to his mother. He remembered too the last sentence before her final farewell to Vivi: *Perhaps I am already an aunt and Emma has a cousin she will never know and I shall never see.*

That, at least, could now be remedied. He pushed the envelope aside and smiled at Mousie. 'So tell me what you think of Dan Crosby,' he said.

EPILOGUE

THE MAY SUNSHINE was hot, the drifting breeze scented with hawthorn blossom, and somewhere high above his head a lark was singing. The donkeys stood together in the shade of the tamarisk trees, heads drooped together as though they were sharing a secret, and he leaned his arms on the warm, rough wooden bar of the gate and smiled to himself.

He'd been to St Endellion, to pay his respects to his great-aunt Madeleine's grave, and now he was going to have tea at Paradise with Emma and Joss.

'After all,' Emma had said to him on the telephone, 'we *are* cousins. We need to get to know each other properly.'

350

He'd been reluctant to impose himself upon them, still guilty at being the agent of such a bombshell, yet the whole family had shown him nothing but kindness when he'd made a brief visit at Easter. Emma had given him his great-aunt's letters to read, suggesting that he should sit in her parlour at the desk where she'd written them, and he'd found the process a deeply moving one. That weekend he'd stayed at the same hotel at Port Isaac, determined not to take any advantage, but this time he was staying for two nights with Joss and her mother at Paradise. The car was down in the quarry—he hadn't quite been able to bring himself to drive up nonchalantly to the front door.

Dan shook his head at his own caution; it was as if he were waiting for something to help him across the invisible barrier that he imagined still lay between him and these people who had made him so welcome. As he stared across the sunlit grass he heard the arched wrought-iron gate open with a clang and saw a young woman pass through, closing the gate carefully behind her. A flowery shirt was tucked into the long denim skirt and she wore a soft-brimmed straw hat.

He straightened up and Joss raised a hand in greeting, walking over the grass towards him, smiling with delight. Gone was the air of wariness he'd first noticed about her and in its place was confidence and joy.

'You haven't been properly introduced to the donkeys, have you?' she asked as she came up to him. 'Rumpleteazer and Mungojerrie. They're rather elderly but they like to meet new friends.'

He laughed, letting himself into the field. 'The names sound familiar—but weren't they cats?'

She shrugged. 'Don't blame us. We just get what we're given by the donkey sanctuary. Are you ready for some tea? Mum's been cooking all morning so I hope you're hungry.'

'How is Emma?' He hadn't forgotten how drawn to her he'd been at their first meeting; that strange sensation of recognition and affection. 'Is she . . . coming to terms with things OK?'

She smiled at him and nodded. 'She's getting used to adjusting to the truth,' she told him. 'We all are. Actually, it's rather liberating. We have you to thank for that. Mum gets very emotional about it all—and sometimes very sad—but I've promised her that when George and I have our first daughter we shall call her Charlotte. Lottie for short.' She shot him a glance. 'Or maybe Charlotte Vivian. What do you think?'

'Sounds a great name to me. Grandma Viv would have been thrilled at the idea.' He grinned. 'Am I missing something here? I thought you told me you and George couldn't hope to be married until the autumn?'

'That's quite right and no, you're not missing anything,' replied Joss. 'I'm just doing a little forward planning. Perhaps you'll be able to get down for the wedding? After all, we *are* family, although we don't know you as well as we'd like to, Cousin Dan.'

'I'm sure that can be remedied, Cousin Joss.' He gave her a little bow. 'There's a whole raft of people out in the States who want to meet you and Emma. And George, of course,' he added quickly.

'And Mousie and Bruno,' she prompted him teasingly. 'And don't forget Rafe and Pamela and Olivia and Joe. You take one of us, you take us all; we're that kind of family.'

'I shall be honoured to.' He answered her with a quaint formality, yet with the joyful feeling that the barrier was finally crossed. 'Thank you.'

They stood together—Madeleine's granddaughter and Vivian's grandson—smiling at each other for a moment in the sunshine, then she led the way across the meadow and he followed her through the gate into the Paradise gardens.

MARCIA WILLETT

Since West Country settings are such an integral ingredient in Marcia Willett's novels, I decided to travel down to meet the author at her home in Devon. As I left the busy motorway and wound my way through attractive country villages, the beauty and the serenity of the scenery began to relax me and I realised why Marcia has such a deep affection for this part of the country.

After a tour of her delightful Devon longhouse, including the tranquil study where she writes, surrounded by the pictures and photographs she has gathered to inspire her current novel, we sit in the garden in the spring sunshine, with a glorious view over Dartmoor in the distance and only the sound of birdsong to disturb us. 'I do so love it here,' Marcia sighs. 'It is the perfect place to write and I am just so lucky. I can hardly believe my good fortune.' As I admire the view, I reflect that Marcia and her husband Rodney bought this house quite recently on the proceeds of her novels and, therefore, it isn't so much a case of luck, really, as one of talent, dedication and sheer hard work.

As ever, chatting to Marcia is a delight, especially as she describes how *The Golden Cup* came into being. 'I could see this woman in my mind—she became Mutt in the novel—who had lived with deception and the burden of her secret. Then there was the appearance of the young man carrying an old black and white photograph. But it took a while before I saw the connection between them.' Over the next few months these visions became more focused until Marcia felt her characters beginning to take shape. At this stage she says it is essential for her to find the right location for them, so she and Rodney, who are a most devoted couple, travel around the West

Country in their camper van, with a handful of Ordnance Survey maps and a Primus stove on hand to keep them supplied with hot drinks. The accurate description of the landscape is very important to Marcia when shaping the lives of her characters within it, and although her stories are completely fictional she is fastidious in her geographical detail.

'For *The Golden Cup*,' Marcia tells me, 'I kne that Paradise would be near cliffs, so off we went to the north coast of Cornwall and eventually found Port Quin and that was perfect. In my mind I could see Paradise and Bruno's folly, the row of cottages and the old boatyard, and I knew that this was the place that would become my St Meriadoc.' Suddenly, remembering the Cornish trip, she casts a loving look towards the kitchen where Rodney is preparing chicken pilau for our lunch, to be followed by apple pie and clotted cream. 'You know, Roddy is my rock. I couldn't write my novels without him,' Marcia said, with a smile. 'Oh yes, you could,' Rodney replies from within. 'You would just do it differently.'

Over lunch, Marcia and Rodney happily regale me with tales of their research trips around the West Country and then joy creeps into their voices as they tell me about their first grandchild, Rufus, born just a few months earlier. On the table beside us are a number of children's books that they have bought for him. 'All our lives Roddy and I have loved reading and we just want to start Rufus off on that path too,' Marcia explains. 'As a child I read and read and read and used to live in the make-believe world of books. And I am really lucky because I still do!'

Jane Eastgate

The
Summer
I Dared

Barbara Delinsky

Julia Bechtel, Noah Prine and Kim Colella are the only survivors of a horrific boating accident off the coast of Maine in which nine people died. For each of them going back to the life they had before the disaster is not an option—for their very survival has changed their view of the world for ever . . .

Prologue

THE *AMELIA CELESTE* was born a lobster boat. An elegant lady, she ran a proud thirty-eight feet of mahogany and oak, from the graceful upward sweep of her bow, down her foredeck to the wheelhouse, and, on a straight and simple plane, back to her stern. True to the axiom that Maine lobstermen treat their boats with the same care as their wives, the *Amelia Celeste* had been doted on by Matthew Crane in much the way he had pampered the flesh-and-blood Amelia Celeste, to whom he had been married for forty years and on whose grave every Friday he continued to lay a dozen long-stemmed roses, even twelve long years after her death.

Matthew had the means. His grandfather had made a fortune logging, not only the vast forests of northern Maine but the islands in its gulf that bore trees rather than granite. He had built the family home on one of those evergreen islands, aptly named Big Sawyer. Two generations later, Crane descendants were equally represented among the fishermen and the artists who comprised the core of the island's year-round residents.

Matthew was a fisherman, and for all his family money, remained a simple man at heart. His true delight, from the age of sixteen on, had been heading out at dawn to haul lobster traps from the fertile waters of Penobscot Bay. When Matthew turned sixty-five and his arthritis made his hands useless in the trade, he fitted the vessel with a new engine and tanks, installed seating for passengers in the stern, and relaunched the *Amelia Celeste* as a ferry. He didn't carry cars; the state ferry did that. Nor did he publish a schedule, because if an islander had a special need, Matthew would adjust his schedule to meet it. This wasn't a job; it was a hobby. He simply wanted to be on the boat he loved, in the bay he loved.

On that Tuesday evening in early June, when his idyll went tragically awry, Matthew—to his deep regret—was not at the helm of the *Amelia Celeste*. She was being piloted by Greg Hornsby, a far younger cousin of his who had spent all his own forty years on the water and was as skilled a fisherman as Matthew.

The *Amelia Celeste* left Big Sawyer at six in the evening. The June waters were cold, and the approach of a warm front brought fog. This was no problem. Fog was a frequent visitor to the region. Between the instruments at hand and Greg Hornsby's familiarity with the route, the *Amelia Celeste* deftly skirted lobster buoys in the shallows leading to inlets at nearby Little Sawyer, West Rock and Hull Island. After taking on a passenger at each pier, she settled into the channel at an easy twenty-two knots, aimed at the mainland six miles away.

Fifteen minutes later, her passengers disembarked at Rockland. Eight others were waiting to board. These eight all lived on Big Sawyer, which meant that Greg would have a nonstop trip home, and that pleased him immensely. Tuesday was ribs night at the Harbor Grill, and Greg loved ribs. On ribs night, the wife and kids were on their own. His friends were saving a booth; he'd be joining them there as soon as he put the *Amelia Celeste* to bed.

He took two bags from Jeannie Walsh and stowed them under a bench while she stepped over the gunwale. Her husband, Evan, handed over their one-year-old daughter before climbing aboard himself. Jeannie and Evan were sculptors; their bags held clay, glazes and tools, all purchased in Portland that day.

Grady Bartz and Dar Hutter, both in their late twenties, boarded with the ease of men bred on the water. Grady worked as dockman for Foss Fish and Lobster, the island's buyer and dealer. Dar clerked at the tackle and gear store. They moved down to the stern for a seat.

Todd Slokum was the next to board. Thin and pale, Todd was the antithesis of a seafaring man. Even after three years on the island, he still turned green on the ferry. Local gossip had never quite got a handle on why he had come to Big Sawyer in the first place. The best anyone could say was that Zoe Ballard was a saint to employ him. Now he stumbled over on rubbery legs to the nearest bench.

Hutchinson Prine was only a tad more steady. A lifelong lobsterman nearing seventy, he still fished every day, but Hutch wasn't well. He had been in Portland seeing doctors. The scowl on his face said he didn't like what they had told him. His son Noah, his face equally as stony, followed him aboard and reached to untie the lines.

The *Amelia Celeste* was seconds shy of pulling away from the dock when a pleading cry came from the shore. 'Wait! Please, wait!' A slender woman ran down the dock. 'Don't leave!' she cried beseechingly. 'I'm coming! Please wait!'

Her jeans were very dark, her blouse very white, her blazer stylishly quilted, and a large leather bag hung from her shoulder. The sandals she wore wedged her higher than any islander in her right mind would be wedged, and as if that weren't odd enough for the setting, fingernails and toenails were painted pale pink. Her hair was a dozen shades of blonde, fine and straight. She was simply made up and strikingly attractive.

'I have to get out to Big Sawyer,' she begged. 'I had my car reserved on the five o'clock ferry, but I missed that. They said I could park back there at the end of the pier for a day or two. Can you take me to the island?'

'That depends on whether you have a place to stay,' Greg said. 'We don't have resorts. Don't even have a b. and b.'

'Zoe Ballard's my aunt. She's expecting me.'

The words were magical. Noah took her bags and tossed them into the pilothouse. She climbed aboard on her own, but when Evan Walsh rose to give her a seat, she shook her head and worked her way along the rail to the bow.

Noah released the stern line and pushed against the piling of the pier. He said something short to his father, but if there was an answer, Greg didn't catch it. As he edged up the throttle, Noah stalked past the wheelhouse and stationed himself on the far side of the bow from Zoe Ballard's niece.

Quiet and graceful, the *Amelia Celeste* slipped through the harbour. The thick fog had drained the world of colour. Only the occasional shadow of a boat at its mooring altered the pale grey. Past the breakwater, the waves picked up and the radar came on, little green dots marking the spot where a boat, rock or channel marker would be. Painted buoys bobbed under the fog, signalling lobster traps on the ocean floor. Safely in the channel, the *Amelia Celeste* throttled up to speed.

The chop was fair to middling, not overly taxing. The boat elicited little noise beyond the soft thrum of her engine, the steady rush of water as the bow cut through the waves, and an occasional exchange of words in the stern.

Far to starboard, a hum simmered before growing into the growl of a motor. In no time, it had grown louder and more commanding, just as its owner meant it to do. That owner was Artie Jones, and he called his boat *The Beast*. It was a long, sleek racer whose aerodynamic purple body shot over the water driven by twin engines putting out a whopping eleven hundred horsepower. It was capable of going seventy-five without effort, and from the rising thunder of those twin Mercs, it was approaching that now.

Noah shot Greg a *What the hell?* look.

Bewildered, Greg shrugged. His radar screen showed *The Beast* tracing a large arc to a point astern of them now and heading off to the north. The rumble of the racer's engines faded.

One hand on the wheel and one on the throttle, Greg kept the *Amelia Celeste* aimed at the island. Dreaming of ribs, he forgot about Artie Jones until the sound of *The Beast* rose again. No mistaking the deep chainsaw growl from the monster tail engines. The racer was headed back their way. Radar confirmed it.

He picked up the handset of the VHF, which was preset to the channel the local boaters used. 'What the hell are you doing, Artie?' No man in his right mind would play chicken in the fog.

Artie didn't answer. The roar of those twin engines increased.

Greg sounded his horn, though it didn't have a chance of being heard above the noise. His eyes went back and forth from the radar screen, which pinpointed the racer, to the GPS screen, which pinpointed the *Amelia Celeste*. If he didn't do something, the boats would collide. Artie wasn't behaving rationally. The radar screen showed him cutting through fishing grounds, ploughing past buoys.

'Artie, what the *hell*—throttle down and get out of the way!' he shouted, sounding the horn again and again, to no avail.

What to do, with the island barely a mile away, the responsibility of nine people in his hands, and Artie Jones a loose cannon in his muscle boat calling on all those horses, shooting off like a bullet, propelled who knew where in the fog at a speed faster than the *Amelia Celeste* could ever hope to move?

Studying the radar screen for a few final seconds, Greg tried to guess where *The Beast* would go based on where it had been. Then he made a judgment call. Unable to outrun the powerful boat, he yanked back on his own throttle to let *The Beast* pass.

It would have worked, had *The Beast* continued along its established arc. But Artie had been hugging the wheel of his machine at the moment his heart stopped and was slumped, frozen against it. As the *Amelia Celeste* made her defensive move, his lifeless body began to slide sideways, pulling the wheel along with it.

Matthew Crane knew what had happened the instant he heard the explosion. He had been in his usual spot on the deck of the Harbor Grill, nursing a whiskey while he waited for the *Amelia Celeste*. His ear was trained to catch the drone of her engine, and he hadn't been able to miss *The Beast*. The horrific boom had barely died when he was hurrying down the steps and scrambling onto the dock, waving and shouting to the handful of men who had just returned from hauling traps.

Those men set off within minutes, reaching the scene quickly enough to fish the first two survivors from the water before they were overcome by smoke from the fire or cold from the sea. The third survivor was picked up by another boat. None of the three suffered more than minor bruises, a true miracle given the fate of the rest.

Chapter 1

JULIA BECHTEL WAS AIRBORNE only as long as it might have taken had a large someone picked her up and heaved her high into the ocean. She went under water in a stunned state, but even before her downward plunge slowed, she was clawing to propel herself back up. When her head broke the surface, she gasped for air. The waves rose around her, but she fought them to keep herself afloat.

Her breath came in shallow gasps, along with a creeping memory of what had happened. She heard in echo the sound of screams, an impact, an explosion. Pushing wet hair from her eyes, she looked around. The waves were littered with pieces of wood, and where the *Amelia Celeste* should have been, there were flames and smoke.

Instinct told her to move away, so she fought the tug of the waves and pulled herself backwards. Her sandals were gone, as was her shoulder bag, and when she felt the weight of the wet quilted blazer dragging her down, she slid her arms from that, too.

'Hey!' came a shout from the smoky haze; then a head appeared. It was the man who had been with her in the bow. He was swimming towards her. 'Are you hurt?' he called loudly enough to be heard above the roar of the flames.

'No,' she called back.

'Hold on to this.' He pulled forward a long seat cushion, clearly buoyant. 'I'm going back in.'

Grasping the cushion, Julia was about to ask if that was possible, when another staggering explosion came. She barely had time to take a breath when the man pulled her under to escape the falling debris. By the time they resurfaced, gasping, sputtering and reaching for the cushion, going back in was a moot point. The flames were louder, the smoke more dense. In obvious anguish, the man stared at the devastation.

'Can you see anyone else?' she asked, breathing hard.

He shook his head, then twisted it towards shore. It was another minute before Julia heard what he had. A small lobster boat emerged from the fog. Julia had never seen anything as welcome in her life.

In no time, she had been helped over the side, wrapped in a blanket, and settled in the cabin under the bow. Once there, though, she began to shake in earnest, because not only were those sounds reverberating in her mind—screams, impact, explosion—but she could see it again: the huge purple point coming out of the fog, right over the side of the ferry.

Unable to sit still, Julia went back up to the deck, where she stood, dripping wet and trembling under the blanket. The smell of smoke was overwhelming. The man who had been with her in the water was also aboard, but he and two others were leaning over the side, peering through fog and smoke as the boat dodged its way between pieces of matter that Julia couldn't identify. Some were burning, some were not.

Another search boat appeared, and when it drew alongside, the man who had been with her in the water climbed into it. Julia didn't ask questions. He was clearly a local, known by the men in both boats, no doubt known by those who had been on the *Amelia Celeste*.

'We're gonna drop you ashore and come back,' the captain explained as her own boat picked up speed.

Within minutes, a darkness materialised, a body of land. The mist thinned to reveal a small fishing village built into a hillside.

The boat pulled up at the dock. Of the islanders already gathered there, one woman ran forward.

Zoe Ballard was Julia's mother's youngest sister, a late-in-life child, barely twelve years older than Julia. That closeness in age alone would have been enough to justify the bond Julia felt. More, though, Zoe was interesting and adventurous, irreverent, independent. She was everything Julia was not but admired nonetheless.

And now here she was, wearing a woven patchwork jacket and frayed jeans, her chestnut hair wind-blown, her eyes filled with tears. But her arms were strong, helping Julia off the boat, then hugging her tightly for what seemed like for ever. Julia couldn't stop shaking.

The crowd closed in, and the questions began.

'What happened?'

'How many were on the *Amelia Celeste*?'

'Did you catch any names?' Zoe asked and Julia understood why. Ferries like the *Amelia Celeste* were casual things. Tickets weren't booked ahead; there would be no list of passengers. Any information Julia could give would be a help to the islanders gathered there.

But Julia could only shake her head. 'I was in the bow. They were in the stern.'

She tried to picture the group she had seen when she boarded the boat, but the image was vague. Running down that dock, she had been tense after a harrowing seven-hour drive up from Manhattan. It should have been an easy drive—*would* have been, had she left when she had originally planned. But her husband had given her a raft of last-minute errands, treating her as usual like a maid, something she had come to sorely resent. Driving out of the city, she had wallowed in that resentment, mentally arguing with Monte as she didn't dare do in person, venting a frustration that had been building for years.

'Her arm's bleeding,' said a man who emerged from the crowd. 'Can I check her out?'

Julia was startled to see blood on the underside of her forearm.

'He's a doctor,' Zoe explained. Stepping out of her clogs, she knelt to put them on Julia's feet. 'His clinic's right around the corner.' Straightening, she slid an arm around Julia's waist and guided her away.

'Now *you* have no shoes.'

'I have socks,' Zoe said, keeping her moving until a large man wearing a khaki uniform stepped in their path.

'I have to talk with her,' he said.

'Not now, John,' Zoe replied. 'She hasn't stopped trembling. She's likely in shock. Jake is taking a look, then I'm taking her home.'

Julia whispered, 'I want to stay here.'

Zoe ignored her and the police chief stepped aside.

Julia was ushered onto Main Street. She was barely over the threshold of the small clinic when she baulked. Something was starting to feel familiar—the same thing she was running from, the sense that she didn't have a mind of her own.

'I am *not* going home right now,' she told Zoe.

'You need to dry off and warm up,' Zoe said.

'I *need* to be down on the dock,' Julia insisted, and something about the sureness in her voice must have registered, because Zoe gave in.

'OK, then. Give me my clogs. While Jake checks you out, I'll drive back to the house for dry clothes.'

Only then did it strike Julia that she had none of her own. No clothes. No shoes. No shoulder bag. No books. No camera equipment. All the things she had so carefully gathered—been putting aside for months, if the truth were told—for her two weeks on the island were gone.

She was grappling with the realisation of all that when Zoe returned. Julia had been judged in fine health aside from the jagged tear on her arm.

'A week for the stitches,' she heard the doctor tell Zoe, while she

363

pulled on dry clothing. 'The shaking will stop. I offered her a sedative, but she refused it. Call me if there's pain.'

Julia zipped the jeans, pulled a T-shirt and sweater on carefully over her bandaged arm, then put on wool socks and sneakers, and a fleece jacket, appreciating the warmth with each layer. Then she joined the others in the front room.

'I'm ready,' she said quietly, and Zoe simply nodded.

The three retraced their steps. The mist over the harbour had thinned, and empty slips and moorings suggested that the entire local fleet had joined the search. Lit by tall torches, the dock itself was crowded with worried people.

Zoe waded right in. 'What's the word?'

'Not good,' said a woman with a cellphone. 'It was Artie Jones's racer. They're picking up purple debris.'

'Artie's up from Portsmouth,' Zoe explained to Julia. 'He has a huge house down on the shaft. You remember.'

Julia did. Big Sawyer was shaped like an axe. It was broadest and most densely populated at its head, which included the harbour, the fishing village and the artists' homes. The shaft, extending southeast, was long and narrow. Seasonal residents lived there, putting a certain distance between the lavishness of their homes and boats and the down-to-earth functionality of the locals'.

'If it was *The Beast*,' Zoe went on, 'Artie's out there, too.'

'Is his family here?' Julia asked softly.

'No,' answered the woman. 'Artie comes alone to open the house and put *The Beast* in the water.' She looked past them. A boat was approaching the dock, drawing the crowd. 'Looks like the *Willa B.* has someone.' She set off.

That someone, Zoe soon told Julia, was Kim Colella. She was standing under her own steam and appeared to be unhurt. Wrapped in a large towel with her hair soaked and her head bowed, she looked to Julia to be little more than a child, but when she voiced this thought, Zoe was quick to correct her.

'Kimmie's twenty-one and tends bar at the Grill. Life hasn't been easy for her. She was raised by her mother and grandmother. They're two tough ladies.'

Julia felt a tug of protectiveness, not only because her own daughter was close to Kimmie's age, but because Kimmie Colella didn't look tough at all. Her chin stayed low as she was helped to the dock, and when a barrage of questions hit her, she recoiled.

'How long can they search?' Julia asked. It was fully dark now.

'A while. They have floodlights.'

By eleven, the fog had dispersed, and the mood of the crowd lifted with the hope that survivors would be more easily spotted. By midnight, that hope waned. By one in the morning, word came back that the Coast Guard had called off the search for the night—but still the local fleet kept at it. By two, however, one boat after another slipped into the harbour. The faces of the men were pale and drawn; they had little to say and simply shook their heads.

Julia searched until she saw the man who had helped her right after the accident. Zoe identified him as Noah Prine. Though he hoisted himself to the dock with the others, he didn't acknowledge any of those waiting, and they, in turn, gave him wide berth.

'He was with his father,' Zoe explained. 'Hutch is missing.'

Julia was horrified. She could only begin to imagine what Noah was feeling, fearing that his father was dead but not knowing for sure.

'I need a phone, Zoe,' she said, feeling a dire need, right then, right there, to hear her daughter's voice. Molly was a culinary student doing a summer apprenticeship in Paris. It would be morning there, though she might still be sleeping.

Zoe produced a cellphone, and Julia quickly punched in the number of Molly's global phone. As it rang, she moved away from the others on the dock. It seemed for ever before a groggy voice said, 'Hello?'

Julia felt such a swell of emotion that she began to cry. 'Oh, baby,' she gasped in a choked voice.

Sounding instantly awake, Molly asked, 'Mom, what's wrong?'

'Nothing. I'm fine,' Julia sobbed, 'but it's a miracle.'

The story spilled out in a handful of sentences, to which Molly injected 'Omigod' with rising frequency. When Julia finally paused, her daughter said with disbelief and awe, '*Omigod!* Are you *sure* you're OK?'

'I am, but there are others who aren't. I'm sorry to wake you'—Julia was crying again—'but with something like this, you need to talk to people like your own daughter. Email doesn't do it. You need to hear a *voice*.'

'I'm *glad* you called. Mom, that's just so awful! When'll they know about the others?'

'The morning, maybe.'

'That's so bad. And you—this was supposed to be your vacation. Are you going right home?'

The question startled Julia. 'No, I'll be at Zoe's. You have her number.'

'Is Dad coming?'

In all that had gone on, Julia hadn't once thought about Monte, which was odd. Or perhaps it wasn't. She had visited Big Sawyer three times since her marriage, and he had opted out each time. Nor had he shown any interest this time. She was sure that he had made other plans for these two weeks, well beyond those he had shared with her.

She hedged. 'I don't know. We'll talk in the morning.'

'Let me know,' Molly rushed on. 'I love you, Mom.'

'Me, too, baby. Me, too.'

Alone, Noah Prine tromped down Main Street, turned left onto Spruce, and began the short climb up the hillside to the house he shared with his dad. It was a fisherman's cottage in a neighbourhood of other fishermen's cottages, clapboards weathered grey by the salt air, blue shutters in need of paint—always in need of paint, because boats and buoys came first. It wasn't a big place, but it was paid for in full.

He bet Artie Jones's place wasn't. He bet that the guy didn't have an ounce of insurance either, because guys like that didn't think past the moment. If eight people turned out to be dead, all the lawsuits in the world wouldn't compensate two orphaned Walsh kids, Greg Hornsby's wife and kids, Dar Hutter's fiancée, Grady Bartz's parents, and whomever Todd Slokum might have left in the world.

Money certainly couldn't bring back his dad—not that Noah was convinced he was gone. Hutch had spent his whole life on the water, survived storms that might have killed another man. Hutch could do it. A night in the sea might even slow the growth of cancer in his blood.

The problem, of course, even beyond that of the initial crash and whatever those mammoth propellers had chewed, was the explosion. Who knew what damage it had done?

Noah turned up the short path. He could smell his mother's lilacs as he went past, though he couldn't make them out in the dark. There wasn't even a light on out front, because he and his father had planned to be back before nightfall. Noah had intended to cook the bass that had come up in a lobster trap the day before. Hutch loved bass, and, sensing that their day at the hospital would be a disaster, Noah had wanted to please him.

Noah hadn't had a clue what the real disaster would be. He had always seen the island as safe and familiar. Yes, death came. They had been through it with his mom three years before, but not with this kind of violence, not with this kind of . . . stupidity.

He opened the door, and a forty-pound creature raced past him. 'Lucas,' he said with dismay. He had forgotten about the dog, shut in all day. He had planned to be back for Lucas, too.

Inside, the emptiness was overwhelming. He hung his head and pushed a hand through his hair. What to do? he asked himself. Was Hutch dead or alive? No one knew anything for sure.

Still, Ian ought to be told. Noah went to the phone. He punched out the number, but hung up before the call could go through. Ian was his son, seventeen years old and difficult. Noah had trouble communicating with him at the best of times. He didn't know what to say now.

He went down the hall in the dark, to the bathroom, stripped off clothes stiff with salt, and turned on the shower. He scrubbed every inch of himself and put on dry clothes, still without lights. He knew enough not to even try to sleep. He had two hours to live through before he went back out in the boat, back to the search. Not knowing what else to do, he did the one thing he did best.

Grabbing an anorak from the coat tree, he went out the door. Lucas was beside him—a surprising comfort—as Noah strode back down the hill to the small shack by the water's edge where he kept his traps. He had already set several hundred in the shallows, where lobsters hid before moulting. Most of the traps he would set now in deeper water were ready to go. But there were a few last casualties in need of attention. He set to repairing them, working by the light of an old oil lamp, because there was no electricity in the shed.

By the time he was done, the two hours were nearly up. He could see it in the whisper of light that came through the window, could feel it in bones that screamed to him, *Get on out there now, man, right now!*

He left the shed, and, with Lucas running every which way ahead, he set off for the harbour. Lights were on up the hillside; people would be down on the dock soon, resuming the vigil.

He reached the Grill. Inside its door, his Thermos was filled with hot coffee, waiting in its usual spot alongside those of the other lobstermen. This time, though, the owner of the Grill was waiting, too.

Rick Greene was a large man with a large mind and a large heart. He had single-handedly turned the Harbor Grill into a destination eatery; summer day-trippers planned expeditions around lunches of mussel salad, lobster chowder or curried cod. Now he pressed a bag into Noah's hand. 'You gotta have food.'

Noah stared at the bag, touched by the gesture.

'Did you sleep any?' Rick asked.

'Nah.' Noah raised bleak eyes. 'Anyone here yet?'

'*Trapper John* left ten minutes ago. Maybe you shouldn't go out alone.'

Noah smiled sadly. 'Lucas'll have to do, since I don't seem to have my sternman.' That would've been Hutch.

Pain crossed Rick's face. 'What can I do?'

Noah looked out at the sea. 'Not a helluva lot,' he said, feeling the kind of despair he hadn't yet allowed himself to feel, but exhaustion did that—poked holes where holes wouldn't normally be. 'Could be we missed something.'

'You need anything, radio it in.'

Noah set off down the dock. The *Leila Sue* rocked gently in her slip, flanked by lobster boats in different sizes and states of repair. Each had a buoy pegged to the wheelhouse roof. Noah's was bright blue with two orange stripes. These were his colours, registered with the state and repeated on every buoy he attached to his traps. Blue-orange-orange— originally his father's colours, for the past ten years his own.

Lowering himself to the deck of the *Leila Sue* seconds before Lucas leapt aboard, he stowed the food, then got the engine going. He didn't look at the yellow oilskins that hung from hooks, one for Hutch and one for himself. He pulled on his Patriots hat. He and Hutch shared their love for the team. The Snow Bowl against the Raiders had been a good day. Driving down to that game, he and Hutch hadn't argued a bit, a rare and memorable thing.

Noah untied his lines fore and aft, then gave the *Leila Sue* enough gas to back her out of the slip and turn her. Throttling up, he headed out. The *Leila Sue* might have been moving forwards, but his thoughts remained in reverse.

No, he and Hutch hadn't argued going to Foxborough that day in the snow, but they sure had bickered yesterday. Hutch had criticised Noah's driving, his choice of a tuna sandwich in the cafeteria, his inability to answer the questions that—Noah countered—Hutch should have asked the doctor himself. By the time they were boarding the *Amelia Celeste,* Noah had had it. When Hutch grumbled that after sitting all day long *he* would stand in the bow during the ride to the island, Noah had baulked.

'Sit,' he'd ordered his father in no uncertain terms. 'I need air.' He had held up a hand in warning. *Stay there!* it said. *Don't argue!* He'd marched up to the bow, and so lived through the crash.

Guided now by the GPS, he pointed the *Leila Sue* towards the spot that had been the focus of the search the night before. With a little help . . . a little luck . . . a miracle . . .

Lucas settled in against his leg. A retriever, Lucas could run himself ragged round the island, but was good as gold on the boat.

Noah held the boat steady at twenty knots and kept his eyes peeled. As soon as his radar picked up the bleeps of other boats near the site, though, he turned off. He just couldn't go there. The best he could do was circle the perimeter and wait for word on the radio, with anger and confusion foremost in his thoughts.

He was a lobsterman. Lobstermen knew that they couldn't control the wind or the waves any more than they could control where lobsters chose to crawl on the ocean floor. But there were certain givens, and Noah loved those. He loved the freshness of the morning air, loved heading out with a boat full of bait and a belly full of breakfast. He loved pulling up a trap that held a breeder loaded with eggs, loved notching her tail and setting her gently back in the sea. He loved knowing that she would drop many thousands of lobster larvae and that in six or seven years he would pull up some of those very same lobsters, now big enough for keeping. He loved knowing that he had some control, however small, over the preservation of the species.

He had no control over people like Artie Jones, though. Artie Jones was a hotshot, bombing around in *The Beast*, polluting the air with its roar, adding its wake to the rock of the sea.

Why in the *hell* had he done what he'd done?

The one person who might have given them a clue wasn't saying a word—not to the fishermen who had pulled her from the sea, nor to the police chief, the doctor, or, with the rising sun now, the families gathering again on the dock. She wasn't talking to friends or to her boss, and certainly not to her mother or grandmother. She wasn't talking, period. To all intents and purposes, the accident had stolen her voice and rendered her mute.

Chapter 2

ZOE BALLARD LIVED in a farmhouse that had been built by an original Crane with the stones taken from his field when he cleared it for sheep to graze. She had updated the electrical and plumbing systems, but where insulation was concerned, the stone was wonderfully effective: the house needed nothing more than a woodstove in winter and open windows in summer. The furniture was large and cushiony, with woven throws everywhere, along with spinning wheels and baskets filled with new-spun yarn, because that was what Zoe did—raised Angora rabbits, plucked their fur, spun it, and dyed it. She sold prime pluck to weavers, spun yarn to knitters, and rabbits themselves to off-island buyers.

Julia was in one of two guest rooms in the house. It had a big double bed topped with a huge quilt of goose down, and before slipping under it in the wee hours of the morning, she had taken a long, hot bath. But a chill remained; all it took was a burst of memory to start her shivering again. She slept poorly, waking every little while to one of those bursts.

Shortly after seven, the phone rang. It was distant and quickly answered. Another call came. Slipping out of bed, she wrapped herself in a robe and, moving gingerly, went down to the kitchen.

The sight of Zoe was a comfort. Totally unadorned, she wore a sweater and jeans and, at fifty-two, was more fit than many women half her age. Standing barefoot, she was at an open window, looking out over the meadow. Fog moved gently through the trees.

'No, I will *not* wake her up,' Zoe was saying into the phone. 'She doesn't need that.' Glancing behind her, she saw Julia but didn't miss a beat. 'No, Alex. She's been through a trauma. Does she need to spell it out for the press? Hey, I have to go.' She ended the call and raised her brows. 'Do you mind?'

'No. *No.* I don't want to talk with the press. How did they know to call here?'

'Alex Brier is local. He saw you on the dock last night. How'd you sleep?'

Julia answered her with a telling look.

Reaching out, Zoe tucked a strand of blonde hair behind her ear in much the way Julia's mother had done when Julia had been very, very young. It was a gesture of affection of the kind that Janet had neither the time nor inclination to show now.

'Did the phone wake you?'

'The phone, my mind, daylight.' Julia wrapped her arms around Zoe and hugged her before dropping into one of the chairs that circled the table. 'Sorry. My legs feel strange.'

'Achy?' Zoe asked, filling the kettle with water. 'How's the arm?'

'Sore. There's word on the search, isn't there?'

Zoe lit the gas. 'There may be nine people gone.'

'*Nine?* So many?'

'Eight from the *Amelia Celeste*, plus Artie Jones. One is the fellow who helps me in the barn. Todd Slokum. He's kind of a lost soul, loves the rabbits. They're his friends. He doesn't seem able to make others.'

Julia held out a hand, which Zoe came and took. 'I'm *so* sorry.'

'So is it worse,' Zoe asked, eyes haunted, 'when someone who is all alone dies, or when someone leaves family and friends? I don't know.'

One of the things Julia had always loved about Zoe was her honesty. Zoe was right out there; what you saw was what you got. Unfortunately, that kind of forthrightness hadn't sat well with her family, which was why, from early adulthood, Zoe had been branded a rebel and distanced from the rest. The ill will remained. Julia's mother, Janet, hadn't even spoken more than a sentence or two to Julia since she had said she was visiting Zoe.

'Does anyone know why the boat ploughed into us?' Julia asked.

'Not yet. They just recovered Artie's body.'

'Do you think he was drunk?'

'Don't know. The medical examiner will do an autopsy.'

'How many others have they found?'

'Three. The captain, Evan Walsh and Grady Bartz.'

'Noah Prine's father?'

'Not yet.'

'Noah and I were the only ones in the bow. Everyone in the stern died, except for that girl.'

'Kimmie.'

'Yes.'

The phone rang. Zoe picked it up. 'Yes?' She rolled her eyes. 'I know you have an investigation to do, John, but can't it wait?' She paused. 'Later, then. Give her a chance to rest.' Zoe politely ended the call and turned in apology to Julia. 'You'll have to talk with our police chief. First, though, you need to call Monte.'

Julia's hopes rose. 'He called?'

Eyes knowing, Zoe shook her head.

'Ah.' Hoped died. 'Well, of course, I guess he wouldn't,' Julia rationalised in an attempt to ease her disappointment. 'He doesn't know about the accident, and we left it that I'd call him. So you're right. That's what I should do.'

Zoe passed her the phone, and Julia carried it out to the porch, punching in her home number as she settled into a rocker.

He picked up after the third ring, sounding groggy. 'Yeah.'

Julia was immediately concerned. 'Monte. Hi. Were you sleeping?' He should have been ready to head off to work.

'It was a late night,' he said in a way that suggested he was stretching. 'Since you weren't here, I figured I'd stay at the office. A group of us went out to dinner, then I worked afterwards. I don't know—maybe I'm getting the flu or something. I'm bushed. I think I'll stay in bed a while longer.'

'Are you running a fever?' Julia asked, because Monte's suggesting that he sleep in, rather than race to the office to monitor the stock market in Japan, was totally out of character.

'No. I'm just tired. What's up?'

Julia told Monte about the accident. By the time she was done, he seemed fully awake. 'You sound OK.'

'I'm alive. Others aren't, and we don't know the extent of it yet.'

'You lost everything? Clothes, books . . . *everything*? Maybe they'll be able to recover some of it. I'll call about the credit cards this morning. How much did you have in cash?'

'A thousand.'

'*That* much? Why that much?'

'That was what you told me to cash. You were going to do it for me, remember? Then you didn't have time.' He hadn't had time to drop his tuxedo at the dry-cleaner, pick up razor blades, or buy a book for a hospitalised client, either—all of which he had asked her to do yesterday morning, and that's why she had missed the car ferry.

'And your camera equipment,' he trotted on like a horse with blinkers, 'there was a *fortune's* worth in that bag. You were signed up for a course with that photographer Himmel.'

'Hammel,' she corrected. She looked up when Zoe joined her with mugs of tea for them both.

'Even if it's recovered,' Monte went on, 'the Nikon is ruined.'

'Monte, they think nine people are *dead*!'

Feeling distant and disconnected, Julia stared at Zoe, who sat on the porch railing. Monte talked on. When she realised he had stopped, she asked, 'I'm sorry, what did you say?'

'I was wondering if you were coming home.'

Had he said something sweet—that he missed her already and really wanted her home—she might have been swayed. But there was nothing. So she said, 'I want to wait here until the searching is done. There are families of people who died. I feel a kind of responsibility.'

'For what? You didn't cause the accident.'

'Not responsibility, then. Connection.'

'OK. That makes sense,' he said. 'So . . . do you think you'll stay for the whole two weeks like you planned?'

'At least,' Julia said. She sensed he wanted that.

'I'll overnight you money and a credit card. And a cellphone. Do you want me to send clothes?'

She looked at her wedding ring. It was an arc of sapphires and diamonds on a platinum band. A matching engagement ring, which she had left in New York, was far too showy for Big Sawyer. But that was Monte—grand and showy. She shuddered to think which of her clothes he might pick from her closet.

'No,' she said. 'I can always buy a few.'

'The car keys!' he exclaimed. 'Where are *they*?'

'In my bag.'

'On the ocean floor. Ah, Christ. OK, I'll send up a set. What else?'

Julia couldn't think of anything. Her life in New York was far removed from this island, this porch, this rocker.

'Call your parents, Julia. You don't want them to read about this in the news. Will you tell Molly?'

'Uh-huh.' There was no point in saying she already had. Monte simply wanted to know he didn't have to do it himself.

'OK, then. Be good.'

'Yes.'

'Bye.'

With the end of the call came a feeling of emptiness that was overwhelming. She didn't understand how she and Monte could be at such opposite ends of the spectrum after living together for twenty years. He had no idea what she was feeling, after surviving an accident like that. Worse, he didn't seem to care.

Setting her tea aside, Julia rose and went to the porch railing. She searched for an ocean view through the trees, but between leaves and the fog, she couldn't see a thing.

'How did I escape it?' she asked in bewilderment. It wasn't guilt she felt, so much as incredulity. Her being in the bow of the boat had been pure chance. 'One of the fellows in the stern offered me a seat. He was the one with the wife and . . .' It hit her then. 'They had a *baby* with them.'

'Kristie,' Zoe admitted solemnly. 'She just turned one. They have two others, ages three and five.'

Julia's heart ached. 'Did any of the others have children?'

'Greg Hornsby, the captain. He had two.'

She tried to process the idea of four children whose lives would be forever changed.

Zoe was suddenly on her feet. She reached inside the kitchen door and pulled out a pair of garden clogs. 'Put these on.' As soon as Julia had done so, she led her down the back stairs and round the side of the house towards the barn.

Julia didn't ask questions. Nor did she baulk when they reached the barn door. Raised to believe that barn animals were dirty creatures, in past visits here she had been content to view them from afar, more out of politeness to Zoe than true interest.

Zoe pushed the door wide. The openings where horses had once hung their heads out for fresh air were now covered by screens. Same with skylights in the roof. Both had shutters on pulleys. A large area in the barn, stalls included, had been taken over by cages. Each looked to have a single rabbit inside. Many were now pushing their noses against the wire, against their food bowls, against the tubes of their water bottles. Julia wouldn't have known these creatures were even rabbits if she hadn't known that Zoe raised them. The traditional bunny ears, eyes and twitching nose were lost in a cloud of fur. Most were white, but others were beige, grey or black. Some had a lilac tinge. Others were mottled.

'Good morning, little sweeties,' Zoe crooned and explained to Julia,

'English Angoras are the smallest of the Angoras. They may look big, but it's all fur. My largest rarely hits eight pounds.' She opened one of the cages. Slipping one hand under the rabbit's belly and another over its ears, she lifted it out and cradled it. 'Gretchen, say hello to Julia.'

The rabbit said nothing, of course. Julia couldn't even tell if Gretchen was looking at her, her eyes were so hidden in fur.

Zoe carried the rabbit to a grooming table lined with carpeting. 'Sit,' she instructed Julia, hitching her chin towards a chair. 'I need to dole out food and water. I want you to hold Gretchen while I do. Put one hand here,' Zoe said, replacing her hand with Julia's on the rabbit's ears, 'and the other by her chest, so that she won't jump off.'

'Does she nip?' Julia sat, feeling a little uneasy.

'Nope. She's my therapy bunny. One of my friends here lives with her grandmother, who is ninety-two and suffers from severe dementia. She can be ranting and raving seconds before I put Gretchen in her lap. Then she calms. Instantly.'

Julia was intrigued by the creature's warmth and softness. She found herself gently stroking the rabbit's ears. 'Is this OK?' she asked Zoe.

'Perfect. She loves it. You're a natural.'

The rabbit actually seemed to relax in her lap. Julia tipped her head sideways and smoothed enough fringe away so that she could see the rabbit's eye. 'Hello,' she whispered.

The creature looked at her, then away. The simple gesture reminded her of Kimmie Colella, but the memory didn't start her trembling again. She did feel calmer, so she kept stroking the rabbit's ears.

'How many of these do you have?' she asked Zoe.

'Currently? Twenty-three adults, twenty-five babies. See the wood boxes in some of the cages? The kits are inside.'

'How do they fit?'

Zoe laughed. 'They are little, Julia. Here, I'll show you.' She opened one of the cages and reached in. Closing the cage again, she carried the baby to Julia. Though she used both hands, the baby would have fitted comfortably in one.

Julia caught her breath in delight. The kit was pure white, with tiny ears, eyes and nose. 'How old is it?'

'Three weeks. It's just beginning to fuzz up.' Zoe carried the kit back to its cage. 'I have to do some cleaning.'

'Let me help,' Julia offered. 'Show me what to do.'

'Is this the woman who was three weeks in replying when I emailed her that I was buying rabbits?'

Julia protested, 'Did I ever tell you not to buy them?'

'No, but you never offered to help with them, either.'

'I never narrowly escaped death before.'

'What does A have to do with B?'

'Todd Slokum, for one thing,' Julia said. 'If he were here, you wouldn't be doing these chores yourself.'

Zoe's shoulders sagged. 'Shouldn't you call your parents?' Julia shrugged. 'I would,' Zoe continued. 'I wouldn't want them getting a call from a reporter. They'd be hurt.'

'They'd be hurt?' Julia cried. 'Know how much support Janet's given me lately?'

'I know,' Zoe said. 'I've been there. Which is why I can't make that call for you.' She sighed. 'With a little luck, she'll have left for work, and George will be the one to pick up the phone.'

Julia didn't need luck. Without fail, Janet was on her way to work by eight. She claimed that the hour before her staff arrived was the most productive of the day, and who was Julia to argue? Janet headed one of the largest charitable organisations in greater Baltimore and was responsible for raising millions of dollars for the underprivileged. From the time Julia was twelve, with brothers nine and seven, she had covered for her mother during those oh-so-important absences. How could Julia possibly object when Janet was doing such meaningful work? Janet couldn't have been more appreciative, and Julia thrived on praise. She became the best homemaker there was, the best helpmate. Only in hindsight, when she looked back on her childhood and her marriage, did she wonder if she hadn't been used more than necessary.

'Hello?' came the wary voice of Julia's father now.

George was a whole other issue, so different from Janet. An accountant by profession, George was introspective and shy. Hearing his voice now, Julia felt a surge of warmth.

'It's me, Dad. Thank goodness I caught you—'

'This isn't a good time. Your mother has a headache.'

Julia was instantly concerned. 'A headache?'

'Just tension,' he said and added in a whisper, 'but it wouldn't help seeing Zoe's name on the caller ID.'

Julia felt chastised. 'I had no choice. This is the only phone I have. I had an awful experience last night.'

'Be right there, Janet,' he called. 'Can I phone you later?'

Julia needed comfort. 'There was an accident. I was on a ferry—'

'Are you hurt?'

'Miraculously, no. But—'

'Thank God. Listen, sweetie,' he said, 'I will call you back. Right now, I need to get your mother some tea. She's late for work. We'll speak soon, Julia.' Without another word, he hung up the phone.

Stunned, Julia held the receiver in midair. Disconnected. And it went beyond the call to her parents, even beyond the call to Monte. She was feeling disconnected from *everything* back in those places she had called home. It was as if the accident had created a barrier between past and present, as if a wall had sprung up and was now separating the two.

Chapter 3

NOAH FELT THWARTED. He needed to blame someone for the accident, and Artie Jones fitted the bill. Big boat, big house, big wallet. Early word, though, ruled Artie out. He hadn't been playing chicken, nor had he deliberately aimed his boat at the *Amelia Celeste*. He'd had heart failure before the crash ever occurred—Noah had no one to blame but fate.

Midday Thursday the Coast Guard recovered his father's remains. With Hutch's death confirmed and no fall guy, Noah was numb. He sat in the stern of the *Leila Sue*, staring out to sea. If there was comfort to be had anywhere, it was here.

His cellphone lay beside him. Determinedly, he dialled his ex-wife's number. Sandi was dean of studies now at a private high school in Washington, DC. He phoned her office, guessing that her responsibilities went on even though the school year was done.

'Sandi,' he said when she picked up. 'It's me.'

There was a brief pause, then a cautious, 'Noah? It doesn't sound like you. Is something wrong?'

'Hutch is dead.'

Sandi had never been particularly fond of either of Noah's parents, but she was a compassionate woman. 'I'm sorry,' she said quietly. 'How?'

'There was an accident.' He gave her the bare outline.

She was appalled. 'How are you? Are you hurt?'

'No, not at all.'

'Were you the only survivor?'

'No.'

There was a pause, then, 'One other? Two?'

'Two.'

'Are they hurt?'

'Not much. One has a small cut.'

'And the other?'

'She can't speak.'

'Is it a physical problem? Crushed vocal cords?'

'No. Trauma, apparently.'

A long moment's silence. Then she sighed. 'Why is it that every conversation with you is like pulling teeth? Is it just with me that you can't say more than three words at a stretch?'

Jaw tight, Noah waited until several seconds passed. When she remained quiet, he said, 'Here's more than three words, Sandi. Hutch died the night before last. I just want to tell Ian his grandfather's gone.'

Sandi was quickly contrite. 'I'm sorry.'

'For his death or the outburst?'

'Both. I'm amazed at how close to the surface everything is, even ten years after the split.'

Noah didn't pretend that she still held feelings for him. The reason was that Sandi didn't like to fail. She had been analysing their marriage since the day it fell apart, and, naturally, she blamed him. He worked unconscionable hours, and was distant when he was home. He excluded her from his thoughts and was insensitive to her needs. Maybe she was right. Maybe it *was* his fault. Just then, though, he couldn't have cared less.

'Where's Ian now?' he asked. At three in the afternoon, the boy would normally be playing baseball.

'He mouthed off to the coach yesterday, so he's warming the bench.'

'Seventeen's tough.'

'*I'll* say.'

'So when'll he be home?'

'Maybe four. Maybe five. He's been somewhat unreliable lately.'

'Have him call me when he gets there?'

'When's the funeral?'

'Tuesday.'

'Do you want him there?'

'Yes.'

'I'll tell him that. It may not hold much weight. Lately, defiance is his middle name.'

Noah was suddenly weary. 'Just have Ian call me, OK. If he doesn't want to come, he won't come. I can bury Hutch just fine without him.'

JULIA didn't get a call from her father, although she did get a call from her friend Charlotte, who had heard about the accident from her husband, who had heard about it through Monte. It wasn't until she was accessing her email on Zoe's computer, exchanging comforting notes with her lawyer friend Donna, that she received one from George.

SORRY I HAVEN'T CALLED, BUT IT'S BEEN A BAD COUPLE OF DAYS, he wrote in the all-caps style he insisted on using. Julia suspected that since Janet didn't use a computer, he spoke loudly on the Web simply because he could.

I GOT YOUR MOTHER SET YESTERDAY AND THEN HAD A MAJOR PROBLEM HERE AT WORK. JANET FEELS YOU OUGHT TO RETURN TO NEW YORK. LET US KNOW.

Stung, Julia didn't reply.

Actually, 'stung' barely covered it. She was angry.

Heart pounding, she put the anger to use and set off for town. There, she bought the makings of half a dozen casseroles and as many batches of cookies. She wanted to take something to the bereaved families. She couldn't do gourmet the way her daughter could, but she was a good cook. She had thrown innumerable parties for Monte's colleagues, and she often gave home-baked cookies as gifts when they went to the homes of clients for dinner. Julia was a pro at making homemade little somethings to satisfy one or another of Monte's professional needs.

So Julia baked. The activity was a comfort at a time when she was feeling unhinged. Monte hadn't helped. Her parents hadn't helped. If her life were a boat that had been torn from its mooring, she was all on her own as far as tying up again went.

Four o'clock came and went, and still Noah waited for Ian to call. He didn't budge from the boat.

Noah grieved, but grief wasn't all. Making plans for the funeral had been eye-opening in a pathetic kind of way. Had he known what Hutch wanted? No. They had never talked about funerals. They had never talked about Noah's divorce. Or about his mother's death. They had never talked about Ian. Or about why Noah had returned to Big Sawyer to haul traps after the divorce, rather than continue on in New York.

What did they talk about? They talked about the weather. They talked about the boat and the traps and the buoys. They talked about the day's catch, the price it would bring. They talked about the lime-grape-lime buoys that were popping up in waters traditionally fished by Big Sawyer lobstermen.

These were the things lobstermen discussed. They interested him.

Small talk did not.

Julia visited the Hornsby house. Nestled not far from the harbour, it was filled with friends. She dropped off a chicken casserole and offered her condolences. She did the same at the homes of Grady Bartz and Dar Hutter. The situation was different at the Walsh house. It stood on Dobbs Hill, where jagged spruce tips grazed the sky, but the face of the hill was an expanse of rolling meadow. There were no crowds, no neighbours milling about. A lone Volvo station wagon sat in front of the barn, which in turn sat not far from a weathered farmhouse.

Julia knocked on the screen door. The woman who appeared was Jeannie Walsh's sister, which Julia knew only because Zoe had filled her in. Ellen Hamilton was single and taught high-school maths in Ohio. With the accident, she had become an instant parent. Despite sandy hair and a face full of freckles, she looked ten years past her age.

When Julia introduced herself, Ellen slipped outside. 'They're both asleep on the sofa,' she whispered. 'They're exhausted.'

'You must be yourself,' Julia said softly. 'I've brought dinner. Is there anything else I can do?'

Ellen smiled sadly. 'No. Thanks, though. Evan's family is handling the funerals. The girls are coming to live with me in Akron. It's really just a matter of packing up this place, and I'm the only one who can do that.' She looked bewildered. 'How do you decide what to take? I'm trying to imagine what might have meaning for the girls when they're grown.' Her voice had begun to waver, her eyes to water. 'Talk about life-changing moments. Little did I know when my phone rang yesterday morning . . .'

Five o'clock came and went without a call from Ian.

Noah pulled a beer from the stash that he kept in the cabin cooler now that summer was coming. A second beer followed the first, and by the time six o'clock came and went with no call, he had mellowed enough so that he wasn't wholly annoyed. It wasn't as if Ian and Hutch had been friends. The boy hadn't been up to the island more than a handful of times. It had always been easier for Noah to visit him on his own turf.

It was nearing seven when the woman appeared on the dock. There was no mistaking the multicoloured angora sweater Zoe wore all the time. Nor was there any mistaking that this woman wasn't Zoe. She stood apart just as she had on the mainland, running down the dock to catch the *Amelia Celeste*. It might have been her blonde hair that was distinctive, or the way she held herself, which was straight, as people did when looking good was part of who they were.

She came up to the side of the boat. 'I'm, uh, Julia. I heard about your father. I wanted to say how sorry I am.'

He nodded.

'And how grateful,' she went on. 'You saved my life. I'm not sure what I'd have done if you hadn't given me that cushion to hold.'

'You'd have been OK. Rescue wasn't long in coming.'

'But would they have spotted the speck that was me without the cushion? Would I have been too close to the ferry when that last explosion came?' Her eyes went out to sea. They were haunted when they found his again. 'I keep stumbling over all these questions. And then there's the big one.'

The big one. 'Why us?' he asked. 'Why not them?'

She nodded, seeming relieved that he knew what she meant. 'I've asked myself that a hundred times. I mean, there's the randomness of what happened. If we'd been in the stern . . . or if the racer had hit the bow . . . I don't know how to explain that.'

Noah didn't either. 'My father wanted to stand in the bow. I made him sit in the stern.'

She didn't blink. 'Evan Walsh offered me his seat. I turned him down.'

Neither of them spoke for a full minute, and he was fine with it. She was easy on the eyes, but it was more than that. With her standing here, something raw in him was soothed.

'Well.' She pressed her lips together, nodded. 'I just wanted to express my condolences. And to give you this.' She passed a foil package down over the gunwale. 'It's dinner. I cooked.'

'Thanks,' he said. 'This is really nice of you.'

'It's the least I can do,' she said with a smile that came and went quickly. 'Have you talked with Kim Colella?'

Noah kept forgetting about Kimmie. 'I haven't. I think she's with her family. How long are you here for?'

'Two weeks. I was supposed to take one of Tony Hammel's courses, but . . .' She moved her hand in a telling arc. 'I've lost my taste for it.'

'And not for Big Sawyer? I'll bet you head back early.'

'No,' she said soberly. 'Don't ask me to explain. I'm feeling . . .' She searched for a minute or two.

'Singled out,' he said. That was what he was feeling.

She nodded. 'Singled out for what? Survival?'

'No,' he said. 'That wasn't it.'

'Singled out by whom? God?'

He felt an instant annoyance. He didn't want to think about God.

'I'm sorry,' she said. 'You have enough on your mind.' She raised a hand in a wave, then started back down the dock.

He didn't stop her. He had nothing to add to the conversation, though he wished he did. He was as confused as she was.

But he felt better now, he realised. Being confused wasn't so bad when someone else felt the same.

The graveyard sat on a hill overlooking the sea. Its headstones were cut of island granite and locally carved.

Of the victims of the accident, the Walshes, Todd Slokum and Artie

Jones were being buried back near family homes on the mainland. The rest were buried on Big Sawyer, and their funerals were attended by just about everyone who lived there. Dar Hutter's was on Monday morning, Greg Hornsby's that afternoon, and Grady Bartz's the next morning, all in fog, reminiscent of how they had died. Julia stood with Zoe, and was as much a part of the community as any stranger could be.

Hutch's funeral was held on Tuesday afternoon at four. Afterwards, Zoe slipped away to meet the ferry. Todd Slokum's brother was coming to take Todd's things back home.

Julia stood at the end of the line of funeral-goers waiting to pay their respects to Noah. The sun had broken through the fog for the first time in two days. Its rays heated the trees on the slope of the hill, sending the fragrance of pine and spruce up into the graveyard.

As she moved slowly forwards over the grass bordering the granite headstones, she thought about the words that had been said about Hutch and found herself wondering what would have been said about her, had she died. Loyal wife. Loving mother. Able homemaker. Obedient woman.

It could be said, she realised as she neared the front of the line, that taking this two-week trip to Big Sawyer without Monte was the most independent thing she had done in her life. Not that he appeared to mind. As promised, he had sent a package containing everything she would need to prolong her stay—money, credit card, a set of car keys and a new cellphone.

Loyal. Loving. Able. Obedient. And . . . what else? She felt there ought to be something. But she couldn't come up with a word.

When the person in front of her moved off, she approached Noah. He wore a sweater and slacks of fine quality, accommodating his significant height. His dark hair was flecked with grey. His eyes, the dark blue of the sea, looked weary.

Still, she felt the same comfort she did each time she saw him. It was especially nice that he managed a small smile. For a few seconds it softened his face.

'My condolences,' she said. 'Again.'

'Thanks. And thanks for the dinner. I ate it all.'

'The heating instructions were OK?'

'I don't know. I didn't bother to heat it up.'

She had to smile. 'Was that laziness or hunger?'

'Hunger.'

'I'm glad it helped.'

Noah suddenly looked over her head. She glanced back to see the police chief, John Roman, climbing the hill to the cemetery. Julia had talked with him over the weekend.

Near enough now, he removed his cap. 'Sorry, Noah. I wanted to be here, but there was a development ashore.' He regarded Julia. 'Did you hear? They brought up some of your things.'

'They did?' She wanted to show excitement, but she felt as distant from her belongings as she continued to feel from her life.

'There's a bag of clothes that's kinda torn apart, but your handbag's intact.' He turned to Noah again. 'I'm coming from the medical examiner's office. They finished the autopsy on Artie. There's a twist.'

'It wasn't his heart?' Noah asked.

'Sure was. The heart was gone before he hit the water, but it wasn't just an ordinary old heart attack.' John Roman shook his head. 'Gunshot wound.'

'Gunshot?' Noah frowned. 'If you're saying that a man's heart stopped because of a gunshot wound, that's murder. We've never had anything like that here before.'

'Don't have to tell *me* that. This is a one-man department. Gear war's the worst it gets.' John gave a mirthless laugh. 'The bullet shattered the shoulder bone.'

'He wouldn't have gone out with a shoulder wound,' concluded Noah, 'which means he was on the boat when he was shot. Was someone with him on *The Beast*?'

'I was gonna ask you that,' John said, broadening his gaze to include Julia. 'Think again. Did you see anything before the collision? Anything at all on *The Beast* to suggest someone else was aboard?'

Julia tried to relive those moments, but the only image that came to mind was the one that continued to wake her in the middle of the night. 'Just that purple bow shooting out of the fog.'

'That fog was thick,' Noah reminded John. 'You know those racers—they're all nose. The cockpit was easily fifteen feet back from the bow. Visibility was less than that.'

'How about noise? Like a gunshot?' John asked.

'Above those engines?' Julia shook her head.

'Divers are going down to look for a weapon. And for another body, in case someone else was aboard.'

Julia asked, 'Did he have any enemies?'

'The wife says no.' John eyed Noah. 'What do you think?'

'Enemies up here? He annoyed lots of us with that boat, but that's all it was, an annoyance. Nothing to kill someone over.'

'What about Kimmie?' John asked. 'Would someone have killed over her?'

Julia was trying to make the connection, when John answered himself. 'Nah. I don't see it. It'd be too much of a coincidence to think that someone shoots Artie for her sake and then she nearly dies on the *Amelia Celeste*.'

'Is she talking?' Noah asked.

'Not yet. I'm going there now.' He put the cap back on his head. 'I was hoping to catch Hutch's service. He was a good man.' Giving a clap to Noah's shoulder, he strode down the hill.

'Kimmie?' Julia asked as soon as he was out of earshot.

'There were rumours she and Artie were an item.'

'So. What do you think? Is there a murderer involved here?'

Noah averted his eyes. 'I've been looking for someone to blame, and that'd do it. But it wouldn't change the outcome any.'

They turned to leave. They were barely past the cemetery gate when a dog bounded up and danced excitedly around Noah's legs.

'Is he yours?' Julia asked.

'Yes. His name's Lucas.'

'He's a striking dog,' she said, admiring the feathered tail, white bib, silky ears and freckled nose. 'What kind is he?'

'A Nova Scotia duck tolling retriever.' Noah bent to scrub the dog's ears. 'Tollers are a breed of dog used as decoys for ducks. They jump around onshore to distract the duck while the hunter takes aim. Since we don't hunt ducks here, it means that this one's forever running back and forth.'

The dog shot off down the hill, where the only two vehicles left were Zoe's little Plymouth and Noah's dark blue pick-up. They started walking again. Noah seemed deep in thought, but the silence was comfortable. They were nearly at the cars when he spoke.

'I keep thinking about what his friends said. You know, about the kind of man he was. I wonder what they'd say if I died.'

Julia wasn't surprised that his thoughts mirrored hers. It went with the territory. 'What would they say?'

'Nothing interesting. I'm an average kind of guy. I could be more.' He frowned. 'What about you? What would they say?'

'Loyal. Loving. Able. Obedient.'

'Obedient?'

'I'm a very docile person. Or was,' she added with a smile. 'I'm not identifying with that woman at this moment.'

'How not?'

'Being here on Big Sawyer, for one thing. Staying for two weeks. I've never left my husband for this long. He's . . . dependent.'

'Physically?'

'No. Custodially.' Not caring to elaborate, she rushed on. 'My mother thinks I should hurry back to New York, because of the accident and all.

But I want my time away.' She smiled in self-deprecation. 'That's out of character. I'm not a very independent sort. But you all are. Maybe there's something in the air here. I'm feeling a little like a stranger to myself.'

'Maybe it's Zoe's clothes,' he suggested.

'The sweater gave me away, huh?'

'Her things are distinctive,' Noah said with respect. 'Maybe you'll feel more like yourself once you have your own clothes.'

But Julia didn't think so. More to the point, she didn't know if she wanted to feel like her old self.

She was saved from confessing more when Zoe's truck rumbled up the road. Bucking erratically, it came to a stop.

'Sounds like gear trouble,' Noah said.

Climbing out of the truck was a petite young woman who, with one marked exception, looked very much like Molly.

'It's not gear trouble. I believe that's my daughter, who doesn't have a *clue* about driving a stick shift.' Julia set off across the grass, walking at first, then running when she realised that, despite the boyish haircut, it really *was* Molly.

By contrast, Molly was frozen in place, her expression registering something akin to horror. By the time Julia reached the truck, her excitement had turned to concern. Molly had Monte's dark eyes rather than Julia's hazel ones, and those eyes were red-rimmed.

Julia took Molly's face in her hands. 'What's wrong?'

'Who's that man?' Molly asked.

'Noah Prine. He survived the accident with me. This funeral was for his father. What's *wrong*, sweetie?'

There was a tiny pause. Then a tense, 'Nothing.'

'Yesterday morning you were in *Paris*!' They had talked then. 'And what is this?' she asked, moving hands lightly over Molly's head.

'It's the rage there. I thought it looked great.'

'It does. I'm just startled. You've always had long hair. I wasn't prepared.'

Molly shot Noah another glance. 'That makes two of us. It's weird seeing you with a man who isn't Dad.' Seeming to simply crumple, she wrapped her arms round Julia's neck and, weeping softly, held on more tightly than she had done in years.

Julia's mind went in a dozen different directions at once. 'What happened? How did you . . . when . . .?'

'Last night,' Molly said, brushing at tears with the palm of her hand. 'I kept thinking that my job stunk, that my boss sucked, and here you were nearly killed, and how could I stay there when someone should be with you? Only the plane to New York was two hours late, and Dad and I had a big fight.'

'About the hair?' Julia asked. Out of the corner of her eye, she caught sight of Noah heading for his truck. He raised a hand; *talk later*, it said.

'About *men*,' Molly cried. 'The things they do. They were just so disgusting at the restaurant, Mom. It's like they were doing me a big favour letting me watch them work—which they were—but they were also supposed to let me work, too. I mean, there I was, their *slave* for the summer.'

'Why didn't you tell me things were so bad?'

'Because I kept thinking they would get better. I'd wanted New York, but Dad kept insisting Paris would look better on my résumé. Well, what's a résumé worth if you're miserable?'

Julia smoothed that short blonde hair. 'I'm so sorry, sweetie. I wish you'd told me.'

'What good would it have done? I probably would have stayed, because *God forbid* Dad should think I'm a quitter. Then you were in the accident, and it changed everything.'

'So how did you get up here?'

'I flew to Portland and took a bus the rest of the way. Dad doesn't know I'm here. I just showered, packed a bag, and left.'

Julia wondered if there was more Molly wasn't saying. 'He's probably worried sick.'

'I doubt it.' With her short hair, and three earrings per lobe, Molly looked uncharacteristically rebellious. 'He has a busy life, and that life revolves around him. Remember the time he was supposed to be vacationing in Washington, DC, with us? Or the time he was supposed to be chaperoning my senior prom?'

'We've been through this before. But he loves you. I'll call him as soon as we get back to Zoe's.' Julia looked again at that hair. It was going to take some getting used to. 'What'll you do now?'

'Go back to New York with you and look for something else,' Molly said. 'I know it's late. But I can talk my way into things.'

'You certainly can.' Molly might have Julia's sensitivity, but she had Monte's drive—and his tongue. 'Only I may stay here a little longer. I'm trying to figure things out. It's been an emotional week.'

Molly glanced up at the cemetery. 'Can we leave now? This place freaks me out. Besides, you need to call Grandpa. I talked with him while I was at the bus station. He said he was waiting for you to call.'

Yes. There had been that order at the end of his email. There hadn't been an email since, though there had been emails from her friends, Donna and Charlotte, and from her brothers.

If Julia's parents felt any of the concern that had brought Molly home from France, Julia saw no evidence of it. Not in them, and not in Monte. Forget concern. If Monte even missed her, Julia saw no evidence of it at all.

Chapter 4

BACK AT ZOE'S, the first call Julia made was to Monte. He picked up with a terse, 'Yes.'

'Hey,' she said, as chipper as could be. 'It's me.' She smiled at Molly, who stood nearby, chewing on a fingernail.

'I've been trying you all day,' he replied, sounding put out.

'I left the new cellphone at Zoe's. I've been at funerals.'

'It'd help if you checked for messages once in a while. Molly's back.'

'I know,' Julia said. 'She's up here now.'

'*There?* How in the hell did she get *there?*'

'She flew to Portland and took a bus to the ferry.'

'A *bus?*' Monte exclaimed. 'Do you know the kinds of scuzzbags who take buses up there?'

'Are they any different from the scuzzbags who take buses down there?'

Molly sniggered. Julia held up a warning hand.

'Ah,' said Monte. 'We're in a mood today, are we? Well, let me tell you, Molly was almost incoherent when she walked in here last night. What did she say to you?'

'She says you're upset that she came home early.'

There was a heartbeat's silence, then an arch, 'Well, aren't *you?* It was a good internship.'

'She didn't think so.'

'She's twenty years old. What does she know?'

Julia bridled on Molly's behalf. Turning away from the girl, she told Monte with a vehemence she didn't often use, 'Let's give her a little credit. We weren't in Paris. She felt that the internship wasn't going to give her the experience she was there to get. She also felt that it would mean a lot to *me* for her to come here and make sure I was OK. And it has.'

'You're OK,' Monte said lightly. 'You're always OK. So you got the package I sent. The credit card, and the cash?'

'Thank you,' she said obediently.

'And the car keys? Have you brought the car over?'

'Not yet.'

'Why not? If you weren't going to be needing it, I could have used it here.'

To go where? she wondered. 'I'll go get the car,' she assured him. 'Especially now that Molly's here, I have reason to do it.'

'She won't find another job now. She might as well stay there another week. Did I tell you that our insurance will cover the camera equipment? She can help you to find out if you can replace it up there.'

'I'll see.'

Monte went on. 'By the way, call your father, will you? He called here wanting to know why you haven't returned his call.'

'He never called,' Julia said, mildly annoyed.

'Maybe you weren't answering your cell. Do me a favour, Julia. Keep it with you, please? It'd be nice to be able to reach you.'

'OK.'

She ended the call, simmering now at the condescension in his voice, and accessed her voicemail, but there was nothing from her father. She was of half a mind to call later, but with Molly still standing close, she'd have to explain herself if she put it off.

Her stomach was jumping as the phone rang. It got worse when her mother's voice came on. 'Hello?'

'Mom, hi.' There was silence on the other end. Quickly, hopefully, she said, 'Talk to me, Mom. Please talk to me.'

But George came right on. 'Julia? We've been trying to reach you. Why haven't you called?'

Julia was deflated. 'Things have been a little busy.'

'Busy? Up there?'

'There was an accident, Dad. Nine people died. When I haven't been at funerals, I've been making meals for families of the ones we've buried, and I've been helping Zoe out, because her assistant died on the ferry. Yes, it's been busy.'

Despite her efforts to stay calm, her voice had risen. Uncharacteristic? Definitely. Even Molly looked startled.

Her father backed off. 'I understand, Julia. It's just that we've been waiting for your call. We're your parents. We worry.'

'If you were worried, why didn't you call me yourself?'

George didn't reply, and Julia felt instantly contrite.

'I'm sorry, Dad, but Big Sawyer's a small place. Everyone knows everyone else. When nine people die, it is *felt*.'

'I can imagine,' he said quietly, sincerely. 'How many more funerals are there?'

'None here. The rest are on the mainland.'

His voice brightened. 'You're coming home, then?'

'Not yet.'

'Why not? What does Monte say?'

387

'He's all for it. He's about as much into the ferry accident as you and Mom are.' The words were so laden with sarcasm that Julia surprised even herself. But she didn't take them back.

'I'm not sure I understand what you're saying.'

'I'm saying that the accident was as traumatic an experience as I've ever had in my life. I'm looking at things differently now, like who I am and what I'm doing with my life. I'm forty, and God willing, I'll have *another* forty years. I need to make the most of them.'

'Are you doubting the first forty?' George asked.

'Yes. Some parts. I wouldn't change a thing about others.'

George said something muffled to Janet.

'If Mom has something to say,' Julia invited, 'why doesn't she pick up the phone?'

'You know why,' George muttered.

'Actually, I don't,' Julia said. 'We all know that she and Zoe had a falling-out, but I'm not sure what it was about. To carry the grudge all this time is absurd. Zoe's her only sister but has she ever picked up the phone and called her?'

'Julia,' he cautioned.

But Julia was on a roll. 'Zoe has friends but no family, and there Mom is, head of a charitable foundation. Her speciality is supposed to be communicating with people, but she won't talk with Zoe and now, because I'm here, she won't talk with me. Charity begins at home, doesn't it? If forgiveness is part of charity, why can't Mom forgive Zoe? What did she do that was so terrible?'

'Ask Zoe.'

Zoe chose that moment to walk in the door. Holding her gaze, Julia said, 'Zoe won't say.' When Zoe arched her brows, Julia mouthed, *Dad*.

George sighed, sounding tired. 'Julia, this has nothing to do with you and your life. You've had a shock. Things will return to normal. You have to move on now. Come home. We'll talk more once you're back in New York.'

Gretchen was waiting for her in the barn. At least, that was what Julia chose to believe, because the instant she approached the cages, of all the rabbits who began their little scrabbles and tugs, only Gretchen moved to the very point where the door could easily open. Reaching in with confidence, Julia lifted her out.

The rabbit settled comfortably on her lap. Gently, she stroked the fringed ears.

'Hello, pretty little one,' she crooned. 'How are you?'

Julia knew if she smoothed back the brow fur, Gretchen might shift her eyes and make contact—which she did now. Under Zoe's tutelage, Julia had learned to accept these small gestures for the shows of affection that they were. She had also learned how to refill water bottles and measure out pellets, how to empty the trays under the cages and fill them with fresh hay.

She held each one of the kits in turn—and all the while, she refused to think about Monte, refused to think about her parents, refused to think about that other, distant life.

Something made her glance back at the barn door. Molly stood there, with Zoe at her shoulder. Startled, Julia said, 'I didn't hear you come in.'

'We've been here a while,' Molly said. She sounded amazed. 'Look at you. Holding rabbits.'

She went to Julia, who held out a baby. Molly took it readily, but remarked, 'Your nail polish is chipping.'

'Now, there's a message,' Julia decided.

'Here's another,' said Zoe. 'This is ribs night at the Grill. I'm not sure we're ribs women, but Rick has a mean salad menu. Lobster salad, shrimp salad, scallop salad, Caesar—you name it. It's been a hell of a day. What do you say we clean up and go?'

The Harbor Grill was as unpretentious as the rest of Big Sawyer. Large banks of glass offered diners a three-sided harbour view that was broken only by a pair of screen doors in the middle. Those doors led to an open deck that stood over the water on thick pilings. In winter, action often centred round the bar. With the advent of warmer weather, though, the deck was the place to be.

When Julia, Molly and Zoe arrived, the sun was still an hour shy of setting. Julia couldn't help but remember that she had arrived on the island at nearly the same hour one week before. The memory was stoked by the grey-haired man who sat alone in a corner, an elbow braced on the wooden rail of a built-in bench that ran round the three open sides of the deck. The other hand, knobby at the knuckles, held his drink. He was staring out past the harbour boats.

Zoe led them to a table, but they had no sooner taken seats when Julia rose again. 'Be right back,' she whispered.

He was nursing his whiskey, seeming preoccupied. 'I'm Julia Bechtel,' she said gently, sitting beside him. 'I was on the ferry the other night.'

The man nodded.

'I just wanted to say . . . well, it's a tragedy, the loss of life. But you lost the *Amelia Celeste*. I'm told she was like a person to you. I just wanted to say I'm sorry.'

He nodded again.

She looked out at the diners. Only one table was left.

'Quite a crowd,' she observed. 'I'm eating with my aunt and my daughter. Would you like to join us?'

'Thanks, but I'll just sit here a while.'

A voice rose at the other side of the deck. It had a tipsy joviality to it and was followed by raucous laughter.

'The fruit guys,' Matthew muttered. 'Insensitive sons of Bs.'

Julia agreed. As charming as the deck was, it didn't erase the week that had been. Loud laughter was out of place. 'Why do you call them the fruit guys?'

'Their buoys are painted like fruit. Green and purple. Lime and grape. It's a problem.'

'The colours?'

'The buoys. They're all over Big Sawyer waters. But they're not allowed.'

'Can't the Coast Guard stop them?'

'It's not federal law.' He started to talk with an ease she hadn't expected. 'Every island has its own territory where its fishermen work. It's an unwritten rule. Outsiders don't sink traps here.'

Julia was intrigued. 'How do you know where one territory ends and another begins?'

'You just know,' Matthew said patiently. 'Oh, the lines smudge some come winter, when you have to go south past the usual turf to catch anything good in your trap. Lobsters don't want to be near the surface cold, so they crawl along the bottom of the ocean into deeper waters.'

'Do you go down south?'

'Nah. I run the ferry.' He looked away abruptly.

Julia ached for him. 'Will you buy another boat?'

He shrugged.

It was time to leave. Julia rose. 'Thank you for talking with me.'

He raised a hand to signal a wave.

Julia headed back to her table and settled into her seat.

'He has to keep staples like burgers and steaks,' Zoe was telling Molly, 'because some of the men here won't eat anything else.'

'Not lobster?' Molly asked in amusement.

'Oh, all the time, but they eat it at home with culls from the catch of the day. Here, they want something different.' She filled Julia in. 'Molly's surprised at how eclectic the menu is, and I was saying Rick Greene is a savvy guy. When he bought this place, it wasn't much more than a fisherman's shack. Then people began building big houses down on the shaft, and luxury boats arrived, and he knew he had to do something different.'

'Up till then,' Molly informed Julia, 'he would cook up whatever the local catch brought in.'

'He still does,' Zoe said. 'That's what the specials are about.'

'We got you iced tea, Mom. Did you want wine?'

Julia smiled. 'Tea is perfect. I'm sorry for that diversion. I invited him to join us, but he wouldn't.'

'Not surprising,' Zoe said. 'He likes being alone. He isn't a big talker.'

Loud laughter erupted from the fruit guys' table. Zoe turned and stared, as did half the people on the deck. Oblivious, the men continued to snigger and snort.

Zoe faced front again, angry now. 'Artie Jones and eight other people are dead. We've just buried four of them right here, yet those guys are laughing away. They're trouble.'

The same sentiment prevailed down the street in the cavernous back room at Brady's Tackle & Gear. A pair of desks stood under fluorescent lights along with assorted old chairs. The men occupying them formed the core of the local lobstermen's association—the trap group, as it was known. They wore T-shirts and jeans. Some held beer cans, others coffee in Styrofoam cups.

Hayes Miller, a full-bearded barrel of a man, ran the *Willa B.* 'They're trouble,' he charged. 'No good's ever come of a West Rock boat down here. West Rockers are supposed to drag for scallops. They got no business hauling traps.'

'Leastways not in *our* waters,' remarked wiry Leslie Crane. He hauled traps from *My Andrea*, named for his wife, who was currently expecting their fifth child. Traps set near his, where they had no right to be, took money from his pocket, bread from his table.

Joe Brady was the unofficial moderator of the group. Dark-haired, with a trim beard, he ran the tackle and gear store. 'So what do we know about them?' he asked.

'Names are Haber and Welk,' said John Mather. A quiet, bespectacled man, he owned the *Trapper John.* 'They're up from Florida. Word is, they bought eight hundred traps.'

'That's legal,' said Elton Hicks, the group's senior member.

'Bet they've gone over.'

'Hayes is right.' Shaven-headed Mike Kling and his father hauled from the *Mickey 'n' Mike.* 'Remember those guys up on Salinica Island year before last? They dropped three hundred traps over the limit, all with forged tags. They'd have got away with it, if the Coast Guard hadn't got a tip. So maybe one of us has to make a phone call. If you ask me, those guys are prime suspects.'

'Prime suspects in what?' Noah set his jaw tight. 'Are we talking lobstering or murder?'

The room was still.

Joe was sombre. 'Both. Think about where the fruit guys have the greatest concentration of traps.'

'Up Little Sawyer,' Mike answered. 'What if Artie ran those twin props right through the fruit guys' lines, and what if Haber and Welk took a shot?'

'Can anyone prove they shot Artie?' Joe asked. 'The medical examiner couldn't tell what gun was used.'

'It's simple,' Mike maintained. 'Search the fruit guys' boat.'

Joe said, 'You're quiet, Noah. What're you thinking?'

'There's one problem with the theory,' Noah said. 'Fog. The fruit guys couldn't have seen who was cutting their lines.'

'They didn't have to see,' Mike insisted. 'They could hear. Everyone knows Artie's boat. What if they took a blind shot?'

'It's a stretch, Mike.'

'So,' Joe reasoned, 'if the shot didn't come from another boat or from land, it came from aboard *The Beast*.'

Hayes looked flummoxed. 'You think he shot *himself*?'

Mike made a face. 'What kind of moron thinks to kill himself with a shoulder shot? I'd say maybe someone shot him before he left his dock, only Artie'd have to be a *double* moron to have left the dock with a gunshot wound.'

Joe sighed. 'I'm beat, I want to get home, so we need to make a decision. What're we going to do about the fruit guys' traps?'

'Want me to cut a few lines?' Mike searched the group.

'Knots are better,' John reasoned, pushing up his glasses.

'That'll only slow them down,' Mike argued. 'We cut their lines, haul their traps and empty them out.'

'Hell, I don't want to spend my day hauling *their* traps,' Leslie argued. 'And I can't get into a fully fledged gear war. It costs too much. Look, I agree with John. Knot the lines.'

Joe looked around. 'Everyone agree?'

No one disagreed. The plan was considered adopted. Feeling suddenly, acutely restless, Noah rose from his chair. He shook hands with Joe and Leslie, nodded briefly at the others, and went out of the door.

Once he started down Main Street, Lucas was by his side. Dusk had fallen. He could hear the muted drone of talk from the deck at the Grill.

As he walked along, he was thinking of Hutch, and of Ian, but he was thinking of Artie, too. It would be convenient if someone had just propped Artie at the wheel and aimed *The Beast* out to sea. There'd be someone to go after. It would be very convenient.

But he had his own theory and it was making him uncomfortable.

He could be wrong. He had been distracted that night, upset about Hutch. He hadn't looked hard at the others in the stern. Taking his venom out on the fruit guys was one thing; they were guilty as sin of trespass. Tossing out accusations that might hurt the innocent was something else.

The one person he could talk to without doing damage was Julia Bechtel. She might have seen something without realising it.

Meanwhile, he couldn't sit and do nothing. So he made for the *Leila Sue*, released her lines, and backed out of the slip. With Lucas near his leg, he steered out of the harbour. Once past its limits, he throttled up, cruised to the spot with the largest aggregation of lime-grape-lime buoys, and began knotting lines—knotting lines for Hutch, even more than for himself. Hutch believed in the law of the seas. He believed that local fishermen had a moral authority when it came to protecting their turf. Noah couldn't think of a more fitting tribute to Hutch, on this day of his burial, than this.

Chapter 5

JULIA DIDN'T WANT to be on the water. She would have been perfectly happy never to set foot on a boat again. Of course, she knew she would have to, since Big Sawyer was an island. There was no other way to leave, and she couldn't stay for ever.

Plus there was Monte harping on at her to get the car. And now Molly wanted her to shop for clothes to replace those lost on the *Amelia Celeste*. Molly wanted a frivolously fun mother-daughter day on the mainland. So what could Julia say? Part of her liked the idea of frivolous fun, and it would force her to face her fear of the ferry.

The accident was indelibly etched on her psyche. She didn't fall asleep without thinking of it, didn't wake up without remembering, and then there were the jolts in the middle of the night, and the restlessness that set in when the jitters eased. The stitches on her arm were gone, but the emotional blow would be slower to heal.

Her stomach was in knots when she woke up on Wednesday morning and saw the fog. Finding Molly and Zoe in the kitchen, she tried to sound nonchalant. 'Should we put it off?'

'Oh, no, Mom, this is a perfect day to go. You need clothes. Think we can make the nine o'clock ferry?'

'Nine o'clock's way too soon,' Julia said. 'I have work to do first.' This was true. She had to help with the rabbits.

'The ten thirty ferry, then?'

Ten thirty it was, though only after Julia had therapy in the barn. Savouring the stillness, she changed the water bottles and measured the proper amount of pellets to add to each bowl. Zoe worked close by, whispering sweet nothings to the rabbits. Finally Julia spoke.

'What about my staying beyond my allotted two weeks?'

'Hey,' Zoe chided with a smile, 'you were the one who set the time limit. If I had my way, you'd be here all summer.'

'What if Molly stays too?' Julia asked.

'I'd love it. But what about you? I had the feeling when you decided to come here that you wanted time away.' She stopped short of saying that Molly's arrival put a chink in that.

But Julia heard. 'I love being with Molly,' she reasoned. 'In the last few years, she's become a friend. Not every mother is as lucky as I am. Besides, Monte didn't rush up here after the accident. Nor did my parents.'

'What's going on with you and Monte?'

Julia pressed her lips together, shook her head. She didn't want to talk about that.

Zoe didn't push it. 'And your parents? What *is* wrong with them? If they didn't want to come here, they could have sent something—clothes, flowers, even just a card.'

Julia smiled sadly. 'To me? But why would they do that? I'm strong. I'm able. I'm the one who takes care of everyone else. They don't have to worry about me.'

'They nearly *lost* you,' Zoe argued.

'Apparently my mother is OK with loss. Look what she's done to you.'

'We're estranged.'

'Estrangement implies a mutual distancing, but you still send her cards and gifts. The door's open on your end.'

'OK. She disowned me.'

'*Why?*' Julia asked. But it was a rhetorical question, asked often in the past. She was startled when an answer came now.

'Way back,' Zoe said, 'we loved the same man.'

Julia gasped. 'But Janet is so much older than you.'

'Men can be with someone far younger, and no one looks twice.'

'Who was it?' Julia asked, scrambling to do the figuring. The maths didn't work out. 'You were twelve when I was born. My parents were

394

married then. You would have been too young before that.'

'It wasn't before. It was after.'

'*After*. My mother fell in love with someone *else*?' The thought was barely out when her eyes widened. Her voice fell to an astonished whisper. 'You and *Dad*?'

'You all used to come here to see me. I was twenty-seven when Janet had a problem at work and had to leave early, but George stayed on. You and the boys kept busy. If the three of you weren't at the beach, you were hanging out at the island store.' She looked up at Julia. 'I'd always thought him *the* nicest man, and then, there he was, trying to adjust to having a wife with a burgeoning career. He was vulnerable.'

'Did anything *happen*?' Julia whispered.

Zoe let out a breath. She nodded.

Julia was stunned. Zoe and her father. 'And Mom found out.'

'Not from me, that's for sure.'

'*Dad* told her?'

'Apparently he couldn't live with the guilt. He's very sweet.'

'Then you don't hate him?'

'Because he chose Janet over me? How could I hate him? Janet is a remarkable woman. And look at the life he had with her. He had the three of you, had the house, had a social life.'

'Oh, Zoe. I'm so sorry.'

'No, Julia. I'm the one who's sorry. If I'd said no, nothing would have happened. And if nothing had happened, you all would still be coming up here to visit, I'd have family, and Janet would be talking with you now.'

Julia felt a burst of anger. 'How *stupid* to be holding a grudge all this time. She got the man. She won. You lost. Doesn't she see that?'

'I'm sure she does,' Zoe said reasonably. 'That's probably why she let you kids keep on coming to visit. But only you kids.'

'It seemed perfectly natural, with us old enough to travel alone. I assumed they used the time to be together.'

'They probably did.'

'With an ulterior motive,' Julia charged.

'Can you blame your mother?' Zoe asked. 'Think about it. She's behaving just like women with straying husbands behave all the time. The affair can end, and be well and truly done. The husband can be attentive and adoring for years, but let him be unexpectedly late coming home from work, and the wife's thoughts shoot off in one direction, and one direction only. Trust can be rebuilt, but it's like a heart. Once there's been an attack, there's always a vulnerability.'

Julia knew that truth all too well. She had been feeling vulnerable with Monte for a very long time.

Fog was hovering still when the ferry motored out of the harbour. Today's ferry was bigger, meaning it should be safer. Heavy and wide, it had an enclosed area with seats, plus benches out front and a small upper deck. Carrying two cars in its stern, it ploughed through the water with remarkable steadiness.

Outside, in the bow, Julia's heart was hammering.

'Mom?' Molly asked. 'You OK?'

Julia took her hand. 'I'll be fine.'

And she was. Another five minutes, the fog began to thin, and Rockland emerged crystal clear, lit by the sun. The ferry dropped her gates and let off the cars. Passengers followed.

Joyful to be alive, Julia was in high spirits. Molly loved to shop, so shop they did. They explored every store in Rockland, then fetched the car and drove north to Camden for more. Molly was in her glory, picking one article of clothing after another from shelves and racks, all for Julia. And Julia indulged. She bought jeans. She bought T-shirts. She bought shorts and slacks, and a quilted blazer not unlike the one she had lost. She bought a fleece robe, a nightgown, and nice underwear.

But she baulked when Molly dragged her inside the camera store.

'I don't think so, Molly.'

'Didn't Dad tell you to replace what you lost?'

'I'm not sure I want to.'

'Why not? He owes it to you.'

Julia felt a twinge. 'Your father doesn't *owe* me anything.'

'Yes, he does. He thinks about work, while you think about everything else. You've given your life to him.'

'And it's not been a bad life,' Julia pointed out. 'I have a beautiful daughter and a beautiful home. Most women would give anything to have a husband who treats her like your father treats me.'

Molly made a dismissive sound.

'*Molly*,' Julia whispered, uneasy now, 'what *is* this about?'

Molly held up a slender hand. 'I'm just annoyed with Dad. OK? I'm just down on men. I still think you should get a camera. You used your point-and-shoot to death.'

The temptation was great. Julia moved to the display case. 'I'd like to see this, please,' she said to the salesman.

Molly laced her fingers in delight. 'Oh, *good*.'

An hour later, Julia drove onto the ferry. Molly wanted to go to the upper deck, where the air was warm. With no fog in sight, Julia went up on top, and though she monitored the nearby boats, she felt quite safe.

The ferry docked. Julia had just driven the car onto Big Sawyer when

Molly said, 'Stop here,' and directed her to a parking space. 'I have to run into the Grill for a minute.' Julia settled back in her seat to enjoy the first quiet moments she'd had in hours. But as quickly as that, the restlessness was back. Opening the door, she swung her legs out. She glanced at the Grill, her watch, the pier.

Then, snatching up her new camera, she climbed out of the car.

She had spotted the *Leila Sue* pulling into its slip when the ferry entered the harbour. Turning down that arm of the dock, she singled it out. Noah was hosing down the boat, cleaning up after a day's work. From midchest down he was covered by wet yellow oilskins. Wide bands cinched them at the shin above big rubber boots.

He didn't see Julia, who stopped just shy of the boat. She was aching to take a picture. The boat was long, with the same up-curved bow and low stern as other boats nearby, the same flat rail and rubber-skidded platform. The wheelhouse was enclosed on three sides, front windows angled open. Steps led to the cabin, and a console housed the throttle, screens and gauges. There was no seat at the wheel. Immediately to the right were long hooks, winches and pulleys. In the centre of the boat, bolted to the floor, was a worktable; Noah was washing that down now.

He happened to look up. For a split second, his face was intent, blue eyes as dark as the North Atlantic. Then, incredibly, he smiled.

'Hi,' he said, and continued with his work.

She smiled and stepped forwards to watch. He was quite handsome—every bit in control of his work. After a minute, he turned off the water and coiled the hose.

'Was the catch good today?'

'Not bad.' He tossed his gloves towards the wheelhouse. 'Pretty good, actually. Most of my traps were full.'

'Not all?' she teased.

'Nope.'

'Why not?'

He shrugged. 'Bad place? Bad bait? Vandalism? You choose.'

'Vandalism? Oh, don't say that.'

'I don't want to say it, but a couple of my traps were bone empty. Two in a string, like someone pulled the line and helped himself.'

'I thought there was honour among fishermen.'

He kicked off the boots and slipped out of the oilskins. 'Once in a while, you get bad guys. We're working on it.' He hung the oilskins inside the wheelhouse and caught up a towel.

'What does "working on it" mean?' she asked.

He stepped into clogs as each foot was dried. 'Trying to get a message to the offending party.'

'The fruit guys?' When he gave her a quizzical look, she said, 'Matthew Crane told me.' She had another thought. 'Is this a gear war?'

'Not yet, but it could become one if they ignore the message. It could get ugly. Part of me's itching for it.' He angled his chin towards her camera. 'Been playing tourist on the mainland?'

'Uh-huh. Clothes shopping, mostly.'

'How'd it feel?' he asked. Those dark blue eyes were sober. He wasn't talking about the mainland or the shopping. This was why she had come to see him.

'The ride out was hard,' she admitted.

'I'm avoiding the place where the boats went down. How're you sleeping?'

'Badly. Dreams wake me.'

He moved closer to the gunwale. 'I wake up restless. Like there's something I'm supposed to do. Like something's unfinished.'

'That is so what I feel,' she said in relief. 'Does your work calm you?'

'There's more to do, working alone. It keeps my mind busy.'

'Where's your dog? Doesn't he go out with you?'

'Sure does, only he runs off when it's time to clean up. There he is.' Two slips down, Lucas sat on a stern platform, looking at Noah. 'He's not much help with cleaning up, or with catching lobster, for that matter.'

'Can I help?' she asked.

He gave her a once-over . 'You're . . . slight. Lobstering takes strength.'

'I'm not a weakling. And I really would like to see how you catch lobsters. Besides, it'll occupy my mind.'

'Until you figure out what you're supposed to be doing?'

She smiled sadly. 'Yes. Until then. Have you seen Kim Colella?'

'No. You?'

'I'm not sure I'd recognise her. I only saw her when they brought her in after the accident.'

'You didn't see her in the boat?'

'No. Do you think she's feeling the things we are?'

He shrugged. 'I don't know. She still isn't talking.'

'Maybe she'd talk with me, my being a woman and all. Is she getting professional help?'

'Counselling? I doubt it. The Colellas wouldn't go for something like that.' His gaze shifted. She followed it in time to see Molly start down his arm of the dock. The girl's cheeks were flushed.

'I did it,' she said with a smug smile as she reached Julia.

'Did what?' Julia asked.

'Convinced Rick Greene to hire me. I told him a couple of things he could do with lobster and said I'd work for free. It was a no-brainer.' She grinned. 'So I'm here for as long as you are, chaperoning.'

'Chaperoning,' Julia repeated quizzically.

'Making sure you're all right.' Molly turned to Noah with something that, to Julia, looked suspiciously like a challenge. 'I'm Molly.' She extended her hand. 'And you're Noah.'

Noah put out his hand. When the handshake was done, Molly said, 'Thank you for saving my mother's life.'

'I didn't do that.'

'She believes you did, and that's all that counts.' Dismissing him, she took Julia's arm. 'I have to go back and shower. I'm starting tonight.'

Julia stood her ground. She pulled the keys from her pocket. 'You go on up. When you get back here, I'll take the car myself.'

'You're staying?' Molly asked. 'Here? On the dock?'

'I want to play with my camera,' Julia said. She gave Noah an apologetic smile. 'Could I photograph the boat?'

'Be my guest. Me, I need a shower and food.' Noah ducked inside the cabin and came up with a logbook and his Thermos, a sweatshirt, and a cooler. Whistling for the dog, he used the rail as a step to the pier, then lifted a hand in farewell.

Noah let himself into the house, picked up the kitchen phone, and punched out Sandi's number.

'Hello?' she said.

'It's me.' He struggled to sound kind. 'Ian never called.'

There was a pause, then a resigned, 'I know. He and I had a big fight about it. I think it really bothered him that Hutch died, but he refused to deal with it. When I said he should go up for the funeral, he argued about all the important things in *his* life that *you've* missed. He didn't understand why he should be there with you.'

'Not me. His grandfather.'

'I told him that. And I told him you wanted him there, but let's face it, Noah. You didn't ask him yourself. You sat and waited for him to call. You could have pestered a little. Sometimes with kids this age, issuing orders is all that works.'

'I'm issuing an order, then. He's to come up next week.'

'Noah, he starts *summer* school next week. I told you that!'

'You said there were two sessions. He can spend three weeks here, then go back for the second session.'

'We were going to look at colleges then.'

'Do it afterwards.'

'Can't. I have faculty orientation programmes to run then. Besides, Ian doesn't *want* to look at colleges.'

'Well, there's your answer,' Noah said. 'If I change his mind, either I'll take him looking, or you can do it in the fall.'

Sandi was silent, before asking a suspicious, 'Why do you want to do this? Ian's going to want to know. Is it because Hutch is gone and Ian's all you have left? Or because you really want to spend time in his company? Or because you need help with the boat and he is free labour?'

Noah hadn't thought out the details. 'He's my son. I want him here. Where is he now?'

'At Adam's for the night. He'll be back in the morning. Elevenish. He won't be pleased, Noah. Do you want him to call you?'

'No. I'll call him.'

Determined, he called on Thursday morning at eleven. What Noah got wasn't so much hostility as indifference. Ian was neutral to the point of being remote. Noah had his work cut out for him.

At the same time that they were talking, Julia was driving to the southern tip of the head. Here, bordering the town beach, were streets of bungalows, all in a row.

Kimmie Colella lived in one of these. It had the same beachy feel as the others, with the same battered shutters, the same rangy lawn. Parking on the street, Julia followed a sandy path through the grass. There was no doorbell, so she knocked.

The woman who answered didn't seem much older than Julia, which made it hard for Julia to decide whether she was the mother or the grandmother. She had pale, strawberry-blonde hair twisted on top of her head and a pair of sunglasses on top of that. She wore a blouse and jeans, and the sun had toughened her skin to a leathery sheen. Brown eyes skewered Julia.

Julia smiled. 'I'm Julia Bechtel, Zoe Ballard's niece. I was in the boat—'

'Uh-huh. What can I do for you?'

'I wondered how Kim is doing.'

'She's doing fine.'

'She isn't fine,' came another voice, and another woman appeared. The family resemblance was there—pale reddish hair, brown eyes, but the face was less hard. 'I'm Kim's mother, Nancy, and this is my mother, June. Kimmie still won't talk.'

'She's stubborn,' June said crossly.

'She needs time.' Nancy looked at Julia. 'She just sits up on the bluff staring out at the water. She has me worried sick.'

'Would she talk to me, do you think?'

Nancy raised her shoulders. 'It can't hurt to try.'

Returning to her car, Julia headed north. The bluff was the highest point at the back of the head, a mass of granite, rearing above a tumble of rock to the sea. An automated lighthouse stood watch, its keeper's house long decayed.

Pulling up beside the ruins, Julia parked behind a small blue Honda. The instant she opened her door, the roar of the surf came full force. Leaning into a stiff breeze, she climbed over a short stretch of granite to the lighthouse, but it wasn't until she was past it that she saw anyone there, and then she wondered if she had the wrong person. The one sitting out on the rocks was small, childlike, knees drawn up to her chest. But it wasn't the pose that was odd.

It was the hair. It was bright red. What was odd was that Julia always noticed hair. She noticed it when she was at the gym, when she was out to lunch, when she was at the theatre. She had always been attuned to hair.

She didn't remember seeing anyone in the stern of the *Amelia Celeste* with red hair. And if Kim had not been in the stern, there was only one other place she could have been.

'Hello!' Julia called loudly enough to be heard over the surf.

Kim looked round quickly. Her face was pale, her eyes blank.

Julia stopped ten feet from the girl. Just as on the night of the accident, she couldn't think of Kimmie Colella as a woman. Then, she had been a sopping figure swathed in a blanket, her hair colour muted by water and night. She now wore jeans and a sweatshirt, but she looked smaller and more forlorn. That vivid red hair was as straight as Julia's, though longer. In the wind, it became a shifting veil.

'I'm Julia Bechtel. I was on the *Amelia Celeste*.'

Kim's eyes held hers for a minute. They fell to her clothes, studying, and went to her car. Then they returned to the sea.

Julia came closer. 'I've been wondering how you are.' She squatted on a nearby rock. 'There are three of us who survived—you, me and Noah Prine. He and I talk every so often. We have this thing in common. It's not often that people survive accidents that take so many other lives.'

Long strands of silky red hair blew over Kim's cheek. She tucked them back behind her ear.

'I'm here to visit Zoe Ballard,' Julia went on. 'She's my aunt, but more like a friend, since we're only twelve years apart. I was initially planning to stay two weeks, but I've extended that. Have you been on a boat since the accident?'

When Kim didn't react, Julia said, 'I was dreading that. But my car was on the mainland, and I needed clothes. There was fog, and I kept waiting for the nose of a purple boat to break through.'

She wanted to ask if Kim woke up with the same image. Only, if Kim hadn't been on the *Amelia Celeste*, but rather on *The Beast*, the question would have been threatening, and that was the last thing Julia wanted to be. Kim might not be speaking, but she was listening. That was something.

'Taking the ferry back, the sun was out, and I was feeling like the ocean might have swallowed me up on Tuesday night and it didn't, so maybe there was a kind of truce between it and me.' Julia paused. With genuine curiosity she asked, 'Do you feel anything like that?'

The girl was somewhere far away. Her eyes were glazed. They suddenly widened. She jerked. Her eyes flew to Julia's.

Oh, yes, she relived the crash. It was there, clear as day.

Gently, Julia said, 'They say that fades with time. I think about why I was spared and what I want to do with my life now. Like I have a chance to be someone different, and I have to decide who that is.' Very quietly, she said, 'Do you feel *any* of that?' Kim met her eyes and there was something so bleak in them that Julia nearly reached for her. She said, 'You and I share something, Kim. We've had an experience that not many people ever have. Talking with you would be therapeutic for me. Maybe you'd get something out of it, too.'

Kim's eyes grew accusatory, and Julia read them well.

'No one sent me here. No one even knows I'm here, other than your mother and grandmother. I guess what I'm saying is that maybe I can help. You're not talking to anyone, but I'm a stranger and an off-islander. If you ever want to talk, I'm as safe a bet as any.' Kim's eyes followed her as she pushed herself to her feet. 'I'm staying at Zoe's. You know where she lives?'

Kim returned to the sea. Not knowing what to do other than momentarily cede defeat, Julia turned quietly and left.

Julia drove back to Zoe's and began to bake. She made Congo Bars this time: brown-sugar batter layered with chocolate and butterscotch bits, coconut flakes, marshmallows and pecans. Julia made them for the Walsh children. As soon as they had cooled enough to be cut into child-size bites and layered in foil, she drove them over.

The children were in the front yard playing in a plastic pool filled with sand. Their aunt sat on the grass nearby. She looked exhausted.

Julia knelt beside her. 'I brought goodies for the kids. How's the packing going?'

'Slow.' Ellen's voice fell to a whisper. 'I'm trying to do it when the girls are asleep. They know they're going to Akron with me, but they think Jeannie, Evan and the baby are meeting us. I try to explain they're in heaven.'

'They're so young. Heaven is only a word.'

A dark-haired three-year-old, Vanessa, climbed out of the sandbox.

She pointed a small finger and asked, 'What's there?'

'Little munchies.'

'I'm hungry.'

Julia unfolded the foil pack. Vanessa watched closely. 'Oooo,' she said, looking up with pretty blue eyes. 'Can I have one?'

'You can.' Julia separated one small bar from the rest. Vanessa bit off a corner, chewed with a thoughtful look, then gave Julia a gooey grin. She pushed the rest of the piece into her mouth.

Her older sister, Annie, joined them. 'What's Nessa eating?'

'It's a Congo Bar,' said Julia, and handed the five-year-old a piece. Then she held the foil pack out to their aunt.

With a tired smile, Ellen shook her head. 'Not much appetite.'

'Want to take off for a little while? I can stay.'

'Would you? There are errands I'd be better doing alone.'

'Go,' Julia said.

For the next two hours, Julia took the girls for a walk through the meadow, read to them, helped them build sandcastles. They were precious children, curious, well behaved and smart. The younger was more physical, holding Julia's hand, sitting on her lap. The older asked questions.

What's this flower? Where's the yellow from? Do you know my mommy? Why's it called a buttercup?

Each in her way, they were needy. They knew something was up. Julia's heart broke for them. When Ellen had returned and it was time to go, Vanessa clung. 'I'll be back,' Julia assured her, holding her tightly for a minute, before whispering in her ear, 'with chocolate chip cookies.'

'I love those,' Vanessa whispered back, but solemnly.

Driving away, Julia thought about love and loss. She hadn't gone far when the thought of her mother loomed before her. Julia couldn't help but think how lucky she was to have her, and how tragic it was they couldn't talk.

Pulling to the side of the road under the shade of an oak, she put down the windows and gave her parents a call.

Her father answered.

'Hi, Dad,' she said tentatively.

'Julia. How's it going?'

'Pretty well, but I need to talk to Mom. Is she there?'

'She's out on the patio.'

'Would you take the cordless to her?'

There was a pause, then a quiet, 'She's relaxing, Julia.'

'Dad, please give her the phone.'

'I'm on your side, Julia. But she's a stubborn woman.'

'Right now, so am I,' Julia decided, and there must have been enough conviction in her voice to give him pause. He put her on hold, and then Janet came on with a curt, 'Yes, Julia.'

Julia's heart beat faster. 'Can we talk?'

'That depends. Is this an apology?'

Julia swallowed. 'If you want it to be.'

Janet was silent.

'I'm sorry, Mom. I don't know what you want me to say. I don't understand why you're so angry.'

'Zoe betrayed me. End of story.'

'Not end of story, because the two of you are still alive. I was just with two little girls who've lost their parents. *That's* the end of a story.'

'Are you trying to reconcile Zoe and me?'

'No. It's me needing to talk, to know you're there and you care.'

'We'll talk when you're back.'

'But I won't be home right away. I need this time.'

'So your father said. Have you told Monte that?'

'He's fine with it.'

'He's your husband. You ought to be with him. Men behave badly when they feel they've been abandoned.'

Exasperated, Julia cried, 'Oh, he *already* behaves badly! Mom, I need to talk about who I am and where I'm going, and what you really think of me, because I haven't done anything like what you've done, and now here I am with half a life ahead of me, and there are things I need to do, only I can't pin them down—and, yes, I want to talk about Monte, because I don't know what to do with my marriage, and you've had experience with this.' She hadn't planned to say the last, would have taken the words back if she could. 'Mom? Are you there, Mom?'

There was no answer. Janet had hung up.

Chapter 6

HEART HEAVY, Julia sat in the car with her hands limp in her lap. A gentle breeze came in one window and went out the other. She felt the breath of it on her skin, but it went no deeper.

She could have used the soothing inside. Everything there was raw, everything in turmoil.

Far down the road, a dark blue truck rounded the curve. It was a recent model, bumpers gleaming even as its tyres kicked back a cloud of dust. It slowed as it neared. Driver's window to driver's window, it stopped.

'Hey,' said Noah, straight-faced as ever. 'You've led me a merry chase.'

Julia felt a tiny lift, a little nudge against the ache in her heart. 'Following me, were you?'

'You look a little down. I'm doing chores. Want to come?'

It was the invitation she needed. Leaving the car without a second thought, she rounded the front of the truck. He had the door open. Lucas slept in a corner of the extended cab. She climbed in and sent Noah a bright smile. 'I'm all set.'

He wagged a finger at the seat belt—which she had forgotten. It got her thinking. 'Here's a question. Would it be possible for us to survive the crash the other night, only to die in a car crash today?'

He shot her a glance. 'Are you feeling immortal?'

'No. But some people who've been through what we have do feel that way. They tempt fate. They take every risk possible.'

'They don't have kids,' he said with some weight.

'I didn't know you did.'

He shifted gears for the cruise down Dobbs Hill. 'I have a son. He's seventeen. He'll be coming up next week.'

'Where does he live?'

'Washington, DC. My ex-wife is an educator.'

'Was she originally from here?'

'No. We met at college. We spent the nine years of our marriage in New York.'

Julia smiled, surprised. 'What did you do in New York?'

'I was an investment banker,' he said.

'You *were*?' Noah was light-years removed in appearance and behaviour from the investment bankers she had met through Monte. 'That's very different from lobstering.'

'Not as different as you'd think. There's the same lone-wolf mentality, the same competitiveness. I was working with MBAs who saw me as a lesser breed because I wasn't one myself.'

Julia knew how that worked. Monte was acutely aware of credentials. And she had no college degree.

'That actually helped me out,' Noah went on. 'If they keep you at arm's length, you can be more independent. I often rowed against the tide, but my instincts were good.'

'Were you always interested in business?'

'Only as it related to lobstering. I figured I'd earn a bundle, invest it, and come back here with no money worries. That's pretty much what I did.'

'What happened to your marriage?'

'I was working nine in the morning to three the next, plus at least one weekend day. When I was home, I didn't have much taste for anything but sleep.'

Julia could see it. Monte didn't work quite those hours, but her friend Charlotte's husband did. Charlotte had bought a boutique precisely to fill the void left by his absence.

'I'm sorry,' she said, feeling oddly responsible, as a New Yorker, for the kind of life that ate people alive.

'Don't be. My marriage was never that strong. My only regret is Ian. I'm never quite sure what to say to him.'

'How long will he be here?'

'Three weeks.'

'Does he come every summer?'

'No. This is the first.'

'Could he not come for the funeral?'

'Didn't *want* to.'

'Oh dear.'

'My fault,' Noah said. 'I should have called him directly and said I wanted him here. I guess I wasn't up for a fight.'

Julia looked out of her side window. They were on a flat road that skirted the far side of the harbour. In the absence of shade trees, the road was bleached by the sun and worn by salty air.

'Tell me about Kim,' Julia said quietly.

'Did you see her?' he asked with what she thought was caution.

'This morning, up on the bluff. I wasn't prepared for her hair.'

'All that red.'

'I don't remember seeing it on the *Amelia Celeste.* I always notice hair. I was thinking maybe she was inside the wheelhouse, but she'd have died in the crash, don't you think?'

'Maybe not. Did she say anything?'

'Not a word.'

He slid her a glance. 'Is that what had you so sad back there?'

'That. And the Walsh girls. Actually, mostly my mother.'

'Is she sick?'

'Oh, no. She's well—and strong-willed as ever. I had been talking with her before you drove up. Talking. That's putting it nicely.'

'You argued. Is it chronic?'

'No. I'm usually the good daughter. Not for the last month, though. She thinks I should be back in New York with my husband. But I came here for me, and I'm staying for me, and I want my mother's support. Why does her opinion matter so much?'

'Because you're a caring person. It's written all over you.'

They were heading in the direction of Hawks Hill, the island's south-ernmost hill. There were no meadows here; it was an ascent through pure forest, heavily shaded. Dark, Julia thought, and felt a chill. 'So what about Kim?' she asked. 'I keep imagining that she wasn't on the *Amelia Celeste* at all. If she was having an affair with Artie, wouldn't it be more likely that she was on *The Beast*?'

Noah took a breath. 'That would mean she was likely the one who shot him. If they were involved, he may have promised to divorce his wife. It couldn't have gone anywhere good. That means she'd have motive.'

'Would she have access to a gun?'

'Probably.'

Letting that reality sink in, Julia watched the road. Every few min-utes, a gap in the trees showed a narrow drive, some were marked by mailboxes, others by name signs. Noah turned right onto a dirt road groomed with sand. At its end stood a house.

It was an A-frame, small with clean lines. Roofed in dark slate, its cedar siding had weathered a natural silver. There were blinds on the windows and a wraparound porch with Adirondack chairs.

A carport was tucked under the trees, a depleted wood bin against its side. Noah backed up to unload his truck bed, but before starting the task, he gestured her towards the house. The air here was dry, lighter, more . . . happy. He had a key out by the time they reached the door.

And suddenly it struck her. 'Is this yours?' It was the feel of the place—appropriate for the setting, yet somehow different. Noah was that way—appropriate, yet different.

He opened the door and stood aside for her to enter. 'I built it when I left New York. I lived here until my mother died. Then my dad needed tending.'

The house was simple. Living room, dining room, kitchen—there were no walls between them, just a comfortable collection of leather chairs, built-in appliances, and a round oak table with ladder-back chairs. A single large rug covered slatted wood floors; she guessed it to be Tibetan, knew it to be expensive. Above were lofts. One had a pair of beds, the other a desk, complete with computer.

'There's more downstairs, built into the hill,' he said. He pointed behind two leather chairs. 'The stairs are back there. Take a look.'

Holding a wide railing, she started down. The flight turned left, and there was suddenly more light than she would have expected. More *room*. There was a bathroom here, and a walk-in closet. Primarily, though, this was a bedroom.

A large bed sat on a rug hooked in myriad shades of blue. It had a simple white spread and enough pillows to prop more than one person up for the view—a wall of French doors with a view of the world. An expanse of sky and sea so seamlessly merged that the horizon was lost. More shades of blue than she could name—blue spruce, blue sky, blue sea, blue land. Gold sunset skimmed in over waves from the west.

She went up the stairs. 'This is a fabulous place. How often do you stay here?'

'Not often enough. I drop by to use the computer.'

'Will you stay here now that your dad's gone?'

'Not yet. I want Ian to know the other place. That's his heritage, y'know?'

'Will he be your sternman?'

'If he can hack it.'

Leaving the house, they went to the back of the truck. Noah loaded his arms with wood, carried it to the bin and stacked it. Julia loaded up her own arms, smiled, and passed him by.

'You'll mess up your nice new T-shirt,' he called.

'It'll wash,' she called back.

Soon enough, they were back on the road. The sun gilded the tips of the spruces as they descended Hawks Hill and headed towards Dobbs Hill and her car. His headlights were on. Dusk was heavy and low.

'About Kim?' she asked softly. 'Do you think I ought to do something? Should we go to the police?'

He was slow in answering, clearly reluctant. 'I hate to do that before Kim starts talking again.'

'If we say nothing, are we obstructing justice?'

'Not unless we know something for sure.' He shot her a glance. 'Why don't you try talking with her again? I'll push John and see what his investigation's turning up. A pistol would be nice, registered to a third party.'

Suddenly he slowed the truck. His headlights picked out several cars haphazardly gathered ahead. It was a minute in the stone blue of dusk before she recognised her SUV and Zoe's truck, along with the little Plymouth that Molly had taken to driving. The police cruiser was parked beside them.

Noah pulled up close behind. Julia was barely out of the truck when Molly started running towards her. She stopped just beyond reach, staring in horror.

'I found your car,' she said in breathless accusation. 'I sat here for ever, waiting for you. I can't tell you what I thought.'

Julia could understand Molly's fear, but only to a point. This was the island, after all, not the city. And she wasn't a helpless ninny. 'What did you think?'

'That you'd been abducted. Or done something strange.'

Julia was taken aback. 'Strange, like what?'

'I don't know. You were supposed to be back. I drove home, and you weren't there.'

Zoe approached. 'She was frightened. She called John.'

'Why were you gone so *long?*' Molly asked.

'My fault,' Noah offered. 'I passed her on the road and conned her into helping me run a few errands.'

Molly's mouth settled into a straight line. Seconds later, she turned on her heel and strode to the Plymouth.

Julia caught up with her. She kept her voice low. 'Molly, what is it?'

'This doesn't look good, that's all. You and him.'

Julia was offended. 'What are you implying?'

'Maybe there's *double* reason Dad's back in New York.'

'Double reason? Did you see something last week?'

Molly drew herself straighter. 'He's lonely. You should go back. You need to be there.'

'Was someone with him?' It wouldn't be the first time.

'You need to *be* there,' Molly repeated, and climbed into the car.

Julia leaned down to window level. 'You didn't answer me.'

'I have to get to work,' she said, and drove off.

Julia walked towards her car, but John Roman said, 'Hold up. I have your things.' At the back of the cruiser, he opened the trunk. Her leather bag was deformed, yet recognisable. She could only assume that the large rubbish bag with it contained the remnants of her other belongings.

The next morning Julia went to the barn early. Zoe had a rabbit on the grooming table and was working a wire brush through its fur. 'Are you all right?' Zoe asked.

Julia crossed the old wood floor and kissed the top of Zoe's head. 'I am. Thank you. How about you? My visit keeps growing more complicated for you.'

'I'm not complaining.'

'Were you up when Molly got back?'

'Um-hmm. She's still angry.'

If anyone has a right to be angry, it's me, Julia thought. She was the one whose integrity had been wrongly questioned.

'So what's going on between you and Monte?' Zoe's eyes were frank.

Zoe had to be suspecting the truth after Molly's behaviour out on the road. Julia let out a breath. 'I'd say that familiarity breeds contempt, only there isn't contempt. Monte and I are perfectly friendly when we're together. It's just that we rarely are. I was hoping it would change after

Molly left. I was hoping there'd be emotional involvement.'

'Are you still in love at all?'

'He's my husband.' Julia didn't know what other answer to give. She didn't hate Monte—should, perhaps, but she didn't.

'Has he been faithful?'

Julia held Zoe's searching gaze, which was answer in and of itself.

'You seem calm,' Zoe finally said.

'Now maybe, but I wasn't always. I cried. I shook. I felt used. I felt *worthless.*'

'Do you still?'

'Sometimes. How not to wonder whether if I'd been a little smarter, a little sexier, a little more of a dynamo, he'd have been satisfied at home?'

'Some men need conquest. Is he in love with someone?'

'I don't think so. He has short flings.'

'Do you confront him?'

Julia made a soft sound of self-derision. Confrontation was something she had spent a lifetime avoiding. 'He knows I've suspected it.'

'Why do you stay?' Zoe asked.

'Because there's been good *reason* to stay. There's Molly. There's financial security. There's a way of life. Monte has been my job for twenty years. He's what I *do.*'

'But you came up here for two weeks, maybe more. That's a longer break than you've ever taken. Is he with someone now?'

'I don't know. I'm afraid Molly saw something when she showed up unexpectedly.'

'Caught him with a woman?'

'Yes.'

'Have you asked?'

'Indirectly. But how blunt can I be? Forget putting her in the position of telling on one parent to the other; if I ask bluntly, it suggests doubt on my part, and once doubt has been voiced, it never goes away. It creates insecurity. I never wanted that for Molly.'

'Is that what you felt when I told you about George and me?'

'Insecurity? No. I'm not starry-eyed, like I was at Molly's age.'

'A jaded lady at forty,' Zoe teased. 'You're like Janet in a way, you know.'

'I am not.'

'Yes, you are. When something is troublesome, you opt out. Isn't that what Janet always did? When raising a family became a nightmare of custodial arrangements, she withdrew into her work and ceded the responsibility to you and George.'

'What responsibility am I ceding?' Julia argued.

'Responsibility for your marriage.'

'Excuse me, Zoe. Monte's the cheater.'

'You're allowing it.'

'By leaving him alone in the house?' Julia asked. 'Well, maybe I'm just giving him just enough rope to hang himself.' Her voice began to rise. 'Maybe I'm begging him to show his true stripes. Maybe I'm ready. Maybe I didn't even know that when I planned this trip. Maybe the accident brought it all out.' She took a quick breath and went on in the same high pitch. 'I don't know. I don't *know*. But I do know that it's my life and I'm not so obedient—or stupid—that I'm oblivious to his affairs, but I'll deal with them in a way that works for me. It might not work for you or for someone else,' she tapped her chest, 'but it's *my* life.'

Zoe smiled. 'That, my dear, is the most force I've ever heard from you.'

Julia exhaled. 'You riled me.'

'I'm glad. You're too nice sometimes.'

'I meant what I said. I will deal with it, but when I'm ready.'

'I know.'

You're *like Janet in a way, you know. When something is troublesome, you opt out.* Julia thought about what Zoe said a lot in the ensuing hours. Molly slept on. It was only when noon neared that Julia realised she was doing precisely what Zoe had accused. Sitting back passively, waiting for Molly to wake up. So she went to Molly's room—and found her wide awake, propped up in bed, reading.

'Hey,' Julia said with a smile. 'And here I thought you were still asleep.'

Molly didn't return the smile. Her eyes said, *So I'm awake. What do you want?*

Julia hadn't seen that look in years. 'How's work going?'

'Fine.' She returned to her book.

'What're you reading?' Julia tried—and realised she was attempting to cajole Molly into speaking her mind, rather than raising the issue herself.

'Stephen King,' Molly said. 'You wouldn't like it.'

Julia went to the bed. 'We need to talk.'

Molly pushed the book down. 'Not you and me. You and Dad. If you're cheating on each other, that's your choice. But it's embarrassing to be told one thing and see another.'

'I am not cheating on your father,' Julia said. 'I have *never* cheated on your father.'

Molly tried to raise her book again. Julia held it down.

'Talk to me, Molly. Tell me what happened last Monday night.'

Molly stared across the room. Julia saw unhappiness, and suddenly the possibility of raising doubt seemed less risky than keeping silent.

'I think someone was there. With him. Your father may not have explained it well—'

Molly's eyes stopped her cold. 'She was in his *bed*. What other explanation could there *be*?'

Julia let out a dismayed breath and sank down on the bed.

'Didn't you *know*?' Molly asked. 'What did you *think* would happen when you went away for two weeks?'

Julia was a minute in processing her daughter's words. This young woman with the boy's haircut and the accusatory look felt like a stranger. 'Are you blaming *me*? Like, if I'd been there, this wouldn't have happened? Do you think this is the first time?' she asked, gloves off now. Molly was an adult, and half-truths were dangerous things. 'Well, it's happened before, Molly, and that's something I have to deal with. Me. Not you. Me.'

Molly's eyes filled with tears. 'Are you divorcing him?'

'I don't know.'

The book fell aside when Molly sat up quickly. 'And you're going to find out *here*? I was right last night. You have to go back. You have to fight for him, Mom. If you want your marriage to last, you're going to have to let him know.'

Quietly, Julia pushed herself up. The pleading on the girl's face nearly broke her heart. Had Molly been younger, Julia would have done almost anything to keep the marriage intact. She *had* done just that, all those years. But Molly was grown, and Julia had to think about herself. Unfortunately, she hadn't had much practice at it.

Stay and argue? Leave and wait?

Unsure, she let herself out of the room, leaving the door ajar.

Molly slammed it shut when she was barely halfway down the hall.

Needing an escape, Julia got in the car and drove to the photography studio of Tony Hammel. Dominated by wide windows and large skylights, it was a rambling contemporary structure high on Dobbs Hill. Small cabins dotted the woods, housing for students who attended week-long workshops. Had it not been for the crash of the *Amelia Celeste*, Julia would have been one of them. Wandering through the studio now, catching bits of lectures given by Tony and others, studying the photographs on the walls, she was inspired.

Late that afternoon, determined to take advantage of the drama of oblique light and long shadows, she drove to the harbour with her camera. By the time she reached it, though, fog had rolled in, which meant that there would be no drama in the pattern of dock pilings, stone walls or wood shingles. These were the kinds of things Tony's students had photographed. Truth be told, Julia was more interested in watching the lobstermen return from a day's work.

Camera hanging from her shoulder, she wandered down the dock.

A pair of lobstermen pulled into a slip. One was grey-haired under a ratty baseball hat, weathered and large in his oilskins. The other was smaller and, even with no hair at all, clearly younger. She pegged them to be father and son.

They secured the boat, produced scrubbing brushes and hoses, and began to clean. Within minutes, a lather was spreading.

Unable to resist, Julia went closer. 'Do you pump fresh water out from shore to do this?'

The older man spoke. 'No sense doin' that. Salt water's just fine.' Words and intonation—both were pure Maine.

'Do you have to use special soap?'

'Well, the wife calls it that when she tries to con me into doin' the dishes.' He looked at the younger. 'What's your mother use? Joy?'

'Dawn,' said the son. 'Dish soap. It'll lather in salt water.'

'Ah,' Julia said with a smile. 'Thanks.'

She would have loved to take pictures of them working, but she was grateful enough for their friendliness not to push her luck. She watched them work a little longer, then she moved on.

Other boats returned, some to slips, some to moorings. Sitting on the edge of the dock, she watched fishermen clean up, toss their coolers and sweatshirts and the occasional lobster trap into waiting dinghies, and motor to the pier.

'That camera work?' asked a voice.

Julia turned to see a man approaching. He wore glasses and a shirt splotched with green paint.

'It does.'

He gestured that she should follow, and led her down an arm of the pier to where several men stood in a clump. Two lobster traps were on the dock, both badly damaged.

'We need pictures for evidence,' said the father from before.

Julia took one picture, then a second. She moved to a different angle for a third, moved in closer and took a fourth.

'See how the net inside's been torn?' asked the bespectacled man. 'Can you get a picture of that?' While Julia did, he talked quietly. 'See the funnel shapes? Ideally, the lobster comes in through the wide part and gets the bait. When he can't go back, he goes through the next funnel into the other part of the trap, and he's stuck here. Problem is, with the net torn, the lobster turns around and walks out. These traps came up empty—no lobster, no bait. When can you get us pictures?'

'Tomorrow morning,' Julia said, thinking to print them tonight. 'Am I giving them to you?'

'No. Give them to Noah.'

Julia knew, in that instant, why the men on the pier had been willing to talk with her. Someone had seen her and Noah together the evening before—John Roman, certainly—and word had spread. These men assumed she would be seeing him again, and soon.

With Molly's accusations still fresh, Julia almost denied it. Then she caught herself. She and Noah were friends in the most innocent of ways. She welcomed an excuse to see him. Besides, she liked it when the lobstermen talked with her. It made her feel part of something. If her connection with Noah won her acceptance, it wasn't such a bad thing.

Chapter 7

JULIA WOKE before dawn. Tiptoeing to the bathroom, she cleaned her face and teeth, brushed her hair, and put on her wedding band. Pulling on a sweatshirt and jeans, she slipped out of the house and headed for town.

She parked at the pier and, camera and tripod in hand, wandered from spot to spot. Choosing the landing at the top of the stairs to the Grill, she set up and took a look.

The harbour was quiet, the water as gentle as she had ever seen it. Lobster boats rocked at their moorings; those in slips seemed simply to rise and fall with each breath of the sea. In this predawn dark, with the headlights of pick-ups raking the dock, the shadows of sleepy lobstermen carrying their gear, and lights going on in one wheelhouse after another, Julia found her drama.

She photographed from the distance, then zoomed in. She captured men rowing to their boats, and those boats motoring out to sea. The light bled from purple to pink.

When she refocused on the dock, she saw Noah. He stood with his hands on his hips, looking directly up at her. She straightened and smiled, feeling inordinately pleased when he left his gear and trotted up the stairs. 'Isn't it early to be doing this kind of thing?'

'Not if you want to photograph the harbour coming to life.'

'Are you always up at dawn?'

'In New York, never. Here, it could become a habit.'

He paused and grew serious. 'About the other night? I'm sorry if I caused a problem.'

'The problem's not your doing.'

'Did you work it out?'

She sighed. 'If you're asking whether my daughter accepts that I'm a grown woman with a right to run errands with whomever I choose, I doubt it. In fairness, though, there are other issues involved.' She reached into her camera bag and pulled out the photos she had printed. 'These are for you.'

'Thanks,' he said with an appreciative smile. 'Actually, the chief of police would love you to email these to him. Think you can?'

'Of course.'

'That'd be great.' He tapped the photos against the rail. 'They found a revolver in the wreck of *The Beast*. It was registered to Artie.'

Julia's eyes widened. 'Was it the one that shot him?'

'They don't know for sure. Short of finding a bullet in debris from *The Beast*, they can only speculate. But there's another twist. Artie was under investigation for smuggling illegal immigrants.'

'On *The Beast*?' Julia asked in disbelief. Forget stealth; a boat like that would announce itself everywhere it went.

'They suspect he arranged for other boats to do the work.'

'Illegal immigrants.'

'Some used as mules. Carrying enough drugs to make it worth Artie's while.'

'Could the shooting have been related to that?'

'They're assuming it. Problem is, there's no other body with the wreck, no sign anyone was with him at the house.'

'At least the gun wasn't Kim's,' Julia said.

'Far as I know, no one but us knows she wasn't on the *Amelia Celeste*.'

'Amazing, if she was on *The Beast*, that she survived the crash.'

'She could have been on the sun platform at the very back of the boat. She'd have gone flying off at the first impact.'

'Maybe it's time I visit the bluff again.'

By the time she got there, the weather had turned, bringing cool air and rain. Until Julia saw the small blue Honda by the ruins of the keeper's house, she wasn't even sure Kim would be there. She finally spotted her tucked in beside the porch. She wore a yellow slicker, but the hood was down. Red hair, pale face, small hands—everything was wet.

Tugging up the hood of her own slicker, Julia took an insulated bag from the car and walked towards Kim.

'Hi,' she called as she approached. 'I figured something warm was called for on a day like this.' Several feet from Kim, she set down the bag, unzipped it, and pulled out a bag of cookies. 'Fresh from my oven,' she said. Extracting two travel mugs filled with coffee, she offered one to Kim. 'I figured if you were anything like my daughter, you'd take it with cream and sugar.'

Kim took the mug. Ignoring the rain, Julia sat down on the ground, opened the bag of cookies, and held it out. Kim took one. Julia sipped her coffee. Kim finished the cookie and took a second. Speaking seemed unnecessary. It was beautiful there on the bluff in the rain.

After a time, quite spontaneously, Julia said, 'This is a special place. It's kind of like you're away from everything up here.'

Kim nodded. She took another cookie.

Julia said, 'I don't know what it is about this island. I've felt something since the first time I was here. I was twelve. Zoe had just moved here, and we used to come for a week or two at a time.'

There had been rainy days then, too, and she hadn't minded at all. She remembered once sitting at the end of the town dock and letting the rain soak her. She was wearing a bathing suit and must have been sixteen.

'Sixteen was a big summer for me,' she reminisced. 'That was when I became aware of men. Boys, actually, but they did look like men to me. Big Sawyer grows them rugged. I remember sitting in the rain in my wet bathing suit and wondering if the boys cared to look. I didn't have the nerve to look and see. I looked at them plenty, even took pictures of them. Do the local boys still have that rope tattooed around their biceps?'

Kim nodded.

'That was a turnon,' Julia mused. 'Where I grew up, only bad boys had tattoos. I kept the pictures all those years. I actually brought them with me. They recovered my shoulder bag from the crash site—but I can't get myself to open it. Everything after feels like a different life.' She paused. The girl was watching her closely. 'You don't feel that, do you.' It wasn't exactly a question.

Kim's head shake was barely a spasm.

'If you could go anywhere,' Julia tried, 'anywhere in the world, where would you go?' The question seemed important. 'I think about that a lot. I always imagined I could stay here for ever.'

Kim shot her a horrified look.

'No?' Julia asked. 'You'd leave?'

Kim nodded.

'Why?' she asked. Then, 'What would you do? Who would you be?' She gave a diffident snort. 'I'm a fine one to ask that. Who would I be? I haven't a clue.'

Julia wished she wanted to be a lawyer. She could see herself doing family law or even legal aid work, either of which would be rewarding enough to compensate for Monte's infidelity. Or she could become an accountant. She was good at maths. Or she could take a job in her friend Charlotte's store.

If she did any of those things, she might craft a life that would allow her to leave her marriage intact. That would please Molly. It might even please Monte. It would surely please her parents.

But would it please *her*?

Shy of an answer, she spent Saturday afternoon alternating between the rabbits in the barn and her photo printer in the house, and spent Saturday evening with Zoe and her friends. These things kept her busy enough so that she didn't dwell on the fact that Molly was coming and going without a word. On Sunday morning, Ellen Hamilton called, desperate for help. Julia was happy to oblige.

Bearing a fresh batch of cookies, she drove to the weathered farmhouse. The front yard was filled with cars. A U-Haul was backed up to the door, and an army of friends was carting furniture and boxes from house to van.

The girls were off in the side yard, playing with a woman Julia had met just the night before with Zoe. Ellen rushed out of the house, sandy hair flying, looking frantic.

'Thank you so much for coming,' she said. 'Deanna's been with the kids, but she has to leave, and the rest of us are trying to finish so I can make the noon ferry, and the girls just love you.' Even as she spoke, Vanessa ran to Julia, tipped her head back, and grinned.

Julia scooped her up. 'How's my little sweetie?'

'Good,' Vanessa said and curled an arm round her neck. 'D'ya bring cookies?'

'I did,' Julia said. 'Ellen, go back to work. We'll be fine.'

Julia took the girls across the meadow, far from the hubbub at the house. Sitting in the tall grass, she gave them cookies and told them stories.

When Ellen came looking for them, Vanessa, who had been sitting snug against Julia's leg, wrapped that little arm again round her neck, so tightly now that Julia had no choice but to lift her. Annie stayed close, as well.

'We're ready to go,' Ellen said. 'The ferry's waiting for us.' She held out a hand to Annie. 'All set?'

Nodding docilely, the child took Ellen's hand. Carrying Vanessa, Julia had a lump in her throat. She doubted the girls were old enough to realise that this part of their life was done. But they did sense something of the moment's import. Annie held back a little when they approached the car with the U-Haul hooked behind it, and Vanessa clutched Julia's neck as though she would never let go.

The lump in Julia's throat grew larger as long-time Walsh friends took turns saying goodbye. Some couldn't speak, simply gave kisses and hugs. They had known these girls since birth.

Annie climbed into the back seat of Ellen's car, but when Julia tried to settle Vanessa there, she refused to go. Wanting to make the leave-taking as easy as possible, Julia offered to drive her to the dock. The little girl played with the long end of the seat belt the whole way. When they arrived, Ellen drove the car with its trailer onto the waiting ferry, before returning for Vanessa.

Vanessa wasn't going. Winding both arms and both legs round Julia now, she started to cry. Ellen tried prising her limbs free. The more she tried, the harder Vanessa held on and the louder she cried.

The deck of the Harbor Grill was crowded with Sunday tourists. Vanessa's cries were shrill enough to draw eyes right and left, but what was there to do? Julia crooned soft words until her own throat closed up, at which point she stroked the little girl's warm hair as she struggled to pass her to Ellen. Large tears streamed down Vanessa's cheeks. She climbed Julia's body with startling strength. Julia's heart positively ached.

In the end, a small child was no match for two healthy adults. They managed to transfer her, twisting and fighting, to Ellen's arms and aboard the ferry with Annie, and still Vanessa held out her arms to Julia, screeching now, 'Nononooo!'

It was when *Nononooo!* turned to *Mamamama!* with little hands opening and closing, trying to grasp what she desperately wanted but was surely losing, that Julia began to cry softly herself. Once started, the tears wouldn't stop—not when the ferry pulled away, nor when its engine drowned out the child's screams.

Sobbing quietly, Julia watched until the ferry was gone. She pressed her lips together to regain control; when that didn't work, she put her sunglasses on. Crossing to a bench at the shore end of the dock, she sank down—and all the while, quietly, she wept.

'Mom?' Molly asked, coming down to the bench beside Julia. 'Did you know them?'

'Enough,' Julia managed, but couldn't say more. She didn't know where the tears had come from and why they refused to stop.

'What can I do?' Molly whispered.

Nothing, Julia said with the shake of her head.

'Want me to drive you home?'

Julia shook her head. She couldn't leave the harbour yet.

'Are you going to just . . . *sit* here?' Molly sounded embarrassed.

'Yes. I'm going to just sit here,' Julia said brokenly. The words were barely out when new tears began to fall.

Molly straightened, then slumped, then swivelled to face forwards, and it hit Julia that her daughter didn't know what to do. Remarkably, she didn't think to give comfort—and that was one more reason for Julia to cry.

'Well, then,' Molly said unsurely, 'I'll be hanging around the Grill. If you want me to do something, come in and get me, OK?'

Julia didn't watch Molly walk away. Elbows on her thighs, she pressed her quivering mouth to laced fingers and closed her eyes. All she had to do was to picture Vanessa Walsh reaching out so futilely, and she began crying again. But it didn't stop there. Julia cried for the failure of her marriage, for wasted heartache and hope. She cried for her life in New York, because, though it was all she really knew, she didn't want it any more.

'Hey,' came a low male voice. She didn't have to open her eyes to know whose hand was holding her knee. She covered it with one of her own. His warmth was a balm.

'That was a rough goodbye,' he said.

She nodded and wiped at her cheeks. 'It just hit me,' she murmured nasally. 'I don't know why.'

'Sure you do,' he said in that same low voice. 'You're sensitive, and you're smart. You know what that little girl's lost.'

His hand on her knee turned up and their fingers linked. She wasn't breaking that contact. She didn't care if people saw; she needed a friend, and he was there.

So was his dog, sitting quietly, facing Julia on her left as Noah was on her right. 'Lucas is staring,' she whispered.

Noah whispered back, 'He's never seen anyone as beautiful before.'

'Beautiful? Omigod. I'm a mess.'

'He doesn't see it that way.'

Julia took some solace in that. Never one for public displays, she figured that anyone passing by must think her a headcase. But she wasn't ready to leave.

'It's more than just Vanessa,' she said, her face inches from his. 'It's every frightening little thing. We think a child is worse off because she doesn't understand what's happening, but an adult *does* understand, and *that* makes it worse. *Plus*, an adult has to act. I'd love to let someone else take responsibility for my life.'

'Right now?' He smiled. 'OK. Are you hungry?'

'No,' she said, then changed that to 'Yes.' There was a definite hole in her stomach. She assumed part of it was from hunger.

'Are you a vegetarian?' he asked.

'No.'

'Then we're golden.' He raised his voice as though summoning a waiter, aimed at the food cart near the line of parked cars. 'Four hot dogs, Alfie—mustard and relish.'

Julia downed every last bit of two hot dogs, and a tall glass of freshly squeezed lemonade. She couldn't remember when she'd had a better lunch. She couldn't remember when she'd had a more companionable one, though neither she nor Noah said much. It was enough that he was with her there on the bench, watching the life of the harbour for an hour that Sunday.

Molly was livid. Julia could see it the instant she pulled up at Zoe's farmhouse and spotted her on the front steps.

Julia tried a smile as she approached. 'I thought you were hanging around the Grill.'

'Well, that was the plan,' Molly said with disdain, 'then you kept sitting there with him and people were commenting, and I couldn't bear it a minute longer.'

'Commenting about what?' Julia asked.

'About what is going on between you two,' Molly said. 'About the fact that Noah hasn't been interested in anyone for ages. About the fact that you're wearing a wedding band. They were asking *me* if you and Dad were separated.'

'Noah and I were sitting on a bench,' Julia argued quietly. '*Sitting* on a bench.'

'You were holding hands. Your heads were together. Anyone watching would have reached the same conclusion.'

'I was crying, Molly. I was upset.'

'But you're married to someone else.'

'Molly, *listen* to me.' Zoe had come to the screen door, but Julia kept her eyes on her daughter. 'Noah Prine is a friend. I have no intention of poisoning that just because some people have small minds. Give me the benefit of the doubt.'

To her credit, Molly looked torn. 'It's just that you're acting so *strange*. You're staying here, even when you know Dad's doing things he shouldn't. You haven't even called him.'

'We've emailed. I've sent him pictures.'

'He doesn't need pictures. He needs *you*.'

'What about what I need? I know it's upsetting to you, but I need this time away, Molly. I *need* this *time*.'

A car approached. Julia had no sooner heard its engine when Molly's eyes flew past her. A dusty red wagon came up the drive and pulled in beside Julia's car.

'That's our taxi,' Zoe said, coming out to the porch. 'Who . . .?' She stopped talking when the back door opened and a man climbed out. Not as tall as he had been in his heyday, nor as slim, he wore a tieless business shirt and pressed slacks.

'Omigod,' Julia cried. 'Dad!' She started forwards, heart pounding as she searched the back seat for her mother. Janet wasn't there, but her disappointment was short-lived. The idea that her father had come through for her after all was enough to warm her heart.

Jogging to the car, she gave him a hug. 'You should have told us you were coming,' she scolded. 'I'd have picked you up.'

'I didn't know it myself. It was a last-minute thing.' He held up a hand, clearly agitated. 'I've been patient. I sat back and followed her lead, but when she goes on and on about Zoe, and you—a man can only take so much. Quite honestly, I've had it.'

Julia felt something turn inside. 'What do you mean?'

'She's done good things—I can't deny her that. Finally, though, I have to look at my own life. I need a break.'

Julia could certainly identify with that. 'A break from?'

'Work. Baltimore. And, yes, your mother. She hasn't been much fun to be with lately.'

'Have you *left* her?' Molly asked, a horrified look on her face.

'I'm here, and she's there,' George said belligerently. 'She needs time alone to think about the effect she has on people, and I need a vacation.' He produced a thin smile.

Slowly and painfully, Julia absorbed the fact that her father hadn't come to comfort her at all. Quite the opposite. He had come so that she could comfort *him*.

Right now, though, she wasn't up for dealing with her parents' problems. She had far more pressing problems of her own. Wary, she asked, 'You're staying on Big Sawyer? For how long?'

He shrugged. 'How long are *you* staying? I'll stay that long.'

Fighting a rising panic, Julia was searching for words when Molly asked, 'Where will you stay? Mom and I are in Zoe's guest rooms.' She paused, then offered a reluctant, 'We could always double up.'

'I'll stay in town,' George said, with Molly quickly shaking her head.

'There are no places, unless you rent a house, and everything decent is booked. Next weekend's the Fourth.'

George was undaunted. 'I'll get something.'

Julia was still struggling with the larger picture—her father coming and going with his problems with her mother, Molly coming and going with her problems with Julia—not to mention Zoe, who would have feelings about George being around.

Suddenly, there was only one choice. 'Stay here,' Julia told her father. 'Take my room. I'll find another place.'

Thirty minutes later, Julia was on her way. If having survived the accident meant that she had been chosen to restructure her life, she couldn't think of a better step than declaring her independence. She packed up her new clothes and camera equipment and the shoulder bag the divers had recovered. Tossing the bag into the SUV, she still didn't waver. She loved Zoe. She loved her father. Lord knew, she loved Molly. Loving herself—respecting her own needs—was something important and new.

Heading first for the harbour, she saw that Noah wasn't on his boat. She drove up Main Street, turned left on Spruce, and cruised past one fisherman's cottage after another until she spotted his blue truck. She was barely out of the car when Lucas loped up and escorted her down the short walk.

Noah opened the door—and for the first time, Julia did waver. He seemed taller than before, perhaps a fact of the darkness behind him. He wore jeans and a T-shirt with the sleeves torn off. She saw broad shoulders and firm biceps. High on one of those biceps was a ropy tattoo.

Noah smiled through the screen. 'How're you doin'?'

'Actually, not great,' she said. 'I have a *huge* favour to ask. After the kindness you showed me earlier, I feel guilty asking for *anything*, but when the problem arose, I could only think of one answer. Of course, I couldn't tell Zoe and Molly and my dad—'

'Your dad's here?'

She nodded. 'Showed up out of the blue, and suddenly there's all this family at Zoe's, and I really want none of it. I packed up my things—just like that. But now I'm in a bind, which is why I'm here on your doorstep. Please feel free to say no. If you're uncomfortable with this, I'm sure there are other options—'

Shhhh, said the finger he put against his lips.

She stopped talking.

'Are you looking for a place to stay?' he asked.

Apologetically, she nodded.

'Want my hill house?'

She took a quick breath. 'Desperately.'

'It's yours. I won't be going there, not with the boy coming tomorrow.'

She exhaled in relief. 'It's just such a perfect location, so out of the way. I need to think. And I'm neat. I'll take good care of the place.'

'I'm not worried.' He smiled. 'There's no one I'd rather have in my bed.'

Julia laughed in delight. Yes, she heard Molly warning her about the way it looked and what people were saying, but if Noah wasn't bothered by the talk, she wasn't either.

'Thanks,' she said, grinning still. She started to turn, paused, looked at Lucas and then at Noah again. 'Um, maybe you can remind me how to get there?'

Noah did one better. He led the way in the truck. He stopped en route at the island store for food basics—which, against Julia's protests, he insisted on paying for but, as he saw it, she was doing him a favour. At a time when he felt the loss of his father, the challenge of his son, and an acute need to do something to justify his having been spared death himself, she was there. Helping her felt right.

Besides, he liked her. She was different from other women. She had a mind of her own and could argue with him quite effectively, but she didn't pretend to have all the answers. *That* was refreshing, after Sandi. And she was married, which made her safe. Nothing could happen.

Lucas, of course, was totally smitten, but Lucas was a dog. What did he know?

Julia Bechtel was a friend and that made it OK for Noah to loan her the hill house. From the minute he opened the door and brought in the first of her things, the place felt warmer. The fact that she seemed to love the house made him feel even better.

She hadn't brought much with her. They emptied her car in no time and put the food away and hooked up her printer so that she could print and email pictures to her heart's delight. Then, since it was only four, he led her through the woods over barely discernible trails to spots that he knew—the ruins of an old cellar, an assembly of peeling white birches, a boulder with a view.

When they returned, he uncorked a chardonnay and sliced French bread, while she washed red grapes and warmed Brie. They took it all out to the bedroom deck and enjoyed the serenity.

Noah didn't know whether it was the wine, the most pleasant social experience he'd had in years, or simply the fact that with Ian due, he couldn't procrastinate any longer, but when he finally returned to his parents' house, he was motivated. For the first time since that fateful Tuesday, he raised the shades, opened the windows, and aired out the house. He put Hutch's things in boxes so quickly that he couldn't dwell on the loss. He scrubbed the bathroom. He cleaned ashes from the woodstove.

By the time he was done, it was nearly midnight. Lying on newly washed sheets in his parents' bed—now his own—he felt more human than he had in days.

Chapter 8

JULIA SLEPT LATE. She had been so late going to bed. One thing had followed the next—a call to Zoe telling her where she was staying, a message left for Monte, a certain amount of unpacking, and then going out on the deck to see the moon and stars between shifting clouds. By the time she had washed up, set her wedding band on the bathroom counter, and pulled back that simple white bedspread, she was flush with adrenaline as she relived the events of the day.

Eventually, it struck her that she had never, ever lived alone. She had gone straight from her family home to life with Monte. For as long as she stayed here, there would be no one else using the bed, no one else drinking coffee from the first pot of the day.

For now, that felt right. It felt like the kind of new experience she was meant to have after the accident. And that raised the dilemma of what to do with her future, which was what kept her awake until three in the morning. She fell asleep with no solution in sight.

She woke after nine, when she heard the doorbell ring in a series of short, urgent trills.

Assuming it was Noah, she slipped on a robe and ran up the stairs. She was startled to open the door and find a visibly guarded Molly—which should have brought back the angst of the previous day, but didn't. Feeling instant pleasure, Julia broke into a smile.

'Molly!' she said, catching the girl's hand. 'You have to see this.' Drawing her into the house, she pulled her down the stairs and onto the deck. 'Isn't this *the* best view?'

Molly looked at it a while. 'It's really nice,' she said quietly. 'So's the house. Zoe said it's Noah's.'

'Yes.' Julia put both hands on Molly's shoulders. 'OK. You just showed up here unannounced. Was he here?'

'No.'

'Do you see any evidence that he was here?'

'You're not wearing your wedding band.'

'I never wear it at night. You know that. Trust me, he doesn't live here, which is the only reason I can. It's the perfect place for me. Don't you think so?'

'I don't know what to think,' Molly answered, losing all semblance of composure. She seemed completely rattled. 'You're here and Dad's there, and now Grampa's here and Gram is there. Of all the people in my life, I thought my family was the most together. What's wrong with Daddy? Doesn't he *know* you're the best woman he could ever have? What is he *looking* for?'

'Adulation? Adventure? Novelty? *Risk?* I don't know, Molly. All I know is that I'm really angry at him.' It had been one thing when Julia was hurt by his affairs. Now Molly had been hurt, too. That changed things.

'I called him this morning,' Molly said. 'It's the first time we've talked since that night, but I wanted him to know you were here, so if he wanted to come, you'd have privacy.'

'You didn't.'

'I did, and he said he might.'

Julia was appalled. 'But this is my time, my place. You had no right suggesting he come.'

'He's my father—'

'You're grown, Molly. You may spend a few more vacations at home, but then you're out in your own place with your own friends. I'm the one who'll be with your father. I'm the one who has to decide what I want. But this isn't only about my marriage. I've been defining myself in terms of other people—Monte's wife, Molly's mother, Janet's daughter. I don't have an identity of my own.'

'Do you need one suddenly now? Because of the accident?'

Julia settled against the rail, turning her back on the view. 'Here I am, spared. For what? Why? There has to be a purpose, something that goes beyond what I've done so far in my life. It has to do with making me a whole person.'

'I think you're a whole person,' Molly said.

'Well, I don't. So maybe I don't value myself enough.'

'Come back to Zoe's?' Molly asked pleadingly.

'This is a good place for me right now. Visit whenever you want.'

'Can I stay here?'

Hel-lo, Julia nearly cried. After all her talk about needing space?

Slipping an elbow through her daughter's, she guided her up the stairs. 'I want you at Zoe's.'

'I want you there, too,' Molly said, and launched in with, 'What is going on between Grampa and Zoe? They had zero to say to each other. I mean, really impolite. I wanted to make them blueberry-stuffed French toast, but Zoe wouldn't even sit and eat with us. I think I'll call Gram.'

'Margaret Marie, do not do that. Let your grandparents work out their own problems. Do you hear?'

425

Driving north from the Portland airport, Noah did his best to engage Ian in conversation. 'So, how's baseball?'

'Done for the summer,' came the reply.

'Was it a good league?'

Ian shrugged. He was a young man with a savvy way about him. He wore the latest in faded jeans and a logo T-shirt. His hair was short, had blond streaks, and stood straight up on top.

'Are you still playing shortstop?'

'Yes.'

'But running cross-country in the fall. Do you like that?'

There was another shrug. 'It keeps me in shape.'

'How are the Orioles doing?'

'Lousy. Nothing's been the same since Cal Ripken retired.'

Tracking the coast, Noah took Route 1 into Wiscasset, where they stopped for lunch at Red's Eats.

'Here?' Ian asked with a dubious glance at the small red building.

'Red's has the best lobster rolls in the state.'

'I don't eat lobster.'

'Maybe you haven't had a good lobster roll.'

'I gag on lobster.'

Noah sighed. 'Do you eat fried clams?'

'Yes.'

'Order fried clams,' he said and got out of the truck.

Ian ordered fried clams and ate them all. When Noah told him to pass a napkin, he passed it. When Noah told him to use the rest room, he used the rest room. He could follow orders. That was something. Noah waited until they were halfway to Damariscotta before trying again.

'How does it feel being a senior?'

'It sucks,' Ian said. 'Everyone's on your back about college. I'm not going.'

'Why not?'

'It'd be a waste. Unless I could play ball, which I can't, because I'm not good enough.'

'Who says?' Noah asked, glancing his way.

Ian returned a defiant look. 'My coach.'

'What does he know?'

'A lot.'

'Pass me my sunglasses,' Noah said. When Ian complied, he asked, 'What colleges are you going to see?'

'I don't know. Mom planned the trip.'

'Ian. This is *your* future. Find some places you like.'

Ian didn't reply.

Patience was one thing, Noah decided, and progress quite another. Standing at the rail as the ferry made the crossing, he wondered if the first would get him the last. He wanted a relationship with his son. Question-and-answer sessions did not make a relationship.

Ian didn't stray far—six feet away. Noah might have pointed out a passing lobster boat, the *My Andrea*, with Leslie Crane at her helm. He might have shown Ian the string of green-and-gold buoys Leslie was tending. He might have shown him where the *Amelia Celeste* had gone down and taken the life of his grandfather with it.

But Noah didn't trust that Ian wouldn't make a disparaging remark, one that might provoke anger in him. That was something he needed to avoid. Better, he decided, to let things unfold slowly.

But it wasn't to be. The ferry had no sooner docked at Big Sawyer and Noah driven the truck off when he was waved down by Mike Kling, whose shaved head gleamed in the sun.

'We got trouble, Noah,' he said. 'Those buoys you set last week up north of Main Mast rock? They're grey.'

'Grey?'

'Painted. You can see blue and orange underneath, but they blend right into the chop.'

'Painted?' That was a new one. Lobstermen didn't carry paint in their boats. Novices might, if they were peeved that their pot warp was tied up in knots. 'As in vandalised?'

'You got it. Haber and Welk most likely.'

And so it went, Noah knew. You invade our turf, we knot your lines, you paint our buoys.

He ran a hand round the back of his neck. He had been expecting good things from the traps near Main Mast rock. They sat on rocky bottom, the bottom of choice for lobsters during the late-June moult, when they were vulnerable to predators. He could still haul the traps; he had notations in his logbook of where each one was. But the buoys would have to be repainted, which meant the loss of a few days' fishing.

'Gotta be done,' he said, as much to himself as to Mike. He thought about continuing on to the house to get Ian settled in. But then he pulled into a parking spot. He still had another few hours of daylight. Before he could decide what to do, he had to know the extent of the damage.

Julia refused to think about anything but the novelty of doing her own thing in her own time. She was reading on the front porch when the second car of the day came out of the woods. If she had been pleased when Molly came, she was delighted now. This car was a small blue Honda with Kim at the wheel.

When Kim simply sat watching her from the car, Julia walked leisurely to the driver's side. Kim bowed her head and looked at her lap, but the window was open, like an ear ready to listen.

'How'd you know I was here?' Julia asked. 'Ah, don't tell me. My father went to the island store for the *Wall Street Journal*, got into a conversation with the owner, and he told your grandmother, who told your mother, who told you.'

The corner of Kim's mouth twitched. In the absence of words, that was progress. Even more so, the fact that she had come at all.

'If the grapevine told you I was here, it must be keeping you up to date on the investigation of the accident.'

Kim swallowed. Julia took that for a yes.

'No one has asked Noah or me about you. Everyone seems to know, though, that you and Artie had a thing.'

Kim studied her hands.

'If that's true,' Julia went on, 'it's only a matter of time before someone will wonder which boat you were on.'

Kim simply stared at her with large chestnut eyes.

'Did you shoot him?'

No reply.

'Do you know who did?'

Still no reply.

'I want to help you, though Lord knows why. Do you know how *wrong* it is to have an affair with a married man? Do you know how hurtful it is for the wife? And for the kids?'

Kim didn't move, didn't blink, didn't speak.

'I ought to hate you, but I can't. We shared something that night. It doesn't matter why you were there. You survived something horrific, just like I did. Don't you ask yourself why?'

Kim moved her head in a deliberate nod and pulled something flat out of her pocket. She gave it to Julia.

It was a bankbook. Uneasy, Julia opened it. The account was in Kim's name, the first deposits dated eight years before—small amounts that represented a teenager's earnings. Several thousand a pop had been deposited recently. The current balance was twenty-three thousand and change.

'Are these big ones from Artie? Did you know he was under suspicion for smuggling illegal aliens?'

Kim stared at her, eyes wide with a plea.

'You want me to hold this? So no one else sees?'

Kim gave a quick nod.

'That makes me an accessory to whatever you did for this.'

Kim eyed her steadily, still with an element of pleading.

'Did you love Artie? Did he give you this money as a gift?'

Her eyes grew distant, then glassy with tears.

'This is your escape,' Julia said, understanding. 'Do you know where you want to go? What you want to do?'

Eyes still brimming, Kim started the car.

'Don't leave, Kim. Tell me these things. I can help.'

But Kim didn't stop. The sound of the blue Honda's motor was soon lost in the woods.

Staring at the bankbook, Julia went inside to the bedroom and tucked it into the mottled leather bag that held her most personal things, still vaguely damp from their time in the ocean. Among them were two envelopes. One held charge receipts and credit card bills that she had so carefully, guiltily gathered. The other held photographs.

Pulling the photos from their envelope, she was relieved to find the basic images intact. One was of the harbour, one captured a stack of lobster traps. A third showed six young men perched on and around the pier piling. They wore work boots and jeans but were bare-chested. Each of the six had a tattoo round his biceps that marked him as part of the local lobster gang.

And there she saw, or thought she did, Noah Prine—less mature in looks and build than he was now, but handsome nonetheless.

The phone by the bed rang. It was the land line. She picked it up.

'Mrs Bechtel, it's Alex Brier from the *Island Gazette*. Zoe said I'd find you there. I have a favour to ask. Those pictures you gave to the Chief? I want them for the paper.'

Julia was startled. She wondered if giving them to the newspaper was permissible. But no one had said she shouldn't. 'Uh, sure,' she managed. 'When do you need them?'

'As soon as you can email them. Got a pen?'

As soon as she hung up, she sent the pictures along. Then she called Noah on his cellphone.

'Yeah,' he answered, sounding irritated.

'It's Julia. I'm sorry, is this a bad time?' She knew he was with Ian. She wouldn't have called if she hadn't felt an urgency.

His voice gentled. 'No more so than another. We're on the *Leila Sue*.' He told her about the vandalism. 'It looks like forty buoys were painted. Someone was busy last night.'

'The fruit guys?'

'Probably.'

'Forty buoys is how many traps?'

'I do pairs, so that's eighty, but I'm not hauling all of them. I have extra buoys. Paint 'em, and they're good for exchange. Everything OK there?'

'I just had a visit from Kim. I need to ask your advice, but not on the phone.'

'Come to the trap shed tonight. You can help paint.'

Julia smiled in relief. 'I'd like that,' she said.

It was lobster night at the Grill. Julia, stopping by to say hello to Molly, saw Matthew Crane in his usual corner, nursing his usual whiskey as he looked out over the foggy harbour towards open ocean.

She slipped down on the bench, but he spoke before she could say a word. 'Know why Monday night's lobster night?' he asked.

She shook her head.

'With no hauling on Sundays, the catch is bigger on Mondays, so the price is lower. It's all about money. It wasn't always that way. Lobster used to be so plentiful it was thought of as charity fare.'

'Charity fare?'

'For widows and children and convicts and servants. Some servants had it written into their contracts that they couldn't be served it more than three times a week.'

Julia smiled. 'You're kidding me.'

Matthew shook his head. He sipped his drink.

'Mrs Bechtel?'

Julia looked up. A fair-haired man with serious eyes and an intense look hunkered down beside her.

'Alex Brier,' he said. 'Thanks for the pictures. I'm using them in this week's paper. Want to take more?'

'Of the traps?'

'Of Noah's buoys and anything else that happens. More will. You can bet on that. I've been doing all the pictures myself, only my wife's expecting a baby in two months and the doctor is making her stay in bed. I've been running back and forth trying to do the newspaper and take care of our other two kids. I could find you a ride out, if you're willing to do it.'

'What fun,' Julia said, grinning. 'I'm willing.'

'Great. Thanks.' Alex stood. 'I'll arrange a ride and give you a call.'

'I'll take her,' Matthew said. 'My nephew's been offering me his Cobalt. Pretty fancy boat for a lobsterman, but not for a lady from New York.'

Noah's trap shed was at the end of Spruce Street, where houses had given way to wild grasses and trees. In the dusk, Julia might have missed the small wood hut, had it not been for a glow in the window. She had barely parked when Noah appeared at the door, and again it suddenly hit her—the way he was now with his hair messed and his

430

jeans spattered with paint. And the way he had looked as a teenager with his buddies and all of them with that ropy tattoo. The way his voice had gentled earlier when she had called on the phone.

Her insides melted. The best she could do was manage a smile.

He stepped aside to let her in. 'I sent Ian home. He was exhausted. I'd say "poor kid", if he hadn't been out until two this morning with friends.'

The oil lamp threw enough light to show dozens of buoys newly painted a bright blue. 'Oh, my,' Julia said, finding her voice. 'Have you done all this tonight?'

'I had no choice. I don't want those traps lost. I'm about to start on the stripes.'

'Give me a brush and show me how you want it done.'

He showed her, and for a time they worked quietly, with Lucas sleeping nearby. They were done with nearly half before Noah said, 'Tell me about Kim.'

Sitting back on her heels, Julia told him about the bankbook.

'Twenty-three thousand over the last eighteen months?'

'She was saving up so that she could leave here. She gave me the bankbook for safekeeping, I guess. But the bank has those same records. Investigators would come up with them in no time. What do I do, Noah? I now know something the police don't. Artie was paying her for something. The question is what.'

'How did she seem?'

'Stricken. Regardless of what she was or was not involved in, she's suffering.'

Noah considered that thought. After a minute, he resumed painting. Julia could see his brow was creased and his mouth had tightened. He would talk when he had something to say.

Sure enough, when the last of the buoys had been carefully hung to dry, he led her outside. There, leaning beside her against her car, he said, 'Let me talk with John. He'll tell me what's going on.'

With the fog obscuring moon and stars, the night was dark. Gently, she asked, 'How was it with Ian today?'

'Awkward. He doesn't initiate anything. First thing tomorrow, we're heading out to replace buoys.'

'I may see you out there. Alex Brier asked me to take pictures of your grey buoys. Matthew Crane is taking me out.'

Noah's voice held a smile. 'You have him wrapped around your finger. Bet you do that to all the men.'

'No. Not all.'

'You've sure done it to my dog. Look at him sitting right by your leg.'

Julia scratched Lucas's head. 'Maybe he's starved for female attention.'

'Nah. There's plenty of females around. He's not interested in them. I told you. He knows beauty when he sees it.'

Julia didn't reply. Noah had said words like this before but words were easily spoken. Yet there was something else here with Noah, something in the thick night air that sent a warmth through her veins. It could have been the way his body touched hers, arm to arm, hip to hip, or the way he looked at her, then away, then back, as though he couldn't control his eyes, any more than she could control the heat she felt inside.

'Oh, boy,' he finally muttered.

She nodded. 'Bad timing.'

'My son, your husband.'

'The accident. Maybe that's all it is? A reaction?'

He shook his head and folded his arms on his chest. She did the same, and all the while good sense was telling her to get in her car and drive away.

'So maybe,' he said quietly, 'this is what the accident was for.'

'You and me?'

'Yes. What's your marriage like? If it's good, I'll back off.'

She unfolded her arms and dropped her chin to her chest. In the next instant, though, she turned into him, and his arms went round her, drawing her close. Cheek settling on his chest, she closed her eyes and breathed in far more than the paint on his shirt. He was beneath it—Noah Prine—heart pounding loudly, limbs trembling slightly. If she wanted to be wanted, the proof was here.

She sighed at the sheer pleasure of it.

'You can say *that* again,' he muttered hoarsely. 'Can I kiss you?'

She shook her head, but her arms were round him.

Taking her face in his hands, he turned it up. His eyes were serious. 'For ten years all I've done is go through the motions—wake up in the morning, work all day, come home exhausted and go to bed. Since the accident, I've been thinking about missed opportunities. I blew it with my parents and now they're gone, but Ian isn't, so I'm working on that. And now there's you. Tell me what you want, Julia.'

Unable to do that, with so much else in her life up in the air, Julia pressed a hand to his mouth. His lips were firm and lean. Her fingers lingered there a minute, then withdrew. Then, slipping out from under him, she rounded the car, slid behind the wheel. After nearly closing the door on Lucas, she eased his head out of the way and started the car.

Noah stood several feet away. She backed around and drove off, alternately watching the road and her rearview mirror. All too soon, the mirror was dark, but his image remained in her mind, a glow that reminded her what it was like to be wanted. She could love him for that alone.

Noah was up before dawn, shaking Ian awake, then monitoring the National Oceanic and Atmospheric Administration weather broadcast while he fried bacon and half a dozen eggs, toasted six slices of bread, and poured large glasses of juice.

Ian looked at the food on the kitchen table and shook his head. 'I hope none of that's for me. I can't eat this early.'

'You're going to be working this early. You'll need energy.'

'Just coffee,' Ian said, and helped himself to a mugful.

Noah didn't argue. It wasn't worth the breath. He ate his own full breakfast while Ian drank his coffee. The boy sat at the table looking at anything but Noah, while Noah made four tuna sandwiches and packed them in a cooler along with canned soda and crisps.

Pulling on a sweatshirt, he suggested Ian do the same. Ian said he'd be fine without. So Noah said, 'Take the cooler.' Logbook in hand, he opened the front door. Lucas bounded out of the deep purple dawn.

Taking the dog's head in both hands, Noah scrubbed his neck. 'Hey, guy, how're you doing?' Lucas's tail wagged wildly.

'The dog hates me,' Ian said. 'He won't come near me.'

'He doesn't know you, so he's cautious,' Noah said.

Ian didn't say anything more, not when they stopped at the trap shed to load up the truck, nor when they transferred the buoys to the boat. To his credit, the boy was no weakling.

Once the truck was unloaded, Noah stopped briefly at Rick's for his Thermos and found two there, along with a bag with a pencilled note: *Something for the boy, in case he suffers withdrawal at ten.*

Smiling, he returned to the boat. He pulled on oilskin overalls and rubber boots, and was relieved when Ian followed suit. Whistling for Lucas, Noah directed Ian to untie the lines while he got the engine humming. Backing out of the slip, he actually felt pretty good. Yes, the gear war was escalating; yes, he was worried about his hankering for Julia Bechtel. But he was going out lobstering with his son, and that was special.

Noah stood at the wheel, absently monitoring the VHF and the intermittent chatter of his friends. Ian was behind him, attaching fresh-painted buoys to the warp of the traps stacked in the stern.

'We'll set those first,' he said when the boy was done. 'Once they're gone, we'll have room to work.'

Ian peered into the fog. 'How do you know where they go?'

'I want them where the lobsters are. This time of year, I want my traps in the shallows. Lobsters are moulting right about now. Once they shed those old shells, they hide in the rocks. Even without the buoy problem, I'd have moved these traps soon anyway.' He brought the engine down to a putter and pointed at one of his screens. 'Eighteen, twenty feet. Let's go.'

Taking traps from the stern, he showed Ian how to balance a pair on the starboard rail, slide the first overboard, then the second, then the buoy. Doubling back, they laid a second string and a third. Further north, they laid another two strings, then another two.

When the stern was free of traps, Noah headed for the grey buoys. He threw the boat out of gear, gaffed one, and pulled it aboard. While Ian exchanged the bad buoy for a newly painted one, Noah threw the line over the hydraulic winch, started the hauler, and pulled each of the two traps aboard. Water splashed up with each; it was North Atlantic cold even at the turn of July.

'You're my sternman,' he told Ian. 'Your job is to empty the trap, measure what's inside, band keepers, and rebait.' He handed him a pair of thick cotton gloves. 'Wear these. And don't get your fingers in the way of a claw.'

Ian was staring at the first trap. 'What's that?'

'Dogfish,' Noah said. 'A small shark. The teeth are sharp and there's poison near the dorsal fins.' Wearing gloves of his own, he pitched the dogfish back into the sea, and did the same with a hermit crab. Three lobsters were left in the trap. He dumped them onto the banding table. 'These two are shorts,' he said, tossing the two smallest back into the ocean. 'Here's a maybe.' He took up a small measuring tool. 'The carapace is measured from the eye socket to where the tail starts. We can't keep anything smaller than three and a quarter inches or larger than five. See? This one's a keeper.'

Taking the banding tool, he showed Ian how to stretch a small, wide elastic band over the claw. 'Come on, bud,' he murmured when the lobster refused to close its claw. He finally blew on the claw, and the lobster complied.

'Cool,' Ian remarked in his first show of animation.

Noah tossed the lobster into a tank. 'Now for the bait. See the bag inside the trap? Take it out.'

Ian got the bag out. It contained nothing but fish bones and small bits of flesh. 'This is gross. What're we supposed to do with this?'

Noah reached in, scooped out what remained of the bait, and tossed it overboard. 'Now, restuff the bag,' he instructed. When Ian had done it, he showed him how to retie the bag in the trap. Setting that trap aside, he turned to the second one. It contained a starfish and a lobster. Noah didn't have to measure it to know it was a keeper, but he had Ian do it anyway.

He let Ian struggle with the bander, which was what he remembered his father doing when he was young and had been learning. Ian eventually had the lobster banded and the trap baited, at which point

Noah put the boat in gear and the traps went back over the transom. As soon as a newly painted buoy was bobbing in the waves, they moved on. They had hauled twenty pairs of traps and were about to gaff the last of the vandalised buoys when the sound of a motor came out of the mist.

Noah was feeling a sense of anticipation even before the Cobalt materialised, and smiled helplessly when he saw the cockpit. Julia stood there with Matthew Crane. She broke into a grin and waved.

He raised an answering hand.

'How's it going?' she called.

'Getting there,' he called back. 'How about you?'

'I've got *terrific* stuff. Now I want you.'

He grinned. 'Want me how?'

'Doing your thing. You know, lobstering.'

'You mean, I should pretend you're not there.'

'Exactly,' she answered and looked past him. 'Is that Ian? Hi, Ian!'

Noah glanced back. His son had taken advantage of the small break to open Rick Greene's bag and was devouring a chocolate croissant. With the bits of seaweed on his oilskins, the wind-blown mess of his spiky hair, and his upper-body musculature, Ian could have been taken for a lobsterman. Noah felt a glimmer of pride.

The boy raised his chin in greeting as he chewed the last of the croissant. Tossing the bag aside, he went to the rail as Noah caught up the last buoy and put the line over the winch. Ian grabbed the first trap, then the second one. While he removed the spoilt buoy and worked at attaching a fresh blue-and-orange one, Noah sorted through the contents of the traps. All the while he did his best to forget Julia was there.

Outwardly, he succeeded. Her camera wouldn't record the fact that his heart was beating faster than normal and his hand was less than steady.

After the Cobalt had disappeared into the mist, Noah worked Ian hard, steaming from one string of traps to the next, hauling, emptying, rebaiting, resetting, and starting all over again minutes later. He demanded a level of stamina from Ian that he doubted any baseball coach had ever demanded, and felt little sympathy when the boy began to flag.

But fatigue caused accidents, and had Noah not looked back at the right moment and lunged to push Ian out of the way, the boy might have gone right over the side.

'What the *hell*?' Ian cried. He was sprawled on the deck, while Noah dropped the second trap over the side.

'Didn't you see the coil of pot warp?' Noah called back. Heart pounding, he dropped the buoy in after the trap. 'There's *always* a coil of rope under the hauler. Put your foot there like you did, and when the line plays out fast, you either lose the foot or go right over the side and down with the trap.'

Ian sat up, a sullen expression on his face.

Noah returned to the wheel. 'I would never have forgiven myself if anything had happened to you,' he said.

'What about *me*?' Ian cried. 'Think I want my life to end up *here*?'

'If your life has to end, you could do a whole lot worse than here. People think here. They care here. They feel here. Your grandparents died here, and your father probably will too. You have roots here, Ian. You may not want to admit that, but that's because you're ignorant.' He had meant to say shortsighted, but the other word had popped out, and Ian was quick to react.

'Ignorant of what? *This*?' the boy asked, shooting a disparaging glance at the marine debris strewn on the deck. 'Am I supposed to care about this? This is what you wanted, not me. You hide here.'

'Hide?'

'You ran here after the divorce and you haven't left.'

'Left to live elsewhere? Why would I? I like it here.'

'But you used to *do* something. This can't compare to that.'

Noah bristled. 'You know nothing about my life, Ian. People do an honest day's work here, and it isn't just physical. There's a lot of know-how goes into successful lobstering. This may not be your choice of work, but there are generations of families who've been lobstering, passing the knowledge on from grandfather to father to son. These people could have gone elsewhere and been successful, but they chose to stay. Just like I chose to return. So don't ever think I'm hiding here. I choose this life.' He was deliberate in his use of the present tense. '*Choose* this life.'

Noah finished hauling the traps he'd set out to haul, and the catch was good, particularly since damage control had taken much of their time. His tanks held 300-some pounds of lobster. Yes, the catch was good.

Even better, he and Ian hadn't argued any more. Granted, they hadn't said much. But they had fallen into a rhythm of hauling that lobsterman and sternman didn't always find.

With the fog finally starting to thin, he directed the *Leila Sue* to a heavy concentration of purple-and-green buoys, then pulled Ian to the wheel. 'See these buoys? Go to one and let her idle.' He threw the gear into neutral to demonstrate. 'I'll be quick.'

'I've never driven a boat,' Ian said.

'No better place to learn,' Noah said, indicating the first buoy. Taking a sharp knife from the cuddy, he leaned over the rail and freed the buoy from its warp with a decisive upward cut.

'Isn't this illegal?' Ian asked as he headed for the next buoy.

'Not by local law.'

'But you're destroying someone's property.'

'That someone is trespassing. Technically, since he's on my turf, it's my property.'

Ian came up on the next buoy. 'What if they bring charges?'

'They won't. There's ten guys who'll testify that they painted my buoys, and zero guys who'll say I was cutting these lines.'

They didn't cut free all of the purple-and-green buoys. The point was for Haber and Welk to find a few tied to traps and know that the rest had been deliberately destroyed. Noah retook the helm and put in for the harbour. At four in the afternoon, he dropped a clearly exhausted Ian back at the house. Then he went back into town to see the police chief.

Julia had come ashore far earlier. She was back on Hawks Hill, sitting at Noah's computer and playing with the pictures she had shot, cropping some, lightening others, sharpening a few. In time, she sent those of Noah and Ian replacing vandalised buoys on to Alex Brier.

Then she drove to Zoe's, fully expecting to find her in the barn, but when she walked in, she found only her father. He was cleaning out trays under cages, refilling hay racks. He wore a furrowed look.

Julia checked out the babies in the nest boxes. 'So,' she said after a bit, 'are you enjoying yourself?'

'Very much,' her father declared with a bit too much zeal. 'It's nice not to be programmed for a change.'

'Are you talking about your work, or Mom?'

'Both.'

'So. Tell me about your day. What'd you do?'

He gave a lopsided shrug. 'Oh, walked around in town, on the dock. I talked with people. You know.'

'Have you called Mom?' Julia asked.

'Not yet.'

'Tell me something, Dad. Why'd you come here?'

'Because you were here. You needed me.'

'What about Zoe? It's clearly hurtful to Mom, your coming here.'

Her father stared at her long enough to see that she knew what had happened between Zoe and him. 'We're talking a one-time thing an awful lot of years ago, Julia. It's time your mother got over it. We've avoided the issue for too long. Maybe facing it will help.' Reaching for two water bottles, he walked off to the cages at the end of the row.

Facing it by walking away? Facing it by refusing to call?

Oh, yes, Julia was guilty of those things herself. What to do? Agonising over that thought, she headed to the house.

Chapter 9

THE POLICE STATION on Big Sawyer was little more than a storefront office. It sat on Main Street, beside the post office and across from Brady's Tackle & Gear.

When Noah walked in, John Roman had his ankles crossed atop a weathered wood desk and his eyes on the computer screen. 'Just the man I wanted to see. Take a look at this.' John pointed at the screen.

Putting thoughts of Kim on hold, Noah rounded the desk. He didn't recognise the face on the screen, but the text beside the picture was clear. 'Kevin Welk,' he read, and perused a short but impressive criminal record. John brought up another page, this one devoted to Curt Haber. Between the two, they had convictions spanning the last dozen years for bank theft, breaking and entering, and assault.

'Their names kept cropping up,' John explained, 'so I decided to check them out. Not your usual lobstermen.'

'Do they have licences to lobster here?'

'Sure do. I checked that first.' John shook his head. 'So, I'm asking myself what they're doing here, and my mind keeps going places it probably shouldn't be going.'

Noah knew those places. He often returned there himself. 'What's the latest theory on Artie's death?'

'For lack of anything better, they're saying he shot himself. The Immigration and Naturalisation Service has gone back to the smuggling part. They're focusing on a guy in Florida who's supposed to be the mastermind shuttling the illegals from large boats outside the two-hundred-mile limit to private docks on the mainland.'

No mention of Kim. 'Haber and Welk are from Florida.'

'Yup. So I ask myself why they're here making public nuisances of themselves. Makes you wonder if lobstering's just a cover.'

Noah agreed. It was almost as if Haber and Welk were going out of their way to let everyone know that they wanted to haul traps. Only wanted to haul traps. Only wanted to catch lobster.

'Still,' he pointed out, 'there's no way they could have·shot Artie in that fog.'

'Unless one of them was on the boat with him.'

'If so, he would have died, too,' Noah tried offhandedly.

'Not necessarily. Who's to say someone couldn't have been thrown off *The Beast* like you were thrown off the *Amelia Celeste*? Who's to say it wasn't maybe even a third person?'

John knew, Noah realised. If he didn't know, he suspected.

'So here's the story,' John went on. His voice held an element of resignation. 'They know Artie was connected to Kim. Could be it was sexual, could be it was something else. There's only one person who knows, and that's Kim. She was at his house, and on his boat. I keep telling her there's nothing to worry about because I'll protect her, but she still won't say a word. I've been out at the house every day for a week now. Most days she isn't there. When she is, she just sits on that sofa and looks at her hands. How long before someone higher than me decides to bring her in?'

Noah decided the computer would give Ian something to do while he and Julia talked to Kim. He called it quits on the water on Wednesday at three, got them both home to shower, and was at the hill house by four. Julia had just taken scones from the oven.

'Scones usually go with tea this hour of the day,' she told Ian affably, 'but I figured you wouldn't be the tea type. So I bought Coke and a Frappuccino.'

Ian's hand hovered over a scone. 'Cool enough to eat?' he asked.

'Should be,' Julia said, handing him a napkin.

Noah led Ian to the loft. At the top of the stairs, Ian's eyes lit. 'Oh, wow. This is really yours?'

'Yes.' Noah turned on the computer, but that was all he had to do. By the time the programs were loaded and the desktop displayed, Ian was on his way to the Internet.

Noah became irrelevant then. He wasn't even sure Ian heard him when he said, 'I'll be back,' and headed downstairs.

On his way out of the door with Julia, he told Lucas to stay with Ian, but the dog wasn't having any part of it. Pushing his way into the back seat of the truck, he sat behind Julia and looked defiantly at Noah.

So Noah caved in, and the dog came along. 'Bluff or beach?' he asked Julia.

'Bluff,' Julia said. 'I just talked with Kim's mom.'

Sure enough, the small blue Honda was there by the keeper's house, shrouded in mist. Even harder to see was Kim, sitting on the rocks beyond it, looking warily back at the truck.

Julia climbed out. 'Hi,' she called over the pounding of the surf as she started over, carrying a small bag of scones.

Noah got out and closed the door.

Kim raised anxious eyes to Julia. They moved to Noah, then returned. 'You know him, he's a friend,' Julia said with gentle insistence. Settling herself close to Kim, she opened the bag and handed her a scone. Noah sat nearby and tried to decide how to begin. What was he supposed to say in a sensitive situation like this?

As carefully as he could, he explained why he had come. 'The Chief is doing everything he can to keep investigators away to give you time to heal. But the investigation is going nowhere. John is afraid that he won't be able to keep them away much longer because they figure you know something. They don't care if you were having an affair with Artie. They want to know other things, like who called Artie, who visited him, what names he used to mention.'

Kim swallowed hard, but said nothing.

'Here's the problem. If they ask you questions and you refuse to answer, they're going to think you're guilty. They won't give you the benefit of the doubt. Talk to us, Kim. John can only hold the others off so long.'

Turning away, Kim put her head on her knees.

'OK,' Noah tried. 'Here's another thought. They know that Artie was involved in bad stuff, with bad people. You may think you're safe as long as you don't talk, but those people are dangerous. If they get nervous enough, they may want insurance that your silence will last. John can protect you, but only if he knows what you know. Artie was working with a man from Florida. Do you know who he is?'

Kim gave a frightened head shake.

'Did he mention Curt Haber and Kevin Welk?'

Another frightened head shake.

'Did he tell you anything about his work?'

A third frightened head shake.

'Were you having an affair with Artie?'

This head shake was firmer.

'Were you on *The Beast* with Artie that day?'

This time there was no head shake at all.

'Have you been on the water since the accident?'

Kim simply stared.

'I didn't think so,' he concluded. 'Me, I've been everywhere else but where the accident happened. Same with Julia. So let's put that demon behind us. We'll go out together, the three of us. Plus my son, who's seventeen. He wants to pretend nothing ever happened.'

And Kim could use the jolt, Noah figured. Even if it didn't help, nothing was lost.

'I'll be at the dock tomorrow at four o'clock. You know where the slip is. Four o'clock.'

Noah pulled off the road into his drive. When the truck made the last turn and the house appeared, there was the little Plymouth of Zoe's that Molly was using, parked by the front door.

The activity inside the house was centred round the kitchen. Molly was there, as was Ian, along with food on the counter, pots on the stove, dishes on the table. Half a dozen things seemed to be in the works. Something smelt divine.

Seeing Julia, Molly said an indignant, 'I came over here thinking you'd be alone and hungry, in which case I'd cook you dinner, since I have the night off. Instead, I found Ian. We're making bouillabaisse and, quite honestly, there isn't enough for four.'

Noah peered into the largest pot. 'What's in it?'

Ian answered. 'Scallops, mussels, clams, monkfish and lobster.'

'I thought you didn't like lobster.'

'Cooked this way, it's palatable.'

'Palatable?' Molly echoed. 'If you don't *love* this, there's something wrong with your taste buds. Could be immaturity,' she added with a smirk. 'Hand me the cayenne, would you?'

Ian handed her the cayenne.

'There's lobster meat in the freezer,' Noah offered. 'If we defrost it, there might be enough in there for four.'

'*Frozen* lobster?' Molly asked. 'I don't think so.'

'What if I drive down to the store for extra ingredients?'

'The store doesn't have the freshest. Rick has the freshest. And Rick's off for the night.'

Noah pulled his cellphone from his pocket. 'How about I call Rick. He'll tell whoever is *on* to give me what we need.'

Julia tried not to grin. It looked like he had her.

But Molly wasn't so easily bested. 'You'll also need another baguette, a leek, and a fennel bulb. And pick up a starter—two orders of escargot and two hearts of palm salad. And a blueberry tart for dessert. Buy the large size. Ian's starved.' She grinned at Noah.

'Thank you,' Julia said several hours later. She and Molly sat on the leather sofa, alone now, both slouched low with their heads on the back of the seat. 'Dinner was fabulous.'

Molly smiled. 'It was good.'

Julia caught her hand. 'Thanks for being civil.'

'Civil?'

'Warm. It wasn't that hard, was it?'

Molly grunted. 'They're OK people. They did the cleanup.'

'What did you think of Ian?'

'Ask me in five years. He's still into adolescent angst.'

'Spoken by a veteran twenty-year-old.'

'You know what I mean. He's angry.'

'So are you lately.'

'I have cause. My life is in chaos. There have been so many changes since high school, and now this—you. You just seem so different. Like I don't know what you're going to do next.'

'Some things never change. I'll always love you. I'll always be there for you.'

'You've had time to think. Do you know where you're going?'

'I'm still working on it.'

'But you're not going back to New York,' the girl said, laying down the gauntlet.

'A year ago, I would have said yes, because that's what everyone there seems to want. But it's not a simple decision. There's nothing win-win about divorce.'

'If you didn't go back to New York,' Molly asked, 'would you stay here?'

'Does it matter?'

'Yes. I feel like you're getting involved in a world I don't know, like I'm going to lose you.'

Julia smiled. 'This feels like the right thing,' she said, 'like I'm heading in the right direction. Actually, it feels good to head in *any* direction. I've been static for too long.' But not since the accident. Like Kim, she felt a jolt, reliving that night. Her past had exploded right along with the *Amelia Celeste* and *The Beast*. The result felt like liberation. 'As for my getting involved in a world you don't know, that doesn't have to be. There's actually someone I'd like you to meet. What time do you start work tomorrow?'

'Two,' Molly said.

'Oh dear. That's too early. We're taking Kim out on the *Leila Sue*. We're hoping it'll give her a little push, maybe some closure. You and she are close in age, and you're so good with people. You could be a real help.'

'What time are you going?' Molly asked.

'Four.'

'I'll be there. Rick's as worried about Kim as everyone else. He'll give me a few hours off.'

Naturally, Julia brought food. It wasn't that this was a party, though it was in fact a rite of sorts, but bringing food was simply what she did. She doubted that part of her would ever change—and in this case it wasn't bad at all. For one thing, Noah and Ian were starved after a day of work. Warm drumsticks, wedges of thick grilled cheese and hot cider hit the spot on a foggy day, when dampness defied the arrival of July and gave the salt air a chill. Rick Greene sent Molly along with bacon-wrapped scallops and grilled portabellas, all hot. They opened the bags on the console and helped themselves while Julia filled cups from the Thermos.

Four o'clock came and went. By 4.05 Noah was glancing at his watch. Pulling his Patriots cap low on his brow, he exchanged a worried look with Julia. By four ten he was scanning the shore through the fog.

At four fifteen, a blue car parked a distance from the pier. Head lowered, Kim hurried down the dock. She wore the same hooded jacket she had worn on the bluff, and presented the same diminutive figure. Under her hood she wore a black watchman's cap, under which she had piled every last strand of her hair.

She didn't want to be seen. Julia could only begin to imagine the courage it had taken for Kim to come. It was when she was hidden half inside the wheelhouse that she finally raised her eyes to acknowledge the others, but those eyes were worried. She shook her head when they offered her food.

Noah backed the *Leila Sue* from her slip and picked his way out of the harbour. Pleasure craft had joined the usual gang of lobster boats at moorings. The summer folk had arrived.

As the boat pitched ahead through the seas, there was no talk, just the thrum of the engine and the sputter of the radio. It wasn't a long ride. The *Amelia Celeste* had been nearly home when *The Beast* hit. Keeping a close watch on the instrument panel, Noah finally said, 'This is it,' and killed the engine.

The boat rose and fell, and the wind whistled over the wheelhouse, but all else was still. Noah went to the gunwale and stood sombrely. Moments later, Ian joined him there.

Julia went to the stern. It was here, on the *Amelia Celeste*, that so many people had died. Julia was instantly transported back to that night, recalling the presence of the eight people who had been lost—felt it so clearly that she shuddered and wrapped her arms around herself. Moments later, Molly was there. Seeming to know what to do this time, she gave Julia a hug.

'Did those people know what hit them?'

'They knew *The Beast* was coming.'

'Did he do it intentionally?' Molly asked.

Julia was about to say she didn't know, when something cold touched her hand. She turned and saw Kim. She had removed the watchman's cap, so wisps of red hair blew round the edge of her hood. Eyes filled with sorrow, the girl shook her head.

'Not intentionally?' Julia asked.

Kim repeated the head shake and touched her own shoulder.

'Because he was shot,' Julia interpreted. 'But why was he still driving the boat?'

Kim shook her head in panic.

'You don't know? But you were there,' Julia whispered.

Panic gave way to something so far beyond regret as to be painful. Julia would have asked more, if it hadn't seemed irrelevant to the moment. Right now in Kimmie's eyes were agony and need.

Julia pulled her close on the right while Molly stayed locked to her on the left, the three of them steadying one another against the roll of the boat as they looked out over the stern.

Noah stood firm at the starboard gunwale. Taking deep breaths, he felt the life of his father consolidate and rise from the depths. Scenes scrolled up over the whitecaps—Hutch working dawn to dusk without complaint; Hutch saving to buy his wife a finer wedding band for their fiftieth wedding anniversary, though she was terminally ill; Hutch standing at the side of the truck when Noah left for college, watching him go, not moving an inch until the ferry was out of sight.

With these memories came the connection Noah sought. He and his father had shared more than an occupation and a house. They may never have said it aloud, but there had been feeling between them. Eyes filling with tears, he took the best of Hutch, tucked it inside, and prayed he could be as good a man.

'I didn't know him,' Ian said.

Noah nodded. He faced the fact that he should have had Ian here every summer. He could try to blame it on his marriage, but it was time he took responsibility for his behaviour. That was another reason why he had survived the accident.

He had three weeks. He was determined to make the most of them.

Returning to the wheel, he started the engine. As soon as the women were in the shelter of the wheelhouse, he turned the *Leila Sue* and headed for shore. The fog remained thick. He had to slow to a crawl inside the harbour markers to avoid hitting other boats, and was relieved when he pulled into the slip.

Kim was off the boat the instant the lines were tied. Head bowed again, she hurried down the dock into the fog. She was nearly at the gauzy bit of blue that was her car when Molly cried, 'Oh, look—she dropped her hat.' Snatching the black watchman's cap from the deck, she ran after the girl.

At the same time, Kim must have realised she had left it, because she had barely closed herself in the Honda and started the motor when she climbed out again. Leaving the car running, she ran back towards the pier. She had just met Molly when an explosion rocked the car, and it burst into flames.

Within seconds, Julia was out of the boat and racing down the dock. Molly had sunk down to the wharf with Kim, the two of them a conjoined shape in the mist. Julia ran with her heart in her mouth. When she reached the girls, she found Molly unhurt, holding Kim, who was sobbing uncontrollably. Molly raised terrified eyes to Julia's.

As people came on the run, some heading for hoses to put out the fire, Julia dropped down and held them both, quaking and tremulous, faces pale and wet with tears.

'Oh God . . . oh God . . . oh God.' The voice was fractured, the words a sobbing whisper, but they definitely came from Kim.

Molly said shakily, 'Someone bombed the car.'

'He wants me dead,' Kim cried between sobs. 'He tried once, but I grabbed the gun. It wasn't supposed to go off—but he just kept holding on—and then it *did*.'

Artie. As stunned as Julia was, the pieces fell into place.

Noah's eyes met hers in the crowd now clustered round. They reflected the same picture. 'Let's get her out of here,' he said softly.

John Roman was running their way. Off to the other side, hoses had doused the worst of the flames.

'My office,' John said.

Noah shook his head. 'My house. It's less threatening.' He helped Kim up. With Ian dashing ahead, he held her against his side and walked her down the dock to his truck.

Julia helped Molly up and then held her, just held her there on the dock for the longest time. People hovered, offering comforting words, a quick touch, the gentle squeeze of an arm. They showed caring and support in a place that, three weeks earlier, had never heard of Julia Bechtel or her daughter.

She wanted to be with Noah and Kim. She wrapped an arm round Molly's waist and started walking. Rick Greene accompanied them to Julia's car and offered to drive, but Julia smiled and shook her head. She needed to feel in control of something. By the time she arrived at Noah's, she was sure enough of Molly's safety to focus on Kim.

They were gathered in the living room, where upholstered furniture and the corner woodstove offered comfort. Kim had sunk deep into the sofa. Her mother and grandmother arrived shortly after Julia, but they stood apart, seeming wary of what Kim might say.

Noah sat on the coffee table near Kim. 'What happened today—that's why you need to tell us about Artie. We can't protect you unless we know what kind of danger you're in. Were you on *The Beast* that day?'

Kim nodded. She held a glass of water braced in her lap, but it was none too steady even then.

'Had you been at the house first with Artie?'

She nodded again, and with that second silent gesture, Julia feared the muteness had returned. But Kim said in a rusty voice, 'I needed him to explain what he was doing.'

'What he was doing with you, you mean?'

She shook her head. 'We never had an affair. It was just supposed to look that way.' Her eyes fell. 'It was supposed to cover up the other.'

'The other?'

'The money.' She shot John a wary look.

'Ignore him,' Noah said. 'What you say here is not any kind of formal confession. Nothing you say can be held against you.'

Kim swallowed. 'I was making cash deposits for him in Portland. He was paying me to do it.' She faltered and took a drink. 'He said he was sheltering it from taxes. I didn't have a *clue* that the money was from smuggling illegals until I overheard a conversation. I was at his house and the phone kept ringing, and we both picked up. He didn't realise I was on the line, and then it was like if I hung up he would think I was snooping. So I listened, and when I went home it hit me that he was using me for something way past evading taxes. So I went back to his house to ask him about it.'

'What did he say?'

'That I had misheard and misunderstood, and why didn't we go out for a ride on the boat, because he really needed some air. So we did, and before I knew it, he pulled out a gun.' Her eyes were wide. 'He didn't say anything, but I knew he meant to kill me. So I jumped at him. The gun went off, and he was, like, totally unable to believe he was shot. He kept touching his shoulder and looking at the blood. By the time he went looking for the gun, I had it back at the sun deck, and I would have killed him if he'd come at me again.'

'Good girl,' said Kim's mother.

Kim turned on her, eyes brimming with anguish. 'I shot him, Ma. I shot him, and I got the gun, and then I was so upset that I looked away at the end, and because I did, we hit the *Amelia Celeste* and nine people died! I'm not good. I don't think I'll *ever* be good!'

Noah's voice soothed. 'What happened wasn't your fault.'

'But I shot him.'

'With *his* gun, which he had taken along on *his* boat, for the purpose of killing you. You acted in self-defence, Kim.'

'Were you aware that he was impaired?' John asked.

Kim looked back in surprise. 'No. I thought the gunshot was nothing from the way he insisted on driving. I was sitting on top of the engines, and the first I knew anything was wrong was when we hit the other boat. I thought he had deliberately run us into the rocks, like he was trying to kill me that way. He *will* kill me. Look at what happened today.'

'That wasn't Artie,' Noah said. 'Artie's dead, Kim. Someone else set that bomb.'

'Who?' Kim asked in bewilderment.

John said, 'I was hoping you could tell us. Do you know who was on the other end of that phone call?'

Kim took a drink of water. 'Dave. No last name.'

John nodded. 'Anyone else?'

'They talked about "the drivers". No names, just "the drivers".'

'Those'd be the men who captain the boats bringing the cargo ashore.'

'Cargo?' Kim cried. 'They're *people*.'

John told Noah, 'The INS figures they're using old trawlers. No one looks twice when a boat like that passes by in the dark.'

'If the authorities know all this,' Julia asked in frustration, 'why don't they make arrests?'

'Unless they catch them in the act, they won't have a case.'

'What about Kim?' Julia asked John. 'If she didn't know about the crime, is she in any way responsible?'

'Not if she helps us out.'

'But if she helps you out, she'll be in worse danger than she already is.'

'We're protecting her now.'

Julia wanted to be alone with Noah. After yet one more incident showing the fragility of life, she wanted to talk about loss. She wanted Noah to hold her the way he had outside the trap shed.

Noah felt the same, if the way he looked at her meant anything. But Ian was there, as was Molly, and somehow the four of them ended up at the Grill, at an inside table out of the rain. There was always someone new drawing up a chair to discuss the explosion and Kim. If it wasn't one of Noah's fellow lobstermen, it was the manager of the island auto shop, the owner of the marina, or Matthew Crane. Several of Zoe's friends stopped by, and Zoe, too, was there for a while.

Alex Brier came by, pulling out the newly printed *Island Gazette*. He pointed to three of Julia's pictures on the front page. She smiled and felt vaguely embarrassed—they were only snapshots. But Molly said they were fabulous, and Ian agreed, and Noah said that they were the best pictures the *Gazette* had printed in ages.

And still Julia wanted to be with Noah. He looked at her often, and she had to settle for that. After the meal was done, Molly wanted her back at Zoe's for a little while, at least.

So Julia went. She found her father bored with the book he was reading, and she talked with him. Mostly she sat with Molly, who wanted to talk about what Julia would have done if Molly had died in the explosion.

'Don't even *think* those words,' Julia scolded.

Molly was determined. 'If I died, would you leave Dad?'

'That's an awful question.'

'Mom. Answer me.'

So Julia said, 'There was a time when you were younger when I would have done most anything to hold my marriage together. I don't feel that way any longer. You're grown. You're strong. I have a feeling that whatever I decide to do, you may not be happy, but you'll understand. So your being here or not is no longer the issue.'

'What is?'

That was the question of the night. Julia thought about it driving back to Hawks Hill, thought about it as she put her wedding band on the counter and showered, brushed her hair, and climbed into bed. She thought about it as she lay in the dark.

The issue was not Monte. She had spent twenty years trying to please him. As she lay there, miles away from him physically and emotionally, what he wanted no longer mattered. What mattered now, at last, was what *she* wanted.

At that moment, only one answer came. She might attribute it to the fact that she was in Noah's bed, but that hadn't been a factor when she had been physically drawn to him at the trap shed and again when she had seen Ian and him out on the ocean. She had been drawn to him all evening. Wanting Noah felt like a necessity.

The telephone rang on the nightstand. Her insides quickened.

'Hello?'

'I just turned onto the road to the house,' he said in a voice that was husky and low. 'Tell me to stop.'

She couldn't do that. Yes, she was Monte's wife. But she was also Julia, a woman whose obedience was stifling, whose loyalty had been ignored along with her needs. Julia was a woman who wanted. Yes, she did.

Out of bed in a flash, she ran up the stairs. She opened the door just as headlights appeared and lit the gossamer nightgown she wore, so innocently purchased in Camden. The truck came to a stop, and Julia didn't hesitate. She had spent a lifetime waiting for others to act.

She reached the truck just as Noah climbed out, and in a heartbeat her arms were round his neck. The sheer relief of it made her cry out. Her mouth was still open when it found his, and the way he devoured her lips said he was as hungry as she.

With remarkable grace, he drew her into the house and down the stairs. Laying her on the bed, in the golden glow of the lamp, he drew the gown over her head—and Julia thought she would die. He said sweet things that set her on fire, and they found a rhythm, eyes open, until the very end, when the surge of sensation was simply too much.

Lying with him in the aftermath, her cheek against the damp hair on his chest, she did think of Monte, because what she was sharing here was like nothing—*nothing*—between Monte and her. Monte didn't say sweet things. He never said her name. She often suspected that he was imagining she was someone else.

Who am I? Monte would have said, *My wife.*

Who am I? I am Julia. She couldn't possibly forget, because Noah said her name over and over. He was making love to Julia. His eyes were on her the entire time.

Who am I? I am appealing. Monte had let her forget this, perhaps as a justification for his affairs, but Noah didn't let it go for a minute. Everything about him spoke of how appealing he found her, from the trembling of his limbs to the hammer of his heart to the sweat on his body. And then there were those husky groans.

By the time dawn approached, she knew more about this man and his needs—knew more about herself and her own needs—than she had learned in twenty years of marriage.

'I have to go,' he whispered. 'Ian will be waking.'

She nodded. He kissed her once, then again. With a groan he tore himself away. He sat on the side of the bed to pull on his trousers. Rising behind him, she snaked an arm over his shoulder and across his chest. The ropy tattoo undulated over muscle as he dressed.

'It's a hemp chain. Know why?' he asked quietly.

'No. Why?'

'Because we are.'

'Are what?'

'Chained. Chained here. Not physically. But emotionally. We're lobstermen, born and bred. We might leave, but it's never for long.'

It was a warning. He didn't look at her as he said it, but silently finished dressing in the predawn light.

He started for the door, stopped, and returned. Catching her up, he held her tightly for a long minute before very gently setting her back on her knees on the bed.

'I love you,' he whispered.

Her eyes filled with tears. He gave her a fierce kiss, then broke away and went up the stairs.

She wrapped her arms round his pillow and held the scent of him, but she didn't sleep. Everything about her body screamed of Noah, but her mind was off on its own trip, headed in the direction she knew she needed to go.

Rising, she showered and dressed in her nicest clothes. Putting on her wedding band was harder today, but she did it.

She had to talk with Monte. It wouldn't wait any longer.

Chapter 10

JULIA TOOK THE FIRST FERRY of the day. Teary-eyed still, she stood at the deck looking back at the island until it was lost in the fog. The chop was rougher than at any other time she had made the crossing, but she and the sea had reached an accommodation after the sinking of the *Amelia Celeste*. It wouldn't take her now.

Once in the car again, she hit the turnpike and drove south. The fog lifted by the time she reached Portland, and her plans congealed. She was able to think of Noah without welling up. From then on, she refused to look back.

She made several phone calls as she passed through New Hampshire, stopped midday in Massachusetts for something to eat, then drove on through Connecticut into New York.

Noah's mood was as lousy as the weather. He had known he was playing with fire; Julia's wedding band stared him in the face whenever he was with her. Now she was gone, left on the morning ferry, information radioed by Leslie Crane. Noah felt he'd been stripped bare and flogged.

Gone for good? He didn't know. And he did care.

Rain had begun at midday and now fell steadily into four-foot waves that had the *Leila Sue* pitching and rolling. Add to that the forecast, which wasn't good, and he had little to smile about. Things got even worse when he neared the traps he had set at the upper ledges north of Big Sawyer and saw a field filled with lime-grape-lime buoys.

'Damn it,' he muttered. 'They just don't learn.'

Ian came to stand beside him. 'Are those the ones you cut?'

'No. These are new ones.'

'What're you going to do?'

Throttling up, Noah pushed the *Leila Sue* ahead until he reached the first of Haber and Welk's buoys.

'We're haulin',' he said and threw the throttle into neutral. 'Gaff the buoy.' As soon as Ian had done it, Noah hooked the line over the winch and started the hydraulic hauler. The first trap came up with two good-sized bugs inside.

'We're taking their catch?' Ian asked, sounding doubtful.

'Nope.' Noah opened the trap, dumped its contents back into the sea, did the same with the second trap, then moved on to the next buoy.

He might be lousy at reading women, but he was good at this.

By late afternoon, Julia entered Manhattan. A teariness returned then, though it was as much from apprehension as anything else. Leaving the car in a garage, she walked along the park and over to Madison Avenue. She headed for the address she had jotted down during the drive south, and the next hour passed in a blur. When she hit the streets again, her stomach was in knots, but she was certainly better informed.

Still she had time on her hands, so she stopped for dinner at a small restaurant far from her usual haunts. She walked around as the evening lengthened. She sat in front of the Plaza, watching the comings and goings. She walked down to Rockefeller Center and did the same. Every few minutes she glanced at her watch. As the time drew near, she grew more committed. That terrified her.

Ten thirty came and went, and she grew edgy. At eleven thirty, praying for calm, she headed uptown again. Shortly before midnight, she reached the address she had called home for fourteen of the last twenty years. Using her key, she let herself in through the service entrance and took the elevator to the top floor. She went down the hall and paused at the door. Quietly, she fitted her key into the lock, opened the door, and slipped inside.

There was Monte's briefcase at the foot of the credenza. A light came from the bedroom hall, and soft music from the bedroom itself. For a split second she had qualms.

Who am I? I'm an ungrateful, disloyal, conniving thief.

No. *No.* This is my home. I have a *right* to be here.

She walked down the Persian runner to the bedroom. Monte was asleep in a tangle of sheets, his arms round a dark-haired woman. Both were clearly naked. Seeing—actually seeing her husband in bed with another woman, the familiarity of him and all that other bare flesh—was

451

like taking a blow to the belly. The reality of it hit her so hard that, for a minute, Julia feared she might throw up. She swallowed once, then again. On the tail of sickness, though, came anger, and anger made her bold.

The music played softly. Monte snored faintly. Julia went right up to the bed. Oddly disengaged, she stared at the twining of bodies. She hadn't slept so close to Monte in . . . in . . . she didn't remember when. He hadn't asked; she hadn't offered.

His low snoring faltered. His lids flickered, then rose. He focused on her without seeing at first. But he did figure it out. Eyes going wide, he bolted up, and it was almost comical, the passage of his thoughts, the way he realised she was there, then realised his mistress was there as well. He pulled at the sheet, as if to cover her up; this woke up the woman, who took one look at Julia and burrowed under the sheet.

He took the offensive. 'You've been away for two and a half weeks with barely a call. What are you *doing* here, Julia?'

Julia was angry but in control. 'This is my home.'

'Why didn't you call? If I'd known—'

'If you'd known, you wouldn't have had her here? I'll wait in the living room.' Feeling a wave of disgust, she turned and walked out.

He appeared in a minute, marginally dressed. 'I never knew you to be a conniver, but this is underhanded. Were you deliberately trying to trip me up?'

'Monte,' Julia cried, 'you were in bed with her. *Naked.*'

He held up a hand. 'It's not what it seems.'

'Oh, please,' she said with some force. 'I want a divorce.'

In a heartbeat's silence, the soft music played on. 'A divorce,' he finally said, sounding stunned. 'Where did this come from?'

'Years of affairs. Years of put-downs. I'm done, Monte. I've talked with an attorney.'

'You aren't serious about this, Julia. On what grounds?'

'I can use irreconcilable differences. Or I can bring an alienation of affection suit against your paramour.'

'You'd never prove that.'

'I would. I have credit card bills and phone bills.'

He went red in the face. 'You had no business going through my files.'

'Our files, Monte. My name's also on the credit card.'

'Julia, this is not *you*.' He shot a look round the room. 'If you think you're going to take all of this, think again. You packed up and moved to Maine. This is abandonment.'

'Not according to my lawyer, Mark Tompkins.'

'Ahhh,' he said snidely, 'the champion of every disgruntled wife in New York. Is he talking you into this?'

'My mind was made up before I ever called his office.'

He lowered his voice to a whisper and hitched his chin towards the bedroom. 'Give me five minutes, and she's history. She doesn't mean anything to me.'

'Well, then, maybe you'll find someone who does.'

'What if I promised—' He stopped short when she held up a hand. She let her eyes say what she didn't want to say aloud. His promises weren't worth a thing. Trust was gone.

'I've felt unloved for too long,' she finally offered.

'I do love you.'

'In your way. But it isn't enough.'

'You said that?' her friend Donna asked a short time later. Donna wore a robe and hair rollers; her face was shiny from soap.

'I did,' Julia confirmed, sinking lower on the sofa, legs sprawled in an unladylike way that she didn't have the strength to change. Walking the five blocks to Donna's small place, she had been hit by the shakes. She was grateful Donna had waited up, grateful for a generous heart and a place to sleep. Terrified by what she had done, she was also suddenly, overwhelmingly exhausted.

'Thank you for the lawyer,' Julia said. 'He might not have taken me on if you hadn't made a call.'

'He'll do right by you.'

'What is right? I'm not sure that I want a whole lot of what Monte has.'

'No.' Donna regarded her thoughtfully. 'You never did.'

Julia yawned. She listened to the city night. She turned her head on the sofa. 'So, did you all know?'

'About the affairs? We suspected.'

Julia reached for her hand. 'And if I leave New York?'

'Leave New York?' Donna cried lightly. 'No one leaves New York. You may live somewhere else, but do you think your friends won't want to visit you wherever you are? Think again, sweetie.'

Julia slept soundly until Donna woke her at the agreed-upon time. She showered and dressed, then picked up her wedding band and turned it in her hand. The stones were shiny, the platinum scuffed— polished outside, bruised inside.

It was time. Tucking the ring in her bag, she joined Donna for a bagel and coffee, but she didn't linger. She had driving to do.

Saturday-morning traffic was light. The trip to Baltimore would take three and a half hours. It was a buffer; she needed the time to sort through her thoughts. She didn't take what she had done lightly. Each time she saw her naked finger, she felt a jolt.

But driving down the familiar route, she focused on Janet. That meant gearing up to buck a pattern of behaviour that had been forty years in the making.

Who am I? she asked over and over again in what amounted to a three-hour pep talk. *I am a strong woman. I am sensible and thoughtful and thorough. I am an independent woman who has her own convictions and is willing to act on them. I have a responsibility to speak up for what I think is right. I won't be minimised any more.*

Her parents' tree-lined street, with its large brick homes and lush green lawns, was as elegant as ever. She parked behind the garage that held his-and-her sedans. She stepped from the car and went up the bluestone walk. Shoulders back, she rang the bell.

The sidelight curtain shifted. The door opened quickly—and, just as quickly, Julia forgot about being aggressive. This was a Janet she hadn't seen before, slim as ever, but wearier and far older. She wore faded knee-length shorts, an untucked blouse and no make-up, and her striking silver hair wasn't combed. Julia couldn't remember the last time she had seen her mother looking anything but perfectly put-together.

Janet's eyes flew to the car. 'Is your father all right?'

'He's fine.'

'Molly, then?'

'She's fine.'

'*You?*'

Julia managed a smile. 'I'm fine, too, Mom. Can I come in?'

Janet stepped aside. 'I was on the patio, just sitting with the paper. It's been a week from hell. This is the first time I've been able to catch my breath.' She closed the door and started down the hall, then turned and eyed Julia with unease. 'Did he tell you to come?'

'No. He doesn't know I'm here.'

'If you've come to argue his case, please don't. He needs to do that himself.' She went on through to the patio and lowered herself into a sun lounger. The paper on the table looked unopened.

Julia's heart broke. Her mother was clearly unhappy. Pulling up a lounger, she said, 'I'm not arguing his case. I just want you to know nothing's going on between Zoe and him. He went up there because he was angry at you and knew that going there would be the most hurtful thing.'

'That was childish of him. How do you know nothing's happening?'

'I've seen them together. Trust me. Dad is bored. Zoe's put him to work in the barn, but she doesn't want to be anywhere near him, so he's there alone, and he has only so much patience for that. He hangs out at the Grill, waiting for Molly to come out of the kitchen and say hello. He hangs out at the dock.'

'He's living in the house with her,' Janet argued, but wearily.

'There was one other place to sleep, and I took it.'

Janet sighed. 'If you're staying somewhere else, how do you know he isn't sneaking down the hall to see her at night?'

'Mom. Zoe's never forgiven herself for what happened. There's no way, no *way* she would let it happen again.'

'If he's bored, why's he staying there?'

'Because you haven't called!'

Her mother met her gaze. 'He hasn't called me, either. What if I fell down the stairs and lay at the bottom needing help? What if I died in my sleep? Doesn't he care?'

'I was in an accident that could have taken my life, but you didn't call,' Julia cried. 'Didn't *you* care?'

'I knew you were well. You called and told us so.'

'I also told you I was upset!'

'Yes. Can we get to this later? We're discussing your father.'

Julia sighed in exasperation. 'Of course he cares.'

'Well, it would be nice to think so, but once a man cheats on his wife, it is hard. You have no idea what it's like to live with that fear all these years.'

'I know what it's like, Mom,' Julia said in a rush of courage. 'I've lived with it myself.' It was time. 'I'm divorcing Monte.'

Janet raised her head off the lounger. 'Divorcing?'

'It isn't working. It hasn't for a while. Monte's had a string of affairs. I walked in last night and caught him in bed with the latest.'

She was braced for an I-told-you-so about having run off to Maine, but Janet said a simple, 'Oh, Julia. A *string* of affairs? Going back how long?'

'Well, I don't know, Mom. I've only documented the past three years—and, yes, I put up with it, for all the usual reasons. But it's got harder to look the other way.'

'And then there's the fear,' Janet said quietly.

Julia realised that Janet was commiserating with her. 'You've felt that fear?'

'I have.'

As Julia relaxed, the pain emerged. 'It was sharpest the first time I realised what was going on. I was convinced he had fallen in love with someone else and would divorce me. I learned to live with the fear, but there was always a new doubt. Did I look young enough? Was I deferential enough and interesting enough? Did I do enough for him, so that he would *need* me?'

Janet slid her feet to the ground and sat up. 'You were far better at all those things than I was.'

'I doubt that,' Julia said. 'I pale next to you. But Dad's different from

455

Monte. He's a background kind of guy. Monte wants to be up there on a pedestal. He likes being *coveted*. I knew that if I became a negative asset, he would sell me off.'

'Buy you off,' Janet corrected.

'That's an awful pressure to live with. After the accident, it just seemed self-defeating.'

'What will you do? Where will you live?'

Julia hadn't thought that far. All she knew was that having slept with Noah, she had to end her marriage. 'For now, I'll stay on Big Sawyer. I met with a lawyer yesterday, before I saw Monte.'

'How did Monte take it?'

'He tried arguing, but I caught him red-handed. Towards the end, he was almost looking sad. I'd say "truly", if I didn't know what a good actor he is. That's the saddest thing of all.'

'The lack of trust.'

'Yes.'

Janet sat back in the lounger again, eyes focused on a pair of tall oaks at the end of the yard. After a bit, without looking at Julia, she said, 'You think you're above it. I run an organisation that deals with people who are down-and-out on so many levels, and it's been easy to feel superior.' She aimed stricken eyes at Julia. 'Suddenly you see that right in your own home, things aren't so good.'

'But we're alive,' Julia countered. This was part of her awakening. 'We're healthy. What a gift that is.'

After a time, Janet faced her. 'You've had reason to think about death.'

'I needed you, Mom. You didn't have to visit. A call would have been enough.'

'I know. I'm sorry.' Janet looked nervous. 'I don't have much time; I'm too busy.'

'Dad feels some of that, you know. Your being too busy. It's the bottom line of why he went to Maine.'

'He was angry that I didn't call you,' Janet argued.

Julia disagreed. 'He was angry that you said you were too busy to do it, because it tapped into his anger about *that*. He's getting old enough to relax some about work, Mom. He wants you to do the same.'

'I'm not sure I want to. Cutting back—it's a whole new stage. Some of my friends are having a hard time.' Janet shot Julia an awkward look. 'You know, being with their husbands all the time.'

'Do you love Dad?'

'Of course. But I'm not sure how it would work. He might hate having *me* around all the time.'

'He wouldn't. He worships you. He would feel *honoured*.'

456

Janet was clearly unsure. 'Well, he needs to tell me that.'

'Maybe he's afraid. You're an intimidating woman.'

'He's my *husband*. He can say what he likes to me.'

'Not always.'

The words lingered. Julia wondered if she had gone too far. Janet hadn't asked for her opinion. Janet had opinions aplenty. Traditionally, Julia did what Janet asked, not the other way round.

But the status quo didn't work for Julia any more.

Noah and Ian were late returning to the dock, not because they chose to work longer, but because the sea was that rough. Even with spindles sticking up, finding lime-grape-lime buoys was a challenge. Same with pulling traps onto the boat. The surf swelled and sucked with enough force to make even emptying the lobster tanks at Foss's harder than usual. Back at the *Leila Sue*'s slip, the shouting went from boat to boat.

'You goin' out tomorrow, Hayes?' yelled Mickey Kling.

'Gonna have to, or I'll lose a bundle. You?'

'We'll move a few, but if it gets much worse, I'm turning round. Hey, Noah! I hear you dumped some rotten fruit!'

Noah raised a hand in acknowledgment and went back to scrubbing his deck. After emptying out Haber and Welk's traps, he had moved a few of his own to deeper water, but there were many more in the path of the storm. Ian's body was still adjusting to the daily rigour of hauling. Noah might take pity on him tomorrow and leave him at home, but he was surely going out himself.

Julia and Janet hung out not doing much of anything at all. For Julia, it was time well spent. Even without talk, she felt closer to Janet. Then came dinner, dressing up some for a restaurant on North Charles. There, surrounded by teak, marble and brass, they shared a bottle of wine and an order of chateaubriand, and it was so startlingly companionable that Julia dared sit back and ask, 'What do you think of me?'

Janet gave her a quizzical look. 'What kind of question is that?'

'I've always felt overshadowed. Irrelevant, often. Do you see me that way?'

'Good Lord, no. You're my daughter.'

'Do you like me?'

'You're my daughter,' Janet repeated, as though that answered the question. But Julia was mellow enough to continue on.

'Are you proud of me?'

'Yes, I'm proud of you.'

'Why?'

'*Julia.*' Janet seemed almost embarrassed.

'I really want to know,' Julia insisted. 'I haven't done anything like you have in life. Are you disappointed? Did you have higher hopes for me? Would you find value in me as a friend?'

Janet seemed startled. 'How could I be disappointed, when you do all the things I can't? I don't have the patience you do. I'm not the agreeable person you are.'

'Maybe being agreeable isn't always good.'

'Turn that round, please. What if everyone were as . . . difficult as I am? You're the grease, Julia. You make things happen.'

'What you do is *important*,' Julia said. For all her resentment of the word, it had to be used.

Janet sighed. 'Not as important as I'd like to think.'

Noah slept fitfully. He kept his cellphone close, thinking he could snatch it right up if she called, which she didn't, but he was in and out of bed anyway, monitoring the weather band. Though the fog remained thick, the wind and rain held off. Reports had the storm approaching from the southeast, but not until noon. He figured he could accomplish a lot before then.

At four in the morning, he began fixing breakfast. He had his cellphone beside him here, too, in case she woke up wherever she was, remembered what they had been doing at this time two nights before, and decided to call. She didn't. The bacon had just begun sizzling when Ian appeared. He wore a sweatshirt and jeans, and appeared to have every intention of coming along.

'You could've slept,' Noah said.

Ian leaned against the doorjamb. 'You can't go out alone.'

'I've gone out alone many a time. I'll be back by noon.'

'I'm coming.'

'Are you sure you want to?'

'I don't think you should go alone, and there's no one else you can take.'

'So you're it by default?'

'Looks that way,' the boy said, folding his arms on his chest. In that instant, everything about him—looks, build, stubbornness—spoke of the grandfather he had barely known.

Feeling strengthened, Noah added extra bacon and eggs to the pan.

Thirty minutes later, they set off. Noah left the cellphone on the kitchen counter. If she hadn't called during the quiet times, she wouldn't now. He tried to close Lucas in the house, but the dog squirmed out of his hands and ran to the truck.

The fog was even thicker at the harbour. Rick met them with muffins at the side door of the Grill. 'Rain's coming, Noah. Are you sure you're game for the ark?'

Noah sniggered, handed Ian a Thermos, and took his own. 'If I'm not back by noon, send the troops.'

Once aboard the *Leila Sue*, he got the engine going and turned on the electronics. He figured he would need all the navigational help he could get. Dawn was barely rising. With Ian and Lucas a muted shadow in the stern, he carefully piloted the boat round moorings. More lobster boats were tied up than gone. The VHF was quiet.

Clearing the harbour, he opened up the throttle and, using the loran, headed full tilt for the furthest traps. They lay forty minutes out, in rocks and ledges. The waves were light, the fog thick enough to wet his windows. He kept his wipers on. Following his instruments, he reached the first of the most distant blue-orange-orange buoys. In no time the first trap was up, then the second. They dumped three keepers in the tank. When the traps were stacked in the stern, ready for deeper water, Noah headed for the next buoy. The traps joined the pile.

Bound for the third buoy, Noah returned to the wheel just as the idle stumbled. He raised the throttle and got a sputter, a surge, a misfire. He shifted back, then forwards. Another sputter came, then the rattle of an almost-catch, then nothing.

'Swell,' he muttered under his breath.

Ian came up beside him. 'You can't be out of gas. We filled up two days ago.'

'It's not gas,' Noah said, heading for the stern.

Ian followed. 'A dead battery?'

'No. The wipers are working.' He began moving traps. 'Give me a hand.' He opened the engine compartment, searched for anything that might be amiss, and saw nothing. Then, on an impulse, he hung over the stern to see the exhaust, and swore softly.

'What?' Ian asked, leaning over beside him.

'Steam,' Noah said in dismay.

'What does that mean?'

'Water in the tank. We're not going anywhere.'

'How'd water get in the tank?'

'The same way my buoys were painted grey.'

Scrambling to his feet, Noah went to the VHF, but when he tried to get it going, nothing happened. He fiddled with the connectors. That usually did the trick. The cut wires came free in his hand.

He swore again.

'Cellphone?' Ian asked.

459

'Back at the house.'

'So how do we get help?'

Noah ducked into the cabin and emerged with a flare kit. He loaded the flare, aimed the gun in the direction of Big Sawyer, and fired. He and Ian stood looking up.

'I don't see anything,' Ian said.

'It's up in the fog. We have six flares. We'll shoot one up every few minutes. Someone will see the glow, or catch us on radar.'

His friends knew where he fished. They would find him if the *Leila Sue* stayed put. For now, anchoring would work.

'The radar's still working,' Ian pointed out hopefully.

'The instruments work off the battery,' Noah said and promptly turned them all off, though not before getting a fix on the *Leila Sue*'s bearings. 'The horn drains less. We'll sound the horn. If anyone's near, they'll come.'

'What if the weather gets bad, and they can't?'

'We'll ride out the storm. Then they'll come looking.'

'Can we ride it out in one piece?'

Noah knew Ian was frightened. He was none too happy himself. He should have made sure the radio worked. No good fisherman left port without a radio. And without a cellphone? *Stupid*, Noah decided in disgust. And with his son aboard? *Stupid and irresponsible*.

He had been on the *Leila Sue* in a storm. She could hold her own in waves up to eight or nine feet, had he power to control his position. Pitching and rolling were one thing, yawing something else. If the *Leila Sue* yawed so much that she ended up broadside to the waves, she could roll right over under a high one.

'Tell you what,' he told Ian. 'Let's take a lesson from Lucas. See how calm he is?' Lucas was sitting in a corner of the wheelhouse, watching Noah with a smile on his face.

'He doesn't know any better,' Ian said.

'Well, neither do we. The sea's not bad right now. It may not get bad at all. Let's give it an hour before we panic.'

It didn't take an hour for the weather to worsen. After one more flare and twenty minutes of bobbing at a tight anchor, the *Leila Sue* began to roll in a rising surf. A third flare and another twenty minutes later, the pull on the boat grew fierce, and still Noah resisted. He liked knowing where he was. The thought of being blown loose around the North Atlantic didn't appeal to him at all.

When another twenty minutes had passed, though, he had no choice. The waves were too large and the wind too strong. Fearing structural damage, he raised the anchor, and for the next few minutes he held his breath. With the fog unremittingly thick, he couldn't see if they were about to hit rock or not. When enough time had passed, he gave the depth finder a quick look. Only when he saw that they were in deeper water did he relax.

Negotiating the roll of the deck, Noah went forwards and pulled life jackets from a bin in the bow. He tossed one to Ian, who put it on just as the boat crested a wave and pitched down.

'It can't get much worse than this, can it?' Ian asked.

Noah gave a half-shrug as he fastened his life jacket. He loaded the flare gun again.

'Do you think it *will*?' the boy asked, sounding impatient.

Noah was wallowing in 'shouldas'—shoulda checked the VHF, shoulda taken the cellphone, shoulda stayed in port, to hell with a few traps. 'Do I look like a weatherman?' he shot back and fired the flare gun, but even as he did, he wondered if it was futile.

'Can't you talk to me? I haven't done this before. You have. Tell me what we're going into.' Ian was staring at him, jaw tight and square. 'I can't read your mind. When you don't say anything, I think the worst. Like, you hate my clothes, hate my school, hate the way I talk and the way I look.'

Noah was startled. 'What are you talking about?'

'You don't *talk*. I don't *know* what you're *thinking*. You don't give compliments. I don't remember your ever saying I did something right. Do you even *like* me?'

Noah was bewildered. 'You do lots of things right.'

'Like what? Name one thing.'

'This isn't the time, Ian.'

'See? I called it wrong. Why isn't it the time? What else are we supposed to be doing?'

'Checking the bilge, for one thing. The pump's not going to work on its own. While I do that, you keep dry.' Grabbing the oilskin at Ian's elbow, Noah pulled him inside the wheelhouse. 'And hold on to something.'

'What about Lucas?'

'Inside the cuddy,' Noah instructed and grabbed Lucas's collar.

One hour passed, then a second. A light rain was falling, and the waves didn't let up. The *Leila Sue* continued to seesaw, but what water she took on ran out of the scuppers, and the bilge remained dry. Noah checked the radar for other boats, but the few blips were easily miles away. He used the fifth flare, then the sixth. They started sounding the horn, but it seemed lost in the waves crashing in on themselves.

Soon, the rain began in earnest. They wore full oilskin jackets now.

Seeming frightened enough to have moved past his snit, Ian asked, 'Do you think we've hit the worst yet?'

'Can't tell,' Noah replied, but he was still annoyed. Ian's accusations hit home—and were all the worse because he thought he had made inroads with the boy. Then there was his own carelessness. And now the same old silence.

He owed the boy more than that. Hell, he owed the people who had died on the *Amelia Celeste* more than that. So, holding the wheelhouse roof for balance, he spoke loud enough to be heard over the commotion of the storm.

'Let me explain something, Ian. I grew up working with my father. He didn't chatter, so I didn't chatter. We were busy hauling, and we were caught in lots of storms. We didn't talk about it, because we knew what we faced, and what we faced was not knowing. The sea has a mind of its own. My guess is we're in for another eight hours.'

'What do we do until then?'

'If we take on water, we bail. If we broach, we pray.'

'Broach?'

'Turn sideways. That's risky.'

'Do you think help'll come?'

'It'll be another hour before anyone thinks we're in trouble. In this fog, a Coast Guard cutter's our best chance.'

'Best chance of survival?'

'Best chance of rescue. We'll live, Ian,' Noah vowed. 'I didn't survive the loss of my father just to go down with him now.'

Chapter 11

JULIA SLEPT LATE in her childhood bedroom. The decor had changed, but the room held memories. The sun streaming in through the blinds was the same, as were house sounds, like the washing machine running in the laundry room. With the rest of her life in flux, she needed the familiarity of these things.

She wondered if it was sunny in Maine, if Noah had to move his traps after all. She wondered if he was thinking of her, if he was wondering why she had left, when she would be back. She was wondering that herself.

Noah wasn't happy. Rain pelted the *Leila Sue*, blowing horizontally at times, and the occasional wave rose up and broke on her deck. The storm continued to worsen. He only briefly turned on the depth finder or the radar. He kept Ian at the horn.

The fog remained opaque, and the *Leila Sue* kept turning. At the rate they were being swept northwest, he guessed they would pass north of Hull in five or six hours. The waters above Hull were littered with rocks. The wind was blowing close to thirty-five knots, definitely gale force. Even the last foolhardy stragglers must have turned round and gone in.

'What time is it?' Ian called.

They were standing side by side, braced against the instrument panel, facing the stern, on the premise that it was less disconcerting to look at the boat than at the nothingness of fog. Even with this shelter, the noise of the storm would have drowned out a quiet remark. Lucas had begun to howl in the cabin.

'Almost twelve. They'll be missing us soon. You feeling OK?'

The boy nodded.

'Not what you expected when you agreed to come up, huh?'

'I thought I'd catch lobsters.'

Noah nodded, then said, 'You do that well.'

Ian shot him a surprised look. 'What'll we do if this boat sinks?'

'There's an inflatable life raft.'

Ian gave him an incredulous look: *Like, we'd survive in an inflatable life raft and not in the boat?*

The ensuing silence was filled with water, wind, and fear.

Julia ate on the patio, more of a brunch than a breakfast. Then she fell asleep in her mother's lounger. Fell asleep. Again.

She woke to find the sun past the midday point. Janet said, 'You were exhausted. Confronting Monte must have drained you.'

It wasn't only that, Julia knew. She had barely slept the night before leaving Big Sawyer. Thinking of that night now, she felt a tingling inside, and suddenly she wanted to talk with Noah.

'I'll be right back,' she told Janet and went into the kitchen, where she had left her cellphone. She dialled his numbers, first cell, then home, and got no answer at either. She was thinking that was odd when her cellphone rang in her hand.

'Mom, it's me,' said Molly. 'Where are you?'

'Gram's.'

'In Baltimore? Oh God.'

'What's wrong?'

'It is storming so bad here, and Noah and Ian aren't back,' said Molly.

'No one's seen or heard from them since they left at dawn.'

Julia's stomach dipped. 'Has anyone gone out to look?'

'They can't. I mean, it's *really* bad. Tonight the Coast Guard's going to try it, but there's a lot of traps and a lot of ocean.'

A lot of traps and a lot of ocean. The ocean depths were real to her now. Likewise, death at sea. Feeling a terrible dread, Julia was holding the phone to her heart when her mother walked in.

'Mom, that was Molly. The weather's bad up there. Two really good friends are lost on the water.'

'Lost, as in *dead*?' Janet asked.

Julia's eyes teared up. 'Lost, as in no one knows where they are. The Coast Guard's going out. I have to leave, Mom. Those friends? They're Noah and his son. Noah is special. I need to be there.'

Janet opened her mouth, seemingly to interrogate. *Special? How? Who is he? What does he mean to you?* Then she closed her mouth for an instant, shifted gears, and said, 'Do you want to fly and leave the car here?'

It made sense, of course—until Julia called the airline and realised that with bad weather in Maine causing air-traffic delays, flying might actually take longer.

'It's a long drive,' her mother warned when Julia made her decision.

'Ten hours. Molly will call with updates. I can do it, Mom.'

She left to pack her things. When she returned, her mother was waiting in the hall with her own small bag. She was coming along.

The waves were fierce, looming six, then eight, then ten feet. The *Leila Sue* was carried along at their mercy, twisting and turning, rising on their crest, then plunging headlong. Each time she turned broadside, waves broke on her deck with greater force. They didn't roll over, but the bilge began taking on water.

Noah pumped by hand. His concern was the weight of water. Enough, and the *Leila Sue* would sink.

They took turns, with the person who was not pumping holding a tether tied to the waist of the other. Noah didn't want Ian or himself washing overboard. Noah's muscles began to scream. He was working ten minutes to the boy's every five, but he figured Ian was hurting, too. He sent him into the cabin to console a howling Lucas. Ian emerged with the tether tied to the dog's collar.

'I can't leave him in there,' he said. 'It's worse than here.'

Noah was frankly pleased that one decision, at least, had been made for him. Actually, another one had. The battery, drained by the horn and brief instrument runs, had just died.

'That's fine,' he told Ian. 'Just hold him good.'

The boat was running before the seas now, being swept up to the crest of a gathering wave, then plunged into the trough, all the while buffeted by wind-driven rain. Noah had never been in anything as bad before. But then, he had never been sabotaged before.

Furious at Haber and Welk or whoever, feeling betrayed by Julia and cursed by the gods, he returned to pumping the bilge with a vengeance. Lacking a villain to yell at, he settled for yelling at Ian.

'I don't disapprove of you,' he shouted over the roar of the sea.

'You don't say positive stuff,' Ian shouted back.

'Do I say negative stuff?'

'You don't come to Washington. You don't phone me much or see me much. You don't want me living with you, you just leave me with Mom.'

'You have more opportunity living there. Your mom agrees.'

'Then summers,' Ian shouted. 'You never ask for those.'

'You're always booked up with things that sound better.'

Neither waves nor rain diluted the disbelieving look Ian shot him. 'Better than my being with my dad?'

'Better than lobstering. Better than hanging out here.'

'I thought you liked it here. You chose to come back.'

'Only after I experienced other things,' Noah called, working the pump. 'I had choices. I want you to have choices, too. That's what going to college gives you.'

Molly called when Julia was driving through Delaware and again when they were in New Jersey. Both calls were discouraging. A third call came shortly before five, after Julia entered Connecticut. Her heart ached.

She relayed the news to Janet. 'There's no sign of them. A Coast Guard cutter is out searching, but something may have happened early in the day, because very few of Noah's traps were moved. The fog is thick, thick, thick.'

'Can't radar cut through fog?'

It certainly could. But if the boat had hit a ledge and broken up, there wouldn't be a blip for radar to catch. Likewise if the boat had *blown* up. Julia fought tears. Kim's car had blown up. If a bomb was planted in Noah's boat, set on a timer to hit when he was far enough from shore so that others wouldn't see . . .

With nightfall approaching, Noah reasoned that the storm would let up, and once that happened, they could drift on the *Leila Sue* until they were found. All they had to do was to hold out until then.

'We need pails.' Snatching two from the cabin, he passed one to Ian, then worked his way back to the bilge hatch and began bailing.

465

Ian joined him, with Lucas still tethered to his waist. They were both soaking wet—Lucas looking sickly thin with his fur plastered down—but there was no fighting that. Absolutely nothing was dry.

'I'm not going to college,' Ian suddenly declared loudly as he heaved water over the side.

'That'd be dumb,' Noah shouted.

'There you go. Calling me dumb.'

'I said not going to *college* would be dumb.' He had a feeling using pails was going to be as ineffective as the pump, but he had to do something. 'If you want me to talk, take the good with the bad.'

The boat angled sharply to port, and another huge wave broke on the deck. Lucas was washed to a corner of the stern before the tether attached to Ian played out. Ian scrambled over and carried him back.

'I need time off. Lots of kids are doing that now.'

'What would you do?'

'I don't know.' He dug the pail into the water. 'But what's the point of college if I don't know what I want to do with my *life*?' He hurled the pail's contents into the sea.

Noah did the same once, twice, five times, while the boat yawed and pulled. With the bilge filling faster than they could bail, it seemed important to keep talking. 'That's what liberal arts programmes are for.'

'I hate the colleges I've seen. The classes are big, the dorm rooms suck, and the weekends are an orgy. You want me to do that?'

'Try small colleges,' Noah said, throwing another pailful over the side.

'Small means selective. My SAT scores stink.'

'Ah.' The bottom line. Noah straightened. 'You're afraid you won't get into the schools you apply to.'

Ian stopped bailing. 'Do you know how embarrassing that would be for Mom?' he shouted.

'No one's asking you to go to an Ivy League college.' The boat headed up another wave. With water in the bilge, they were riding deeper now.

Ian braced himself for the descent. 'You went to one.'

'You're not me.'

'Not as smart.'

The *Leila Sue* crested the wave and soared down. '*Just* as smart,' Noah shouted, bracing himself as Ian was doing. 'Maybe smarter, only growing up in a different time and place.'

They hit the trough. The bow went under, water poured up against the wheelhouse, then rose to the roof—it seemed for ever that the *Leila Sue* hung there, for ever that Noah waited in horror, until the whole thing reversed and the bow was buoyant again.

Then he heard a strangled cry. He looked back at the stern in time to see Ian off the boat on the tail of a wave—boy and dog both—and Noah whirled, lunged for the end of the tether, and grabbed it tight. Losing his footing, he slid all the way into the stern before his boots caught, but he came up pulling the rope. Ian was ten feet behind the *Leila Sue* and being dragged right along into the next wave.

Keeping his eyes on the boy, Noah pulled at the rope; the water fought him, or maybe it was the weight of boy and dog, but he kept at it. He pulled harder, pulled faster, saw Ian moving closer, but at the same time felt the upward surge of the boat. He just pulled. When the boy was close enough, he reached down, grabbed his wrist, and hauled him up and aboard, all six feet, 170 pounds of him, as though he were a child. Lucas was next. Noah got him aboard seconds before a huge wall of water hit the deck.

Just south of Boston, the rain began. Julia put on the wipers and tightened her hands on the wheel, but she didn't slow down. Mind, heart, soul—all were on Big Sawyer with the rest of the people who were gathered at the Grill, anxiously awaiting word on the *Leila Sue*—and when mind, heart and soul weren't at the Grill, they were out in the storm.

'He must be something,' her mother remarked gravely.

Returning to reality with a start, Julia shot her a blank look.

'Noah,' Janet said. 'We've been out of Baltimore all this time, and you haven't once asked how I feel about going up there. It's not going to be easy. Seeing your father is only the first challenge. The bigger one is seeing my sister. I'm sitting here remembering everything, before and after. You haven't asked about that.'

No. Julia hadn't. Nor did she plan to. 'I'm sorry, Mom. I'm on overload here.'

'That's why I say he must be something.' Janet paused. 'Is he the reason you're divorcing Monte?'

'No. I'm divorcing Monte because our marriage has no meaning. Because he's a hopeless cheater. I deserve better.'

'Where does Noah come in?'

'He is . . . just . . . a breath of fresh air.'

'That could mean anything. What about him is so fresh?'

'The way he looks at me,' Julia offered without having to think. 'The way he talks. The way he smiles. It's all genuine.' She did think then. 'We don't have to be talking. There's stuff up there that takes the place of words. Life there is rich.'

'You were enthralled with the place from the first. Could you live there?'

'I think so.' Actually, she knew so, all the more the nearer they came.

She was returning to a place she wanted to be. As frightened as she was for Noah, there was room for that knowledge.

'What if Noah's not there?'

'Dead, you mean?'

'Would you want to stay there then?'

She teared up. 'He'll be fine,' she insisted and brushed a tear from her cheek. 'He won't die. He'll be fine.'

Darkness snaked into the fog. There hadn't been a monster wave in a while, and though the boat continued to turn and rise and duck, Noah was too numb with relief to do anything but sit in the wheelhouse with Ian. Their backs were against the console, their sides were touching. Ian had lost his boots to the sea, but he was alive. Lucas lay sprawled, trembling, across their legs.

In a situation that was grossly surreal, Noah picked up where he had left off. Quietly now, lacking the strength for more, he said, 'The thing about Ivy League schools? It's OK.' He breathed, shooting for greater calm. 'Barely a third of my high-school class went to college, and none of those applied to the ones I did. That gave me an edge in the admissions process. I know that competition is bad in your class. But opting out is worse.'

Ian was totally drained. 'What am I supposed to do?'

Noah felt an inkling of strength. 'Apply to different schools from those your friends choose. Pick ones you like. Don't be pressured, not by me or your mother, and certainly not by your friends. Here's a chance to do what you want, for a change. Go for it.'

'If we live.'

'We'll live,' Noah said, feeling suddenly calm. 'We've come this far, haven't we? If you didn't die back there in the water, you won't die now.'

Nor would Noah, he realised. He had been spared dying on the *Amelia Celeste* so that he could mend his relationship with his son, and he was on his way to doing that. There were things they could do together, things that went beyond lobstering. And then there was Julia. For a little while, he let himself think about her. It started with images of the night they'd shared and went on to more innocent ones. Work, play, travel, family, sex—he could share it all with her, could do it in a heartbeat. He had let his marriage die of attrition. Julia was his second chance. Wasn't this another reason why he hadn't died with Hutch?

Go for it, he had told Ian. The same applied to him. Realising that, he felt conviction, and feeling conviction, he suddenly felt calm.

Then he realised that the calm wasn't only internal. The *Leila Sue* continued to roll, but the waves were no longer as angry. Sure enough, as night fell, the storm waned.

Thirty minutes shy of Rockland, Julia got word from Molly that the weather had begun to improve and Matthew Crane would meet her. By the time she parked at the pier, the rain had stopped. Even in the dark, the fog had lifted enough for her to see Matthew and his nephew's Cobalt waiting to take Janet and her to Big Sawyer.

Matthew helped Janet board. Julia asked, 'Any word?'

'Not yet. The others are heading out to search.'

The waves were hearty, but the Cobalt cut neatly through. The fog continued to lift. Increasingly, Julia could see the running lights of other boats, lobster boats that would never be leaving port this late at night if one of their own weren't in trouble.

In less than fifteen minutes, Matthew steered into the harbour. Of all the people gathered along the dock, front and centre were Molly and George.

Julia glanced at her mother. She looked unsure of herself, which was so uncharacteristic that Julia moved close and said, 'He's waiting for you. He loves you.'

Janet didn't answer. Eyes brimming, she simply swallowed.

The lines were tied. So many hands were there helping them from the boat that Julia didn't know whose was whose, but she did know Molly's arms when they wrapped round her and held her with a desperate need.

Julia looked around. George was hugging Janet, and the hug was mutual. Janet's arms held George as tightly as his held her.

Julia spotted Zoe through a hole in the crowd. She stood alone, arms folded in a gesture of self-protection. Julia wanted to go to her, but she wasn't the person Zoe needed.

Suddenly, there was Janet, separating herself from George and the rest, and walking down the dock.

Zoe dropped her arms as her older sister approached.

Julia would never know what words were said. It was not her business to know. She saw Janet stop several feet away, saw her stand there for a minute, then move closer, raise a hand, and touch Zoe's cheek.

Julia looked away, then. It was a beginning, and it was between Janet and Zoe. More crucial now, Julia needed to know about Noah.

They drifted, exhausted as much by the aftermath of terror as by the physical exertion of keeping the *Leila Sue* afloat. In short bursts of strength, they bailed enough water from the bilge to avoid sinking. For the most part, though, they sat in the wheelhouse and rode the gentled ocean swells. For all the times Noah had wondered what to say to his son, there was no wondering now. They didn't have to talk to know what they had shared.

It was a bond. Noah didn't need words to say that. He could feel the knowledge in Ian, who was working with him now, not against him—feeling with him now, not against him—thinking with him now, not against him. As initiations went into the brotherhood of lobstermen, Ian had suffered trial by fire. He'd made Noah proud.

At ten o'clock, after seventeen hours on the water, the first lights emerged from the lifting fog. They let out whoops of relief and stood at the gunwale, shouting and laughing. In his exuberance, Ian threw his arms round Noah, and the rescue was complete.

Leading a parade of lobster boats, the Coast Guard cutter entered the harbour shortly before eleven. Torches blazed on the dock. Noah and Ian were off the cutter the instant it docked, as was Lucas, looking damp but glad to be on his home turf. Friends converged on Noah and Ian in a circle of backslapping and hugs.

Breaking out of the circle, Noah was intercepted by John Roman.

'You're sure it was water polluted the tank?' he asked.

'I'm sure,' Noah said. 'And the radio wires were cut.'

'Haber and Welk?'

'Got another suspect?'

'Not me. We'll pay them a visit with Charlie Andress, whenever you want.'

'I want now,' Noah said. 'I'm not ready to sleep, but they should be. Your boat has radar. Give me ten to change clothes, and we'll take a ride to West Rock.'

'I'm game,' John said.

It was a plan. Noah felt good.

In the next instant, he stopped walking. As if to compensate, his heart began to race. Julia stood not ten feet away, breathlessly beautiful with her hair shining in the night. She had a hand pressed to her mouth and tears in her eyes, and she didn't move towards him.

I've lost her, he thought. She's come back to say goodbye.

Then he noticed the strangeness of the hand that was pressed to her mouth. A handful of steps took him to where she stood, and all the while she looked at him with a kind of fearful yearning.

He touched her hand—touched the spot that looked so odd without its wedding band. He brought her hand to his heart so that she could feel its thud, and she smiled through her tears.

What that smile did to him!

'Dad?' Ian came up behind him. 'John's waiting.'

'We're going to West Rock,' Noah told Julia softly. 'Bearding the lion in his den.'

'I'm coming.' She was holding his eyes like she would never let them go, holding his hand the same way.

'No, ma'am. And neither is Ian.'

'They nearly got me killed,' Ian argued. 'I have a right.'

'These are criminals, Ian,' Noah said, though the message was meant for Julia, as well. 'John and Charlie have guns.'

'But—'

'I messed up bad with the boat. No radio, no cellphone—and it nearly got you killed. Stay at the house with Julia. That way, I'll see both of you when I get back.'

In the end, Ian came. For a boy who had been sullen and silent, he wouldn't stop talking now, and he was eloquent. *It's my fight, too*, he said. *If it had been your dad and you when you were seventeen, would you have gone?* And once Noah said Ian could come, Julia looked ready to rebel. It took a quiet moment with her, and the sharing of bits of his heart and his hopes, before she acquiesced.

John's boat made the crossing in seven minutes. Charlie Andress, the West Rock police chief, met them at the dock and drove them to a fisherman's cottage as run-down as any on the road. Not so the black Porsche sitting in front.

'Whoa,' said Ian. 'Cool car.'

'A little out of character for a lobsterman,' John remarked.

Charlie said, 'The car's registered in Florida.' He parked by the house.

'No lights on,' observed John. 'They must be sleeping.'

Charlie took the lead, since this was his jurisdiction. He knocked on the door loudly while the others waited. A light came on. The door opened. One man stood there and was joined seconds later by another, but neither had been asleep. Both were wide awake, and both wore rain jackets. Of average height and build, they were bearded, as many lobstermen were. One had a shaved head, the other did not.

'You know me,' Charlie said in a lazy way. 'This here's John Roman from over Big Sawyer. We need to talk with you.'

'Bad time, man,' said the hairless one—Welk, Noah decided, recalling the picture on John's computer. 'It's kinda late.'

'Doesn't look to me like you were in bed,' Charlie remarked.

'We just got back.'

'Oh? Where you been?'

Welk gave a halfhearted shrug. 'Here and there.'

Charlie grunted. 'Not in that car. I touched the engine cover just now. It's cold. If you ask me, though, I'd say you're on your way out. Where you headed?'

'To bed, as soon as you leave,' Haber said.

'Well, now, that may be a while,' Charlie said. 'Like I told you, we need to talk. How 'bout inviting us in?'

'How 'bout getting a search warrant?' Welk snapped back.

'I'm not searching anything. Just wanting to talk. We can either do it here or back in the office.'

'In the morning,' Welk said anxiously. He checked his watch and, with a calm that said he wasn't calm at all, lowered the wrist. 'OK, man?'

'Actually,' Charlie mused, 'it's not OK. I got folks here who've come all the way over to see you. My friend Mr Roman thinks you sabotaged his friend Mr Prine's boat. He's prepared to bring charges.' Charlie looked to be enjoying himself. 'And I got witnesses that say you go out in the boat at night, and I'm asking myself why you do that. Are you pulling traps in the pitch-black? Or sliding up to the dock at Big Sawyer and fouling the fuel tank of its most respected citizen?'

'They also cut the radio wires,' Ian charged.

Noah was just rarin' to go. 'Fouled the tank and robbed me of my radio when a storm's about to hit—which resulted in our being out on the ocean in a disabled craft through the whole of that storm. Bottom line? That's attempted murder.'

'Why look at us?' Haber asked. 'We're just lobstering for the summer. You guys don't like outsiders. That's your problem, not ours.'

'Wrong,' Noah said. 'You trespassed on *my* property when you disabled my boat. Wilful destruction of property is a state crime.'

'I want a lawyer,' Haber said.

Charlie smiled right back. 'Maybe in the morning.'

'OK,' Welk said quickly. 'Morning's fine. Come on, Curt.' He seemed eager to close the door.

'You sure you guys aren't heading out?' Charlie asked.

'At twelve twenty?' Haber countered. 'If you're gonna charge us, do it, man. If not, get the hell off my doorstep.' Both he and Welk seemed on the edge of panic.

'OK, Charlie,' John said. 'I think we've imposed on these gentlemen enough. Let's let them get their sleep. We'll all be fresher in the morning.'

'I was just getting started,' Charlie protested.

But John gestured him back to the car. As soon as they were all four inside, John said, 'Go round the corner, Charlie, then park and put out the lights.' Pulling a notebook from his pocket, he flipped through it in the cast-off light of the dashboard.

'Are you thinking what I am?' Noah asked.

'That there's a reason one checked his watch and the other knew the exact time? I'll bet I am.' He took his cellphone and dialled a number.

'What?' Ian asked Noah as Charlie pulled round the corner.

'Haber and Welk are heading off to do business.'

'In the middle of the night?' Ian asked sceptically.

'That's when smuggling is done,' Noah replied.

'But why would they do all the rest?'

Noah snorted. 'Stupidity? Artie let people think he and Kimmie were having an affair as a cover. Haber and Welk might have used lobstering as theirs. They unwittingly set traps in our space. When we called them on it by knotting their lines, they tried to best us.'

'Why?'

'Because they're no good. Violence is all they know.'

'There's the Porsche,' Charlie said as a black car sped past.

John ended his call. 'Follow it, Charlie. We're witnesses on this end. The INS has already boarded the big boat. The crew is in custody. Now they want the drivers of the smaller boat.'

Ian leaned forwards. 'They're smuggling illegals in a *lobster boat*?'

Noah confirmed the possibility. 'Their boat's a forty-five-footer. They could easily pack thirty or forty people on each night, and God knows how many kilos of smack.'

'Smack,' Ian echoed. 'Wow.'

Noah asked John, 'Do we think they bombed Kimmie's car?'

'They know how,' John remarked. 'They haven't spent the last ten years in a church choir.'

Once they saw Haber and Welk park at the pier, board their boat, and head to sea without running lights, and once that information had been duly reported to John's INS contact, there was no point in hanging around West Rock. John guided his own boat in the other direction, and just in time. Ian dozed off, and Noah wasn't in much better shape. They had been up for nearly twenty-two hours.

Noah still had one thing to do. When he arrived back at his parents' house, he found that one thing to do sound asleep on the sofa. Her body was covered by an afghan his mother had crocheted years before; her feet were covered by Lucas, who was sound asleep as well.

'She's been cooking,' Ian whispered, sniffing the air.

'Go take a look,' Noah said softly.

Momentarily revived, Ian left for the kitchen.

Noah hunkered down beside the sofa and just looked at Julia. He guessed he could do that for hours any day, but all the more so now, sluggish as he was with exhaustion. He could watch her sleep. He could look at every one of her features, could trace every curve, but the beauty he saw went beyond that. She was peaceful. She was together, and reasonable, and compassionate. She was a giver, which was both a gift and a challenge. She was generous to a fault.

And she was smiling.

He smiled back. 'Hi,' he whispered, not knowing what else to say.

A hand came from under the afghan and touched the stubble of his beard, then his mouth. 'Did you get them?'

He nodded. 'We got 'em good. No one hurt.'

She let out a pleased sigh. 'I'm sorry I fell asleep.'

Ian appeared. His mouth was full. He said to Noah, 'Wait'll you see what's in the kitchen.' To Julia, he said, 'It's all *so* good.'

'All?' Noah asked. 'You didn't eat it *all*, did you?'

'Nuh-uh. This is for you.' He passed Noah a napkin filled with brownies and cookies and went down the hall to his room.

Noah sat back on his heels. Suddenly ravenous, he ate a cookie, then a brownie. 'I could be spoilt,' he finally said.

'Everyone needs spoiling from time to time.'

He took her hand. 'I know. But you want to take it slow.'

'I have to. I'm at the bare beginnings of a legal process, and I want things as easy as possible for Molly.'

'But you came back here.' He clung to that thought.

She squeezed his hand tight. 'How could I not?'

Noah's heart swelled. 'If it weren't for the boy, I'd climb up there with you.'

She actually blushed. After what they had shared the Thursday night before, that blush came as a surprise. But it was honest and sweet, one more thing for him to love.

Epilogue

JULIA GAVE HERSELF A YEAR. She figured she wouldn't need half of that time to realise that she loved Noah, but she was gun-shy. She had loved Monte, too. Older and wiser now, she understood that defining herself in terms of one man or another wasn't enough. Nor was defining herself in terms of her parents or her daughter. She needed an identity of her own and the confidence that would bring.

July was a month to coast. Everything was new, from the freedom of being with Noah, to the pleasure of watching him with Ian, watching her mother with her father, and watching Janet with Zoe. Even the sun felt new. It returned following the storm and stayed, bringing days that were warm but relieved by breezy nights.

Julia's camera became her entrée to parts of Big Sawyer that she mightn't have otherwise explored. She meandered around the marina where boats were being repaired, around Foss Fish and Lobster while the day's catch was tallied, around the dock when lobstermen were doing the myriad little chores of their trade.

Noah still refused to let her haul traps, but Julia spent many days photographing Ian and him at work aboard the *Leila Sue*. Other days she spent with Molly, who was truly unbalanced now that the divorce was real, and who needed coddling. And then there was Kim. She was determined to reshape her life in the aftermath of what had happened. She wanted to go to New York, and Julia hatched a plan that began with Julia's friend Charlotte hiring Kim to work in her boutique, and went on to include helping her find a small apartment and signing up for courses at City College.

August was a month of legal doings, most notably a formal separation agreement. Monte's infidelity became a given. He did argue about almost everything else, though, starting with the contents of the apartment and ending with investments made over the years. Julia wanted a settlement that would give her a nest egg, assets enough to enable her to live with total independence. Part of that meant having money to spend on Molly. For all his other faults, Monte was desperate to have his daughter in his life, and he bent over backwards to reach out to her.

Noah did reach Ian. The boy agreed to look at colleges before the start of school, but only if Noah came along.

September was the prime lobstering month, the time when lobsters were fully grown in their shells. With Ian in school again, Noah chose to work alone, though Julia often went along. The local paper was regularly printing her photos now, so she had excuse enough to take pictures. And she pitched in to help with whatever Noah allowed. The more she handled well, the more he let her do the next time. He absolutely refused to call her his sternman, but she didn't need the title.

October produced a phone call to Julia from a man who was writing a book on lobstering.

'A book? I can't do a *book*,' she told Noah. 'This is more serious than working for the *Island Gazette*.'

'That's why you should do it. Your pictures are good, Julia, and you've already taken most of the ones he needs. What's the downside here?' After grappling with her own insecurities, Julia agreed.

Molly came up to visit during her fall break. She loved seeing Julia, Noah and Zoe, but was nearly as excited to see her friends from the Grill.

Monte claimed that some of his major investments had soured. Julia's lawyer put a forensic accountant on the case.

Come November, Noah pulled his traps for the season and trucked them to the trap shed for cleaning and storage. Julia kept the home fires burning—largely at Noah's house in town, though she worked at the hill house. She rose each morning at dawn for breakfast with him, then headed out to help Zoe with the rabbits, or simply to visit. She was back at the house before him at night.

December was for family. With the traps stacked in tall piles behind the shed and the *Leila Sue* out of the water, Noah went to Washington. He visited the school where Ian studied. He sat in the bleachers cheering the varsity basketball team, of which Ian was a member. He helped Ian with college applications.

Julia spent this time in New York. The accountant had uncovered the heftiest of Monte's hidden investments, which was reason enough for Monte to give up the fight. Julia was more rooted elsewhere now, and seeing him wasn't as painful as it had been at the start. The apartment went on the market. Julia sorted through her things, deciding what to save and what to toss. She saw friends. She saw Kim. And the treat at the very end? Ten days' skiing in the Canadian Rockies with Noah, Ian and Molly.

In January, Janet turned sixty-five, so George threw her a party. It wasn't a surprise—Janet would have never stood for that. She had loosened up since her time on Big Sawyer, but she still felt *very* strongly that there had to be *plenty* of hors d'oeuvres, because you didn't call a party for seven o'clock with plans for dinner at nine and *not* feed people during the interim.

She also requested that Zoe come.

Zoe was apprehensive. This was a family shindig and she hadn't been part of family for years. She feared she would be on display and come up short.

'How could Zoe possibly come up short?' Noah asked in disbelief.

Julia cleared her throat. 'Excuse me? Who was it who agonised over what clothes to wear visiting his son's school? Who wanted to look totally urbane?'

'I didn't want to embarrass him.'

'You could never do that. Ian was so proud to have you there. I think he was actually disappointed that you looked so urbane. He would have preferred you wore an old T-shirt, so that his friends could see the tattoo.'

Noah winced. 'His mother hasn't forgiven me for that.'

'For your tattoo or Ian's?'

'Either one. But Ian earned it. After what he went through that day in the storm, how could I say no?'

February was bleak. A cold ocean wind rushed up the hillsides. Noah had warned Julia. But she didn't complain—because February, it turned out, was for *them*. There were no kids, no parents, no aunts. Julia and Noah moved up to the hill house and burrowed in. They had books and food and a fire in the hearth.

March brought work thoughts. For Noah, that meant fixing latches, replacing hog rings, painting buoys. It meant deciding what the *Leila Sue* needed to get in tiptop shape. For Julia, it meant helping organise twenty-some local artisans for a show in Boston and producing a publicity flier. Midmonth, Janet and Molly made a surprise appearance.

Then came April, and Julia found herself wondering where winter had gone. The days were longer, and with the *Leila Sue* tuned up and back in the water, Noah set the first strings of the year.

Julia went along for the ride, giving Noah a hand with ease. Alex Brier marked the start of the season by printing four of her pictures on the front page of the *Gazette*.

In May, the lobstering book was published. It was reviewed prominently by the Portland press, one member of whom happened to be putting together a book on Maine culture. He called to ask if Julia would illustrate it.

'I do lobstering,' Julia reasoned. 'I don't do potato farming, or innkeeping, or blueberry growing.'

'You do spinning, and weaving, and rabbitries,' Noah said. 'You just bought a second camera—'

'A small one for my pocket.'

'It packs four megapixels, and you bought a telephoto lens for the bigger camera. Seems to me you're perfectly set up to do the job. Unless you don't want it,' he added.

'I *want* it,' Julia said with more than a glimmer of excitement. She wasn't a professional photographer, but she was a survivor. She rarely woke in the morning without thinking, *Here's a new day*. Life was fragile. Happiness and fulfilment, even success, weren't things to postpone.

She took Noah's hand. 'Yes, I could do this,' she said.

In June, with the first anniversary of the accident approaching, Noah turned the tables and took her hand. She kept saying that he had saved her life, but the opposite was true. For knowing Julia, he was more open and relaxed. He communicated better than he had. His relationship with Ian continued to solidify, and he was in love.

He waited until her divorce was final, but not a day longer. A whole year had shown him how perfectly Julia fitted into his world. But he knew of the fragility of life, too.

So, the very first morning she was formally free, he forwent lobstering in favour of sleeping in with her at the hill house. Then he brought her breakfast on the bedroom deck, and, with sea, sky and trees looking on, he put three stones in her hand. They were diamonds, set vertically in platinum, and they hung from a chain that was as elegant and as delicate as she was.

'The two small ones at the top are from earrings my father bought my mother. She didn't live long enough to enjoy them, so I want you to do that in her stead. The big one, here, is from me. If you'd like all three put into a wedding band, I'd love that. But a simple gold band would work, too. Whatever you want. It has to be different this time. For both of us. Y'know?'

She did.

BARBARA DELINSKY

Over the past twenty-five years, Barbara Delinsky has written seventy-three novels, most of which have been translated into twenty-five languages and published in twenty-eight different countries. 'I know these numbers are mind-boggling,' Barbara says, 'and when I go through an airport or a hotel lobby and see someone with one of my books, I'm stunned. But I've always wanted to reach as many people as I can and I think perhaps my books touch chords in people.'

Barbara Delinsky draws inspiration from the lives of real people who live in real places. 'I read the newspaper daily and watch news shows. I have also been inspired by a song lyric, a movie, or even by another book. I always do a lot of research, because each story has got to have a certain amount of background. I use the Internet and I talk to people. In *The Summer I Dared*, I "dared" write of two topics about which I knew absolutely nothing—Angora rabbits and lobstering—but I learned. First from a rabbit breeder in Massachusetts and then from someone who had helped me to research maple-syrup production for an earlier book, who turned out to know lots about lobstering too!'

As well as supporting her stories with carefully researched material, Barbara Delinsky often describes earthshaking personal events. 'At the age of eight, I concocted complex scenarios to explain my mother's death from breast cancer. I did not really know her, but I've spent the better part of my life doing things that I hope would have made her proud. Very often we let the past haunt us and slow us down. Until we face it, we can't move ahead.'

Moving ahead is just what the author has done in her own life, having herself suffered from, and survived, breast cancer. Following the trauma, she wrote the only nonfiction book of her writing career. Titled *Uplift*, it draws on the experiences of many different women and takes a practical and humorous approach to living well and long after breast cancer. 'I wanted it to offer all the practical little secrets to survival that have nothing to do with doctors, machines or drugs and everything to do with women helping women,' Barbara says. All proceeds from the sale of the book go directly to her own charitable foundation for breast cancer research. The foundation's first gift was to Massachusetts General Hospital, where Barbara's mother was treated more than fifty years ago, and where the author received her treatment.

Now, seven years on and aged fifty-nine, Barbara Delinsky intends to keep writing for as long as she enjoys it. 'I don't like doing nothing. I started writing when our twin sons were four. It's a lot of busywork, raising kids. I had one son, then the twins five years later. Your mind feels like it's going to atrophy. Like a washing machine going round and round. I needed something. I read an article about three women who wrote romance novels. They all had lives that were similar to mine. So I thought to myself, If they can do it . . .' She wrote her first book, *Hills of Eden*, in three and a half weeks and by the time it sold, she was in the middle of her second book. 'And aren't I lucky now to have the kind of a career where I don't have a mandatory retirement age?'

Anne Jenkins